My Last Summer with Cass

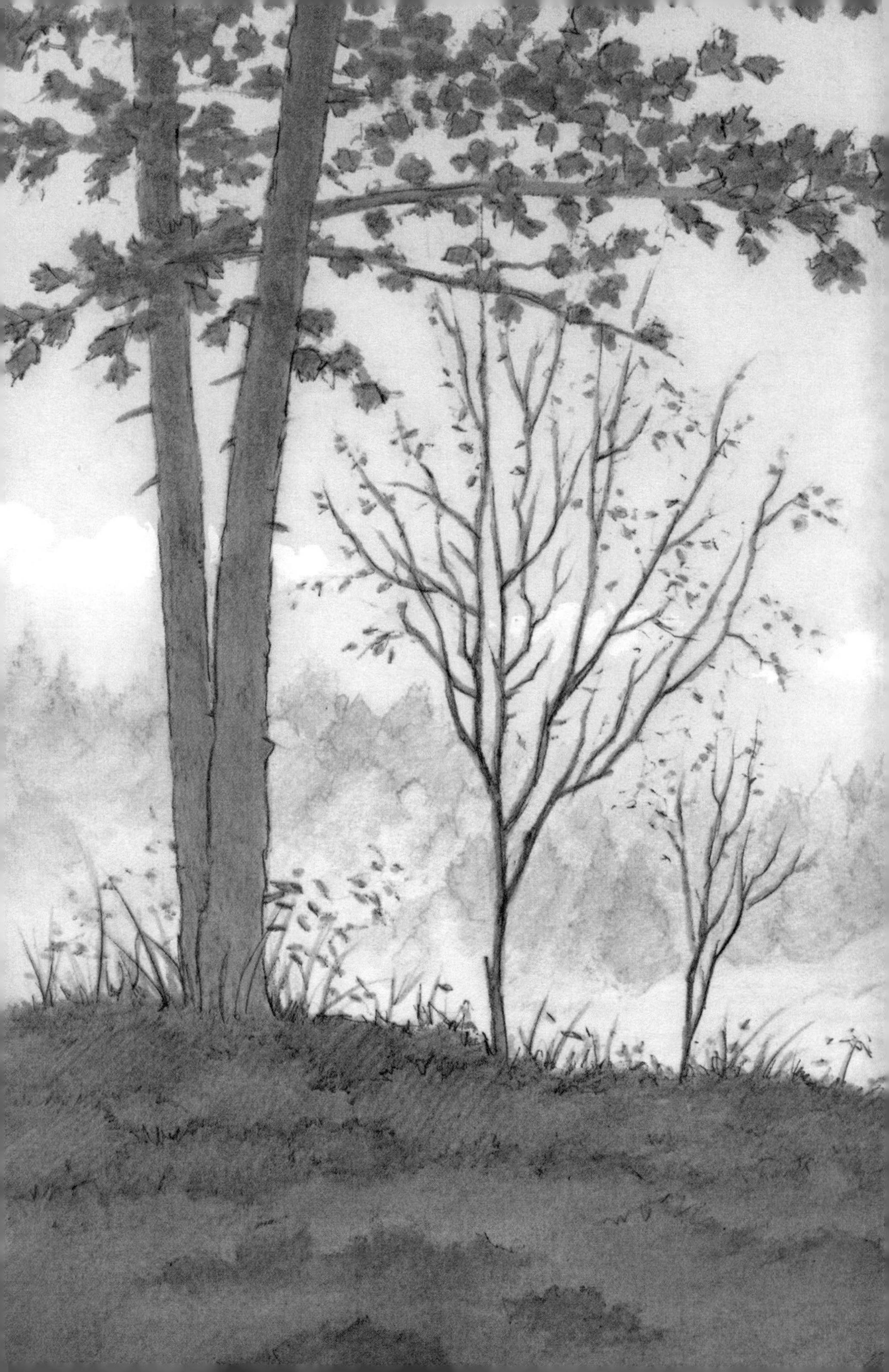

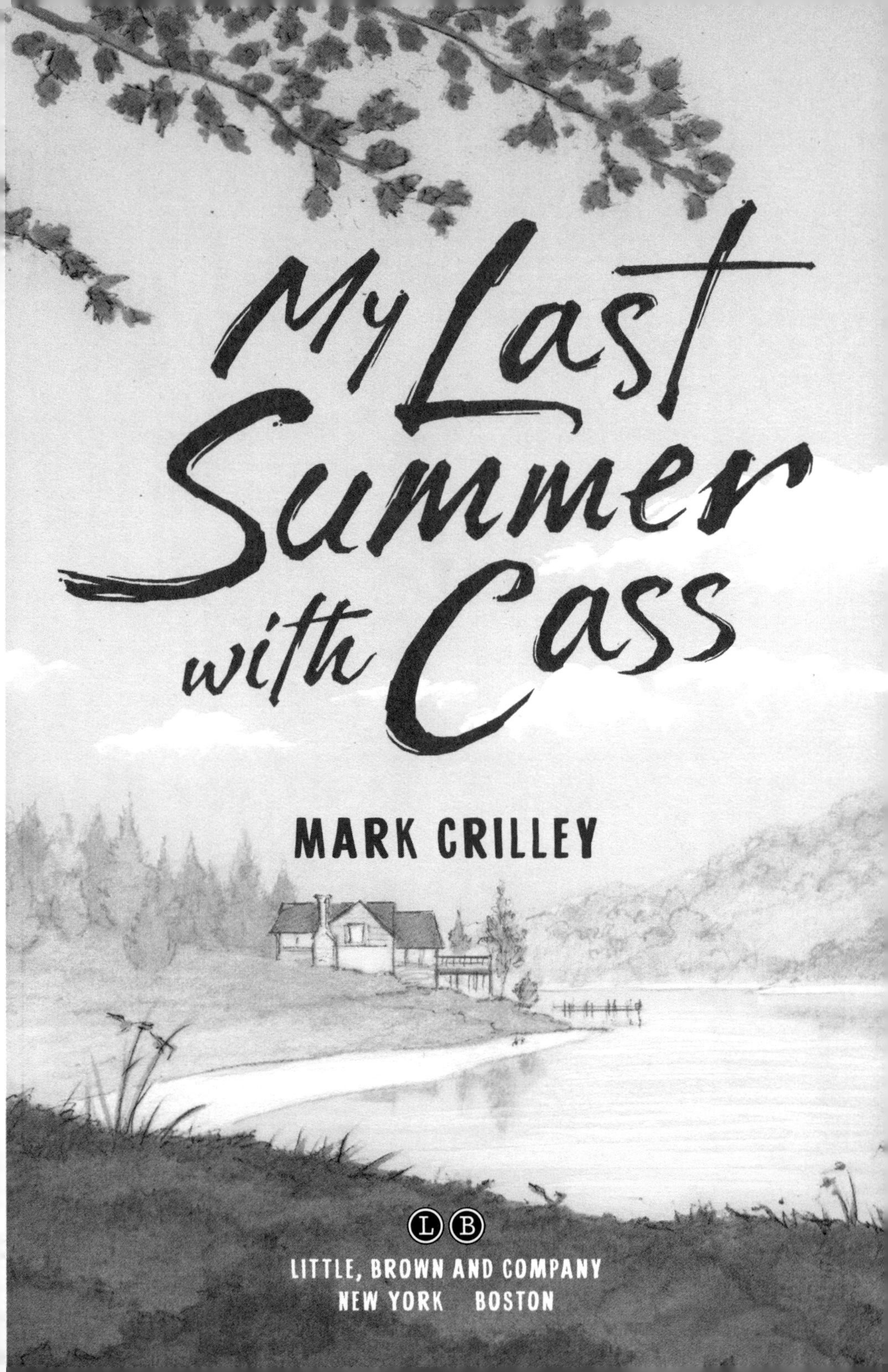

My Last Summer with Cass

MARK CRILLEY

LB

LITTLE, BROWN AND COMPANY
NEW YORK BOSTON

About This Book

This book was edited by Emily Meehan, Hannah Allaman, and Andrea Colvin and designed by Jenny Kimura. The production was supervised by Bernadette Flinn, and the production editor was Lindsay Walter-Greaney. The text was set in CC Wild Words Lower, and the display type is Hillstone Regular.

Little, Brown and Company
Hachette Book Group
1290 Avenue of the Americas, New York, NY 10104
Visit us at LBYR.com

First Edition: March 2021

Little, Brown and Company is a division of Hachette Book Group, Inc. The Little, Brown name and logo are trademarks of Hachette Book Group, Inc.

The publisher is not responsible for websites (or their content) that are not owned by the publisher.

Library of Congress Cataloging-in-Publication Data
Names: Crilley, Mark, writer, illustrator.
Title: My last summer with Cass / Mark Crilley.
Description: First edition. | New York : Little, Brown Books for Young Readers, 2021. | Summary: "Megan and Cass are at a crossroads in their lives and in their art. Will this summer make or break their friendship?"—Provided by publisher.
Identifiers: LCCN 2020015189 (print) | LCCN 2020015190 (ebook) | ISBN 9780759555464 (hardcover) | ISBN 9780759555457 (paperback) | ISBN 9780316705479 (ebook) | ISBN 9780316705448 (ebook other)
Subjects: LCSH: Graphic novels. | CYAC: Graphic novels. | Friendship—Fiction. | Summer—Fiction.
Classification: LCC PZ7.7.C75 My 2021 (print) | LCC PZ7.7.C75 (ebook) | DDC 741.5/973—dc23
LC record available at https://lccn.loc.gov/2020015189
LC ebook record available at https://lccn.loc.gov/2020015190

ISBNs: 978-0-7595-5546-4 (hardcover), 978-0-7595-5545-7 (pbk.), 978-0-316-70547-9 (ebook), 978-0-316-70558-5 (ebook), 978-0-316-70546-2 (ebook)

Printed in the United States of America

LSC-C

Printing 1, 2020

To John Walter,
whose friendship really is a work of art

Part One

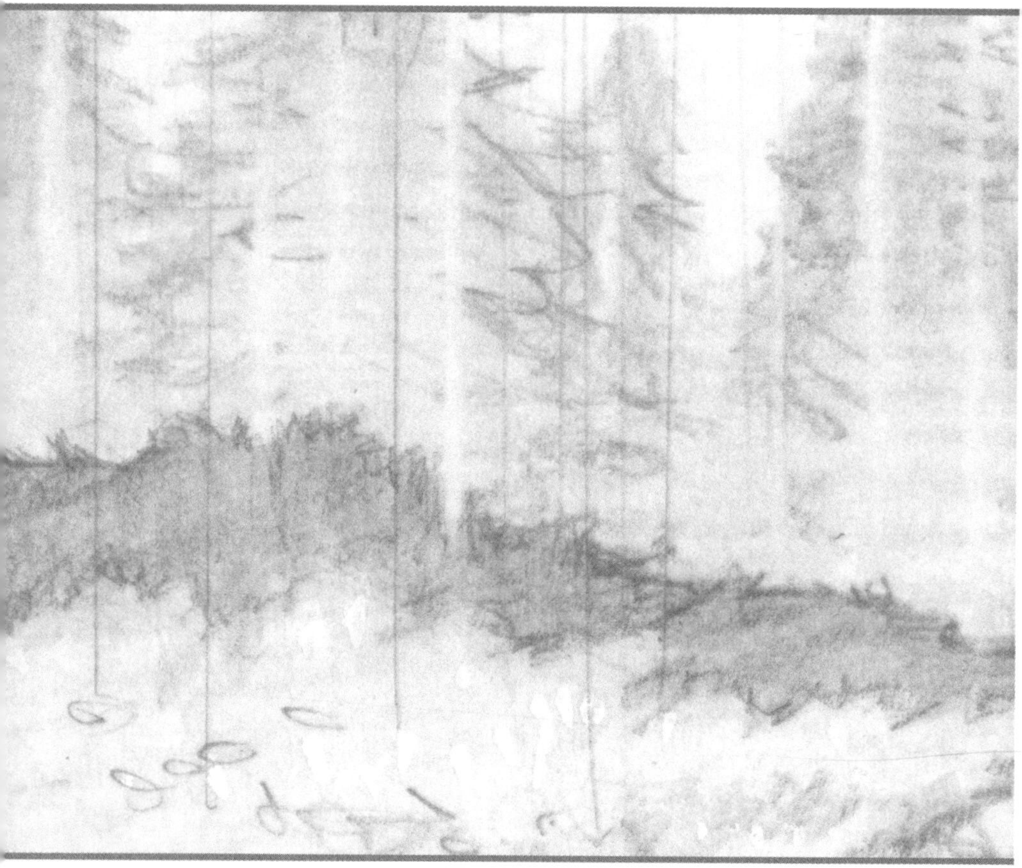

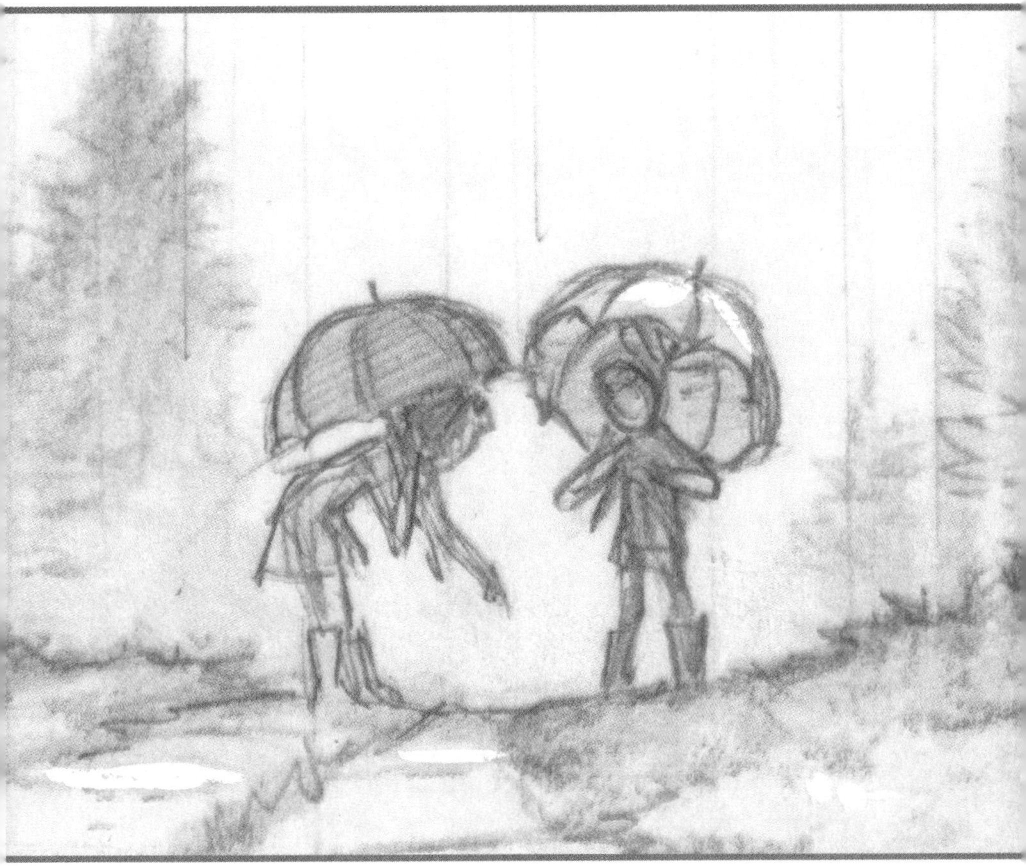

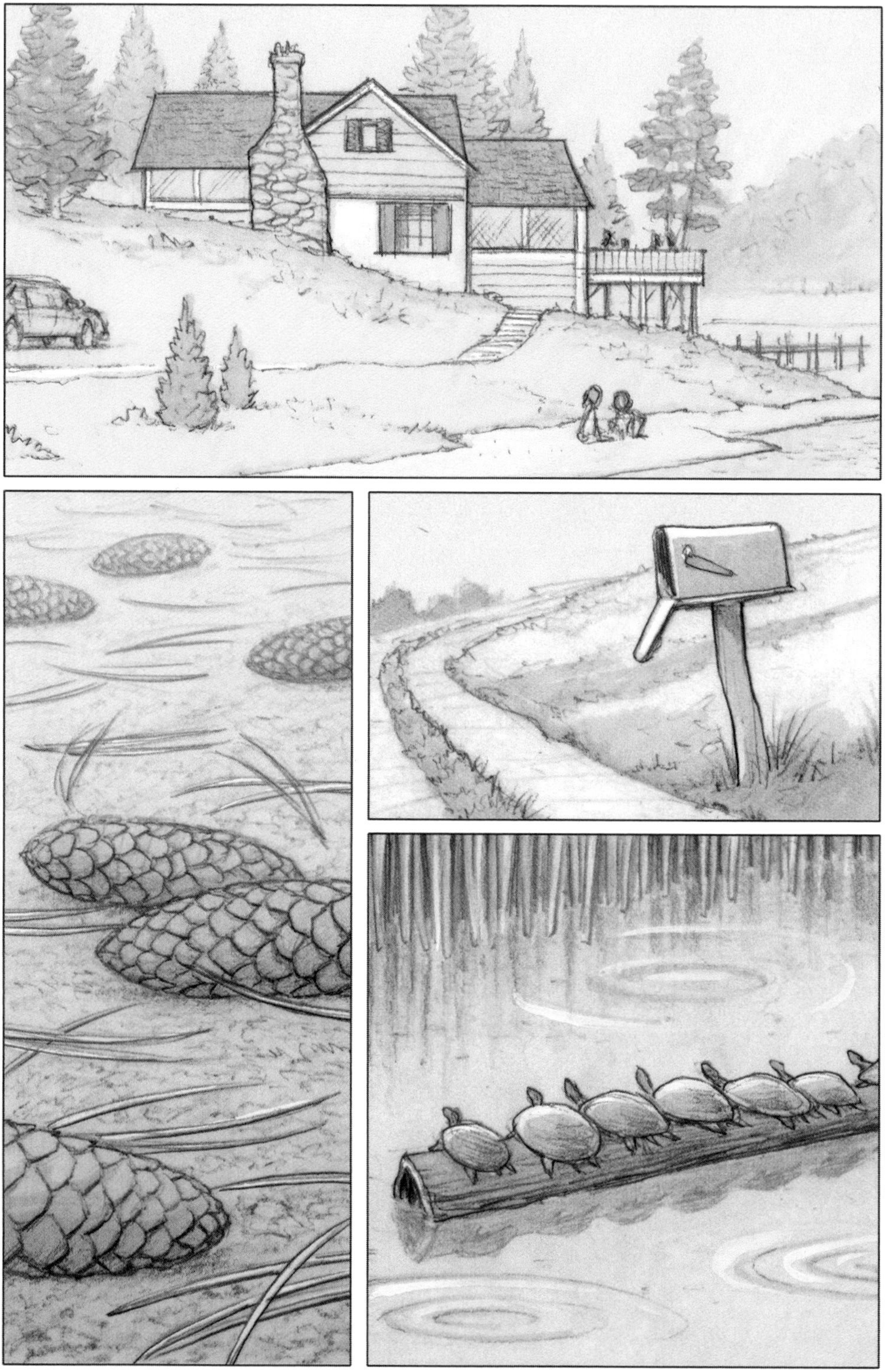

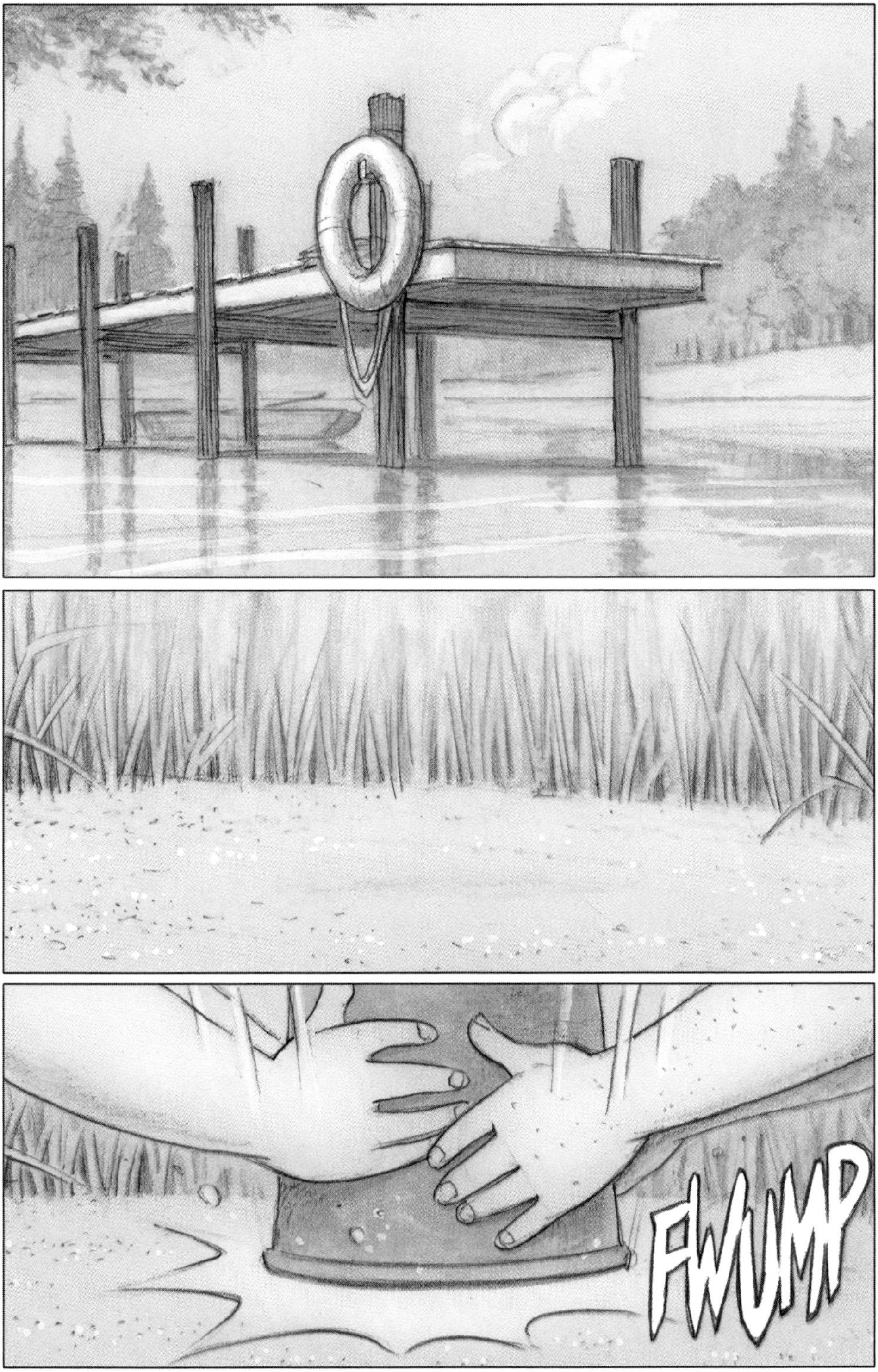
FWUMP

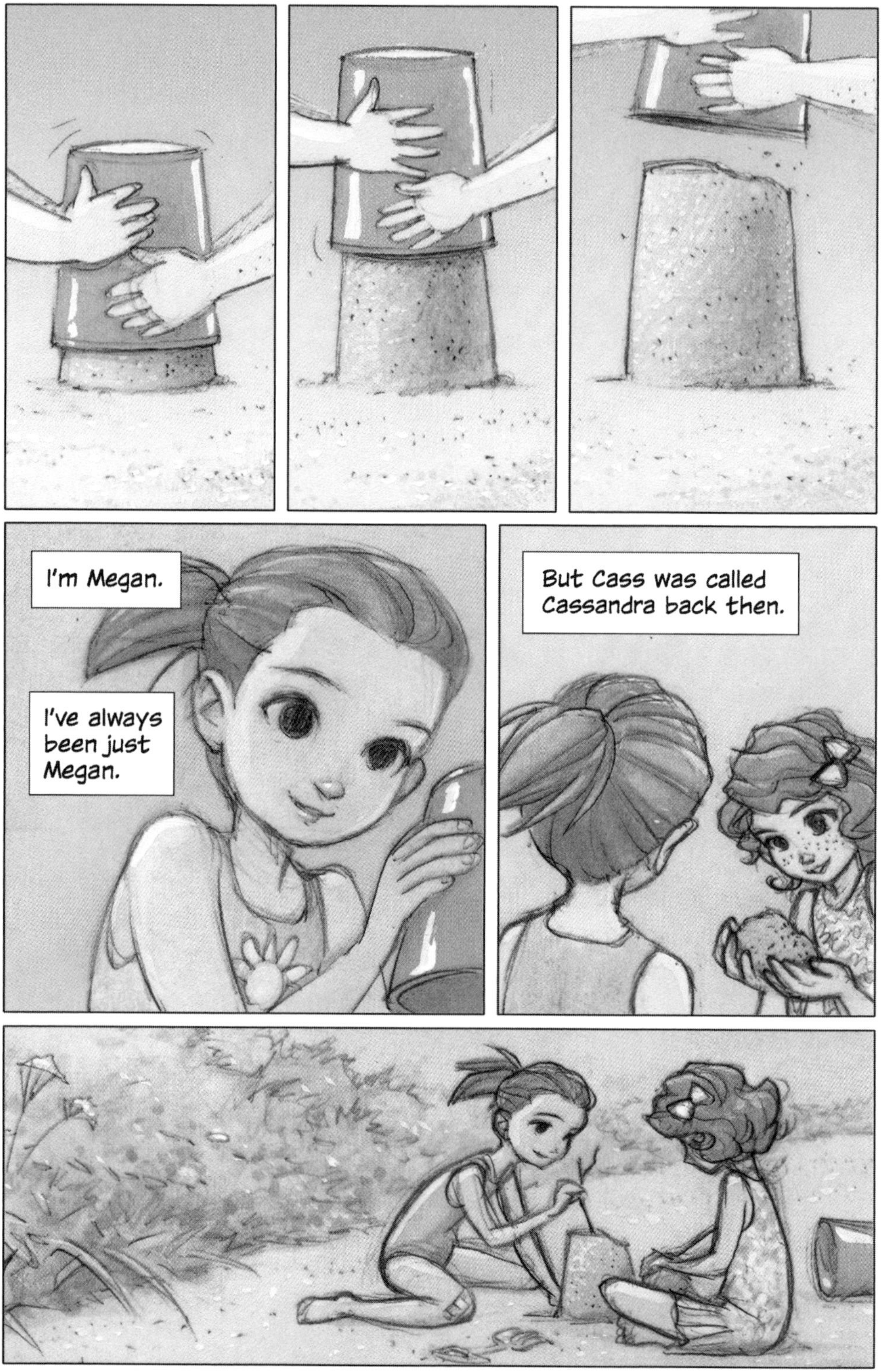

I'm Megan.
I've always been just Megan.
But Cass was called Cassandra back then.

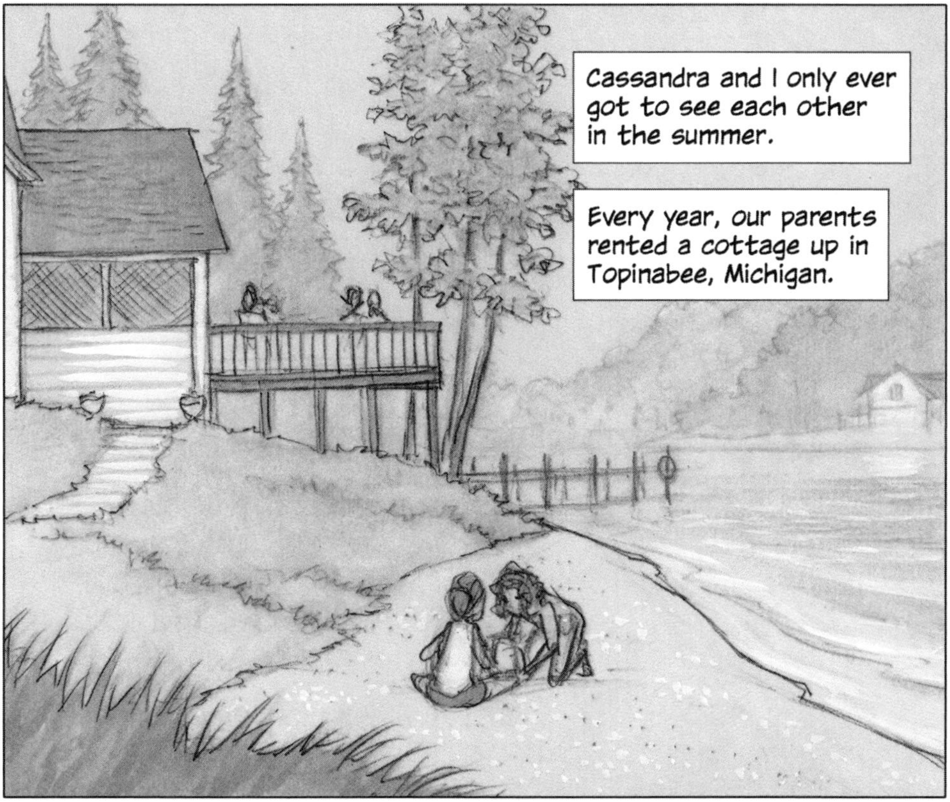
Cassandra and I only ever got to see each other in the summer.
Every year, our parents rented a cottage up in Topinabee, Michigan.

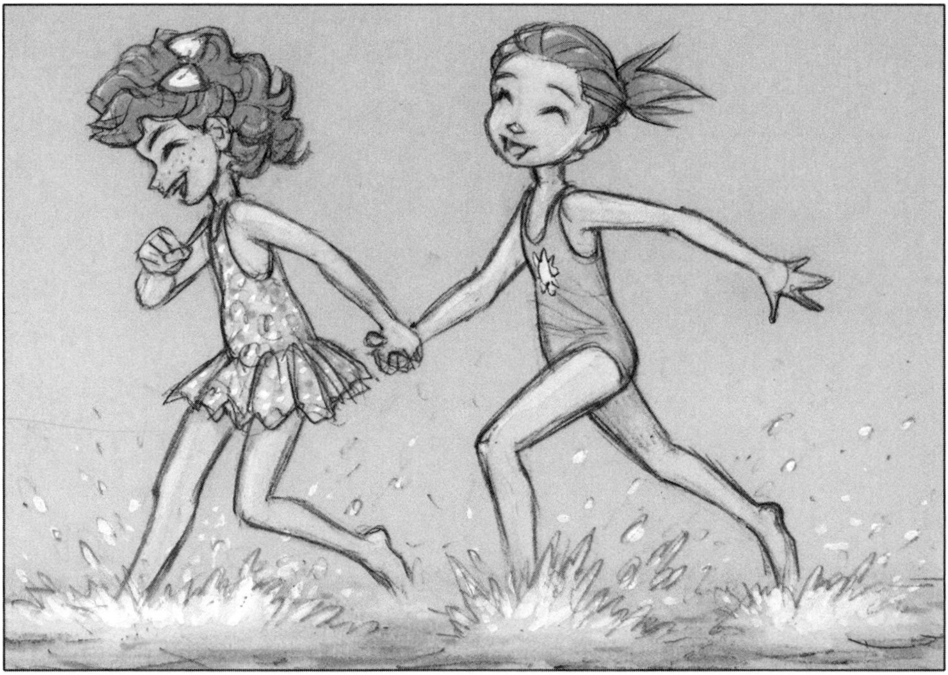

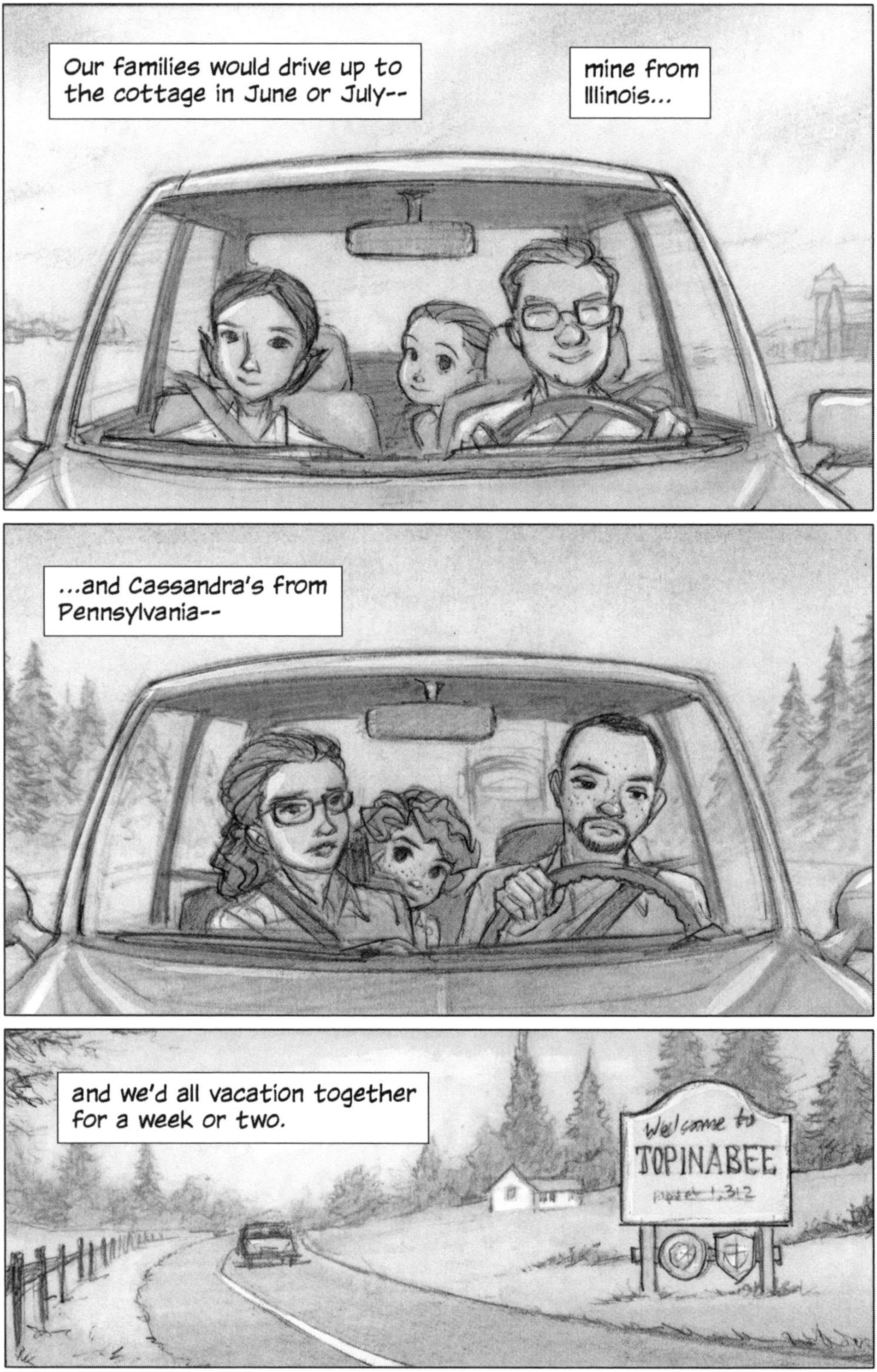
Our families would drive up to the cottage in June or July--
mine from Illinois...
...and Cassandra's from Pennsylvania--
and we'd all vacation together for a week or two.
Welcome to
TOPINABEE

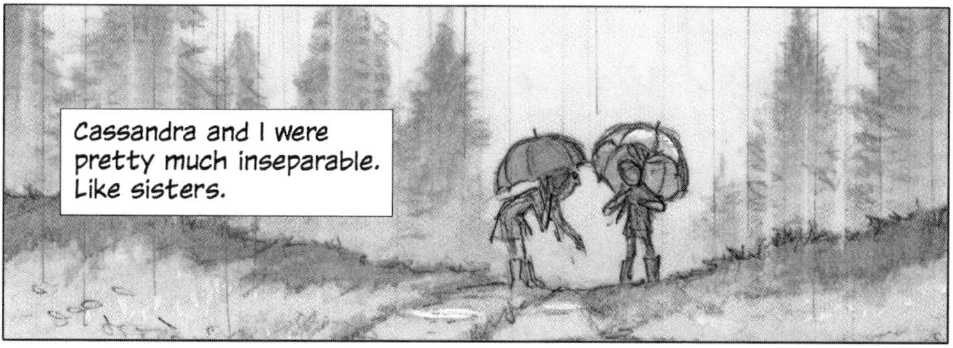
Cassandra and I were pretty much inseparable. Like sisters.

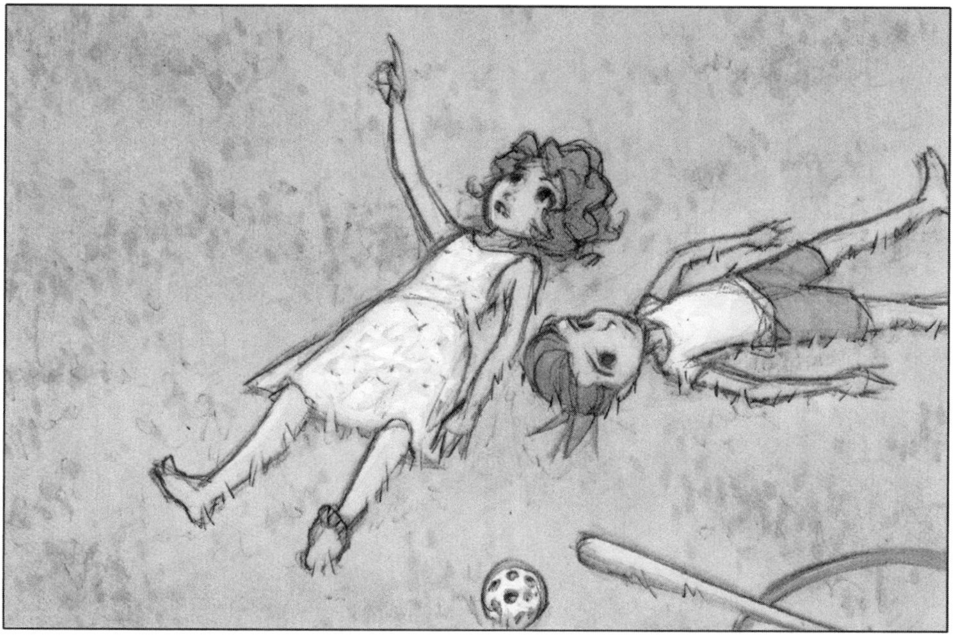

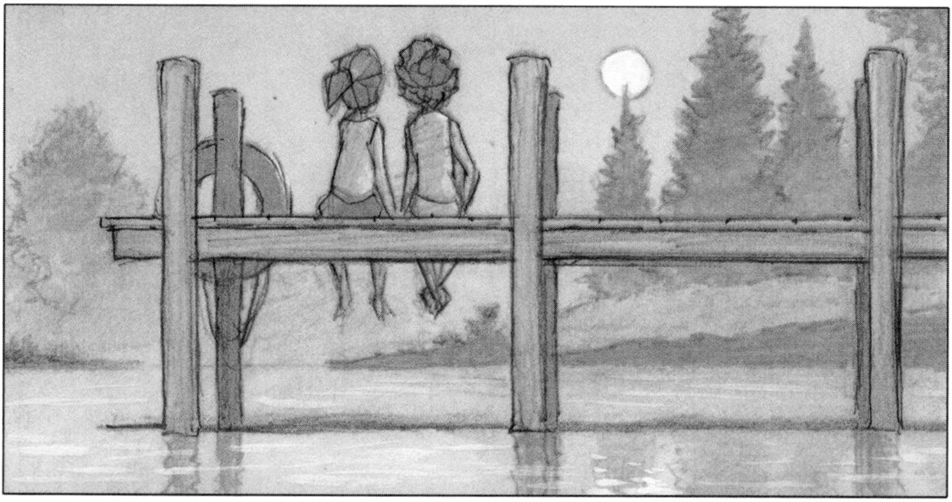

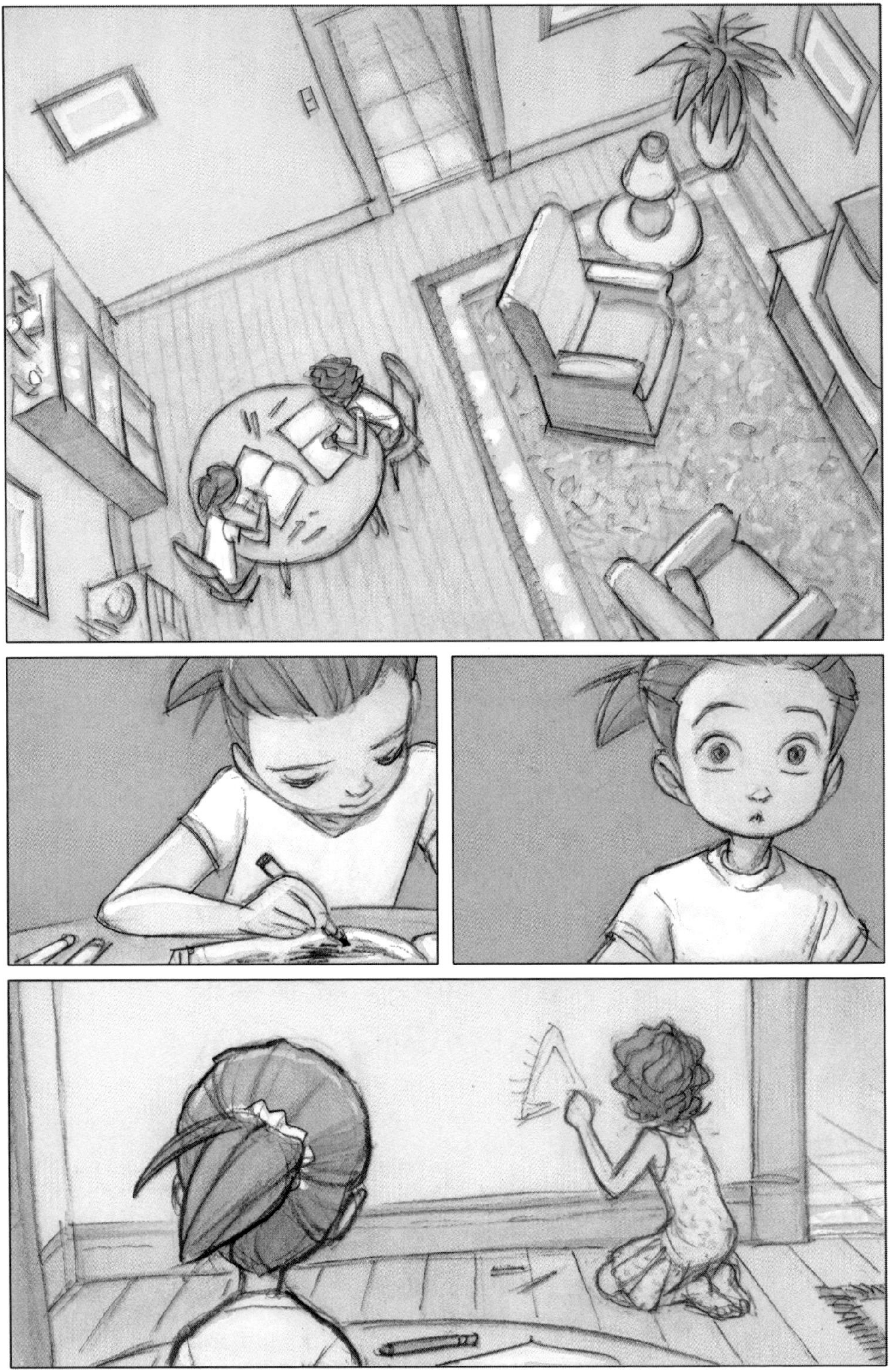

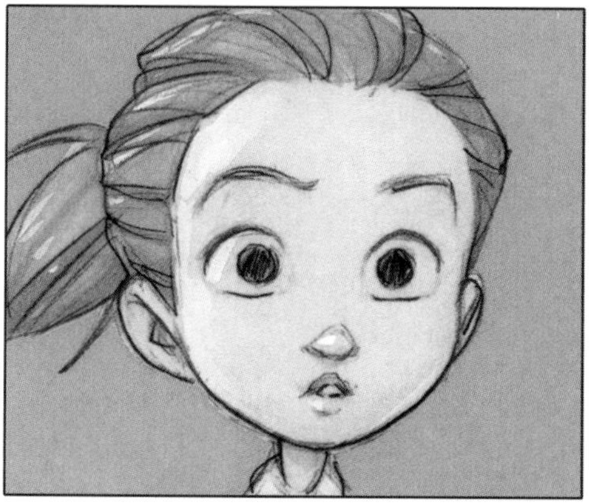
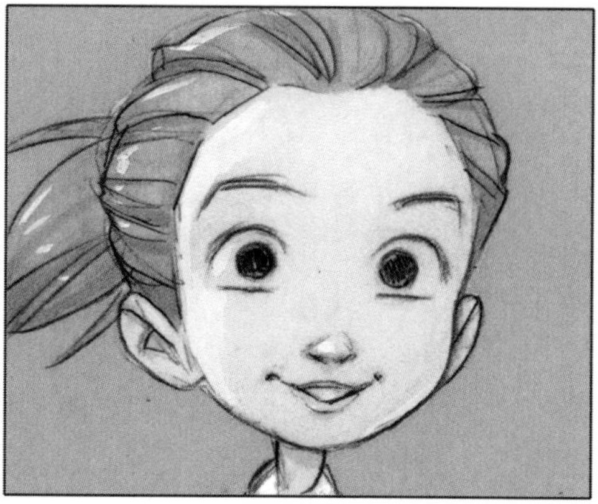
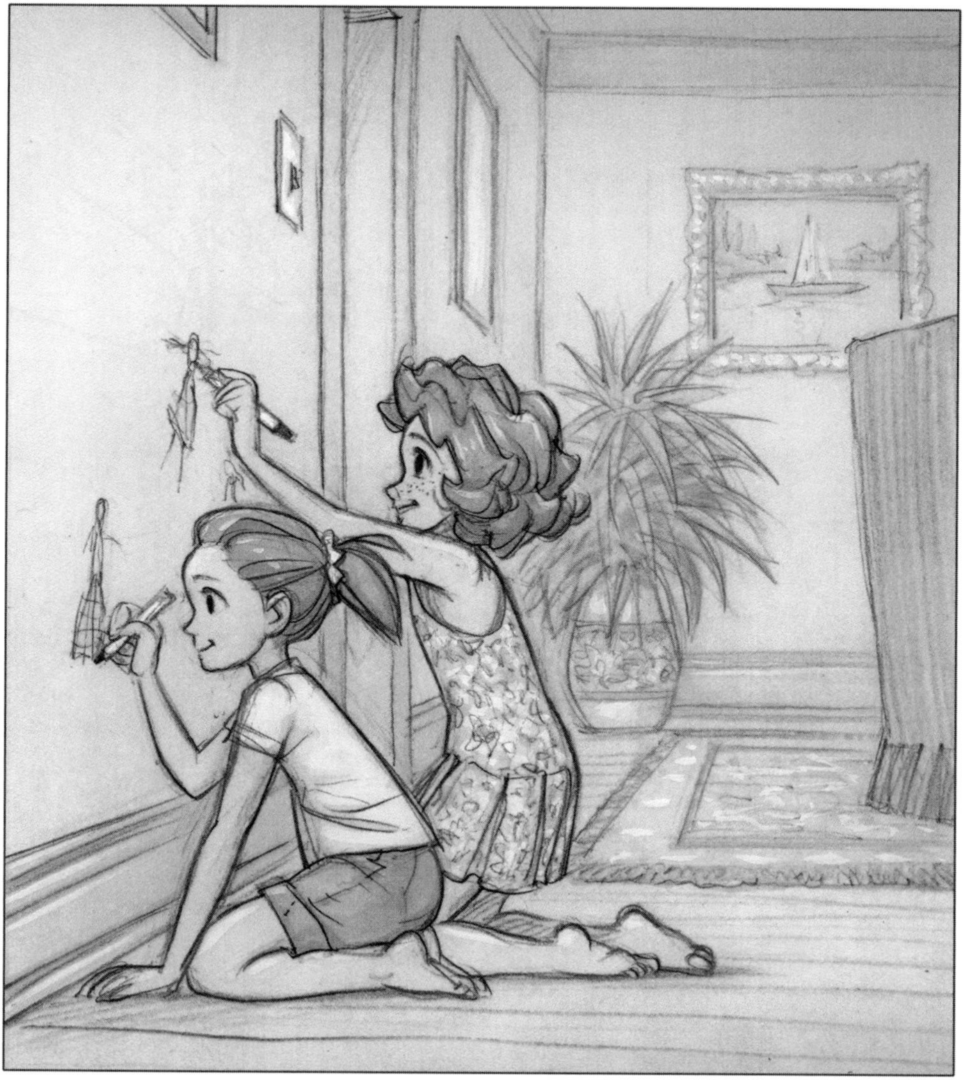

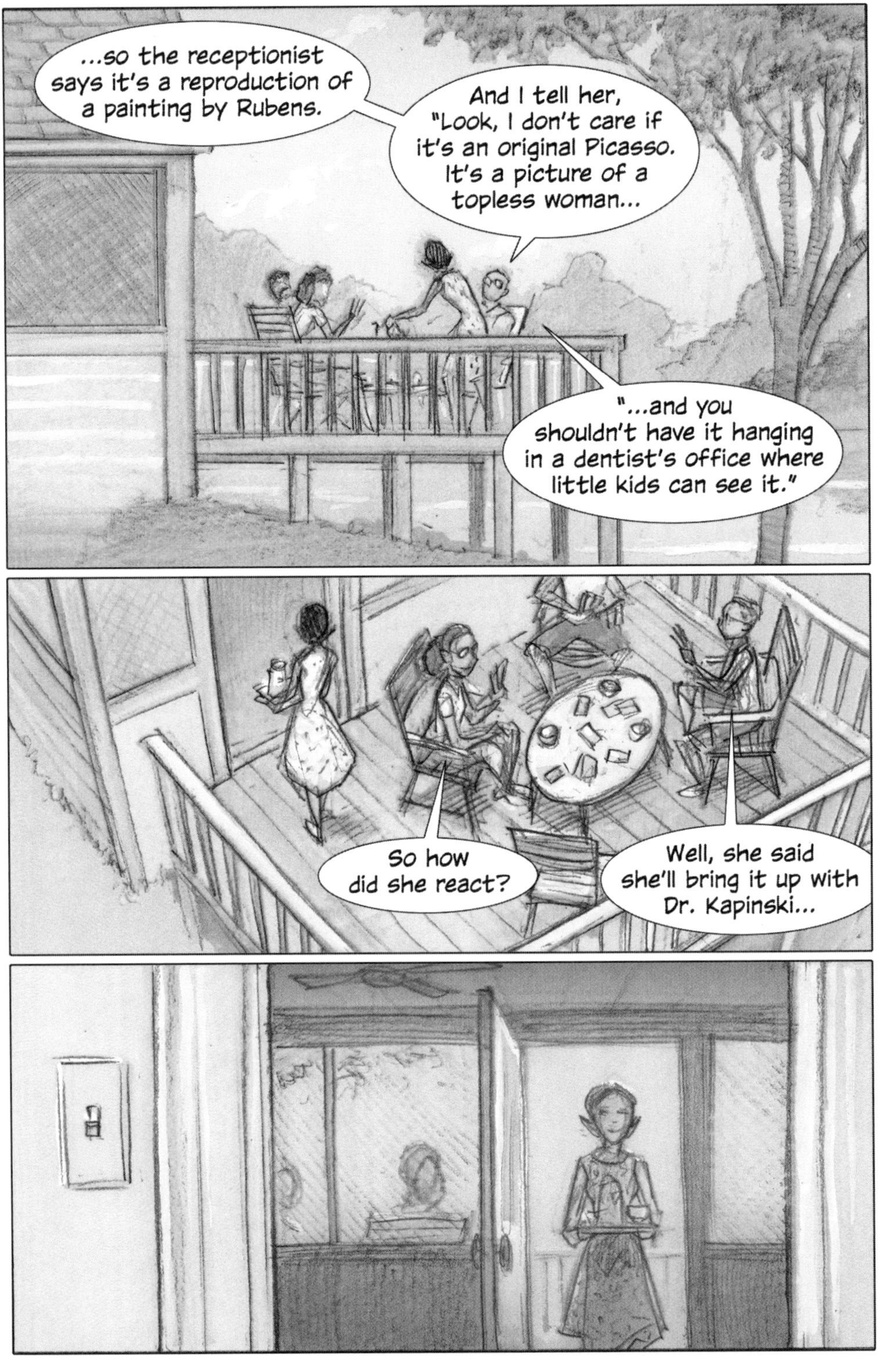
...so the receptionist says it's a reproduction of a painting by Rubens.
And I tell her, "Look, I don't care if it's an original Picasso. It's a picture of a topless woman...
"...and you shouldn't have it hanging in a dentist's office where little kids can see it."
So how did she react?
Well, she said she'll bring it up with Dr. Kapinski...

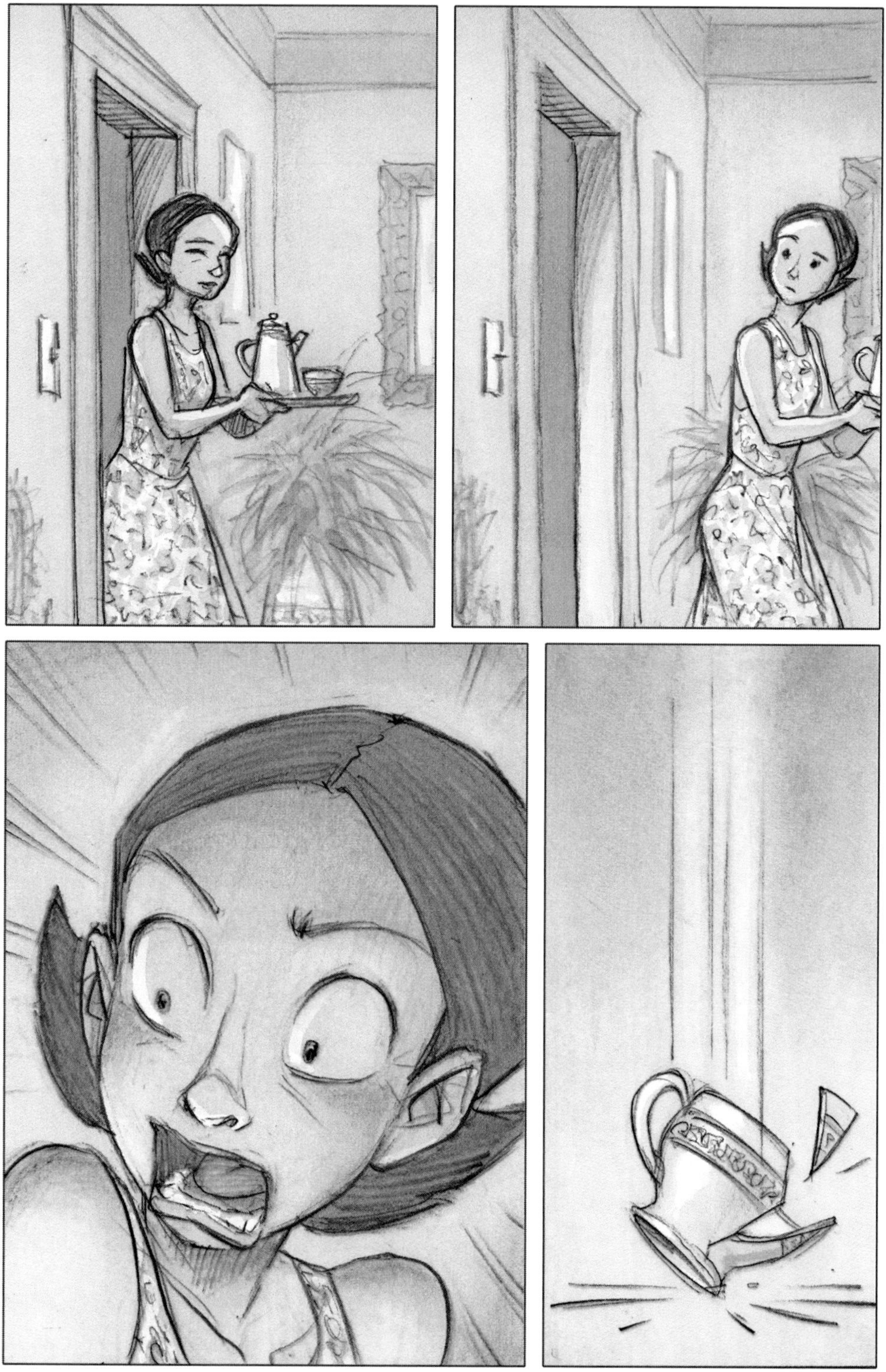

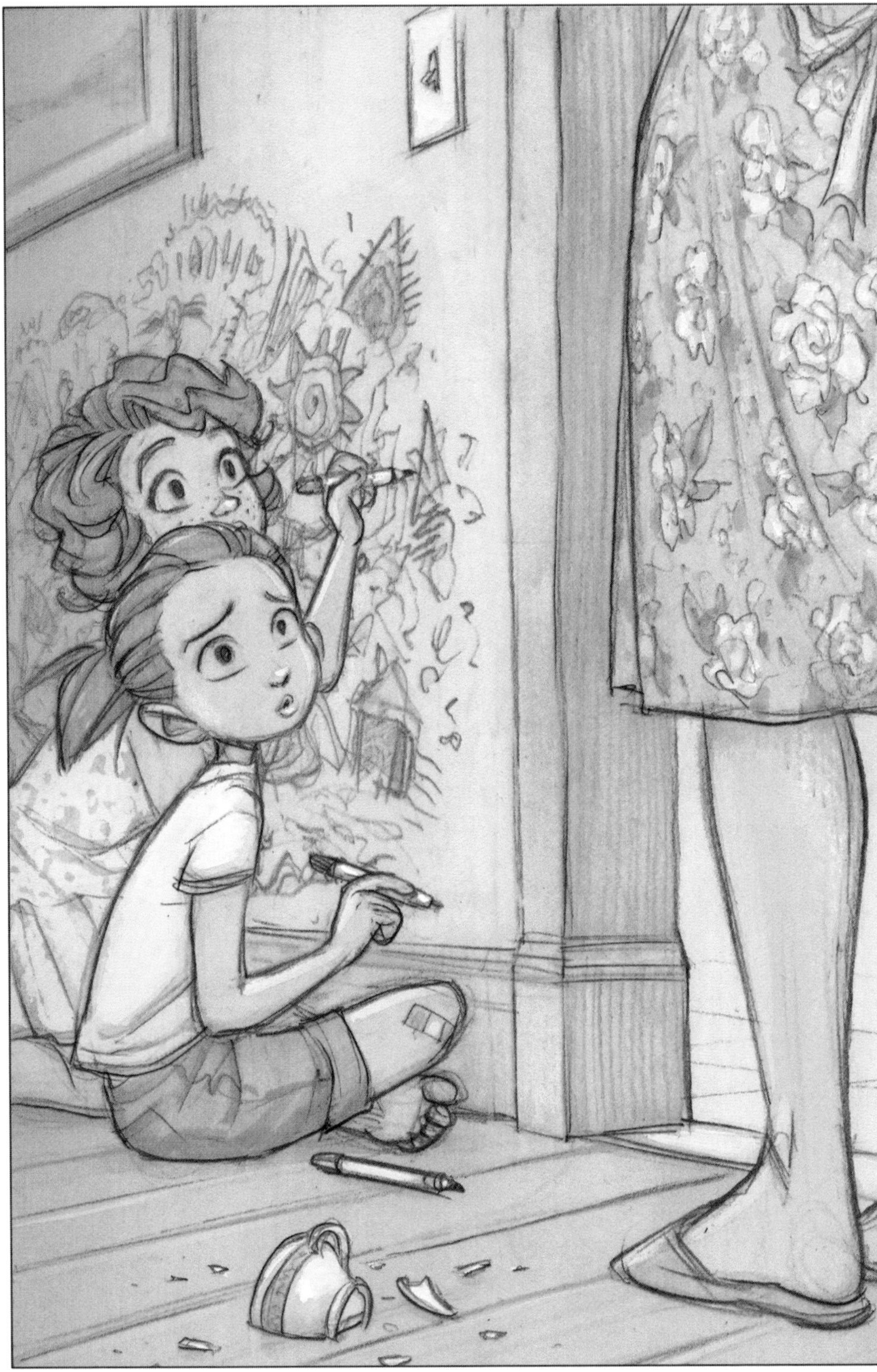

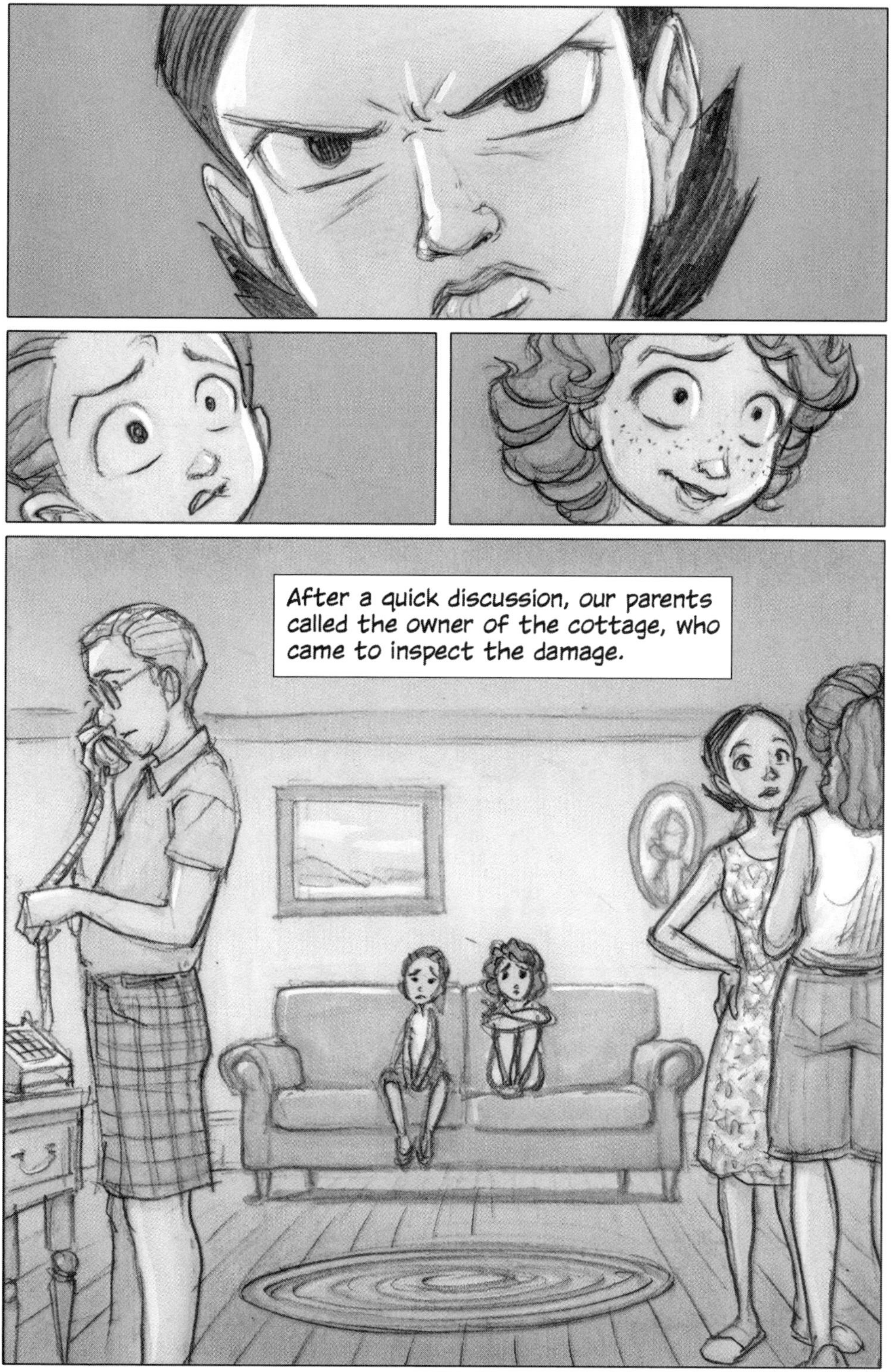
After a quick discussion, our parents called the owner of the cottage, who came to inspect the damage.

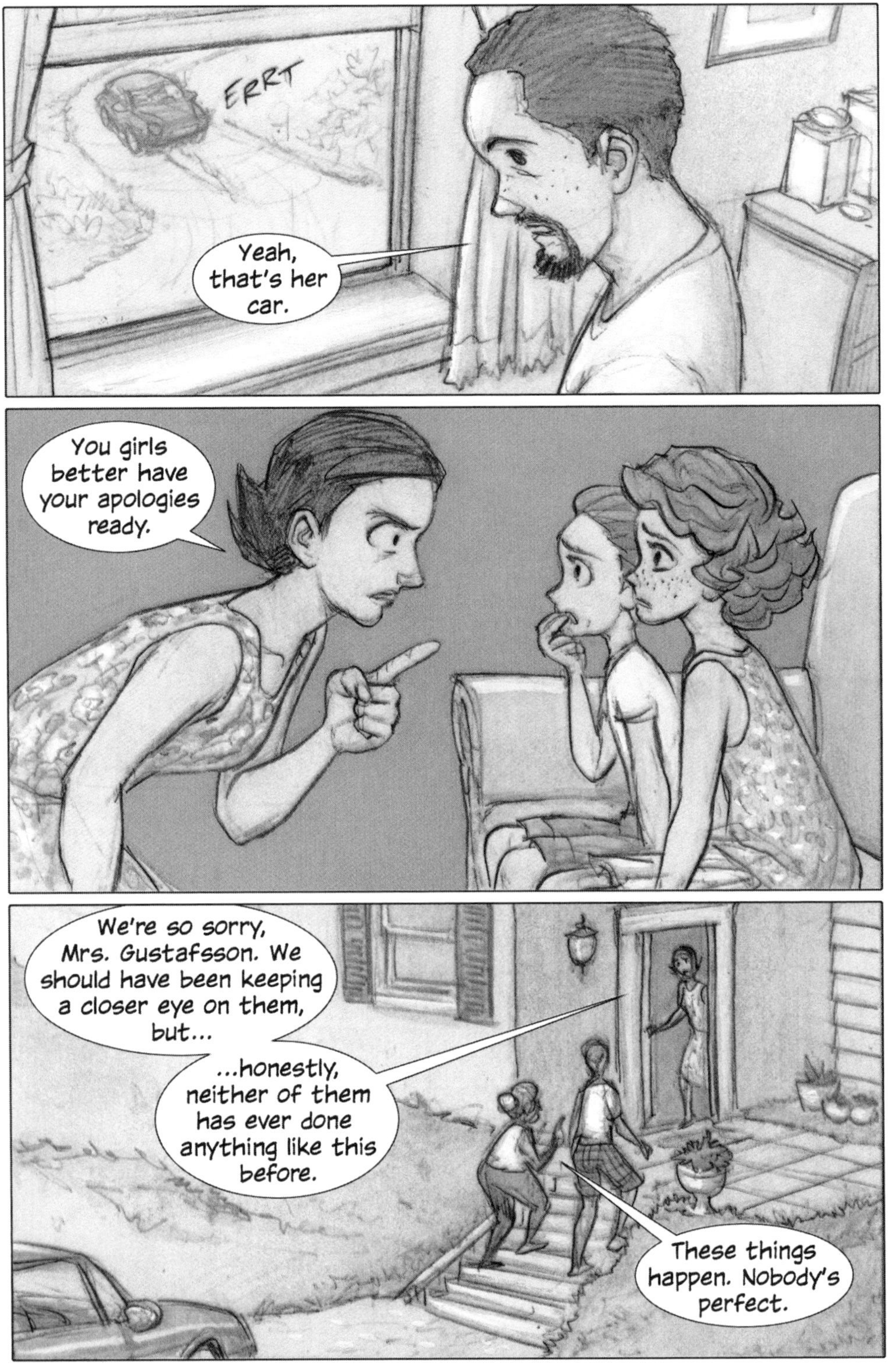
ERRT
Yeah, that's her car.
You girls better have your apologies ready.
We're so sorry, Mrs. Gustafsson. We should have been keeping a closer eye on them, but...
...honestly, neither of them has ever done anything like this before.
These things happen. Nobody's perfect.

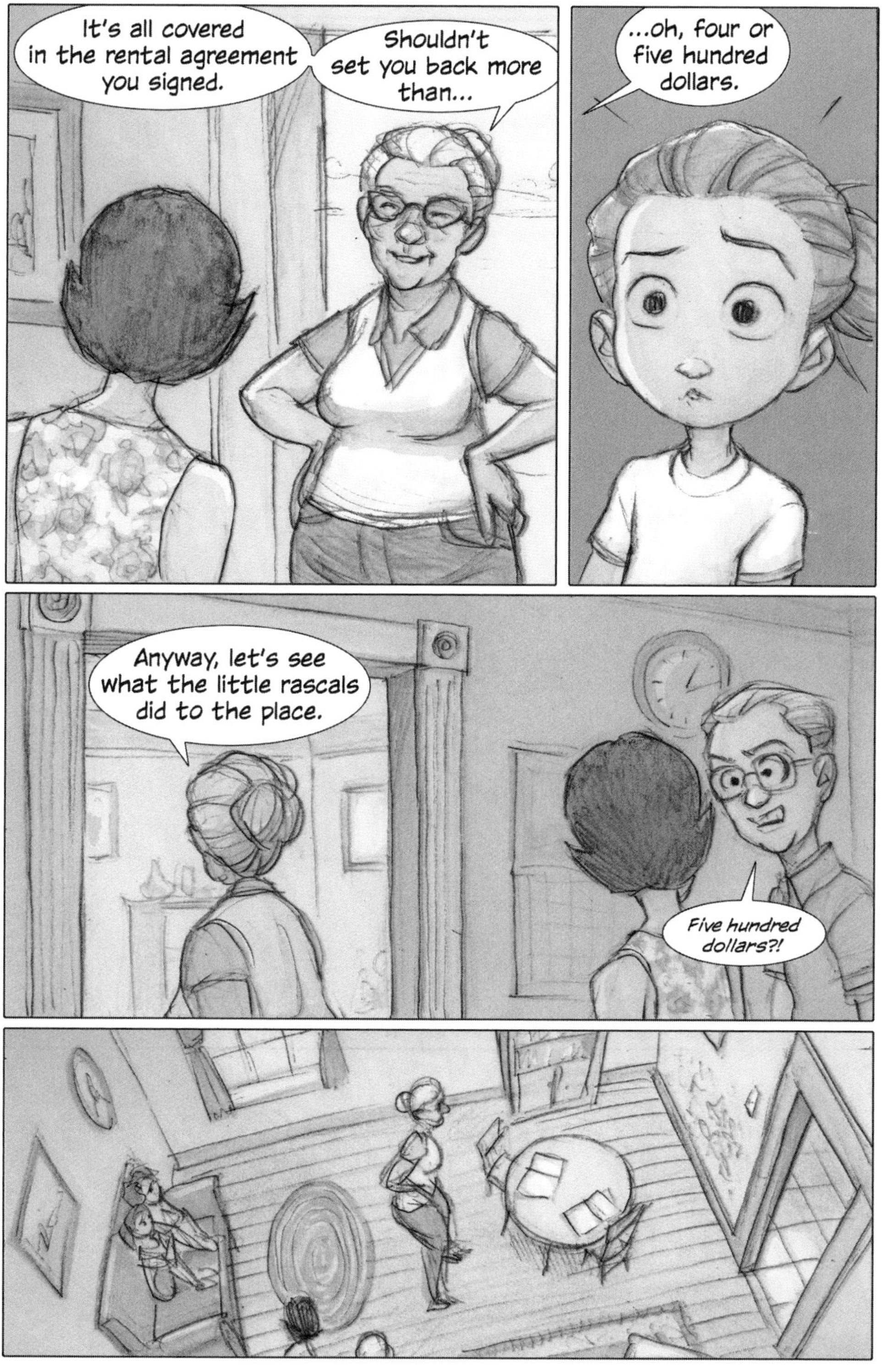
It's all covered in the rental agreement you signed.
Shouldn't set you back more than...
...oh, four or five hundred dollars.
Anyway, let's see what the little rascals did to the place.
Five hundred dollars?!

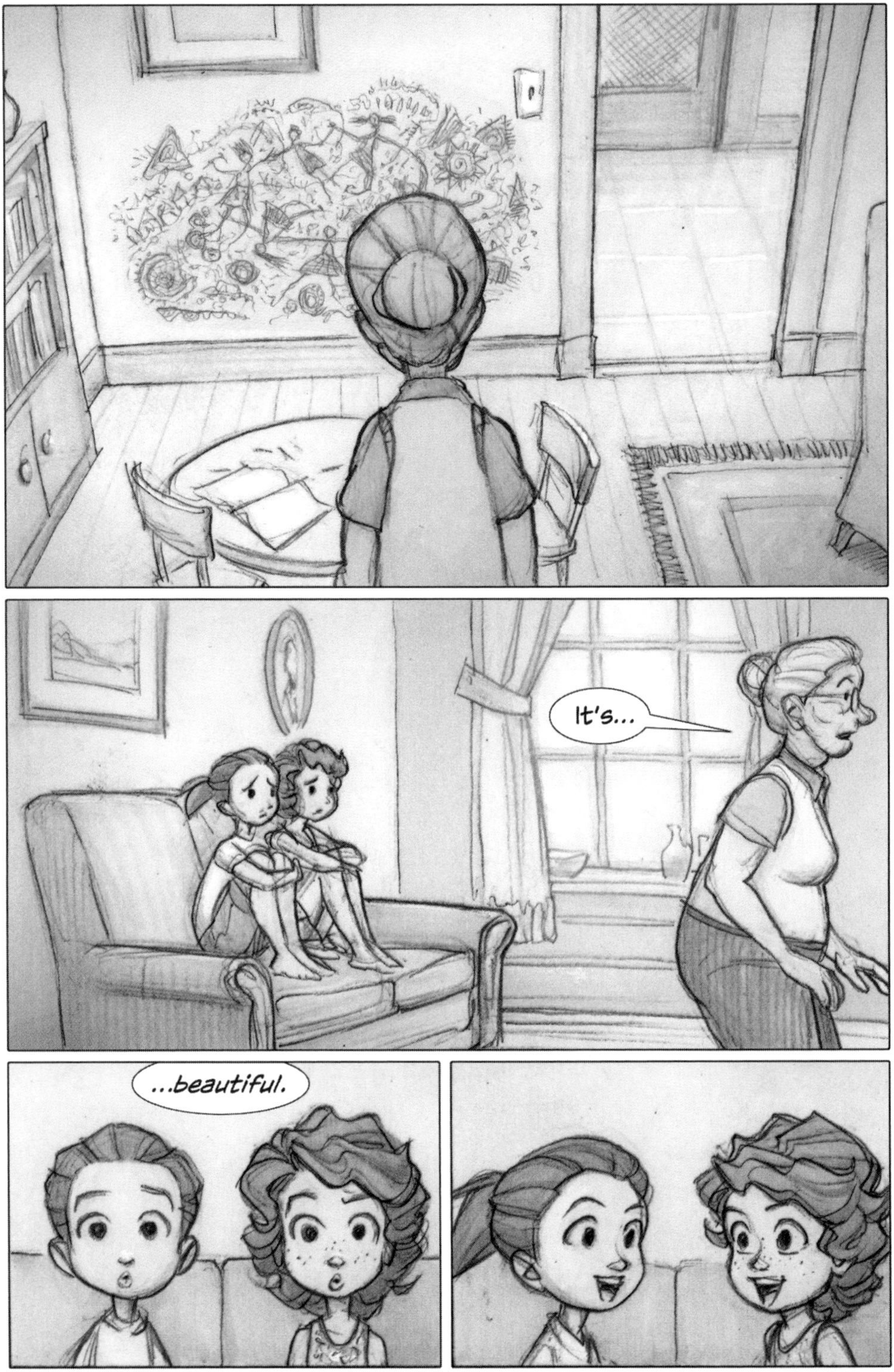
It's...
...beautiful.

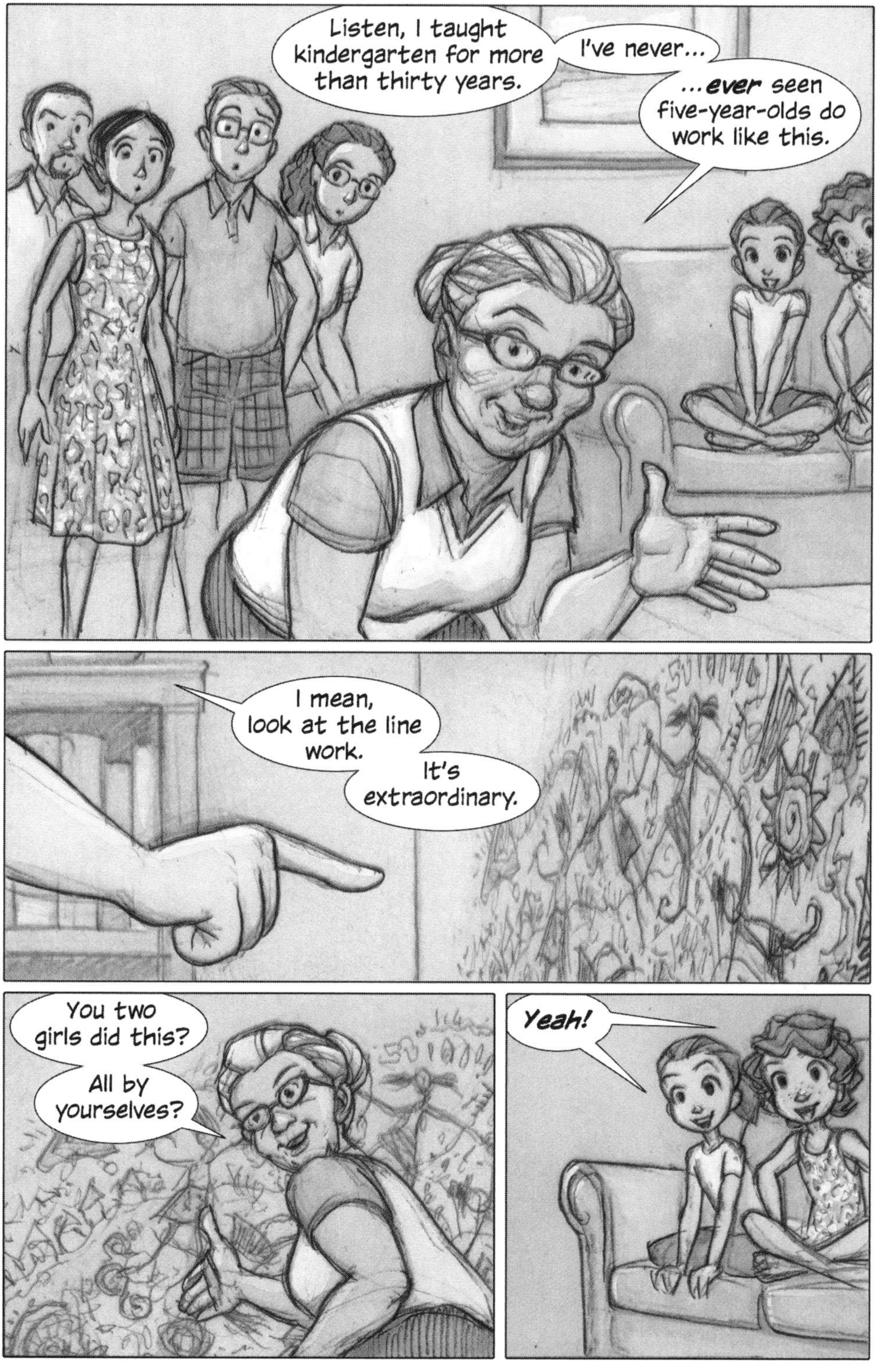
Listen, I taught kindergarten for more than thirty years.
I've never...
...ever seen five-year-olds do work like this.
I mean, look at the line work.
It's extraordinary.
You two girls did this?
All by yourselves?
Yeah!

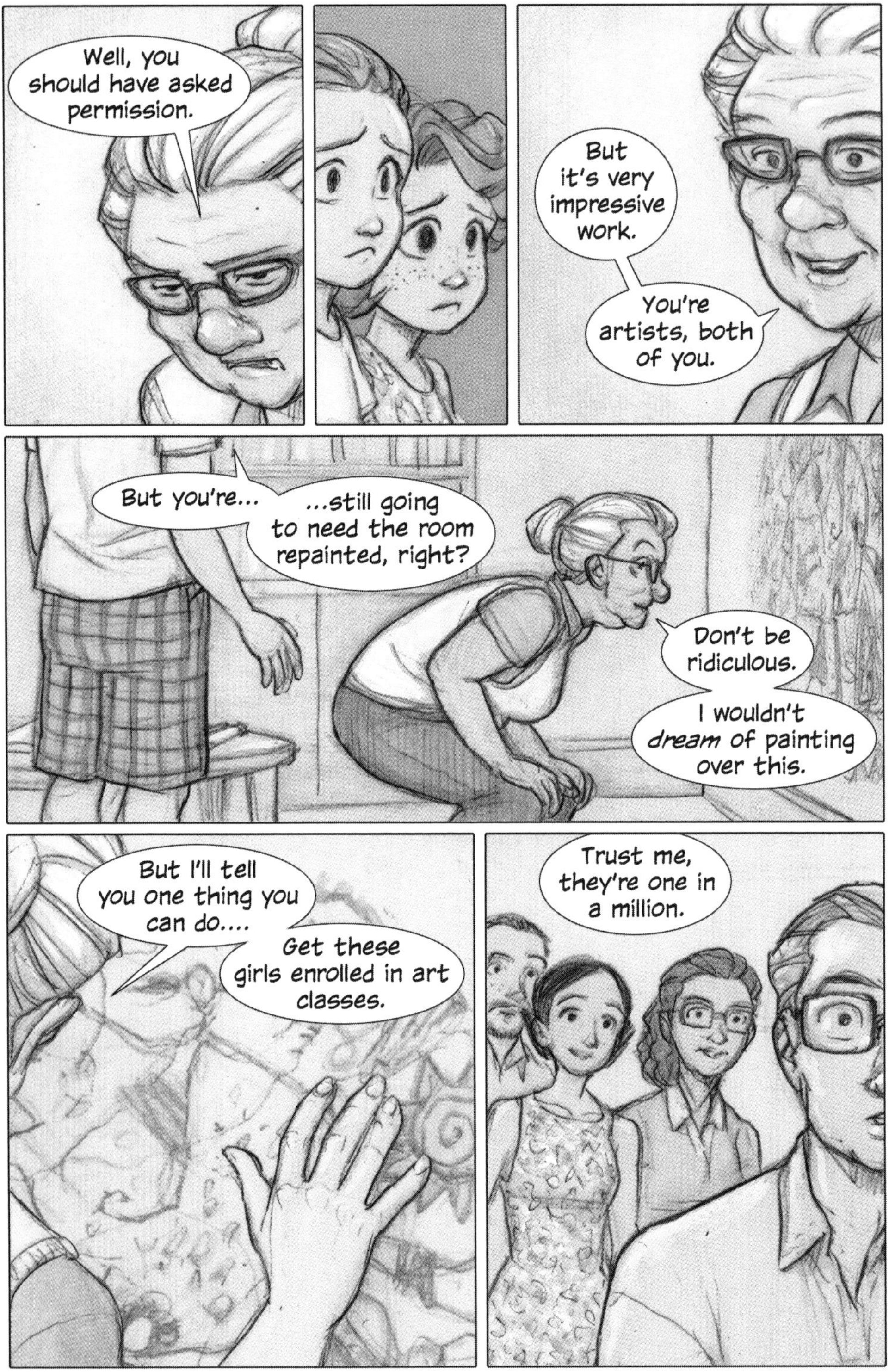
Well, you should have asked permission.
But it's very impressive work.
You're artists, both of you.
But you're...
...still going to need the room repainted, right?
Don't be ridiculous.
I wouldn't *dream* of painting over this.
But I'll tell you one thing you can do....
Get these girls enrolled in art classes.
Trust me, they're one in a million.

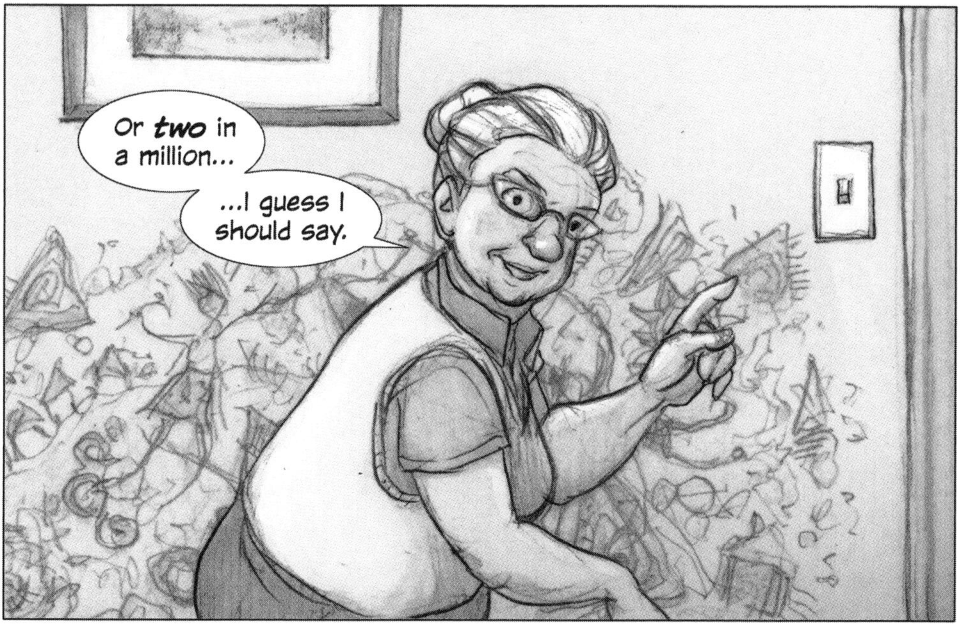
Or **two** in a million...
...I guess I should say.

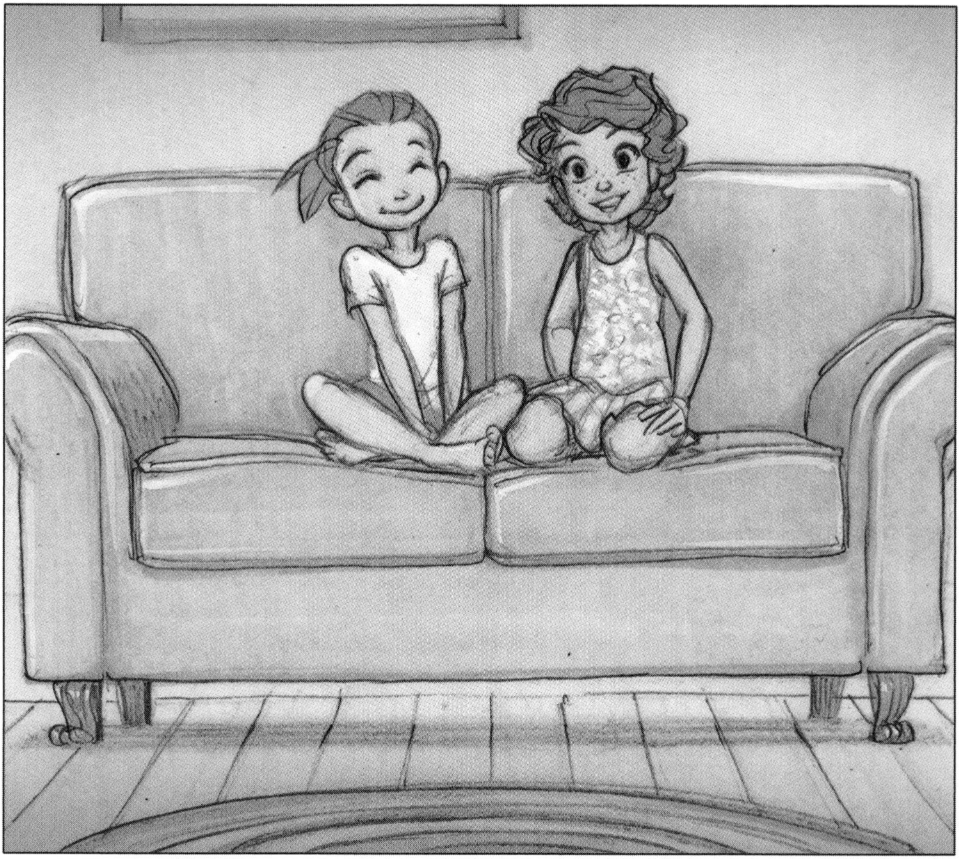

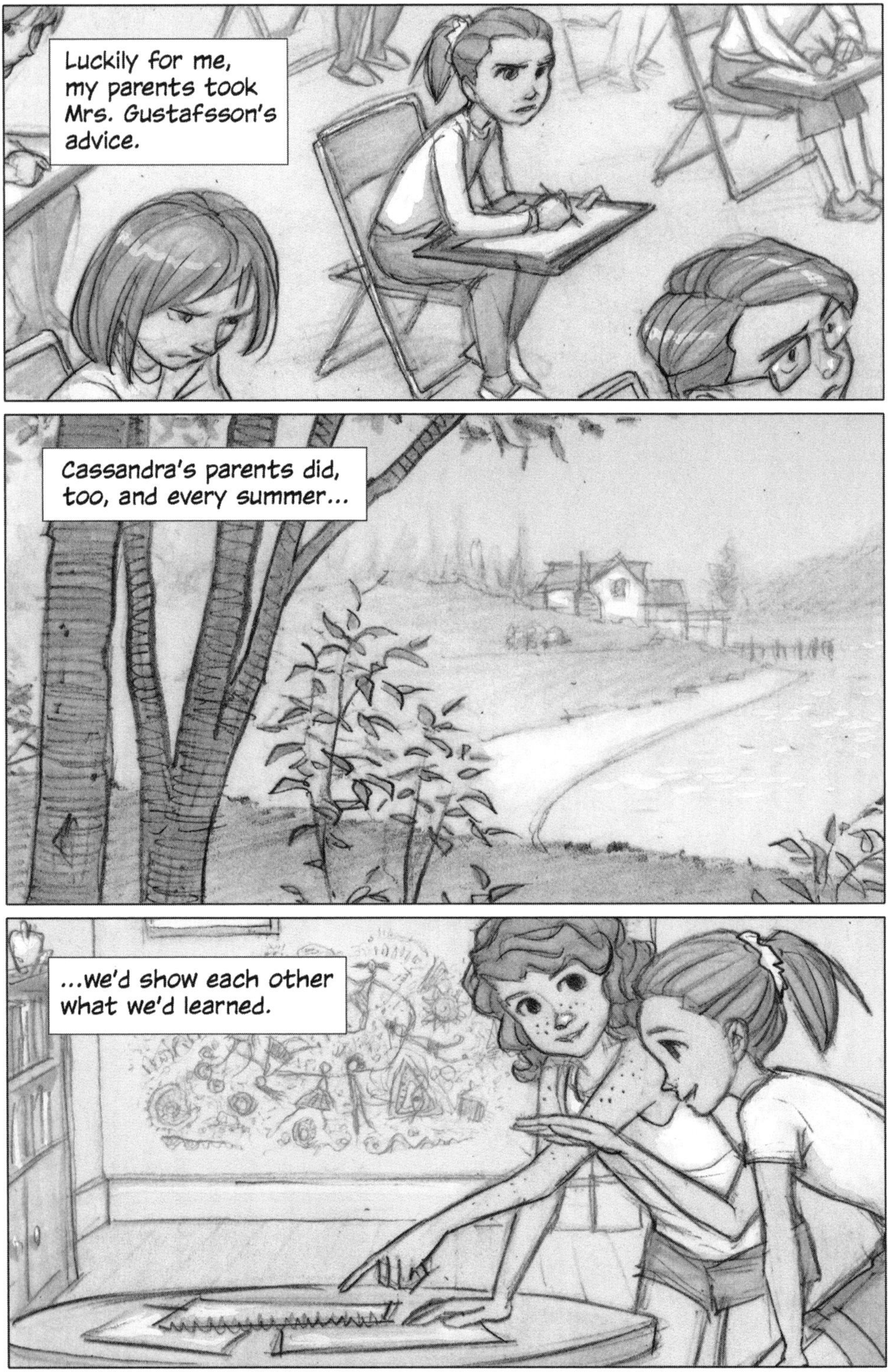
Luckily for me, my parents took Mrs. Gustafsson's advice.
Cassandra's parents did, too, and every summer...
...we'd show each other what we'd learned.

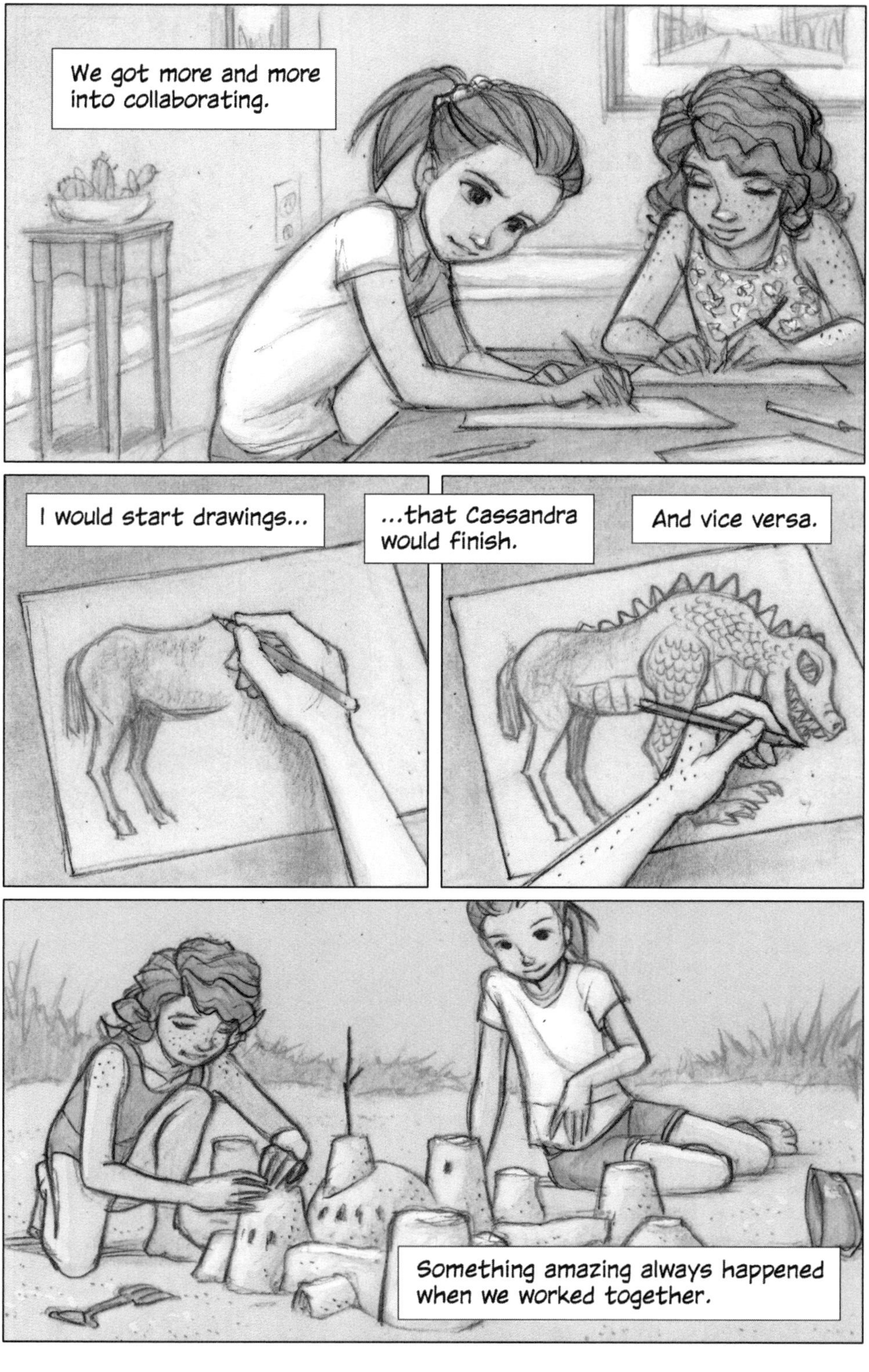
We got more and more into collaborating.
I would start drawings...
...that Cassandra would finish.
And vice versa.
Something amazing always happened when we worked together.

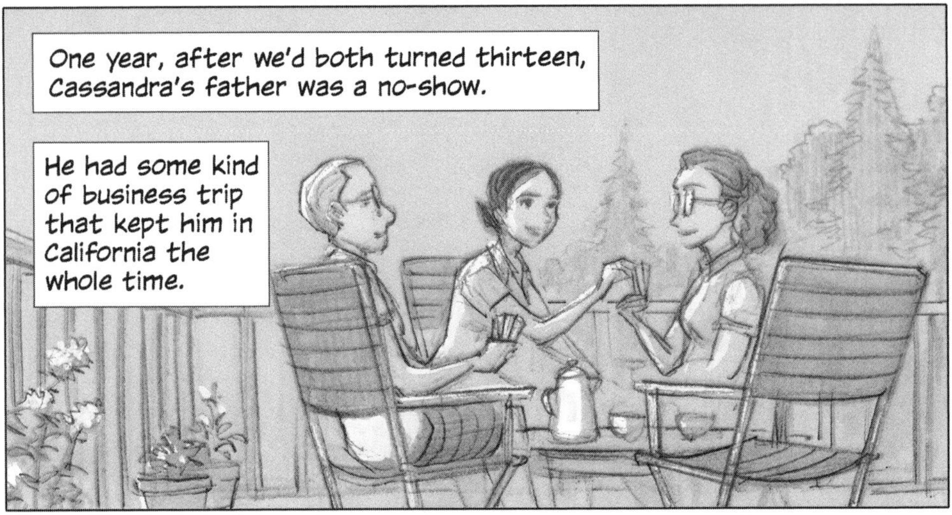
One year, after we'd both turned thirteen, Cassandra's father was a no-show.
He had some kind of business trip that kept him in California the whole time.

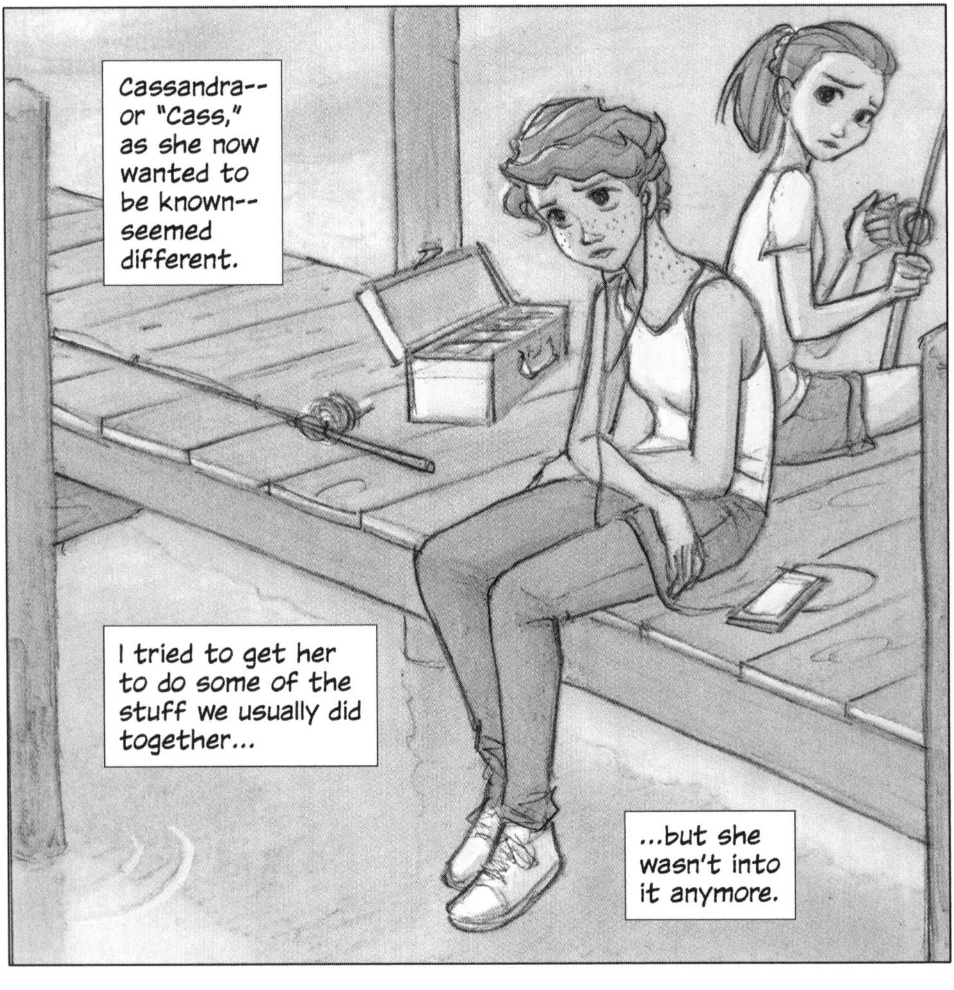
Cassandra--or "Cass," as she now wanted to be known--seemed different.
I tried to get her to do some of the stuff we usually did together...
...but she wasn't into it anymore.

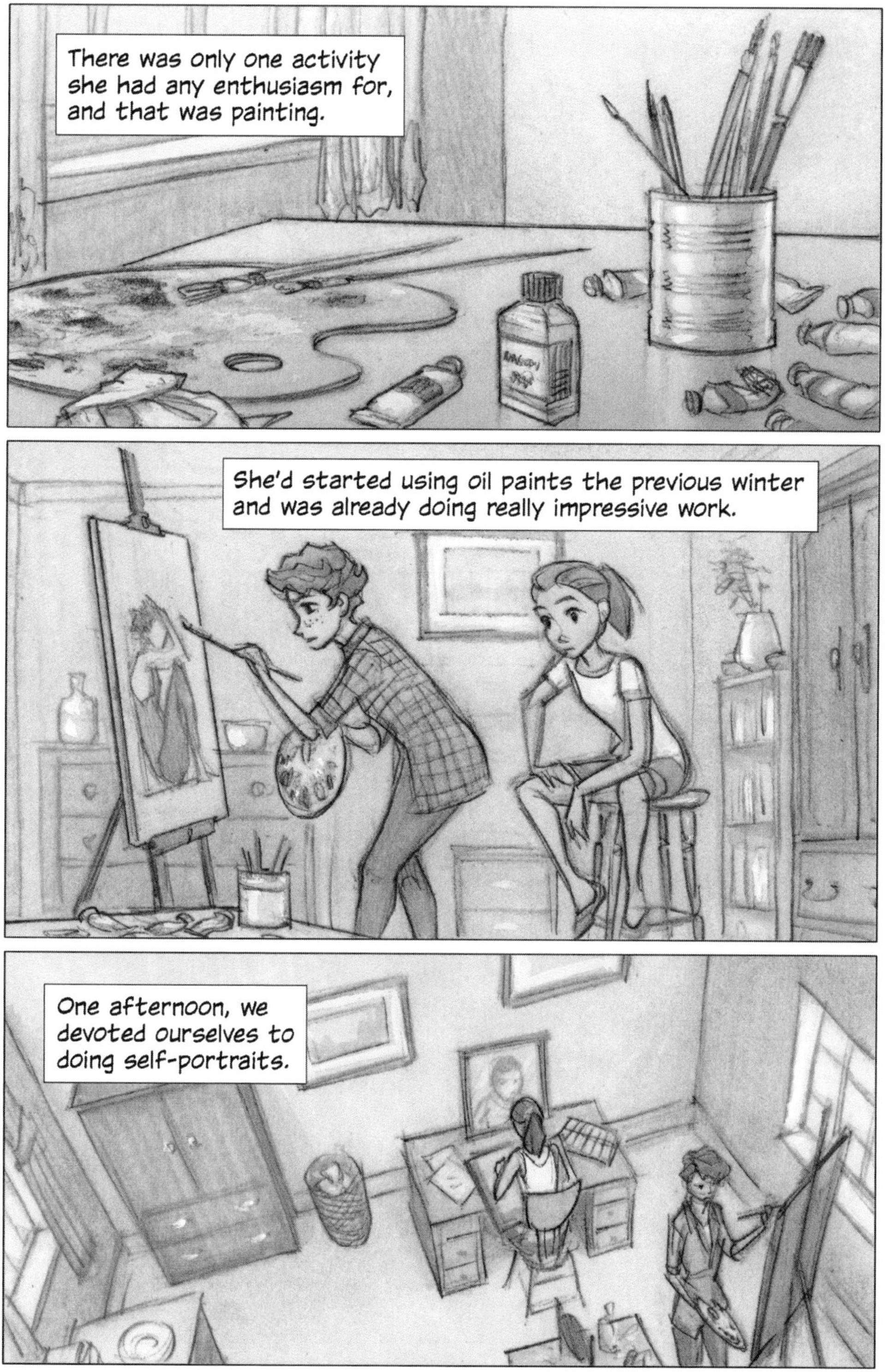
There was only one activity she had any enthusiasm for, and that was painting.
She'd started using oil paints the previous winter and was already doing really impressive work.
One afternoon, we devoted ourselves to doing self-portraits.

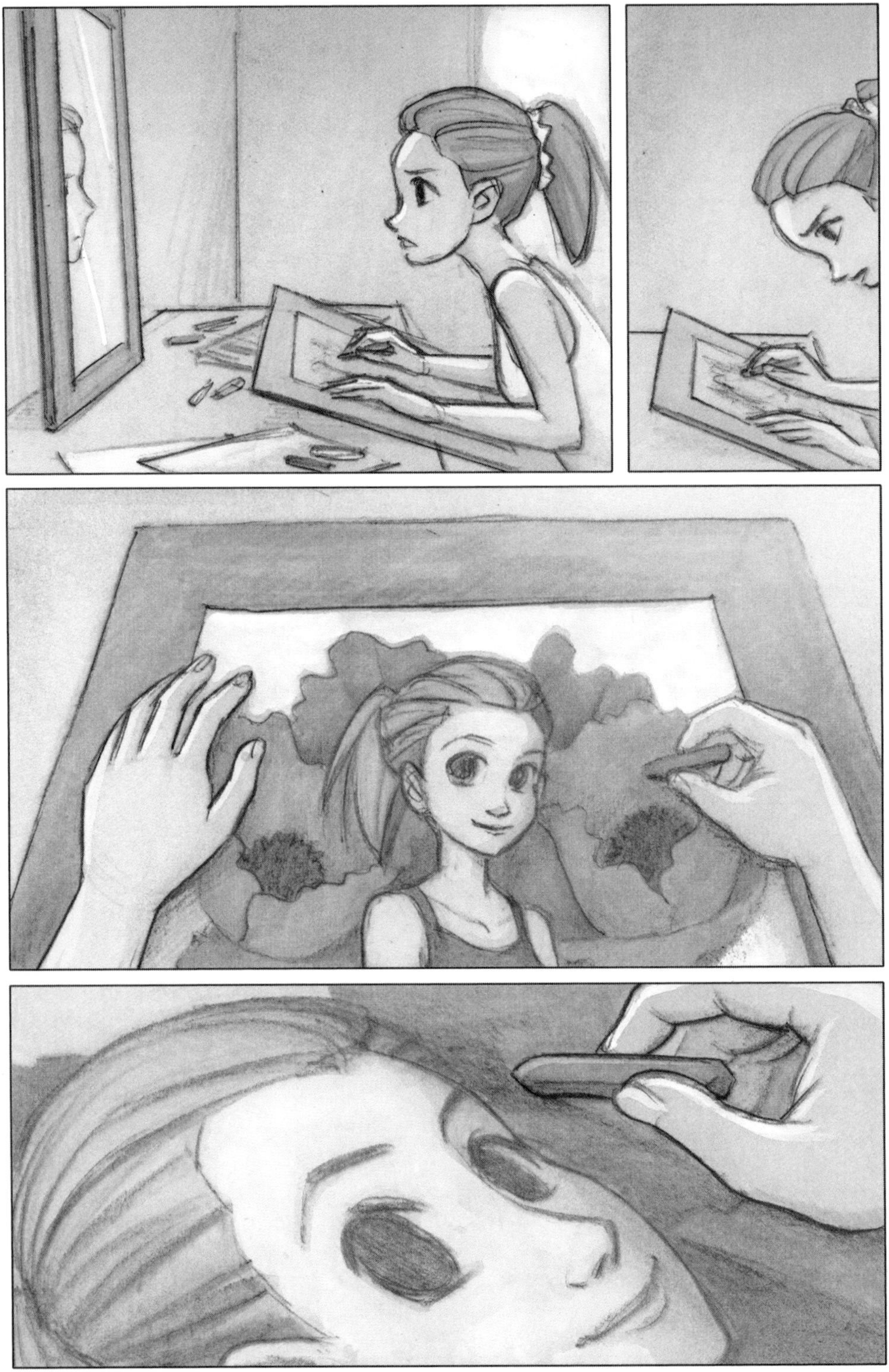

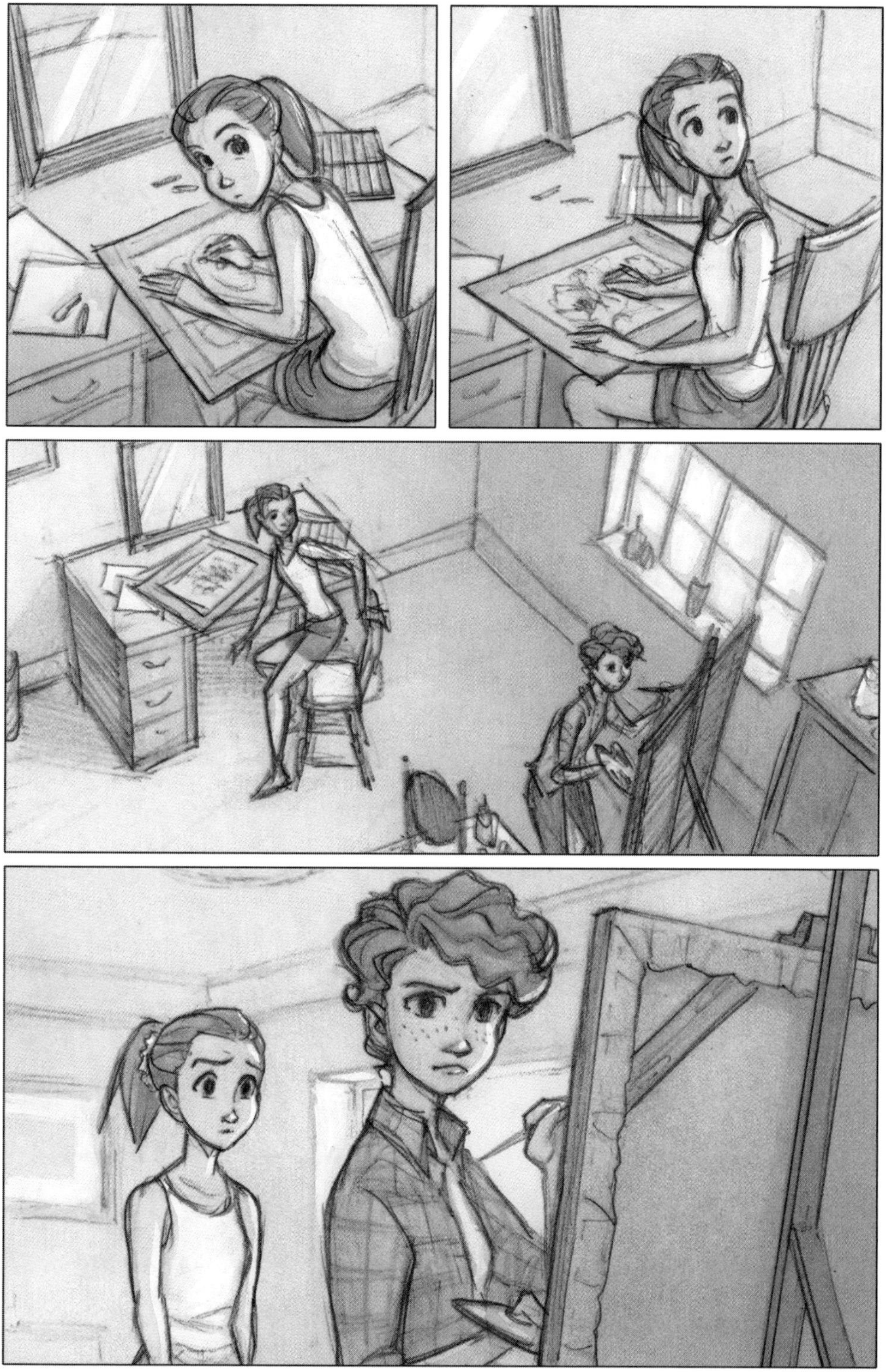

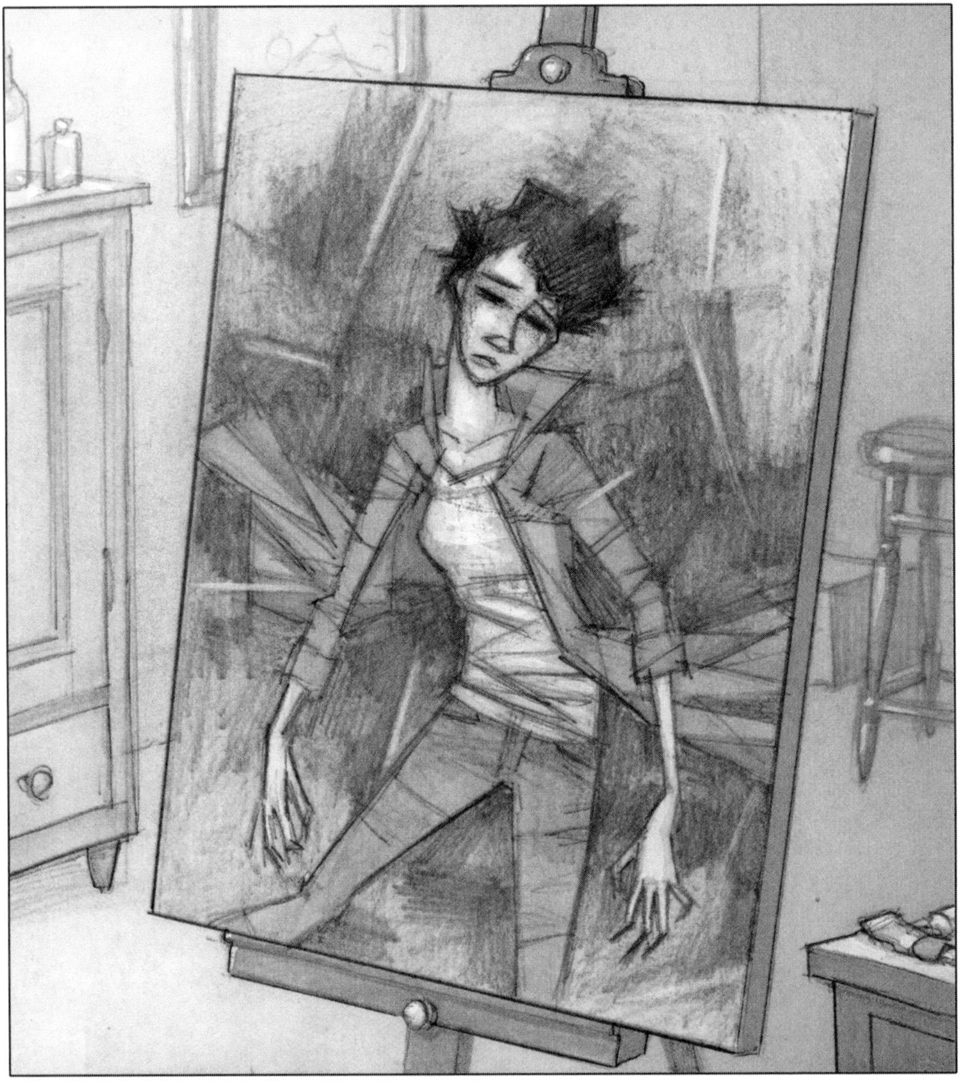
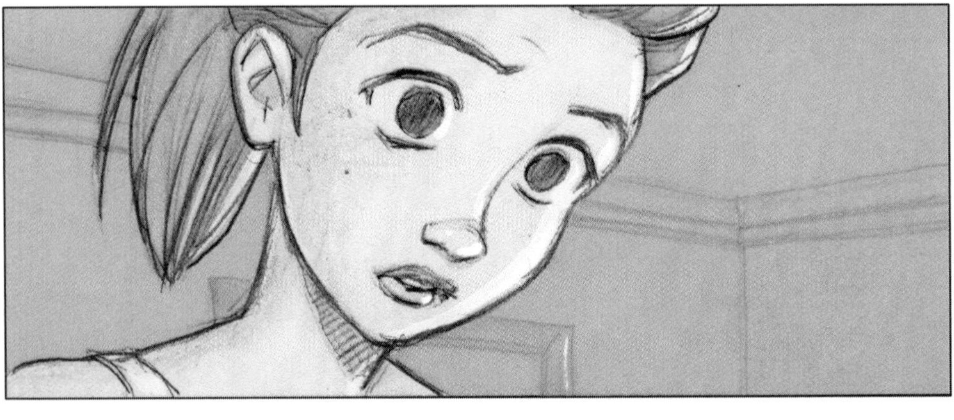

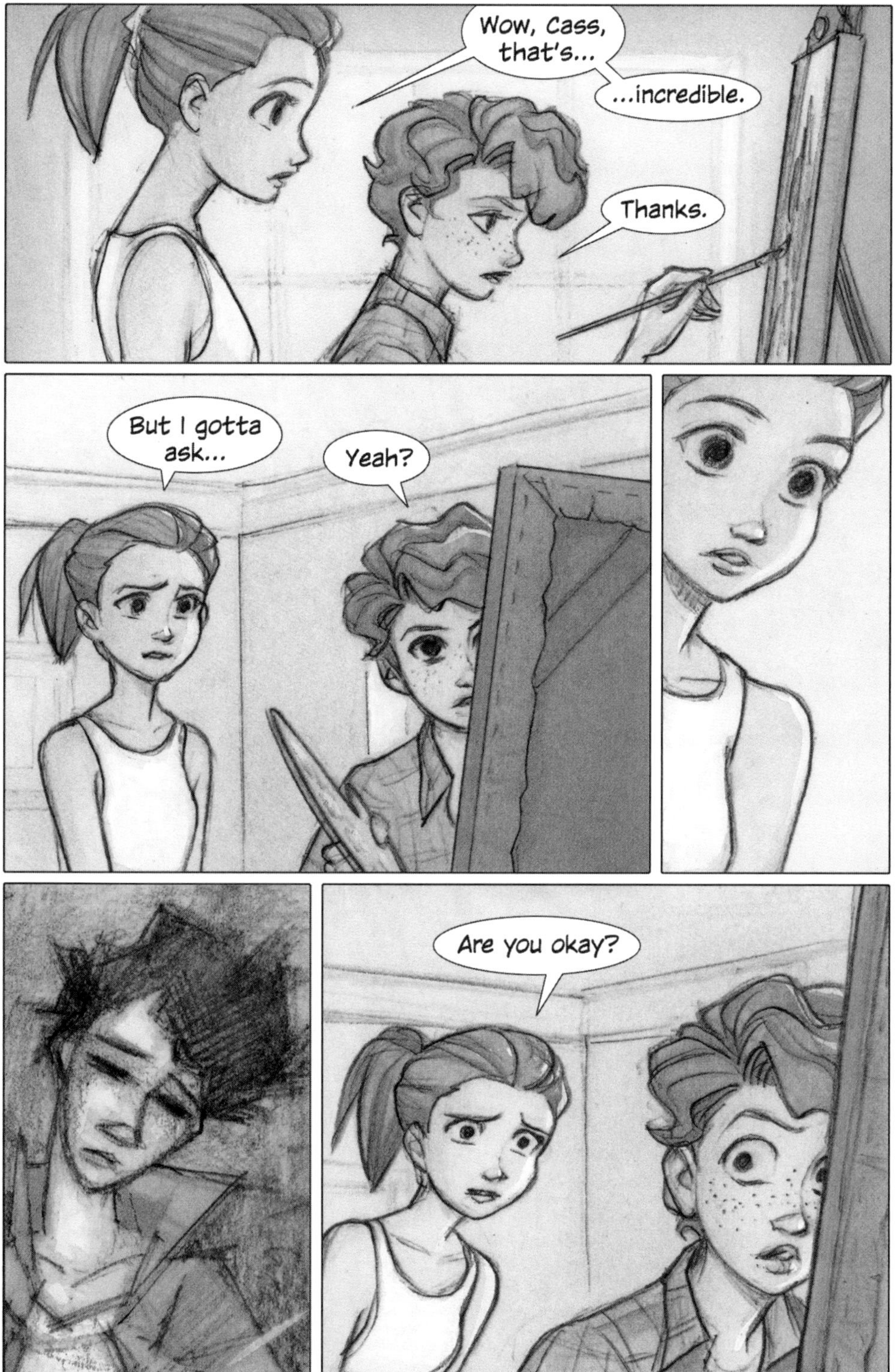

Wow, Cass, that's...
...incredible.
Thanks.
But I gotta ask...
Yeah?
Are you okay?

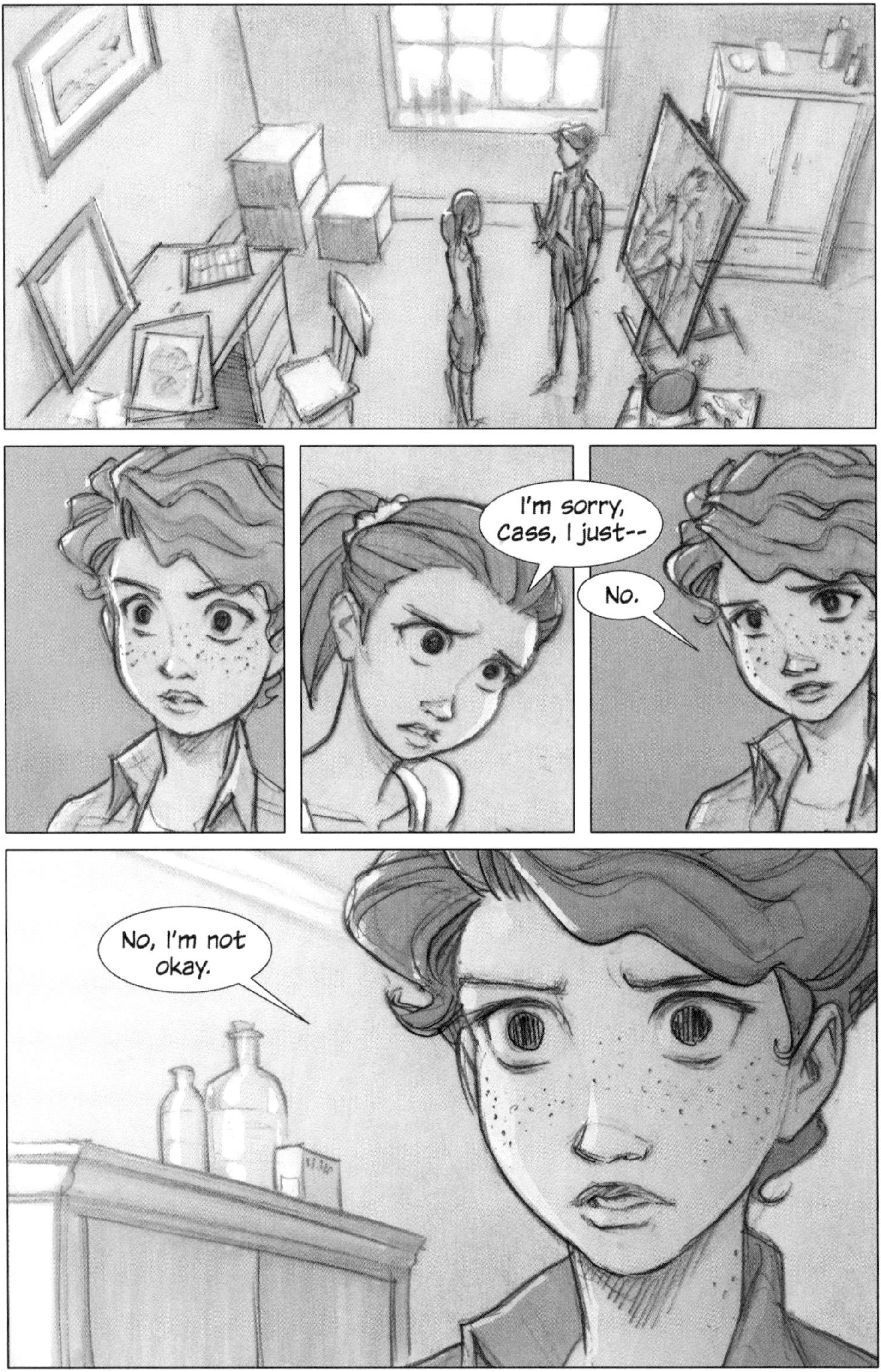
I'm sorry, Cass, I just--
No.
No, I'm not okay.

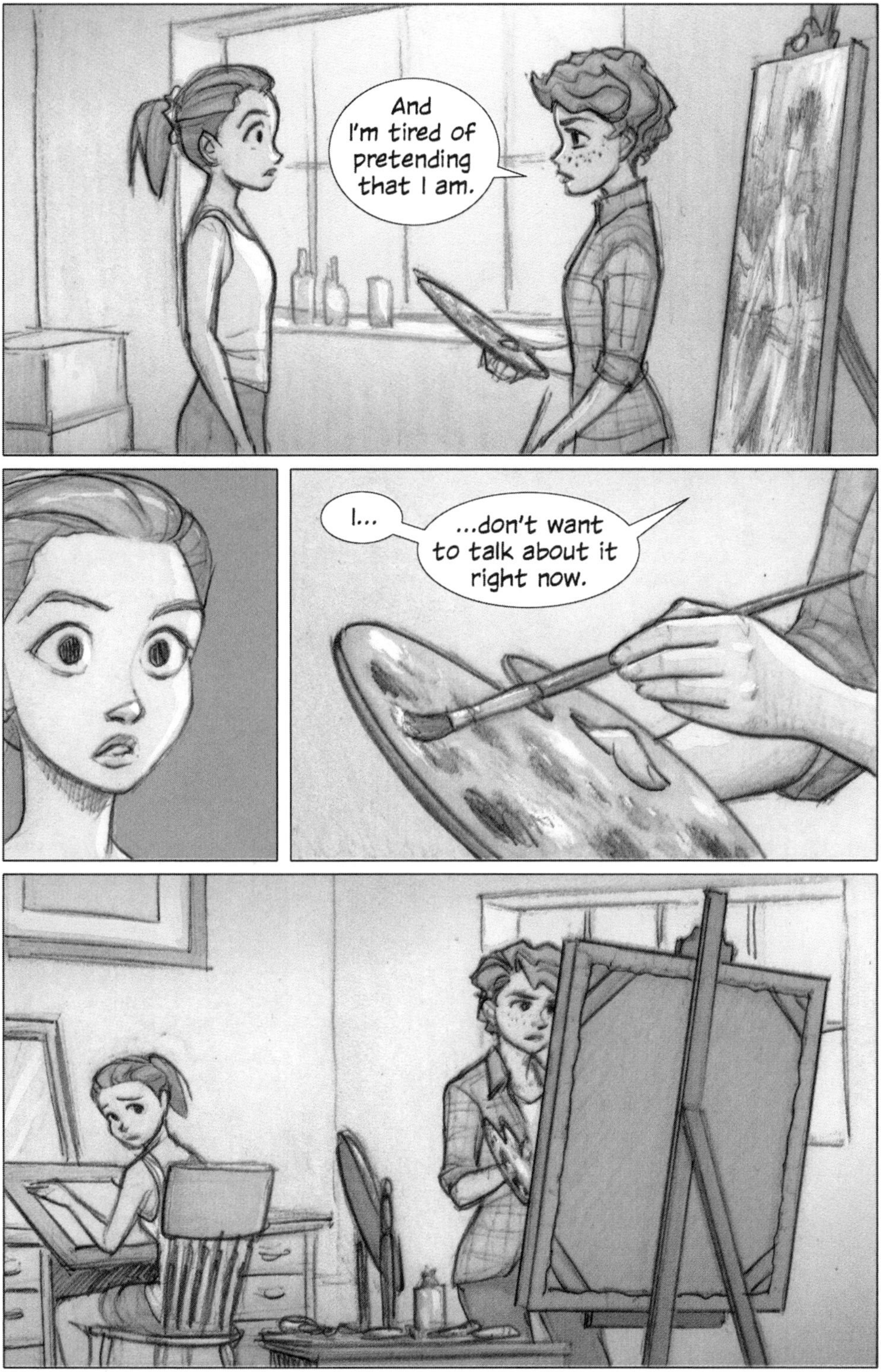
And I'm tired of pretending that I am.
I...
...don't want to talk about it right now.

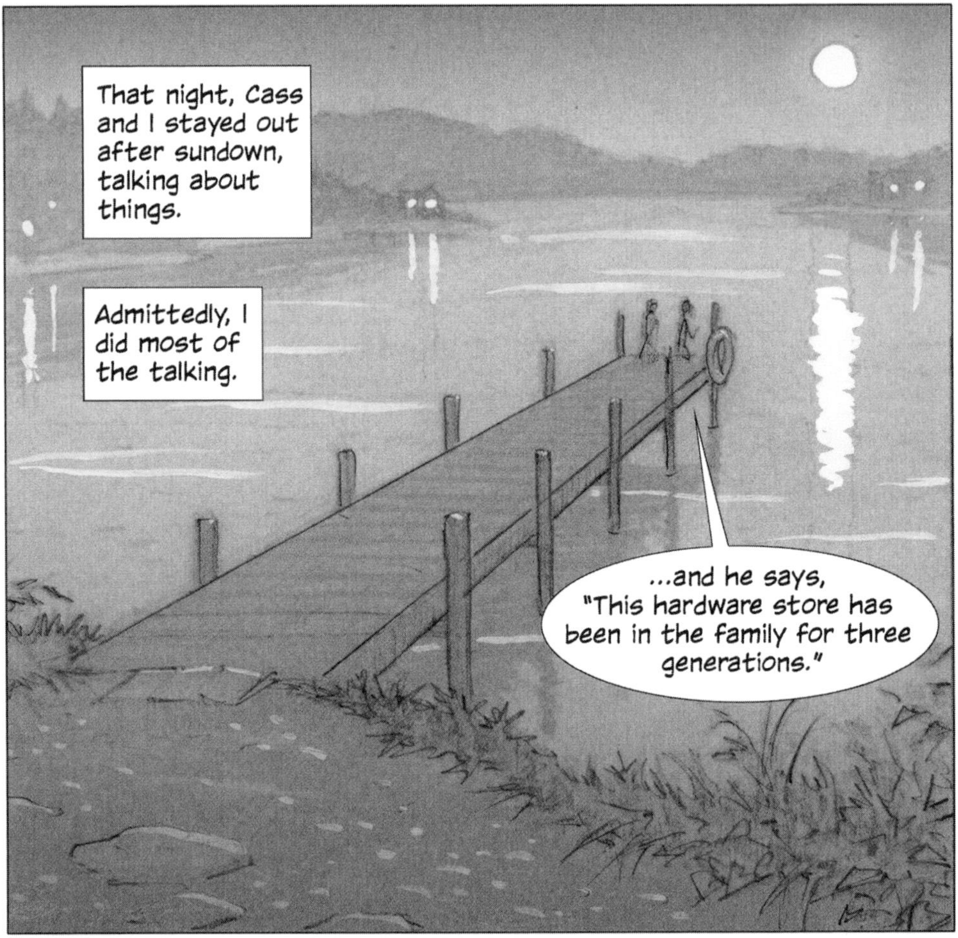
That night, Cass and I stayed out after sundown, talking about things.
Admittedly, I did most of the talking.
...and he says, "This hardware store has been in the family for three generations."

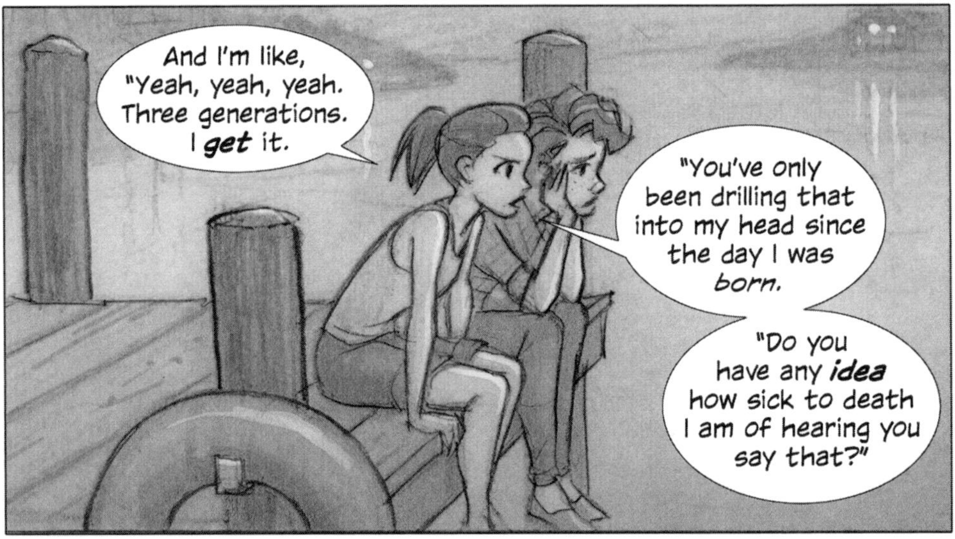
And I'm like, "Yeah, yeah, yeah. Three generations. I **get** it.
"You've only been drilling that into my head since the day I was *born*.
"Do you have any ***idea*** how sick to death I am of hearing you say that?"

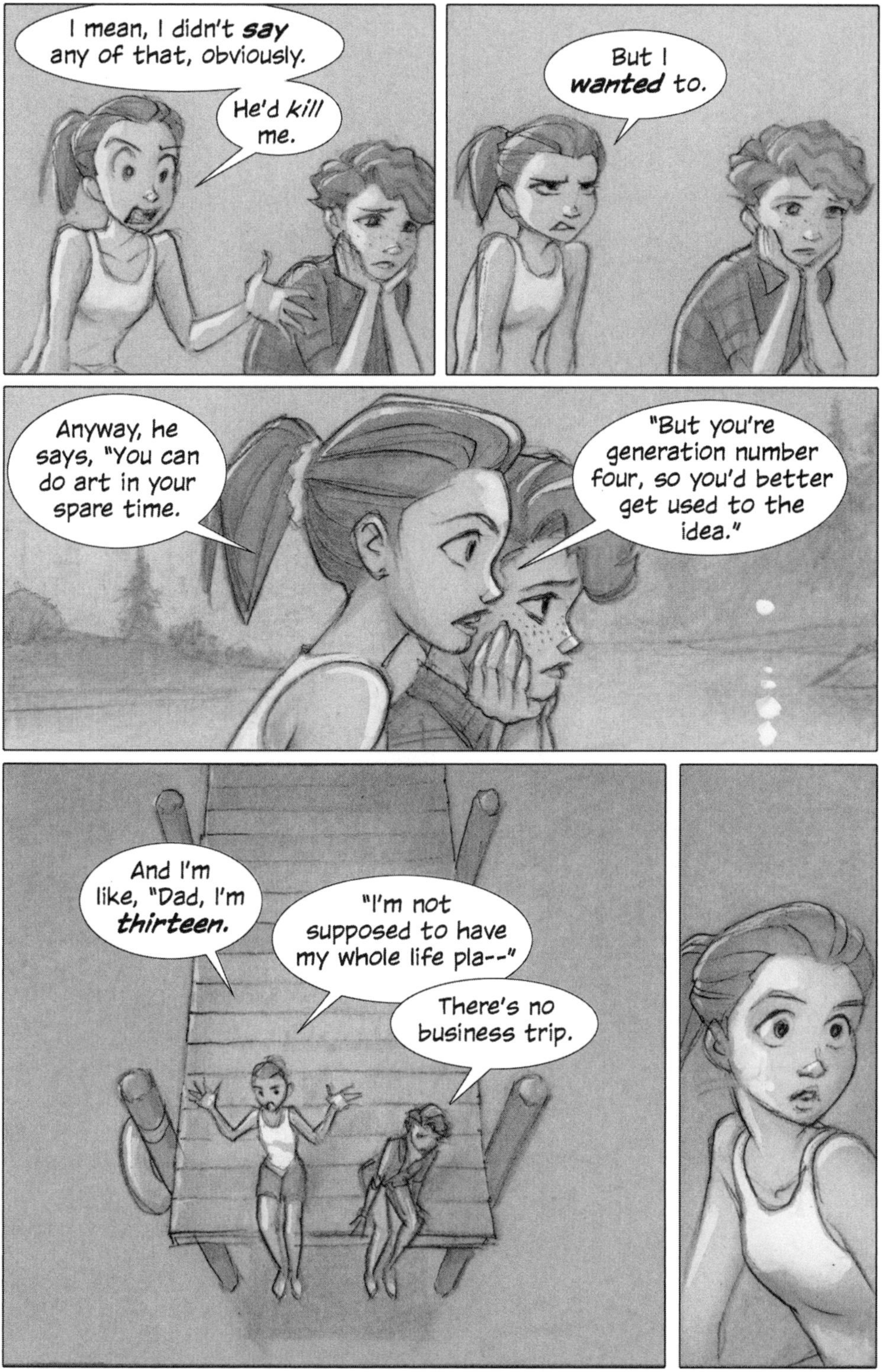

I mean, I didn't *say* any of that, obviously.
He'd *kill* me.
But I *wanted* to.
Anyway, he says, "You can do art in your spare time.
"But you're generation number four, so you'd better get used to the idea."
And I'm like, "Dad, I'm *thirteen.*
"I'm not supposed to have my whole life pla--"
There's no business trip.

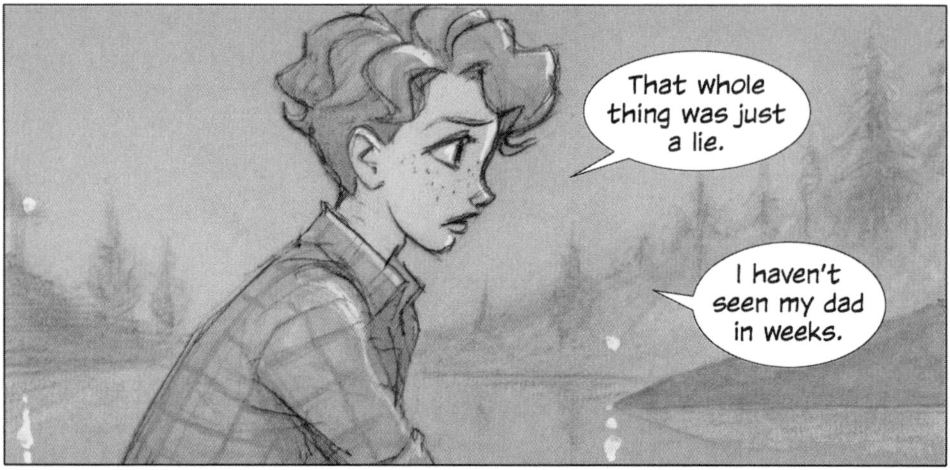
That whole thing was just a lie.
I haven't seen my dad in weeks.

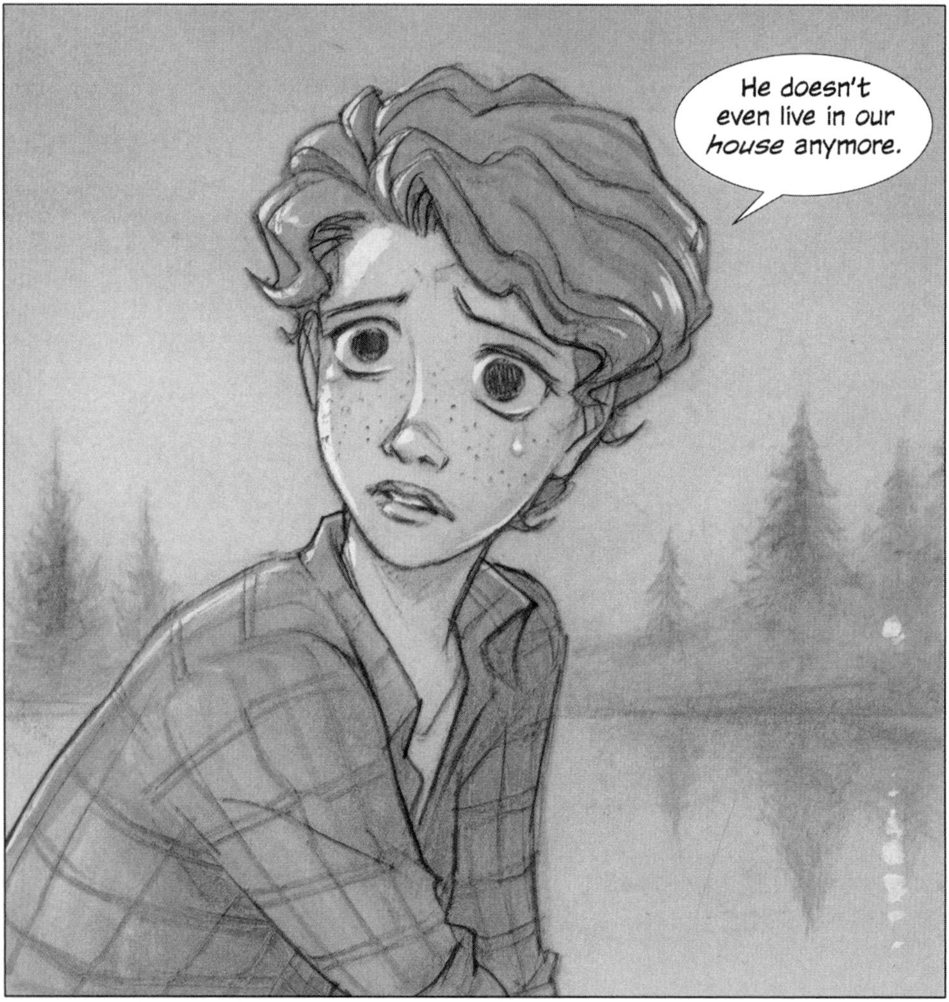
He doesn't even live in our *house* anymore.

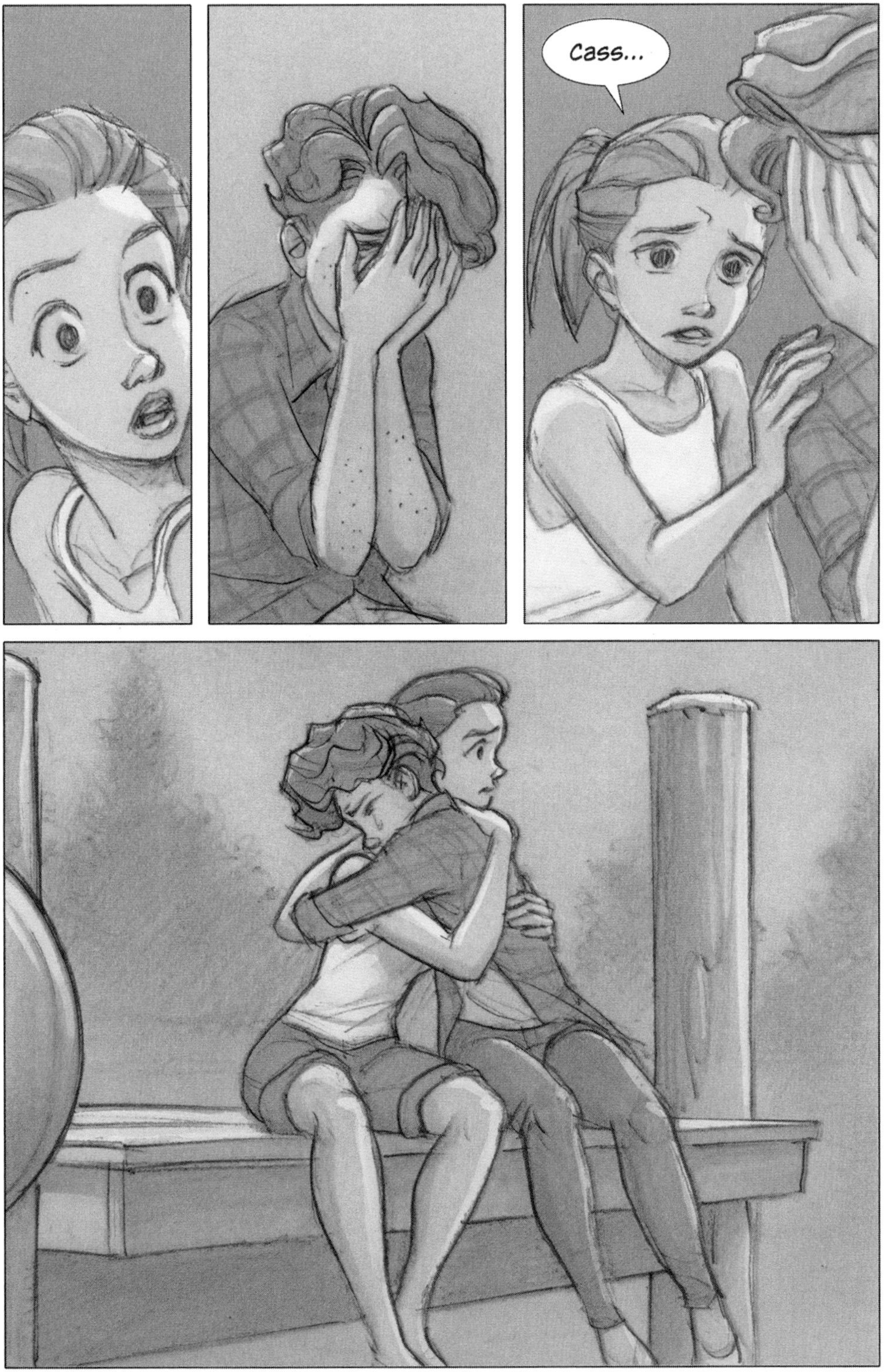
Cass...

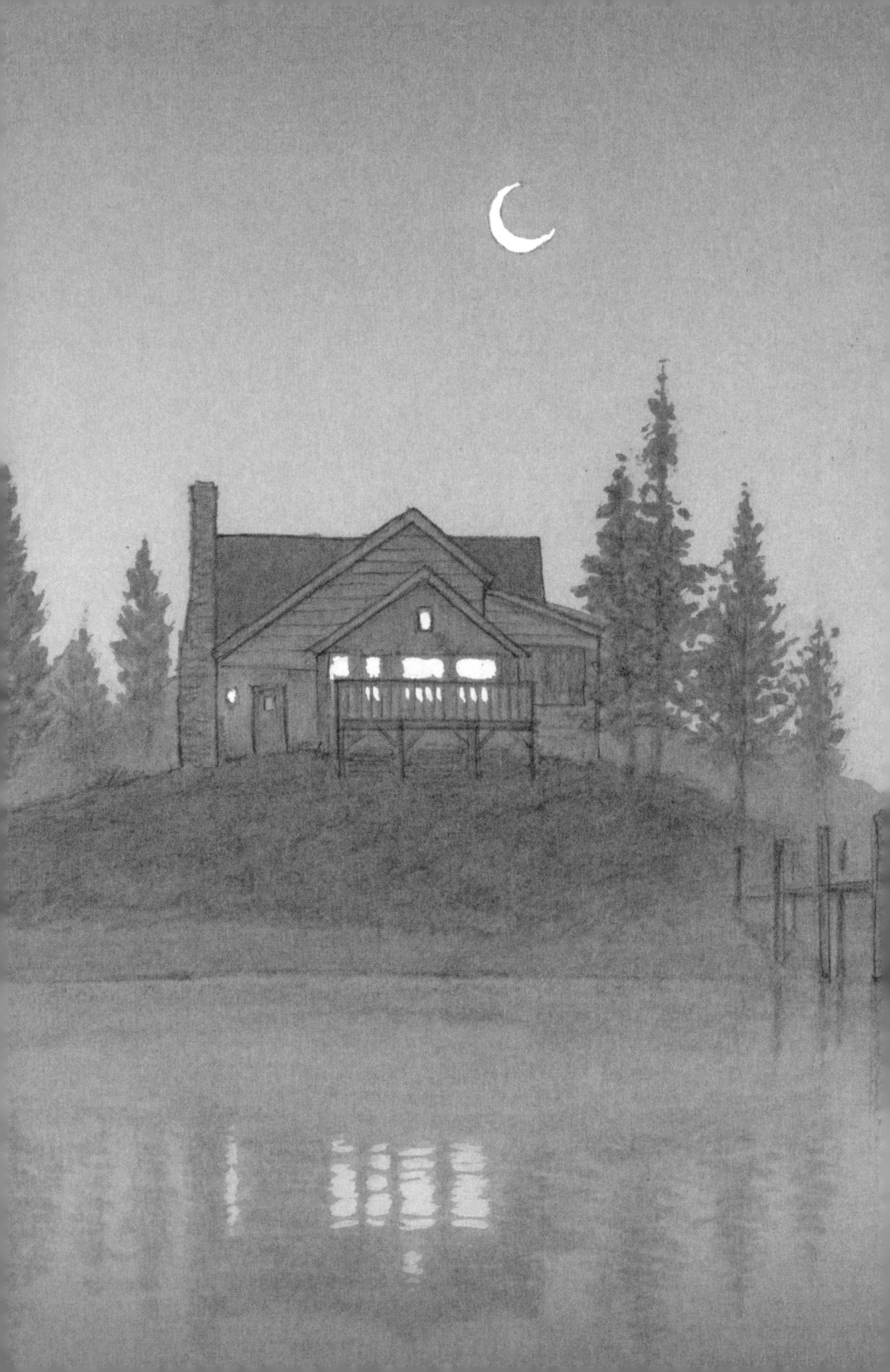

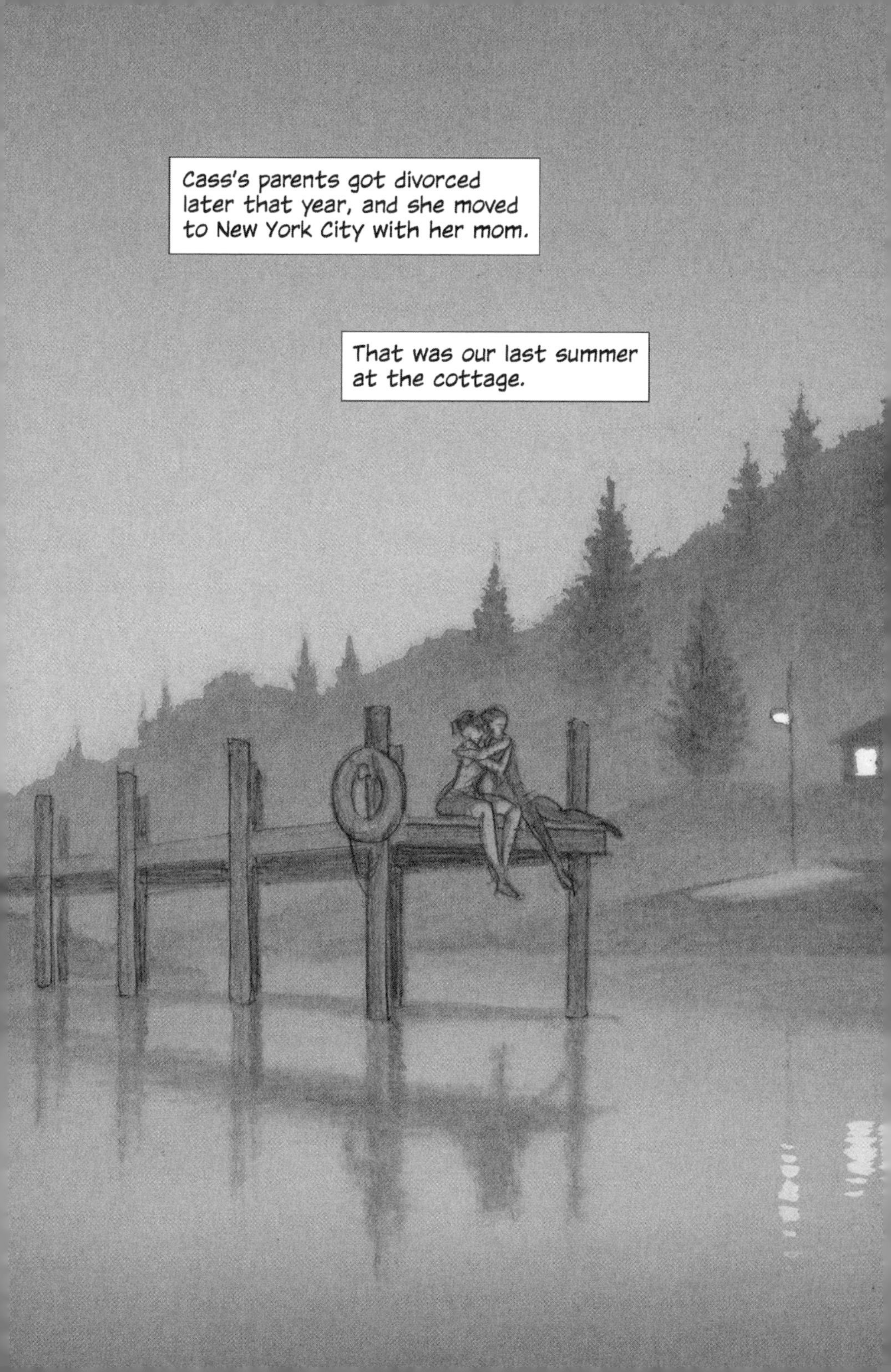
Cass's parents got divorced later that year, and she moved to New York City with her mom.
That was our last summer at the cottage.

Part Two

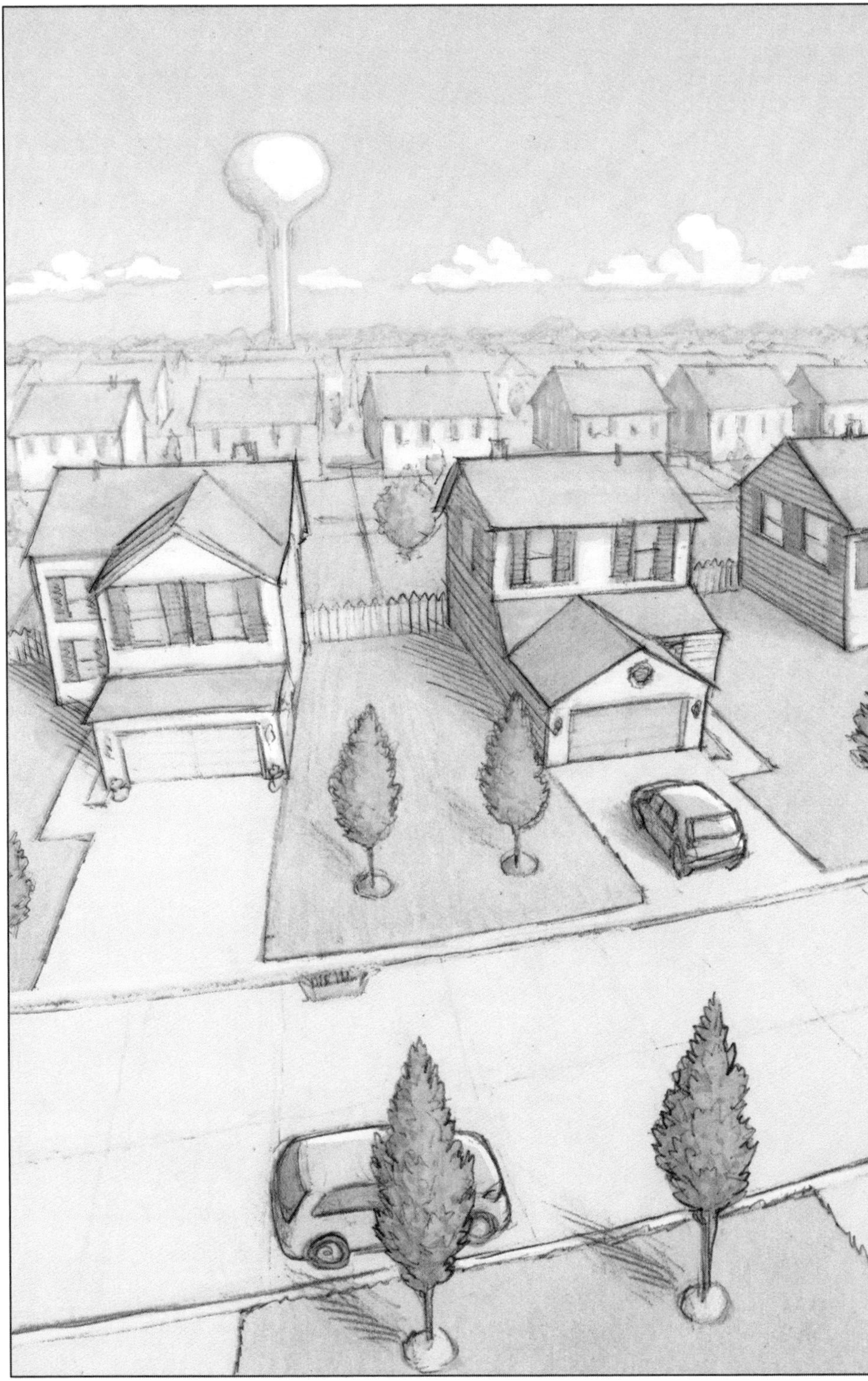

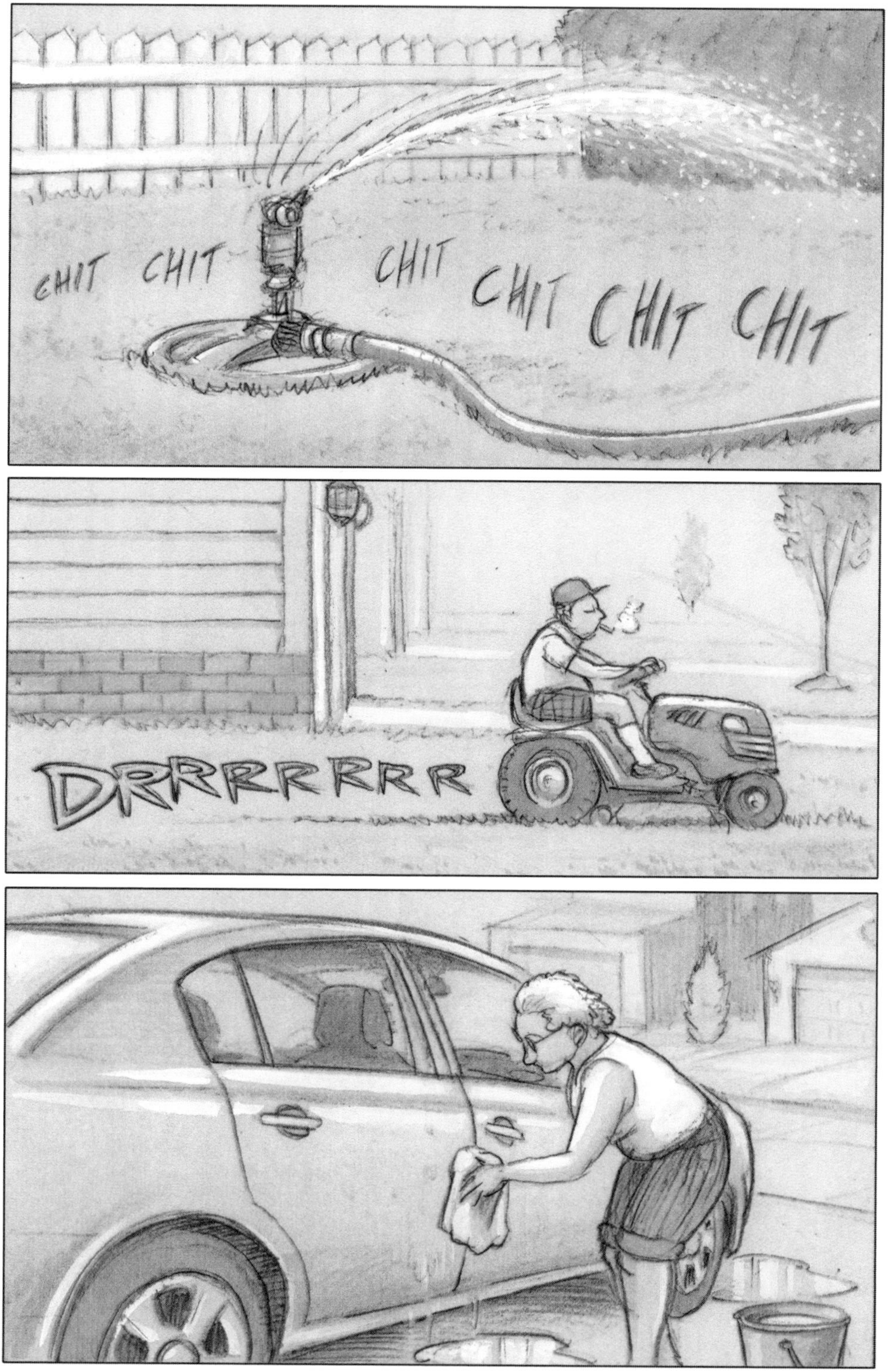
CHIT CHIT CHIT CHIT CHIT CHIT
DRRRRRRR

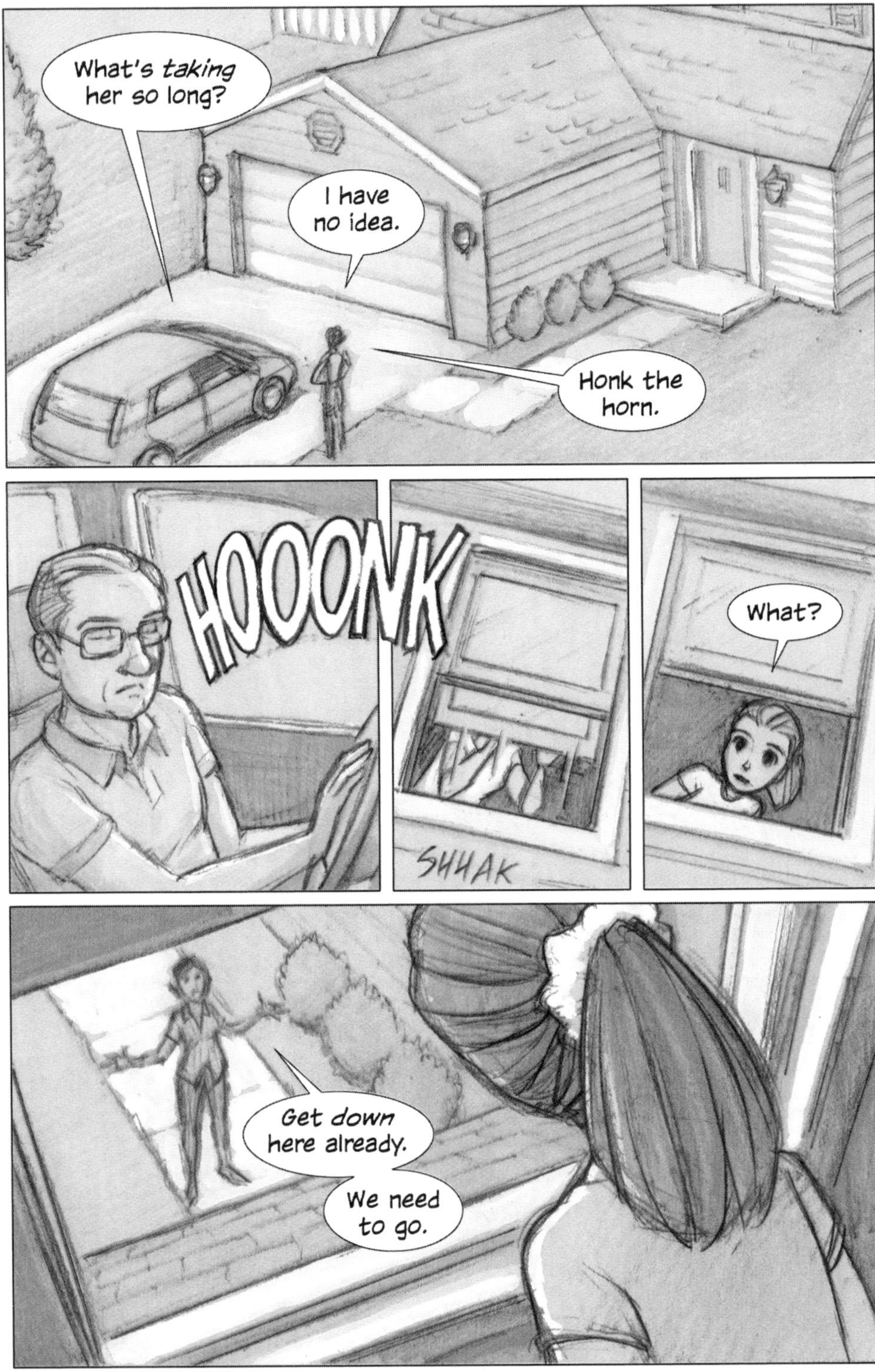
What's *taking* her so long?
I have no idea.
Honk the horn.
HOOONK
SHUAK
What?
Get *down* here already.
We need to go.

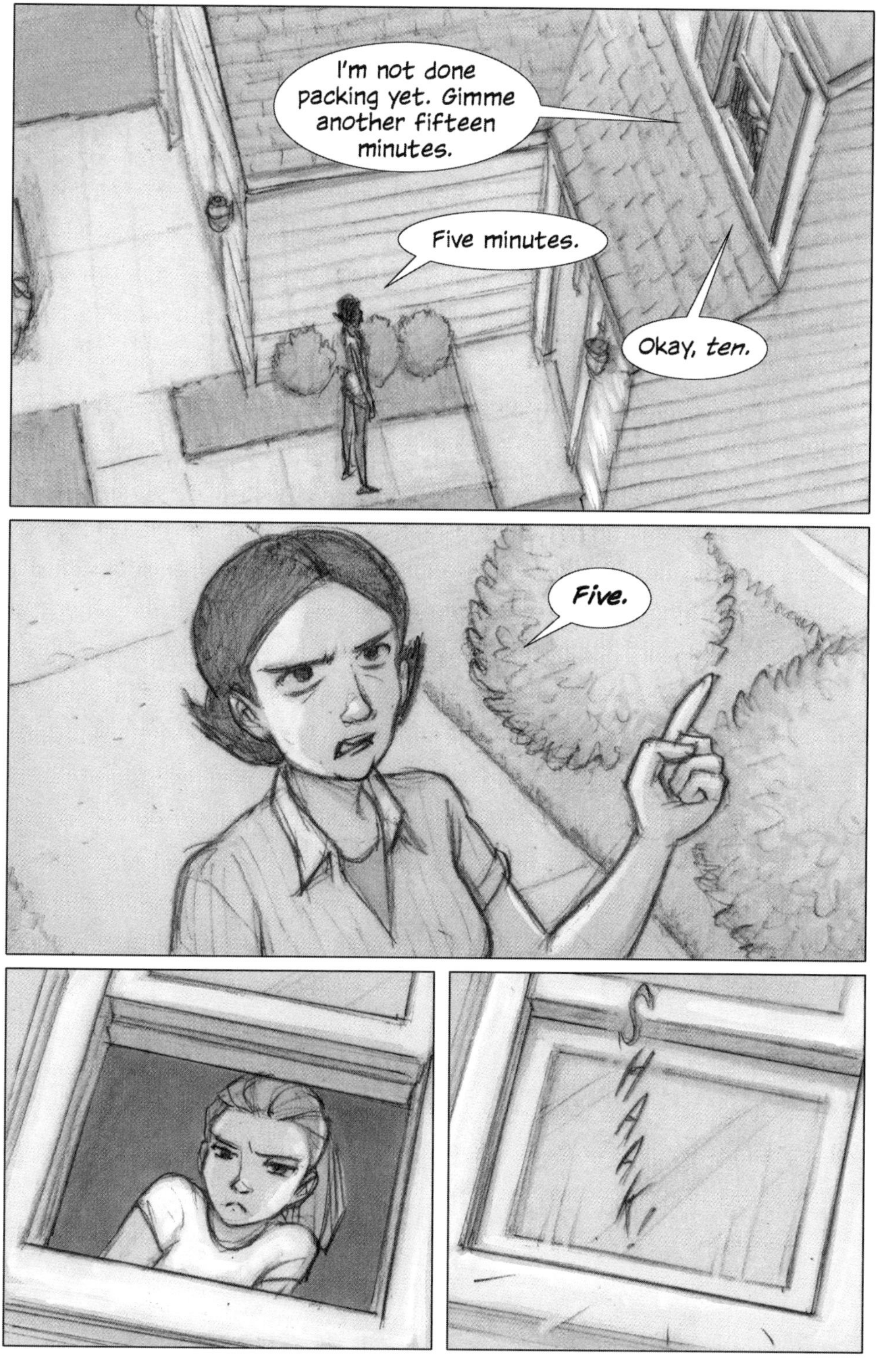

I'm not done packing yet. Gimme another fifteen minutes.
Five minutes.
Okay, *ten.*
Five.
SHAAK!

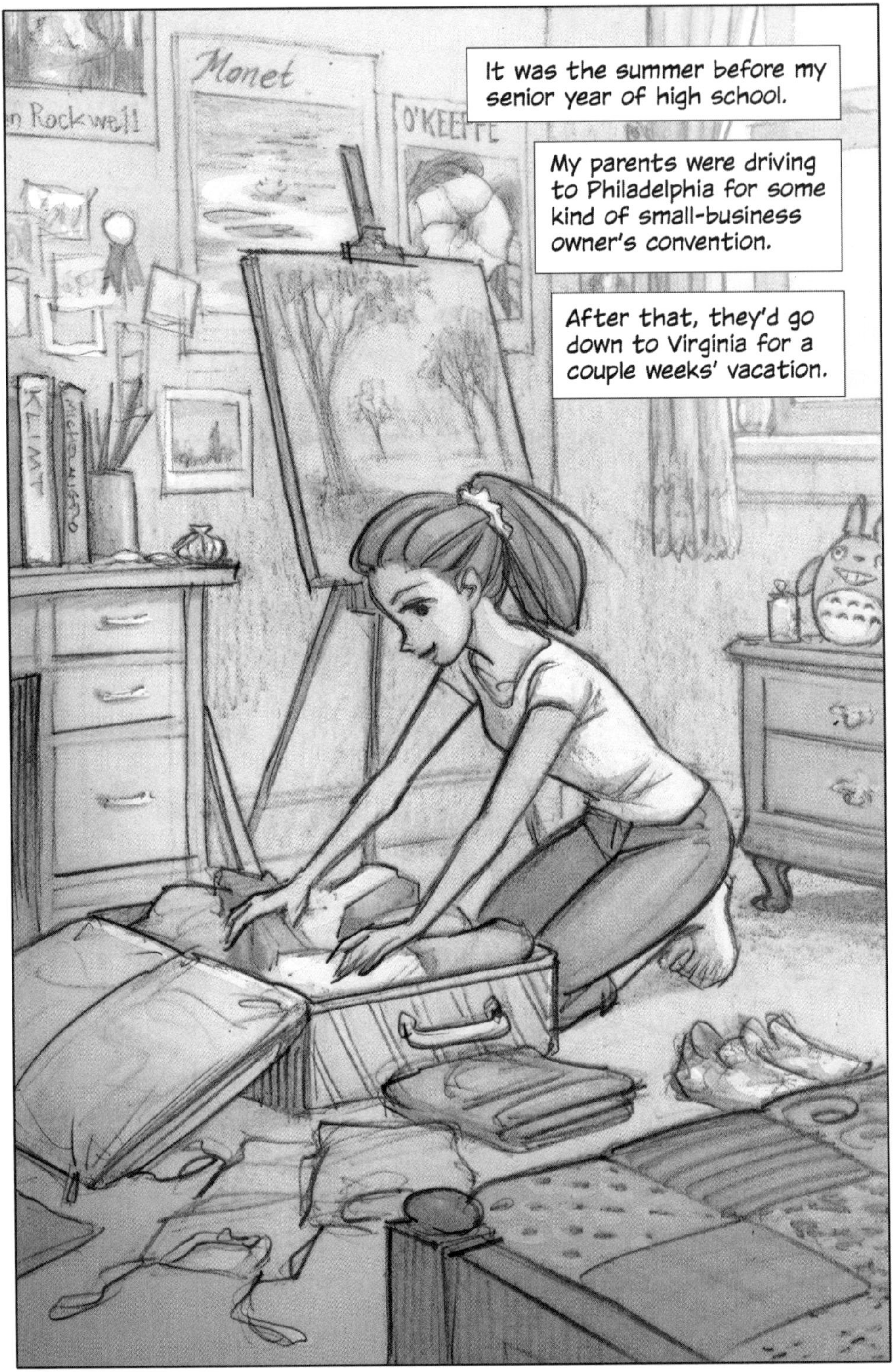
It was the summer before my senior year of high school.
My parents were driving to Philadelphia for some kind of small-business owner's convention.
After that, they'd go down to Virginia for a couple weeks' vacation.
Monet
O'KEEFFE
KLIMT

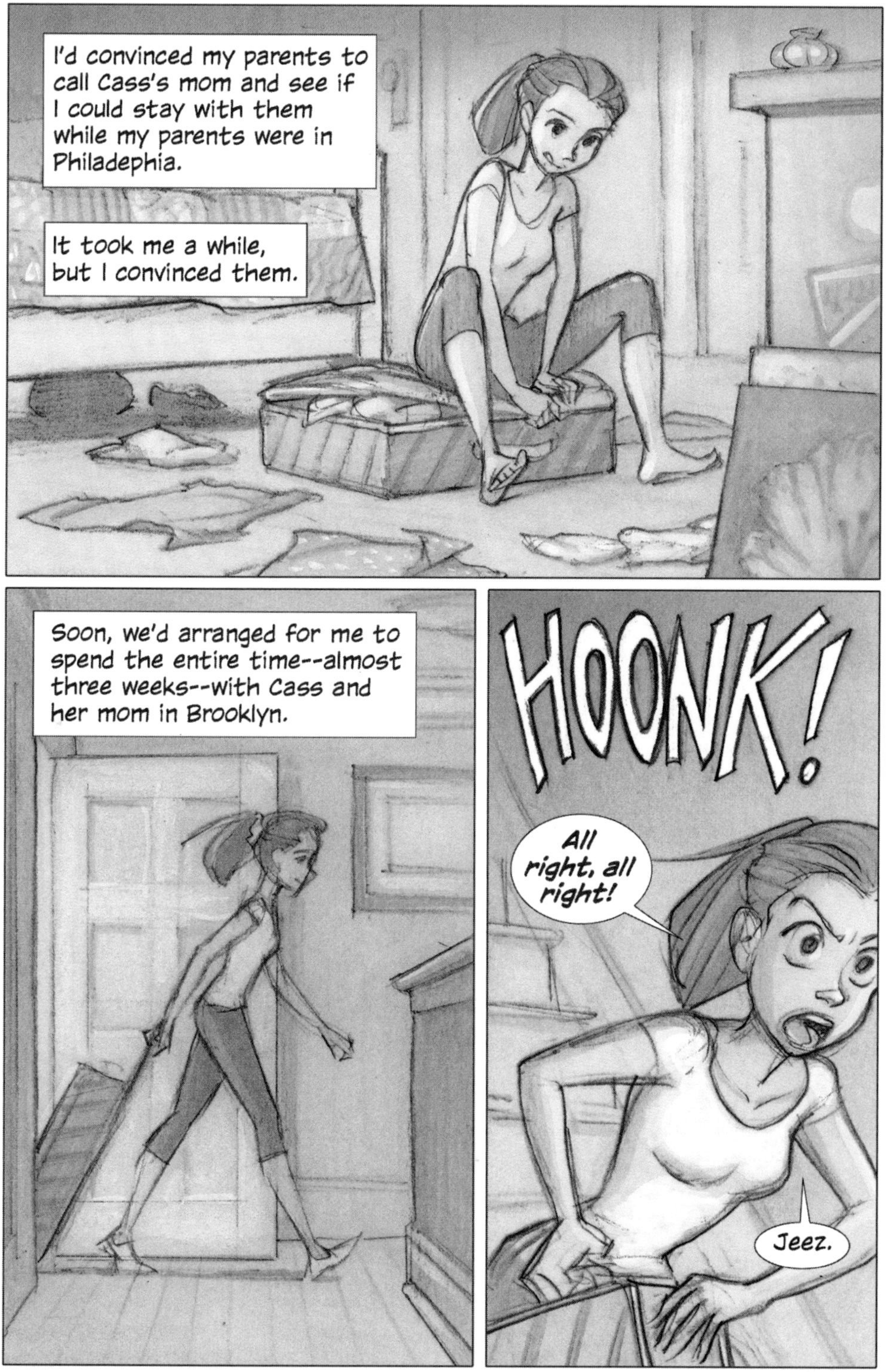
I'd convinced my parents to call Cass's mom and see if I could stay with them while my parents were in Philadephia.
It took me a while, but I convinced them.
Soon, we'd arranged for me to spend the entire time--almost three weeks--with Cass and her mom in Brooklyn.
HOONK!
All right, all right!
Jeez.

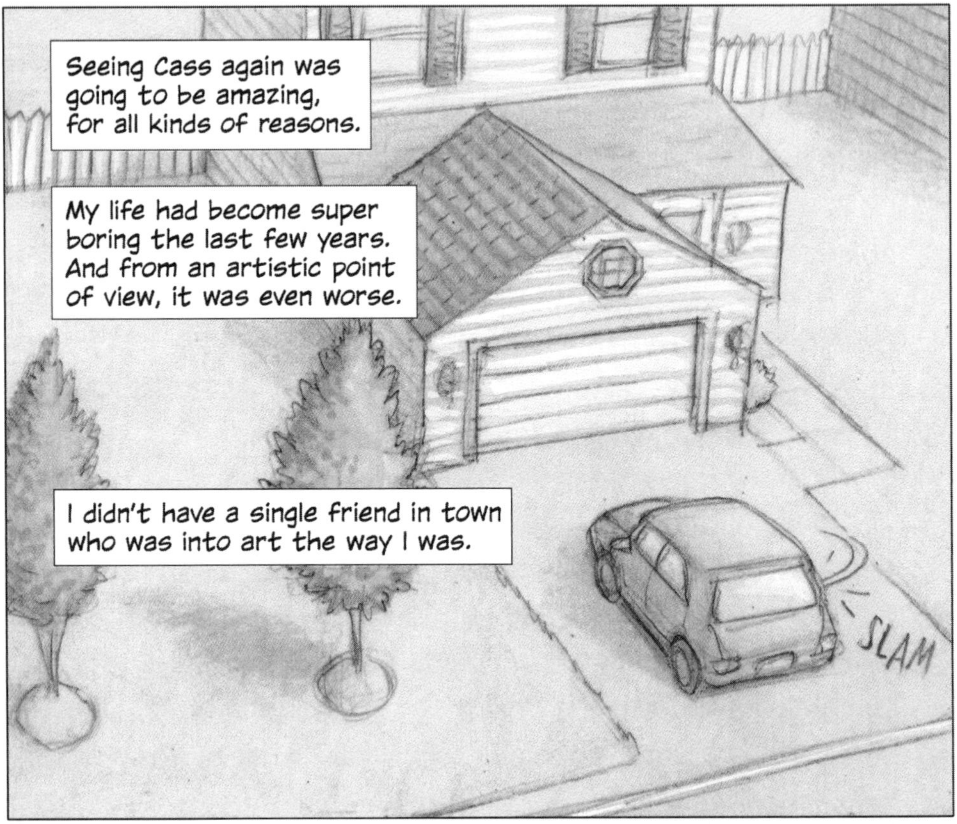
Seeing Cass again was going to be amazing, for all kinds of reasons.
My life had become super boring the last few years. And from an artistic point of view, it was even worse.
I didn't have a single friend in town who was into art the way I was.
SLAM

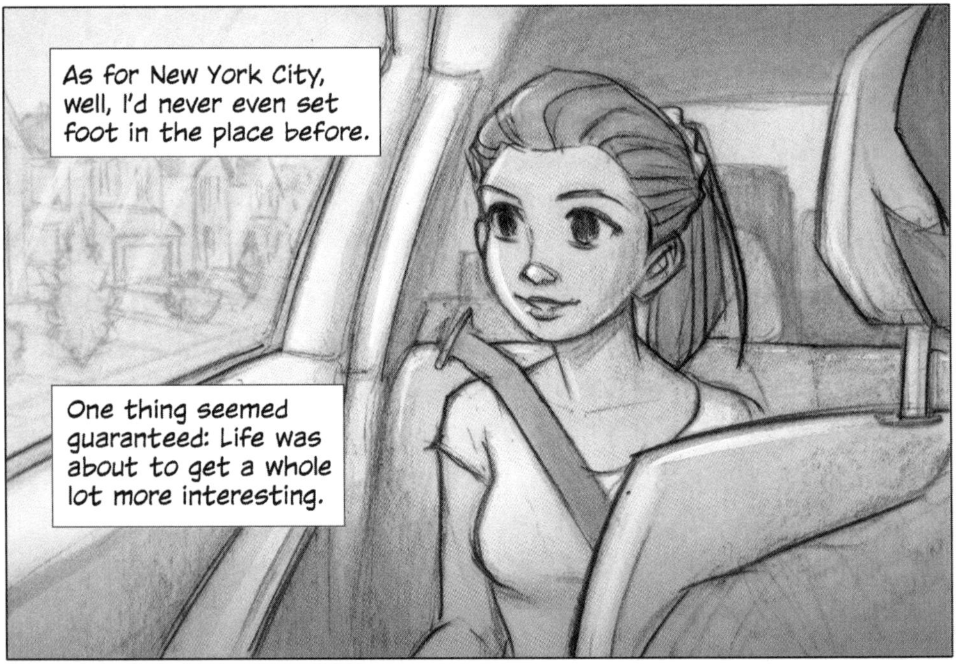
As for New York City, well, I'd never even set foot in the place before.
One thing seemed guaranteed: Life was about to get a whole lot more interesting.

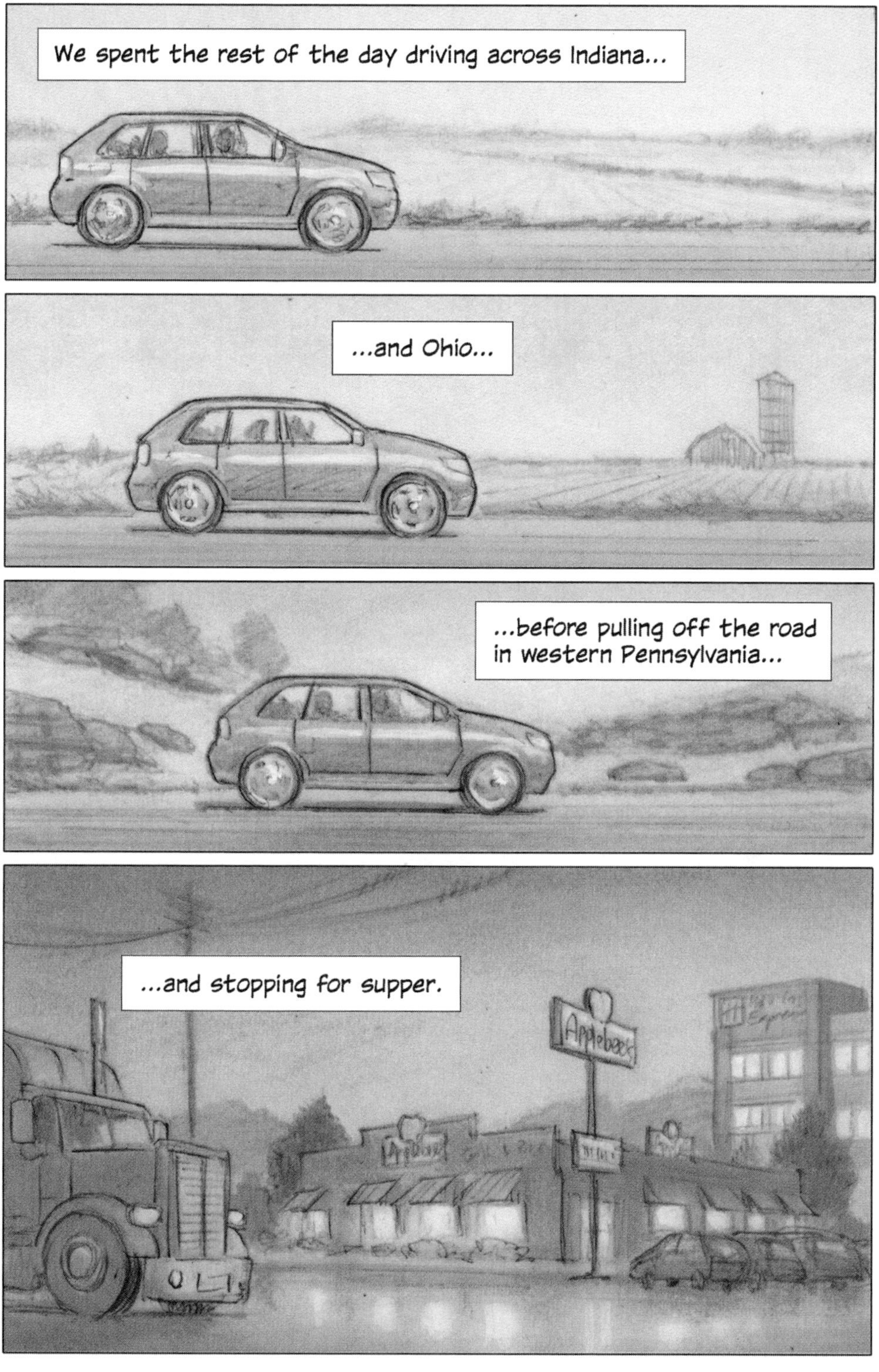
We spent the rest of the day driving across Indiana...
...and Ohio...
...before pulling off the road in western Pennsylvania...
...and stopping for supper.

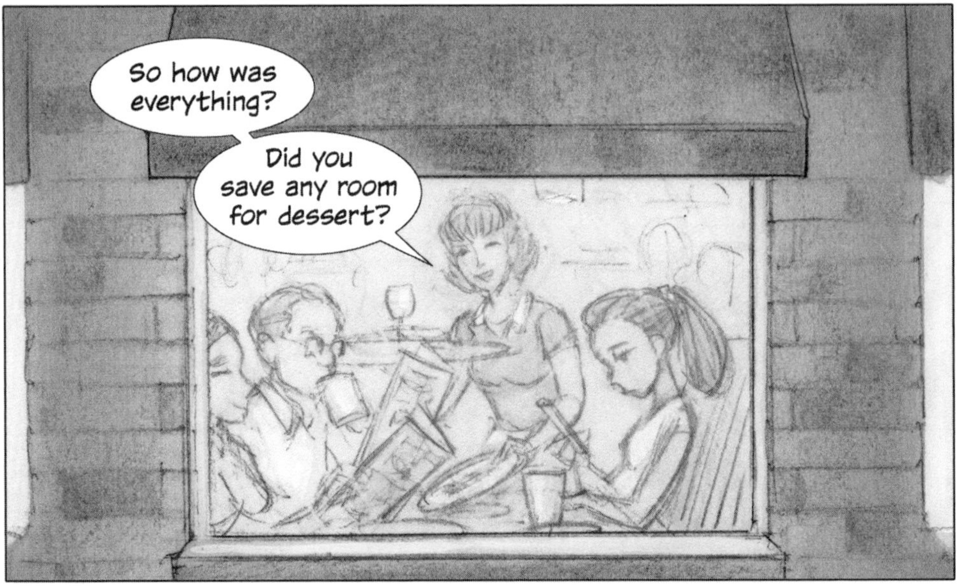
So how was everything?
Did you save any room for dessert?
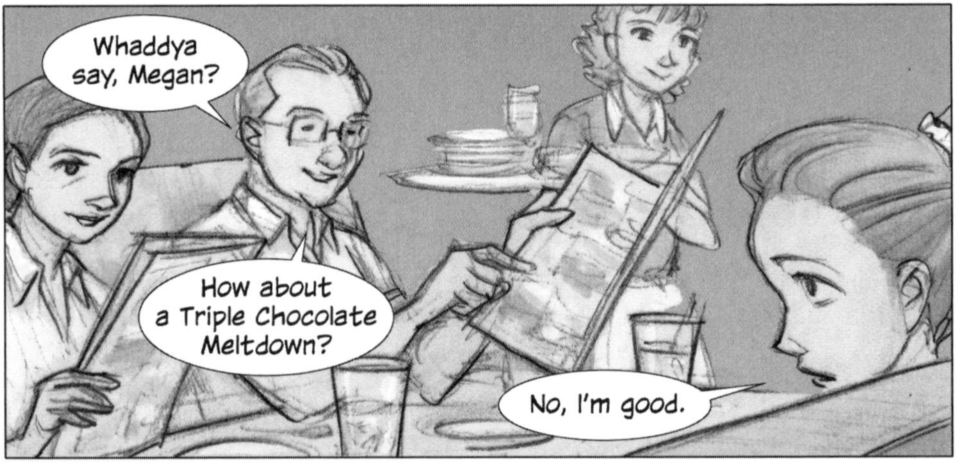
Whaddya say, Megan?
How about a Triple Chocolate Meltdown?
No, I'm good.
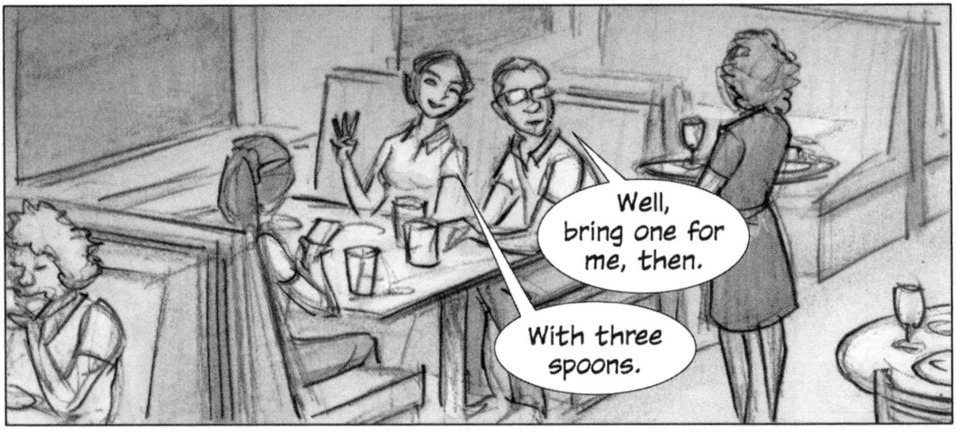
Well, bring one for me, then.
With three spoons.

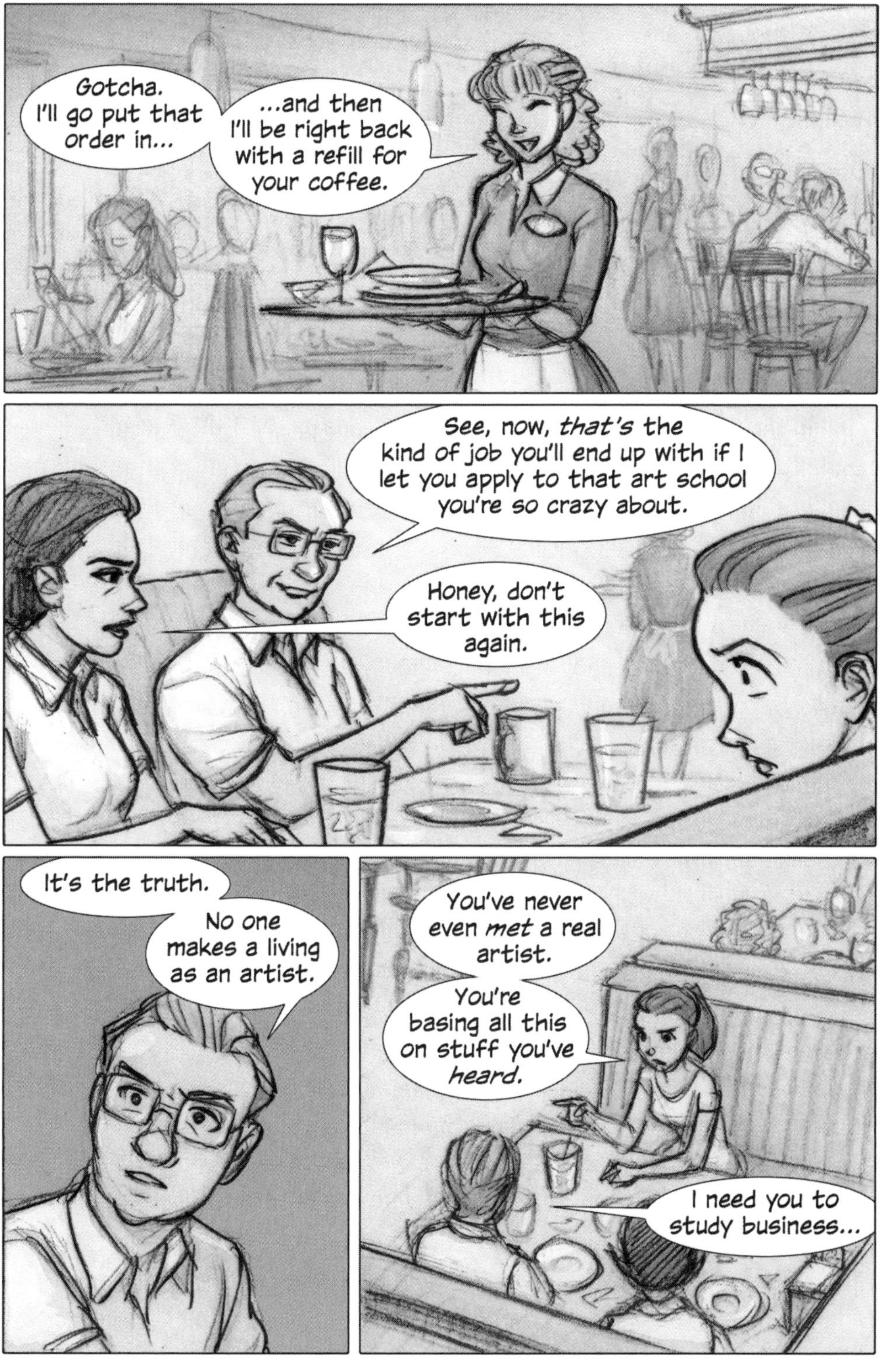
Gotcha. I'll go put that order in...
...and then I'll be right back with a refill for your coffee.
See, now, *that's* the kind of job you'll end up with if I let you apply to that art school you're so crazy about.
Honey, don't start with this again.
It's the truth.
No one makes a living as an artist.
You've never even *met* a real artist.
You're basing all this on stuff you've *heard.*
I need you to study business...

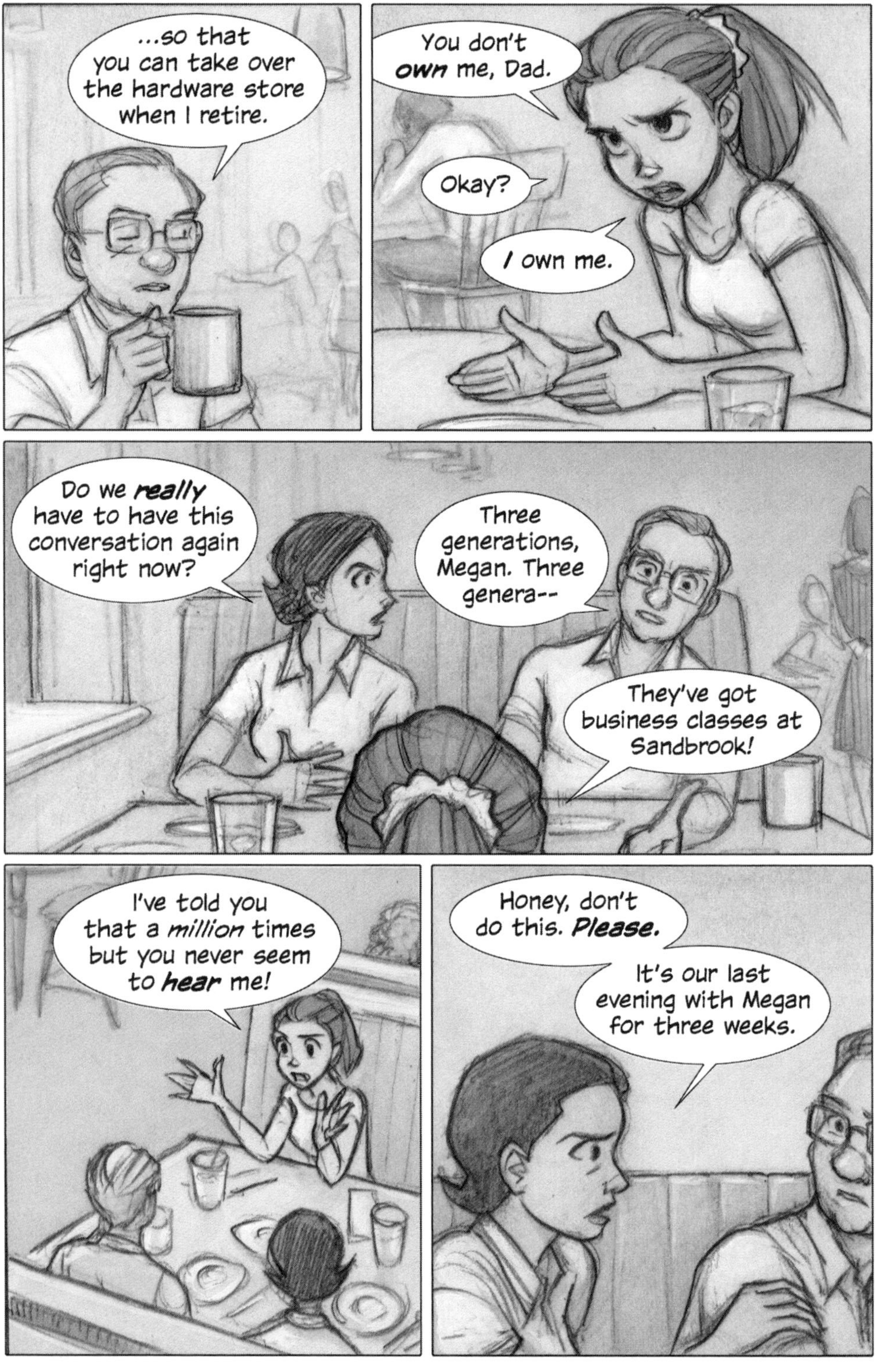
...so that you can take over the hardware store when I retire.
You don't *own* me, Dad.
Okay?
I own me.
Do we *really* have to have this conversation again right now?
Three generations, Megan. Three genera--
They've got business classes at Sandbrook!
I've told you that a *million* times but you never seem to *hear* me!
Honey, don't do this. *Please.*
It's our last evening with Megan for three weeks.

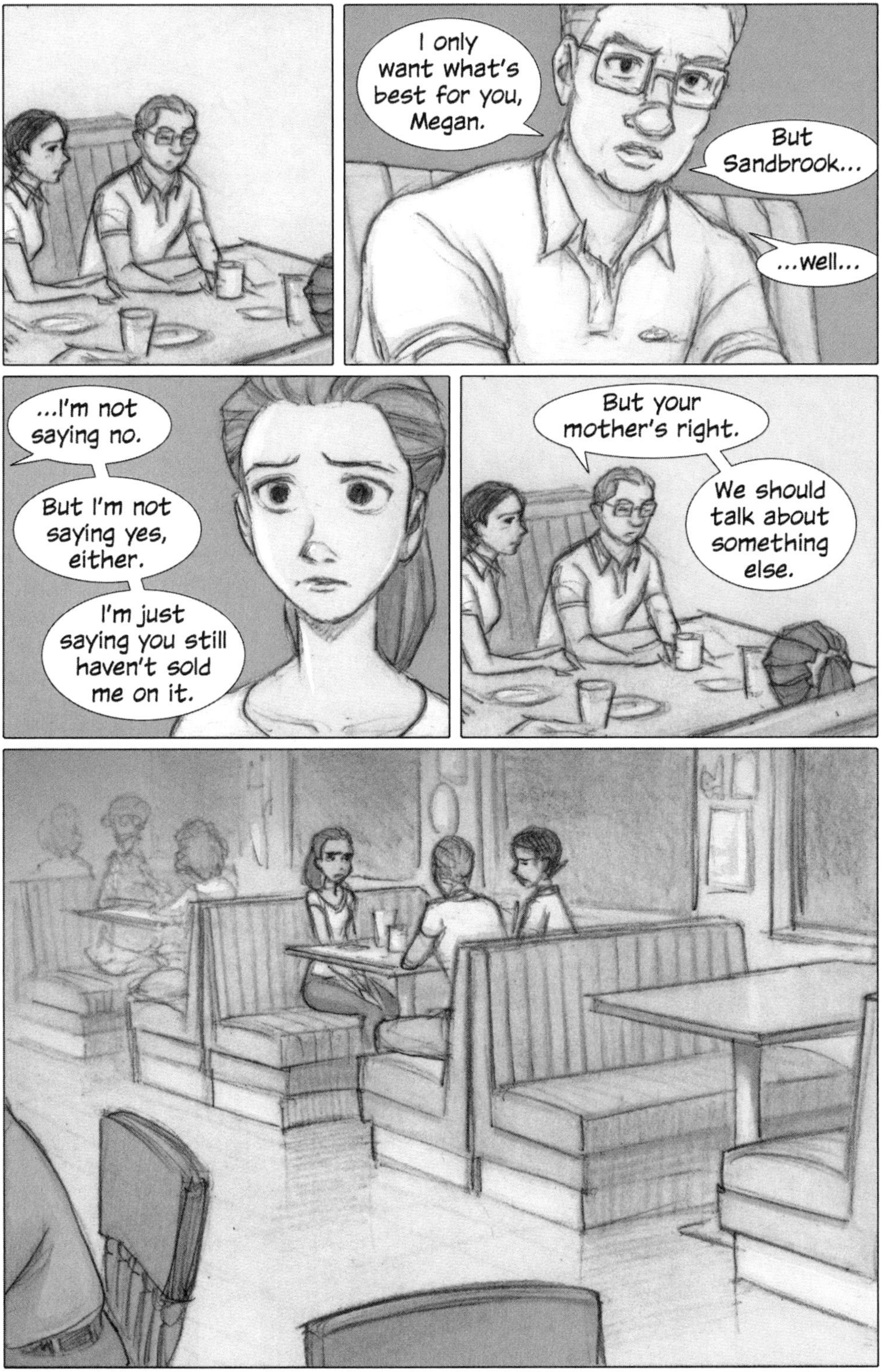
I only want what's best for you, Megan.
But Sandbrook...
...well...
...I'm not saying no.
But I'm not saying yes, either.
I'm just saying you still haven't sold me on it.
But your mother's right.
We should talk about something else.

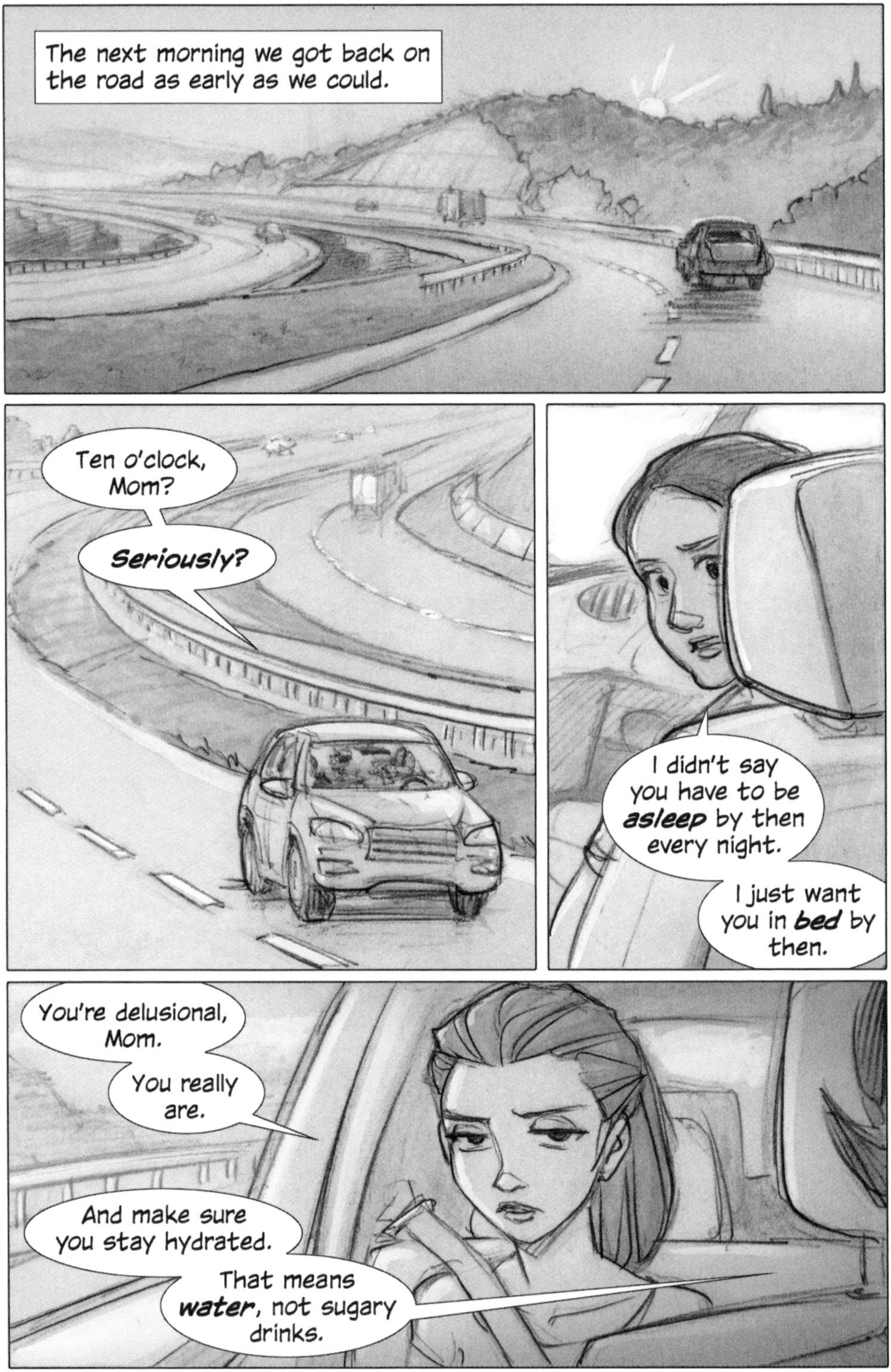
The next morning we got back on the road as early as we could.
Ten o'clock, Mom?
Seriously?
I didn't say you have to be ***asleep*** by then every night.
I just want you in ***bed*** by then.
You're delusional, Mom.
You really are.
And make sure you stay hydrated.
That means ***water***, not sugary drinks.

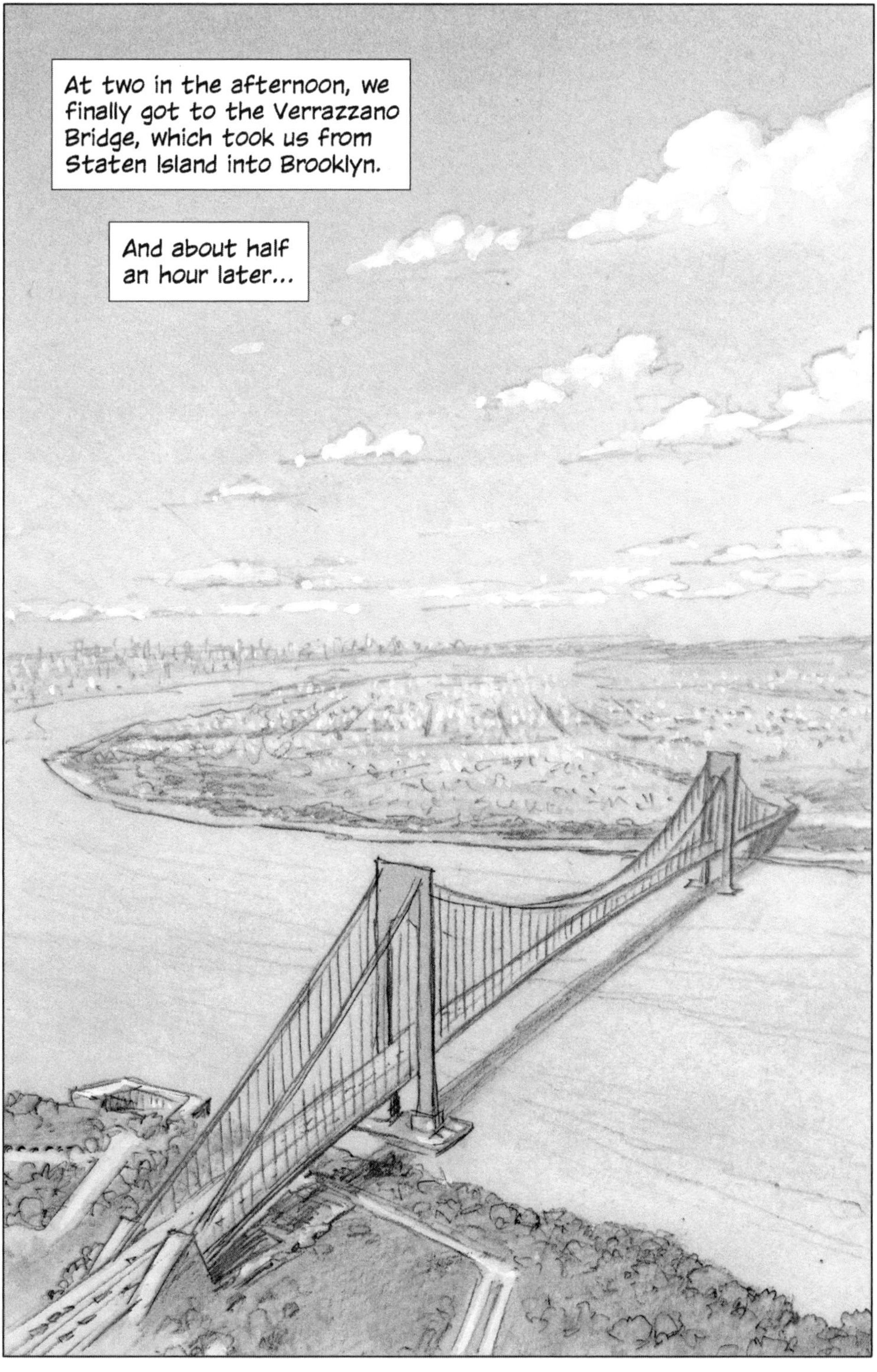
At two in the afternoon, we finally got to the Verrazzano Bridge, which took us from Staten Island into Brooklyn.
And about half an hour later...

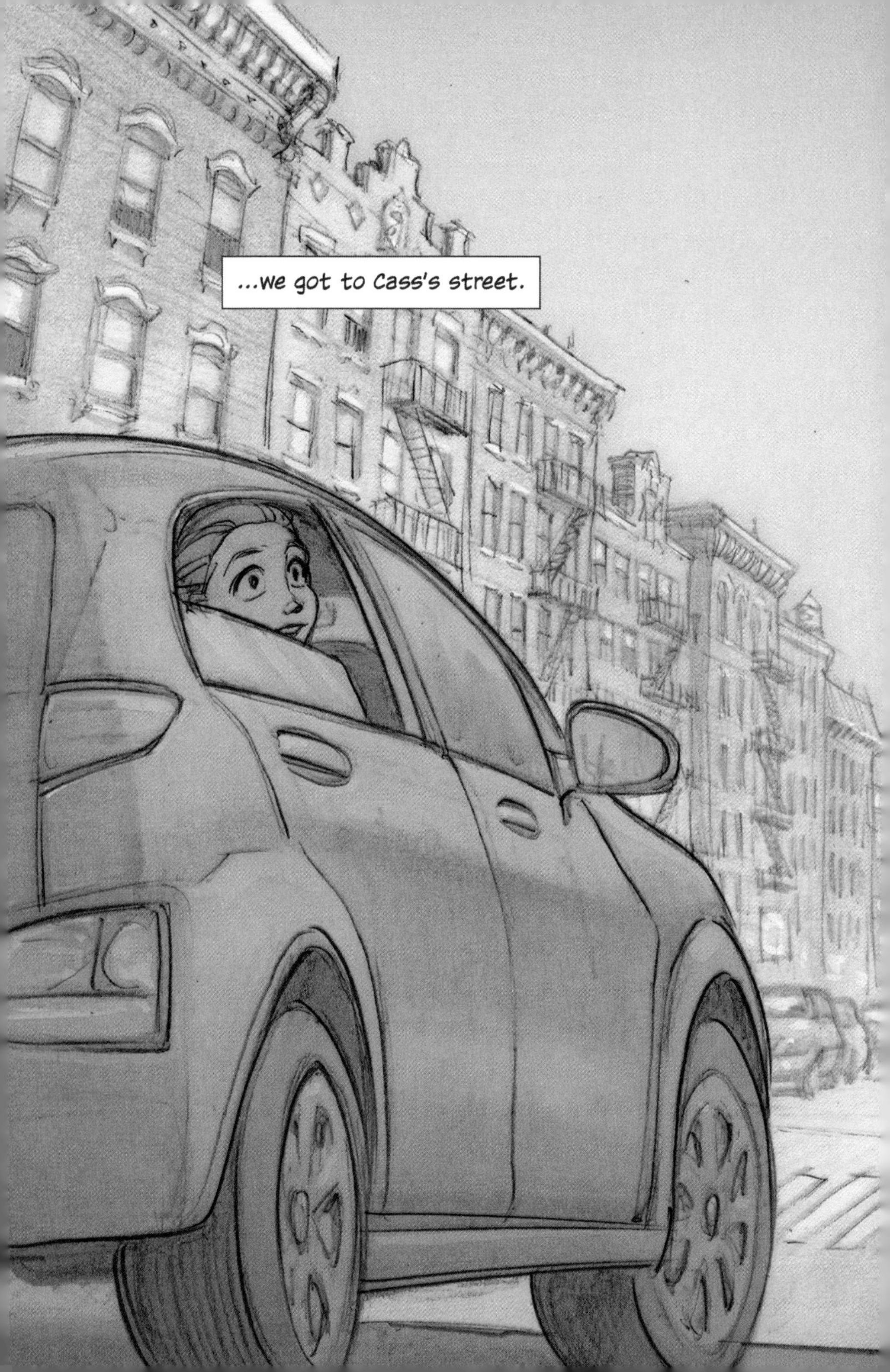
...we got to Cass's street.

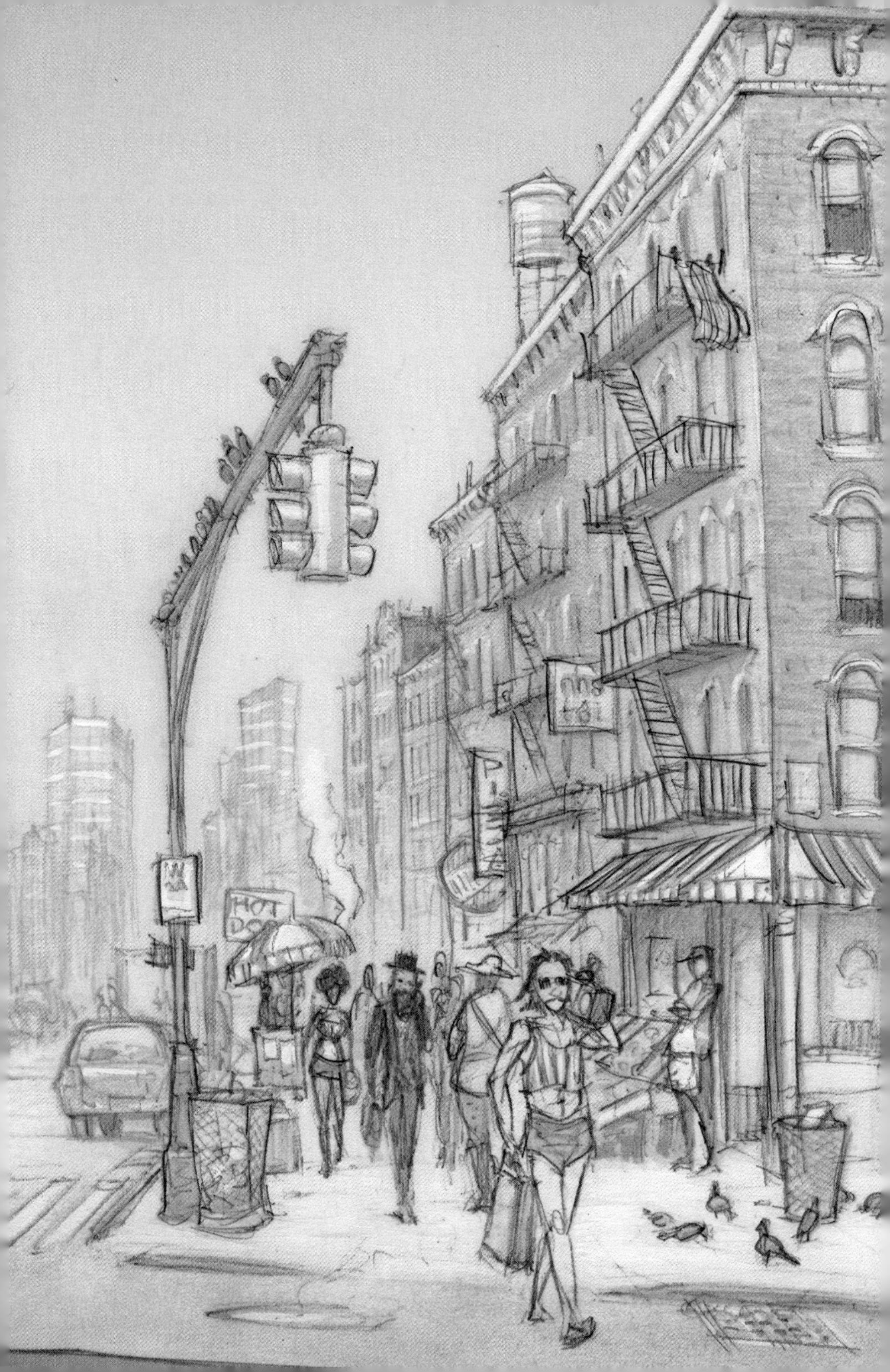
HOT

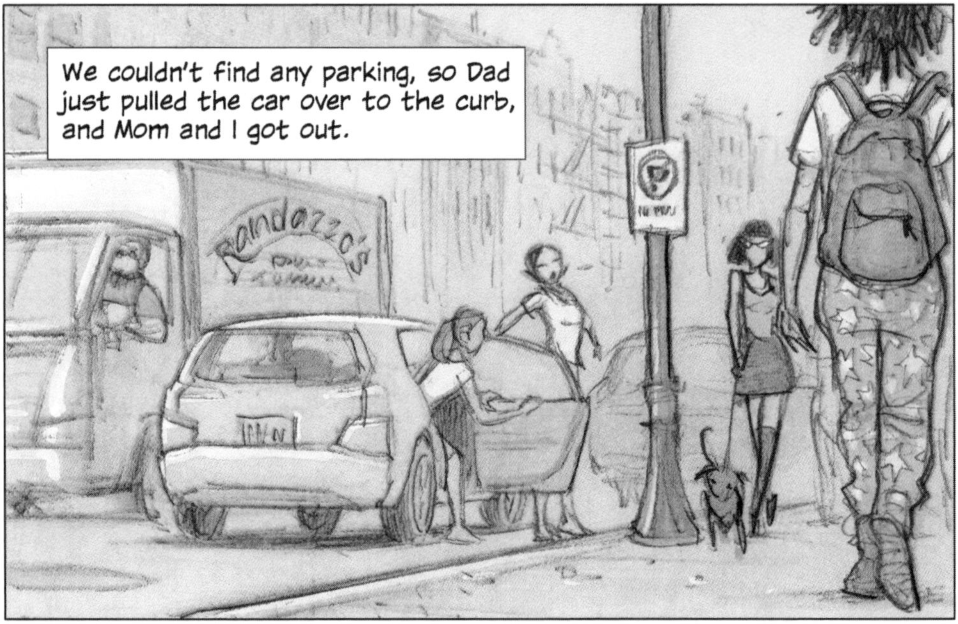
We couldn't find any parking, so Dad just pulled the car over to the curb, and Mom and I got out.
Raindazzo's

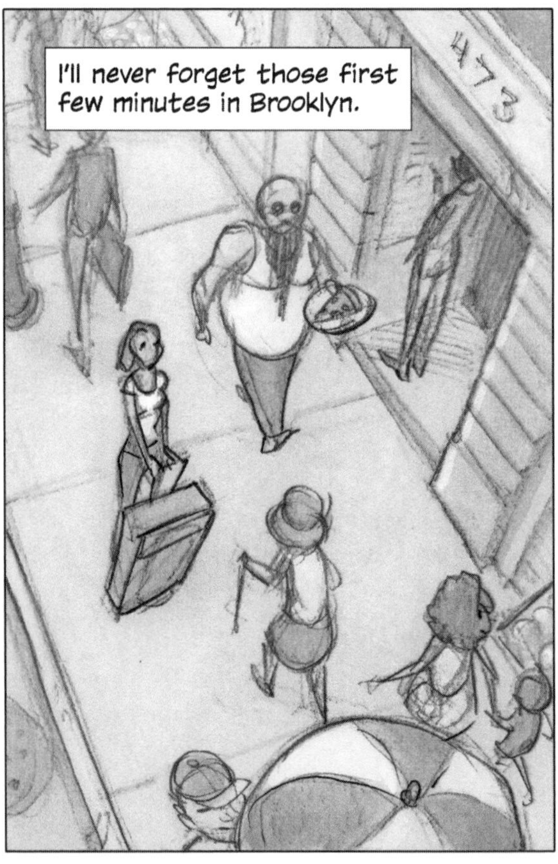
I'll never forget those first few minutes in Brooklyn.
473

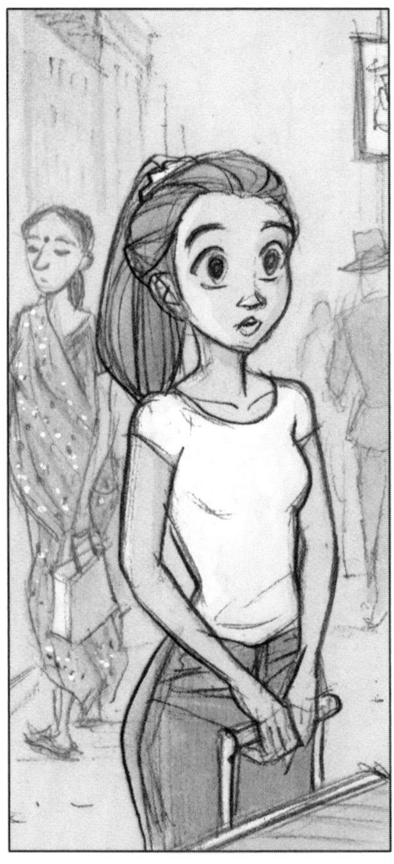

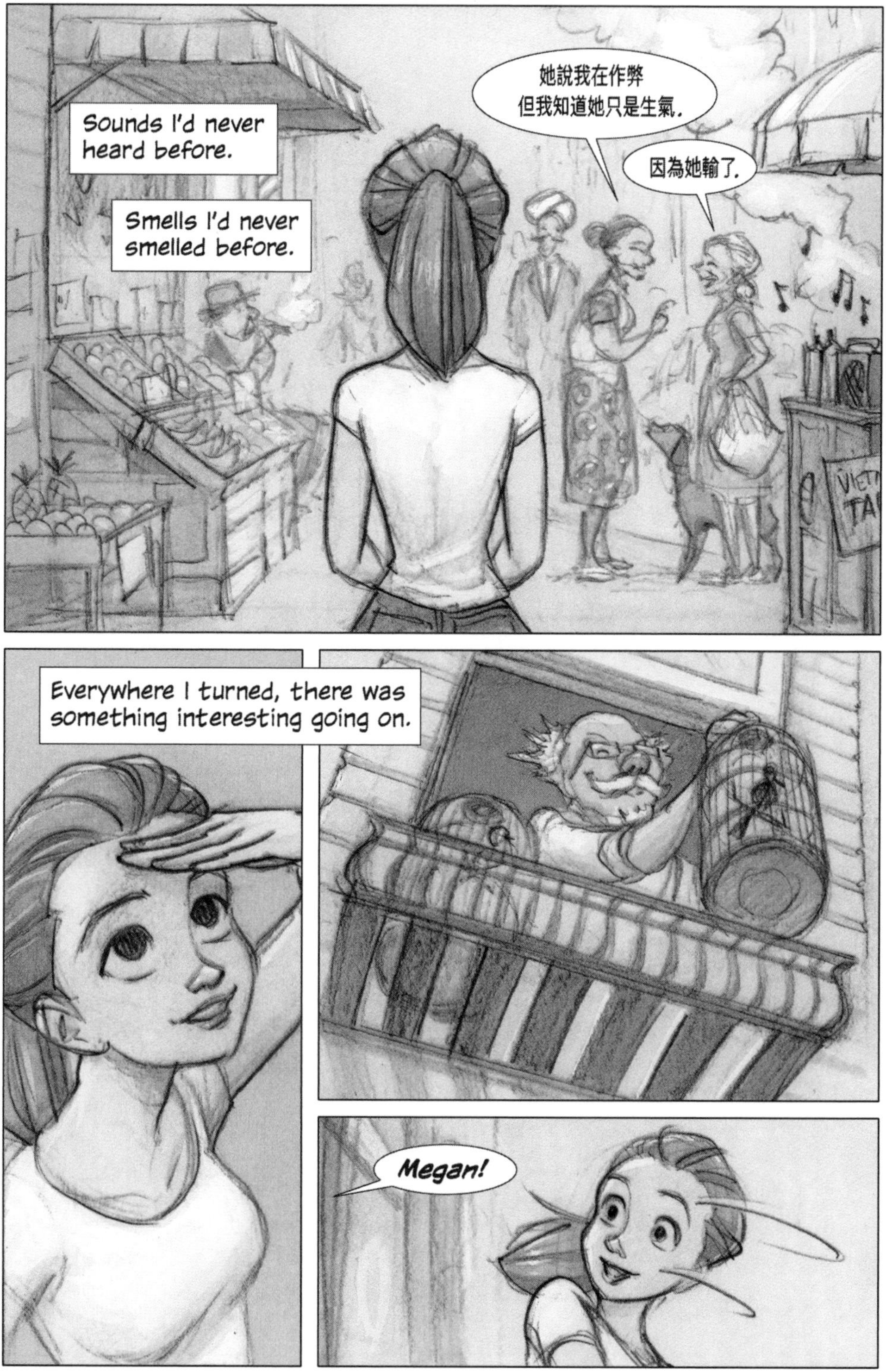
Sounds I'd never heard before.
Smells I'd never smelled before.
她說我在作弊
但我知道她只是生氣.
因為她輸了.
Everywhere I turned, there was something interesting going on.
Megan!

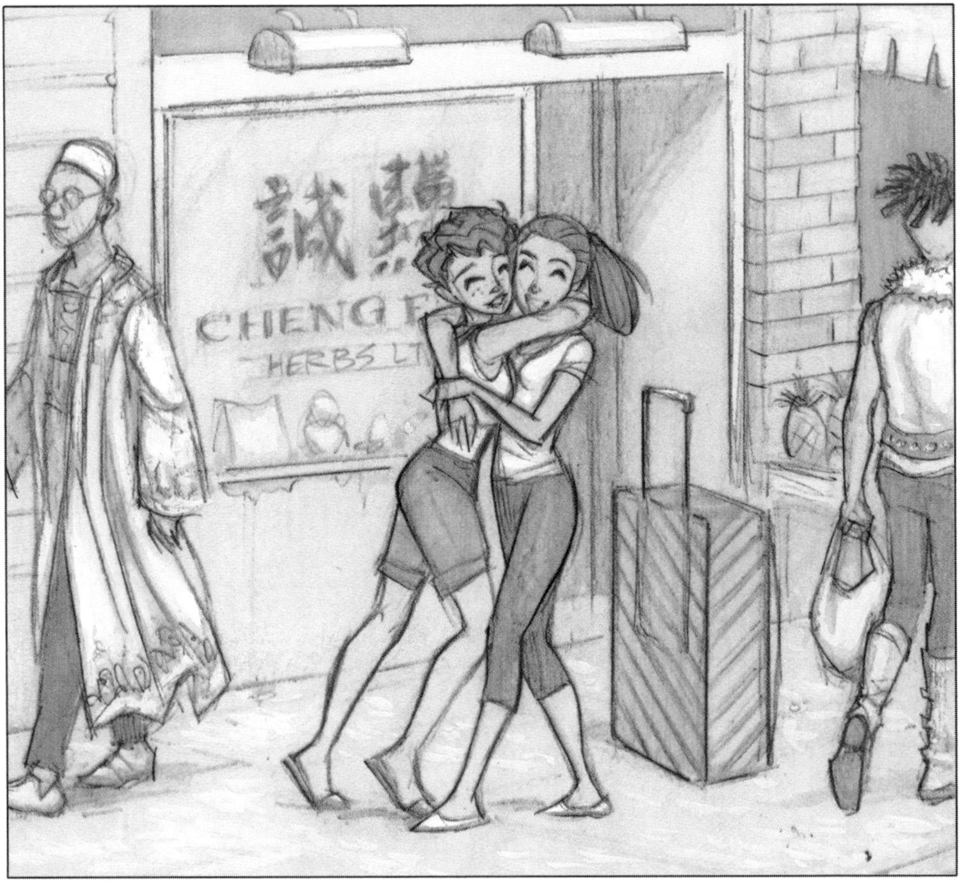
CHENG
HERBS

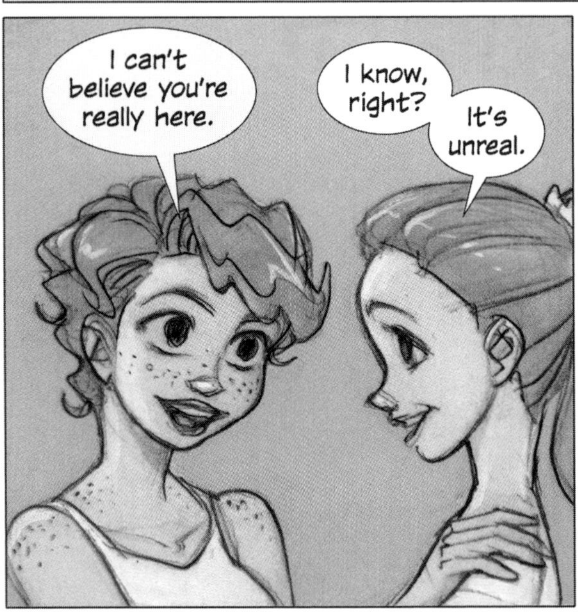
I can't believe you're really here.
I know, right?
It's unreal.

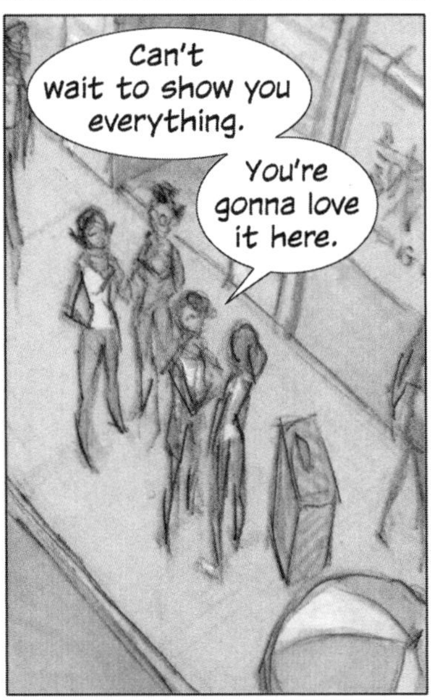
Can't wait to show you everything.
You're gonna love it here.

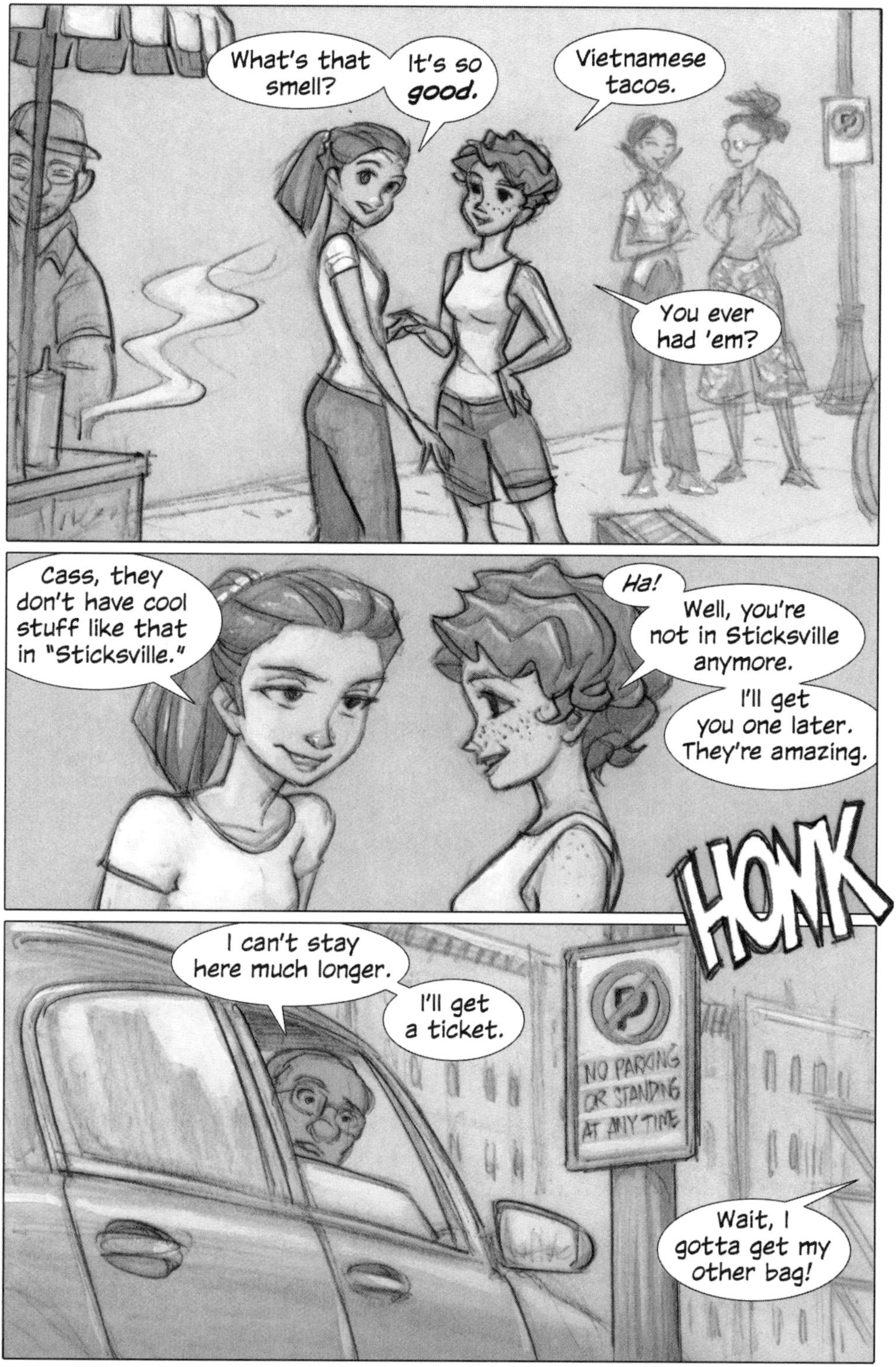
What's that smell?
It's so *good.*
Vietnamese tacos.
You ever had 'em?
Cass, they don't have cool stuff like that in "Sticksville."
Ha!
Well, you're not in Sticksville anymore.
I'll get you one later. They're amazing.
HONK
I can't stay here much longer.
I'll get a ticket.
NO PARKING OR STANDING AT ANY TIME
Wait, I gotta get my other bag!

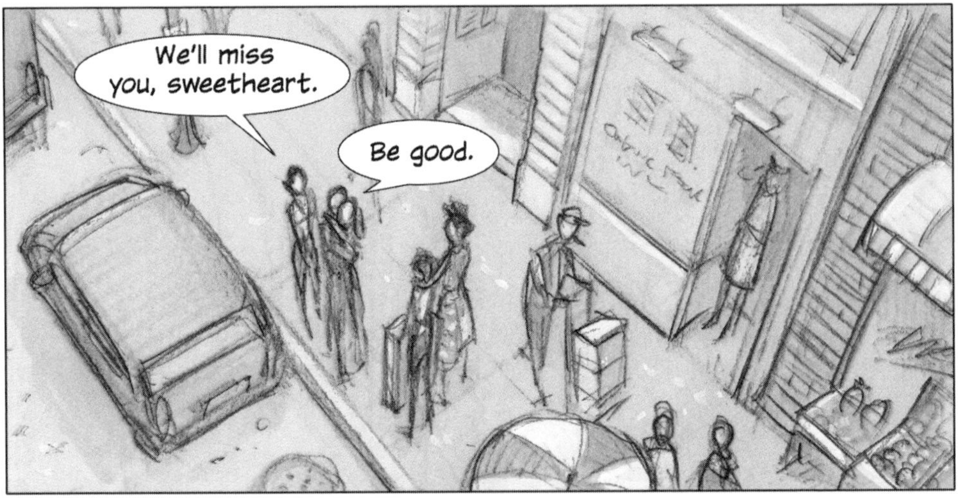
We'll miss you, sweetheart.
Be good.

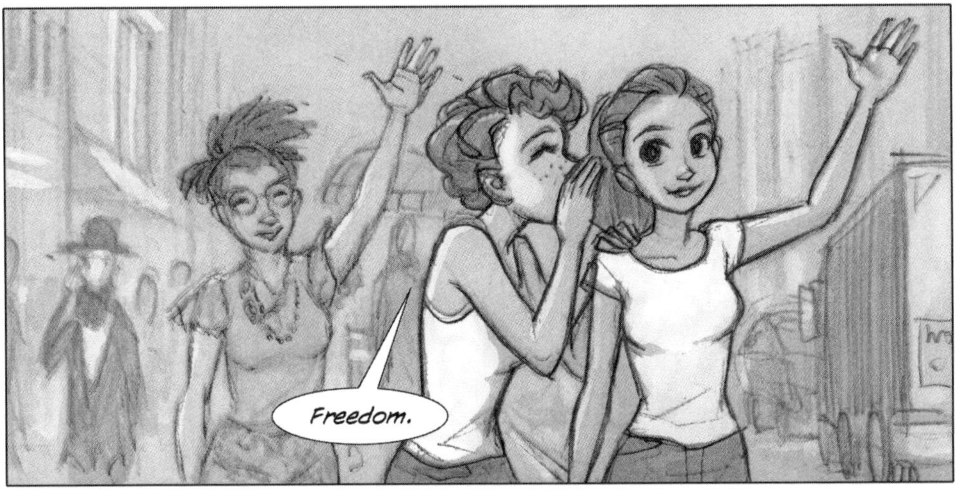
Freedom.

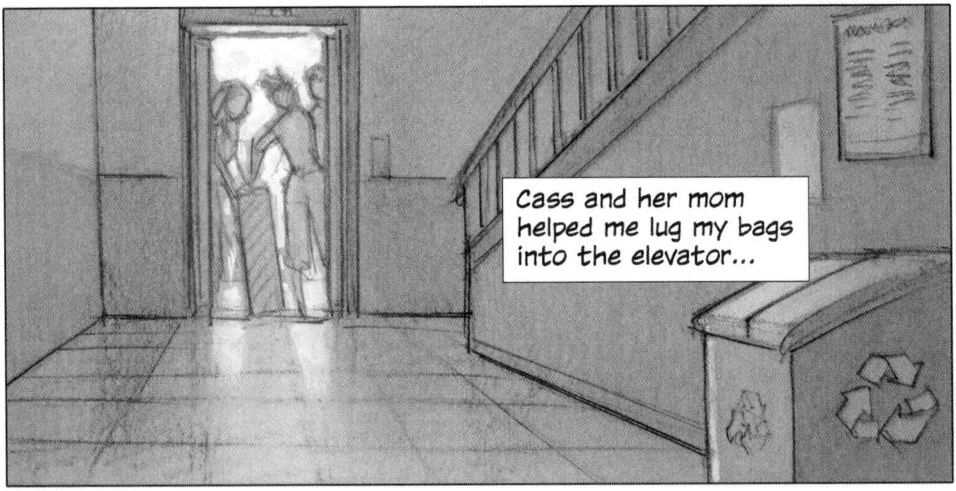
Cass and her mom helped me lug my bags into the elevator...

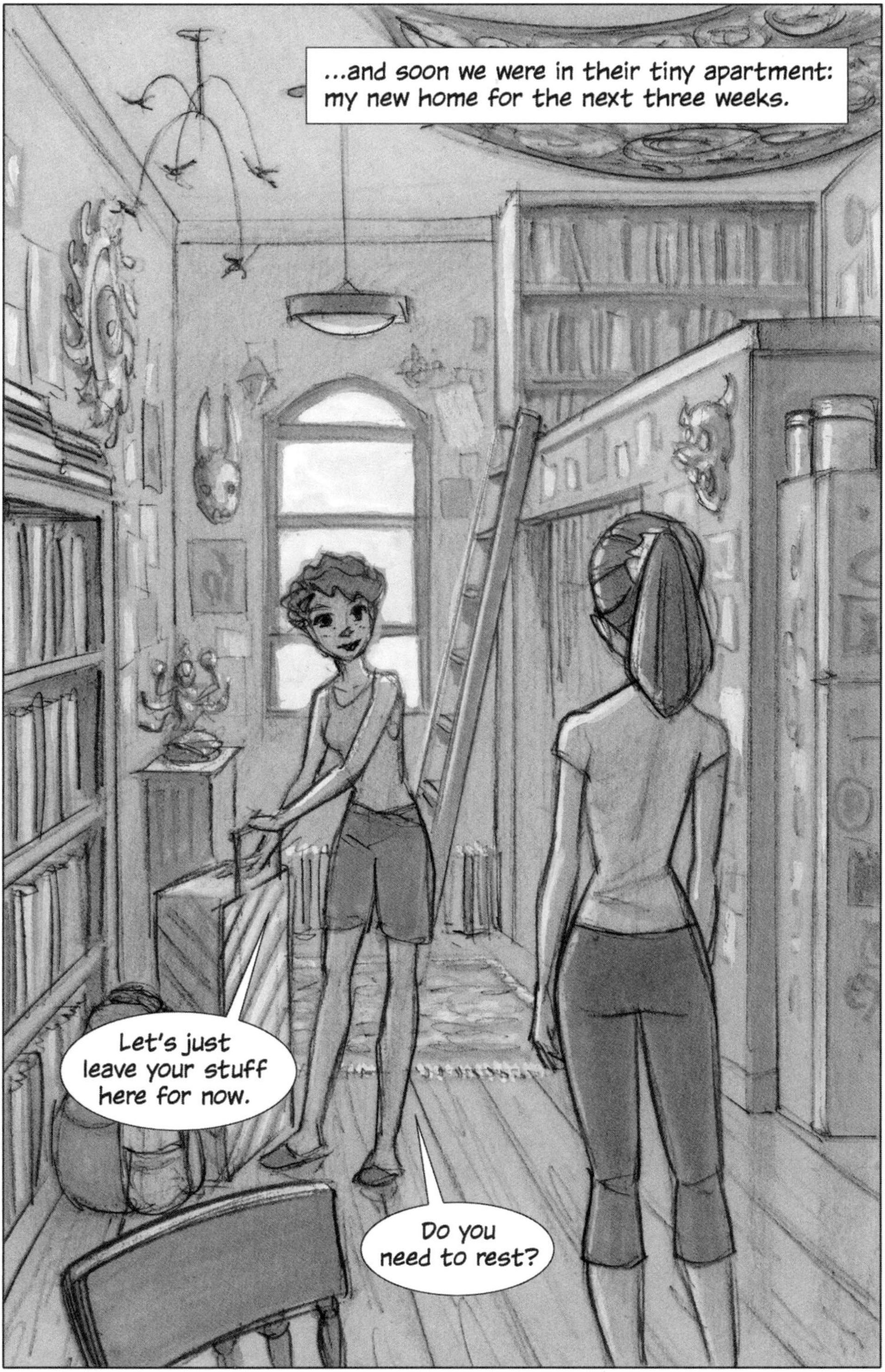
...and soon we were in their tiny apartment: my new home for the next three weeks.
Let's just leave your stuff here for now.
Do you need to rest?

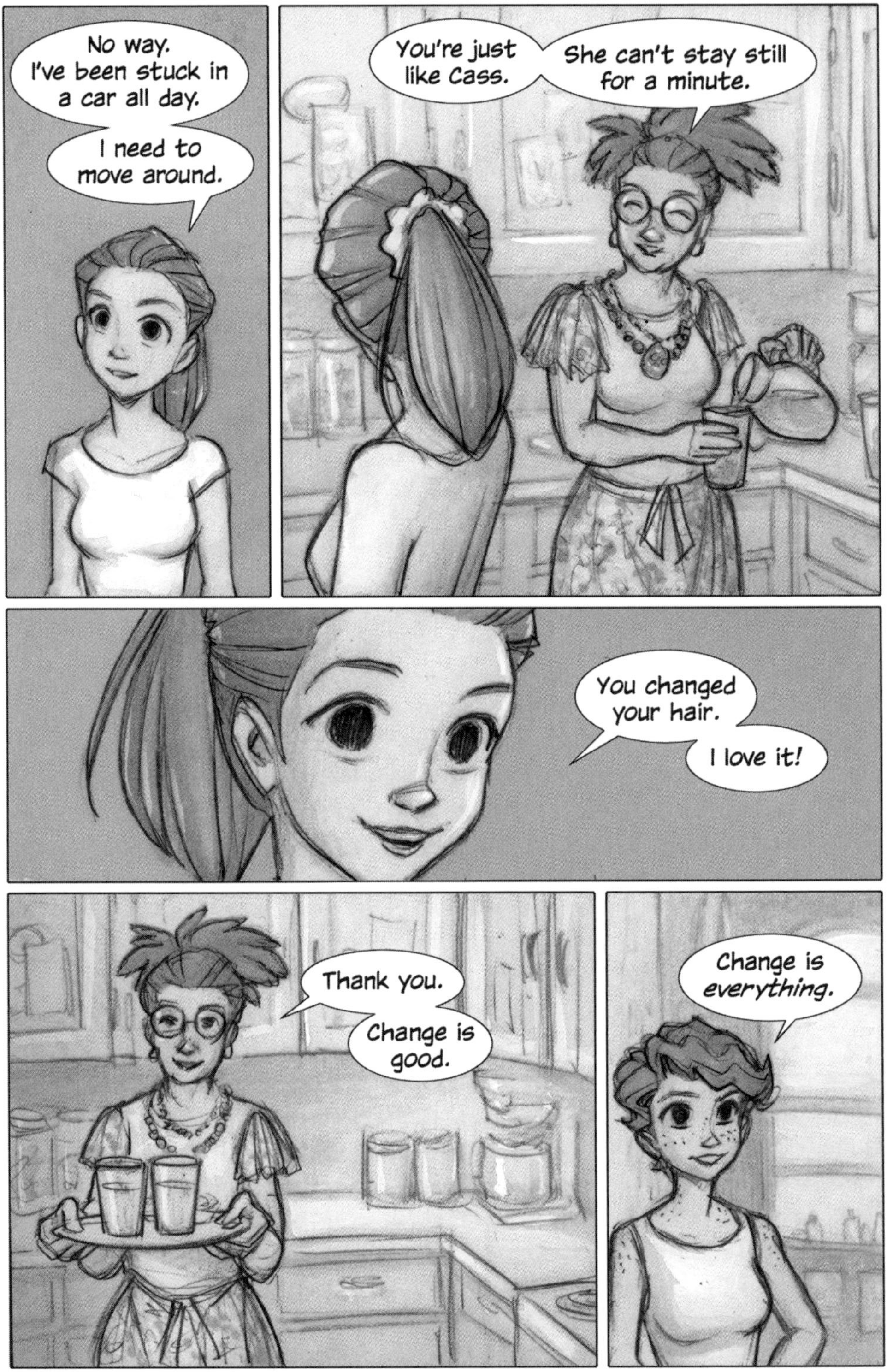
No way. I've been stuck in a car all day.
I need to move around.
You're just like Cass.
She can't stay still for a minute.
You changed your hair.
I love it!
Thank you.
Change is good.
Change is *everything.*

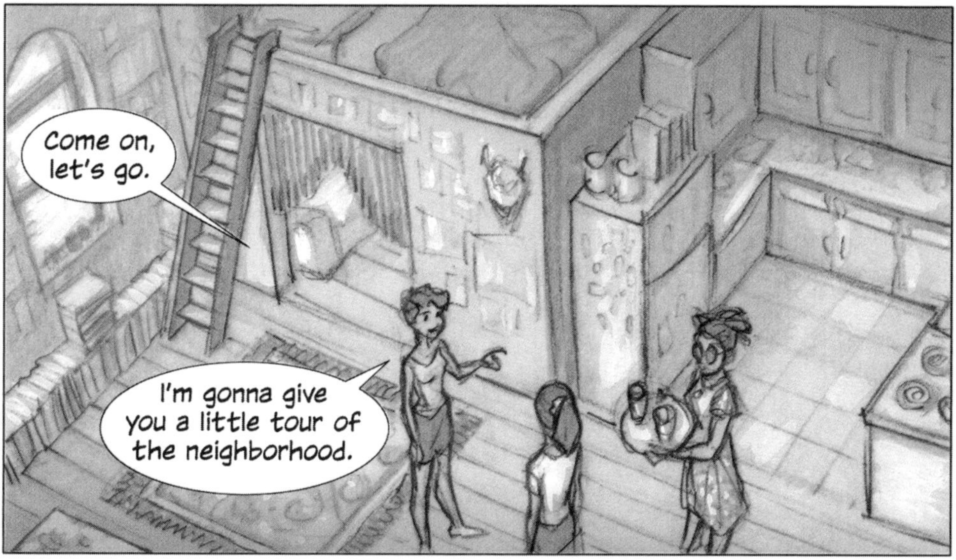
Come on, let's go.
I'm gonna give you a little tour of the neighborhood.

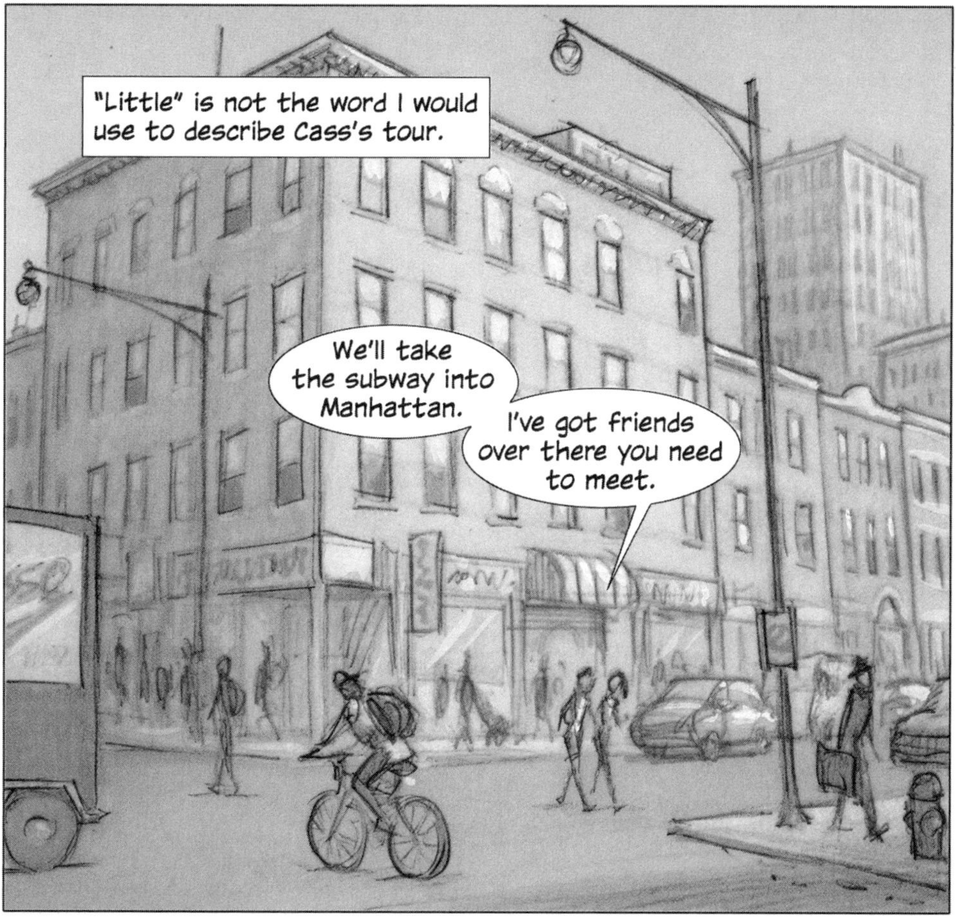
"Little" is not the word I would use to describe Cass's tour.
We'll take the subway into Manhattan.
I've got friends over there you need to meet.

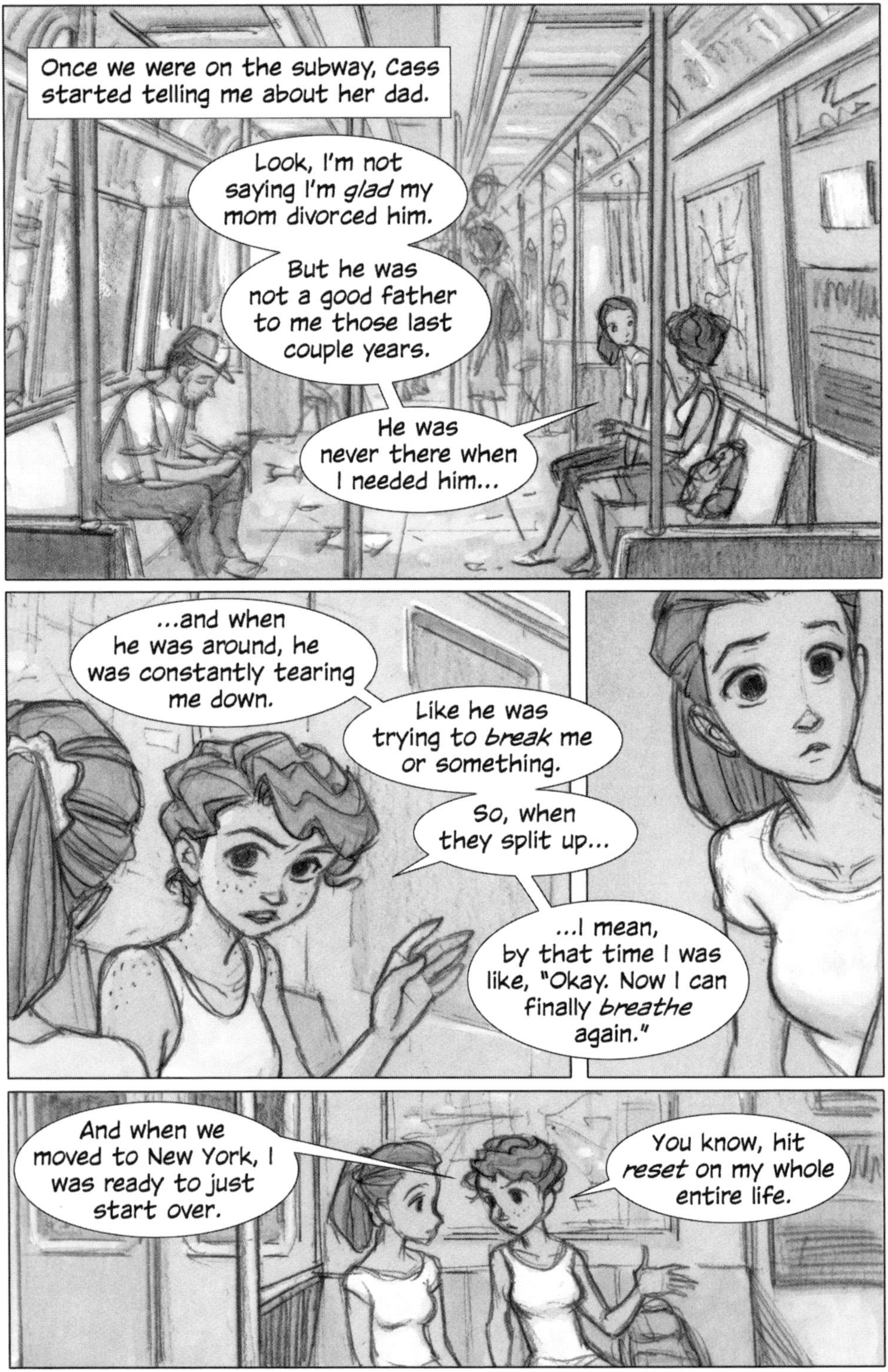

Once we were on the subway, Cass started telling me about her dad.
Look, I'm not saying I'm *glad* my mom divorced him.
But he was not a good father to me those last couple years.
He was never there when I needed him...
...and when he was around, he was constantly tearing me down.
Like he was trying to *break* me or something.
So, when they split up...
...I mean, by that time I was like, "Okay. Now I can finally *breathe* again."
And when we moved to New York, I was ready to just start over.
You know, hit *reset* on my whole entire life.

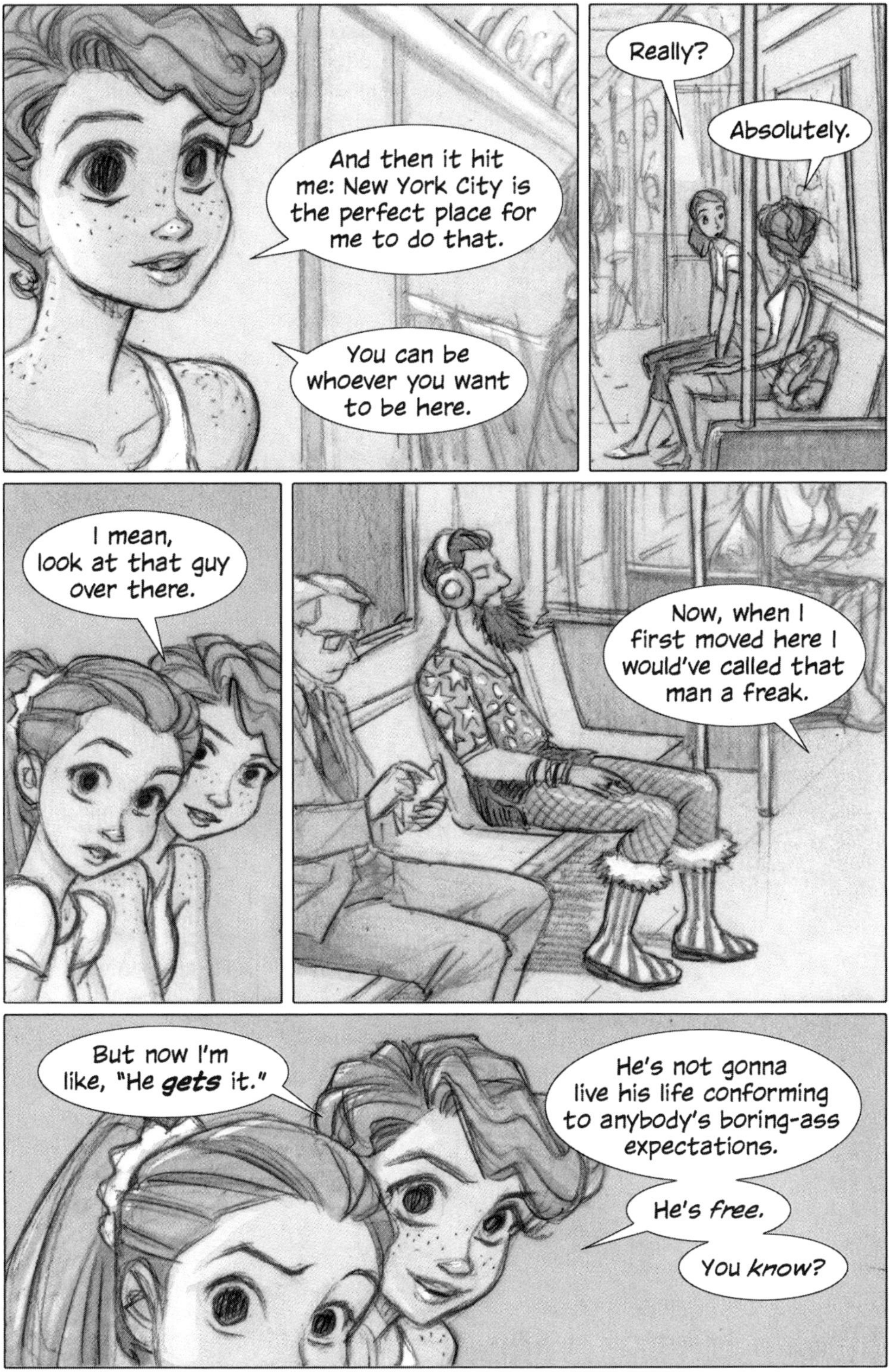
And then it hit me: New York City is the perfect place for me to do that.
You can be whoever you want to be here.
Really?
Absolutely.
I mean, look at that guy over there.
Now, when I first moved here I would've called that man a freak.
But now I'm like, "He **gets** it."
He's not gonna live his life conforming to anybody's boring-ass expectations.
He's *free.*
You *know?*

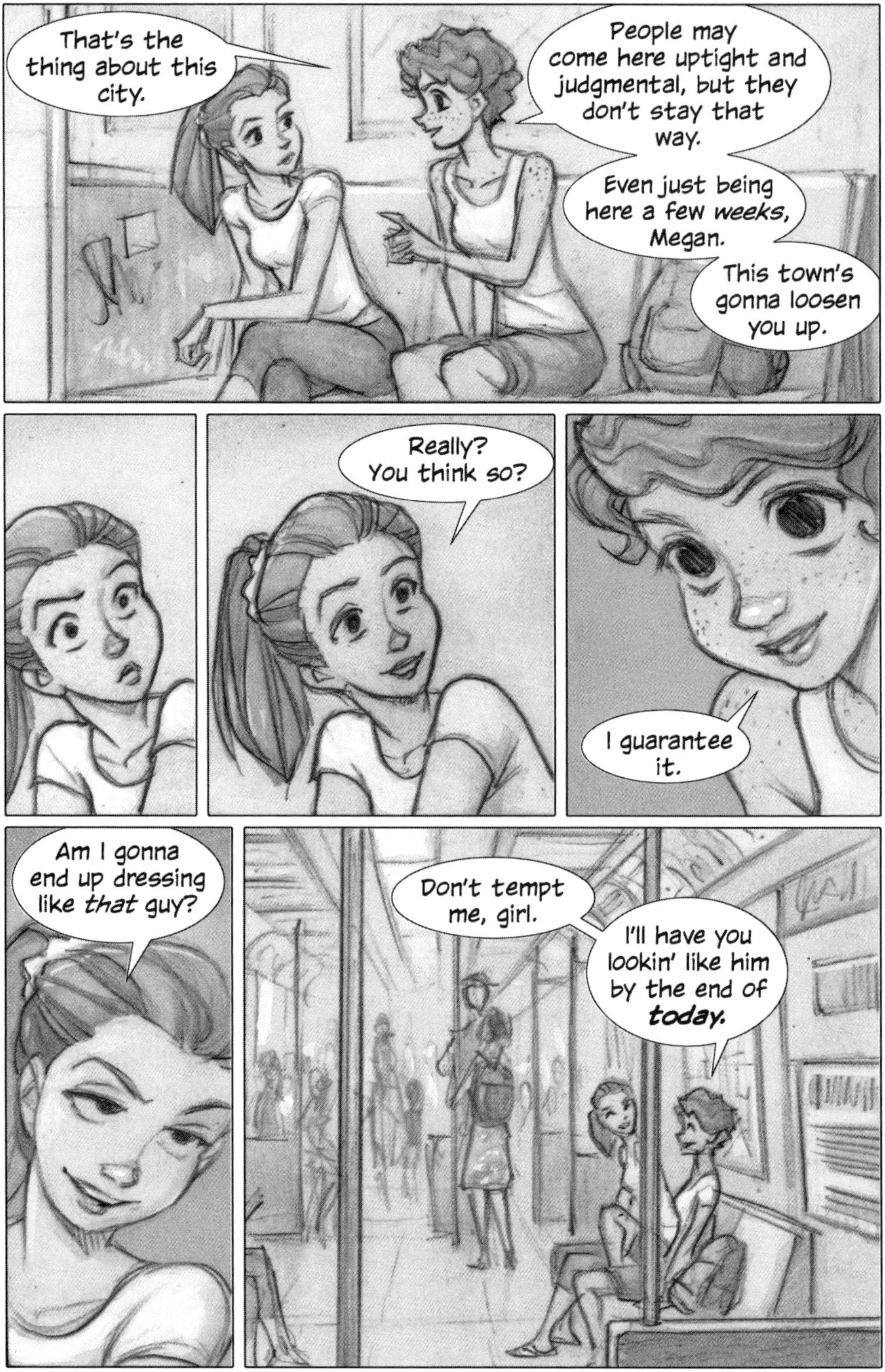
That's the thing about this city.
People may come here uptight and judgmental, but they don't stay that way.
Even just being here a few *weeks*, Megan.
This town's gonna loosen you up.
Really? You think so?
I guarantee it.
Am I gonna end up dressing like *that* guy?
Don't tempt me, girl.
I'll have you lookin' like him by the end of ***today.***

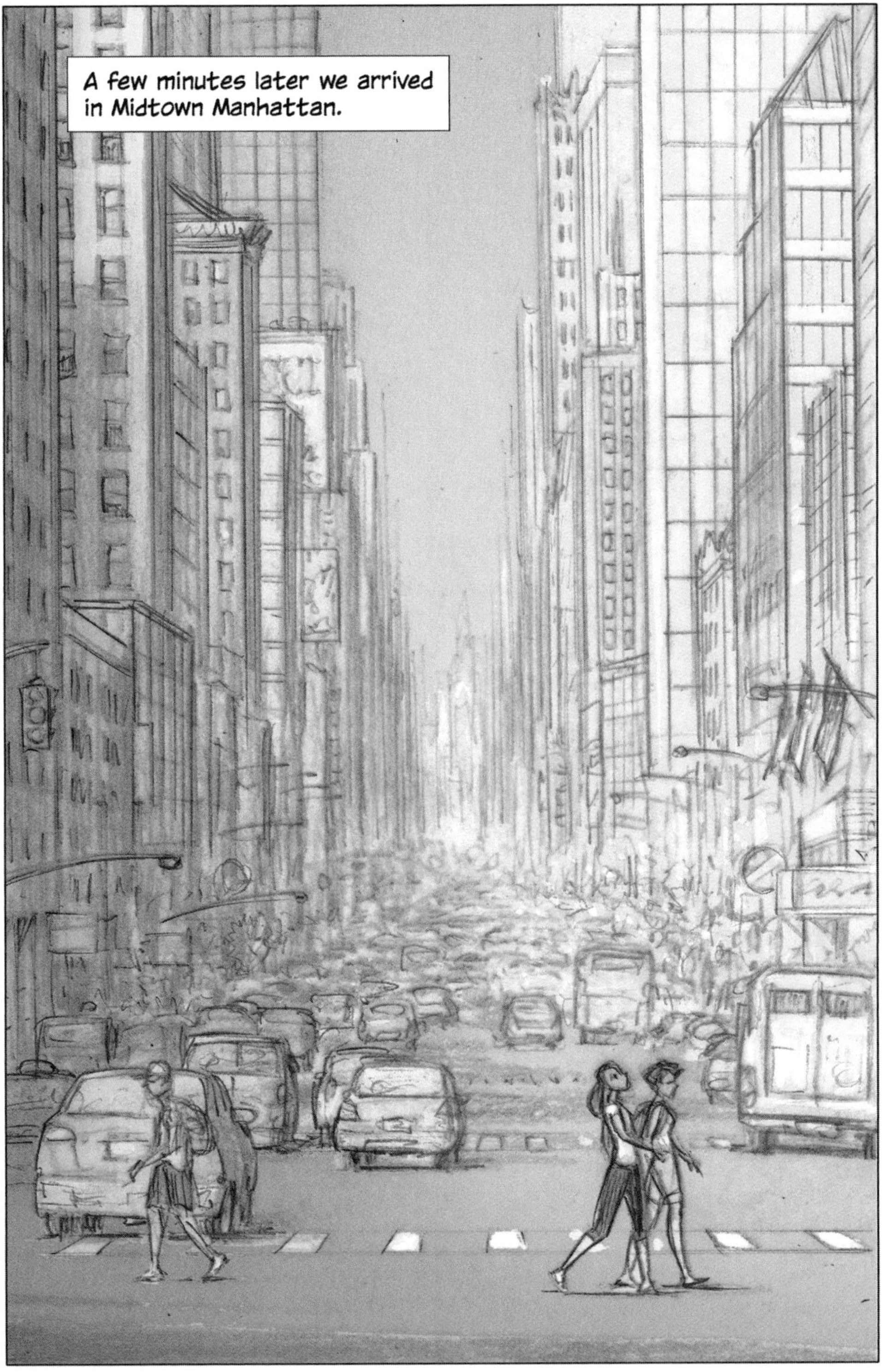
A few minutes later we arrived in Midtown Manhattan.

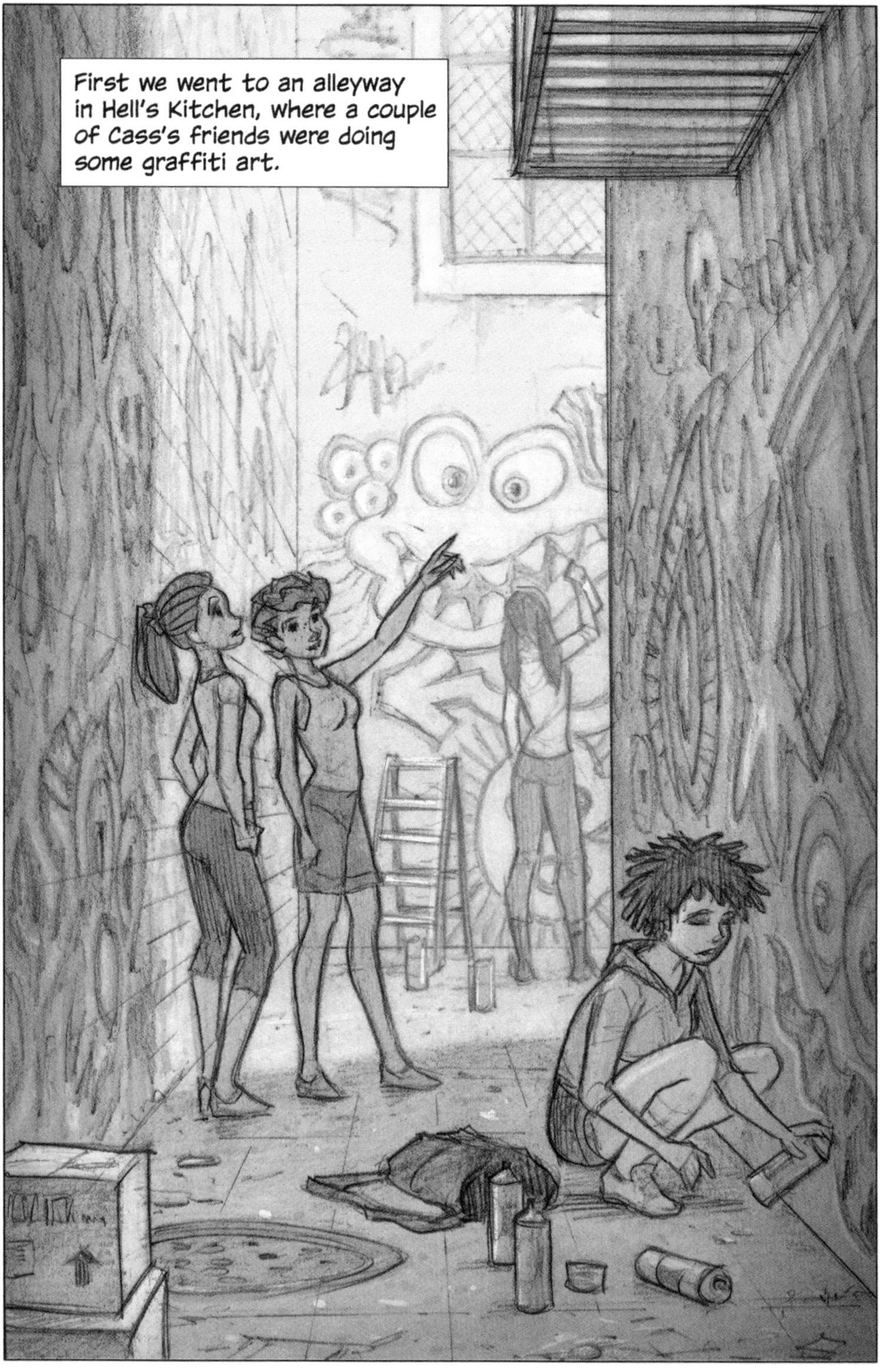
First we went to an alleyway in Hell's Kitchen, where a couple of Cass's friends were doing some graffiti art.

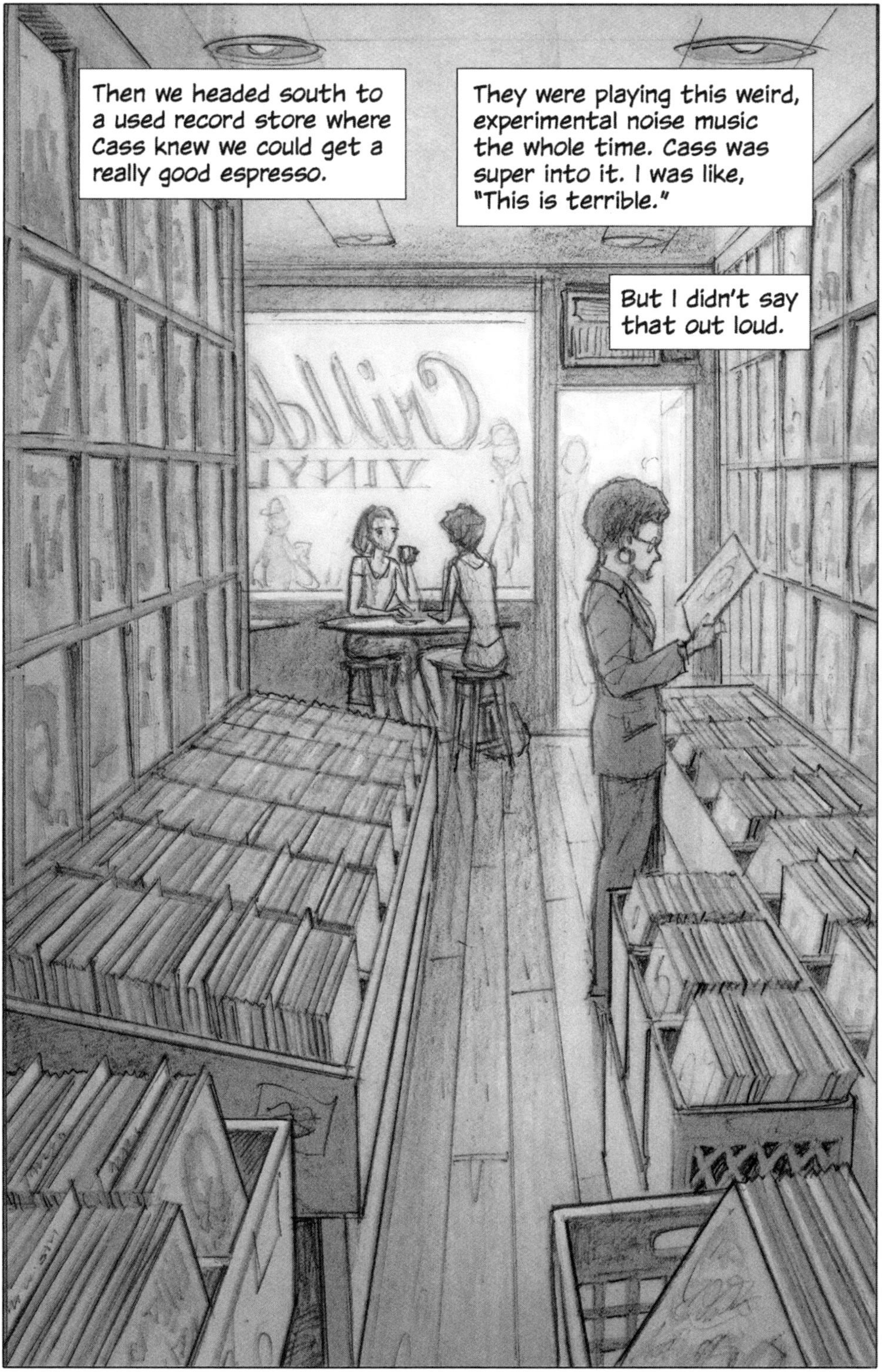
Then we headed south to a used record store where Cass knew we could get a really good espresso.
They were playing this weird, experimental noise music the whole time. Cass was super into it. I was like, "This is terrible."
But I didn't say that out loud.

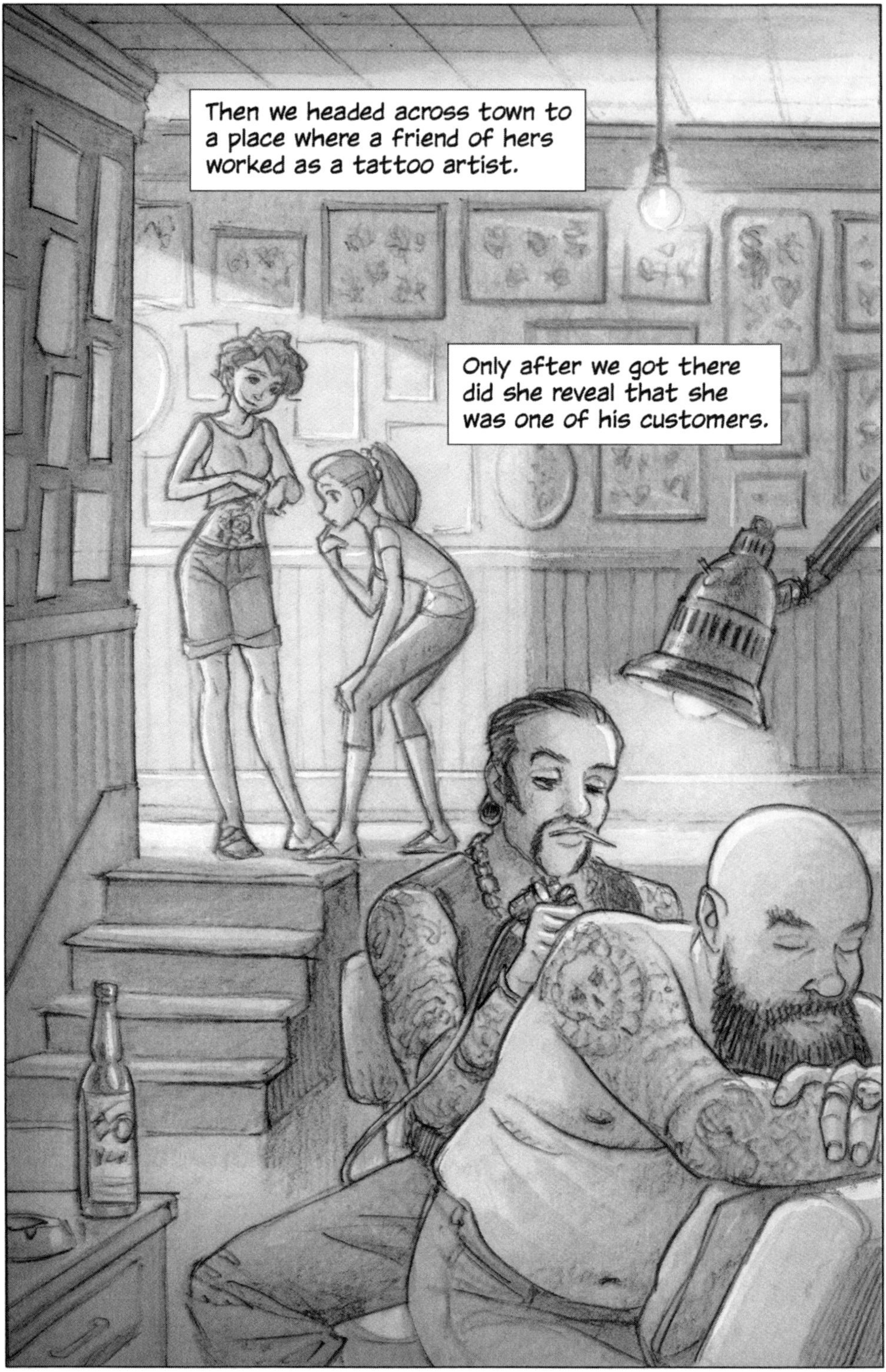
Then we headed across town to a place where a friend of hers worked as a tattoo artist.
Only after we got there did she reveal that she was one of his customers.

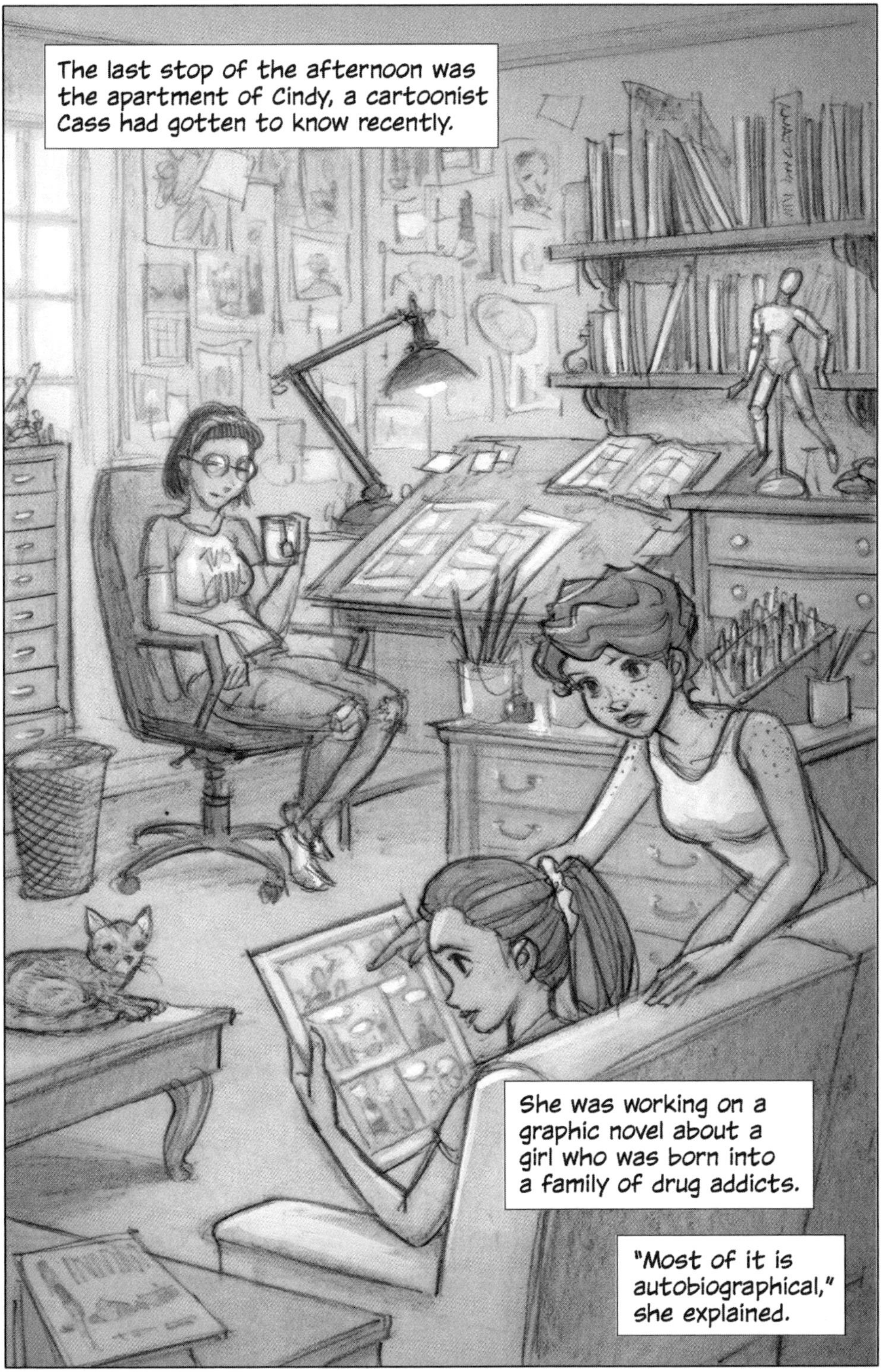
The last stop of the afternoon was the apartment of Cindy, a cartoonist Cass had gotten to know recently.
She was working on a graphic novel about a girl who was born into a family of drug addicts.
"Most of it is autobiographical," she explained.

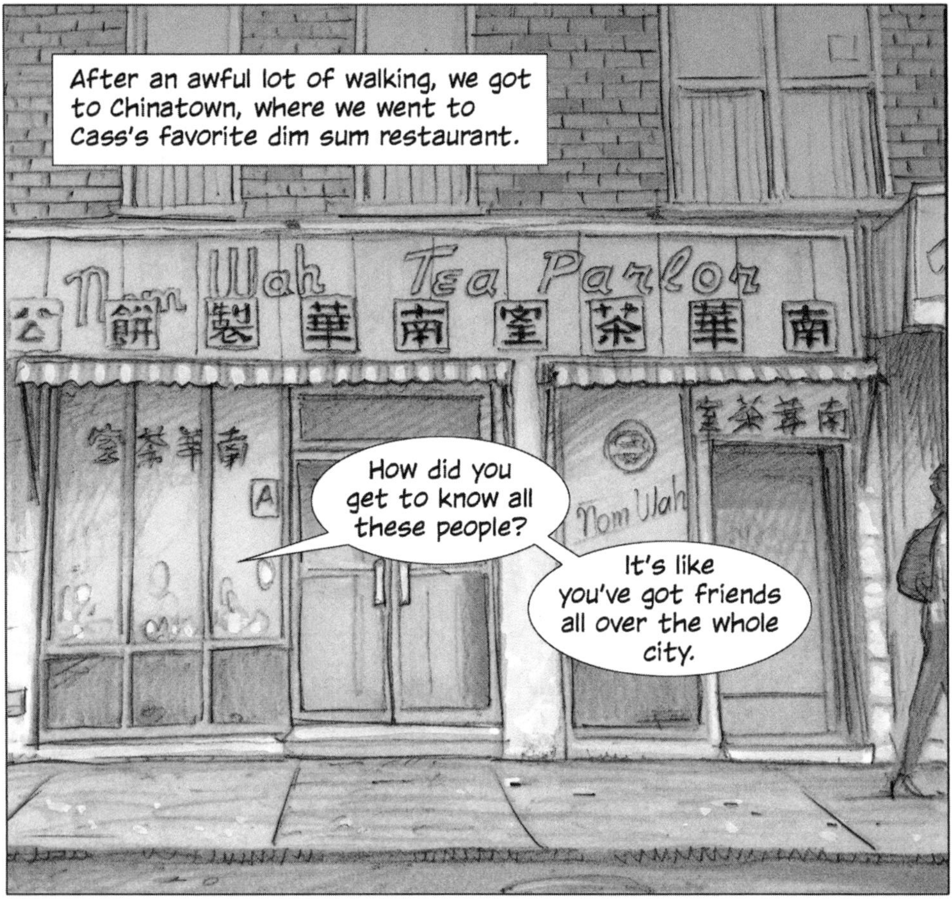
After an awful lot of walking, we got to Chinatown, where we went to Cass's favorite dim sum restaurant.
Nom Wah Tea Parlor
南華茶室
How did you get to know all these people?
It's like you've got friends all over the whole city.

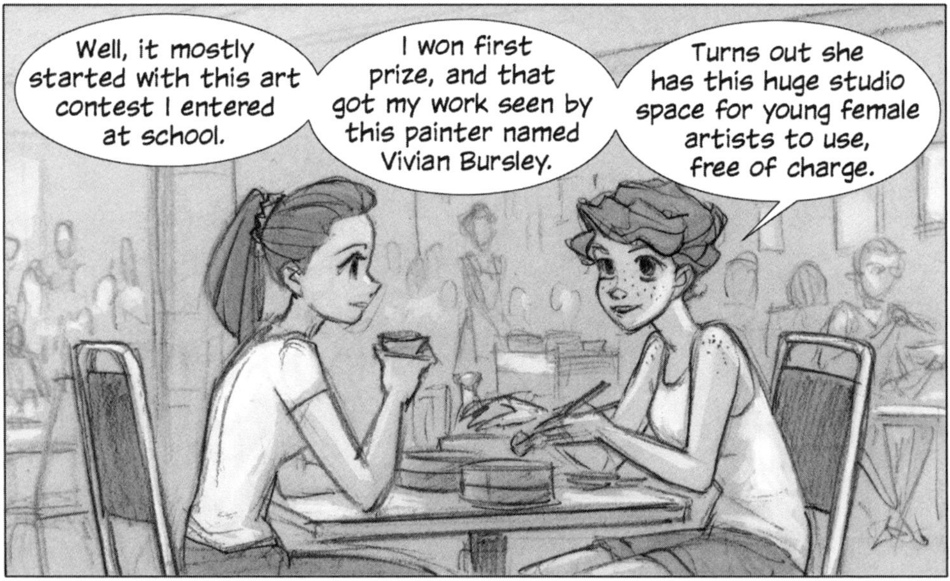
Well, it mostly started with this art contest I entered at school.
I won first prize, and that got my work seen by this painter named Vivian Bursley.
Turns out she has this huge studio space for young female artists to use, free of charge.

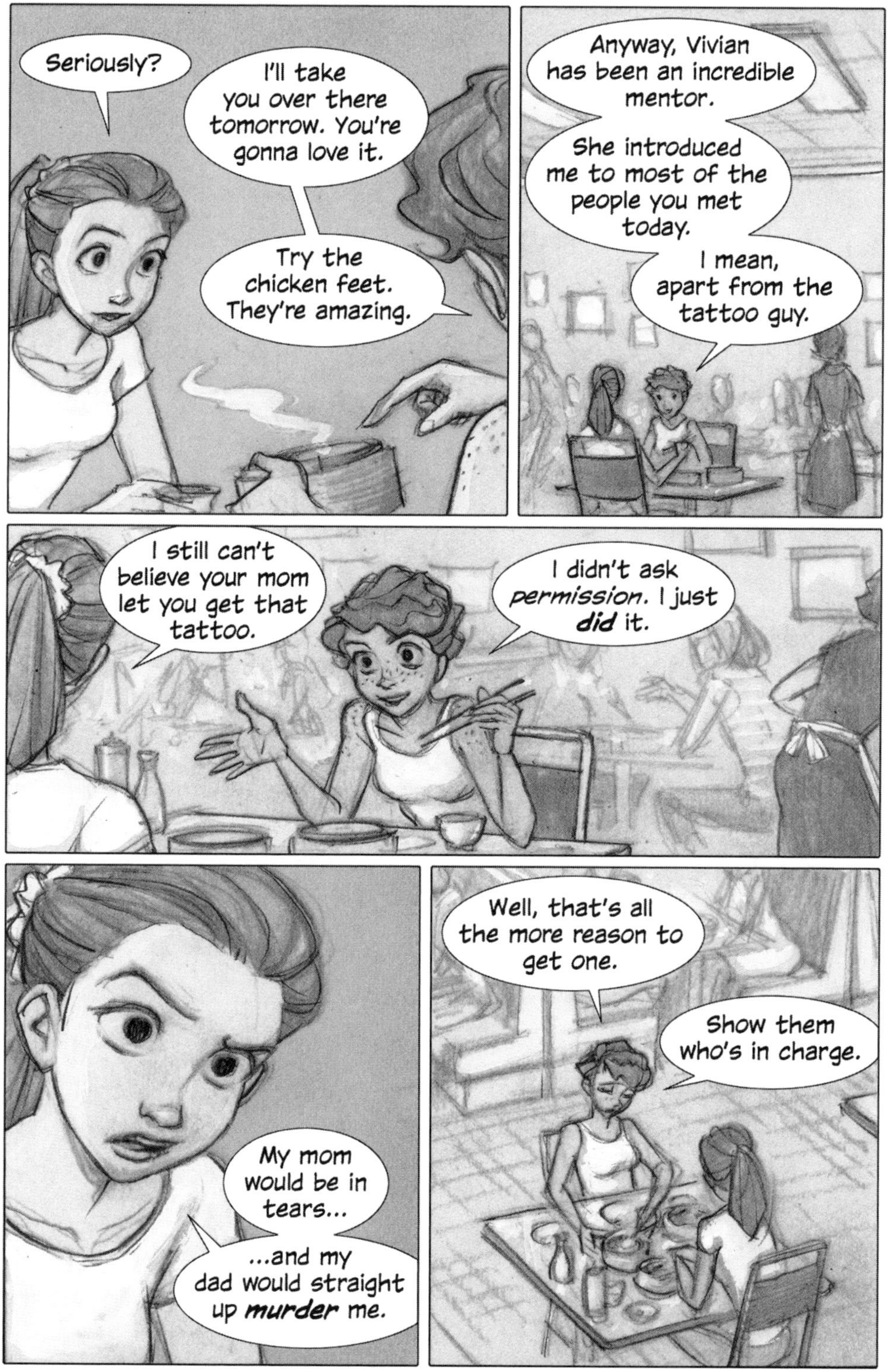
Seriously?
I'll take you over there tomorrow. You're gonna love it.
Try the chicken feet. They're amazing.
Anyway, Vivian has been an incredible mentor.
She introduced me to most of the people you met today.
I mean, apart from the tattoo guy.
I still can't believe your mom let you get that tattoo.
I didn't ask *permission*. I just ***did*** it.
My mom would be in tears...
...and my dad would straight up ***murder*** me.
Well, that's all the more reason to get one.
Show them who's in charge.

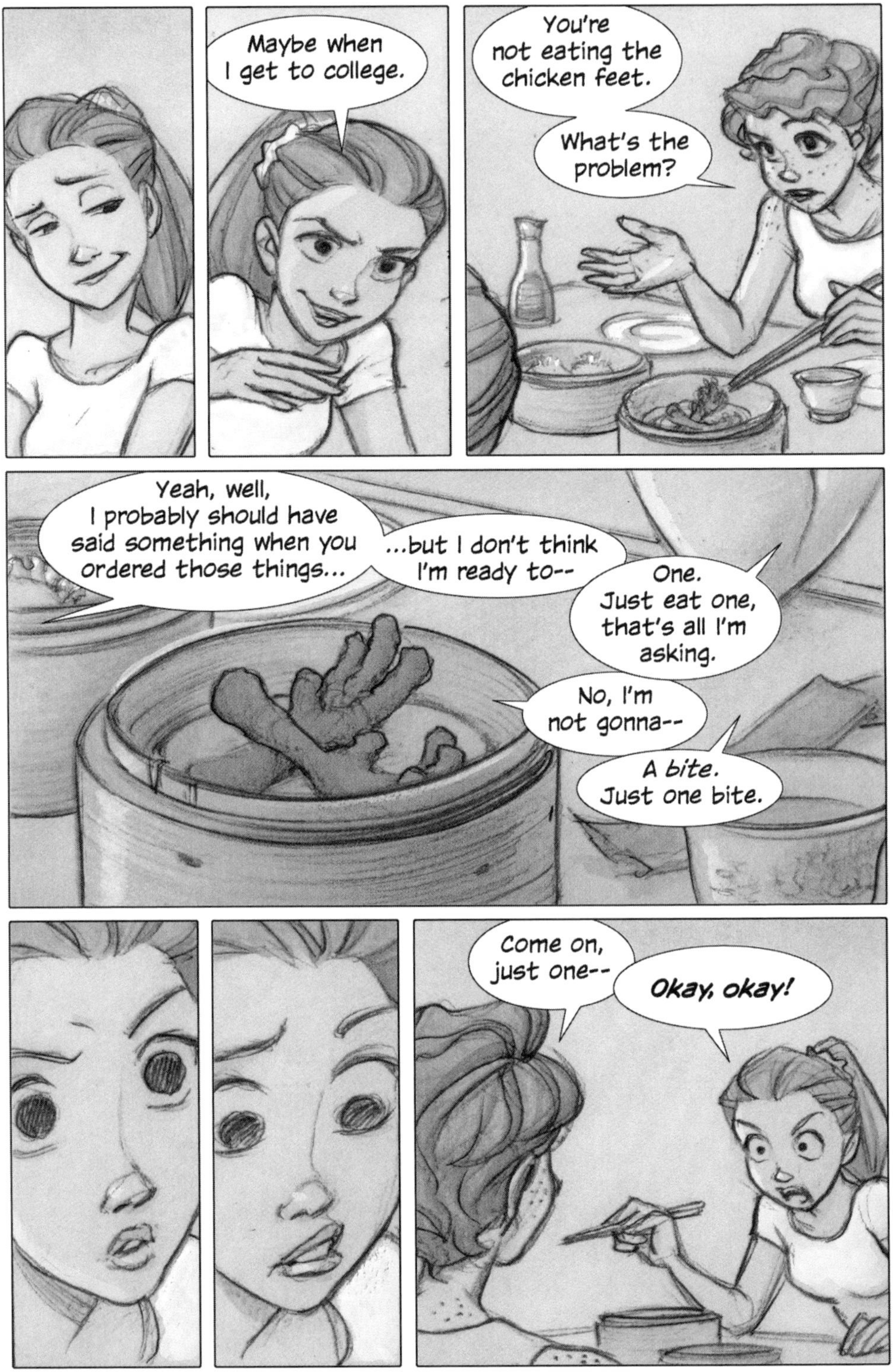
Maybe when I get to college.
You're not eating the chicken feet.
What's the problem?
Yeah, well, I probably should have said something when you ordered those things...
...but I don't think I'm ready to--
One. Just eat one, that's all I'm asking.
No, I'm not gonna--
A *bite*. Just one bite.
Come on, just one--
Okay, okay!

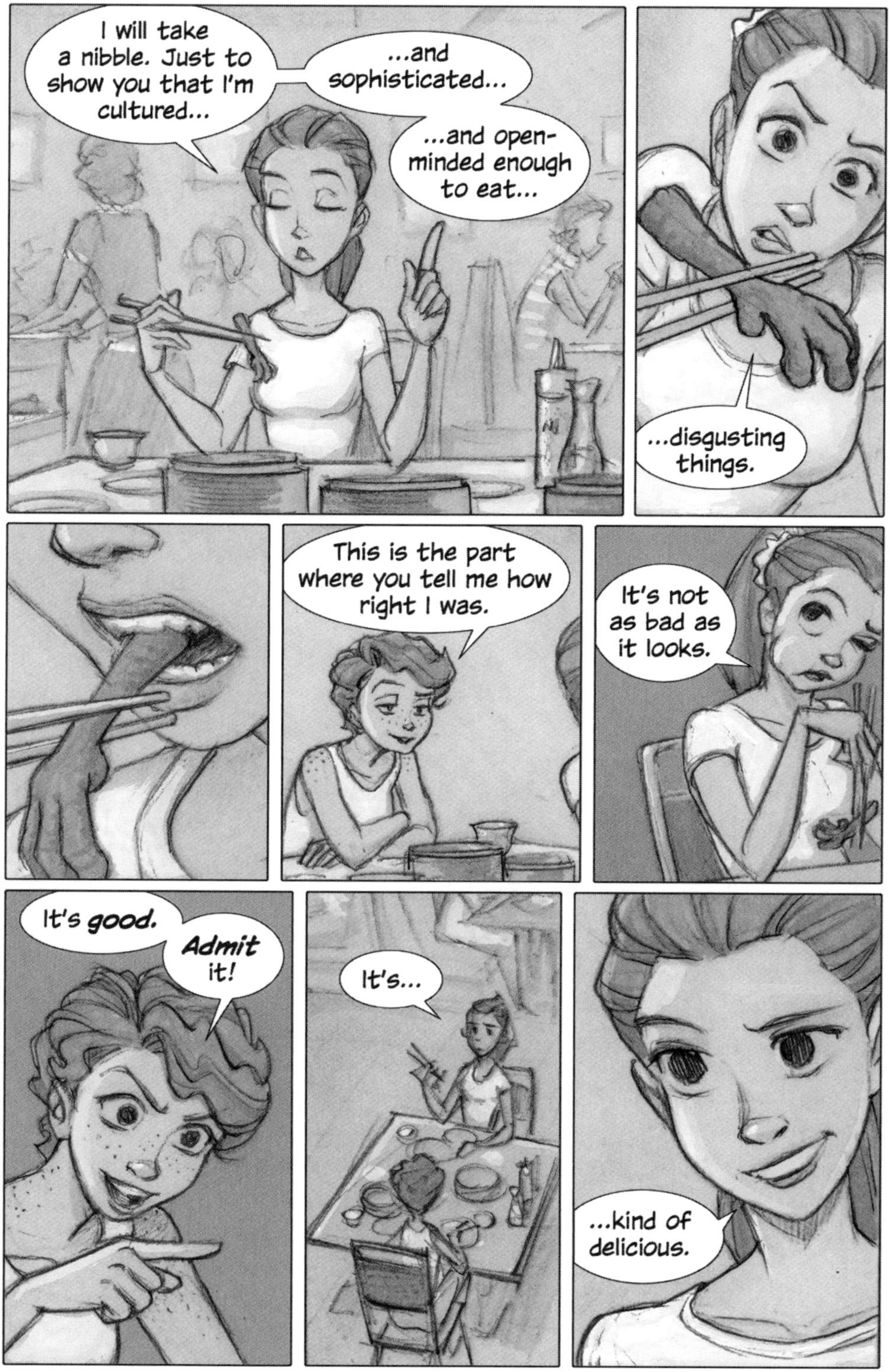
I will take a nibble. Just to show you that I'm cultured...
...and sophisticated...
...and open-minded enough to eat...
...disgusting things.
This is the part where you tell me how right I was.
It's not as bad as it looks.
It's *good.*
Admit it!
It's...
...kind of delicious.

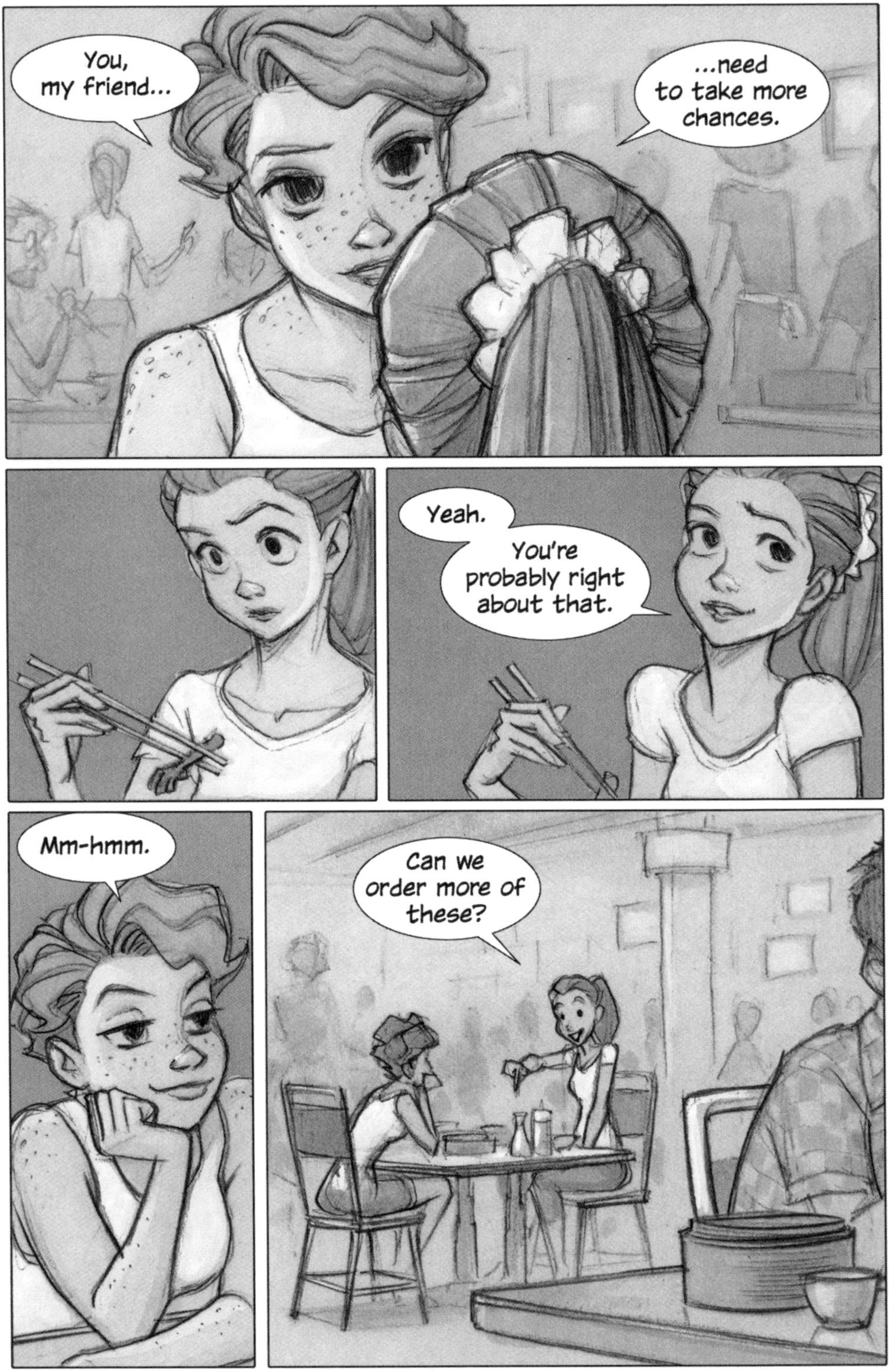
You, my friend...
...need to take more chances.
Yeah.
You're probably right about that.
Mm-hmm.
Can we order more of these?

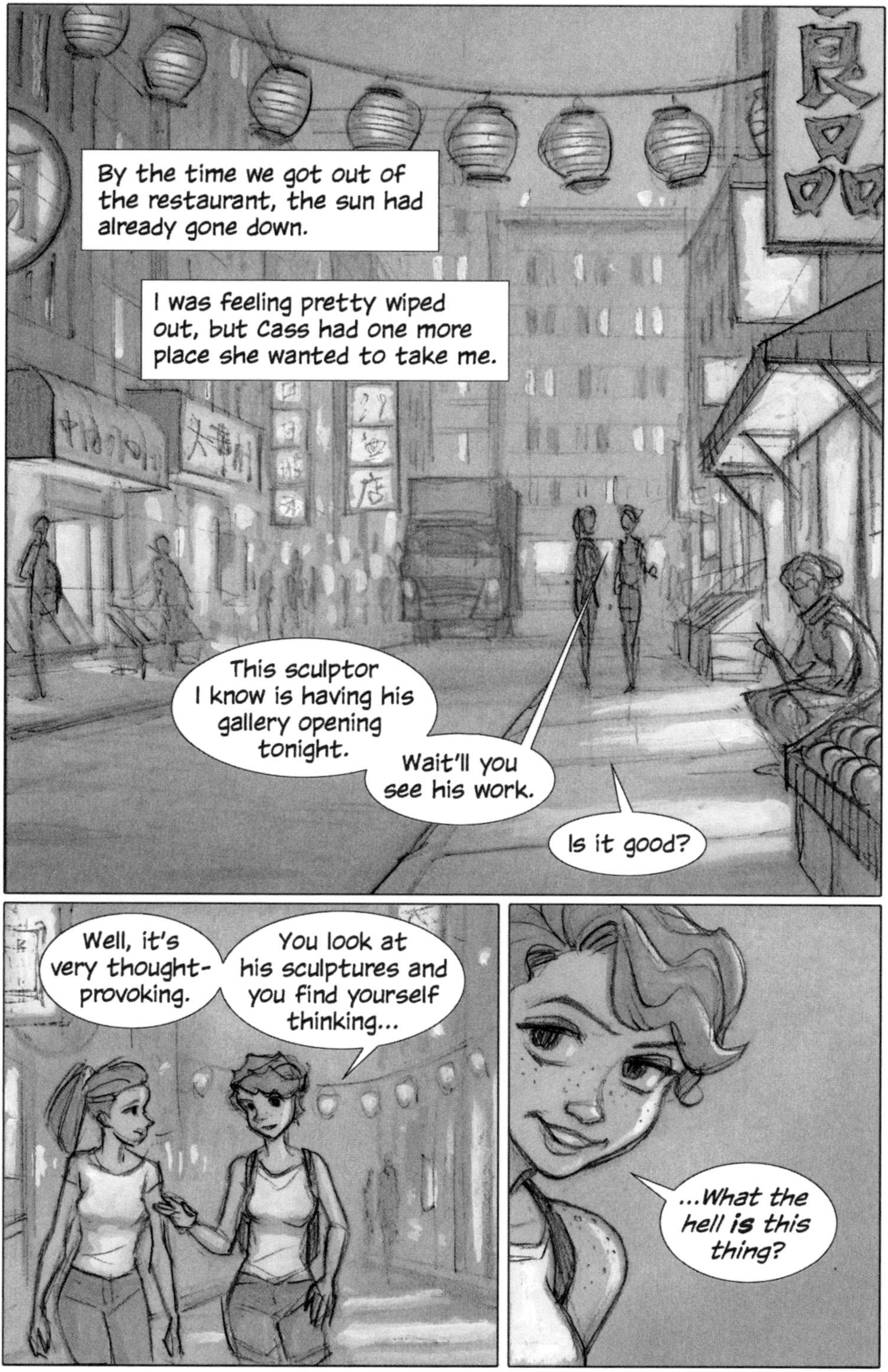
By the time we got out of the restaurant, the sun had already gone down.
I was feeling pretty wiped out, but Cass had one more place she wanted to take me.
This sculptor I know is having his gallery opening tonight.
Wait'll you see his work.
Is it good?
Well, it's very thought-provoking.
You look at his sculptures and you find yourself thinking...
...*What the hell* ***is*** *this thing?*

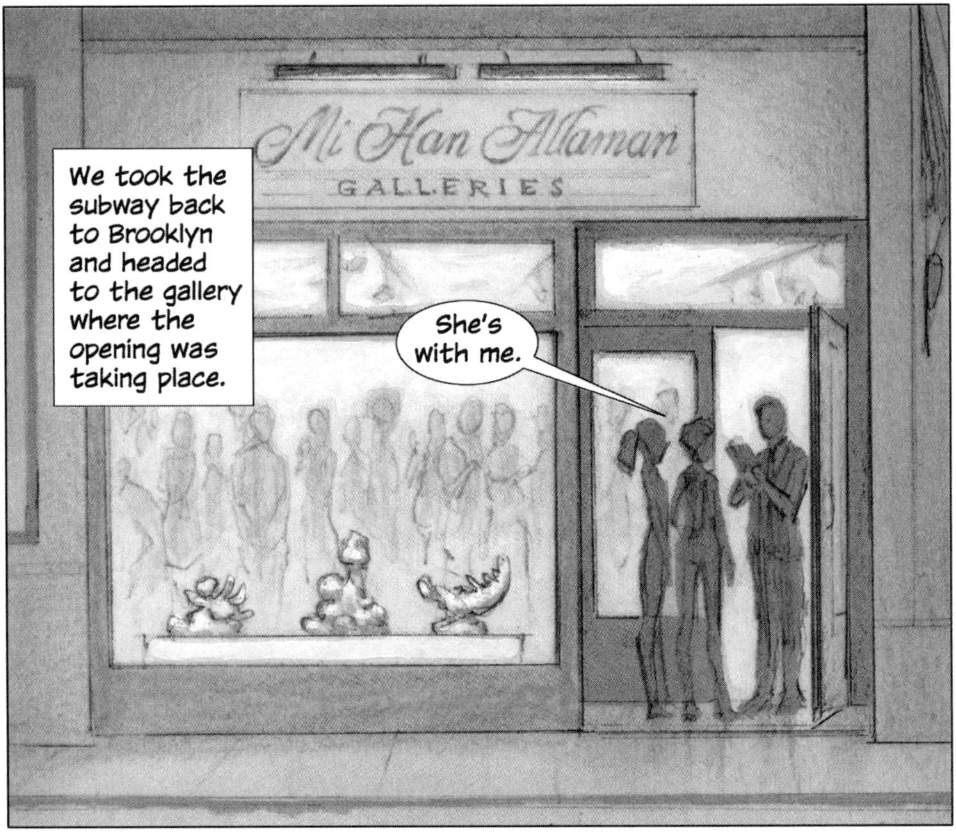
Mi Han Allaman
GALLERIES
We took the subway back to Brooklyn and headed to the gallery where the opening was taking place.
She's with me.

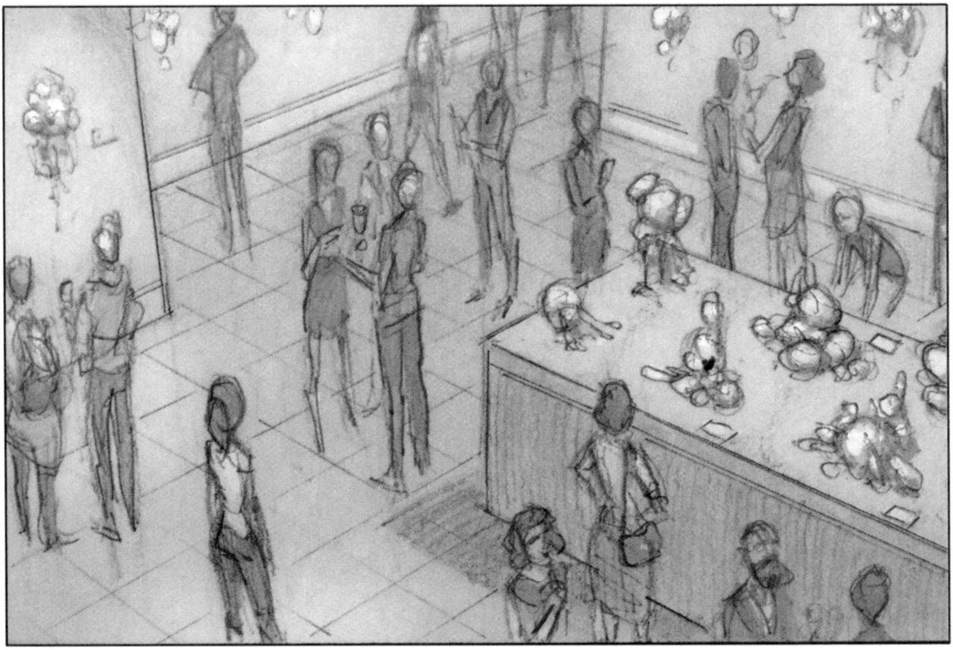

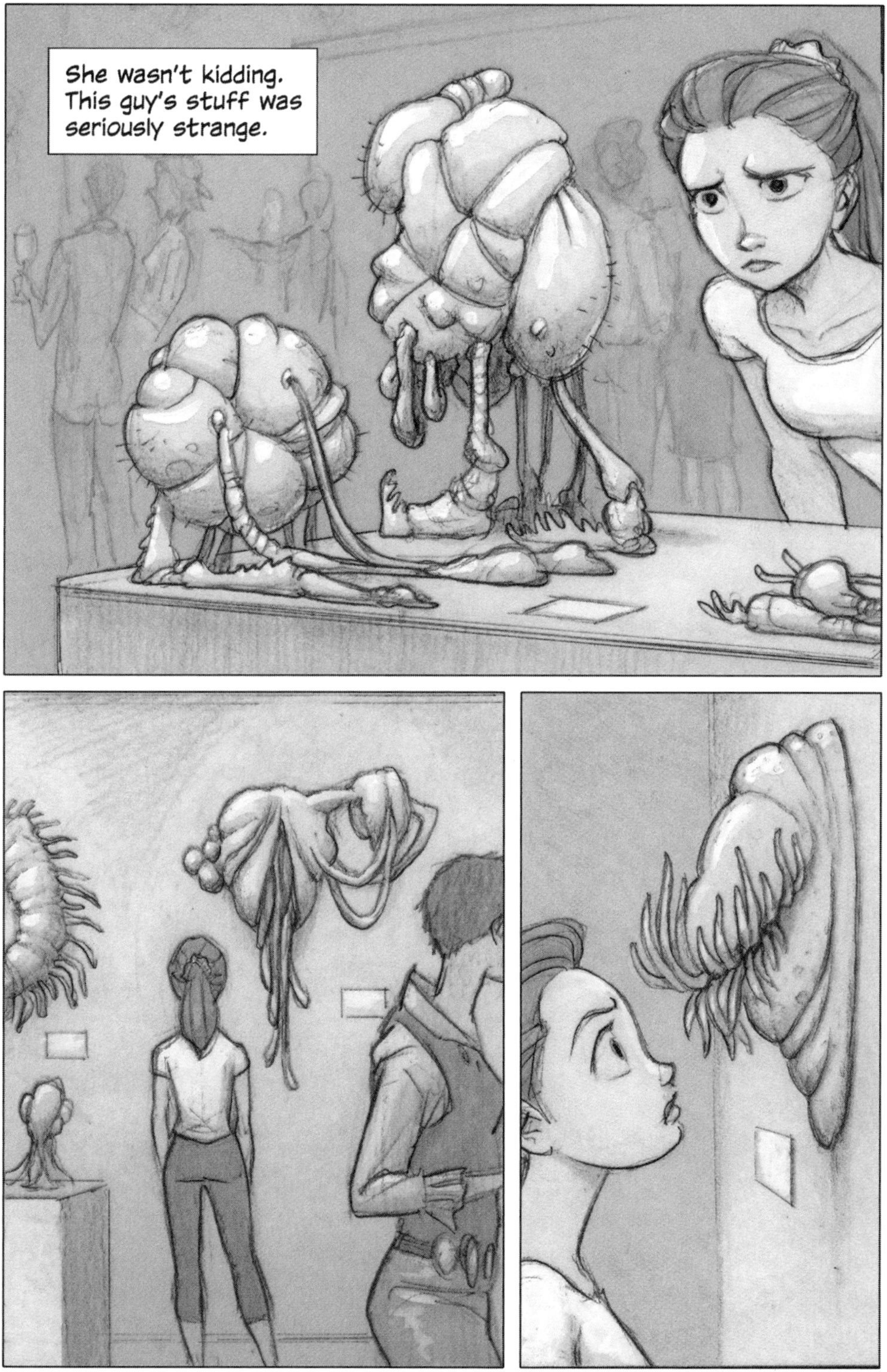
She wasn't kidding. This guy's stuff was seriously strange.

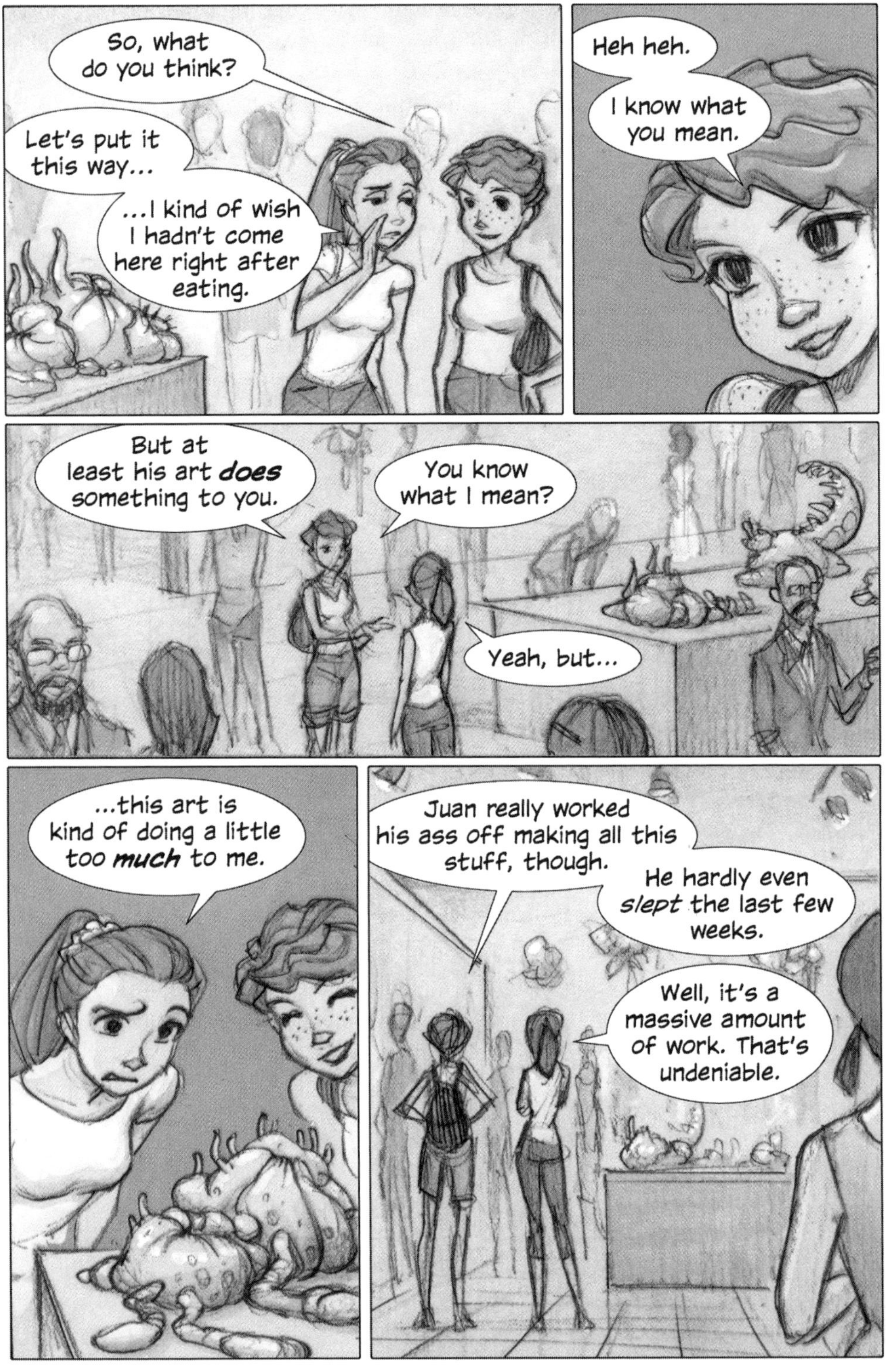
So, what do you think?
Let's put it this way...
...I kind of wish I hadn't come here right after eating.
Heh heh.
I know what you mean.
But at least his art *does* something to you.
You know what I mean?
Yeah, but...
...this art is kind of doing a little too *much* to me.
Juan really worked his ass off making all this stuff, though.
He hardly even *slept* the last few weeks.
Well, it's a massive amount of work. That's undeniable.

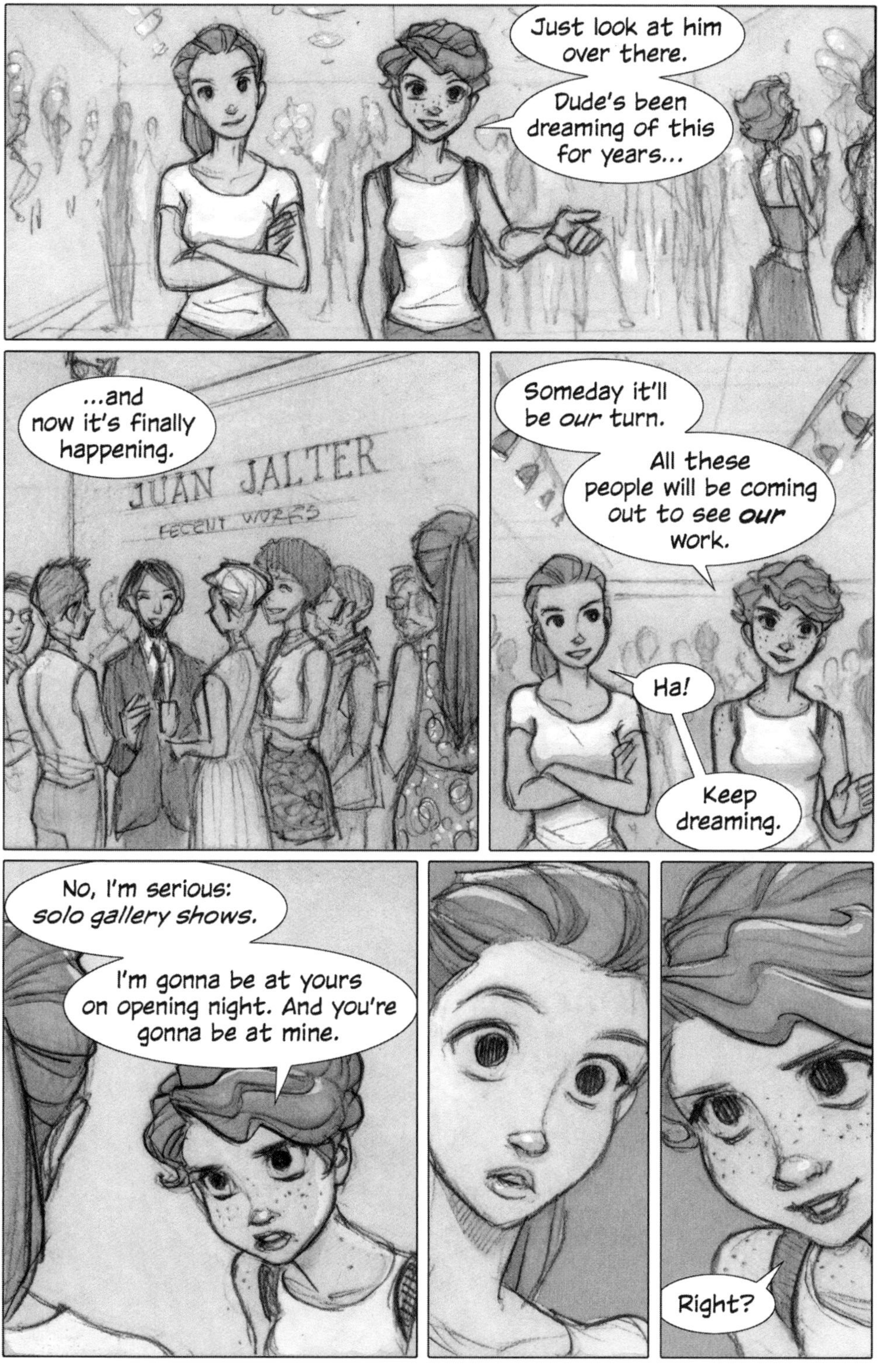
Just look at him over there.
Dude's been dreaming of this for years...
...and now it's finally happening.
JUAN JALTER
Someday it'll be *our* turn.
All these people will be coming out to see ***our*** work.
Ha!
Keep dreaming.
No, I'm serious: *solo gallery shows.*
I'm gonna be at yours on opening night. And you're gonna be at mine.
Right?

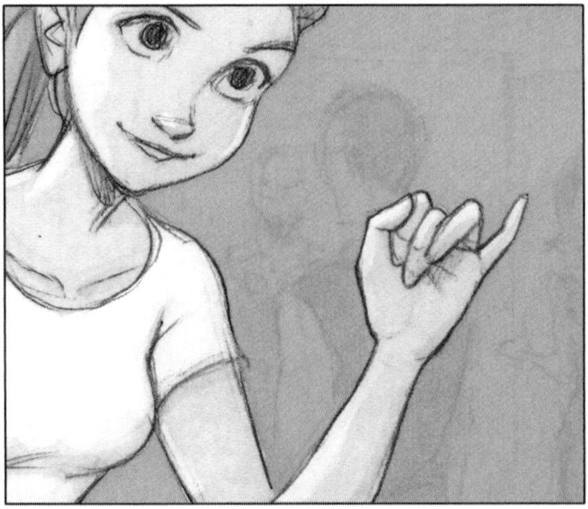

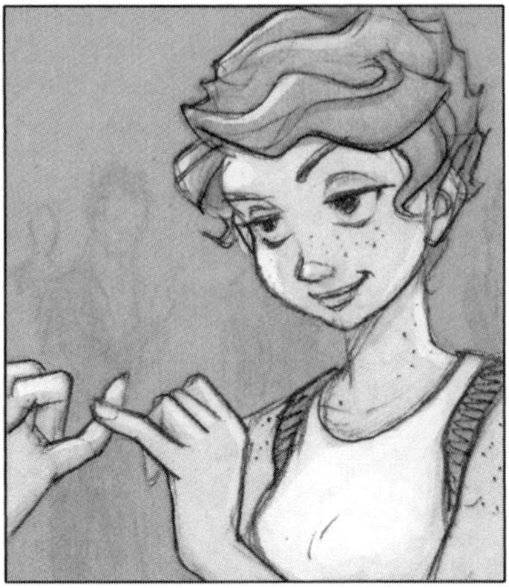

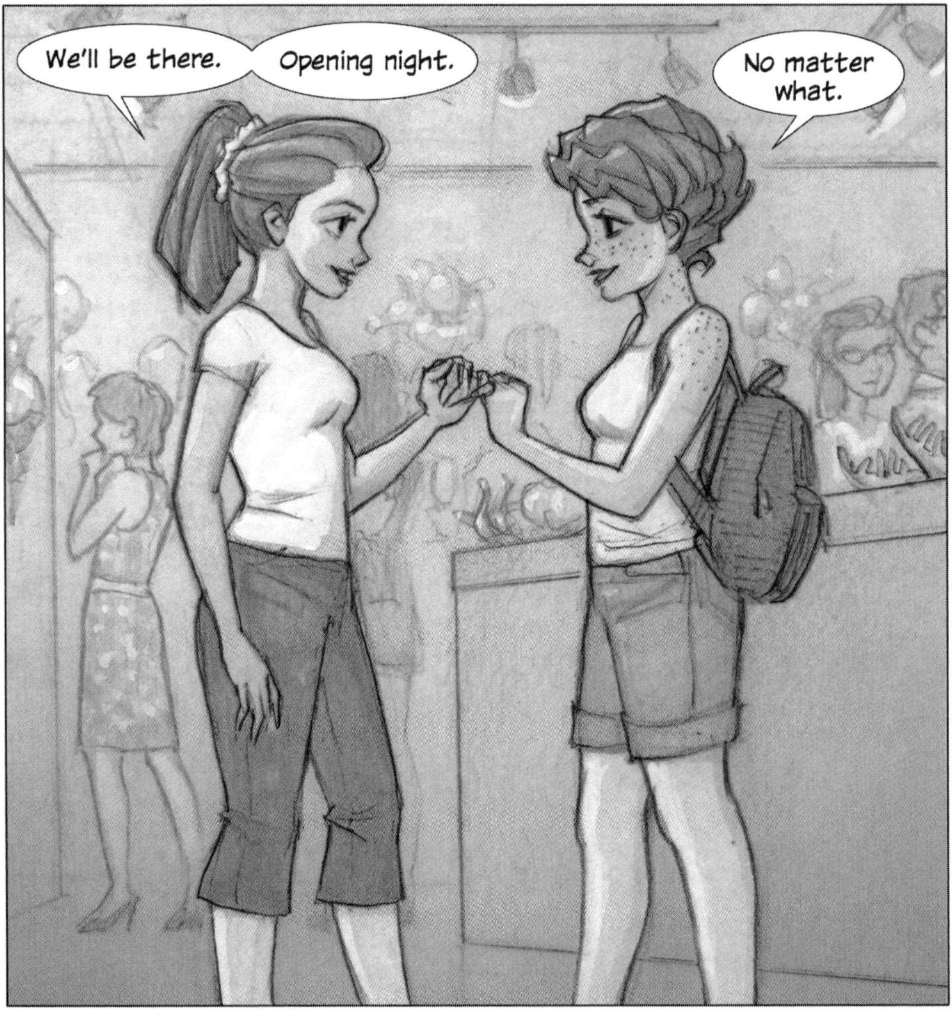
We'll be there.
Opening night.
No matter what.

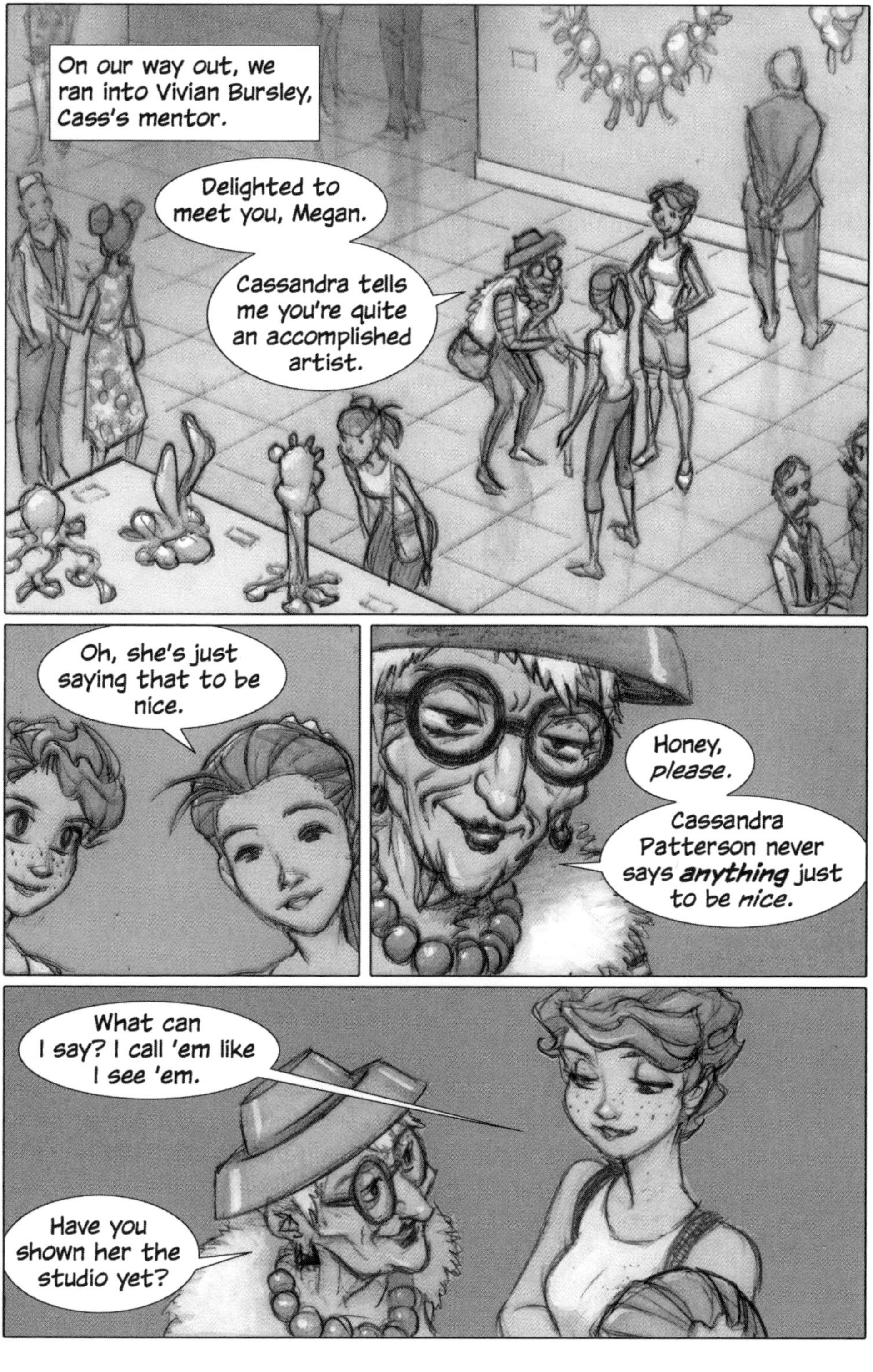
On our way out, we ran into Vivian Bursley, Cass's mentor.
Delighted to meet you, Megan.
Cassandra tells me you're quite an accomplished artist.
Oh, she's just saying that to be nice.
Honey, *please*.
Cassandra Patterson never says ***anything*** just to be *nice*.
What can I say? I call 'em like I see 'em.
Have you shown her the studio yet?

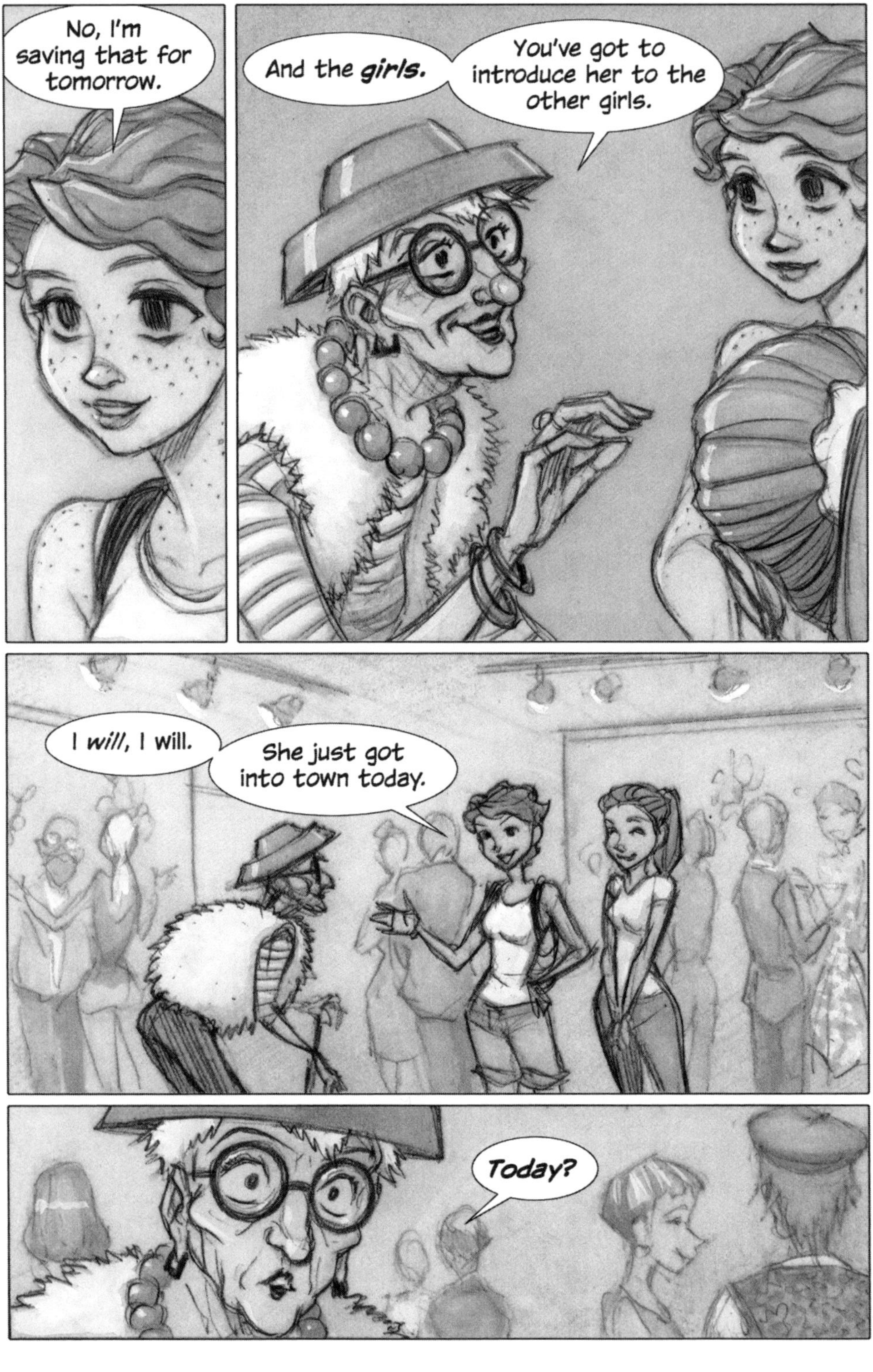
No, I'm saving that for tomorrow.
And the *girls.*
You've got to introduce her to the other girls.
I *will*, I will.
She just got into town today.
Today?

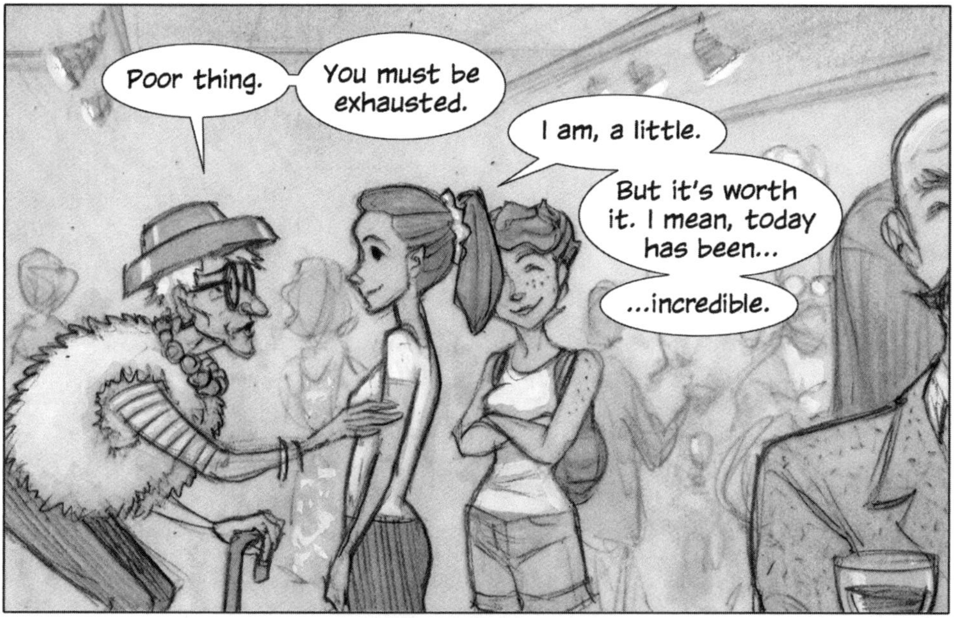
Poor thing.
You must be exhausted.
I am, a little.
But it's worth it. I mean, today has been...
...incredible.

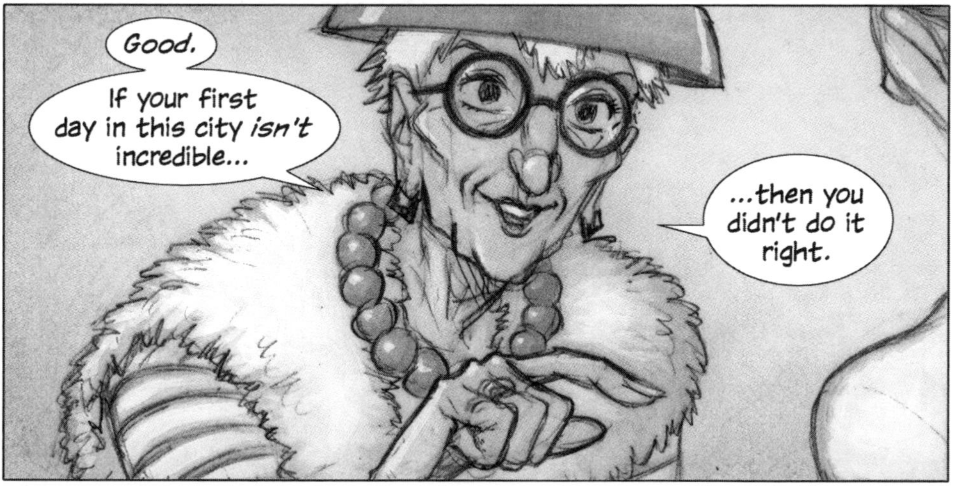
Good.
If your first day in this city *isn't* incredible...
...then you didn't do it right.

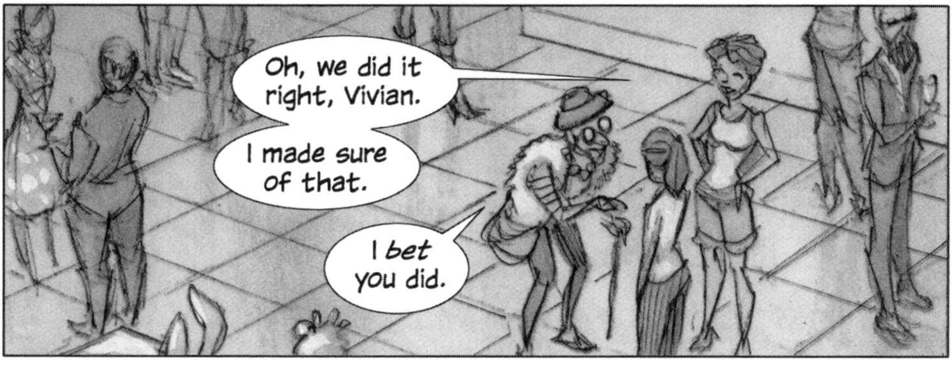
Oh, we did it right, Vivian.
I made sure of that.
I *bet* you did.

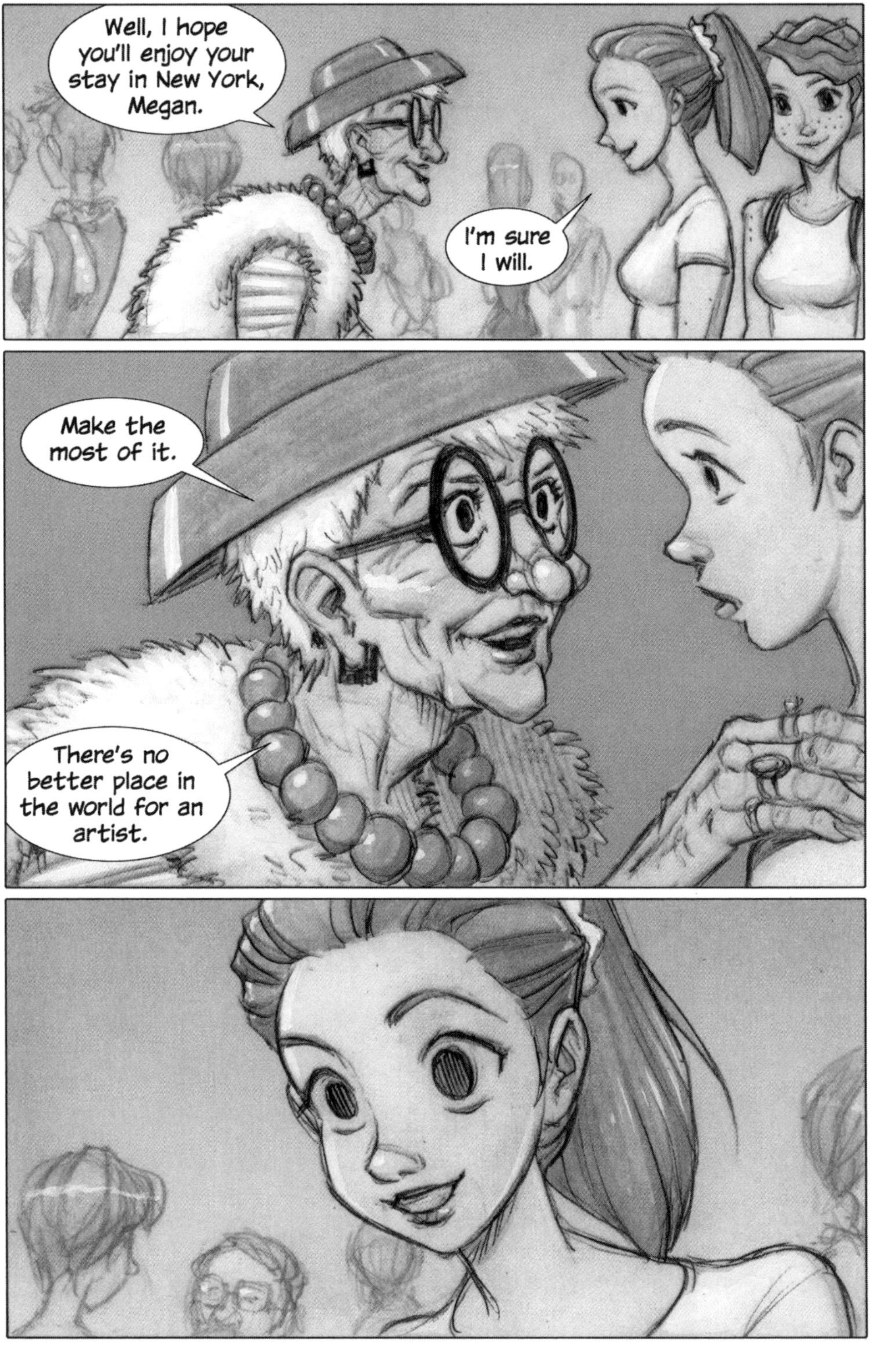
Well, I hope you'll enjoy your stay in New York, Megan.
I'm sure I will.
Make the most of it.
There's no better place in the world for an artist.

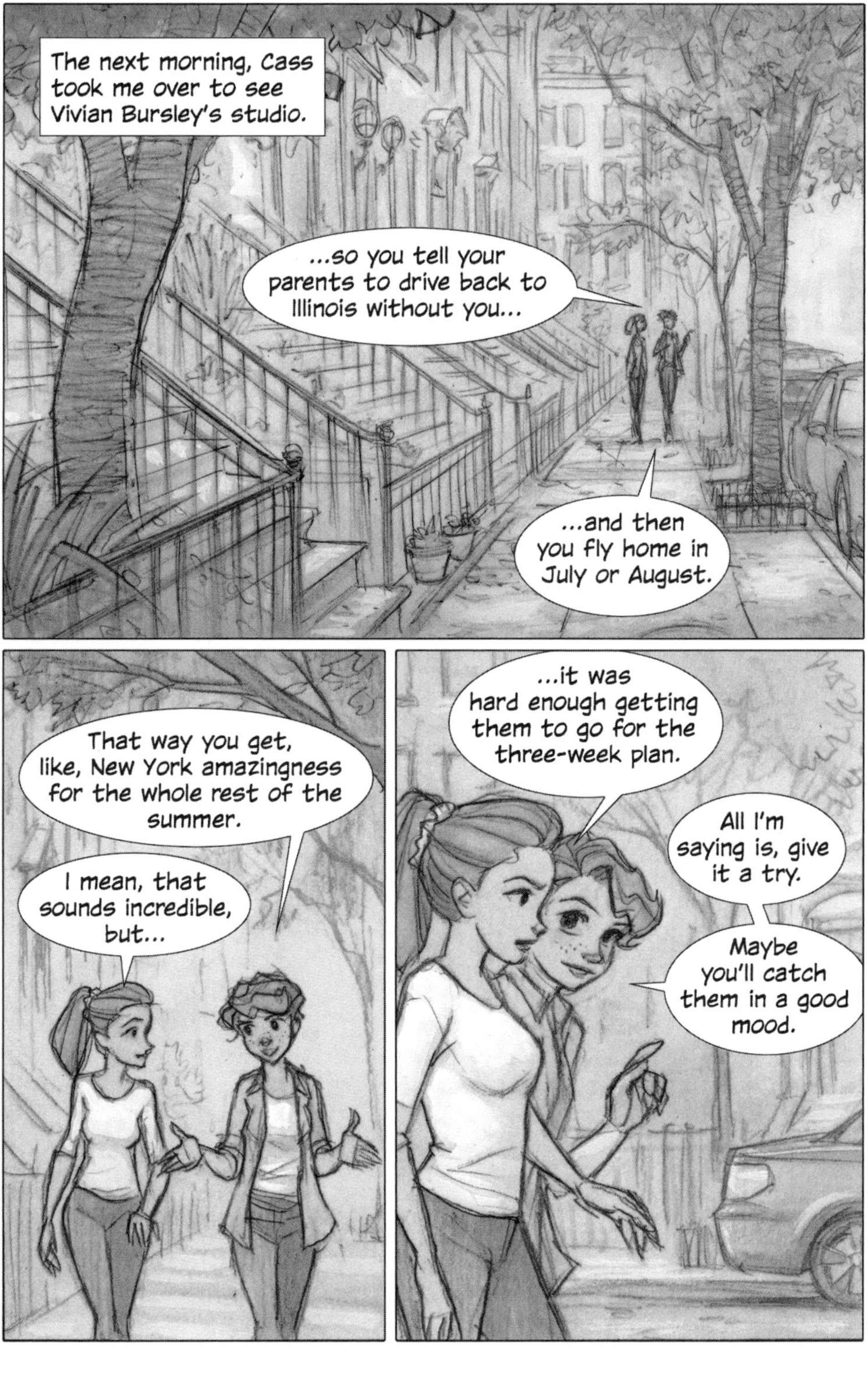
The next morning, Cass took me over to see Vivian Bursley's studio.
...so you tell your parents to drive back to Illinois without you...
...and then you fly home in July or August.
That way you get, like, New York amazingness for the whole rest of the summer.
I mean, that sounds incredible, but...
...it was hard enough getting them to go for the three-week plan.
All I'm saying is, give it a try.
Maybe you'll catch them in a good mood.

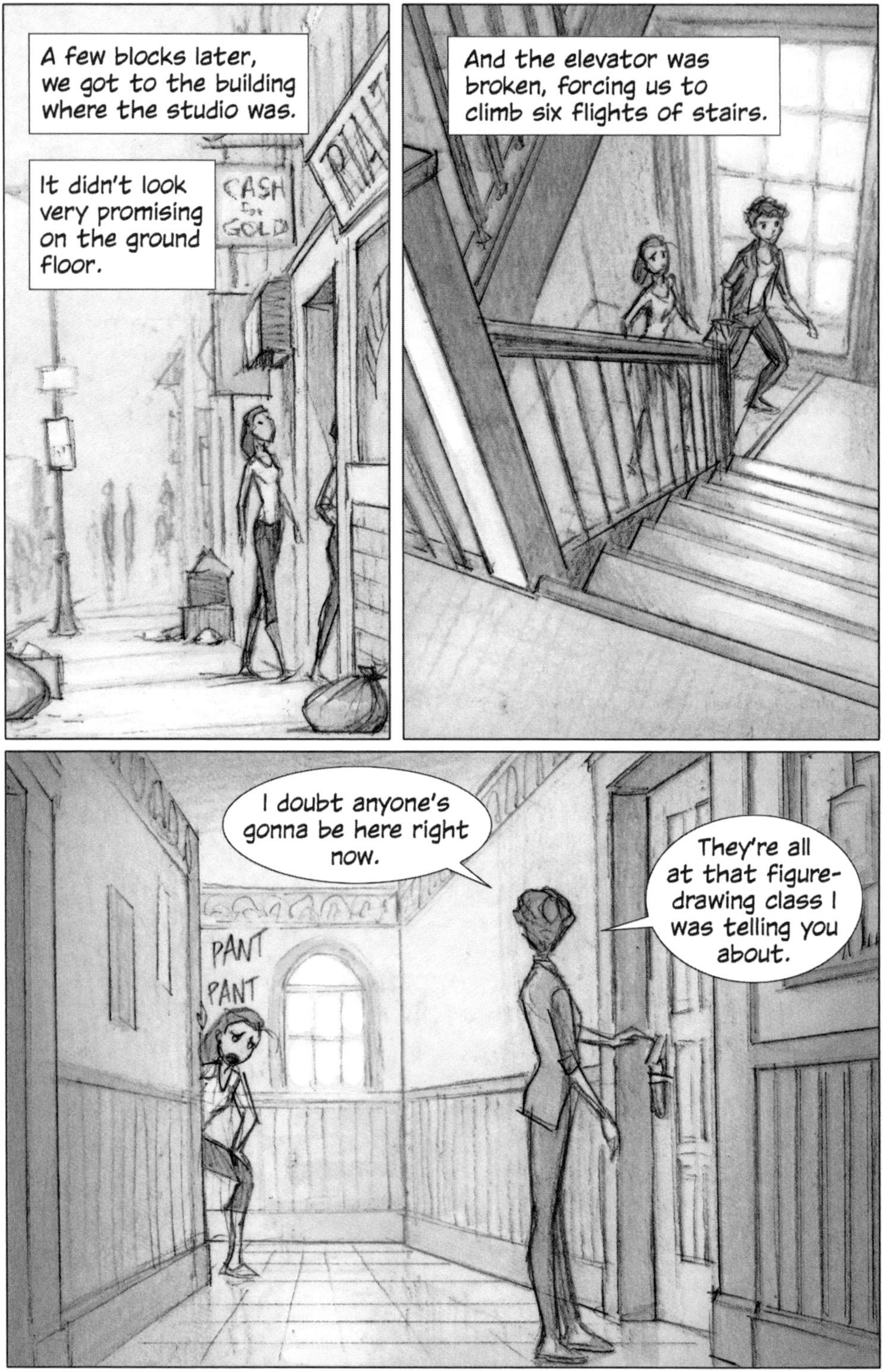
A few blocks later, we got to the building where the studio was.
It didn't look very promising on the ground floor.
CASH for GOLD
And the elevator was broken, forcing us to climb six flights of stairs.
I doubt anyone's gonna be here right now.
They're all at that figure-drawing class I was telling you about.
PANT PANT

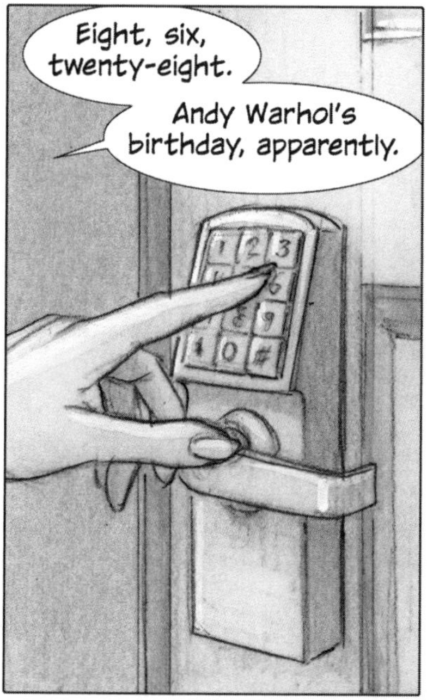
Eight, six, twenty-eight.
Andy Warhol's birthday, apparently.

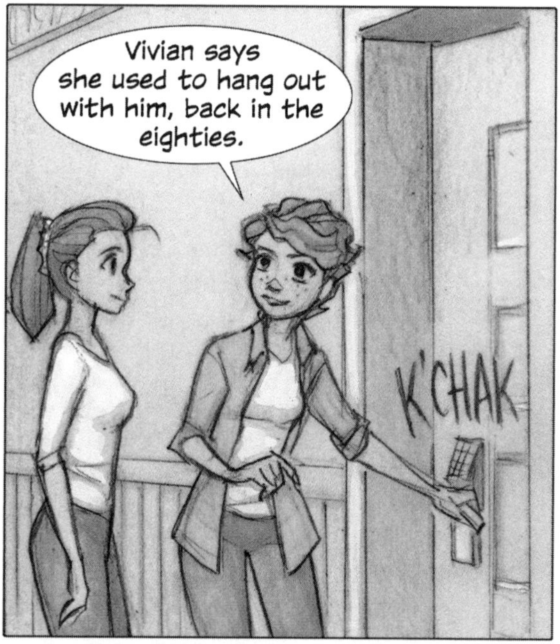
Vivian says she used to hang out with him, back in the eighties.
K'CHAK

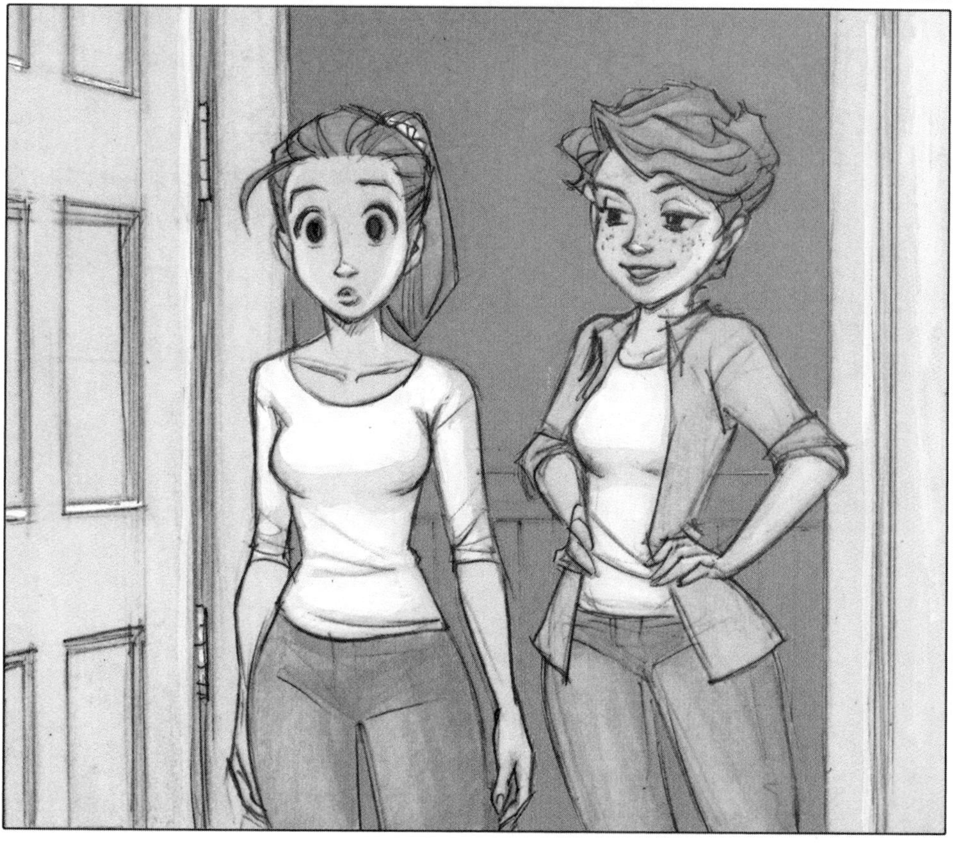

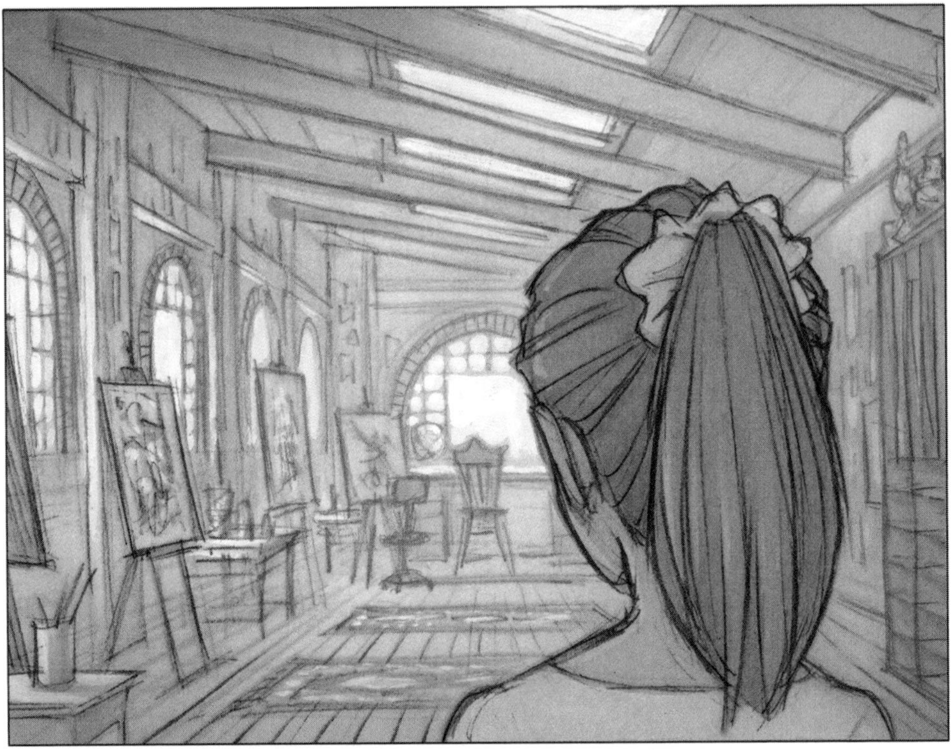

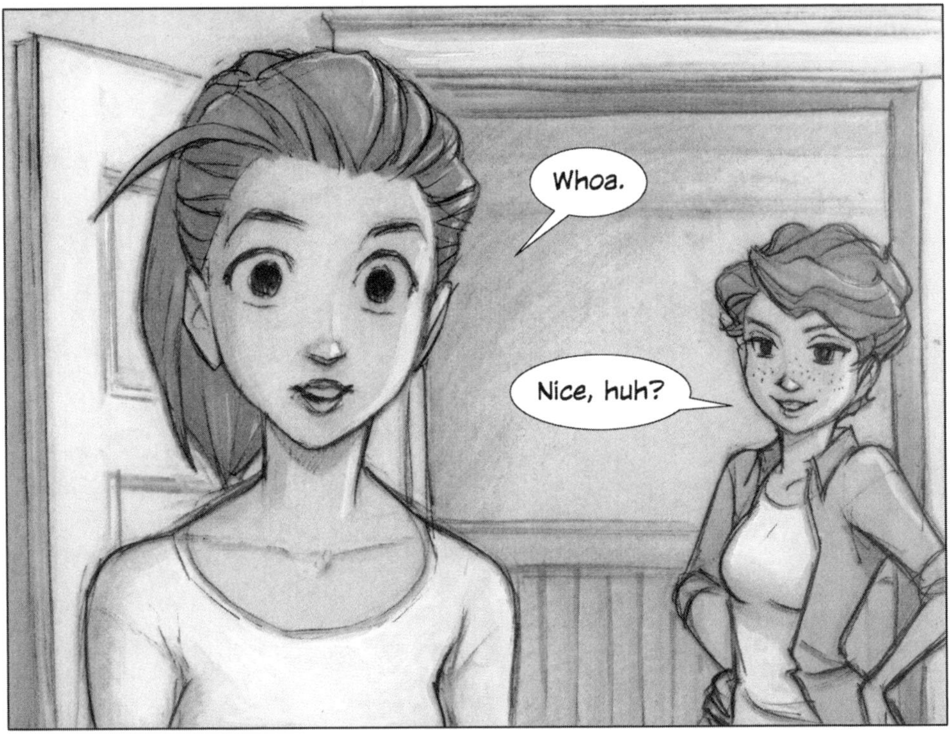
Whoa.
Nice, huh?

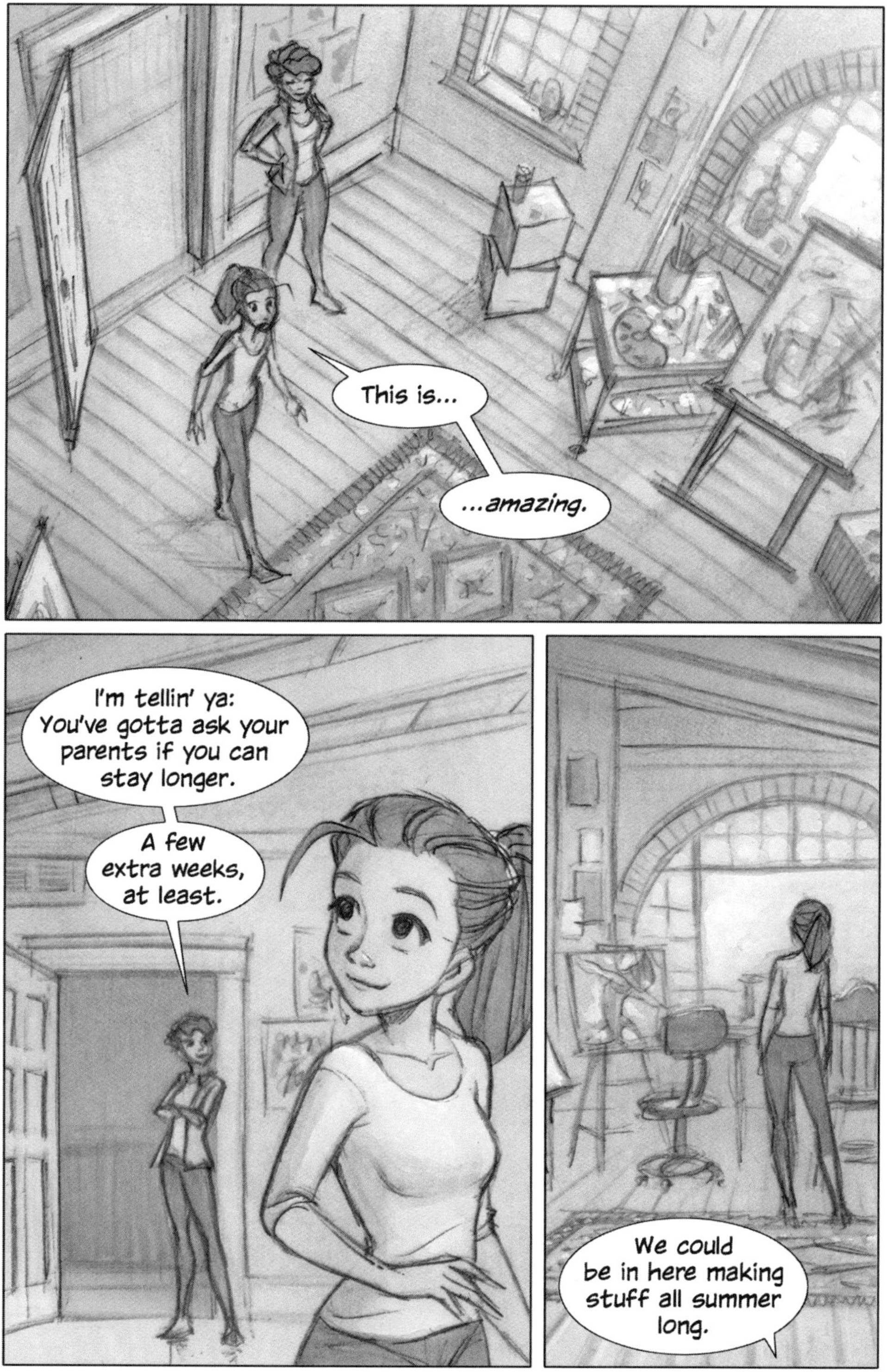
This is...
...amazing.
I'm tellin' ya: You've gotta ask your parents if you can stay longer.
A few extra weeks, at least.
We could be in here making stuff all summer long.

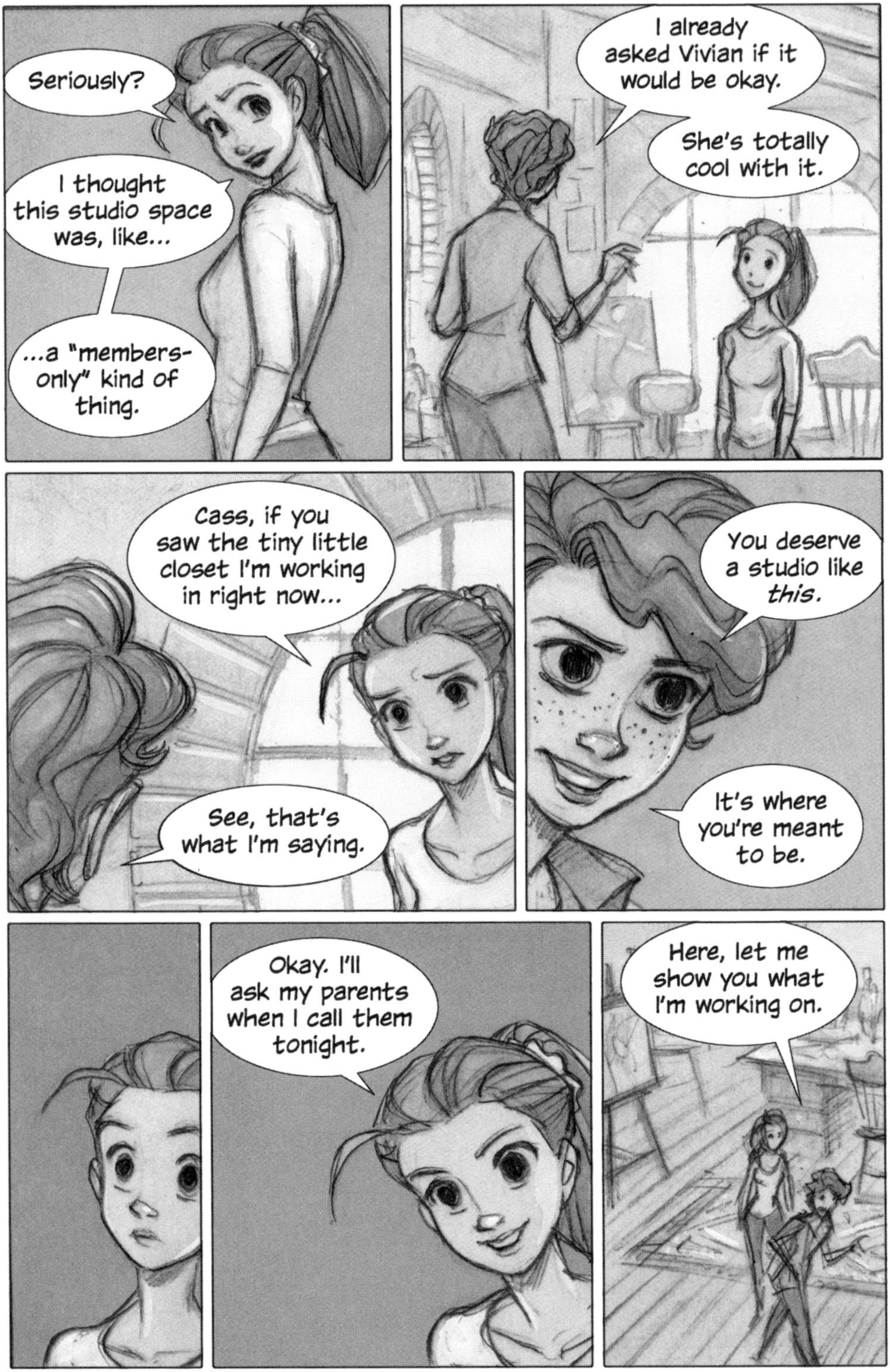
Seriously?
I thought this studio space was, like...
...a "members-only" kind of thing.
I already asked Vivian if it would be okay.
She's totally cool with it.
Cass, if you saw the tiny little closet I'm working in right now...
See, that's what I'm saying.
You deserve a studio like *this.*
It's where you're meant to be.
Okay. I'll ask my parents when I call them tonight.
Here, let me show you what I'm working on.

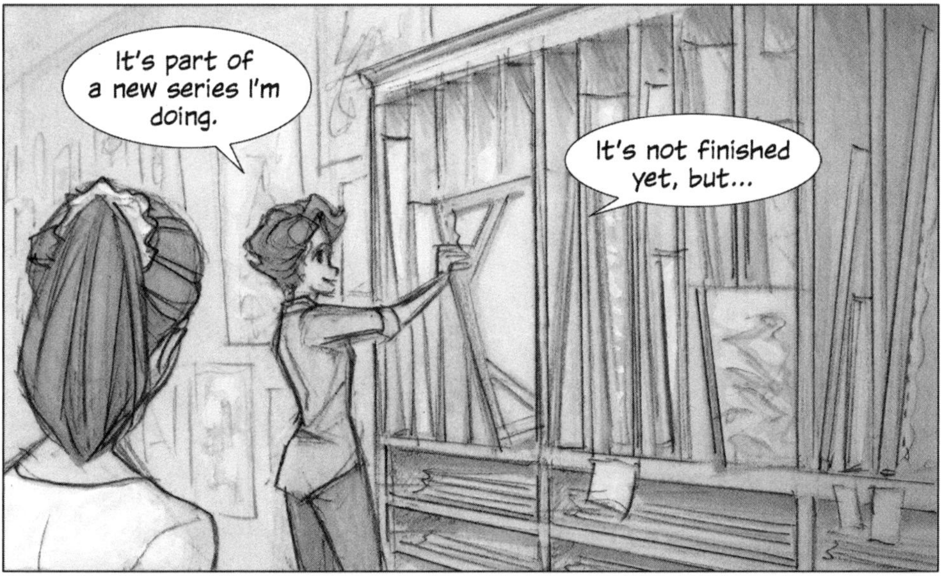
It's part of a new series I'm doing.
It's not finished yet, but...

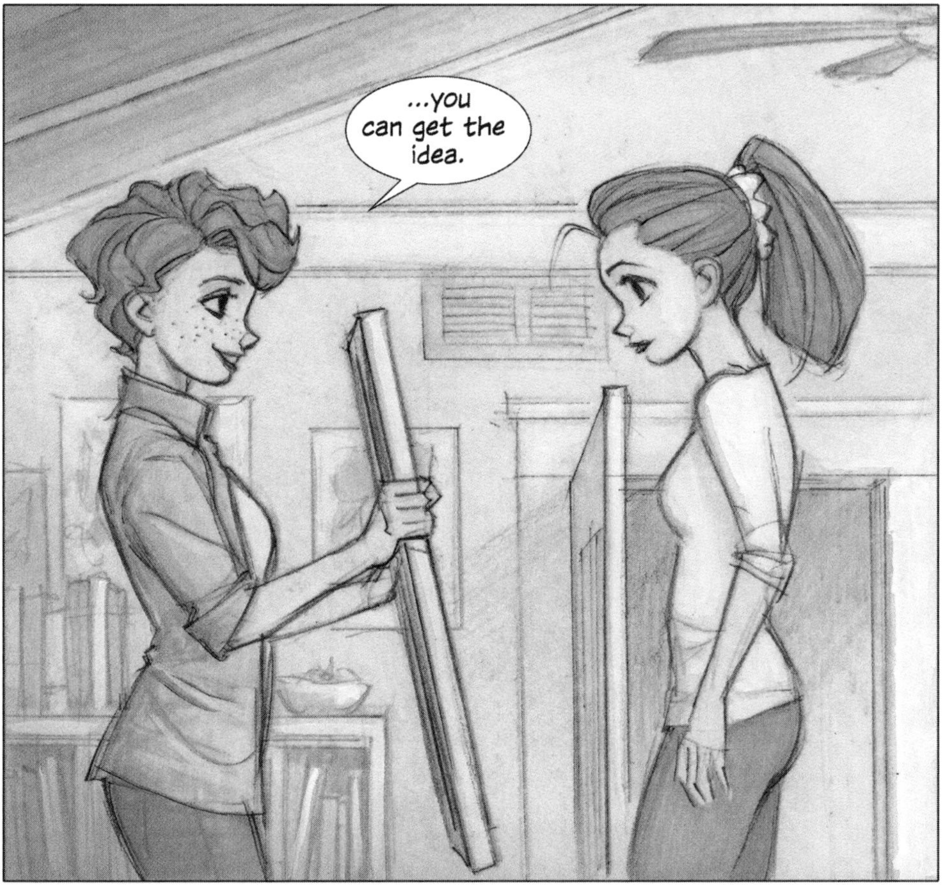
...you can get the idea.

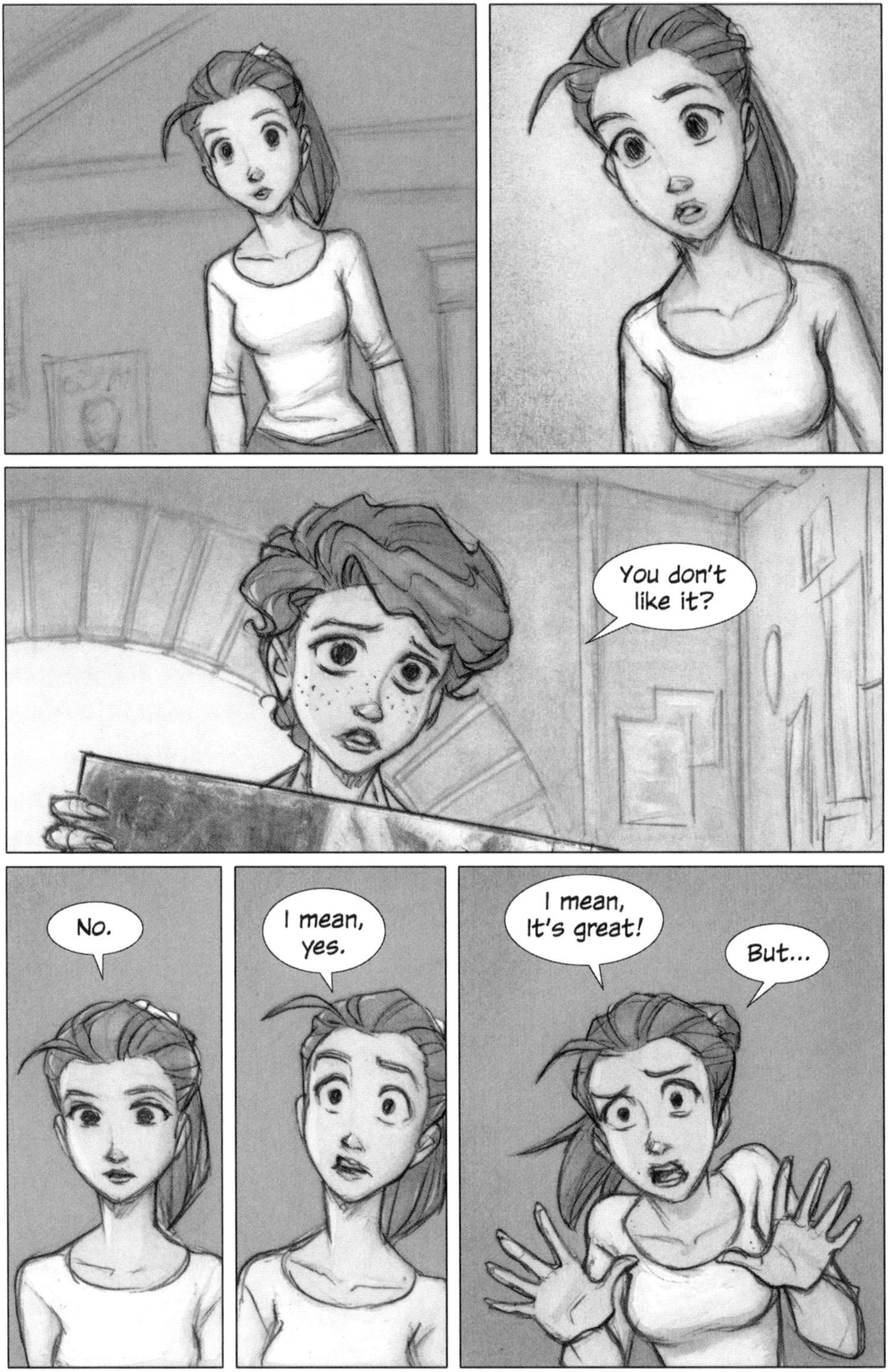
You don't like it?
No.
I mean, yes.
I mean, It's great!
But...

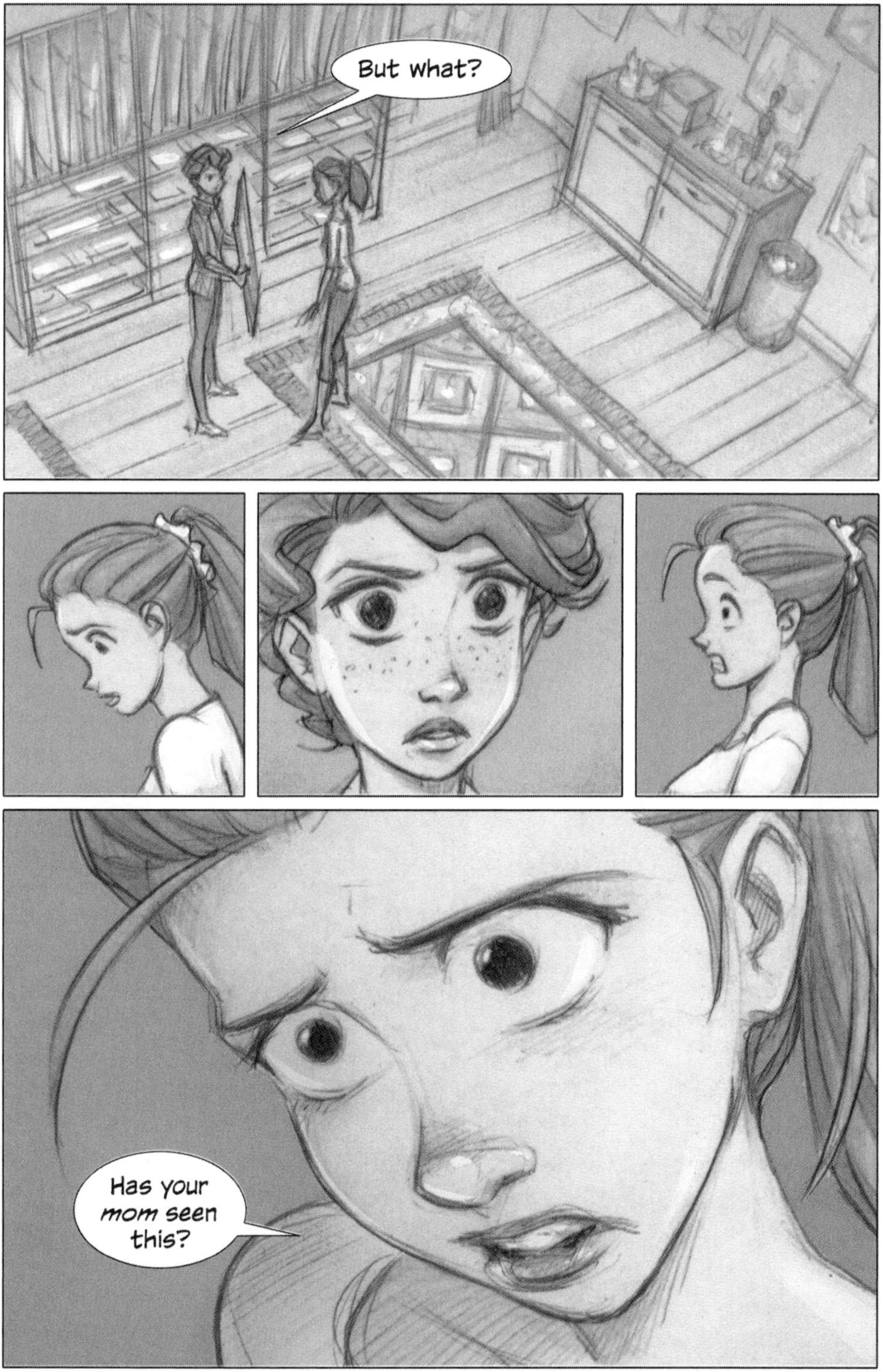
But what?
Has your *mom* seen this?

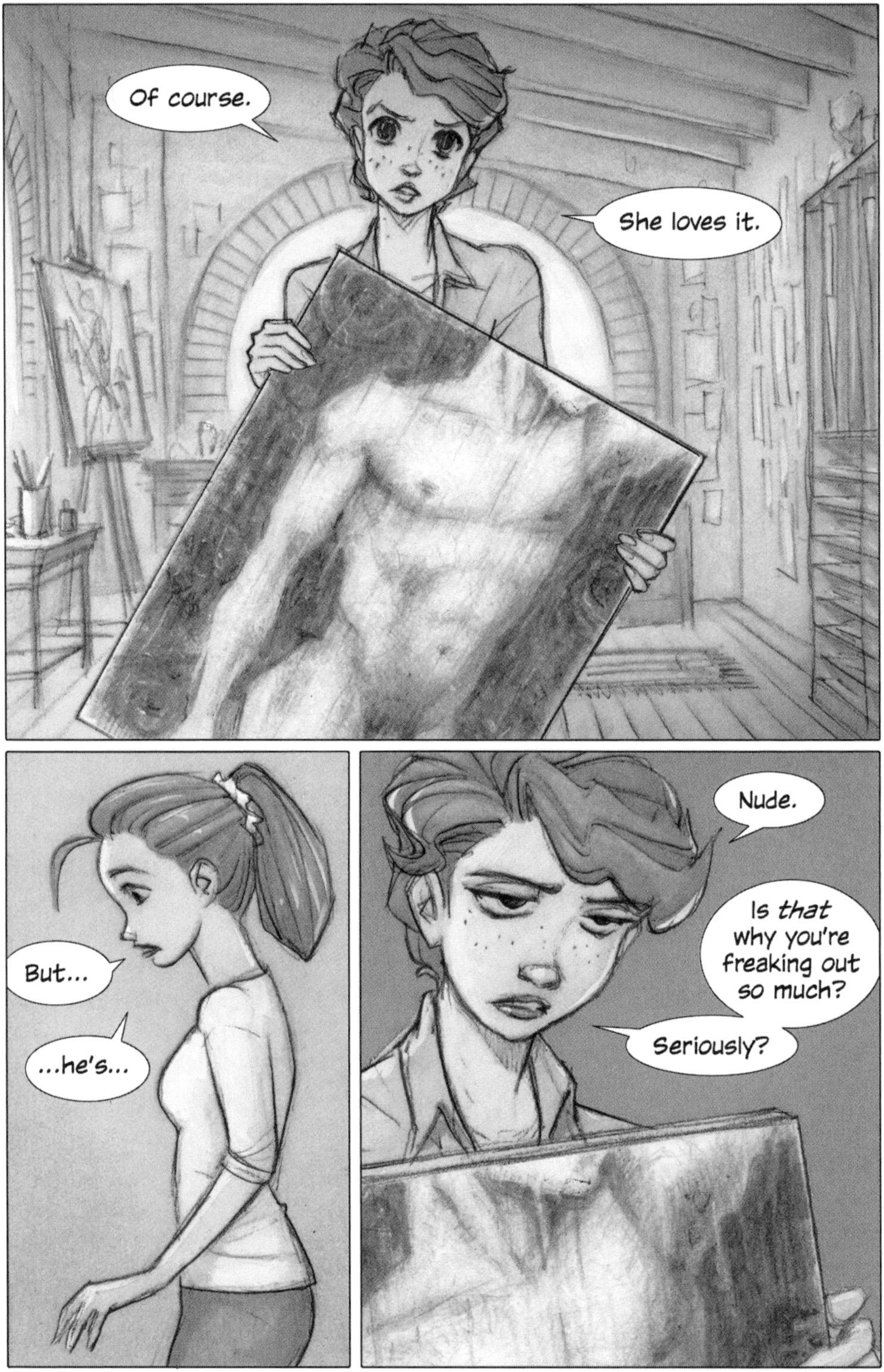

Of course.
She loves it.
But...
...he's...
Nude.
Is *that* why you're freaking out so much?
Seriously?

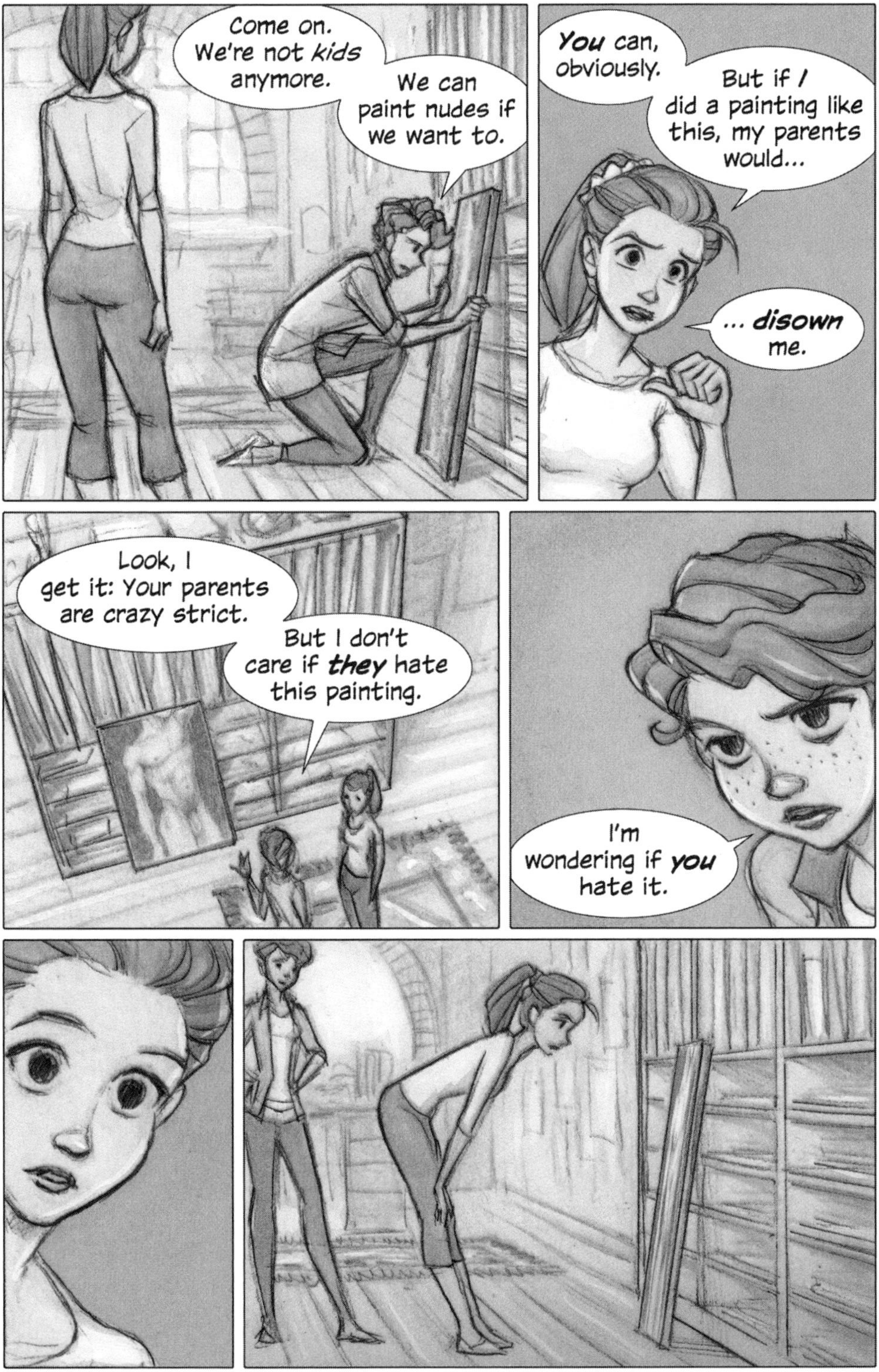
Come on. We're not *kids* anymore.
We can paint nudes if we want to.
You can, obviously.
But if *I* did a painting like this, my parents would...
... ***disown*** me.
Look, I get it: Your parents are crazy strict.
But I don't care if ***they*** hate this painting.
I'm wondering if ***you*** hate it.

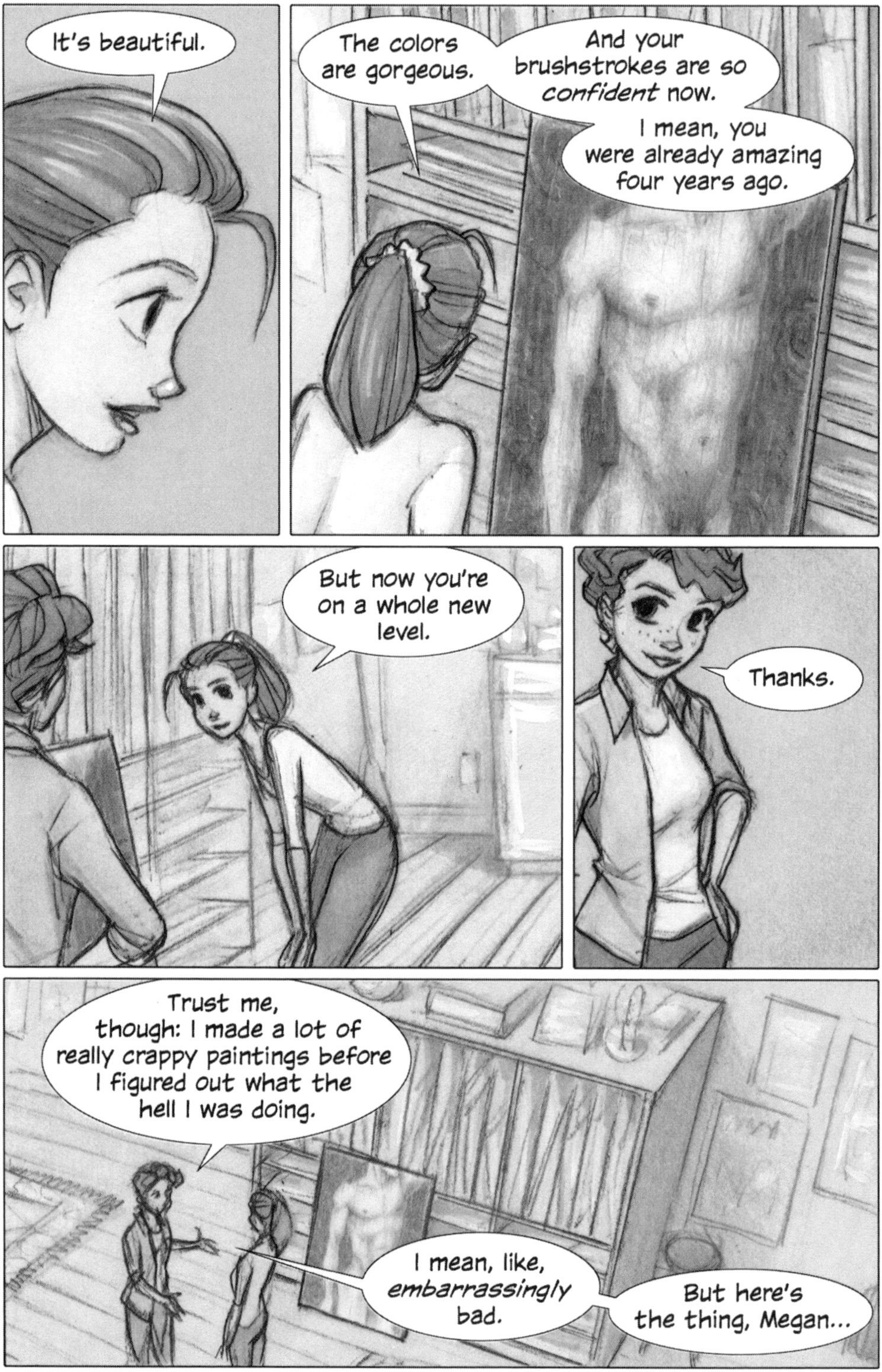
It's beautiful.
The colors are gorgeous.
And your brushstrokes are so *confident* now.
I mean, you were already amazing four years ago.
But now you're on a whole new level.
Thanks.
Trust me, though: I made a lot of really crappy paintings before I figured out what the hell I was doing.
I mean, like, *embarrassingly* bad.
But here's the thing, Megan...

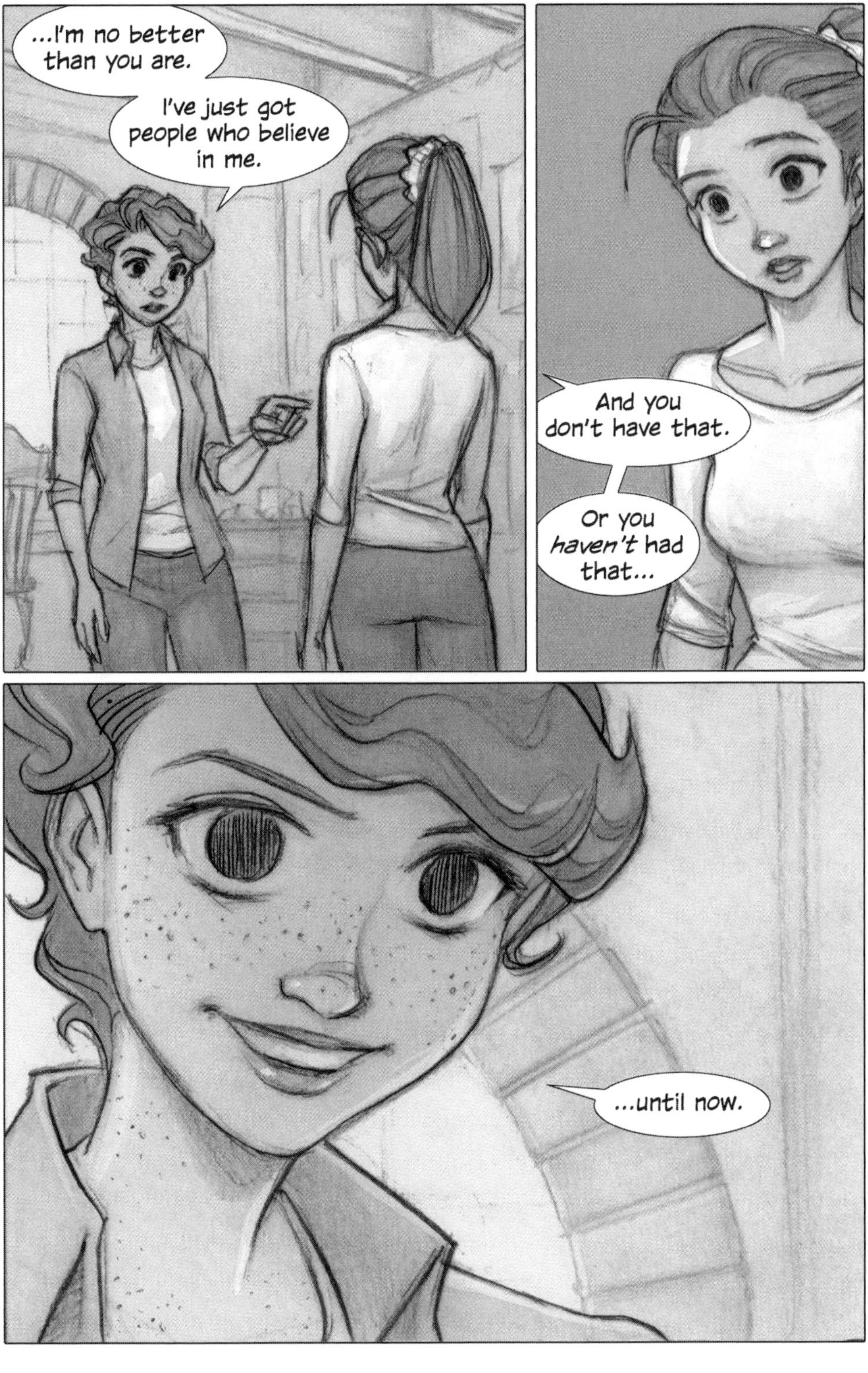
...I'm no better than you are.
I've just got people who believe in me.
And you don't have that.
Or you *haven't* had that...
...until now.

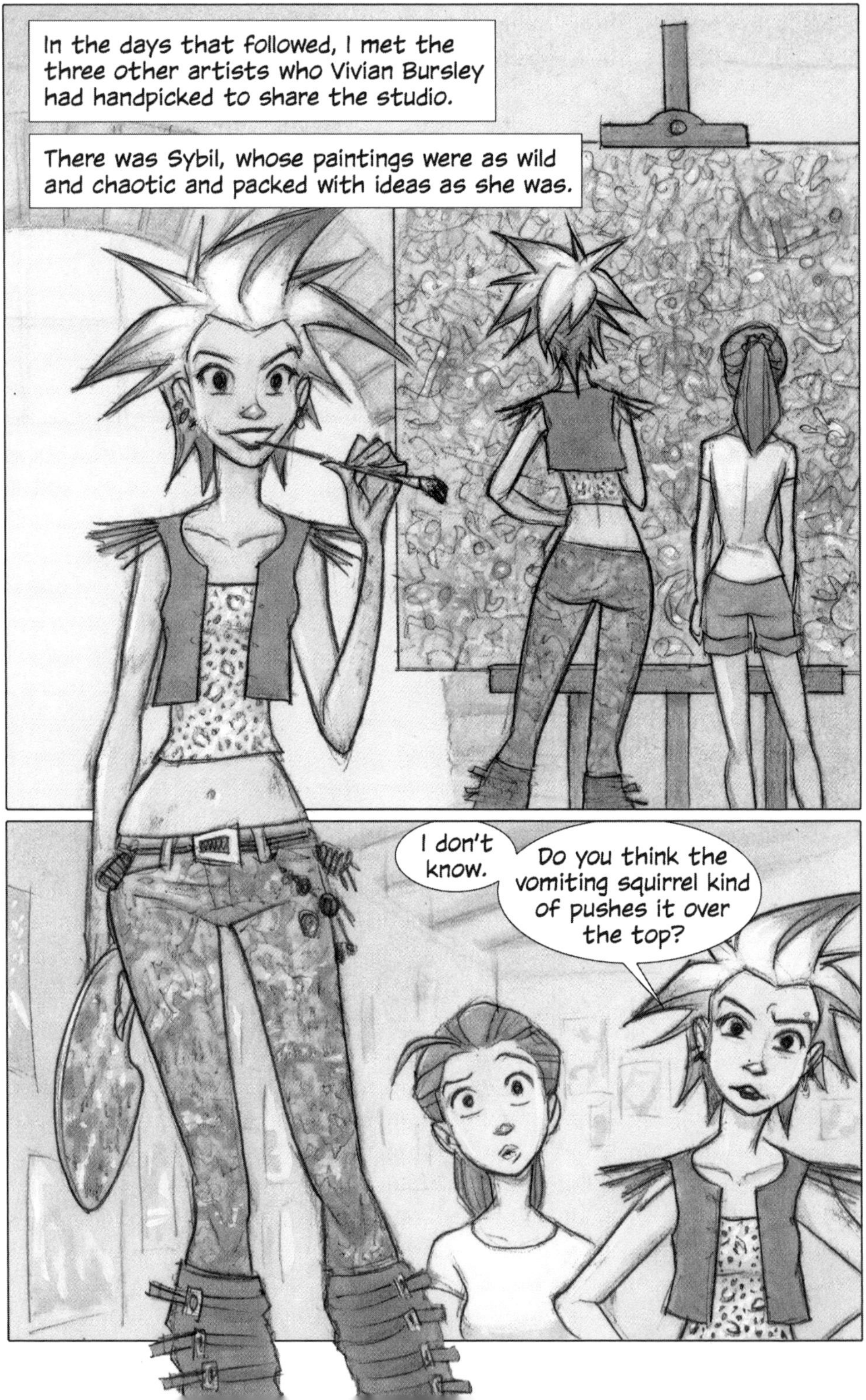

In the days that followed, I met the three other artists who Vivian Bursley had handpicked to share the studio.
There was Sybil, whose paintings were as wild and chaotic and packed with ideas as she was.
Do you think the vomiting squirrel kind of pushes it over the top?
I don't know.

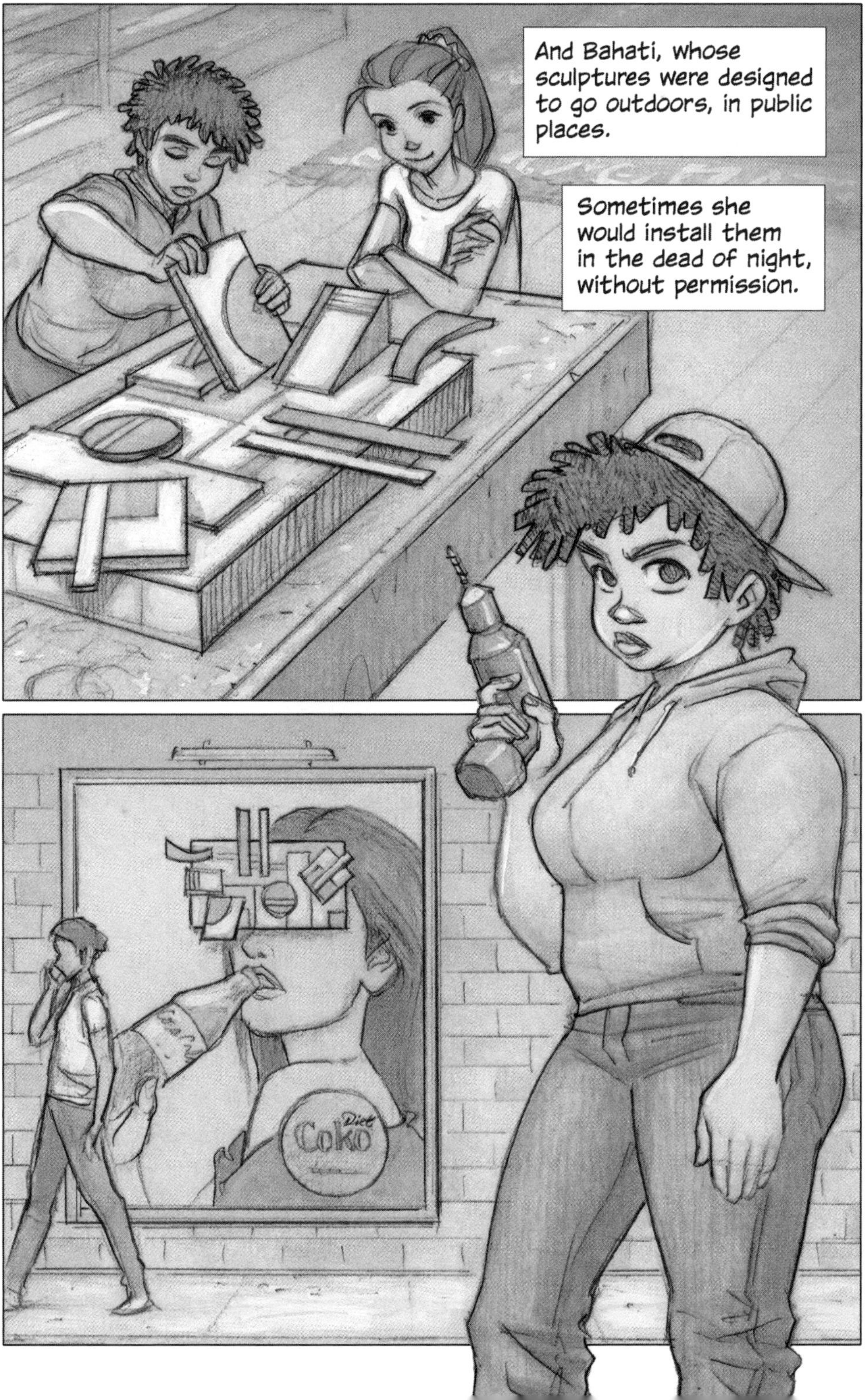
And Bahati, whose sculptures were designed to go outdoors, in public places.
Sometimes she would install them in the dead of night, without permission.
Diet
Coko

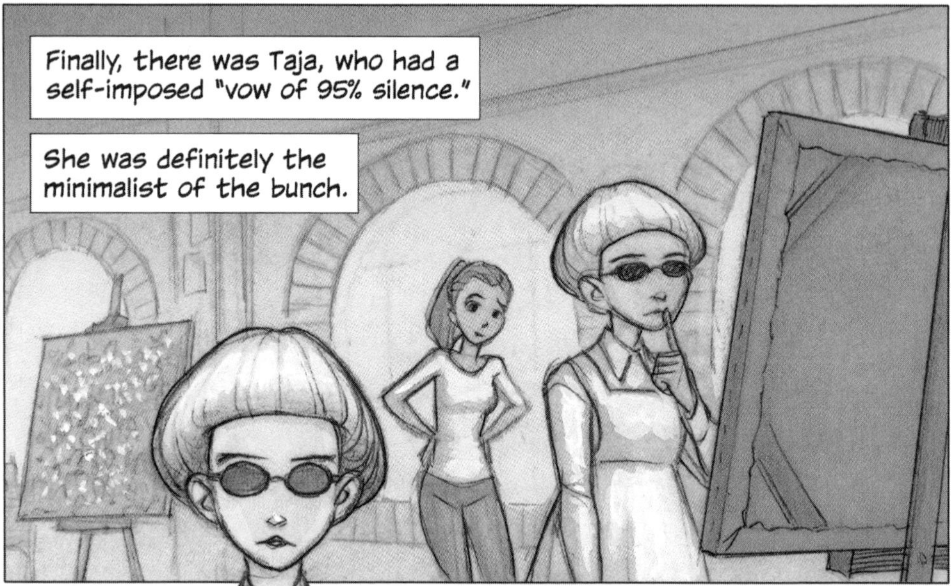
Finally, there was Taja, who had a self-imposed "vow of 95% silence."
She was definitely the minimalist of the bunch.

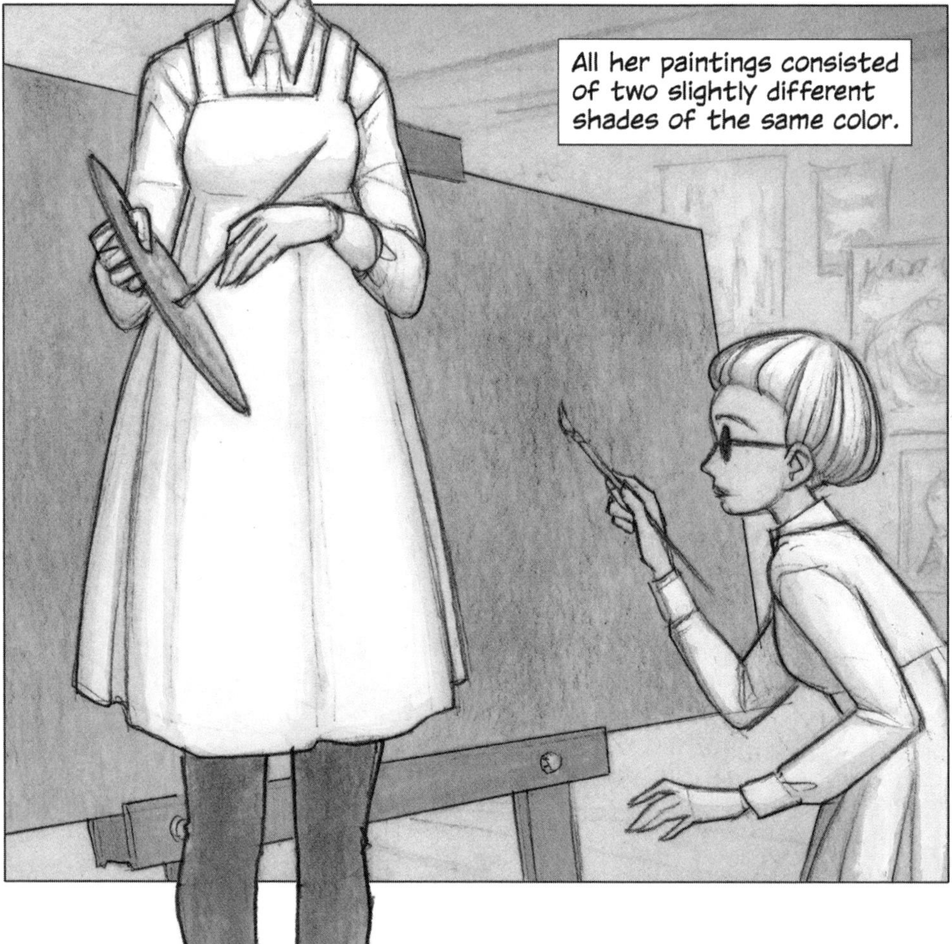
All her paintings consisted of two slightly different shades of the same color.

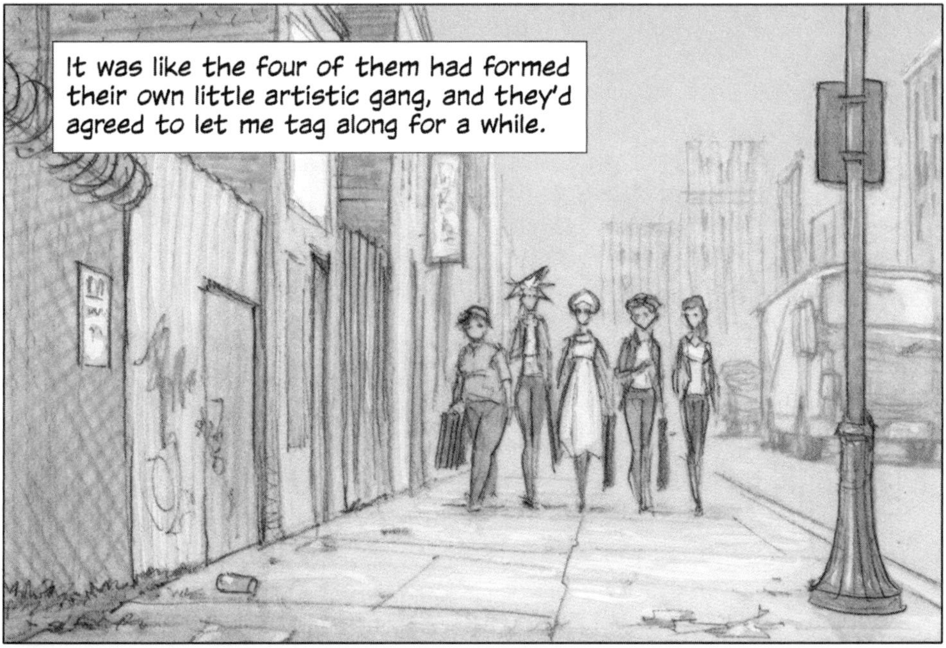
It was like the four of them had formed their own little artistic gang, and they'd agreed to let me tag along for a while.

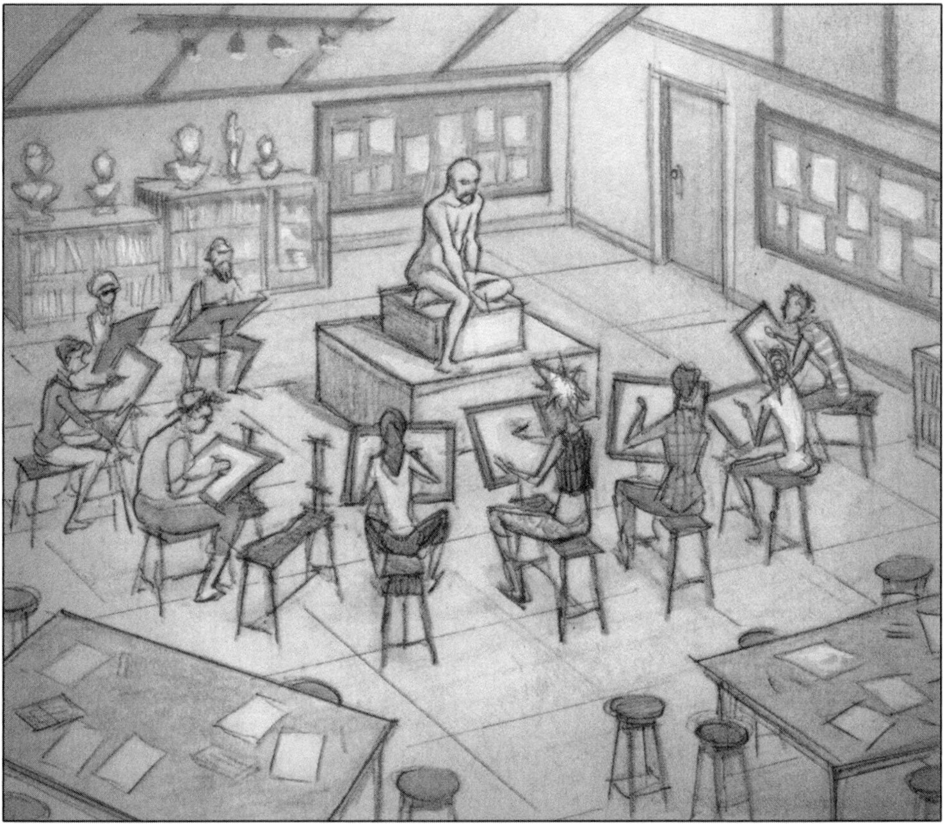

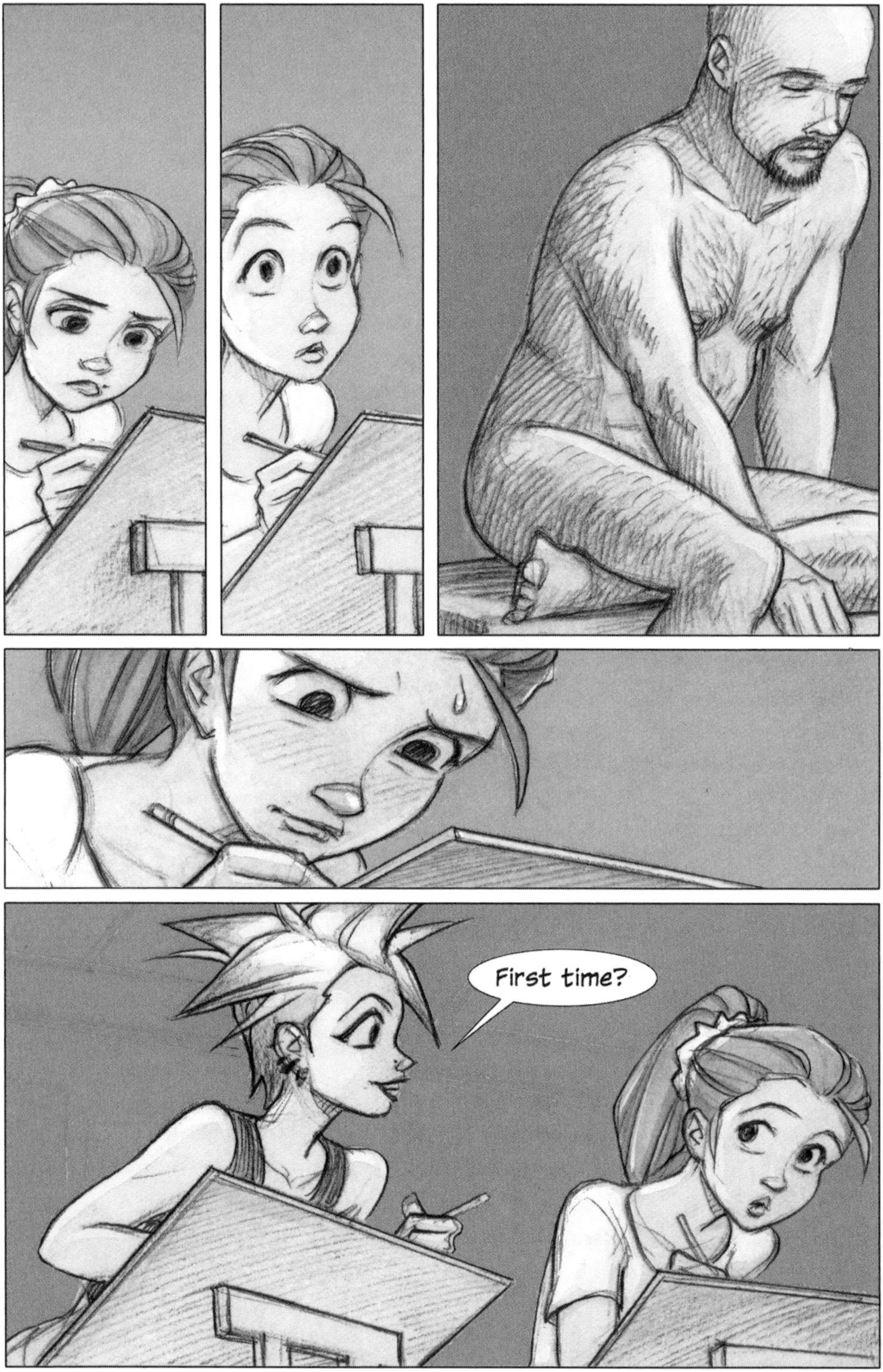
First time?

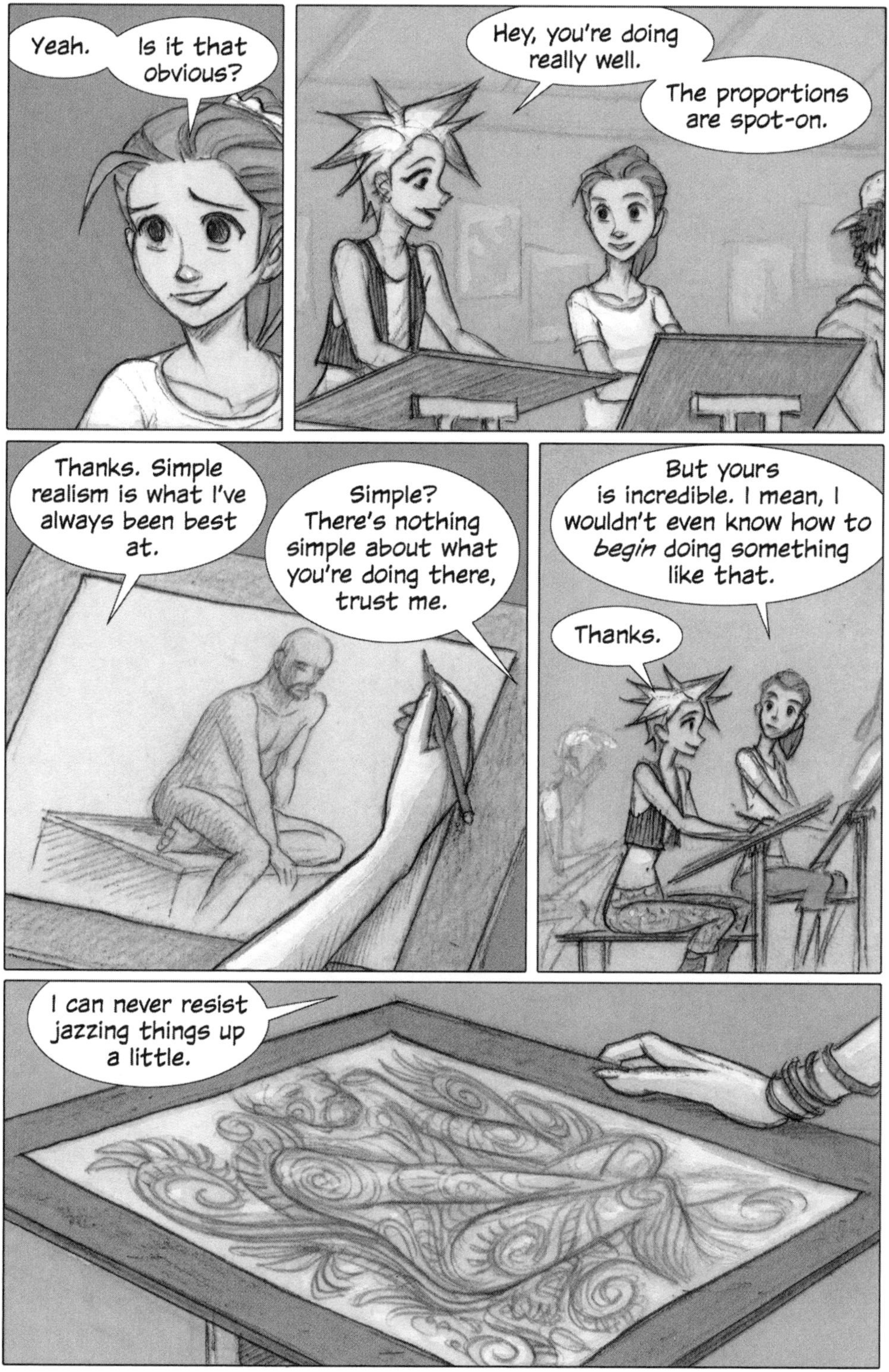
Yeah.
Is it that obvious?
Hey, you're doing really well.
The proportions are spot-on.
Thanks. Simple realism is what I've always been best at.
Simple? There's nothing simple about what you're doing there, trust me.
But yours is incredible. I mean, I wouldn't even know how to *begin* doing something like that.
Thanks.
I can never resist jazzing things up a little.

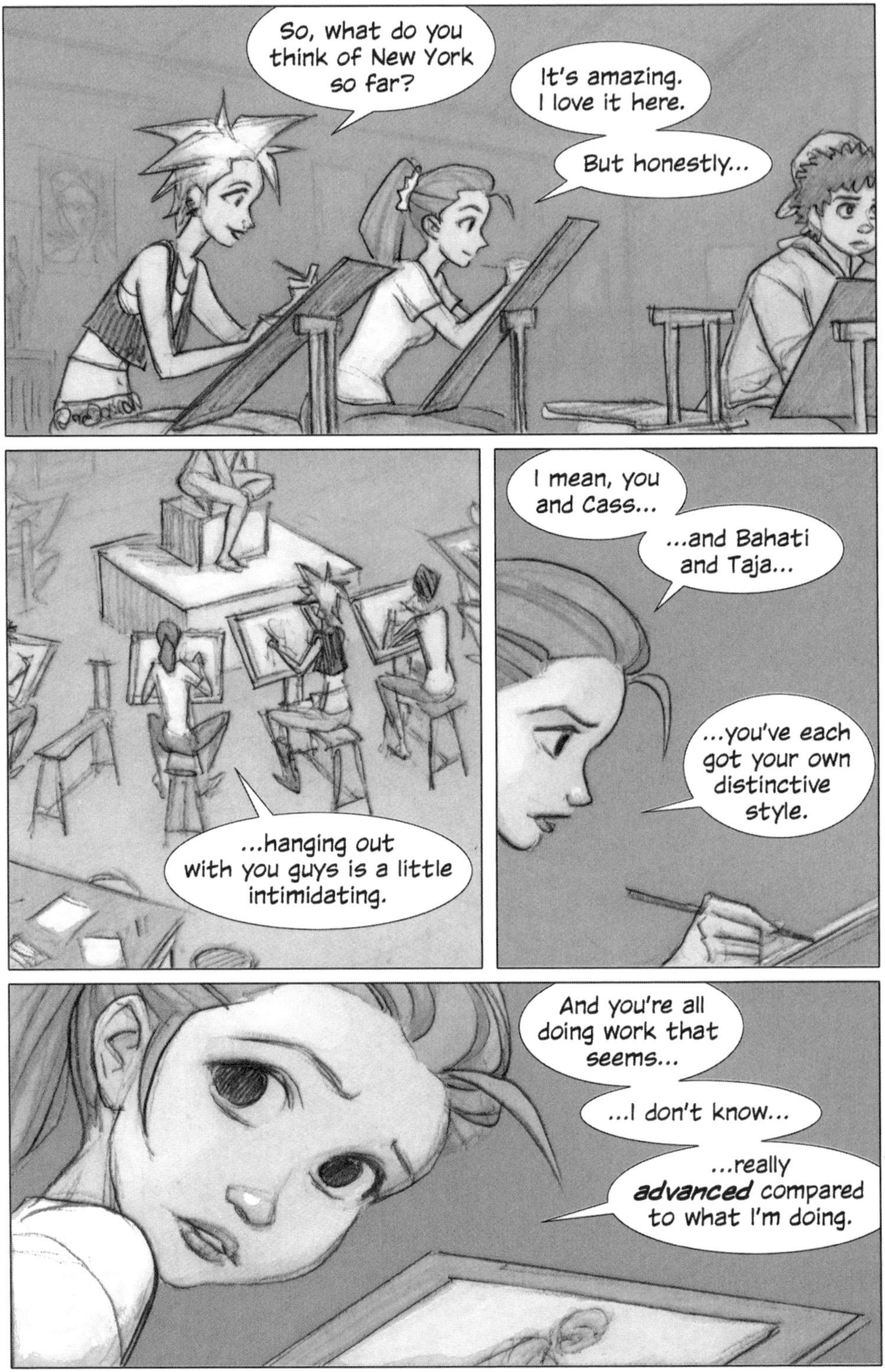
So, what do you think of New York so far?
It's amazing. I love it here.
But honestly...
...hanging out with you guys is a little intimidating.
I mean, you and Cass...
...and Bahati and Taja...
...you've each got your own distinctive style.
And you're all doing work that seems...
...I don't know...
...really *advanced* compared to what I'm doing.

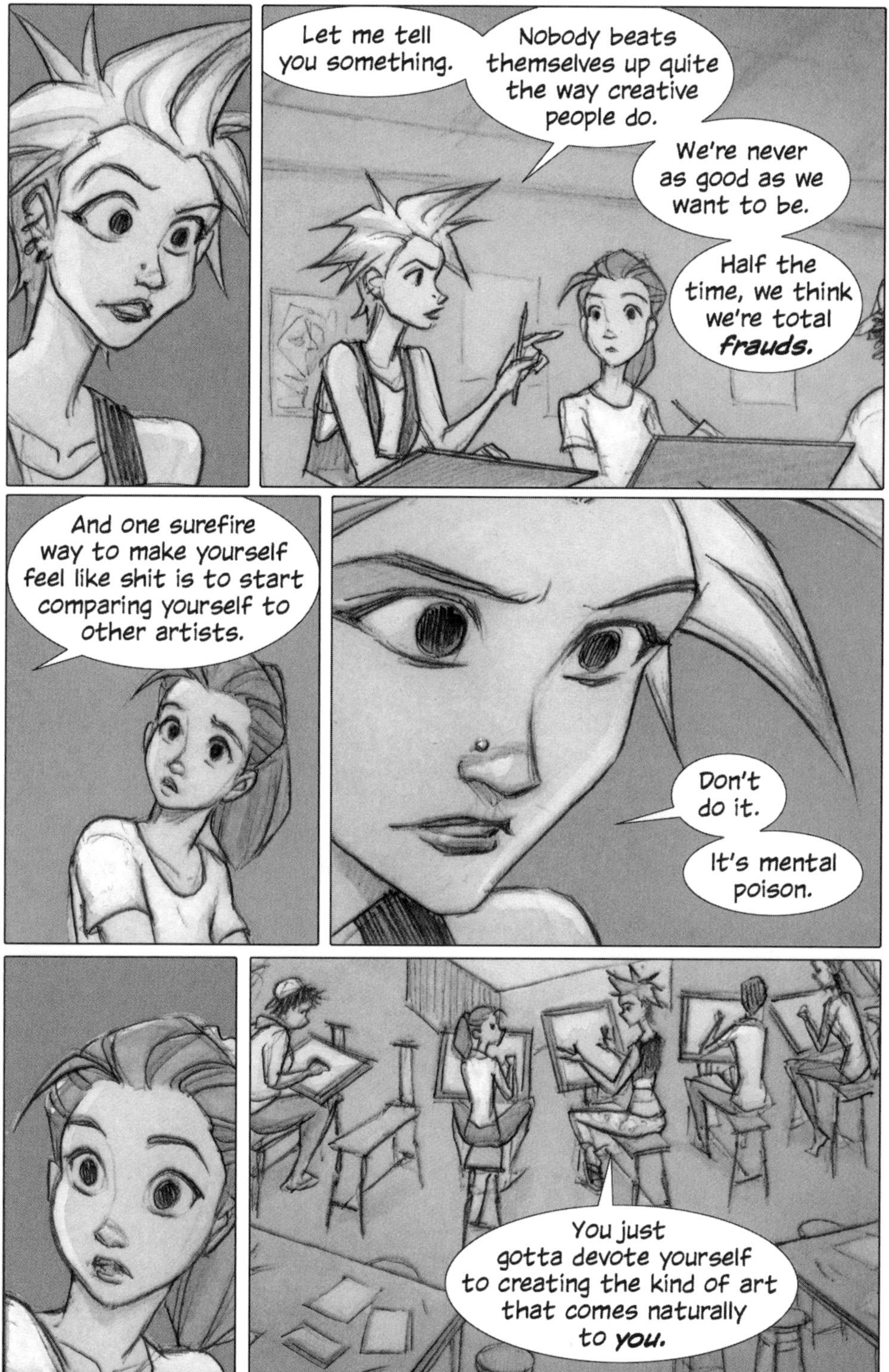
Let me tell you something.
Nobody beats themselves up quite the way creative people do.
We're never as good as we want to be.
Half the time, we think we're total *frauds.*
And one surefire way to make yourself feel like shit is to start comparing yourself to other artists.
Don't do it.
It's mental poison.
You just gotta devote yourself to creating the kind of art that comes naturally to *you.*

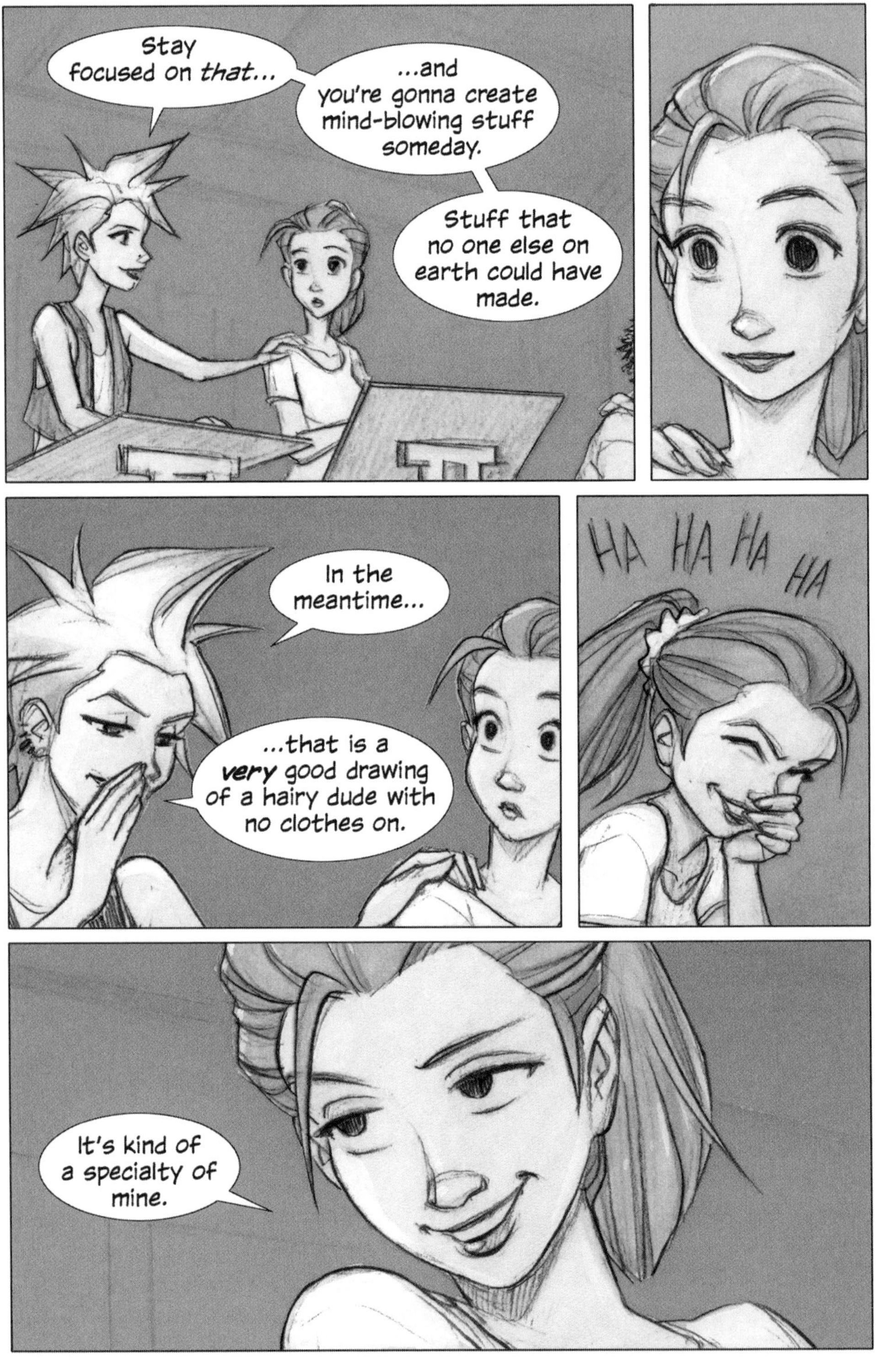
Stay focused on *that*...
...and you're gonna create mind-blowing stuff someday.
Stuff that no one else on earth could have made.
In the meantime...
...that is a ***very*** good drawing of a hairy dude with no clothes on.
HA HA HA HA
It's kind of a specialty of mine.

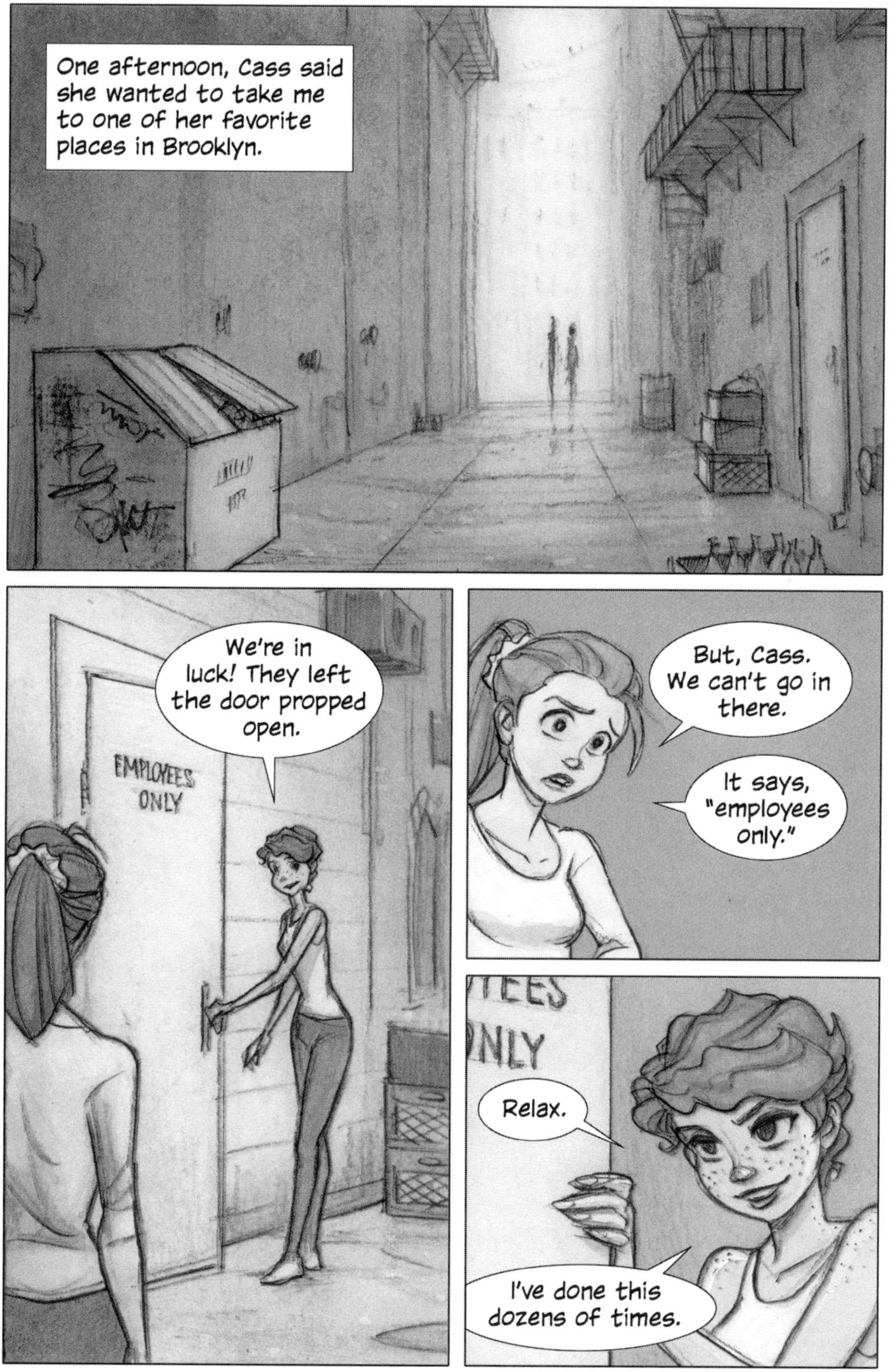
One afternoon, Cass said she wanted to take me to one of her favorite places in Brooklyn.
EMPLOYEES ONLY
We're in luck! They left the door propped open.
But, Cass. We can't go in there.
It says, "employees only."
Relax.
I've done this dozens of times.

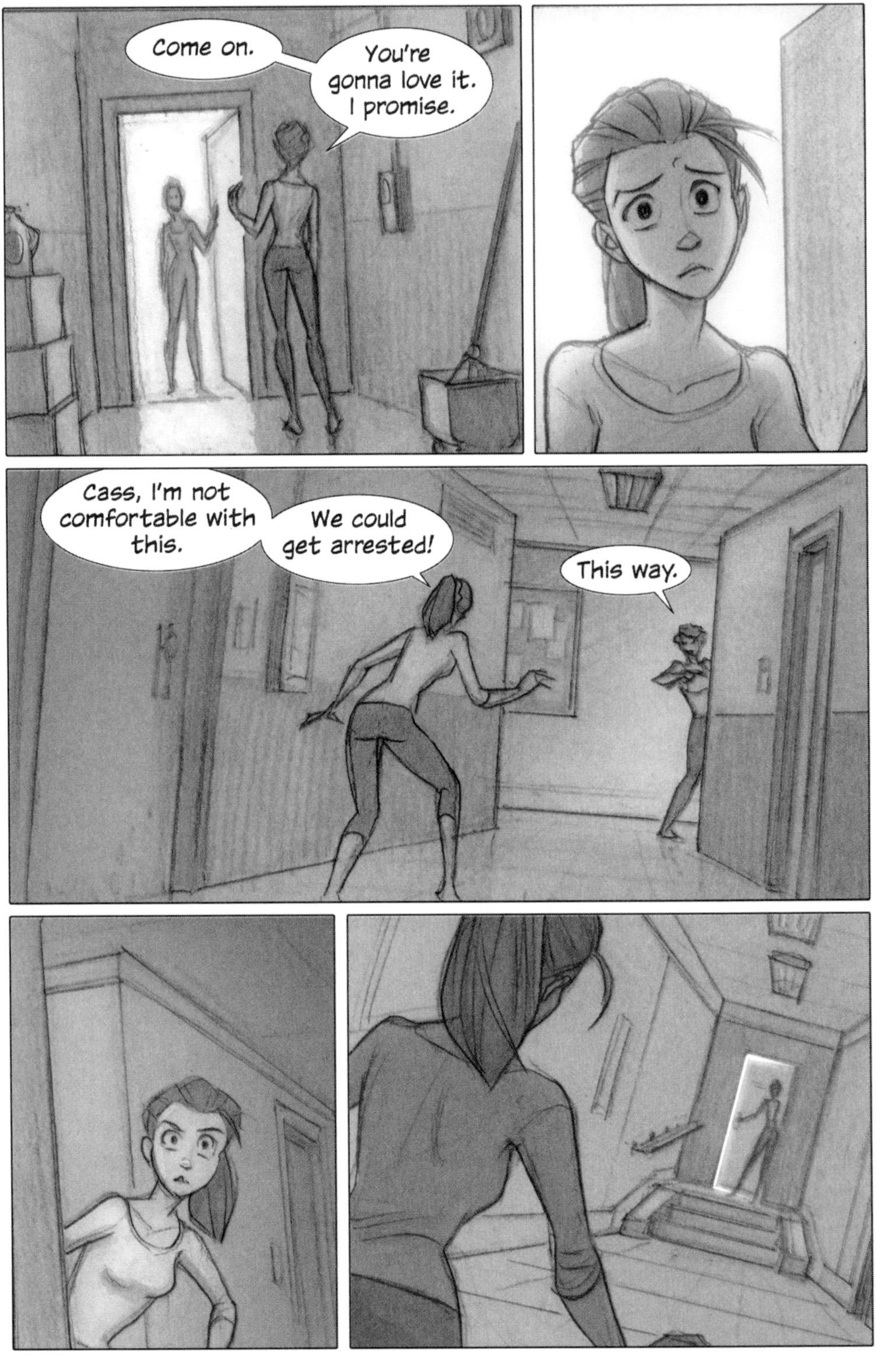
Come on.
You're gonna love it. I promise.
Cass, I'm not comfortable with this.
We could get arrested!
This way.

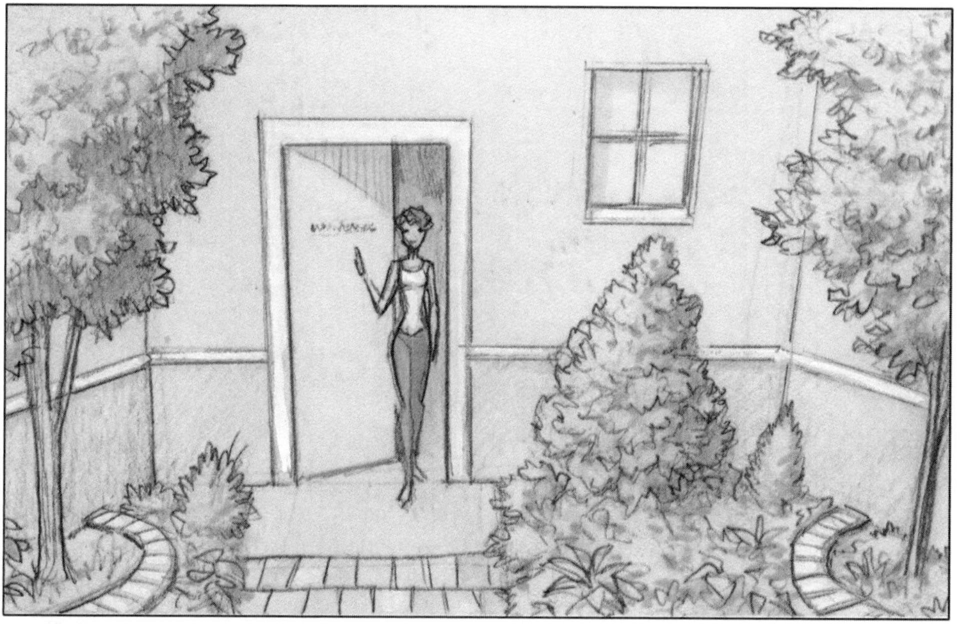

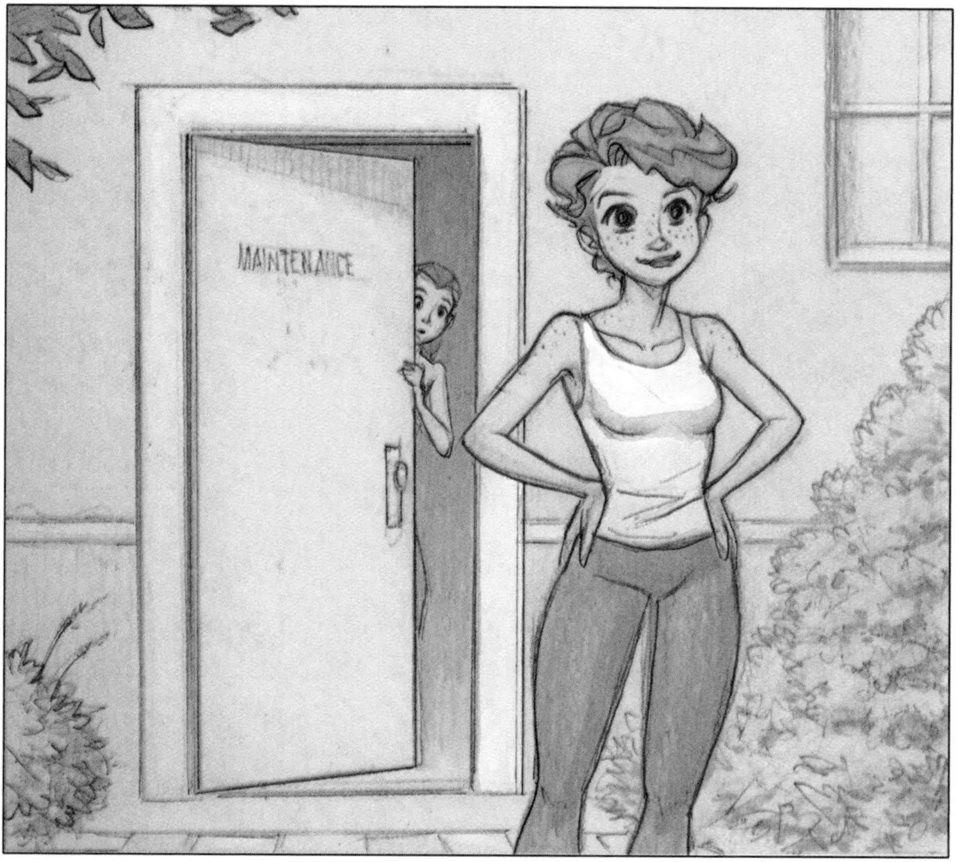
MAINTENANCE

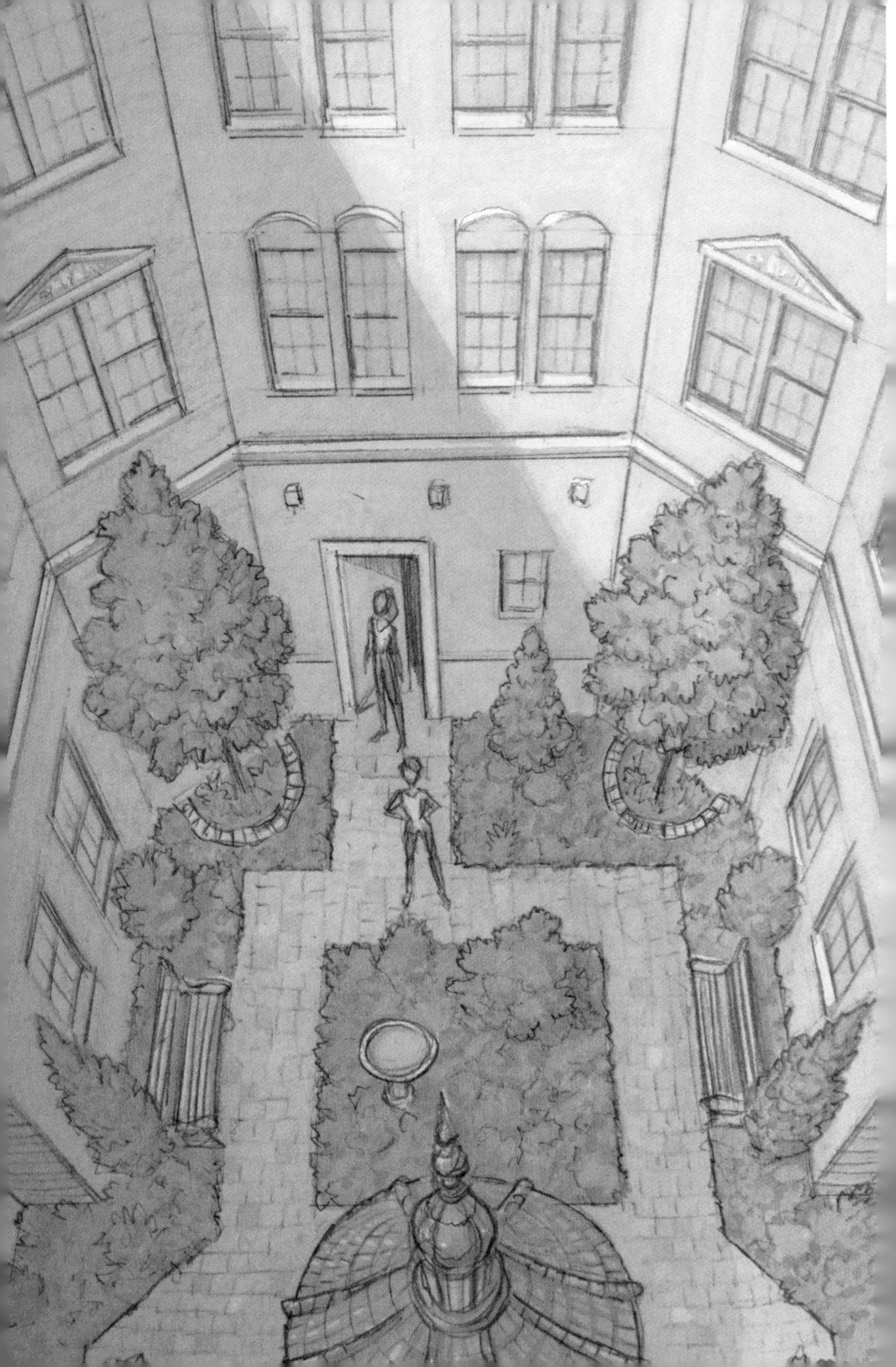

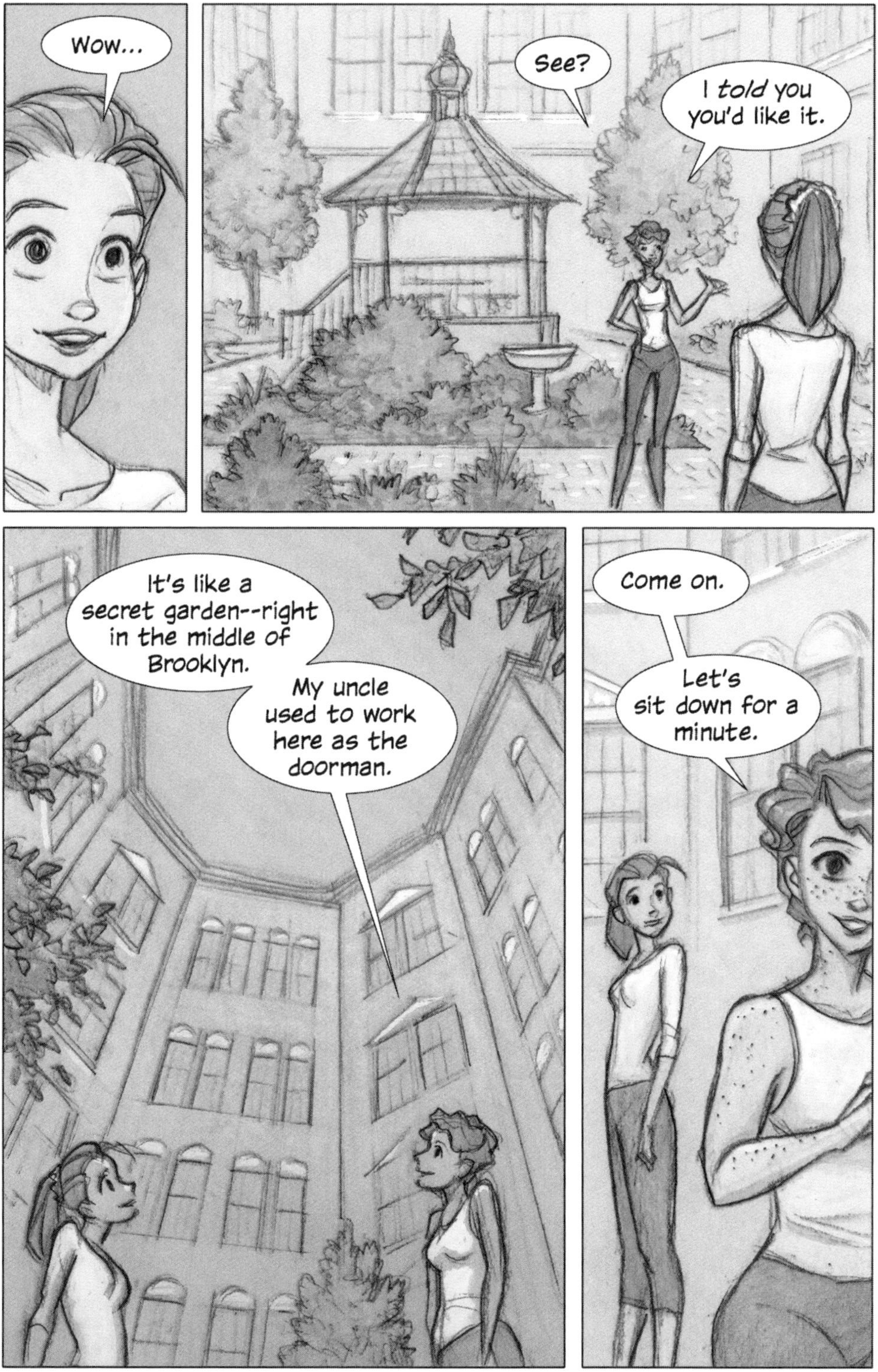
Wow...
See?
I *told* you you'd like it.
It's like a secret garden--right in the middle of Brooklyn.
My uncle used to work here as the doorman.
Come on.
Let's sit down for a minute.

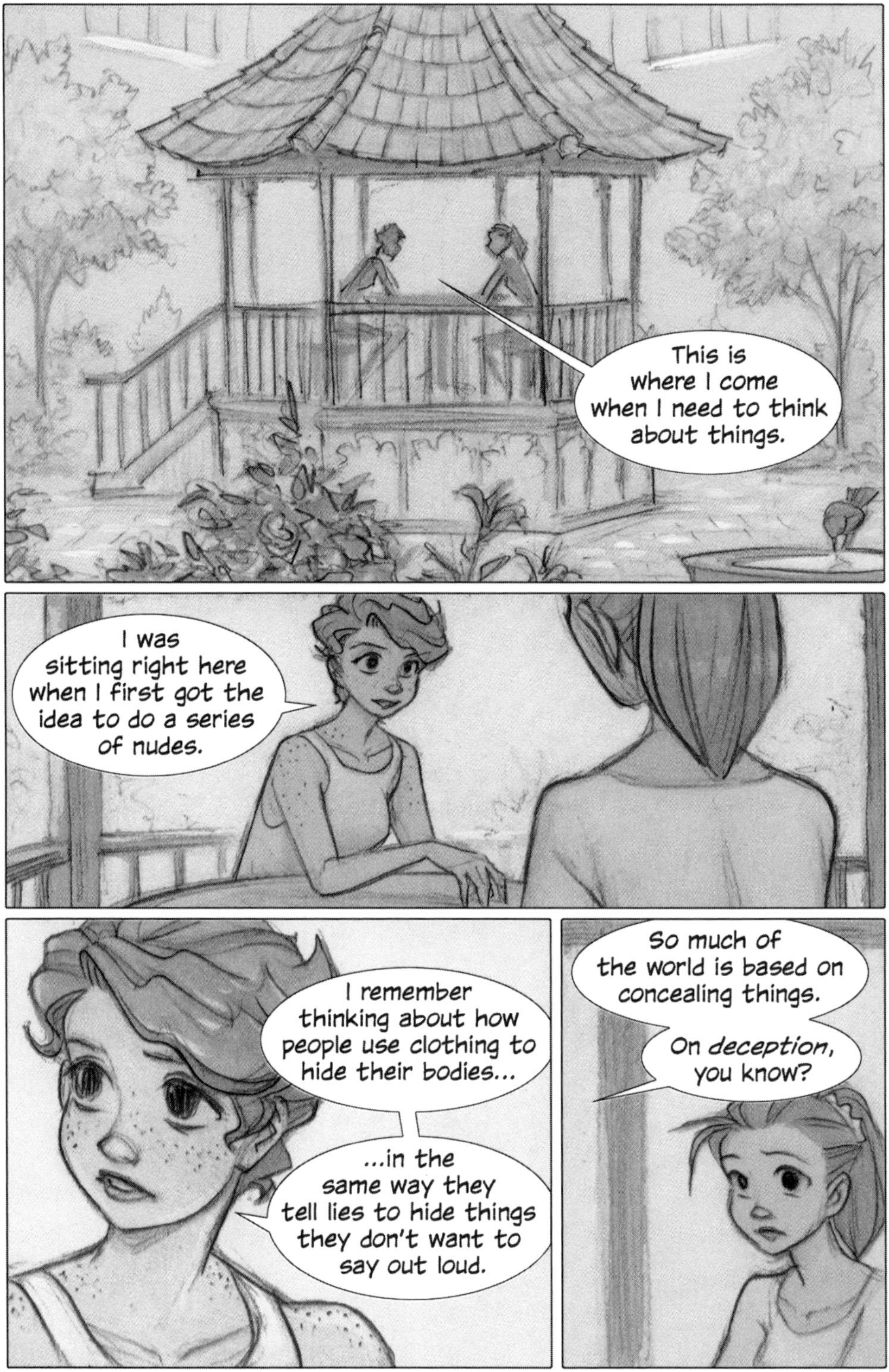

This is where I come when I need to think about things.
I was sitting right here when I first got the idea to do a series of nudes.
I remember thinking about how people use clothing to hide their bodies...
...in the same way they tell lies to hide things they don't want to say out loud.
So much of the world is based on concealing things.
On *deception*, you know?

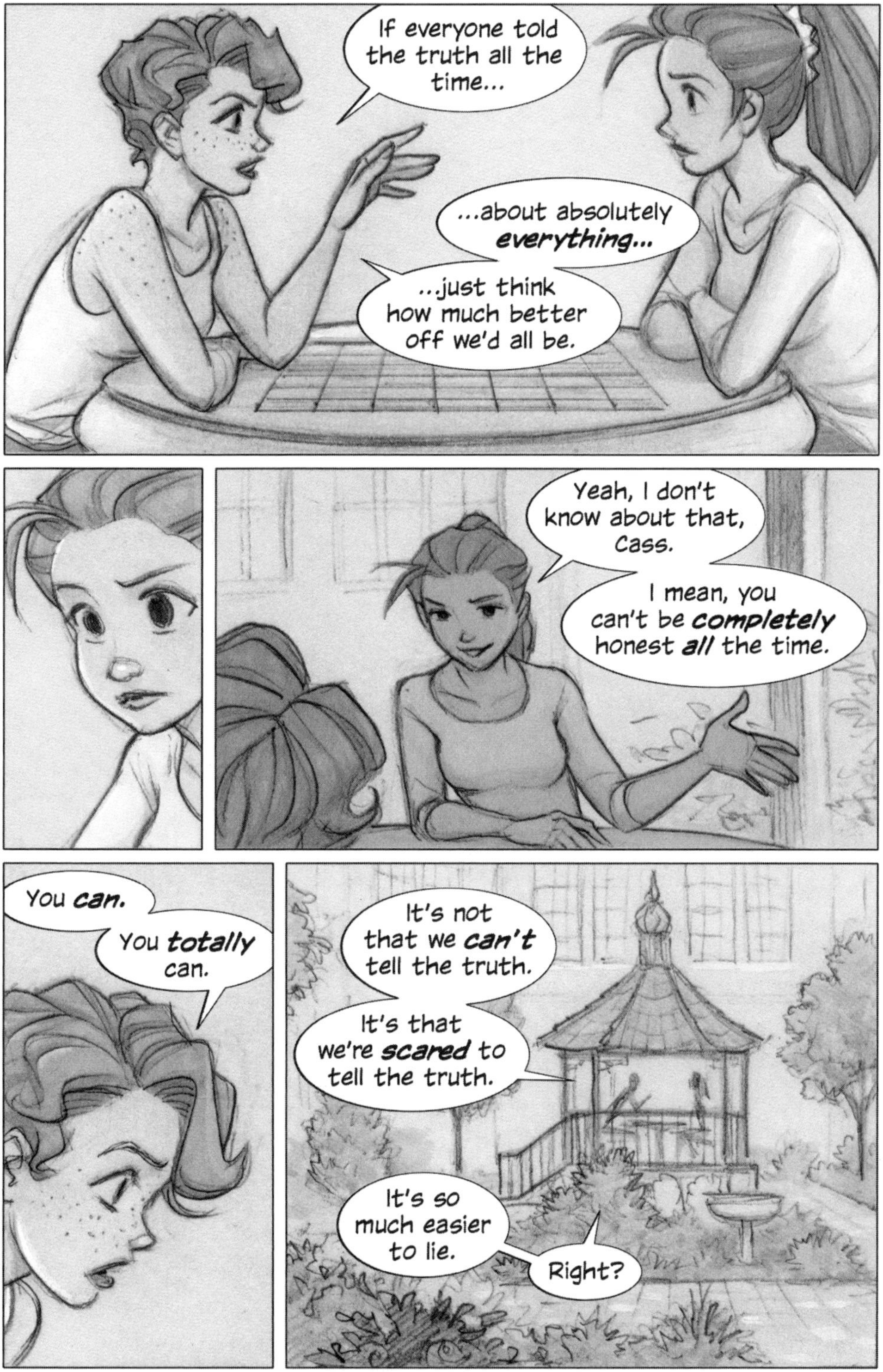
If everyone told the truth all the time...
...about absolutely *everything...*
...just think how much better off we'd all be.
Yeah, I don't know about that, Cass.
I mean, you can't be *completely* honest *all* the time.
You *can.*
You *totally* can.
It's not that we *can't* tell the truth.
It's that we're *scared* to tell the truth.
It's so much easier to lie.
Right?

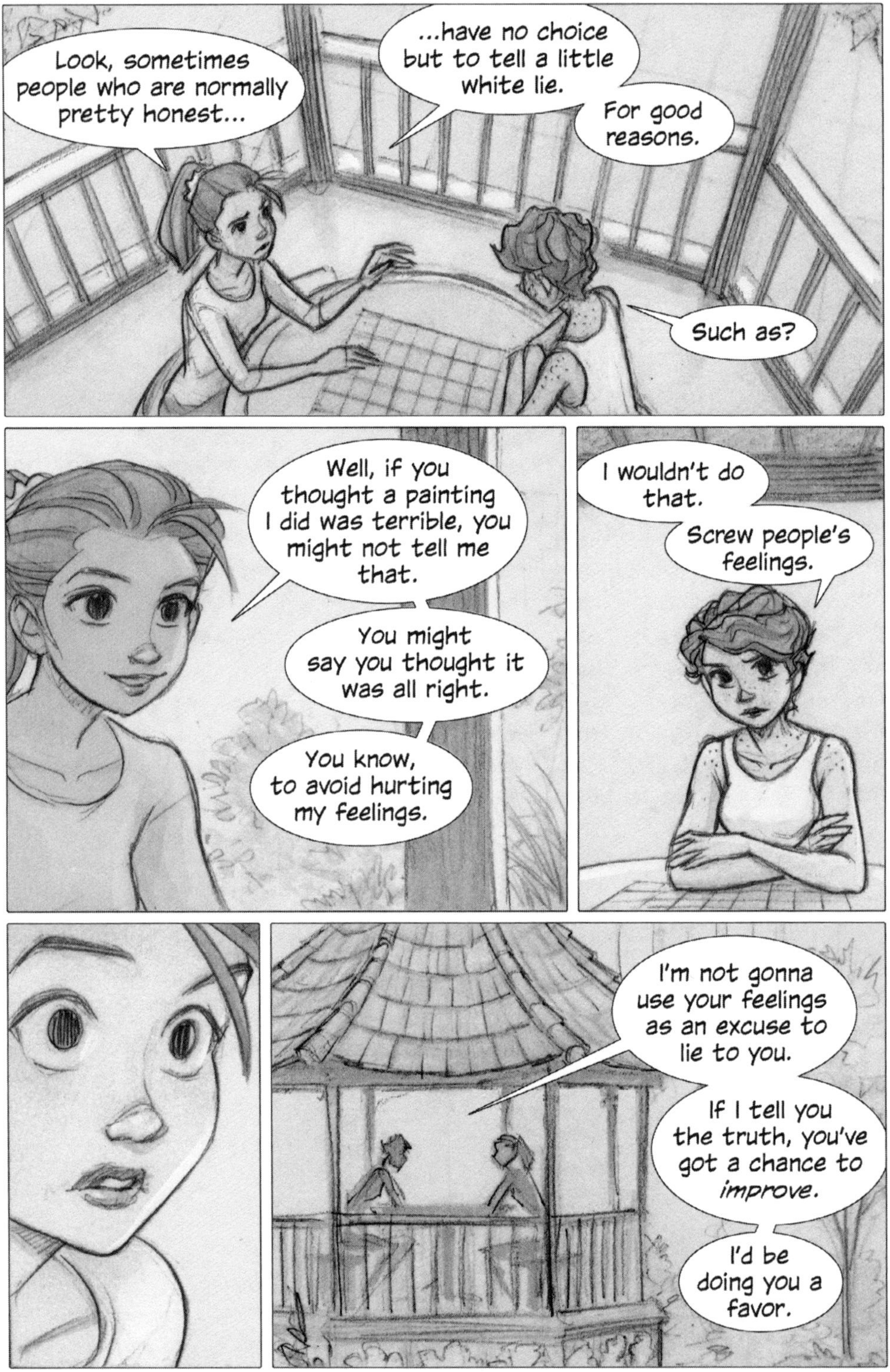
Look, sometimes people who are normally pretty honest...
...have no choice but to tell a little white lie.
For good reasons.
Such as?
Well, if you thought a painting I did was terrible, you might not tell me that.
You might say you thought it was all right.
You know, to avoid hurting my feelings.
I wouldn't do that.
Screw people's feelings.
I'm not gonna use your feelings as an excuse to lie to you.
If I tell you the truth, you've got a chance to *improve*.
I'd be doing you a favor.

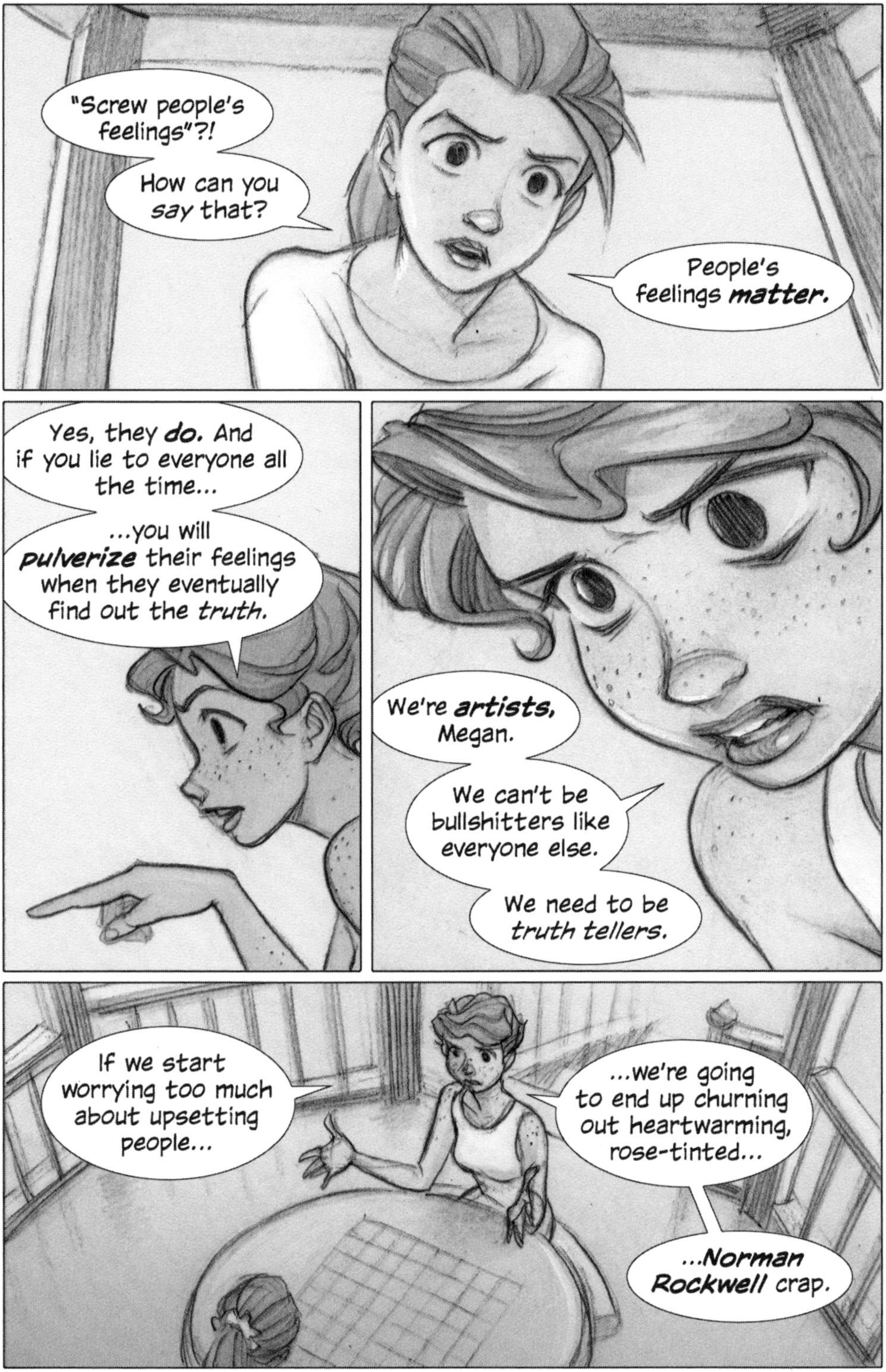
"Screw people's feelings"?!
How can you say that?
People's feelings matter.
Yes, they do. And if you lie to everyone all the time...
...you will pulverize their feelings when they eventually find out the truth.
We're artists, Megan.
We can't be bullshitters like everyone else.
We need to be truth tellers.
If we start worrying too much about upsetting people...
...we're going to end up churning out heartwarming, rose-tinted...
...Norman Rockwell crap.

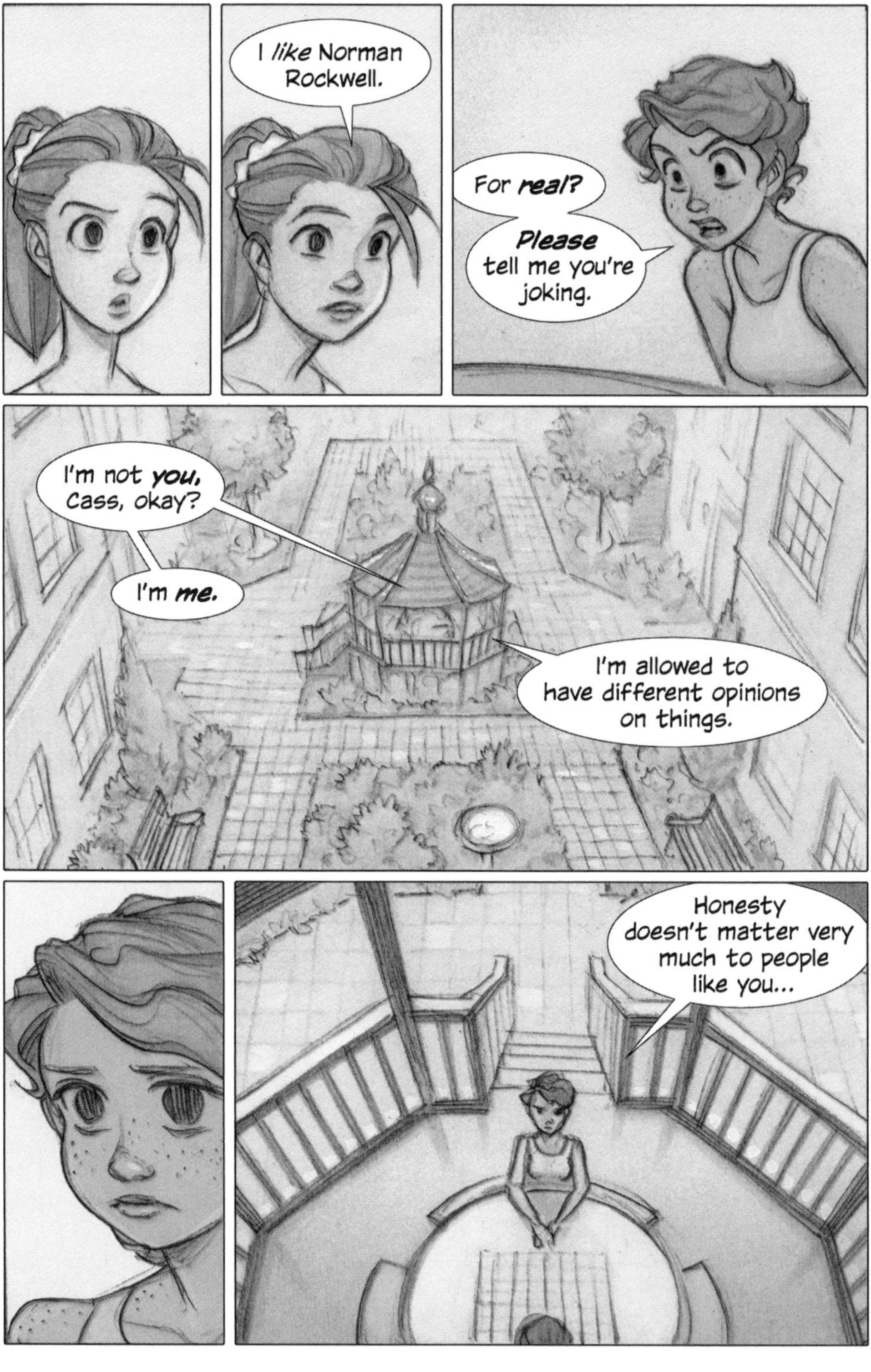
I *like* Norman Rockwell.
For ***real?***
Please tell me you're joking.
I'm not ***you,*** Cass, okay?
I'm ***me.***
I'm allowed to have different opinions on things.
Honesty doesn't matter very much to people like you...

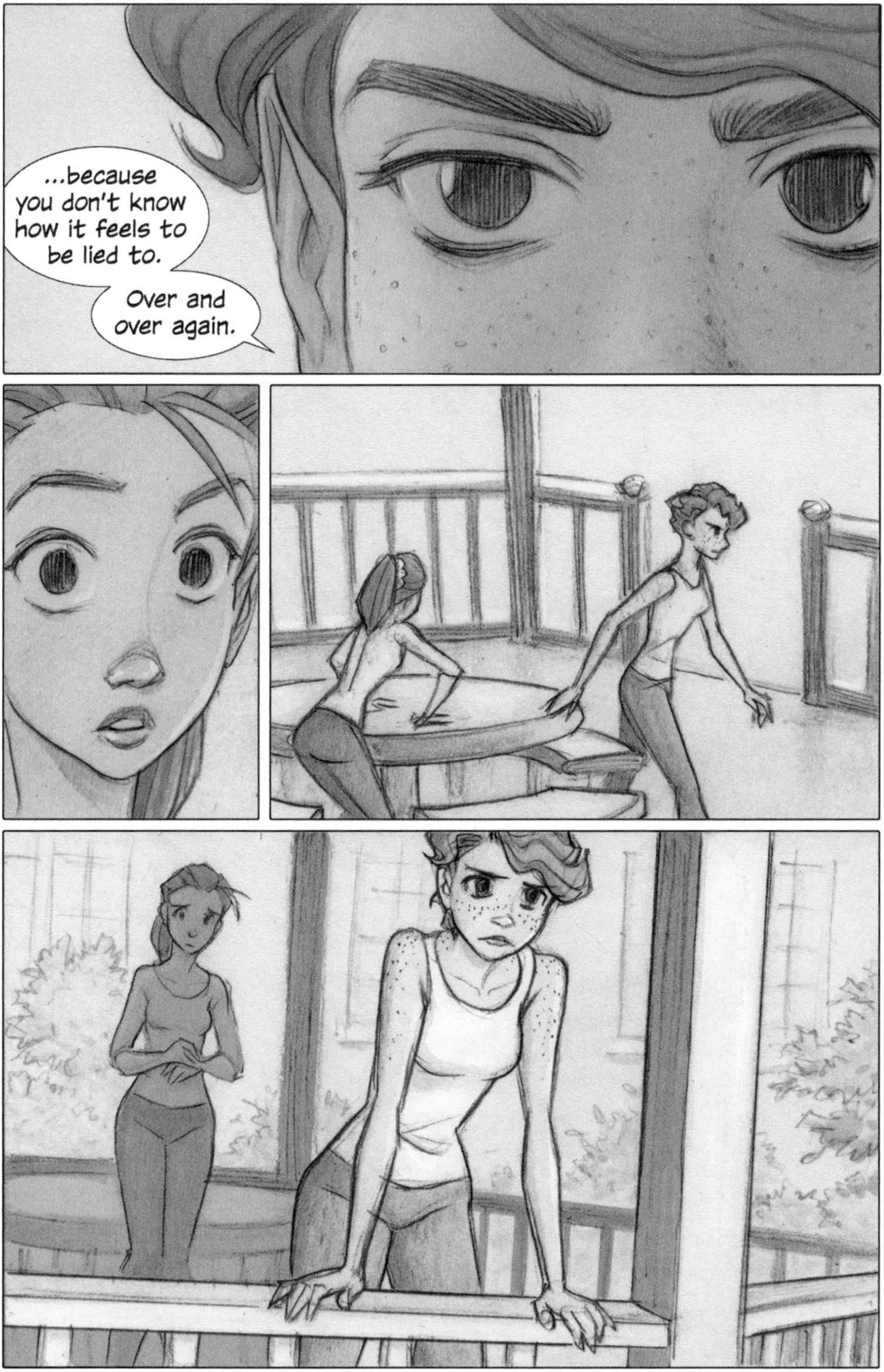
...because you don't know how it feels to be lied to.
Over and over again.

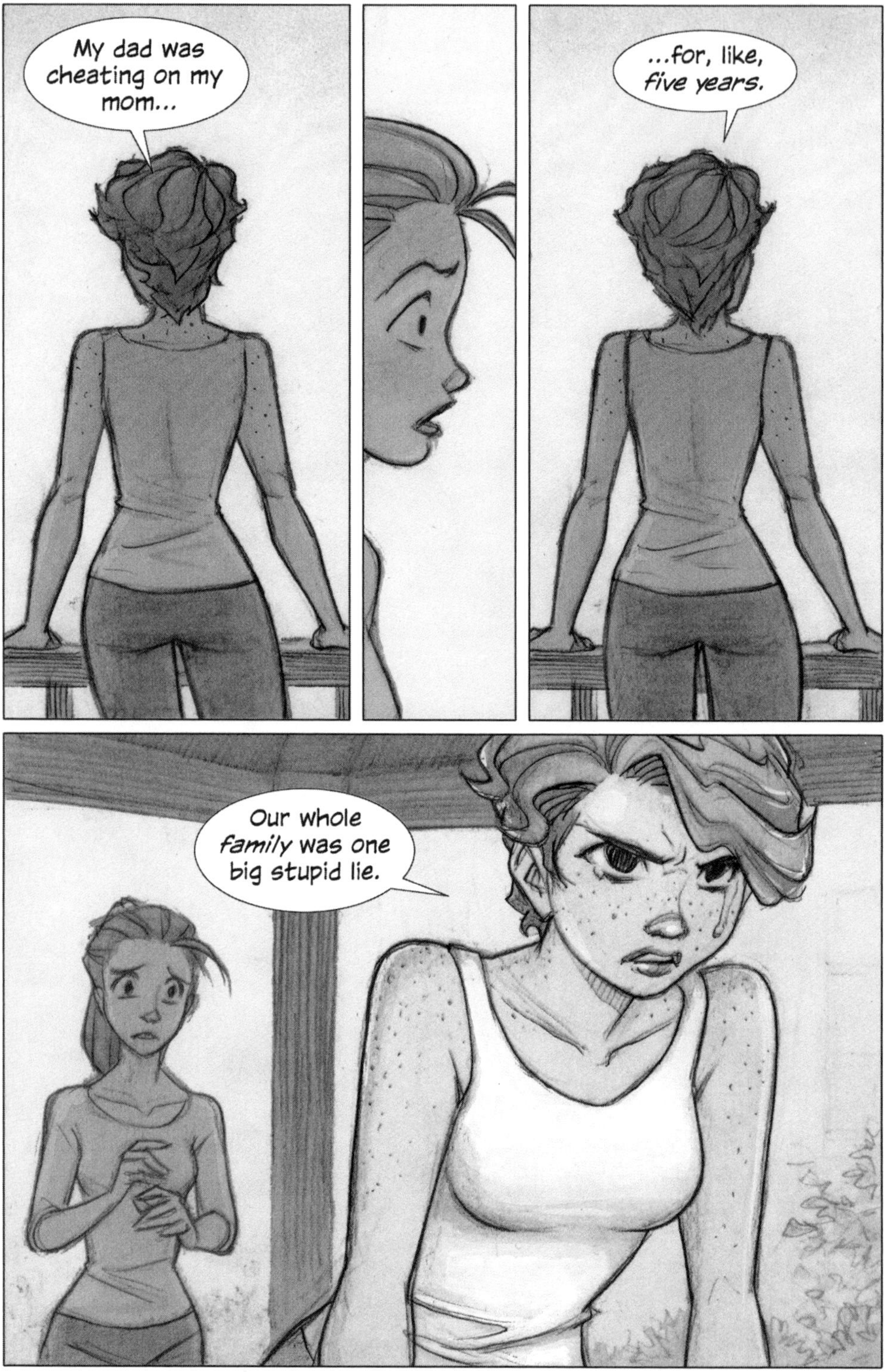
My dad was cheating on my mom...
...for, like, *five years.*
Our whole *family* was one big stupid lie.

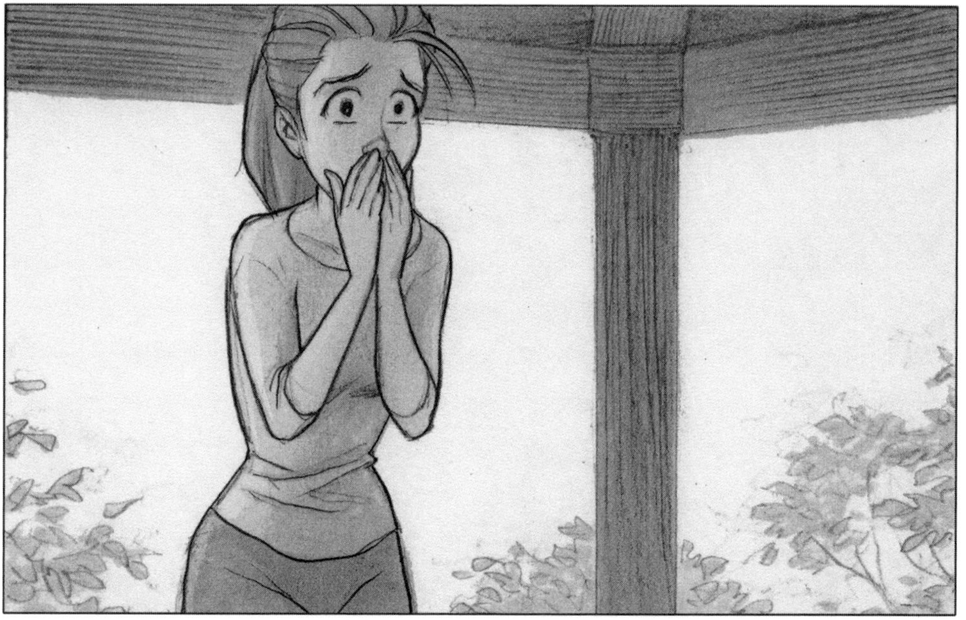
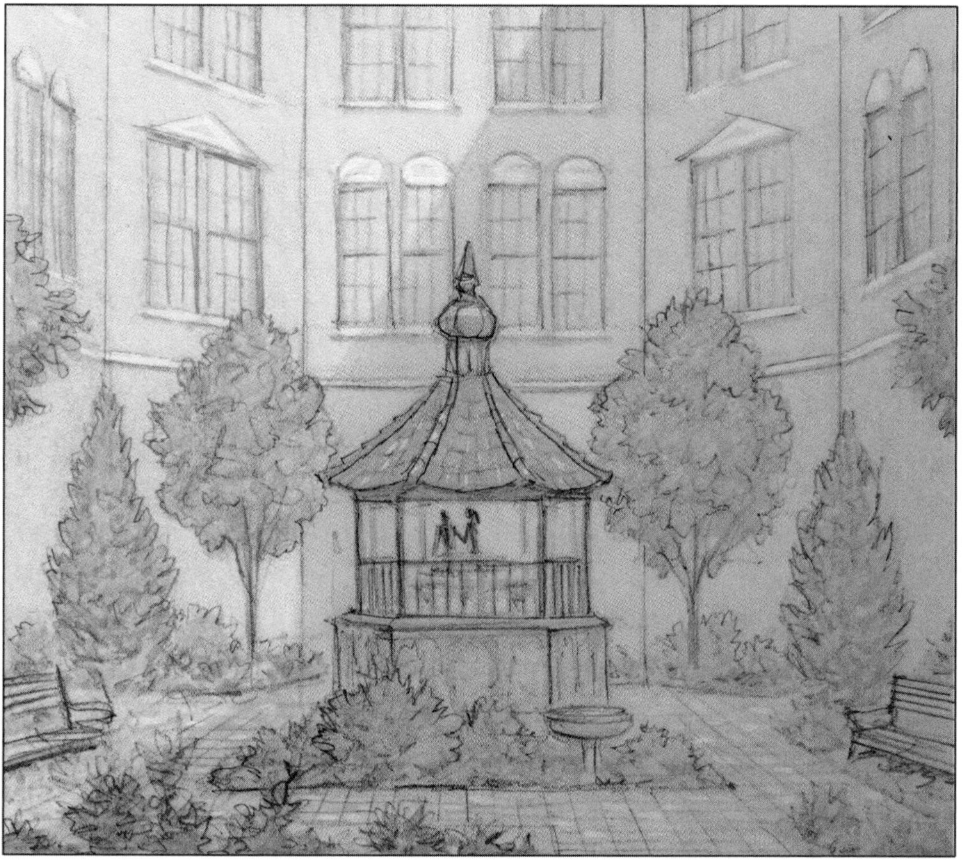

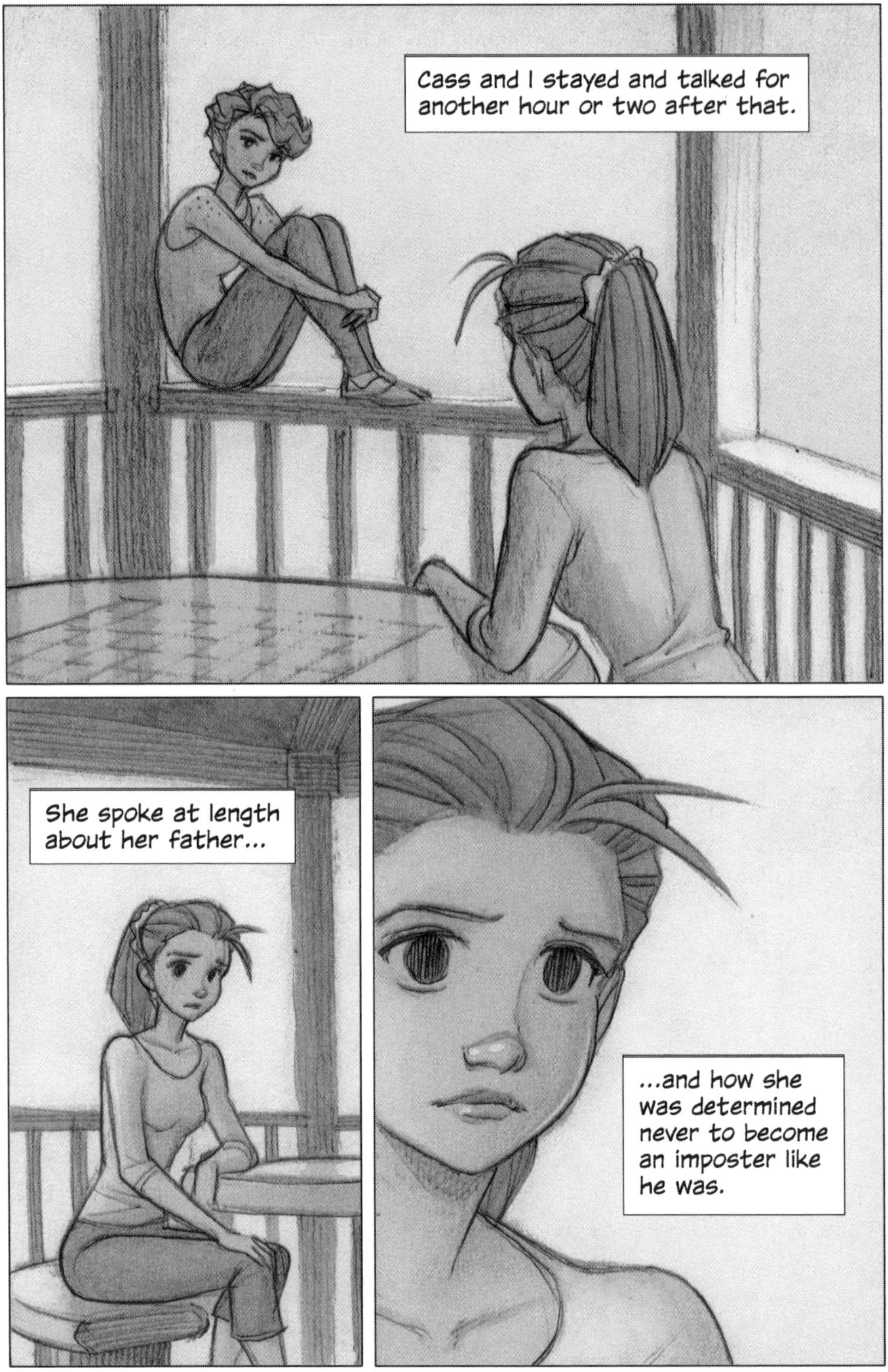
Cass and I stayed and talked for another hour or two after that.
She spoke at length about her father...
...and how she was determined never to become an imposter like he was.

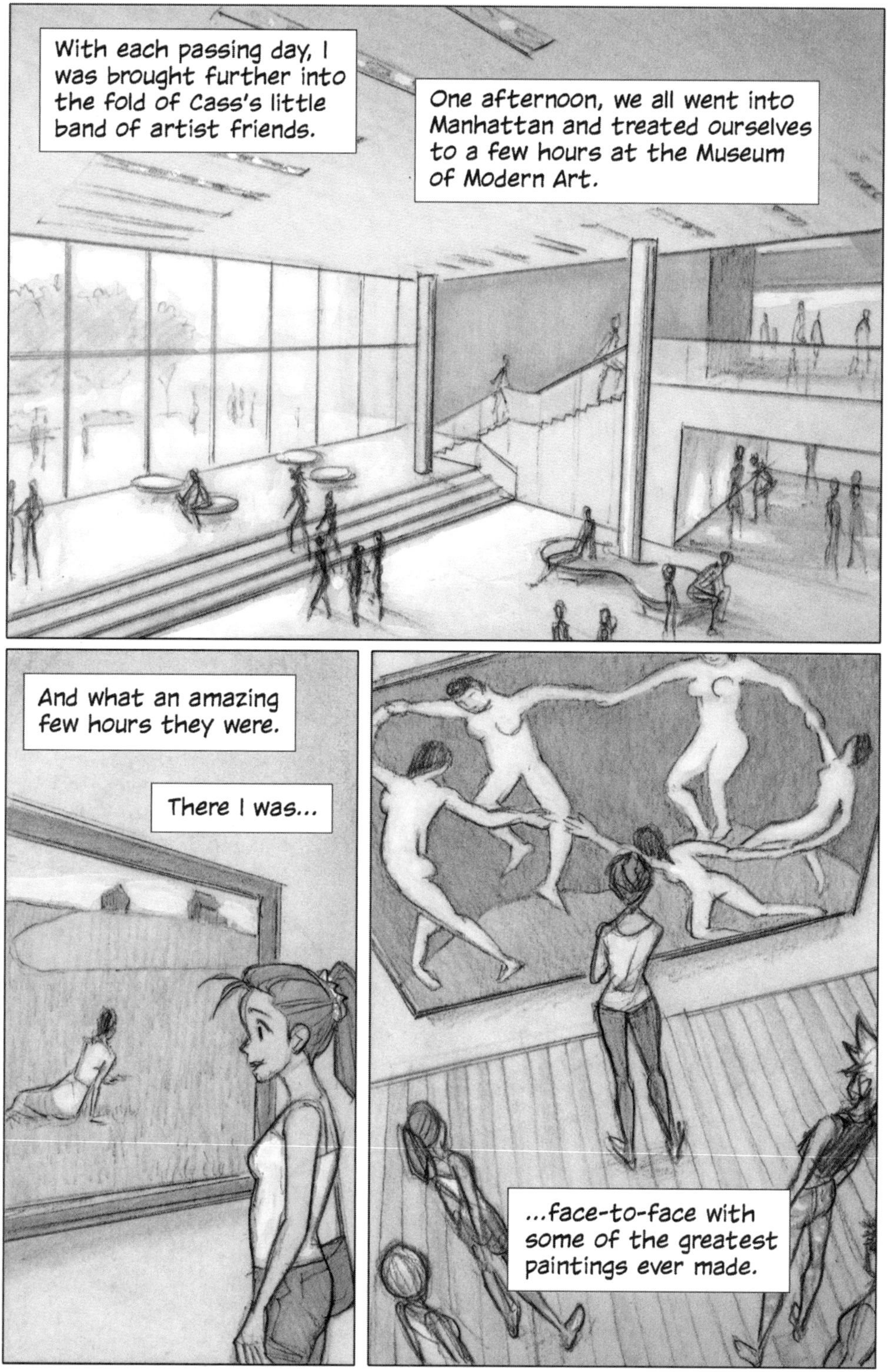
With each passing day, I was brought further into the fold of Cass's little band of artist friends.
One afternoon, we all went into Manhattan and treated ourselves to a few hours at the Museum of Modern Art.
And what an amazing few hours they were.
There I was...
...face-to-face with some of the greatest paintings ever made.

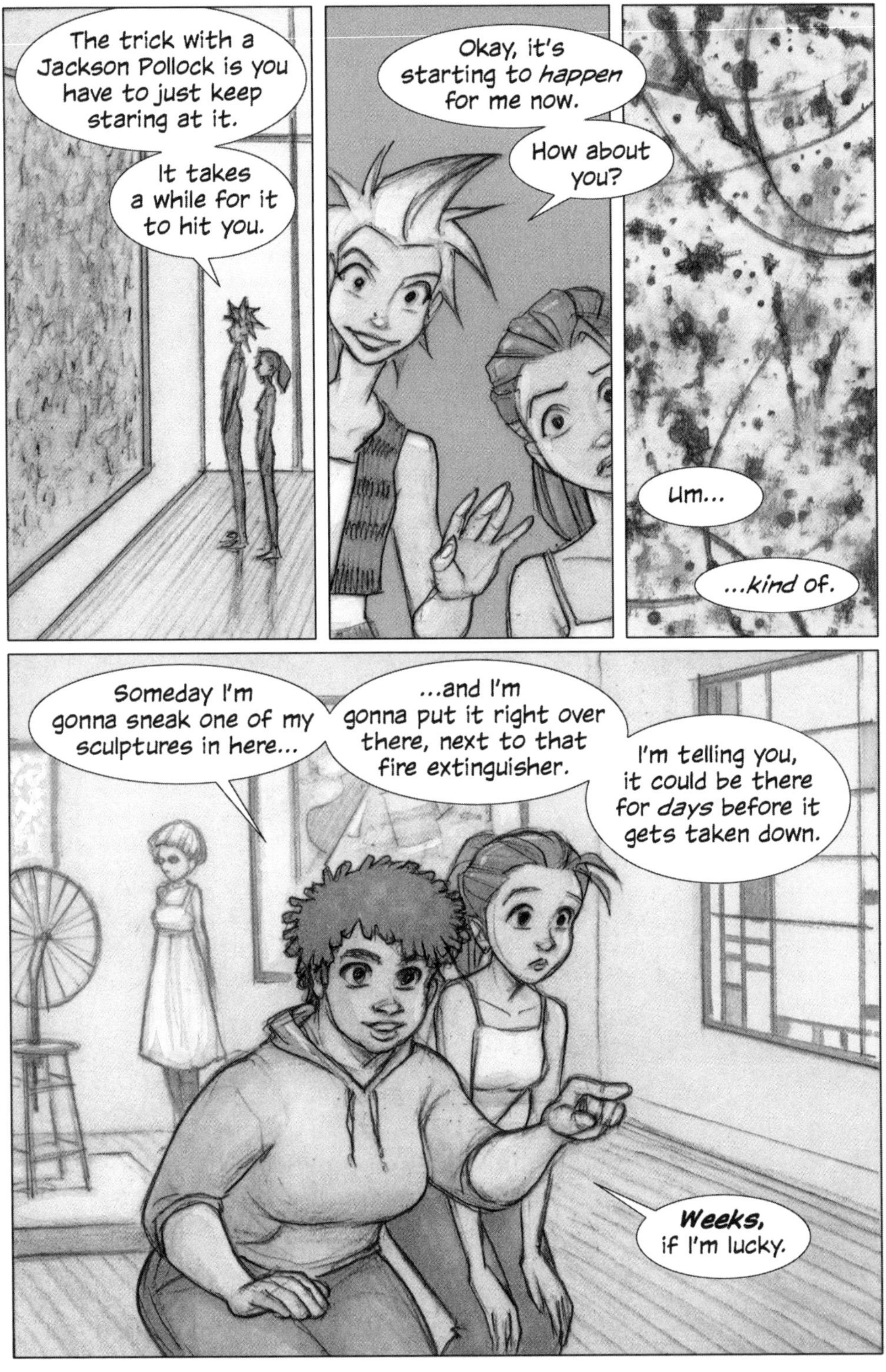

The trick with a Jackson Pollock is you have to just keep staring at it.
It takes a while for it to hit you.
Okay, it's starting to *happen* for me now.
How about you?
Um...
...*kind* of.
Someday I'm gonna sneak one of my sculptures in here...
...and I'm gonna put it right over there, next to that fire extinguisher.
I'm telling you, it could be there for *days* before it gets taken down.
Weeks, if I'm lucky.

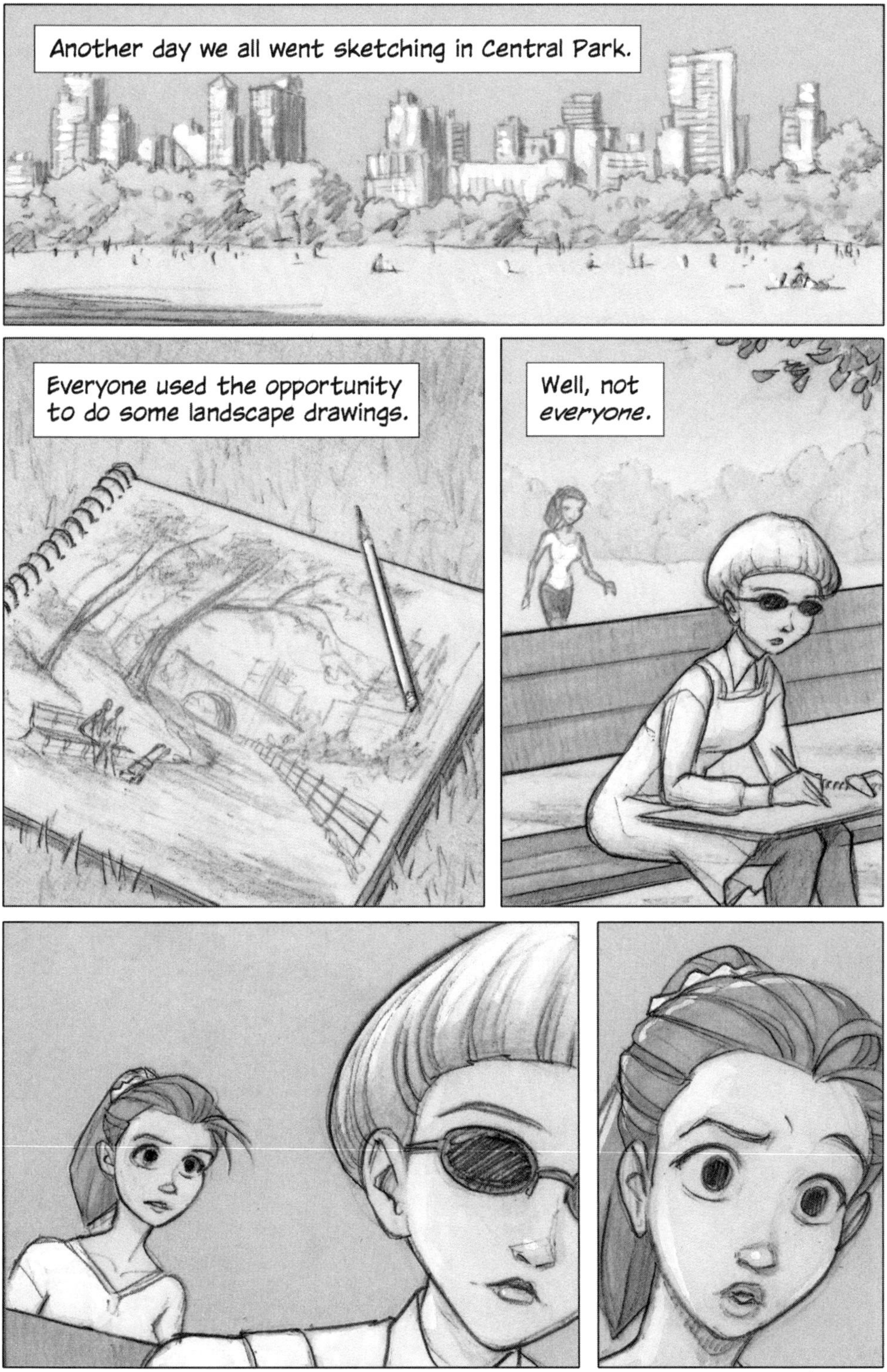
Another day we all went sketching in Central Park.
Everyone used the opportunity to do some landscape drawings.
Well, not *everyone*.

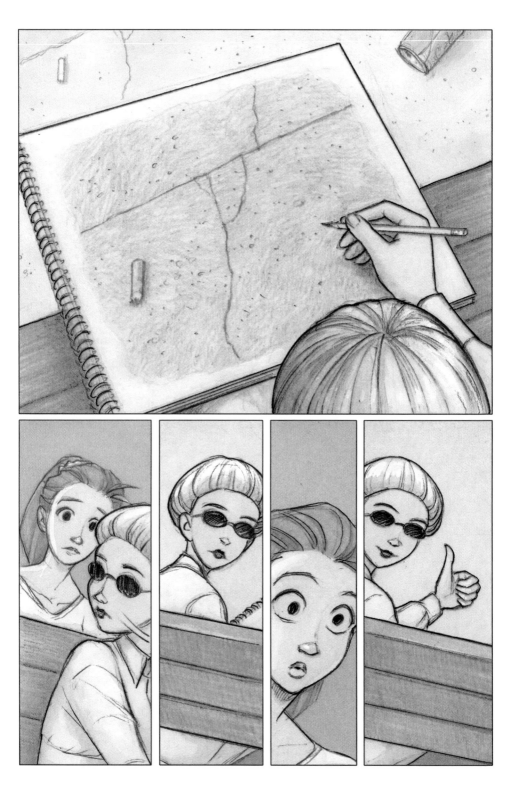

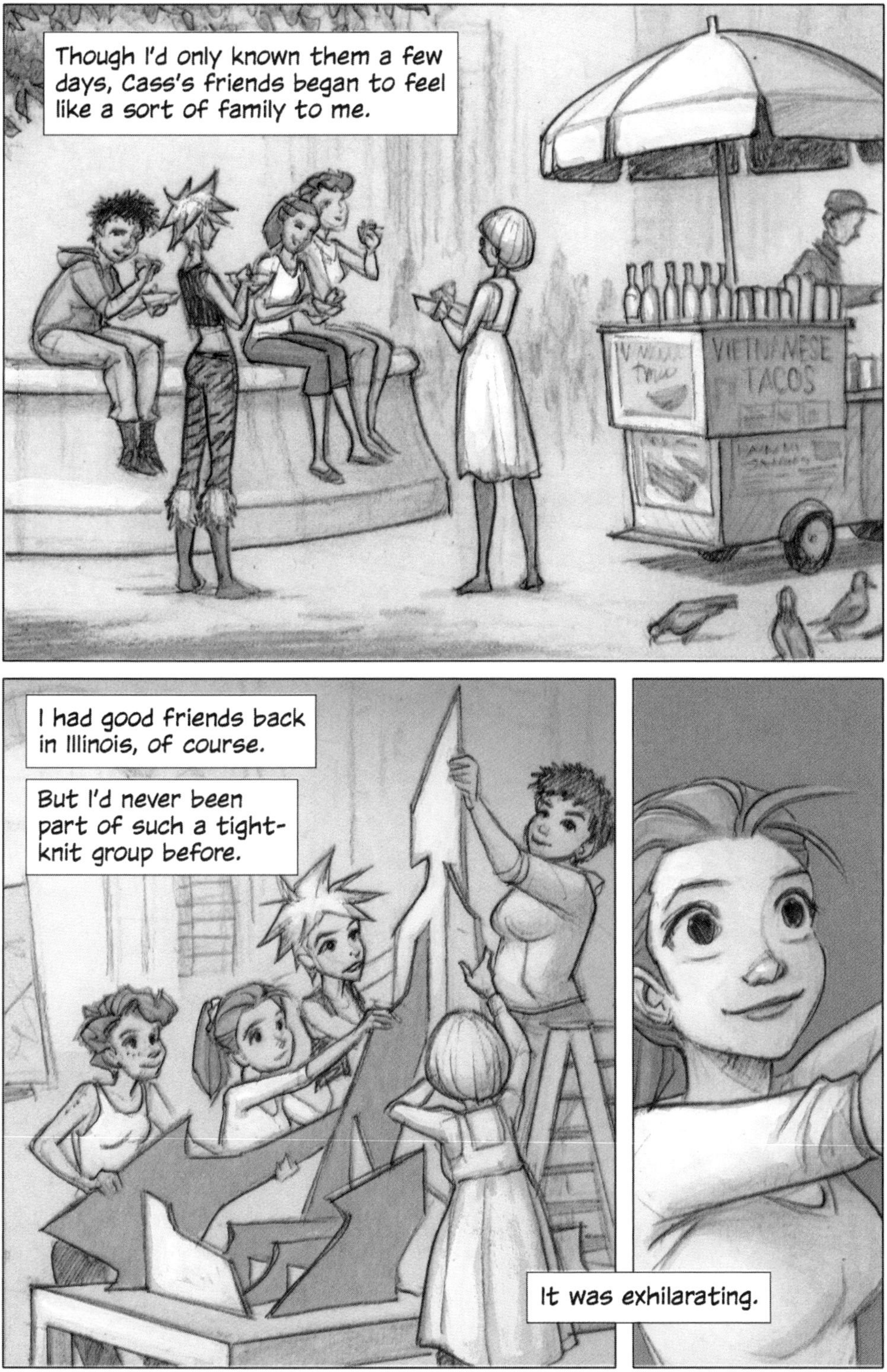
Though I'd only known them a few days, Cass's friends began to feel like a sort of family to me.
VIETNAMESE TACOS
I had good friends back in Illinois, of course.
But I'd never been part of such a tight-knit group before.
It was exhilarating.

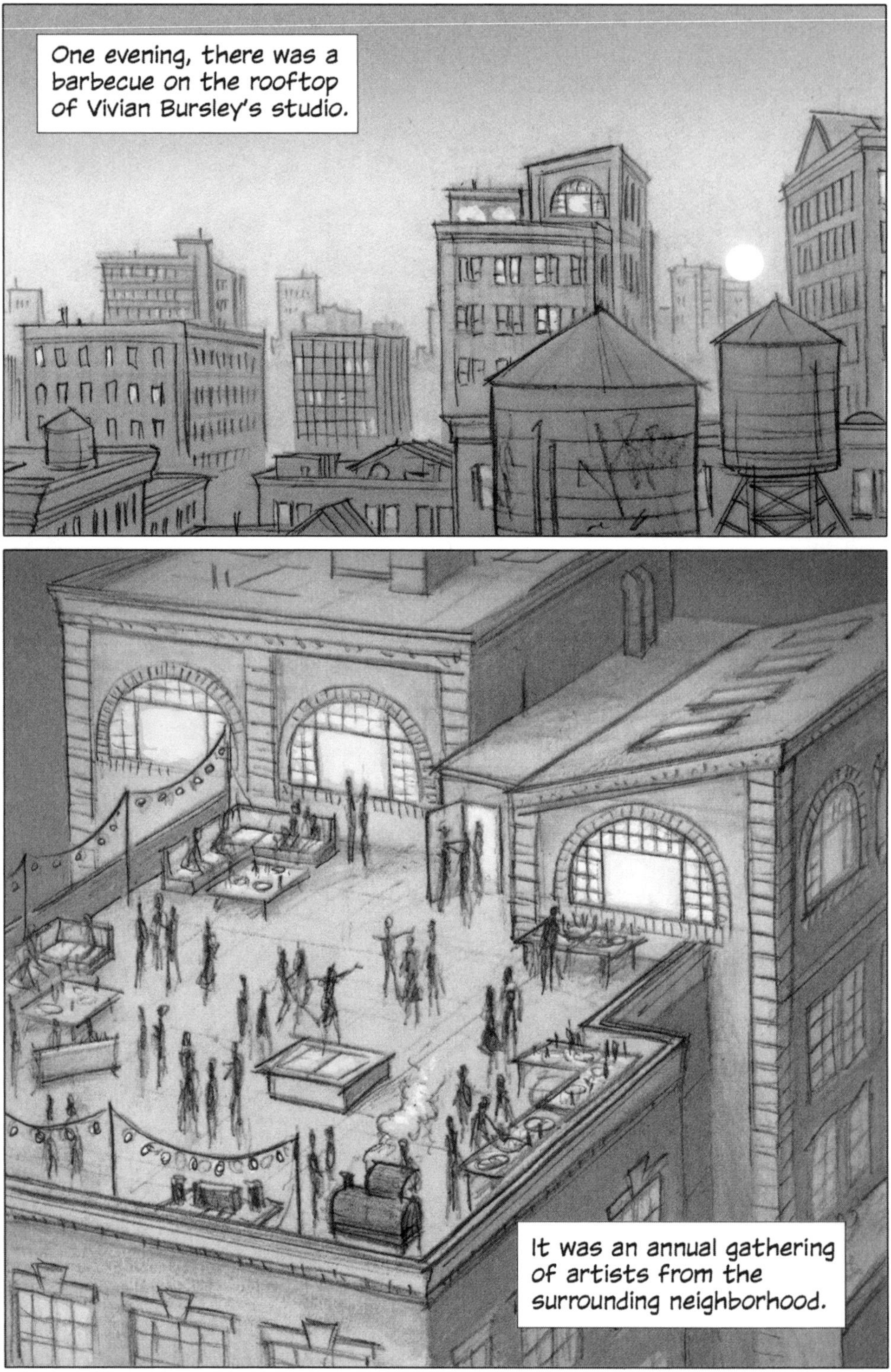
One evening, there was a barbecue on the rooftop of Vivian Bursley's studio.
It was an annual gathering of artists from the surrounding neighborhood.

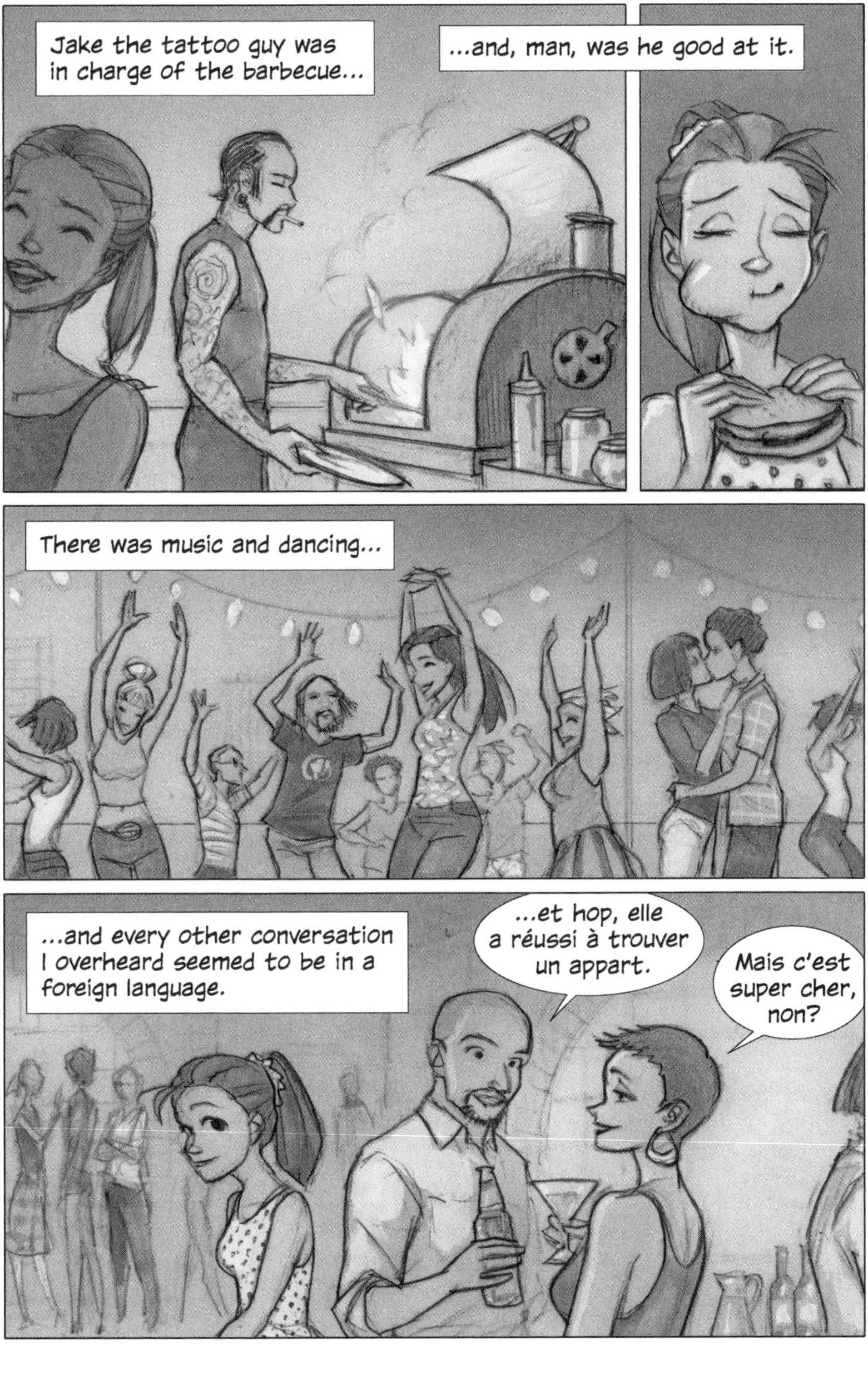
Jake the tattoo guy was in charge of the barbecue...
...and, man, was he good at it.
There was music and dancing...
...and every other conversation I overheard seemed to be in a foreign language.
...et hop, elle a réussi à trouver un appart.
Mais c'est super cher, non?

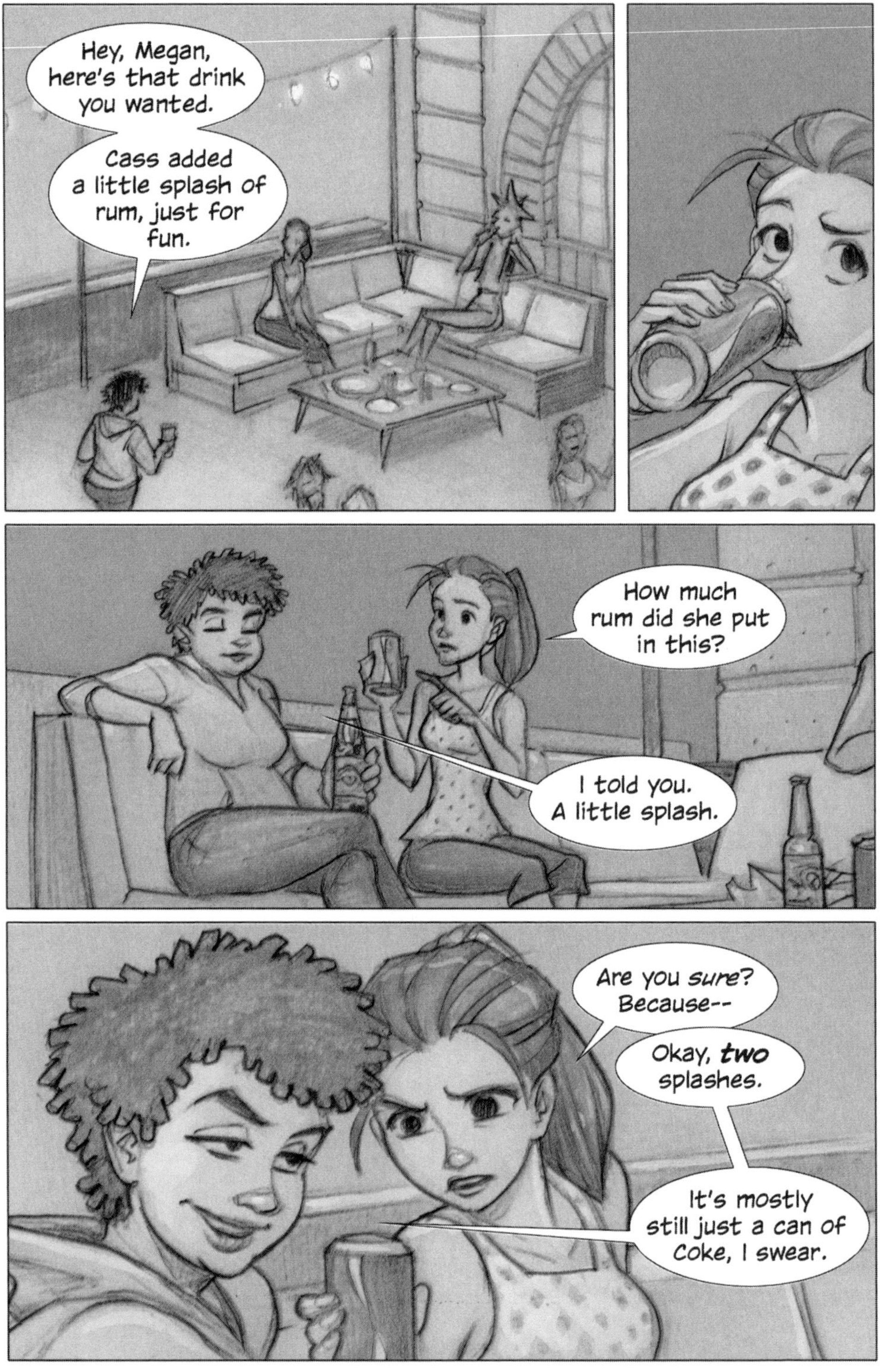
Hey, Megan, here's that drink you wanted.
Cass added a little splash of rum, just for fun.
How much rum did she put in this?
I told you. A little splash.
Are you *sure*? Because--
Okay, ***two*** splashes.
It's mostly still just a can of Coke, I swear.

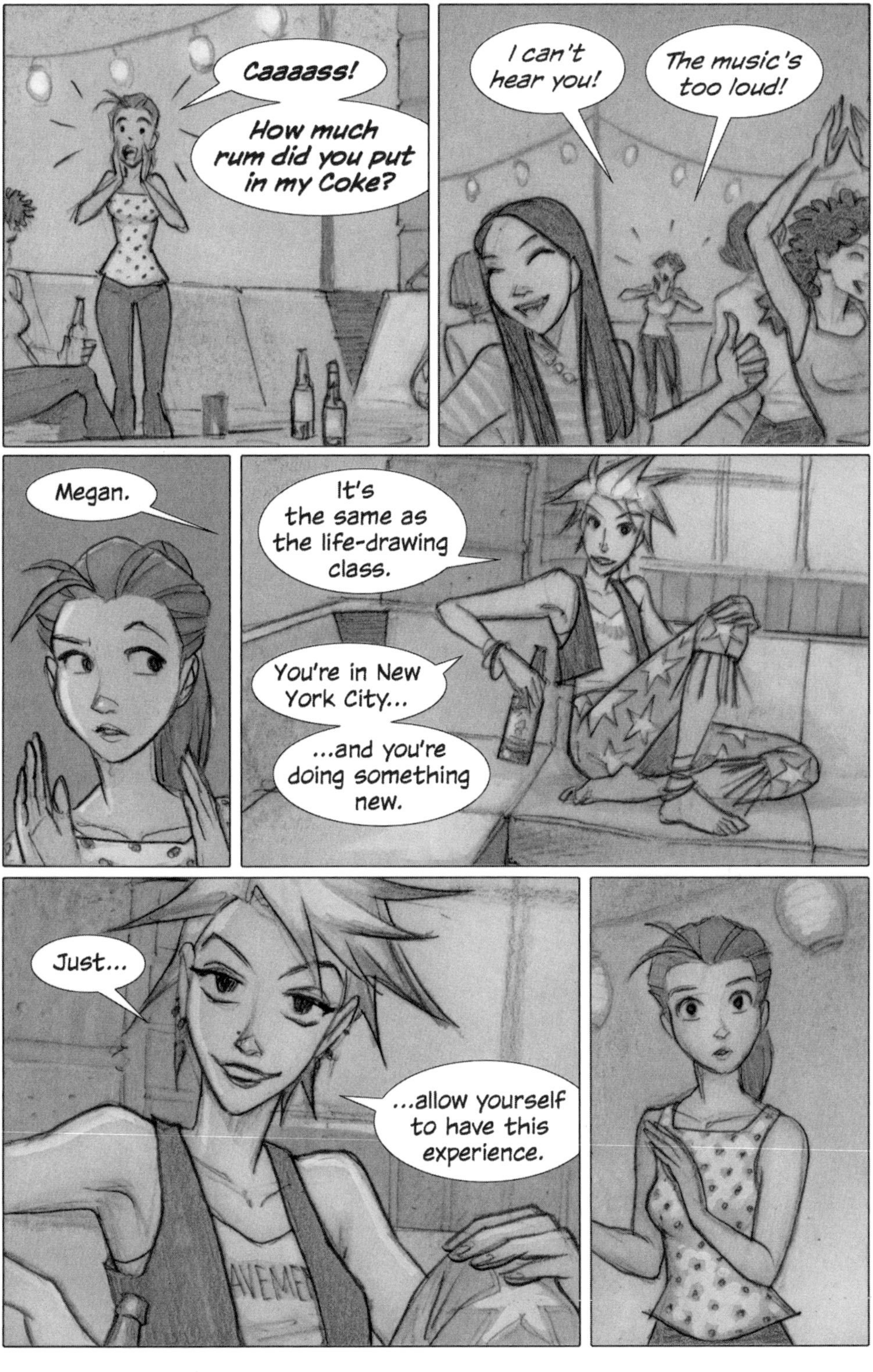
Caaaass!
How much rum did you put in my Coke?
I can't hear you!
The music's too loud!
Megan.
It's the same as the life-drawing class.
You're in New York City...
...and you're doing something new.
Just...
...allow yourself to have this experience.

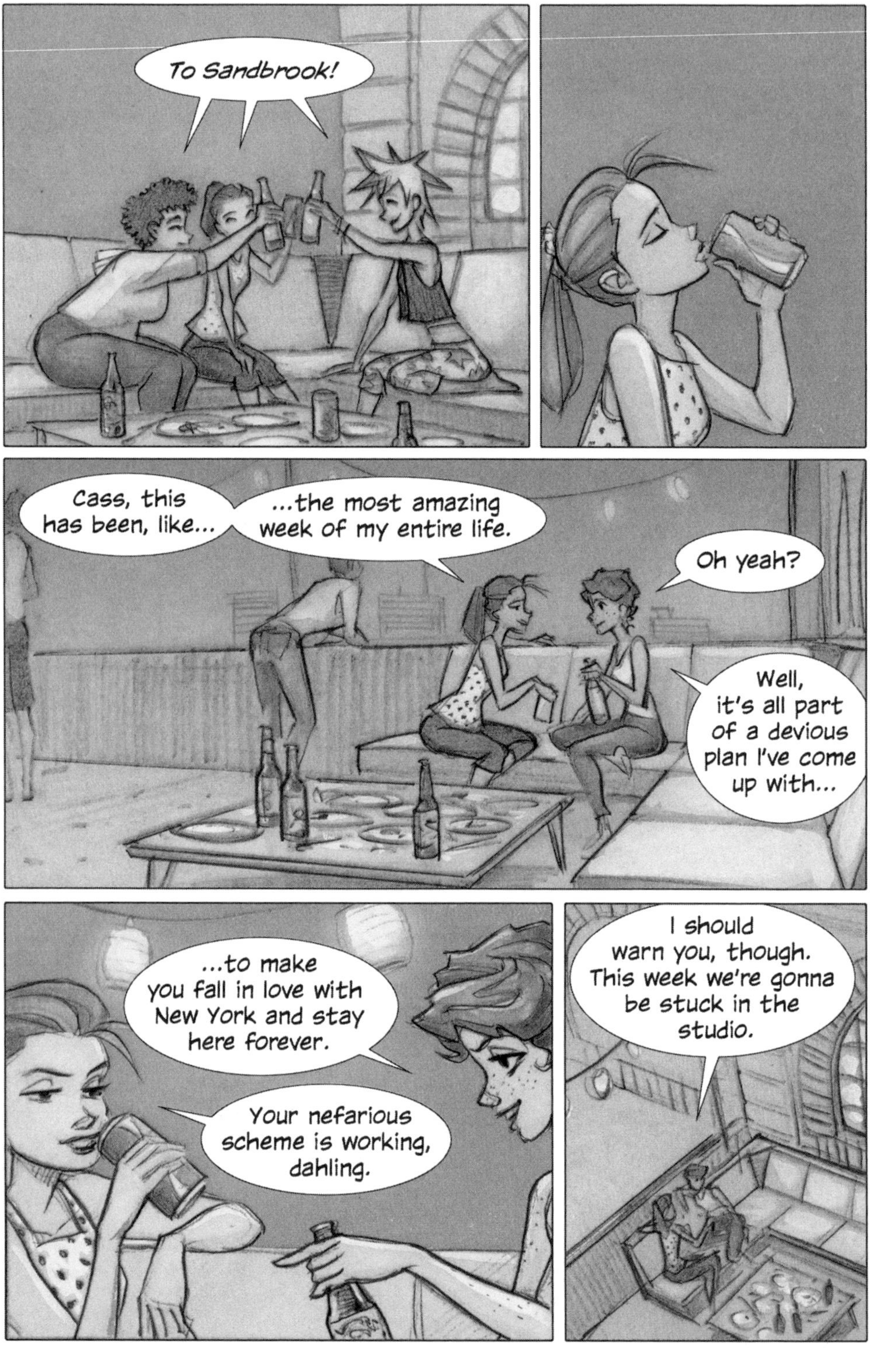
To Sandbrook!
Cass, this has been, like...
...the most amazing week of my entire life.
Oh yeah?
Well, it's all part of a devious plan I've come up with...
...to make you fall in love with New York and stay here forever.
Your nefarious scheme is working, dahling.
I should warn you, though. This week we're gonna be stuck in the studio.

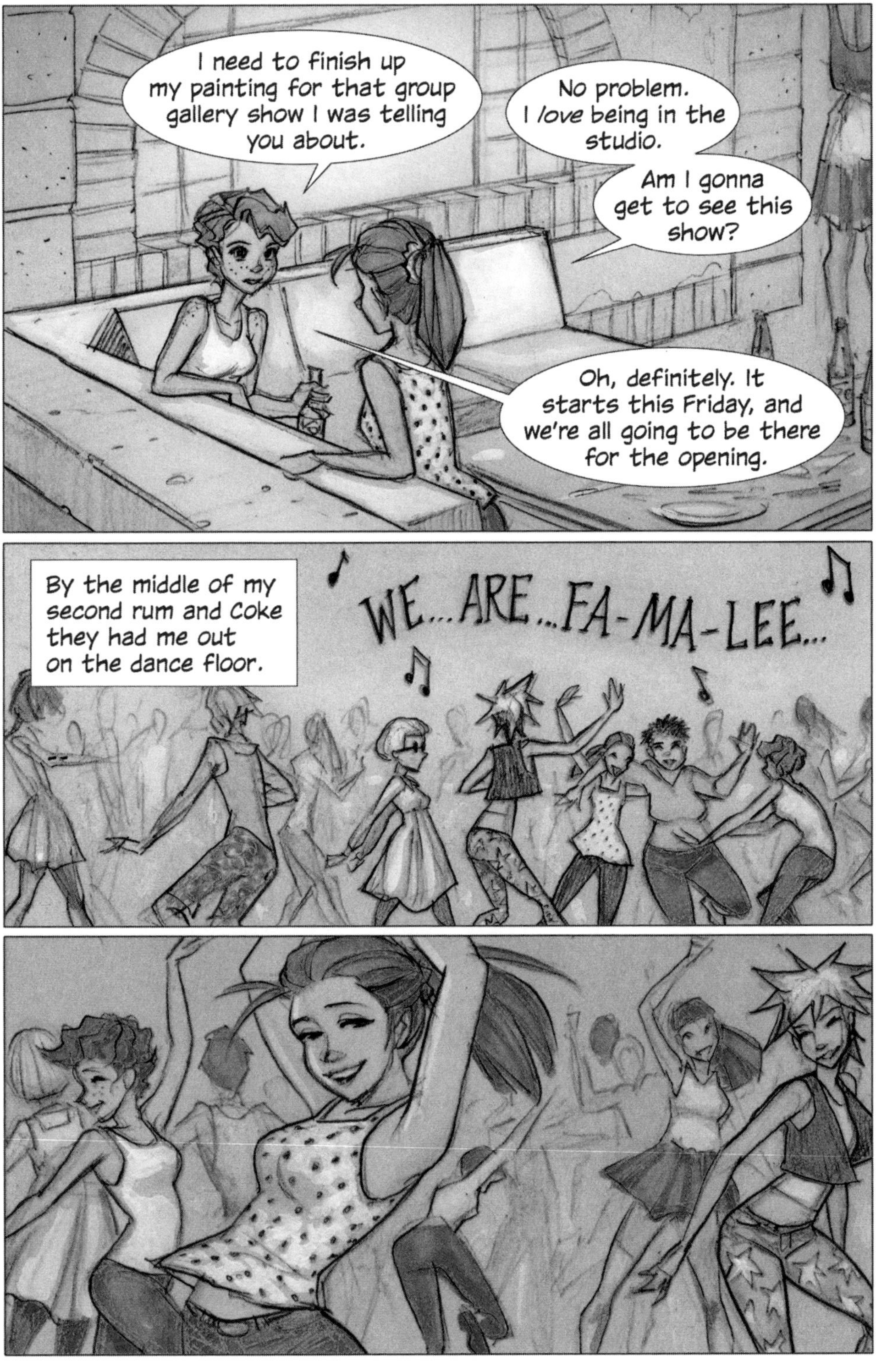
I need to finish up my painting for that group gallery show I was telling you about.
No problem. I *love* being in the studio.
Am I gonna get to see this show?
Oh, definitely. It starts this Friday, and we're all going to be there for the opening.
By the middle of my second rum and Coke they had me out on the dance floor.
WE...ARE...FA-MA-LEE...

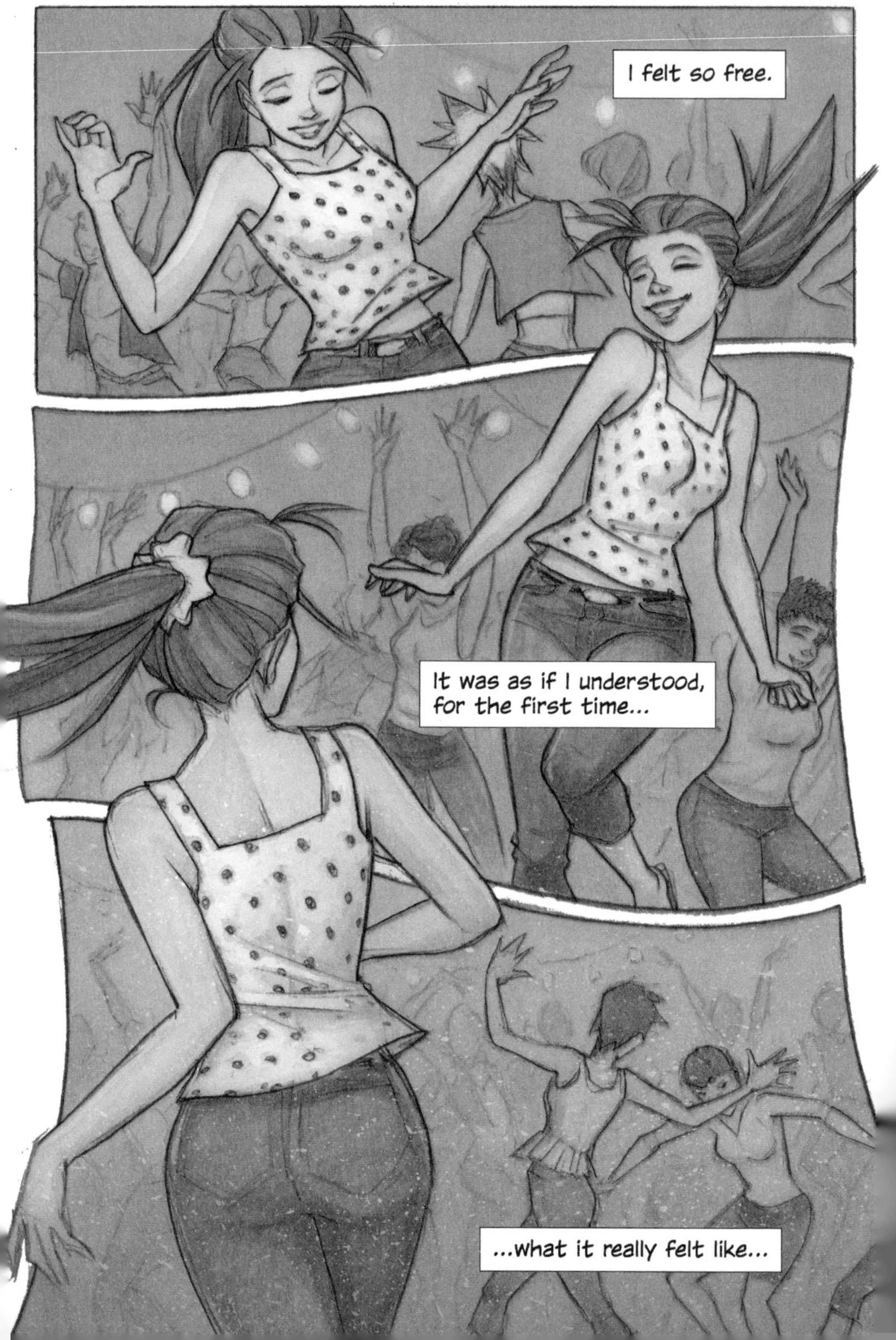
I felt so free.
It was as if I understood, for the first time...
...what it really felt like...

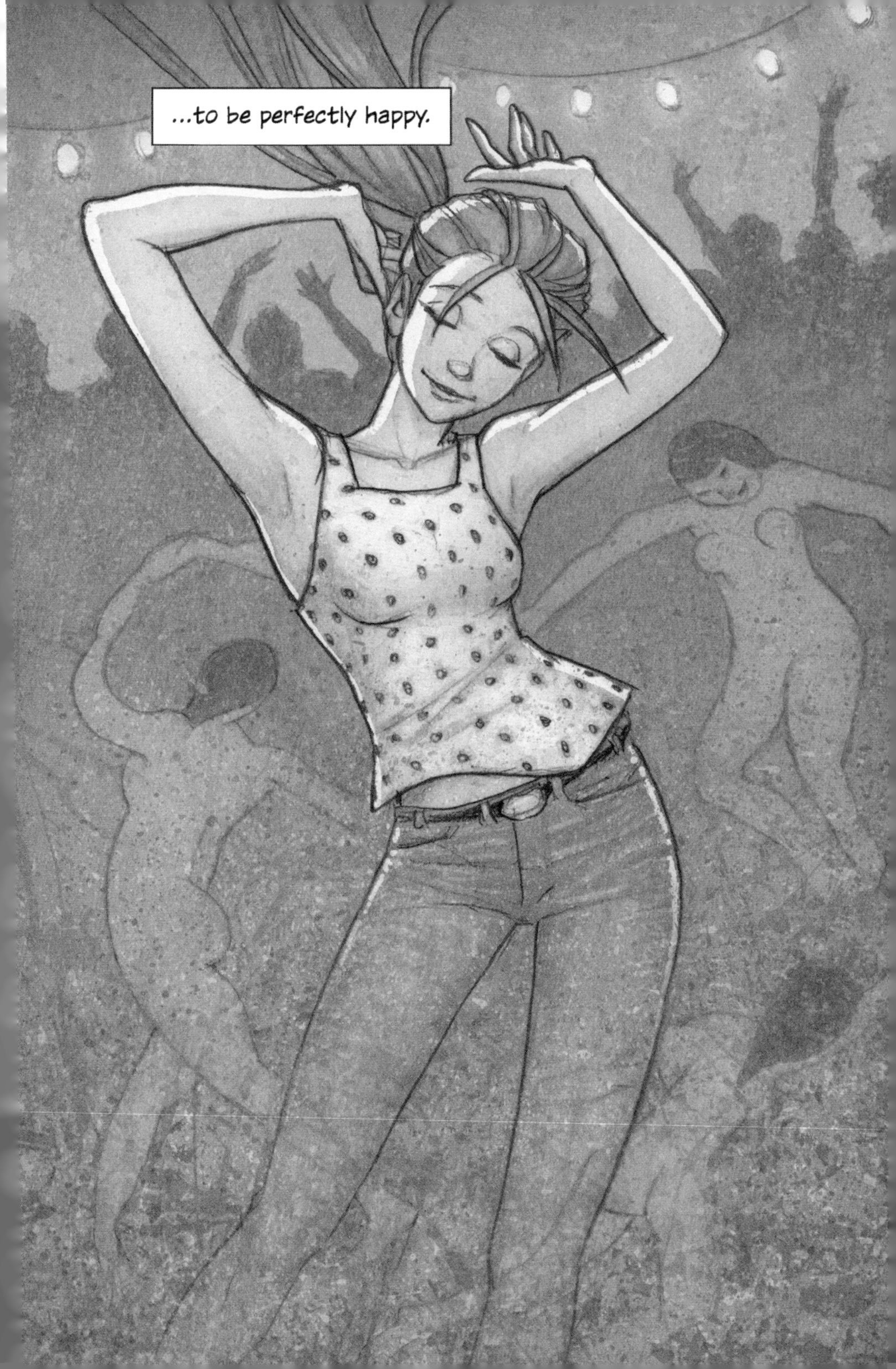
...to be perfectly happy.

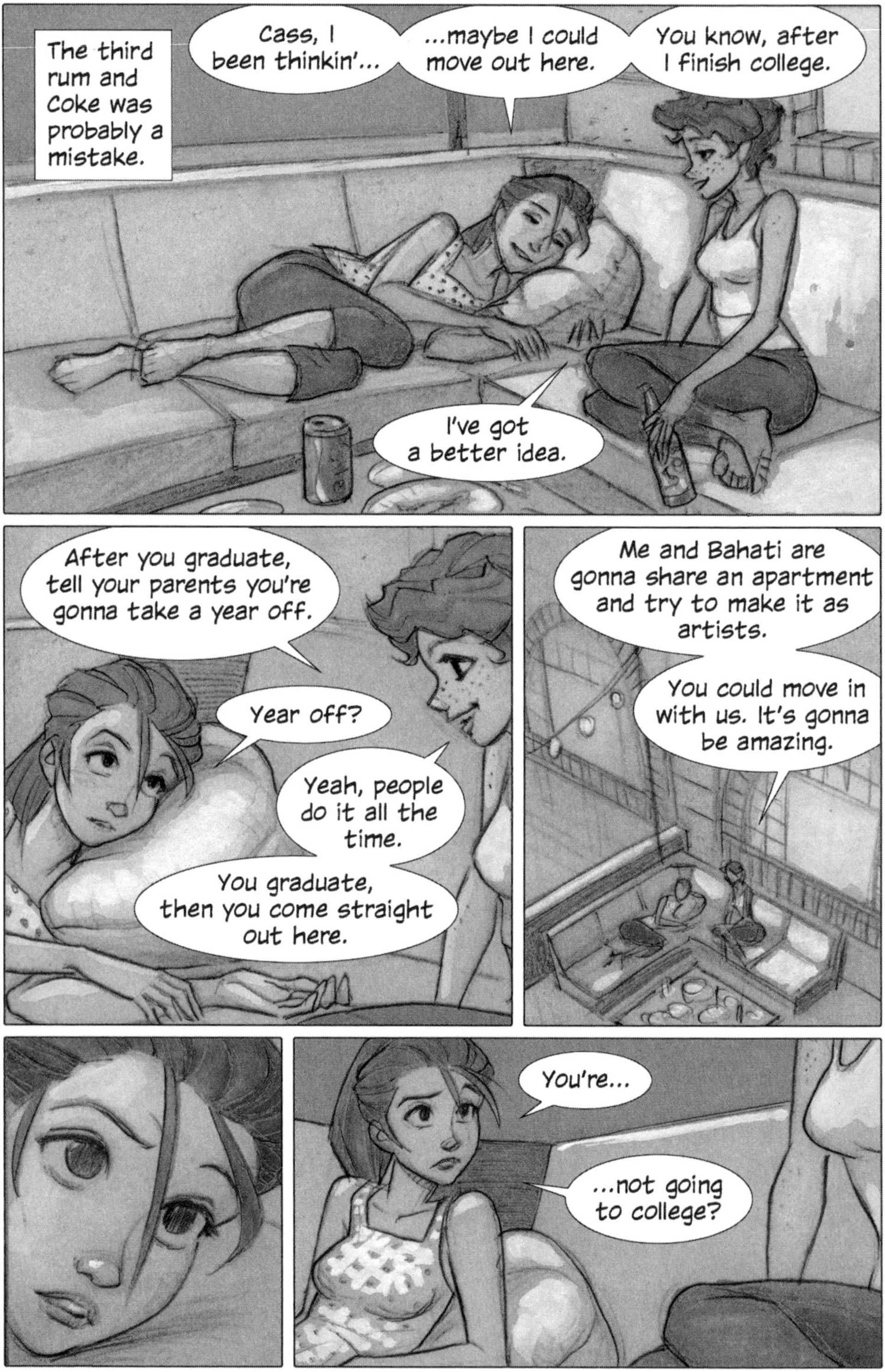
The third rum and Coke was probably a mistake.
Cass, I been thinkin'...
...maybe I could move out here.
You know, after I finish college.
I've got a better idea.
After you graduate, tell your parents you're gonna take a year off.
Year off?
Yeah, people do it all the time.
You graduate, then you come straight out here.
Me and Bahati are gonna share an apartment and try to make it as artists.
You could move in with us. It's gonna be amazing.
You're...
...not going to college?

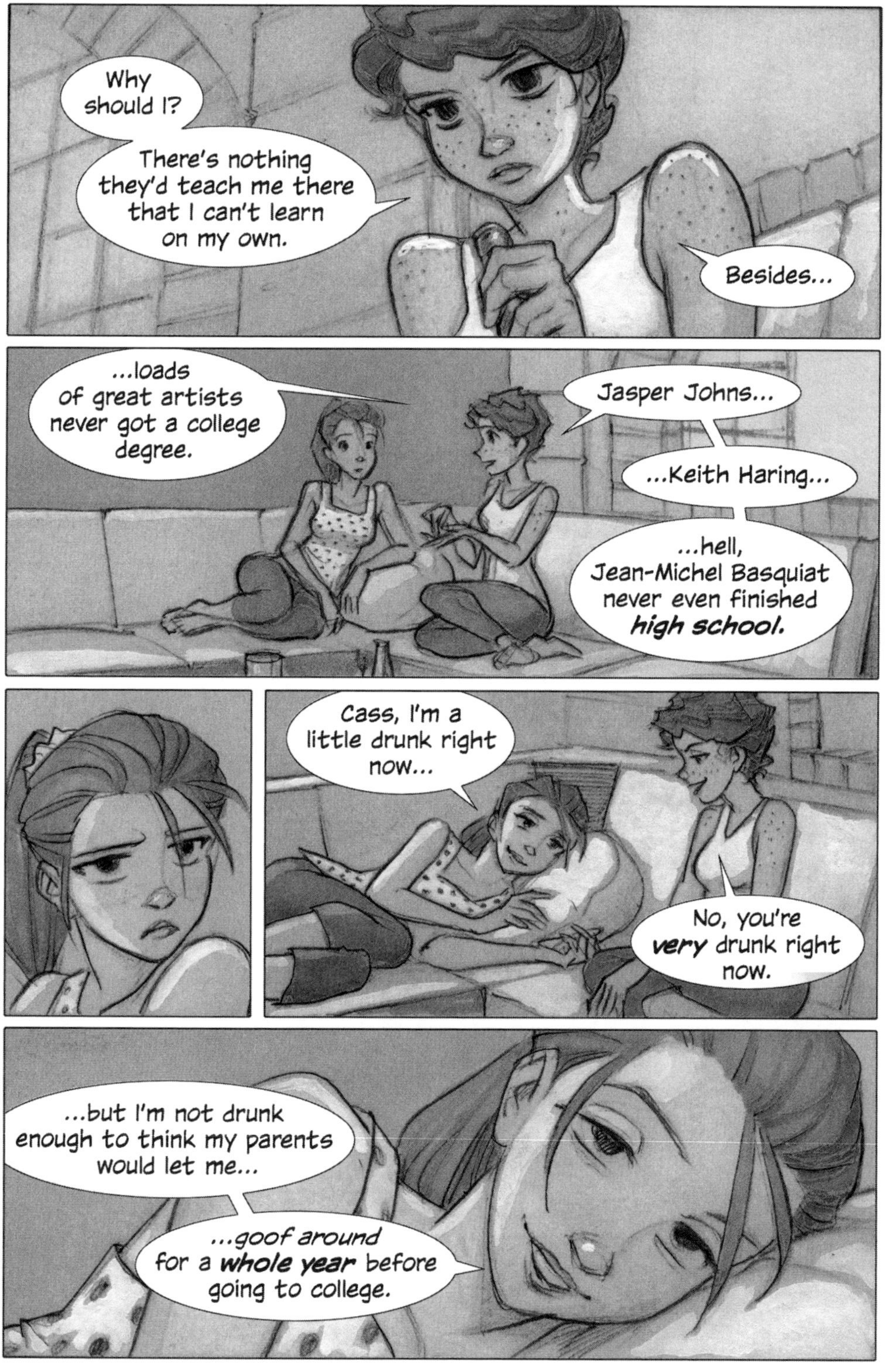
Why should I?
There's nothing they'd teach me there that I can't learn on my own.
Besides...
...loads of great artists never got a college degree.
Jasper Johns...
...Keith Haring...
...hell, Jean-Michel Basquiat never even finished ***high school.***
Cass, I'm a little drunk right now...
No, you're ***very*** drunk right now.
...but I'm not drunk enough to think my parents would let me...
...goof around for a ***whole year*** before going to college.

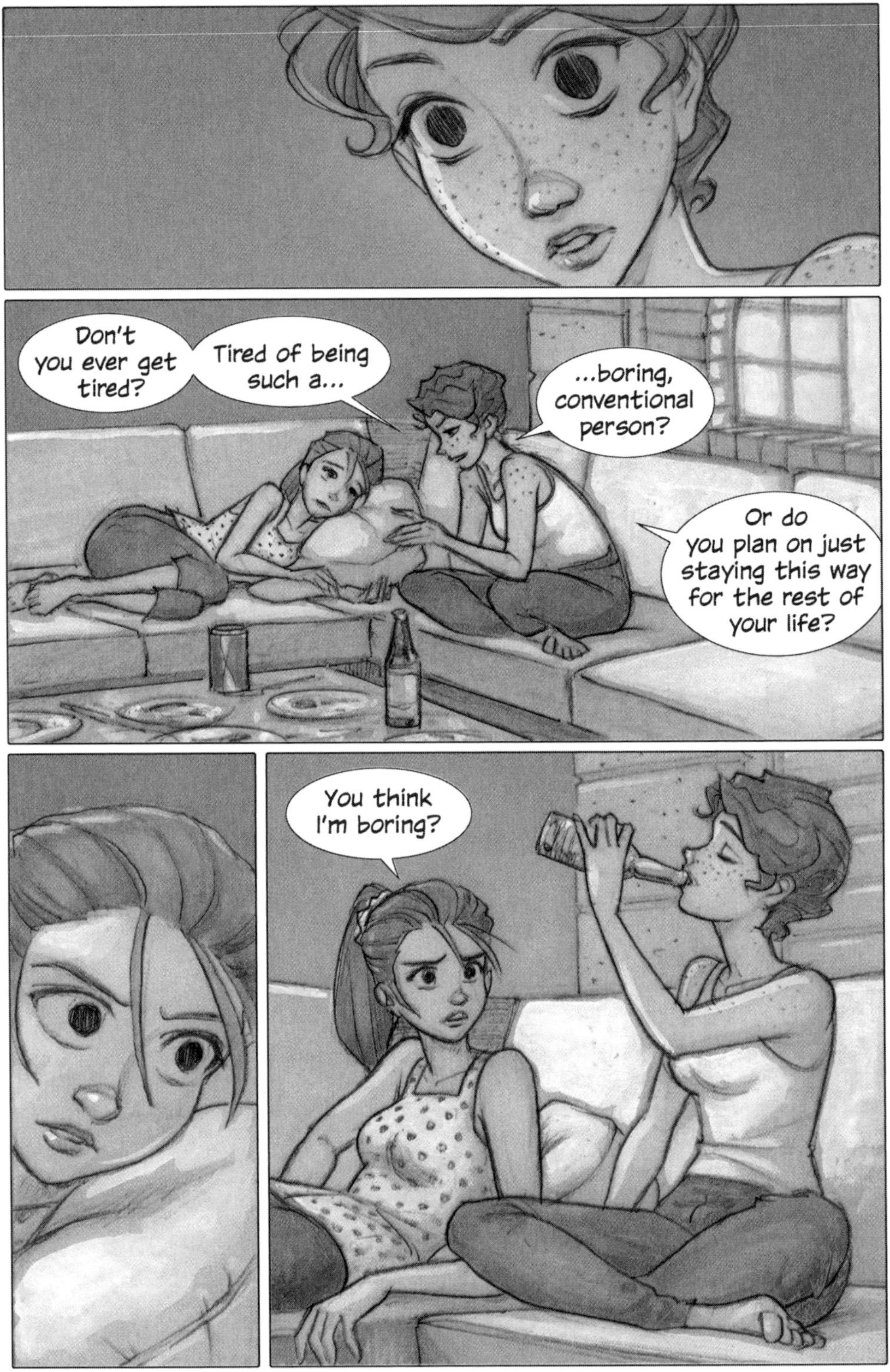
Don't you ever get tired?
Tired of being such a...
...boring, conventional person?
Or do you plan on just staying this way for the rest of your life?
You think I'm boring?

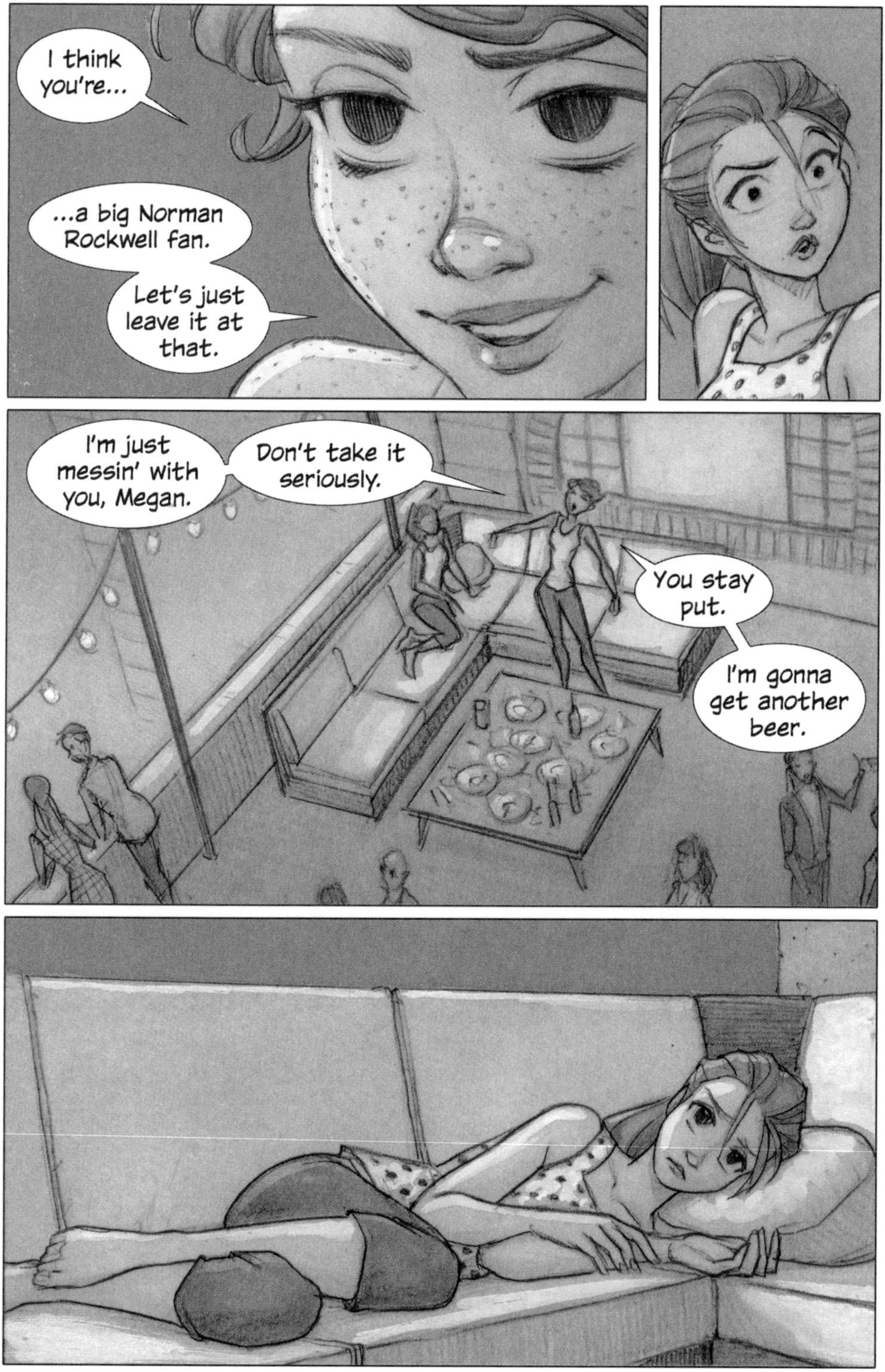
I think you're...
...a big Norman Rockwell fan.
Let's just leave it at that.
I'm just messin' with you, Megan.
Don't take it seriously.
You stay put.
I'm gonna get another beer.

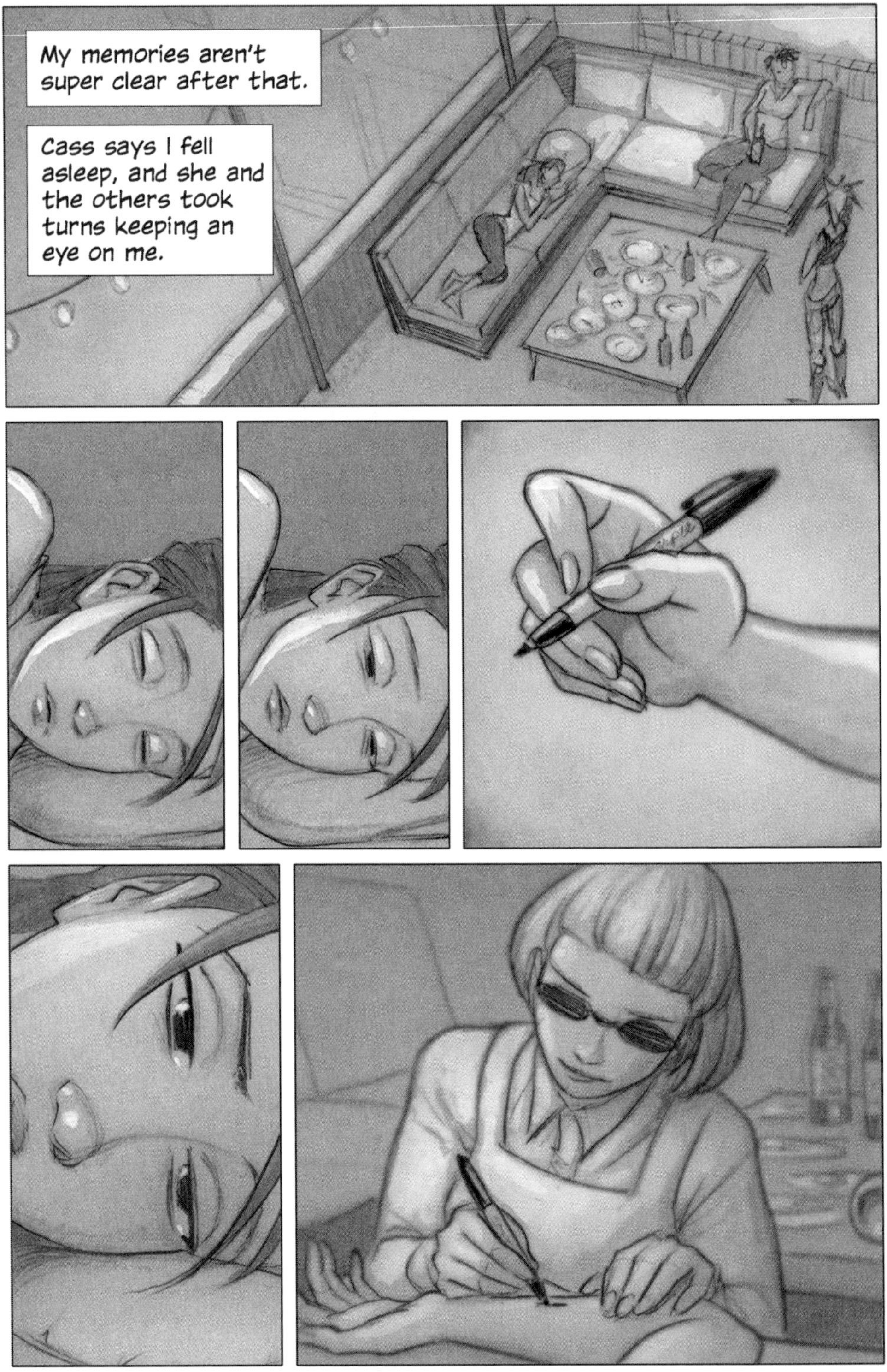

My memories aren't super clear after that.
Cass says I fell asleep, and she and the others took turns keeping an eye on me.

Taja...
...what're ya doin'?

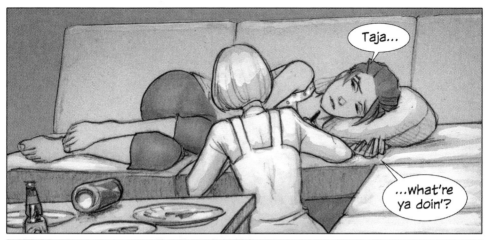

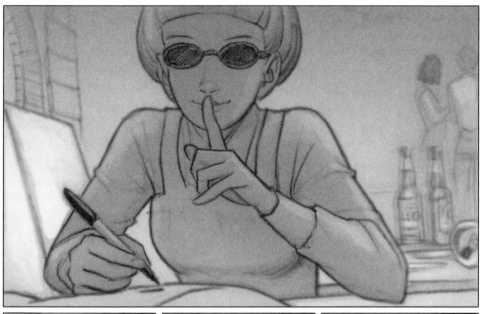

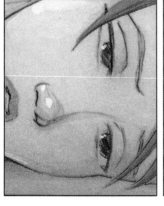

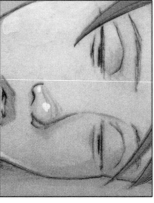

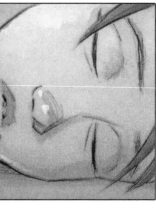

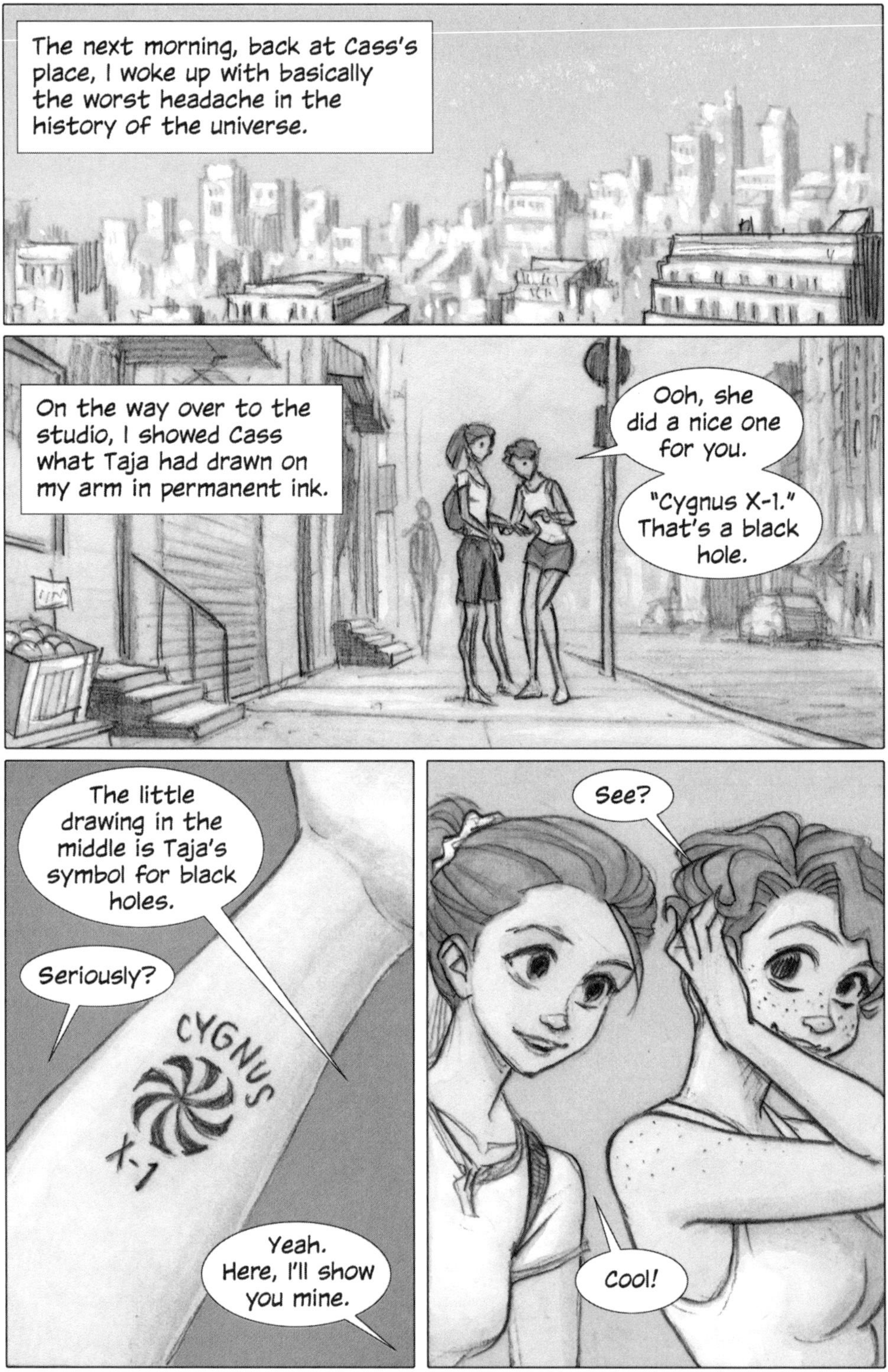
The next morning, back at Cass's place, I woke up with basically the worst headache in the history of the universe.
On the way over to the studio, I showed Cass what Taja had drawn on my arm in permanent ink.
Ooh, she did a nice one for you.
"Cygnus X-1." That's a black hole.
The little drawing in the middle is Taja's symbol for black holes.
Seriously?
CYGNUS X-1
Yeah. Here, I'll show you mine.
See?
Cool!

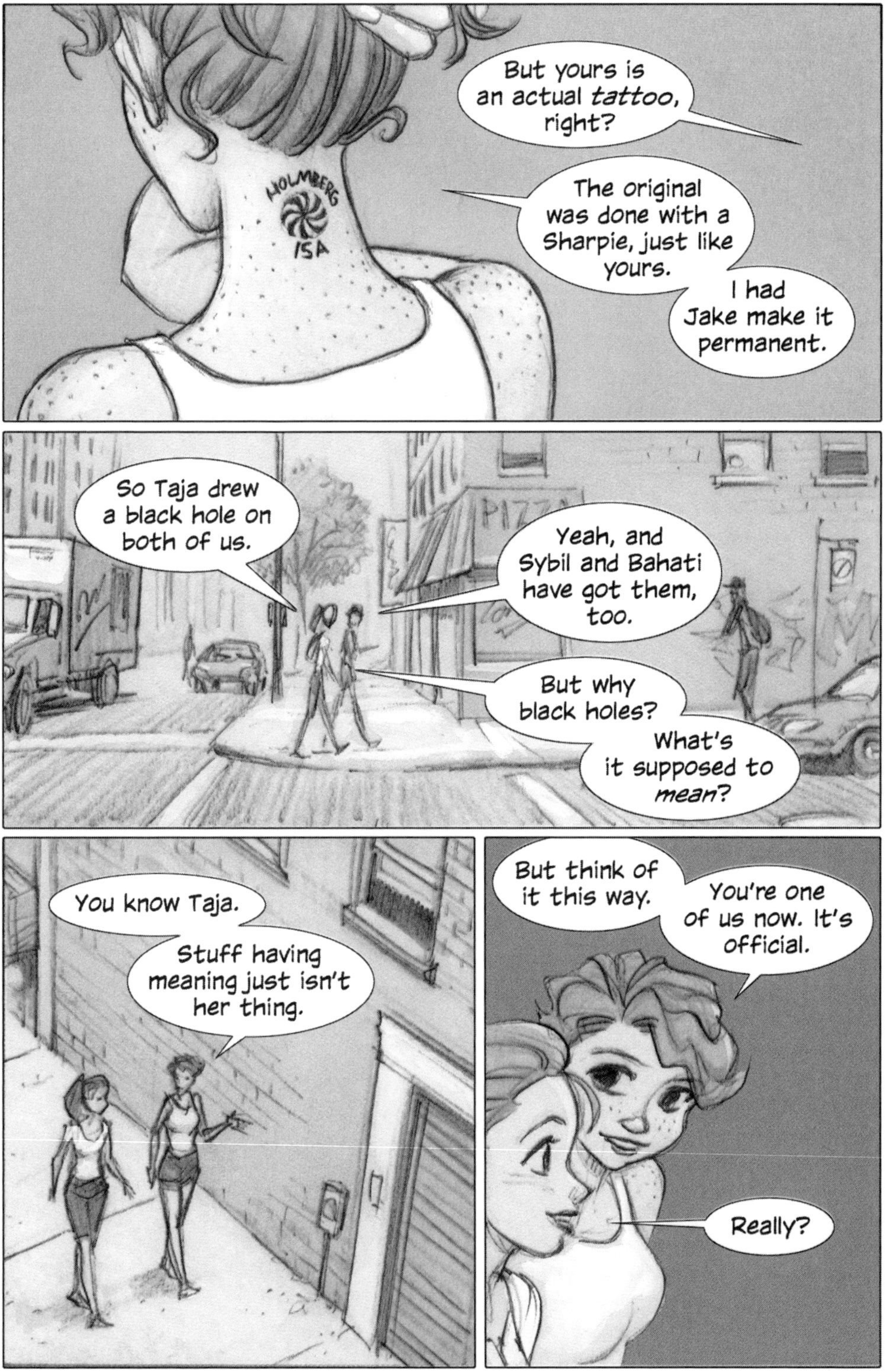

But yours is an actual *tattoo*, right?
HOLMBERG ISA
The original was done with a Sharpie, just like yours.
I had Jake make it permanent.
So Taja drew a black hole on both of us.
Yeah, and Sybil and Bahati have got them, too.
PIZZA
But why black holes?
What's it supposed to *mean*?
You know Taja.
Stuff having meaning just isn't her thing.
But think of it this way.
You're one of us now. It's official.
Really?

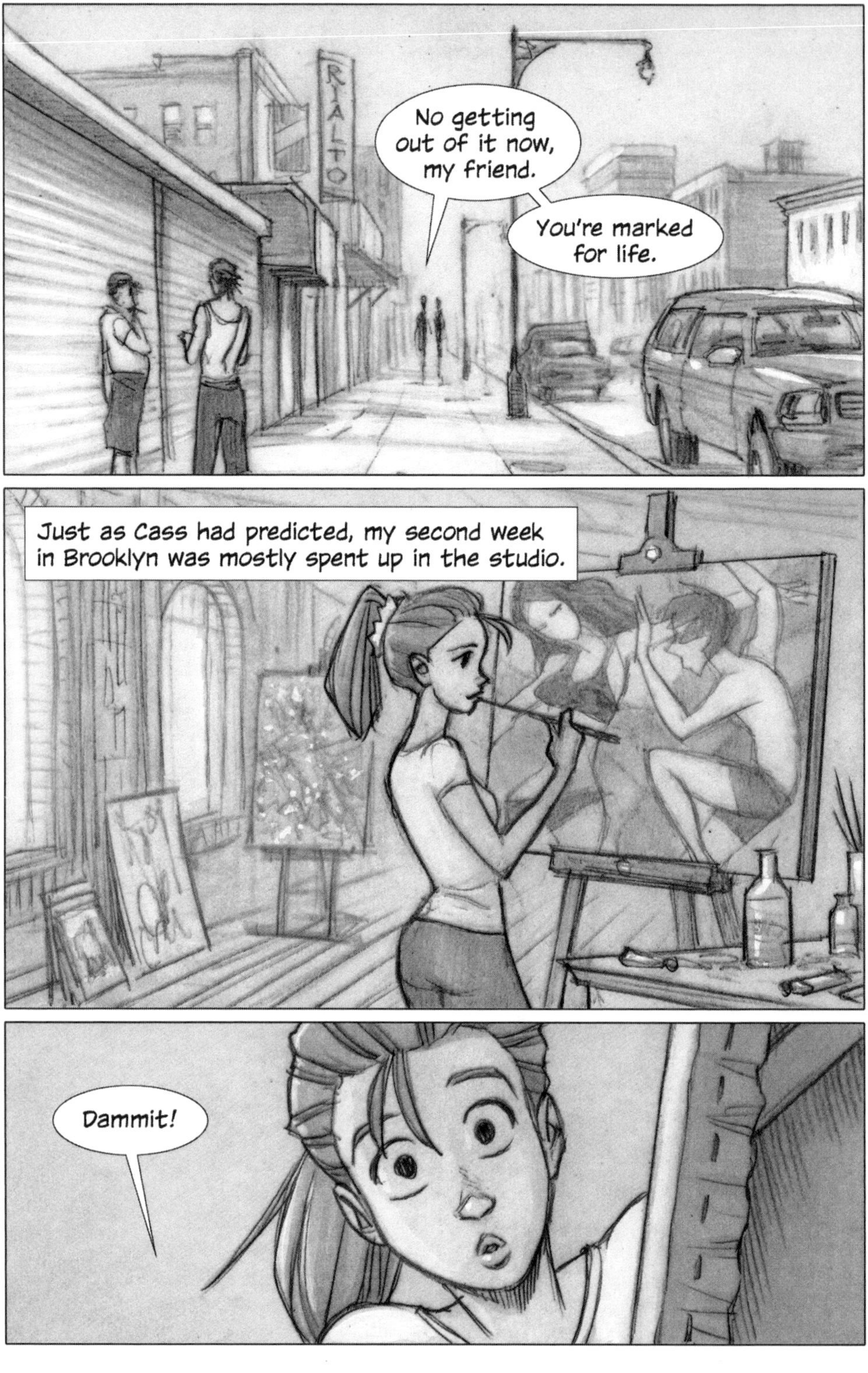
RIALTO
No getting out of it now, my friend.
You're marked for life.
Just as Cass had predicted, my second week in Brooklyn was mostly spent up in the studio.
Dammit!

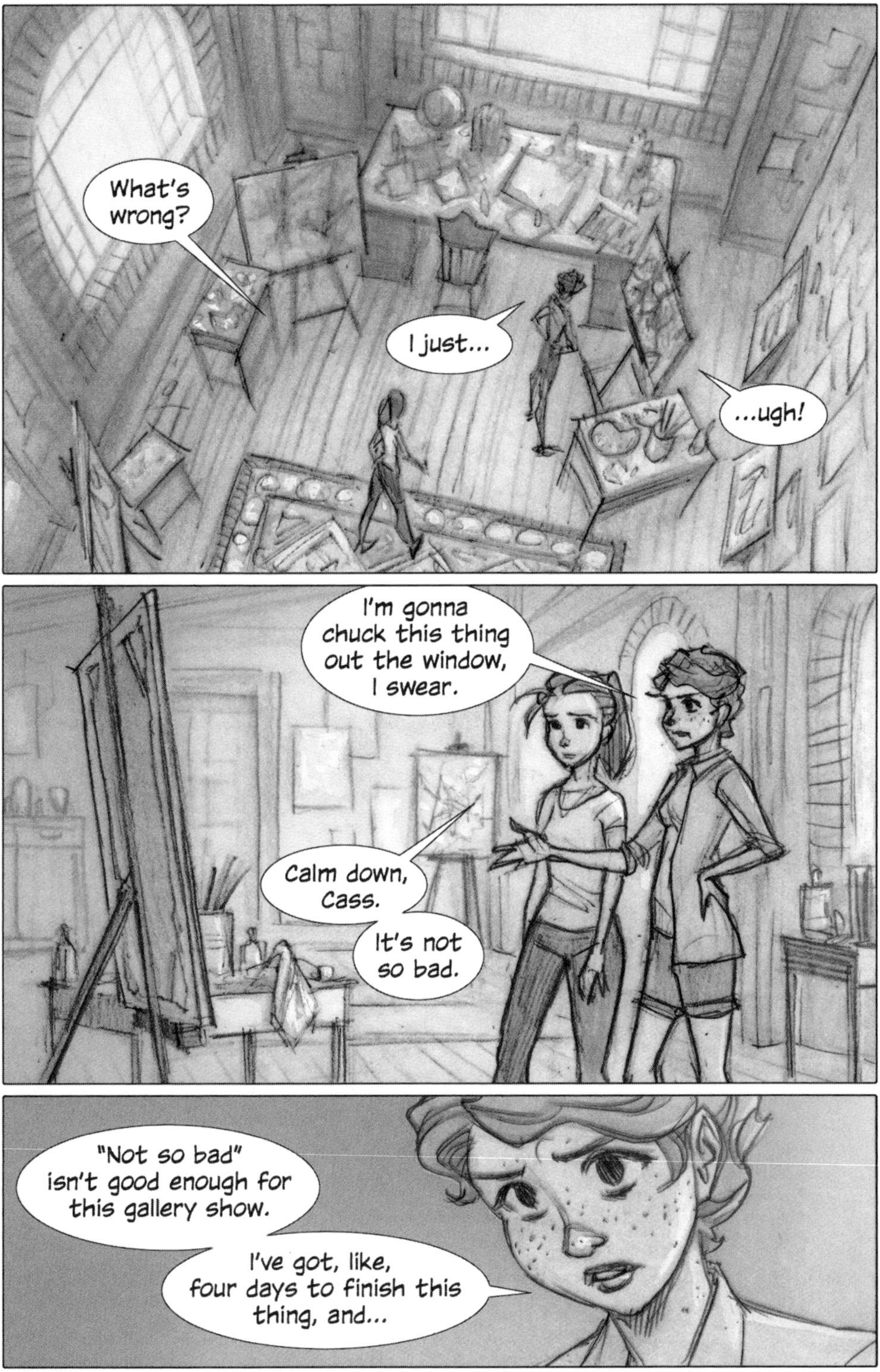
What's wrong?
I just...
...ugh!
I'm gonna chuck this thing out the window, I swear.
Calm down, Cass.
It's not so bad.
"Not so bad" isn't good enough for this gallery show.
I've got, like, four days to finish this thing, and...

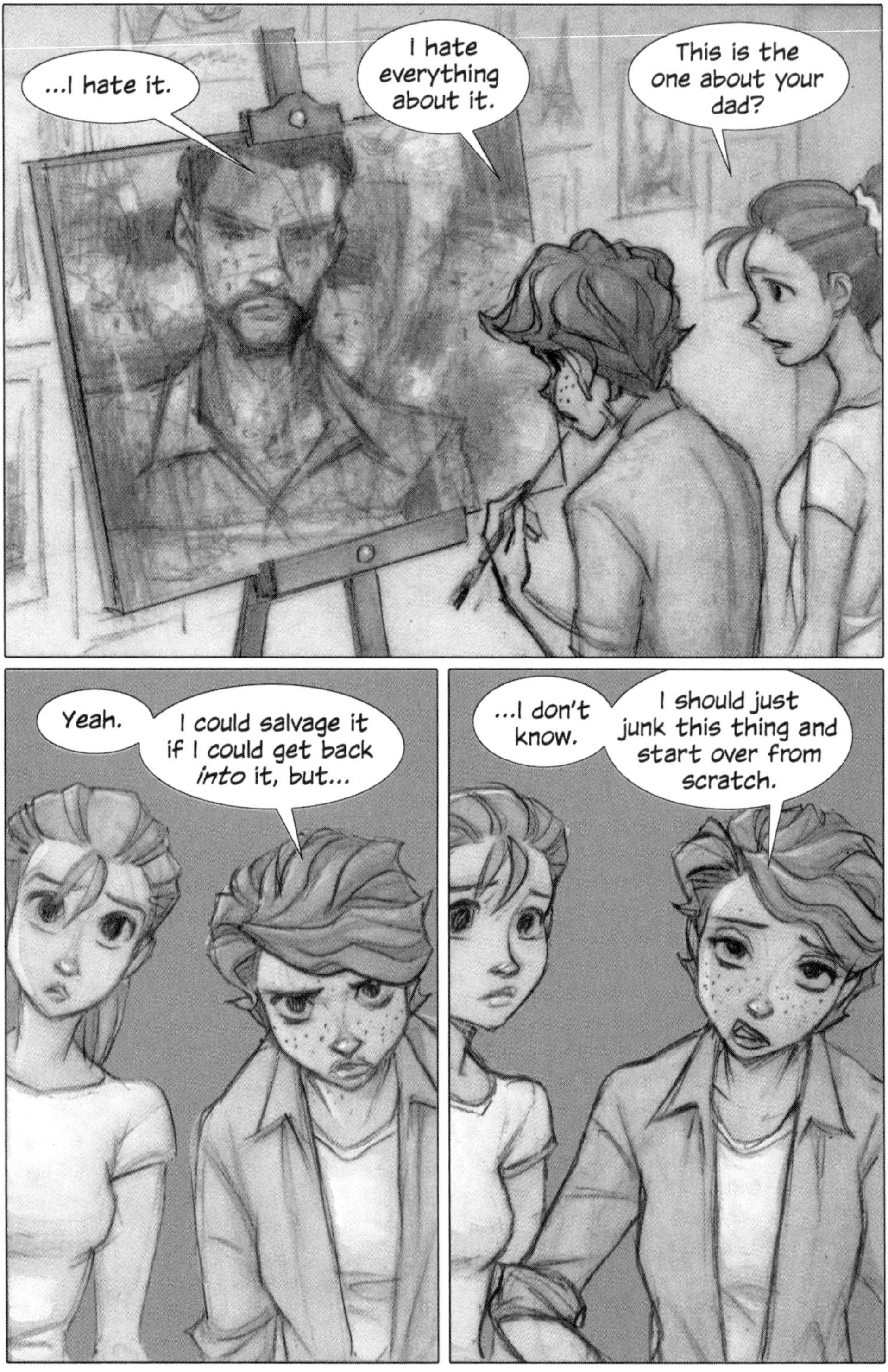
...I hate it.
I hate everything about it.
This is the one about your dad?
Yeah.
I could salvage it if I could get back *into* it, but...
...I don't know.
I should just junk this thing and start over from scratch.

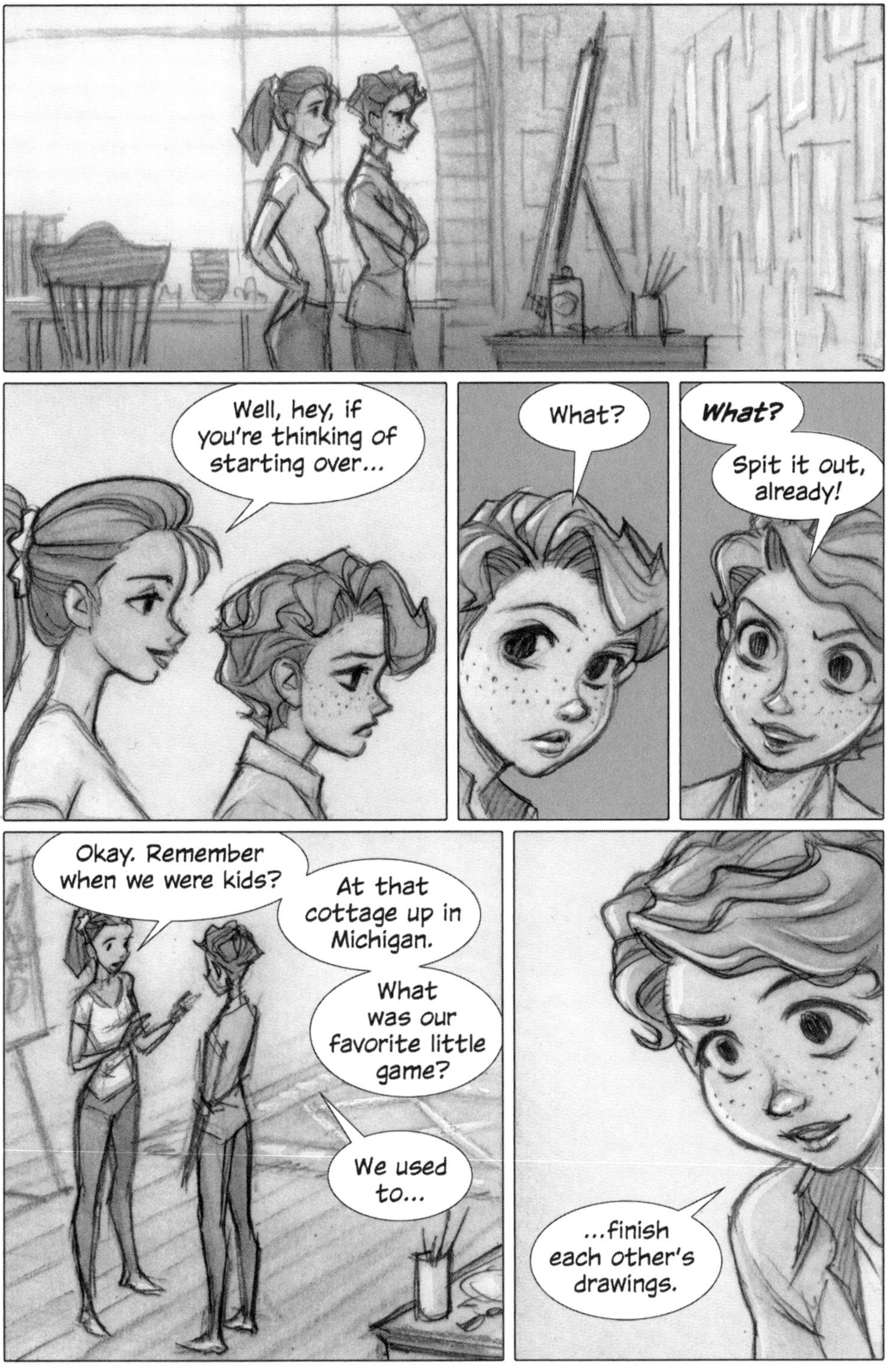

Well, hey, if you're thinking of starting over...
What?
What?
Spit it out, already!
Okay. Remember when we were kids?
At that cottage up in Michigan.
What was our favorite little game?
We used to...
...finish each other's drawings.

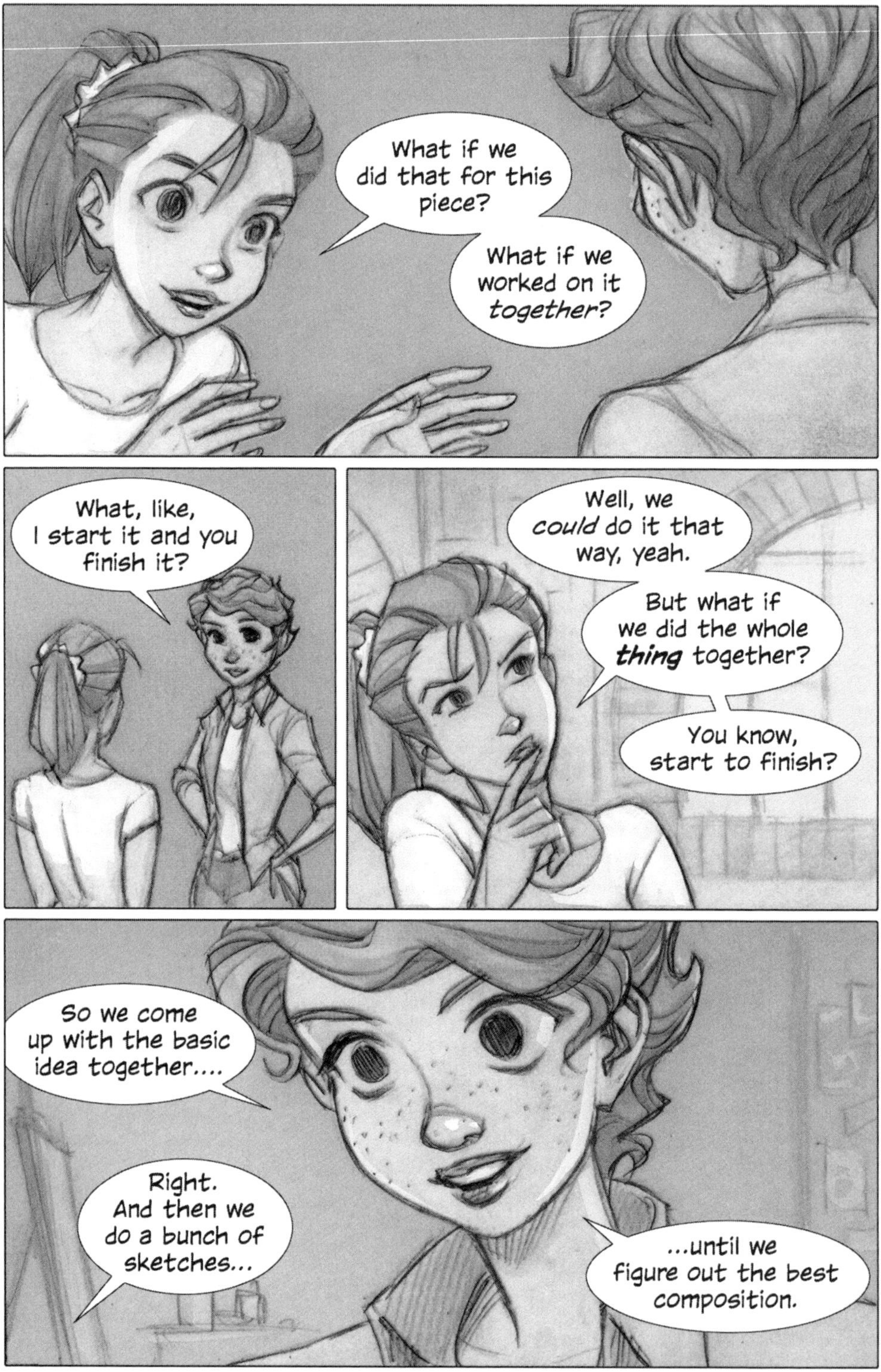
What if we did that for this piece?
What if we worked on it *together?*
What, like, I start it and you finish it?
Well, we *could* do it that way, yeah.
But what if we did the whole ***thing*** together?
You know, start to finish?
So we come up with the basic idea together....
Right. And then we do a bunch of sketches...
...until we figure out the best composition.

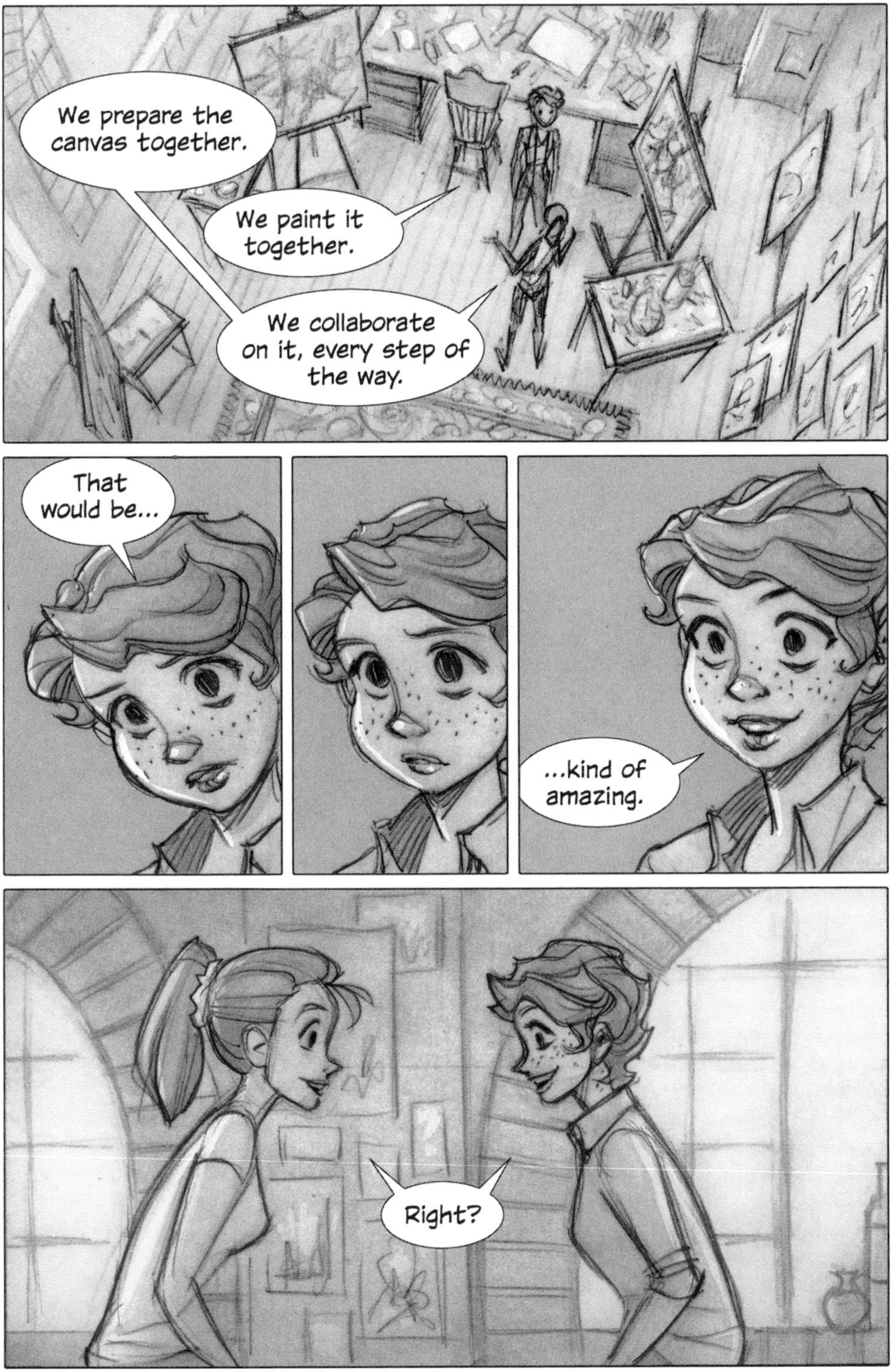
We prepare the canvas together.
We paint it together.
We collaborate on it, every step of the way.
That would be...
...kind of amazing.
Right?

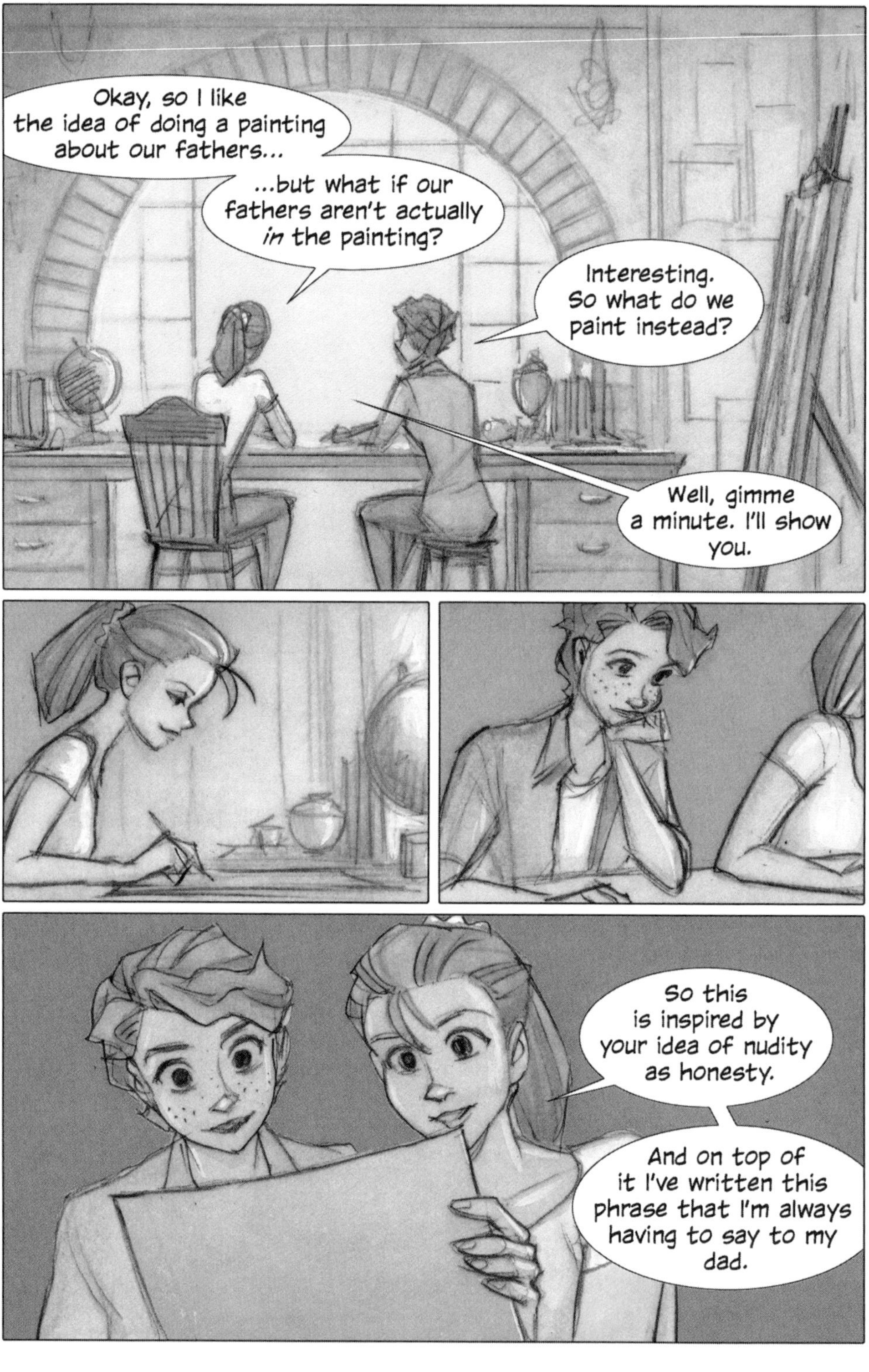
Okay, so I like the idea of doing a painting about our fathers...
...but what if our fathers aren't actually *in* the painting?
Interesting. So what do we paint instead?
Well, gimme a minute. I'll show you.
So this is inspired by your idea of nudity as honesty.
And on top of it I've written this phrase that I'm always having to say to my dad.

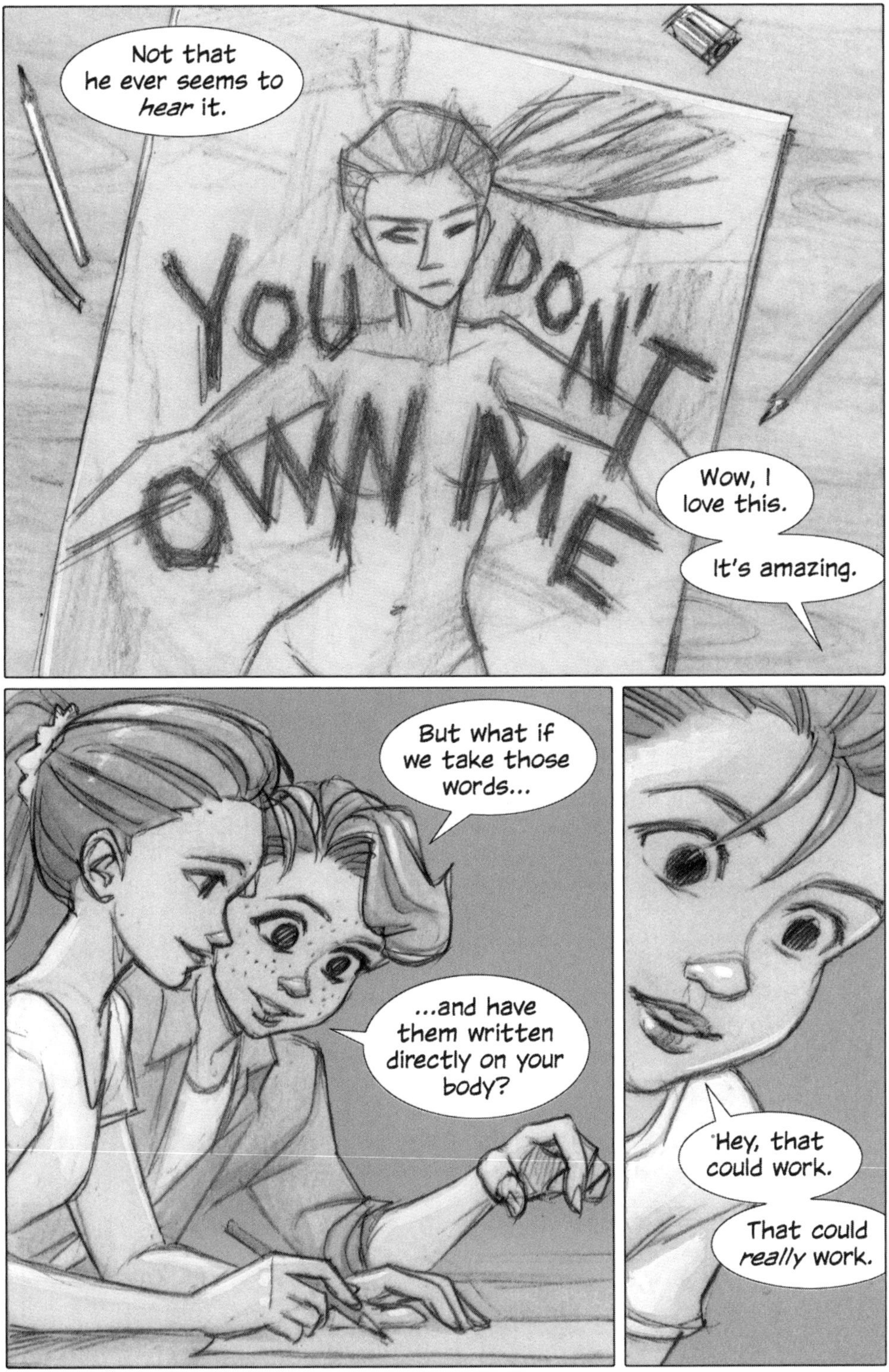
Not that he ever seems to *hear* it.
YOU DON'T OWN ME
Wow, I love this.
It's amazing.
But what if we take those words...
...and have them written directly on your body?
Hey, that could work.
That could *really* work.

Yeah, yeah. This is it. This is the right direction.

But hold up.

I wanna try something.

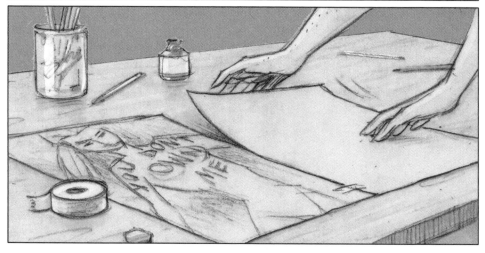

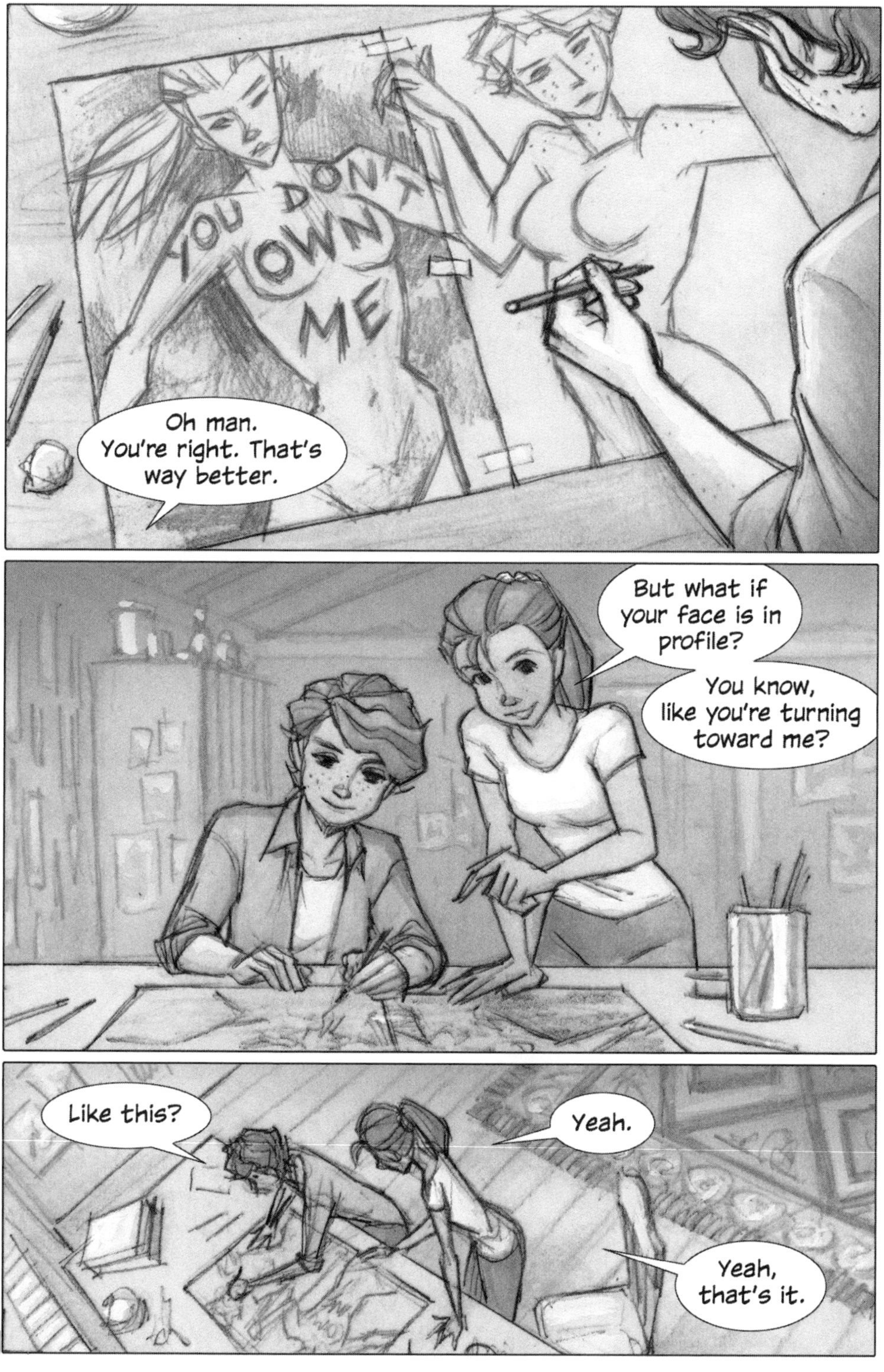
YOU DON'T OWN ME
Oh man. You're right. That's way better.
But what if your face is in profile?
You know, like you're turning toward me?
Like this?
Yeah.
Yeah, that's it.

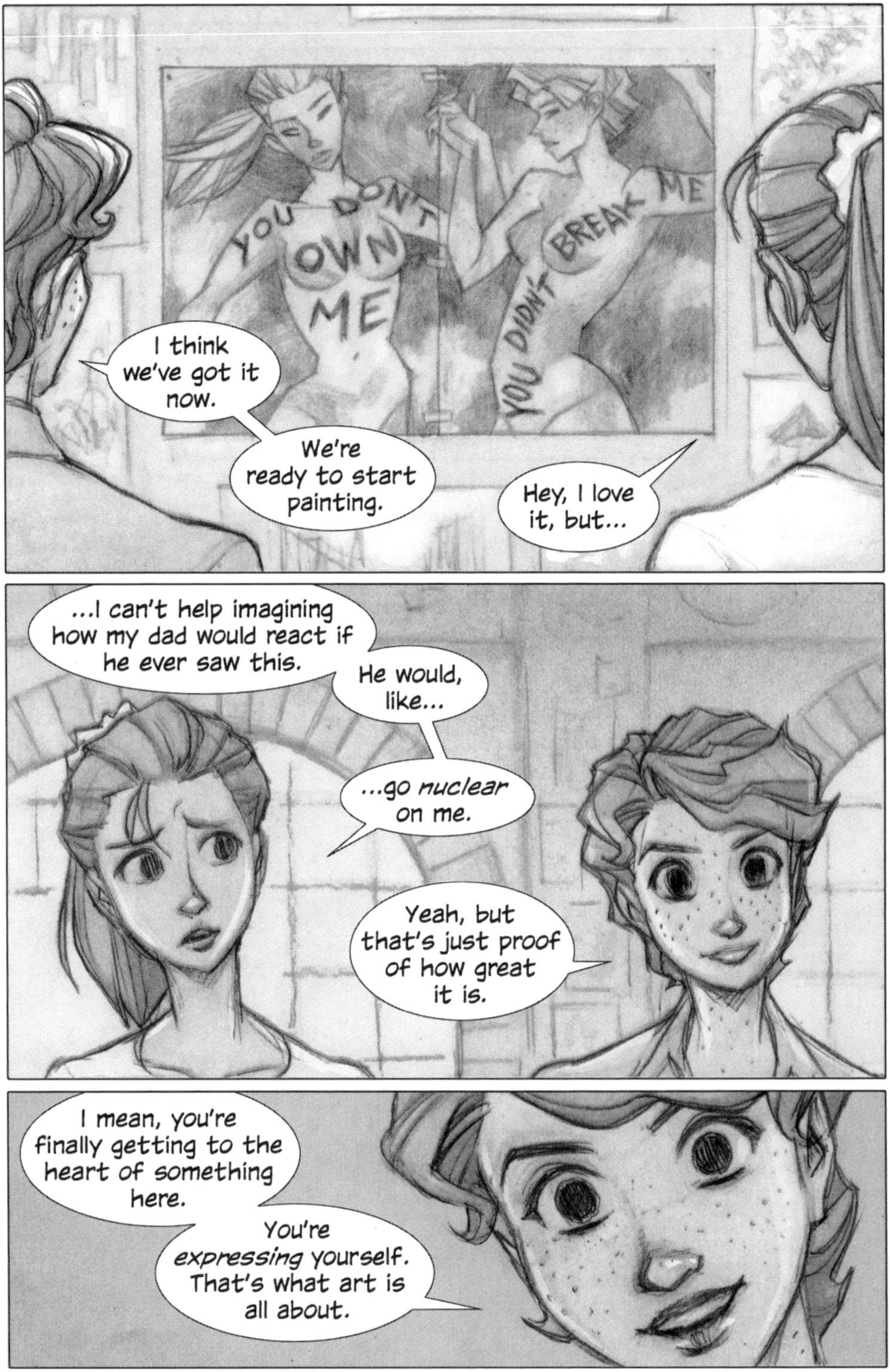
YOU DON'T OWN ME
YOU DIDN'T BREAK ME
I think we've got it now.
We're ready to start painting.
Hey, I love it, but...
...I can't help imagining how my dad would react if he ever saw this.
He would, like...
...go *nuclear* on me.
Yeah, but that's just proof of how great it is.
I mean, you're finally getting to the heart of something here.
You're *expressing* yourself. That's what art is all about.

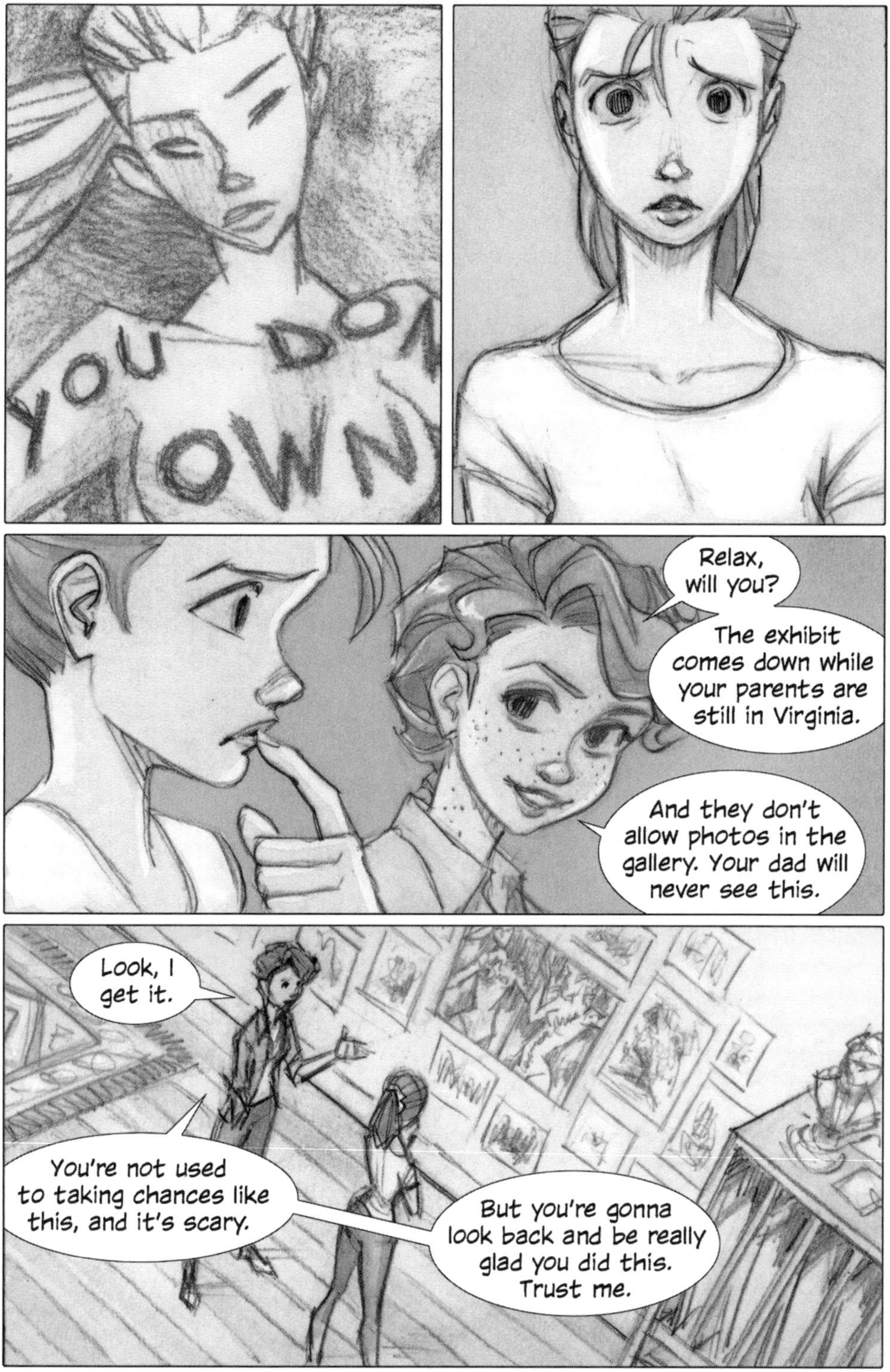
YOU DON
OWN
Relax, will you?
The exhibit comes down while your parents are still in Virginia.
And they don't allow photos in the gallery. Your dad will never see this.
Look, I get it.
You're not used to taking chances like this, and it's scary.
But you're gonna look back and be really glad you did this. Trust me.

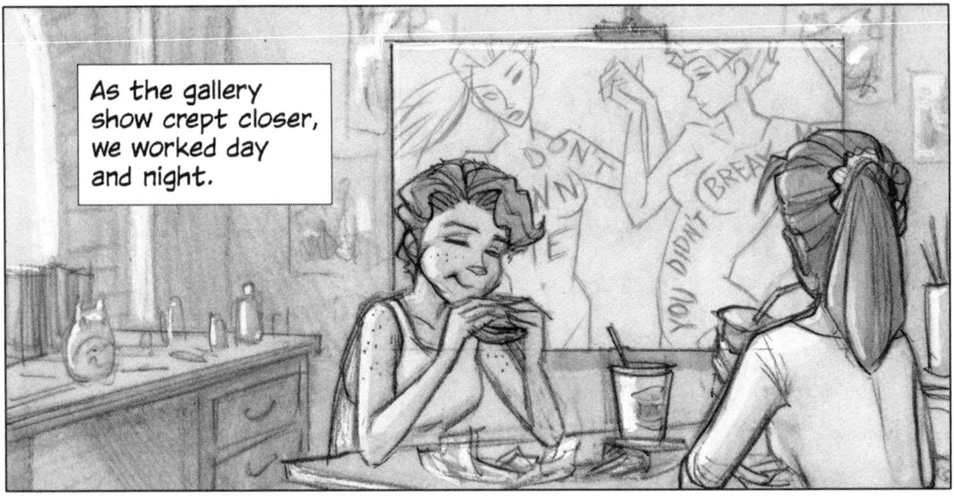
As the gallery show crept closer, we worked day and night.

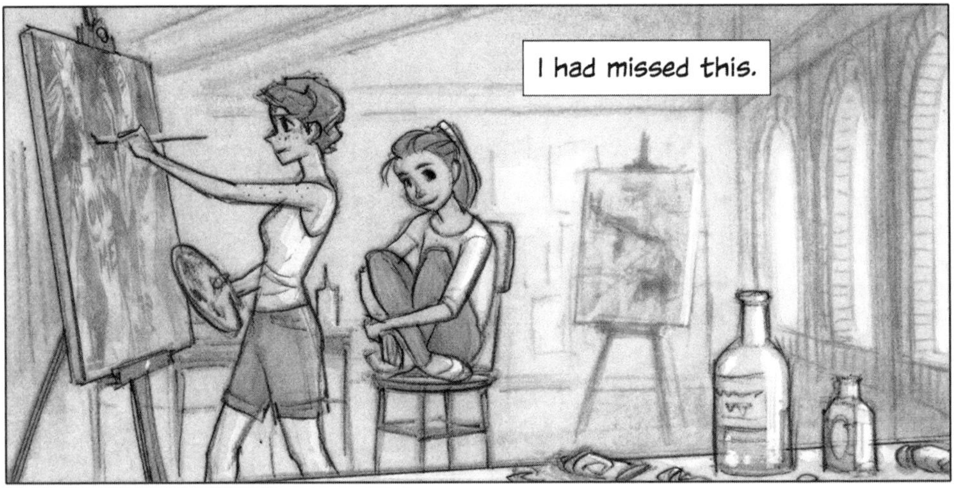
I had missed this.

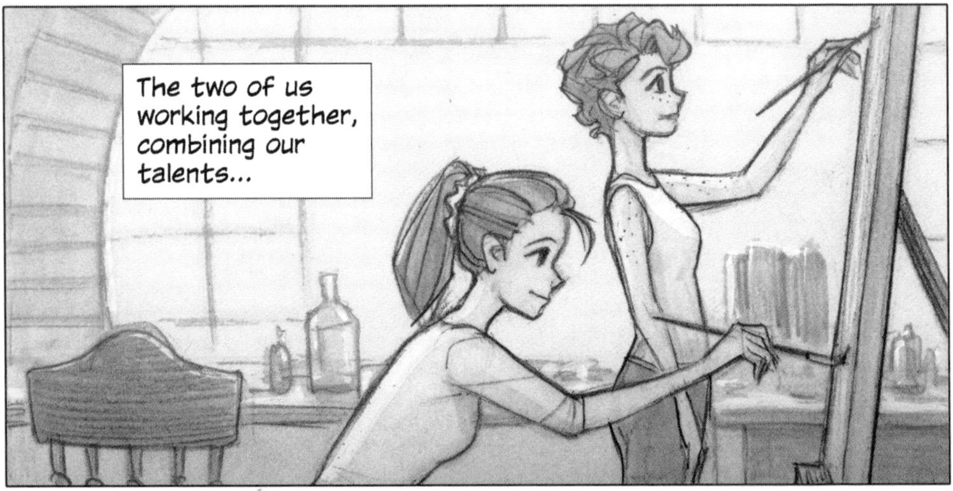
The two of us working together, combining our talents...

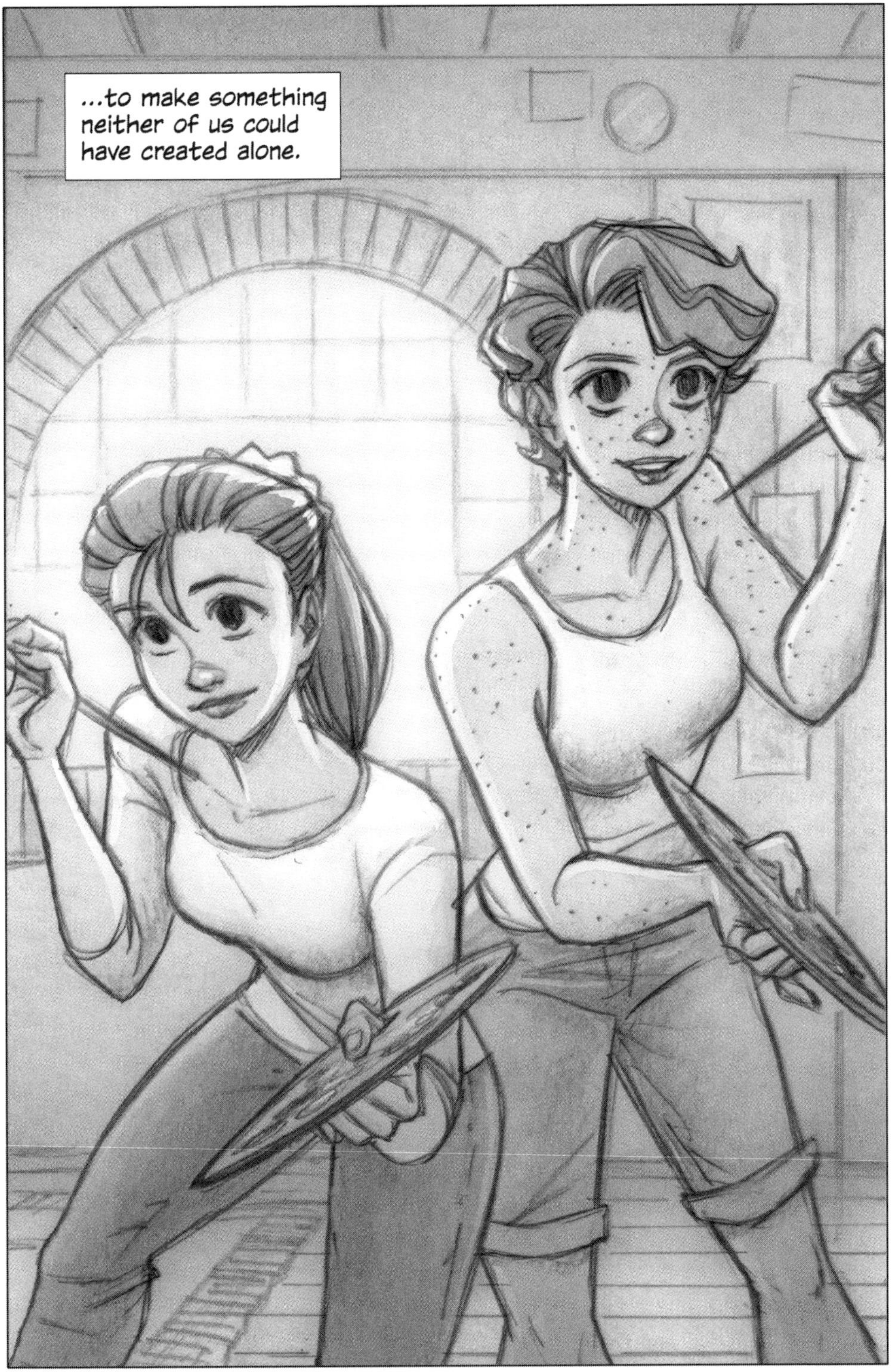
...to make something neither of us could have created alone.

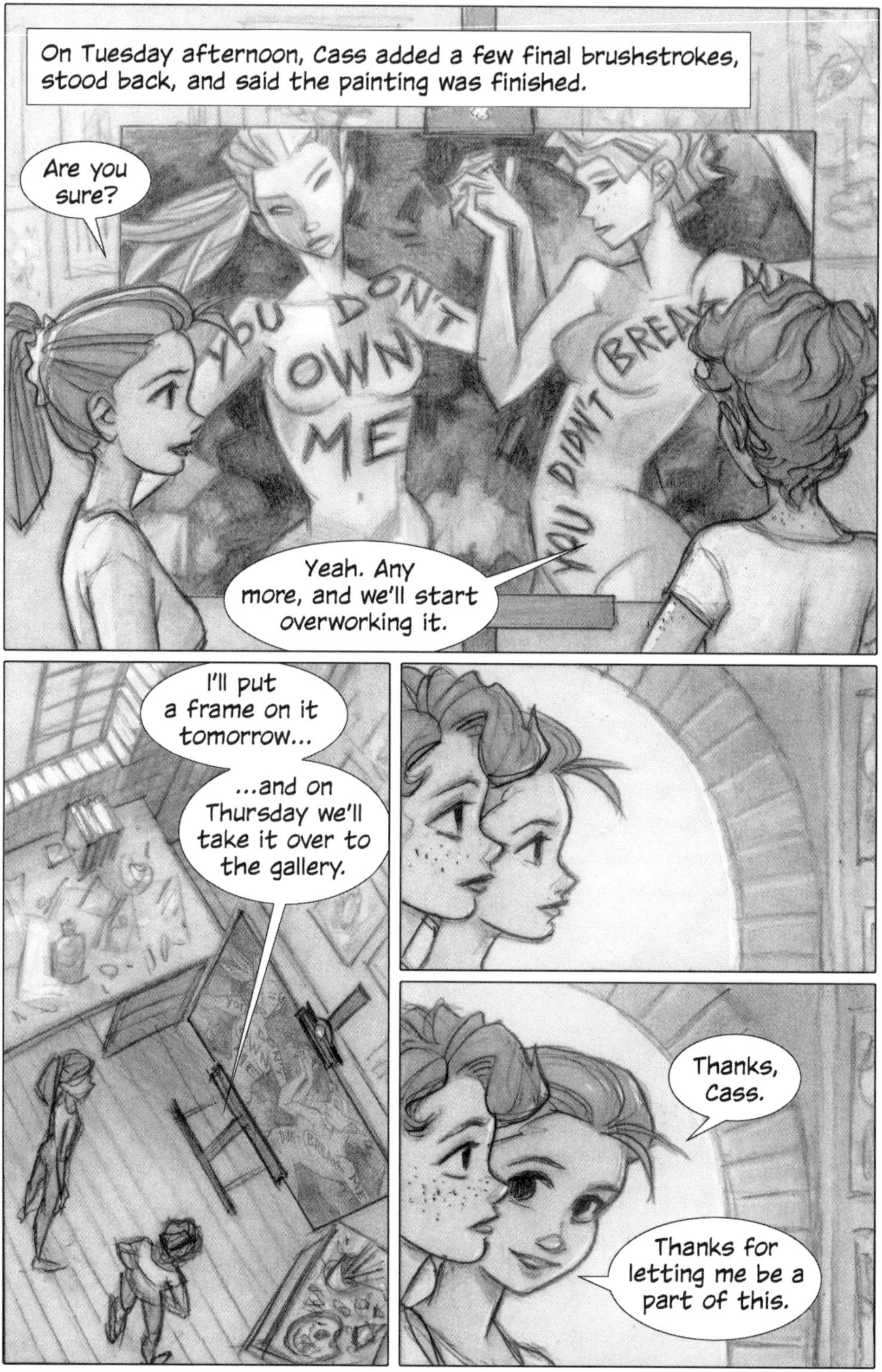
On Tuesday afternoon, Cass added a few final brushstrokes, stood back, and said the painting was finished.
Are you sure?
YOU DON'T OWN ME
YOU DIDN'T BREAK
Yeah. Any more, and we'll start overworking it.
I'll put a frame on it tomorrow...
...and on Thursday we'll take it over to the gallery.
Thanks, Cass.
Thanks for letting me be a part of this.

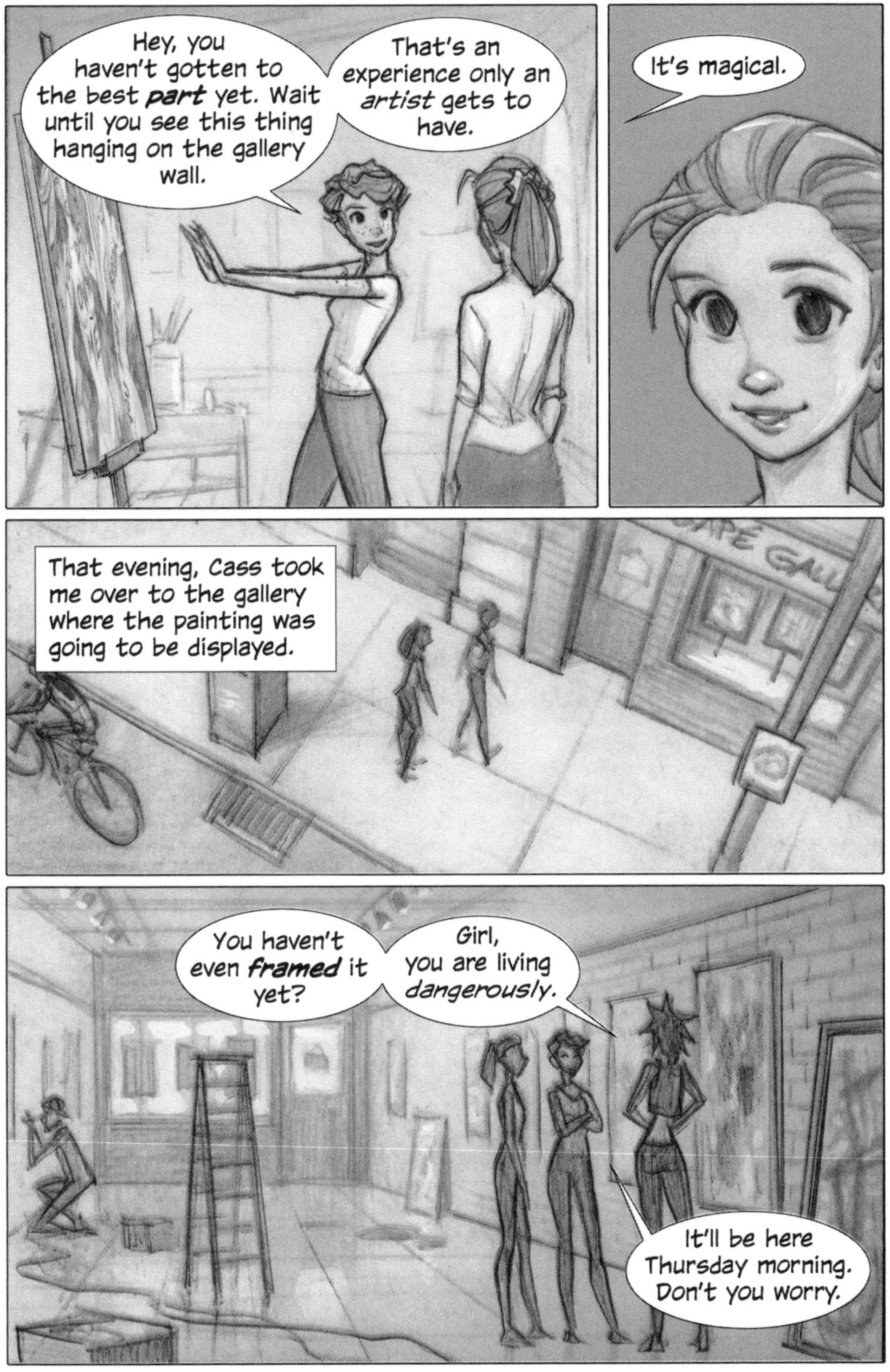
Hey, you haven't gotten to the best part yet. Wait until you see this thing hanging on the gallery wall.
That's an experience only an artist gets to have.
It's magical.
That evening, Cass took me over to the gallery where the painting was going to be displayed.
You haven't even framed it yet?
Girl, you are living dangerously.
It'll be here Thursday morning. Don't you worry.

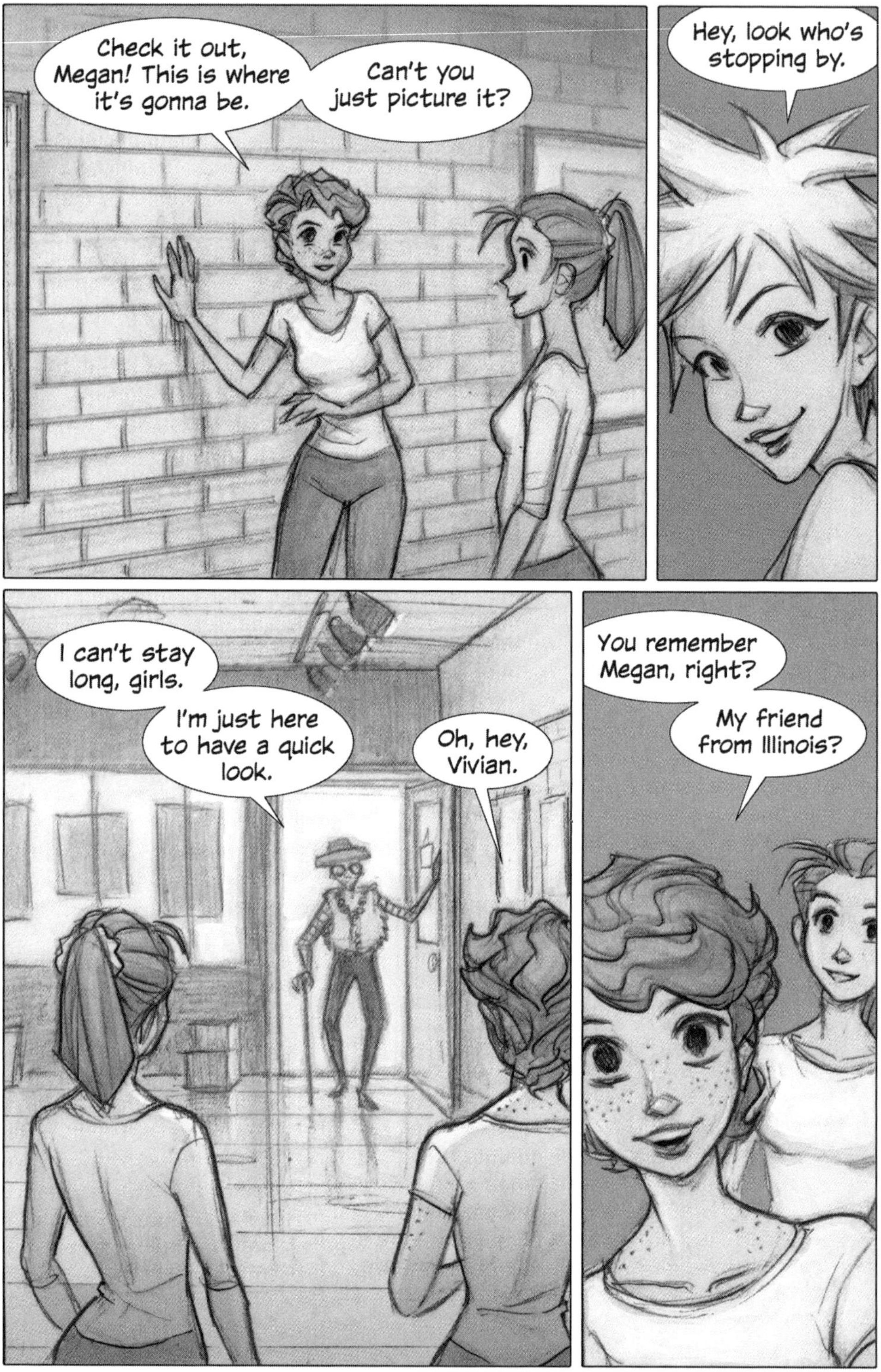
Check it out, Megan! This is where it's gonna be.
Can't you just picture it?
Hey, look who's stopping by.
I can't stay long, girls.
I'm just here to have a quick look.
Oh, hey, Vivian.
You remember Megan, right?
My friend from Illinois?

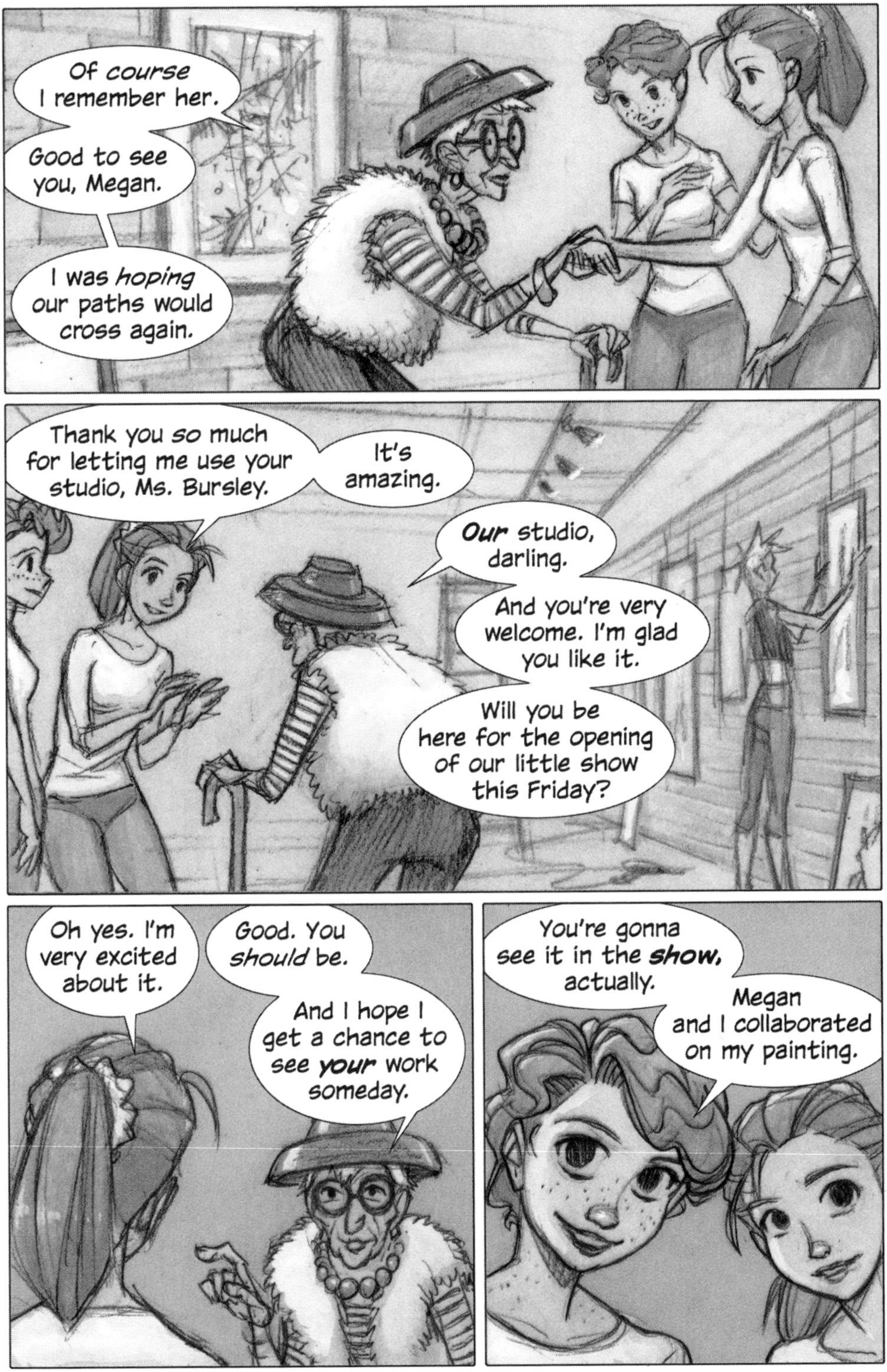
Of course I remember her.
Good to see you, Megan.
I was hoping our paths would cross again.
Thank you so much for letting me use your studio, Ms. Bursley.
It's amazing.
Our studio, darling.
And you're very welcome. I'm glad you like it.
Will you be here for the opening of our little show this Friday?
Oh yes. I'm very excited about it.
Good. You should be.
And I hope I get a chance to see your work someday.
You're gonna see it in the show, actually.
Megan and I collaborated on my painting.

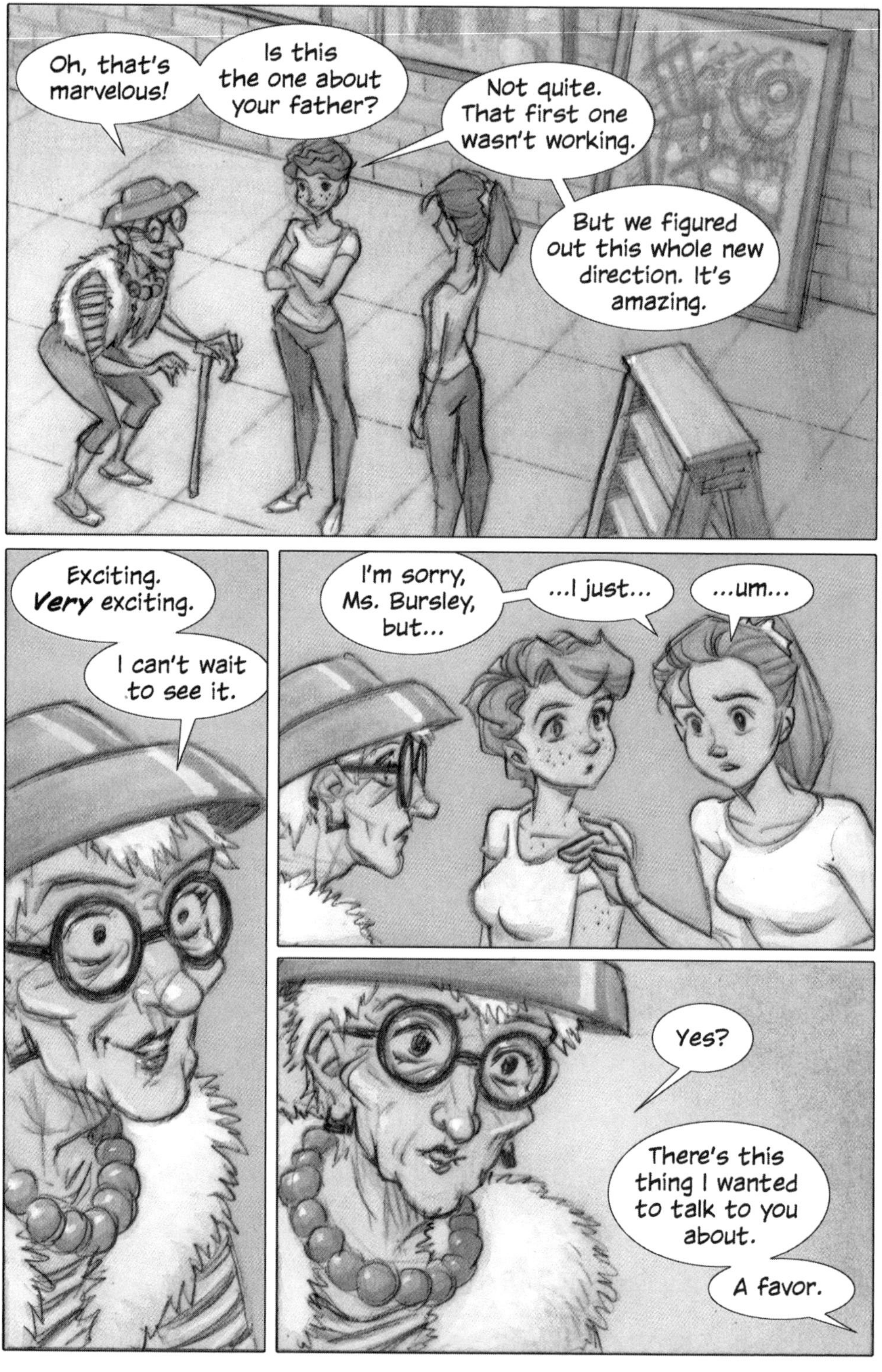
Oh, that's marvelous!
Is this the one about your father?
Not quite. That first one wasn't working.
But we figured out this whole new direction. It's amazing.
Exciting. *Very* exciting.
I can't wait to see it.
I'm sorry, Ms. Bursley, but...
...I just...
...um...
Yes?
There's this thing I wanted to talk to you about.
A favor.

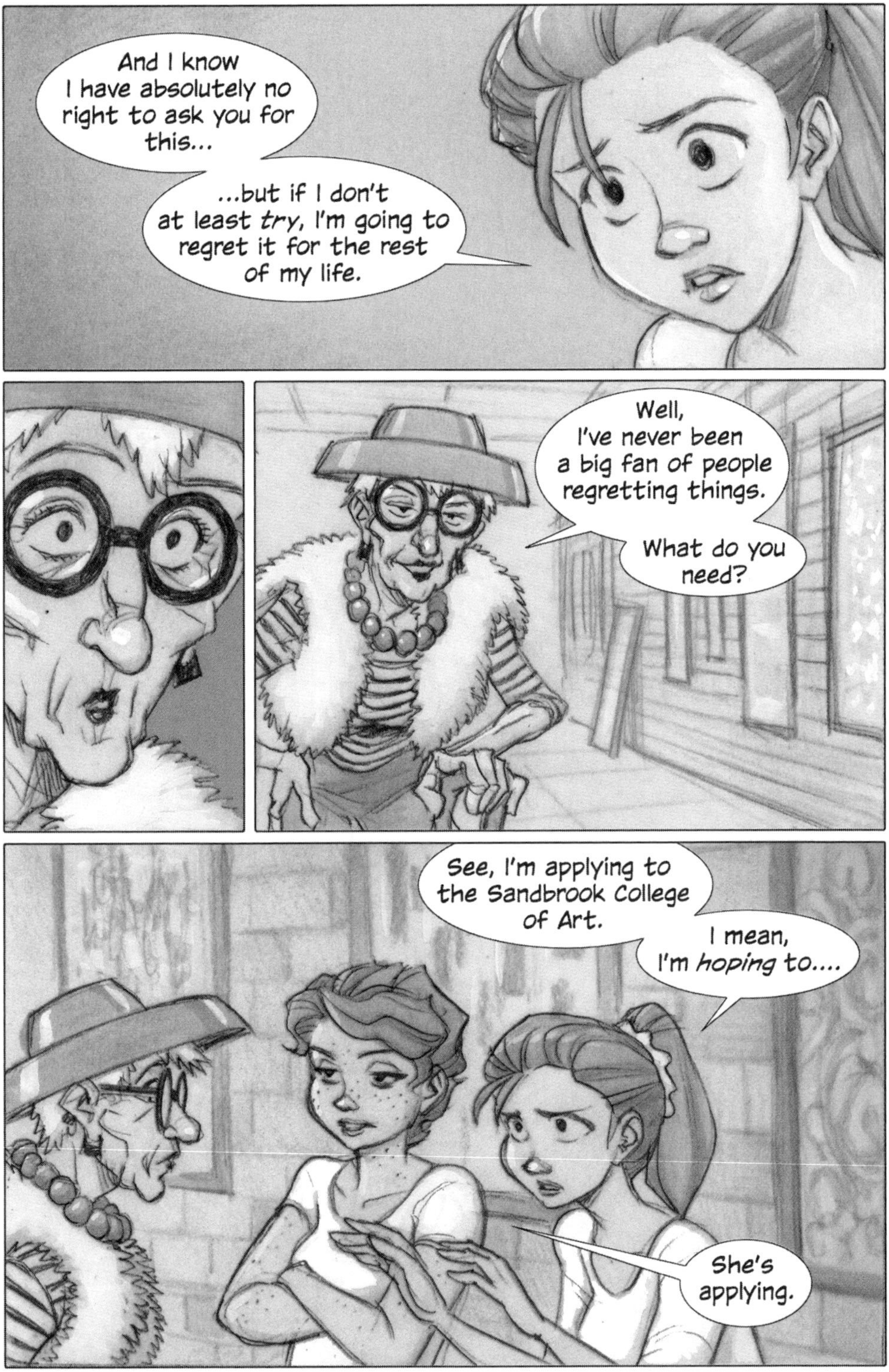
And I know I have absolutely no right to ask you for this...
...but if I don't at least *try*, I'm going to regret it for the rest of my life.
Well, I've never been a big fan of people regretting things.
What do you need?
See, I'm applying to the Sandbrook College of Art.
I mean, I'm *hoping* to....
She's applying.

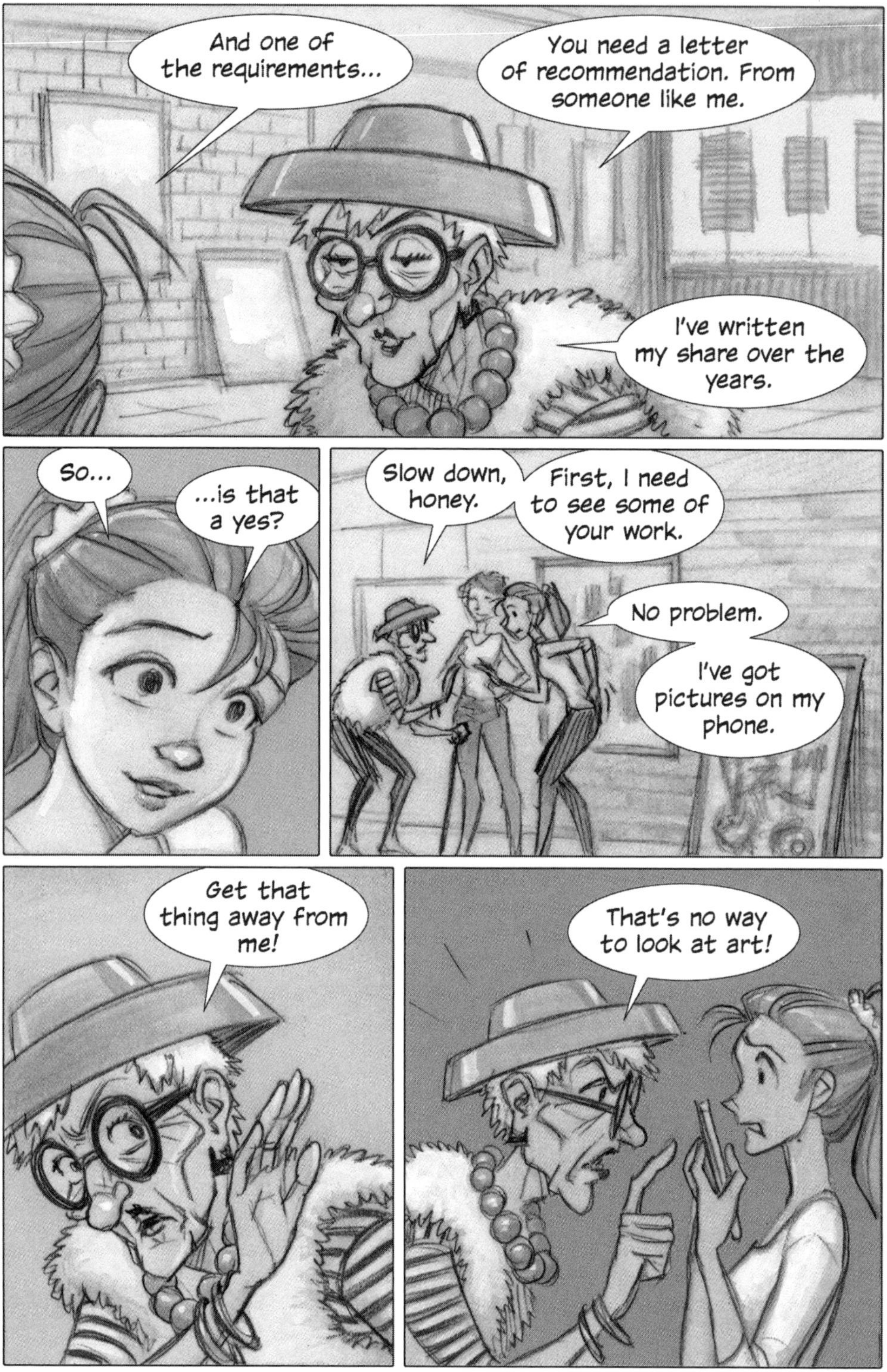
And one of the requirements...
You need a letter of recommendation. From someone like me.
I've written my share over the years.
So...
...is that a yes?
Slow down, honey.
First, I need to see some of your work.
No problem.
I've got pictures on my phone.
Get that thing away from me!
That's no way to look at art!

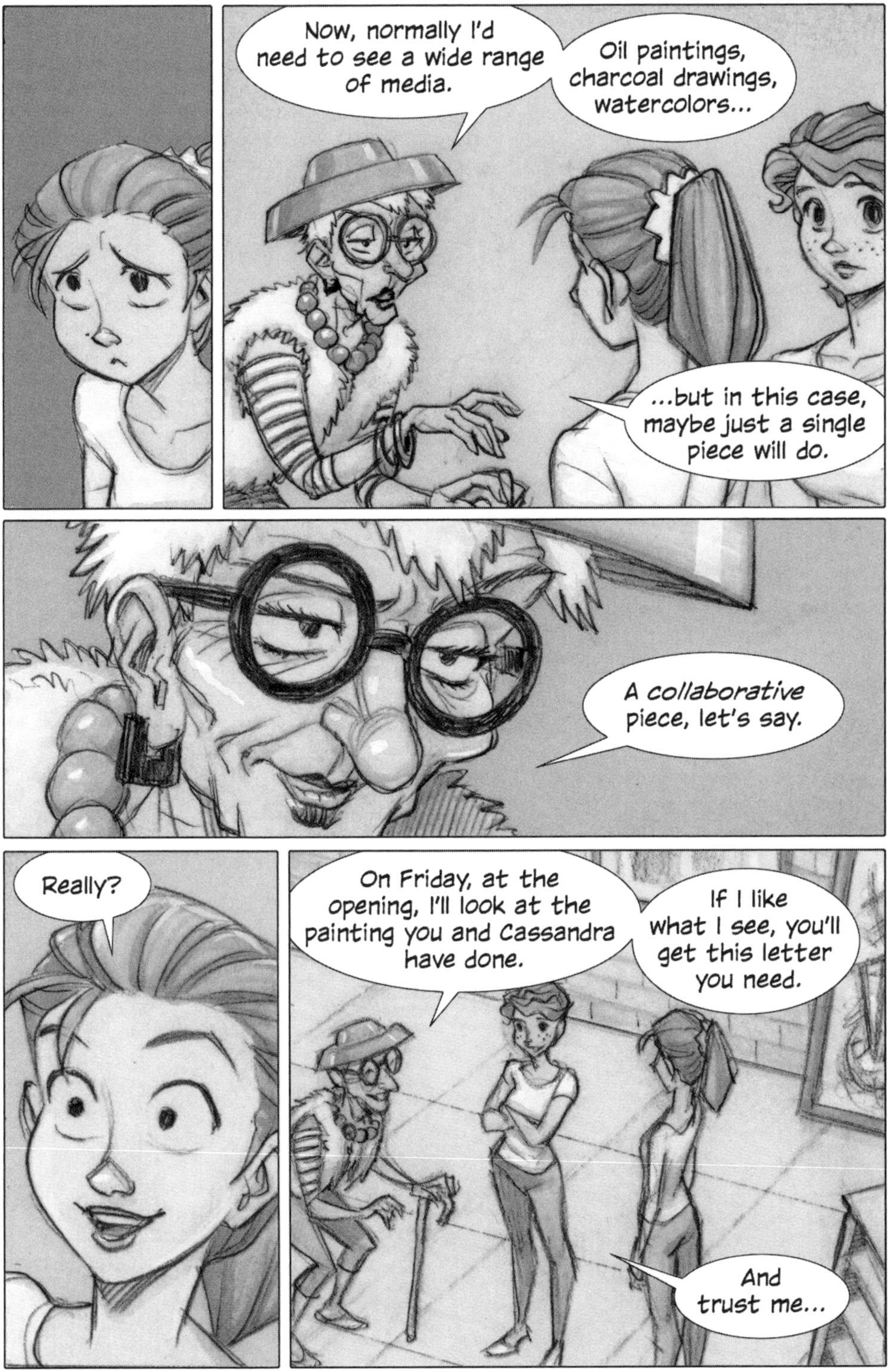
Now, normally I'd need to see a wide range of media.
Oil paintings, charcoal drawings, watercolors...
...but in this case, maybe just a single piece will do.
A *collaborative* piece, let's say.
Really?
On Friday, at the opening, I'll look at the painting you and Cassandra have done.
If I like what I see, you'll get this letter you need.
And trust me...

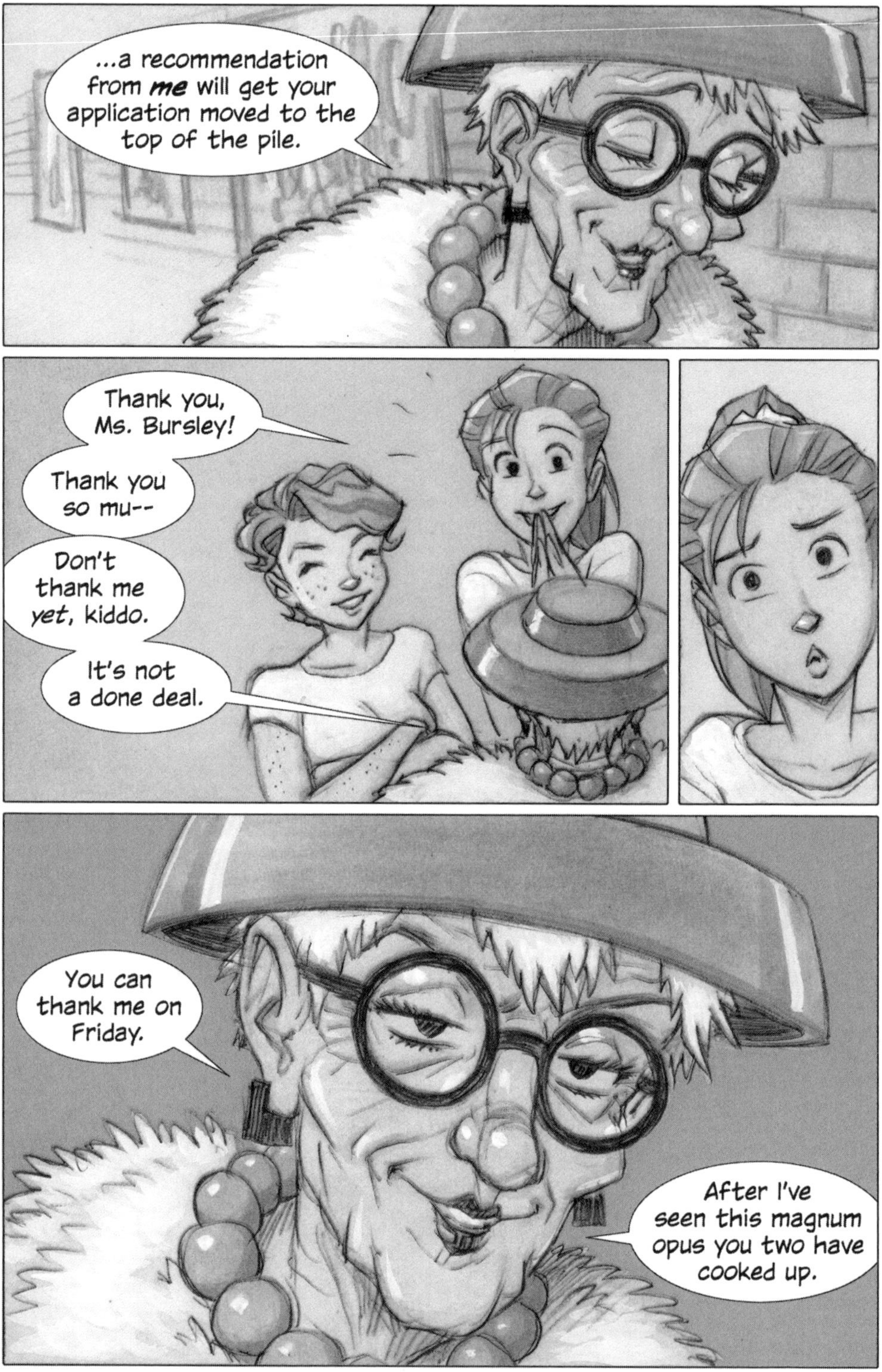
...a recommendation from *me* will get your application moved to the top of the pile.
Thank you, Ms. Bursley!
Thank you so mu--
Don't thank me *yet*, kiddo.
It's not a done deal.
You can thank me on Friday.
After I've seen this magnum opus you two have cooked up.

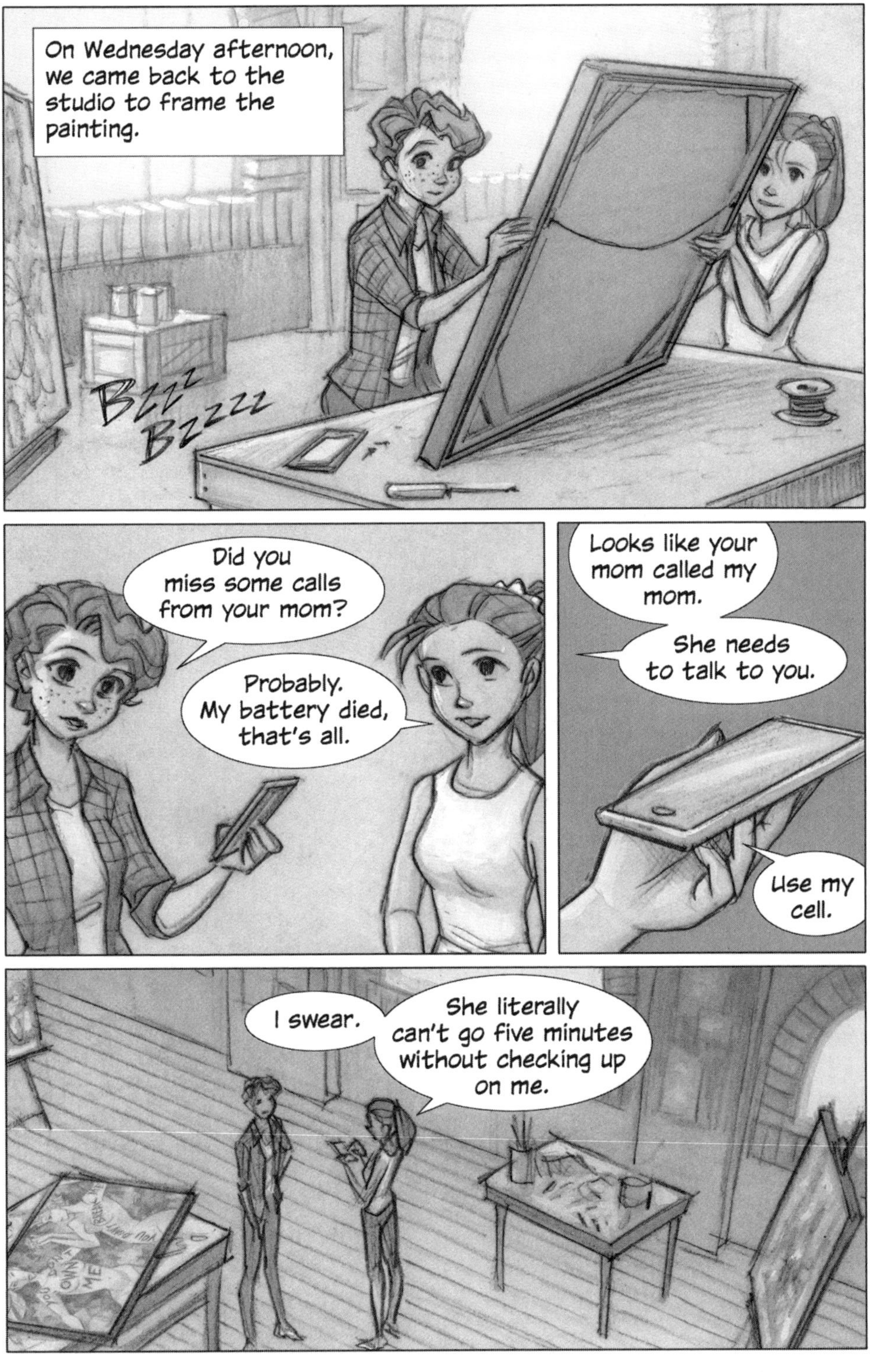
On Wednesday afternoon, we came back to the studio to frame the painting.
Bzzz Bzzzzz
Did you miss some calls from your mom?
Probably. My battery died, that's all.
Looks like your mom called my mom.
She needs to talk to you.
Use my cell.
I swear.
She literally can't go five minutes without checking up on me.

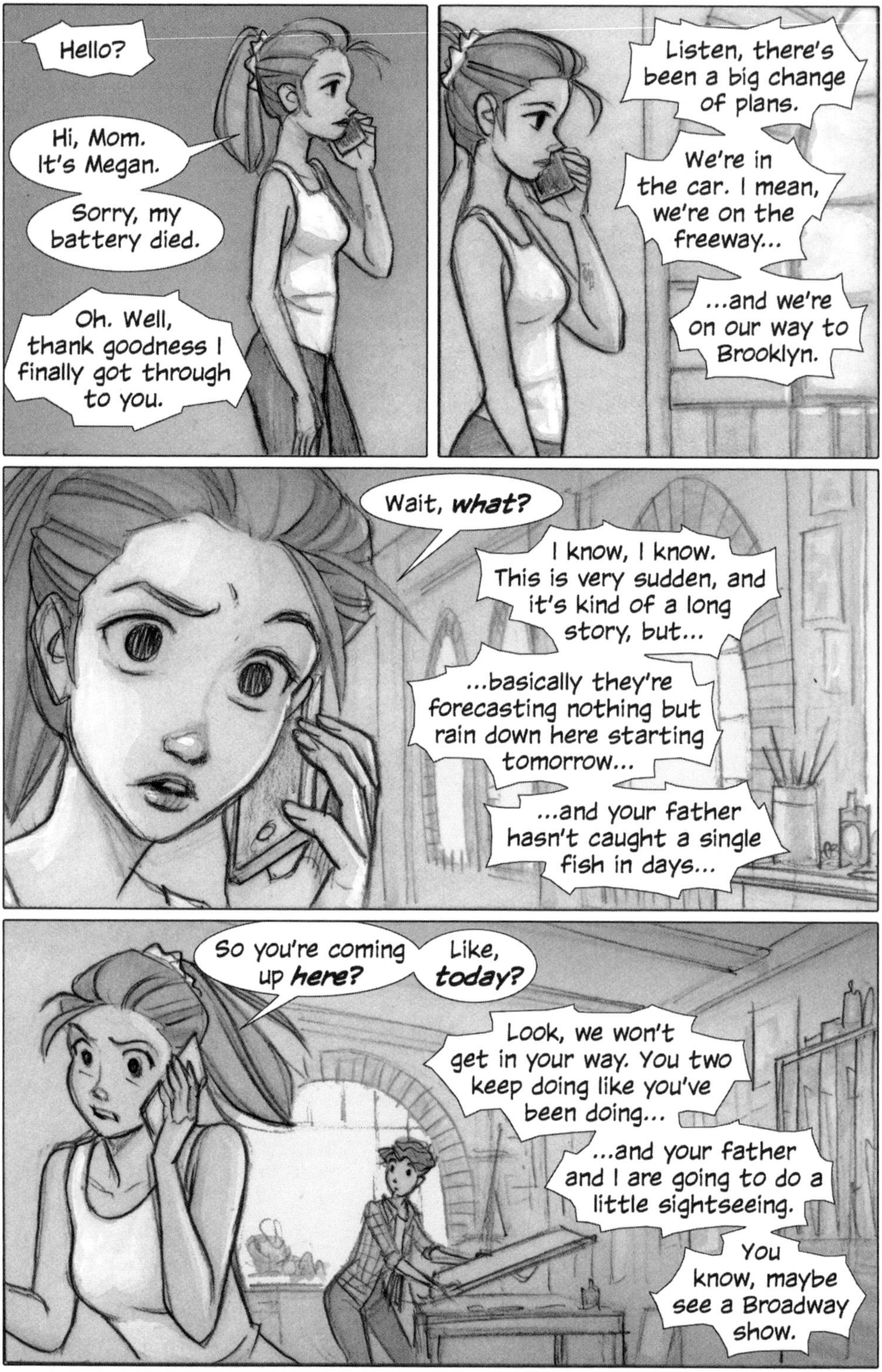
Hello?
Hi, Mom. It's Megan.
Sorry, my battery died.
Oh. Well, thank goodness I finally got through to you.
Listen, there's been a big change of plans.
We're in the car. I mean, we're on the freeway...
...and we're on our way to Brooklyn.
Wait, *what?*
I know, I know. This is very sudden, and it's kind of a long story, but...
...basically they're forecasting nothing but rain down here starting tomorrow...
...and your father hasn't caught a single fish in days...
So you're coming up *here?*
Like, *today?*
Look, we won't get in your way. You two keep doing like you've been doing...
...and your father and I are going to do a little sightseeing.
You know, maybe see a Broadway show.

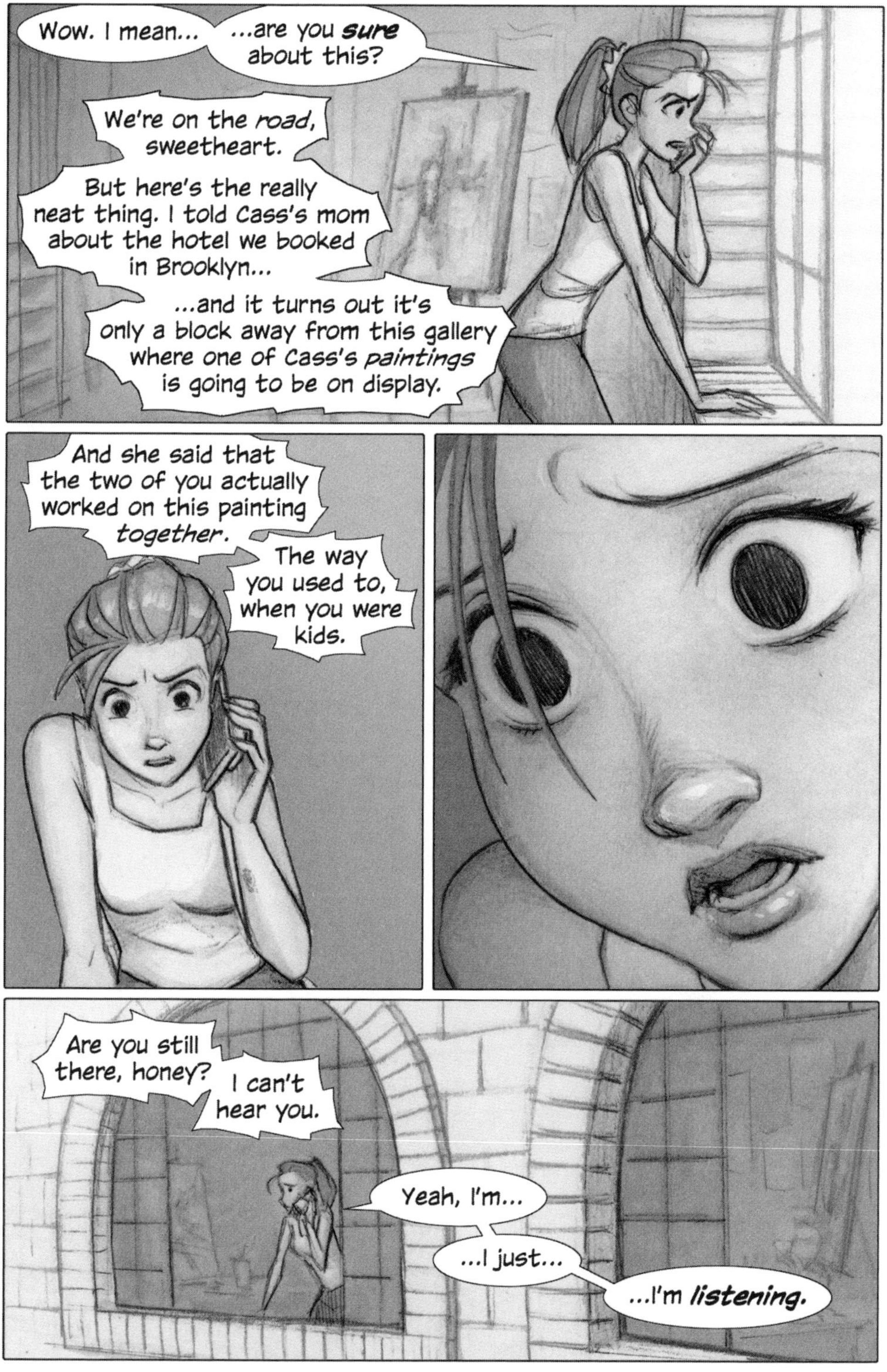
Wow. I mean...
...are you *sure* about this?
We're on the *road*, sweetheart.
But here's the really neat thing. I told Cass's mom about the hotel we booked in Brooklyn...
...and it turns out it's only a block away from this gallery where one of Cass's *paintings* is going to be on display.
And she said that the two of you actually worked on this painting *together*.
The way you used to, when you were kids.
Are you still there, honey?
I can't hear you.
Yeah, I'm...
...I just...
...I'm *listening.*

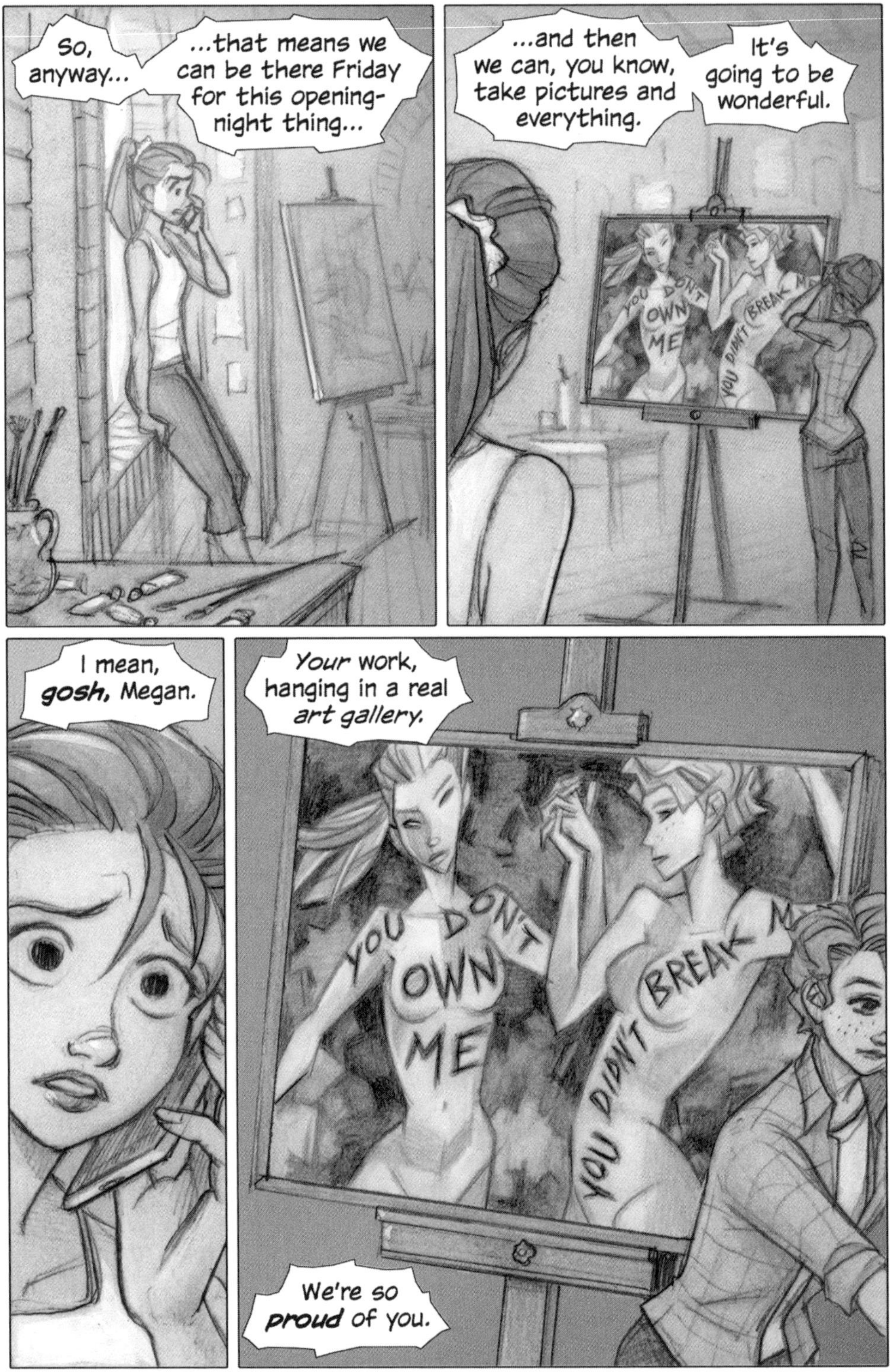
So, anyway...
...that means we can be there Friday for this opening-night thing...
...and then we can, you know, take pictures and everything.
It's going to be wonderful.
I mean, **gosh,** Megan.
Your work, hanging in a real *art gallery.*
YOU DON'T OWN ME
YOU DIDN'T BREAK M
We're so ***proud*** of you.

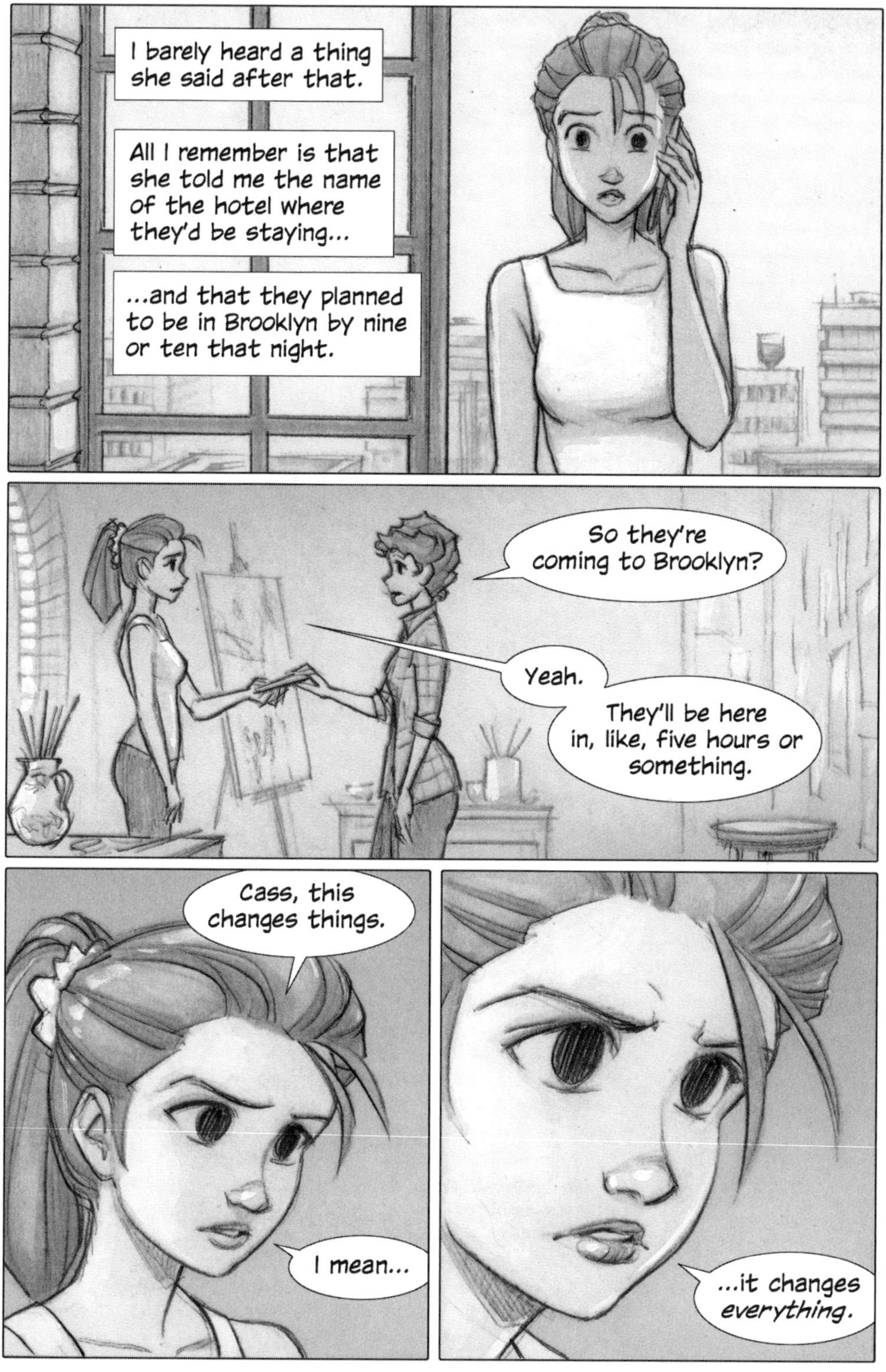
I barely heard a thing she said after that.
All I remember is that she told me the name of the hotel where they'd be staying...
...and that they planned to be in Brooklyn by nine or ten that night.
So they're coming to Brooklyn?
Yeah.
They'll be here in, like, five hours or something.
Cass, this changes things.
I mean...
...it changes *everything*.

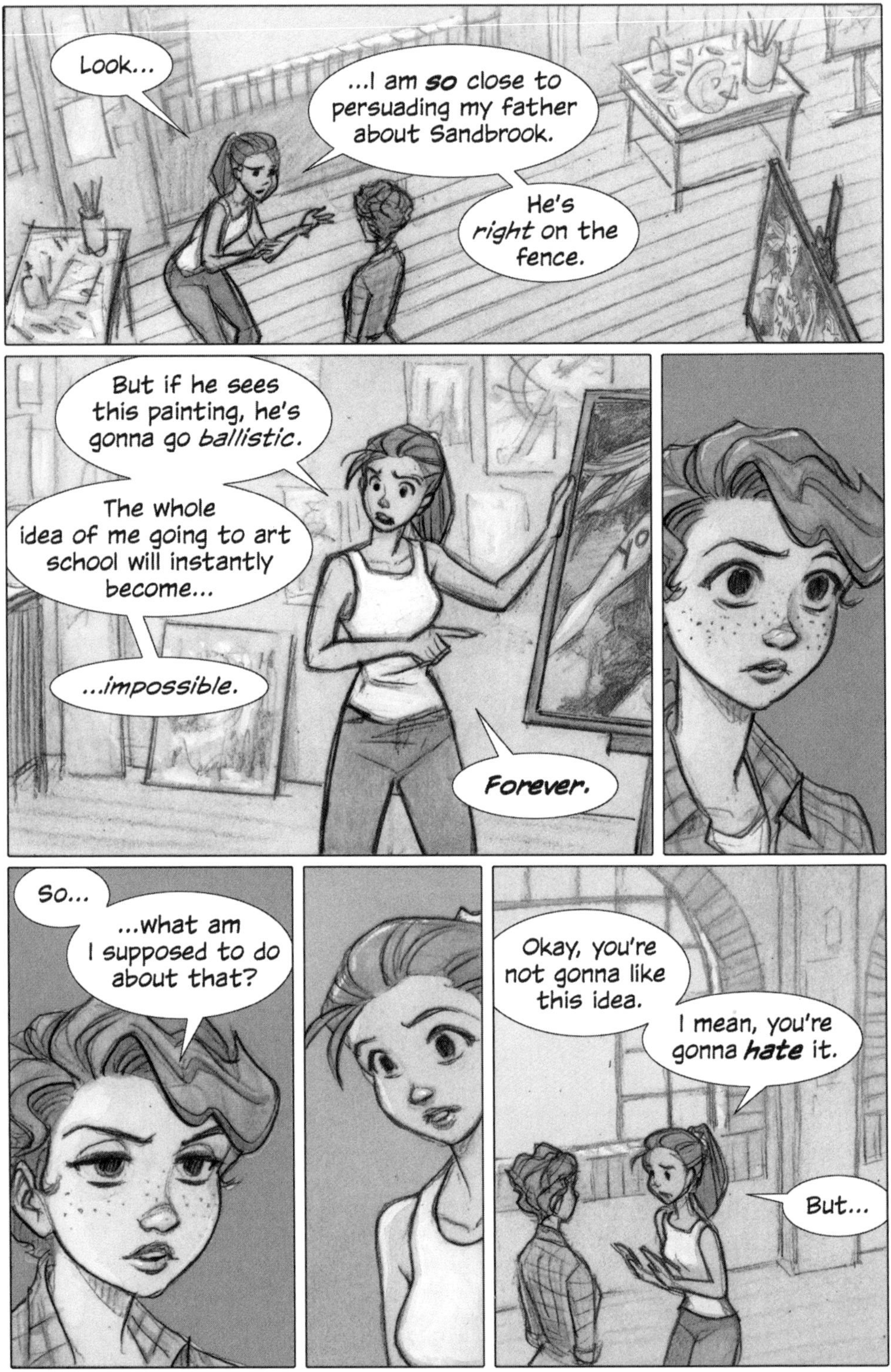
Look...
...I am *so* close to persuading my father about Sandbrook.
He's *right* on the fence.
But if he sees this painting, he's gonna go *ballistic*.
The whole idea of me going to art school will instantly become...
...*impossible*.
Forever.
So...
...what am I supposed to do about that?
Okay, you're not gonna like this idea.
I mean, you're gonna ***hate*** it.
But...

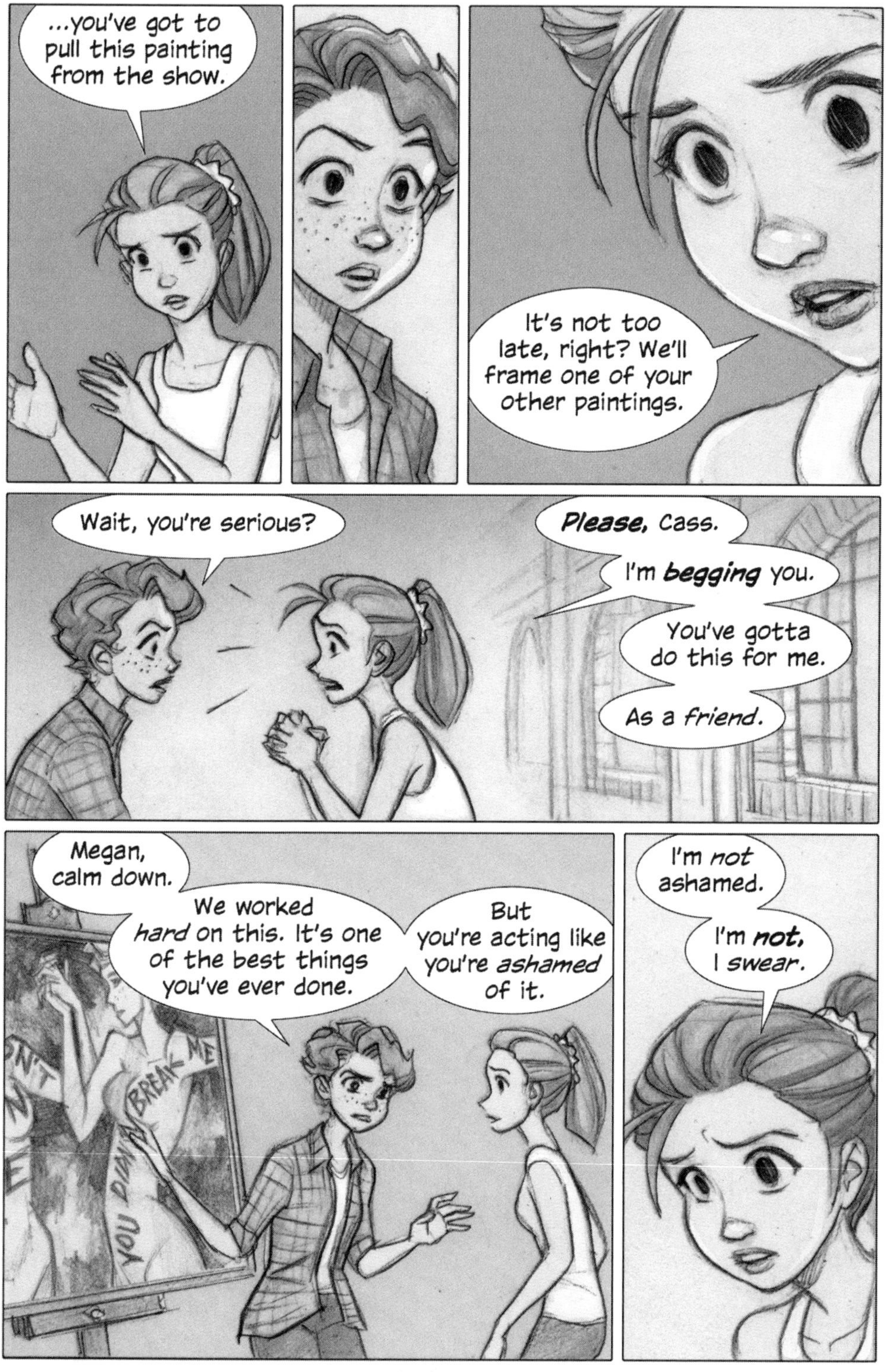
...you've got to pull this painting from the show.
It's not too late, right? We'll frame one of your other paintings.
Wait, you're serious?
Please, Cass.
I'm ***begging*** you.
You've gotta do this for me.
As a *friend*.
Megan, calm down.
We worked *hard* on this. It's one of the best things you've ever done.
But you're acting like you're *ashamed* of it.
YOU DIDN'T BREAK ME
I'm *not* ashamed.
I'm ***not,*** I *swear*.

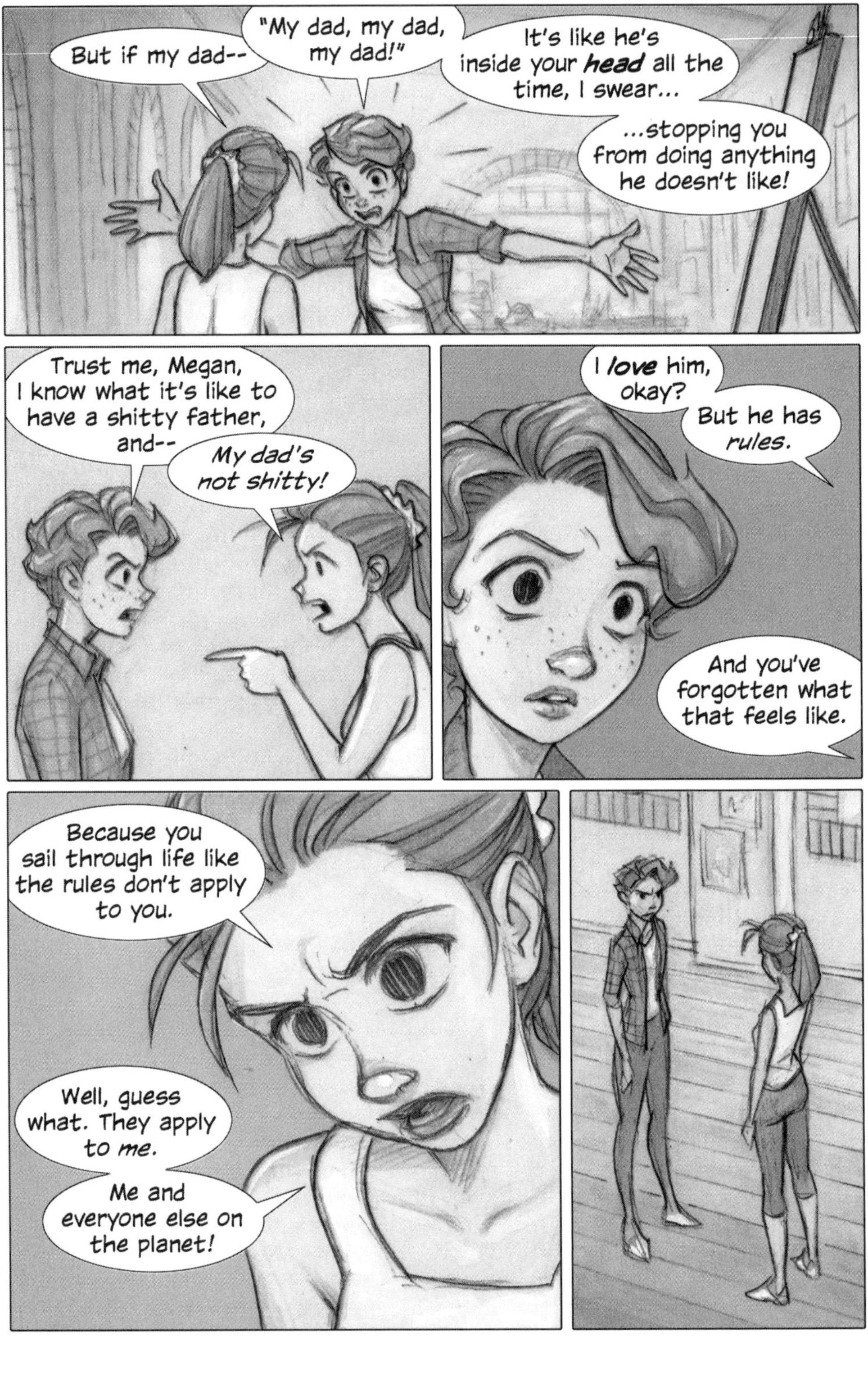
But if my dad--
"My dad, my dad, my dad!"
It's like he's inside your *head* all the time, I swear...
...stopping you from doing anything he doesn't like!
Trust me, Megan, I know what it's like to have a shitty father, and--
My dad's not shitty!
I *love* him, okay?
But he has *rules.*
And you've forgotten what that feels like.
Because you sail through life like the rules don't apply to you.
Well, guess what. They apply to *me.*
Me and everyone else on the planet!

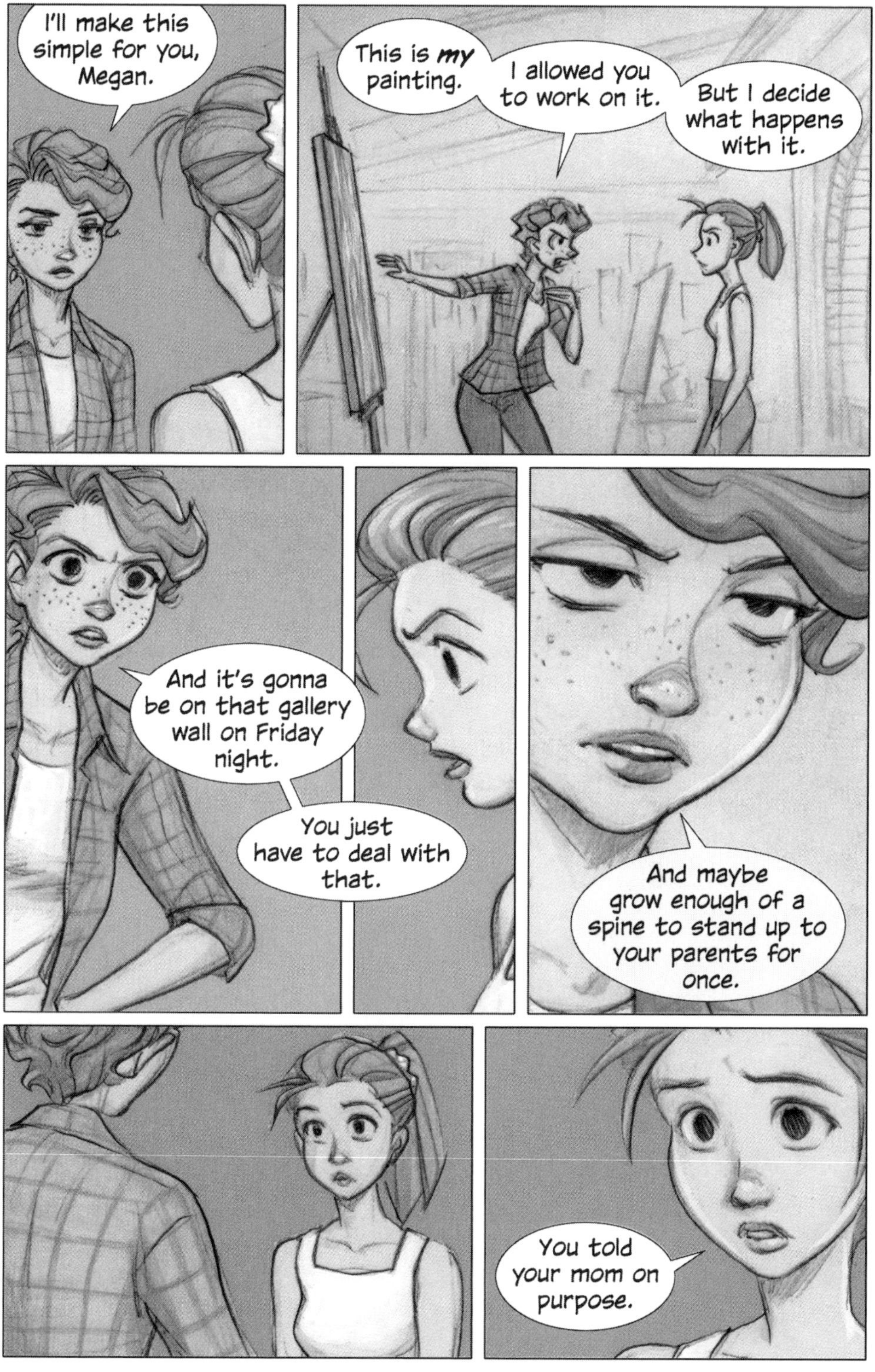
I'll make this simple for you, Megan.
This is *my* painting.
I allowed you to work on it.
But I decide what happens with it.
And it's gonna be on that gallery wall on Friday night.
You just have to deal with that.
And maybe grow enough of a spine to stand up to your parents for once.
You told your mom on purpose.

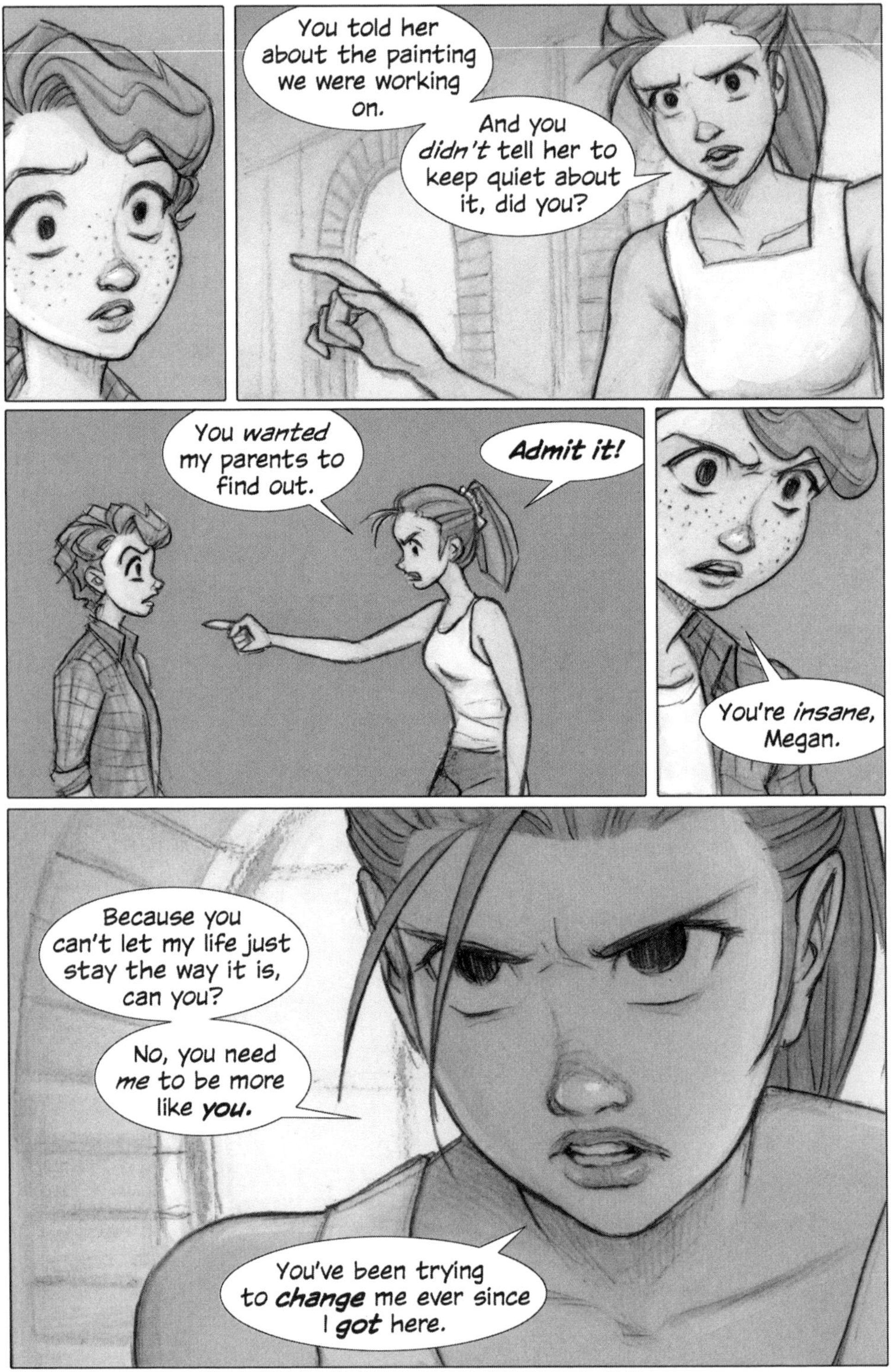

You told her about the painting we were working on.
And you *didn't* tell her to keep quiet about it, did you?
You *wanted* my parents to find out.
Admit it!
You're *insane,* Megan.
Because you can't let my life just stay the way it is, can you?
No, you need *me* to be more like ***you.***
You've been trying to ***change*** me ever since I ***got*** here.

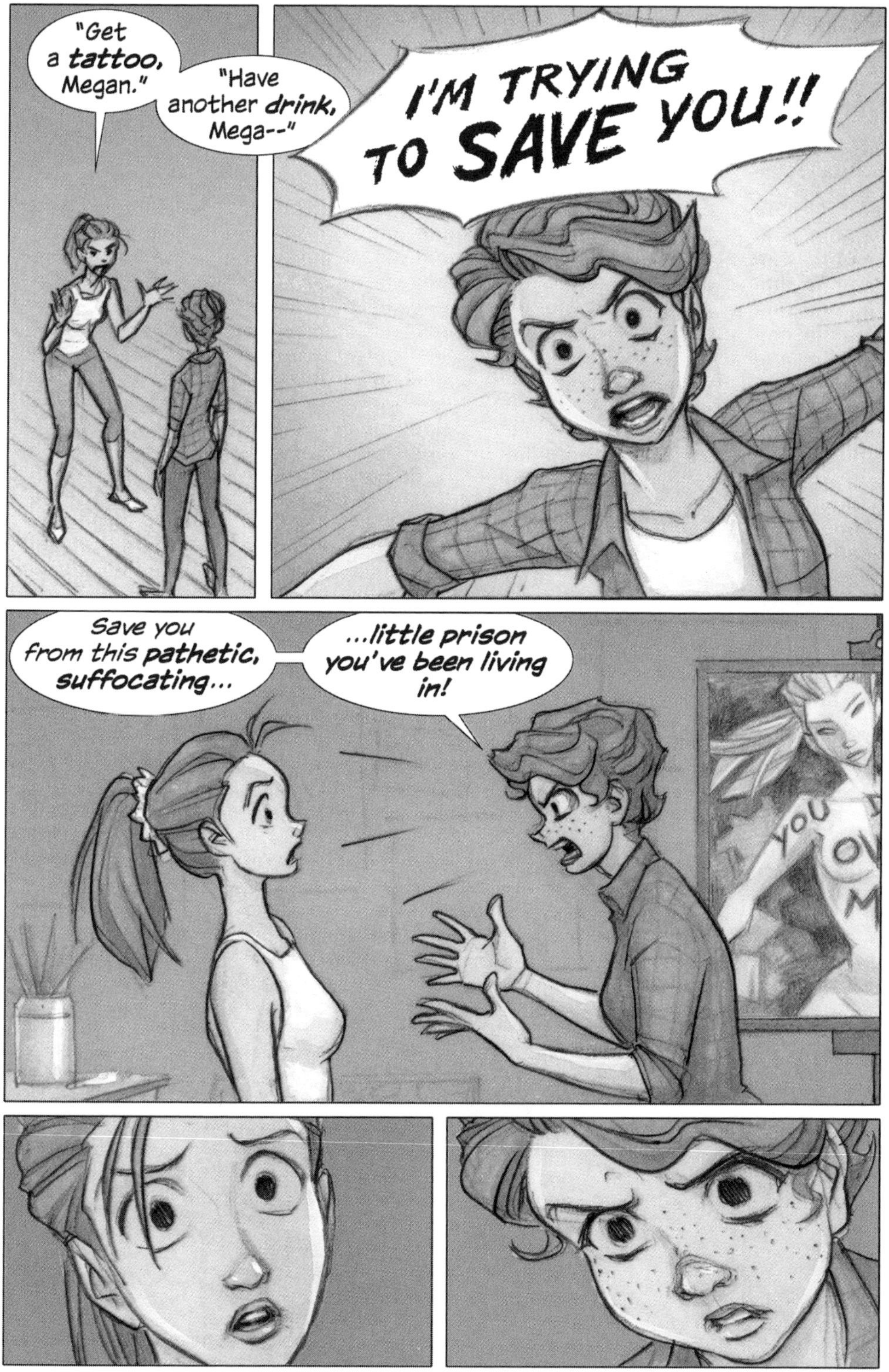
"Get a tattoo, Megan."
"Have another drink, Mega--"
I'M TRYING TO SAVE YOU!!
Save you from this pathetic, suffocating...
...little prison you've been living in!
YOU

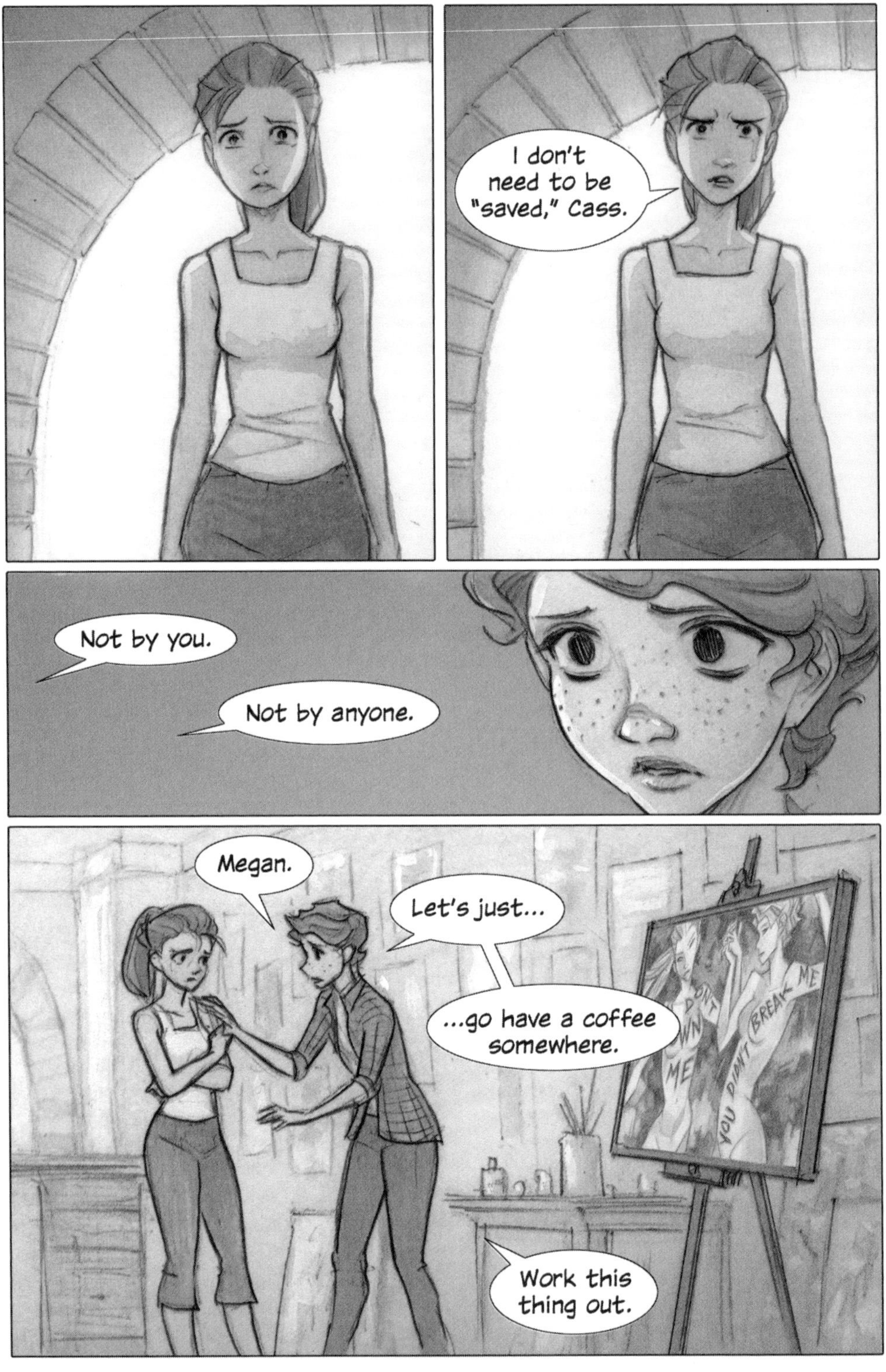
I don't need to be "saved," Cass.
Not by you.
Not by anyone.
Megan.
Let's just...
...go have a coffee somewhere.
Work this thing out.

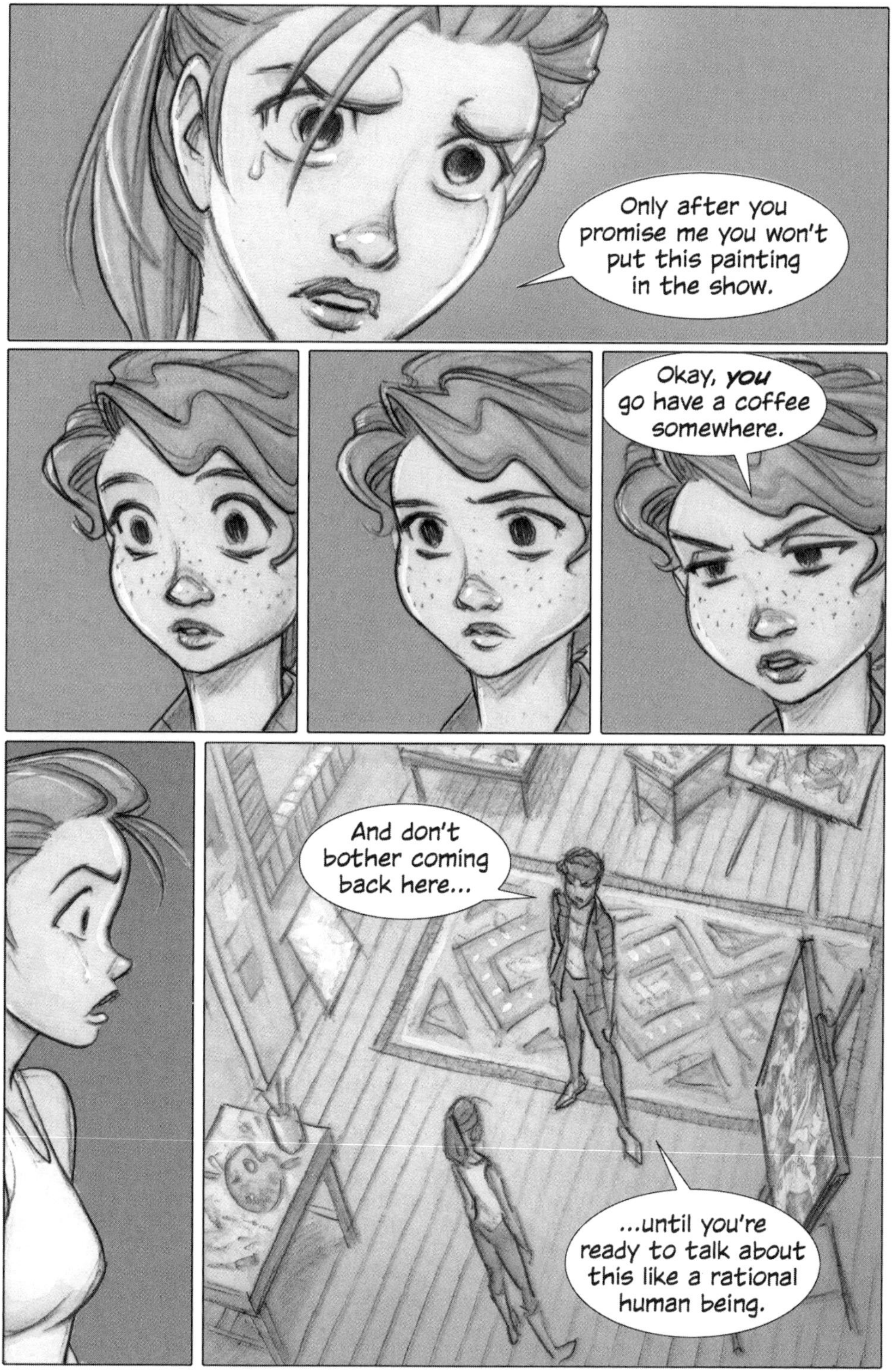
Only after you promise me you won't put this painting in the show.
Okay, ***you*** go have a coffee somewhere.
And don't bother coming back here...
...until you're ready to talk about this like a rational human being.

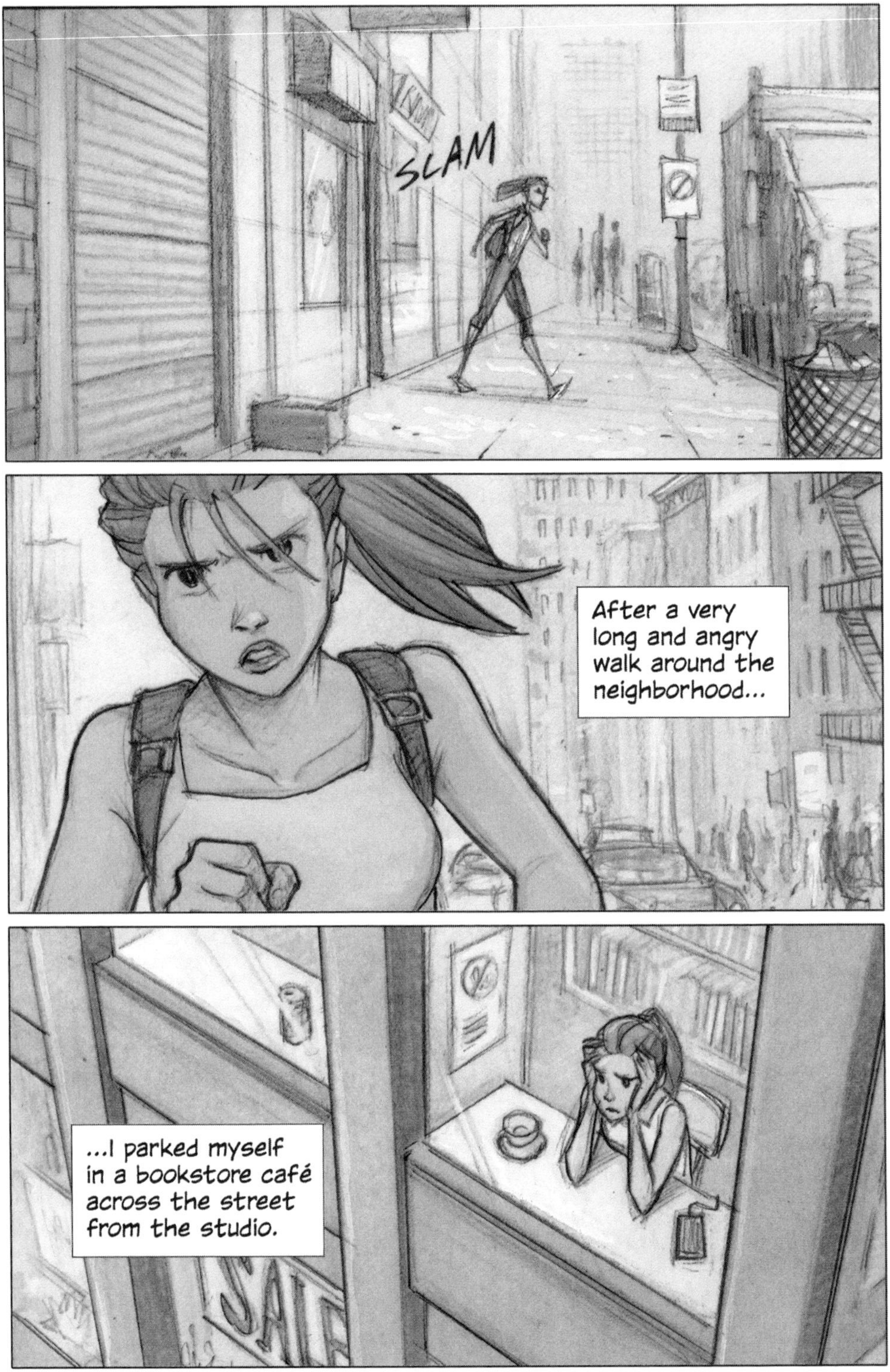
SLAM
After a very long and angry walk around the neighborhood...
...I parked myself in a bookstore café across the street from the studio.

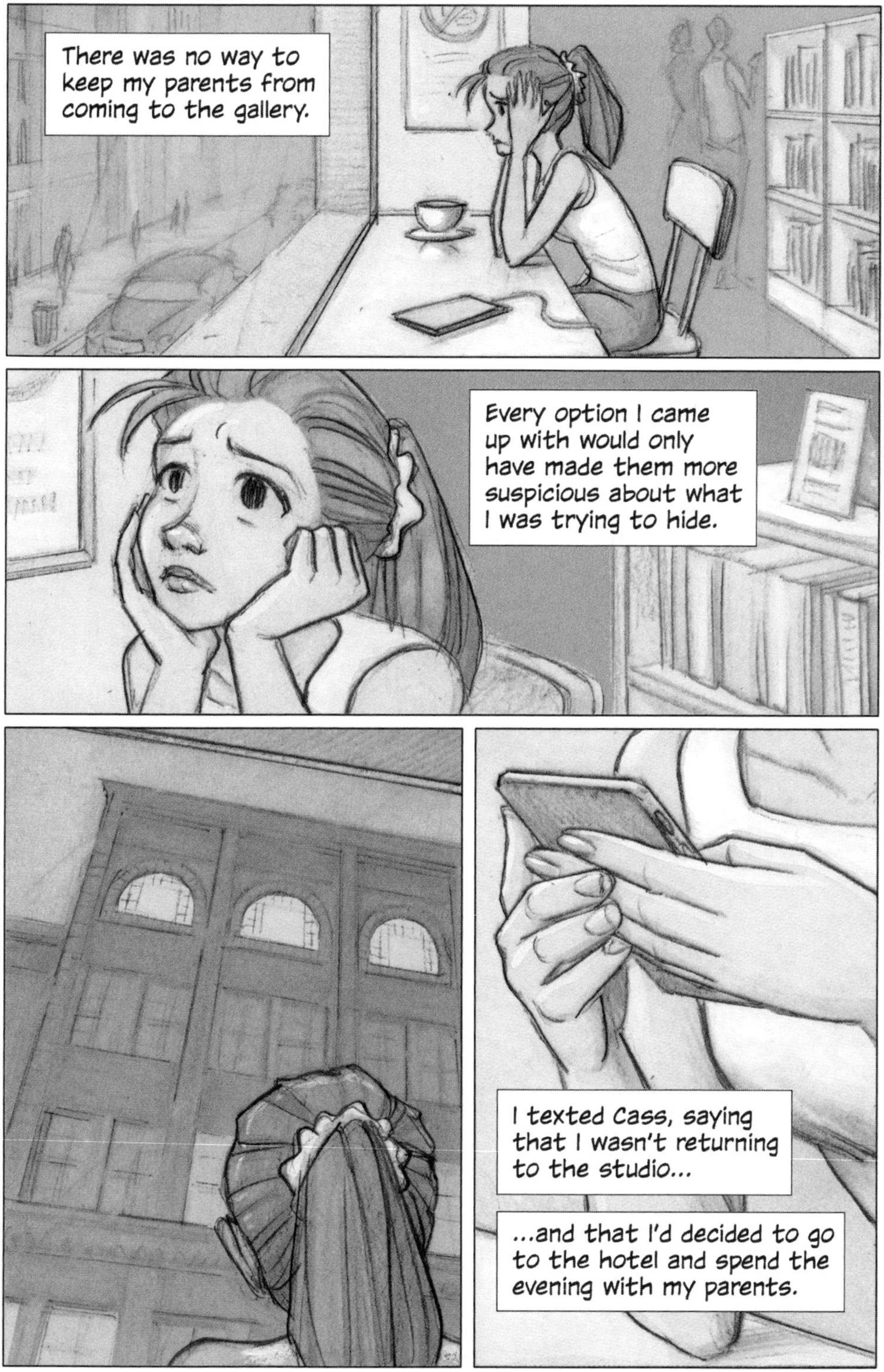
There was no way to keep my parents from coming to the gallery.
Every option I came up with would only have made them more suspicious about what I was trying to hide.
I texted Cass, saying that I wasn't returning to the studio...
...and that I'd decided to go to the hotel and spend the evening with my parents.

Was Cass right?

Was it time to stand up to my parents?

To let them see the painting and just deal with the fallout, whatever it may be?

Or was there still...

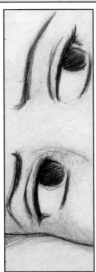

...another way?

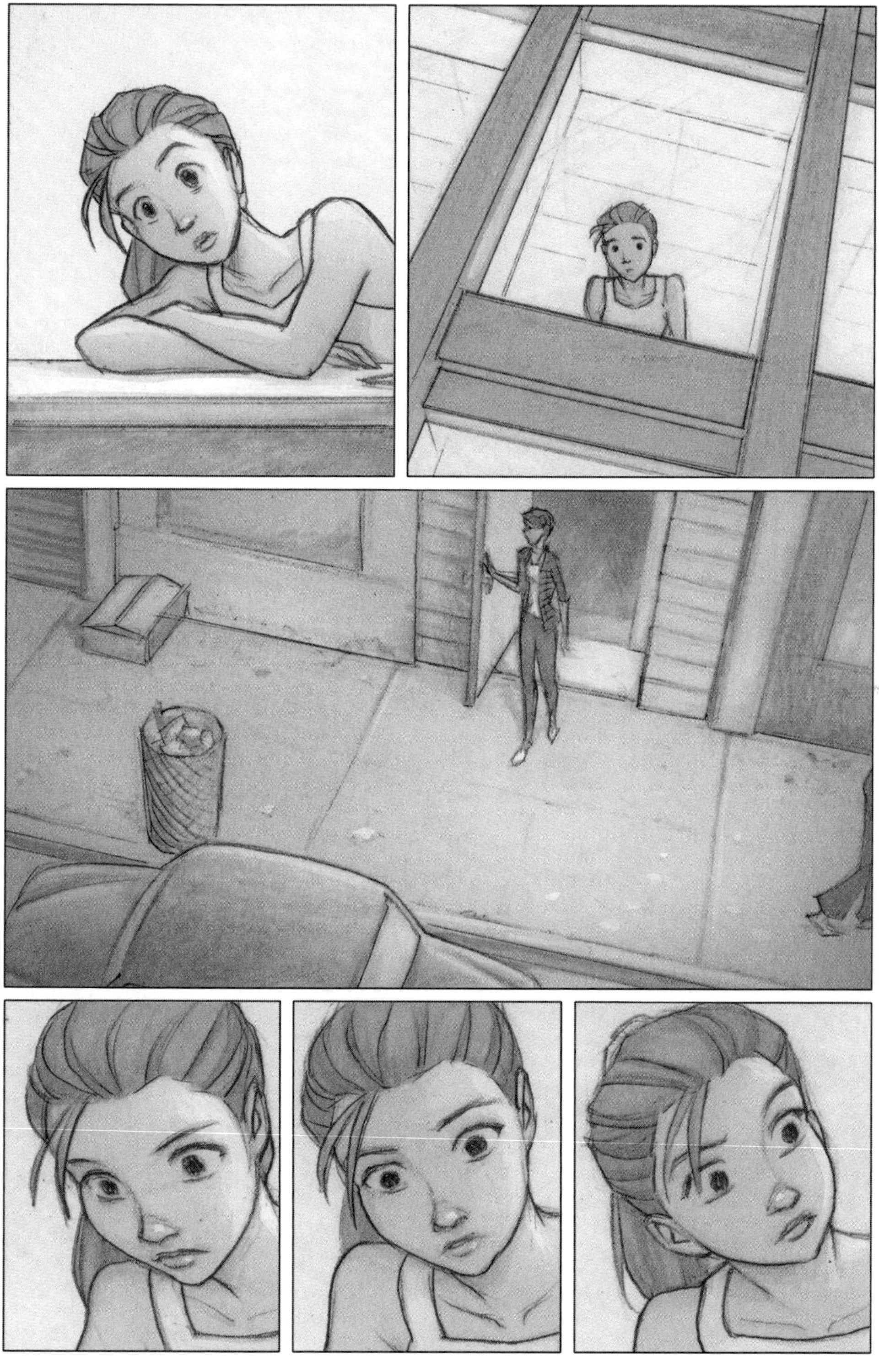

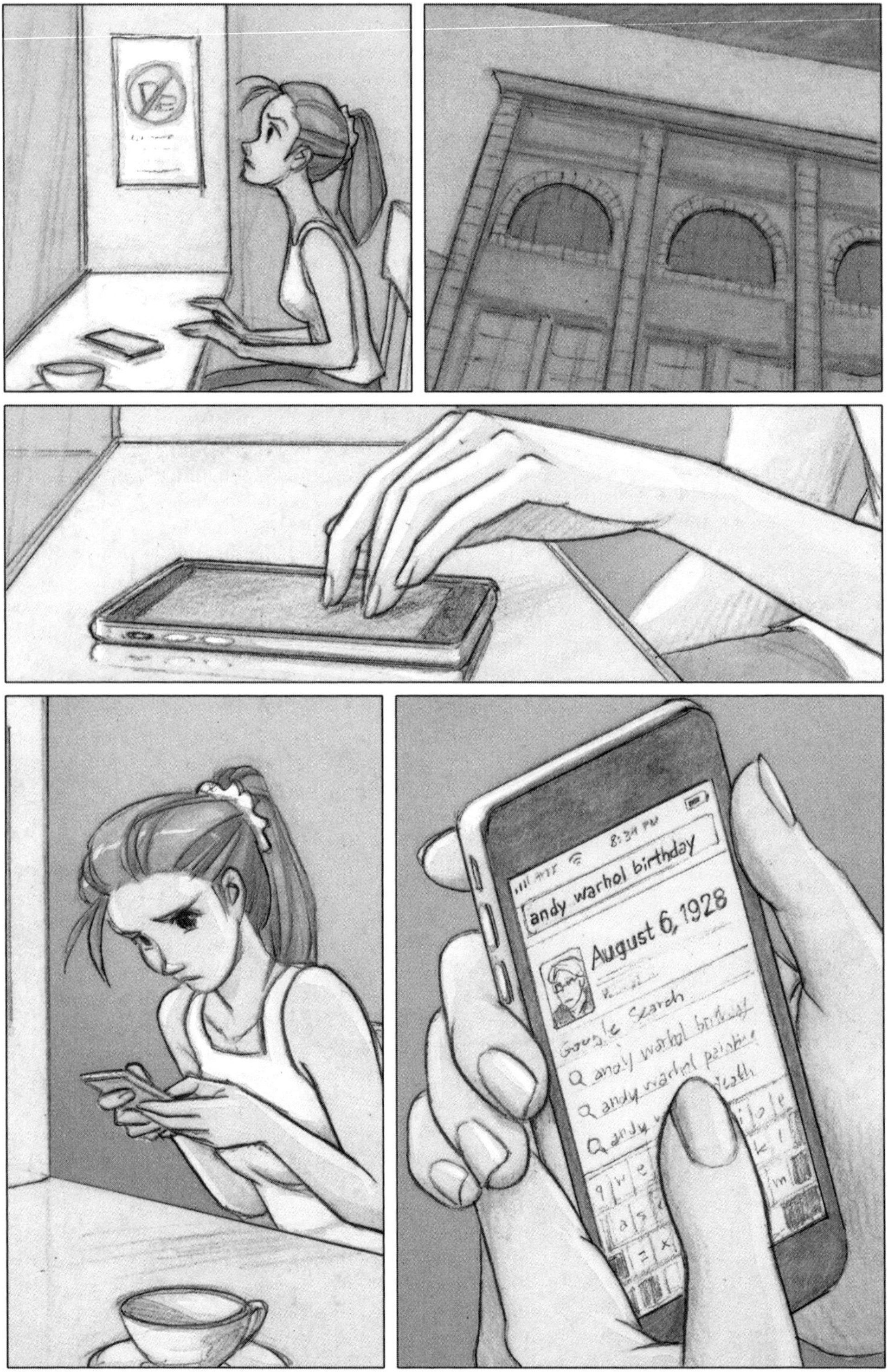
8:34 PM
andy warhol birthday
August 6, 1928
Google Search

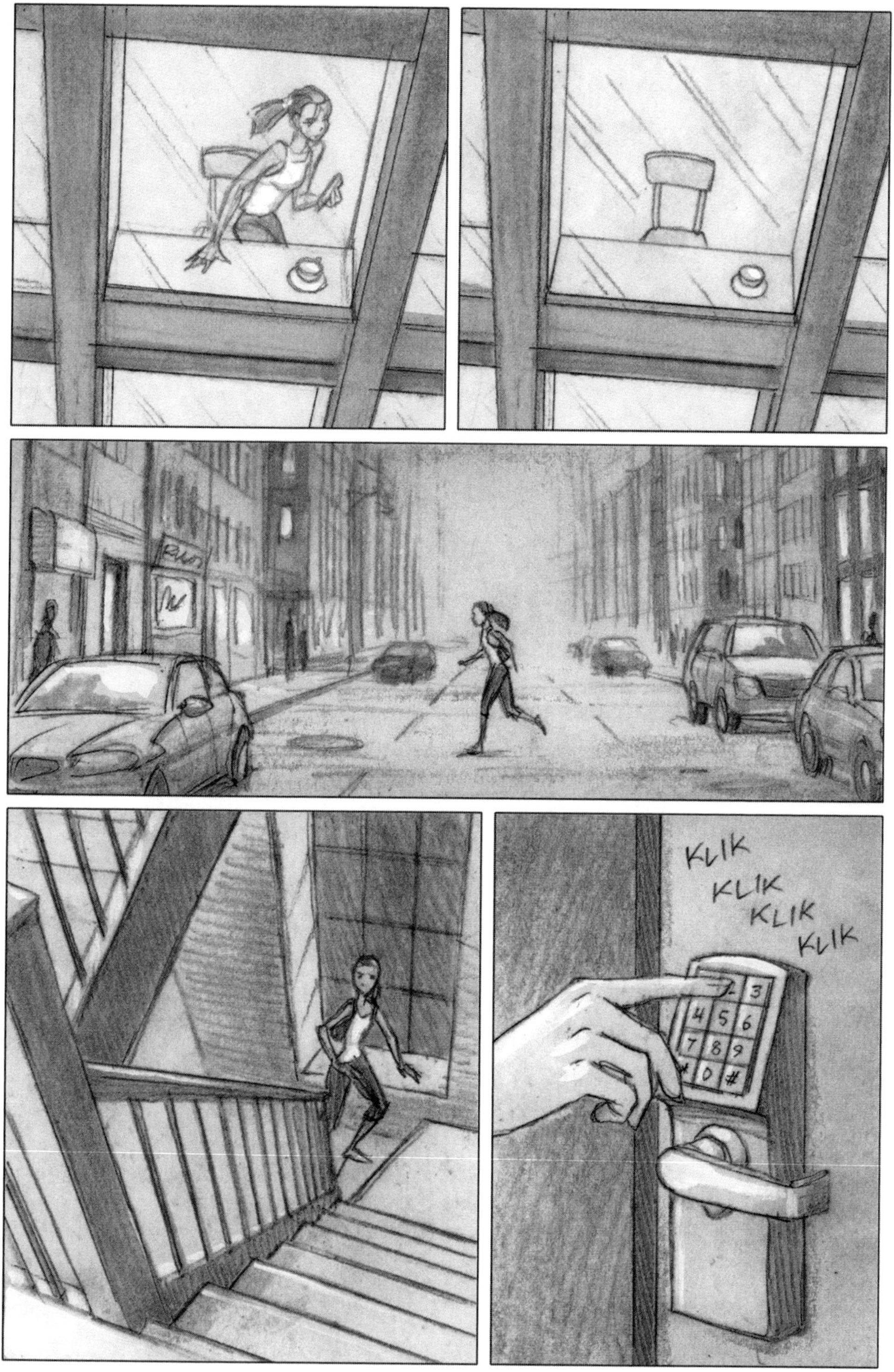
KLIK
KLIK
KLIK
KLIK

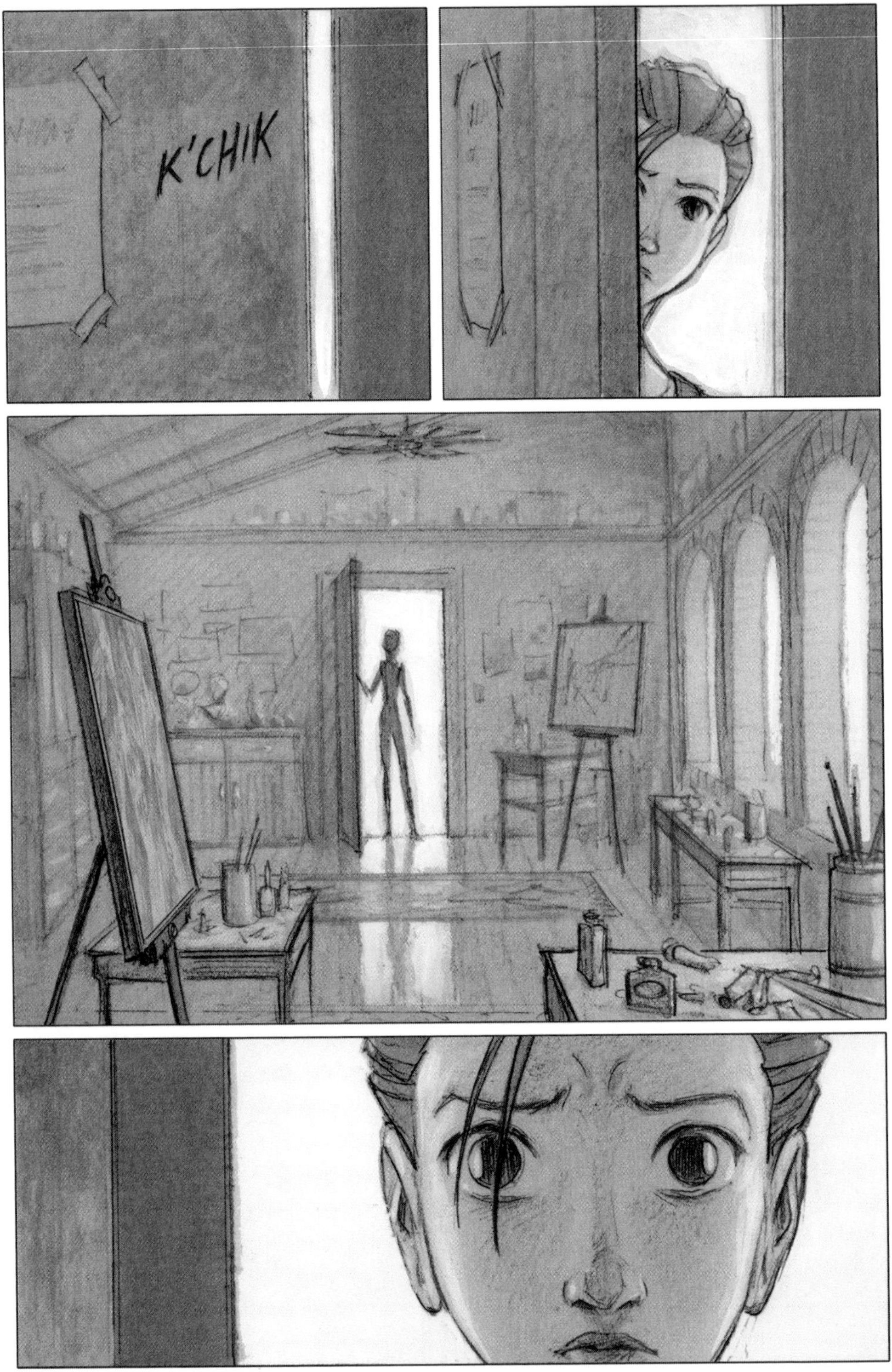
K'CHIK

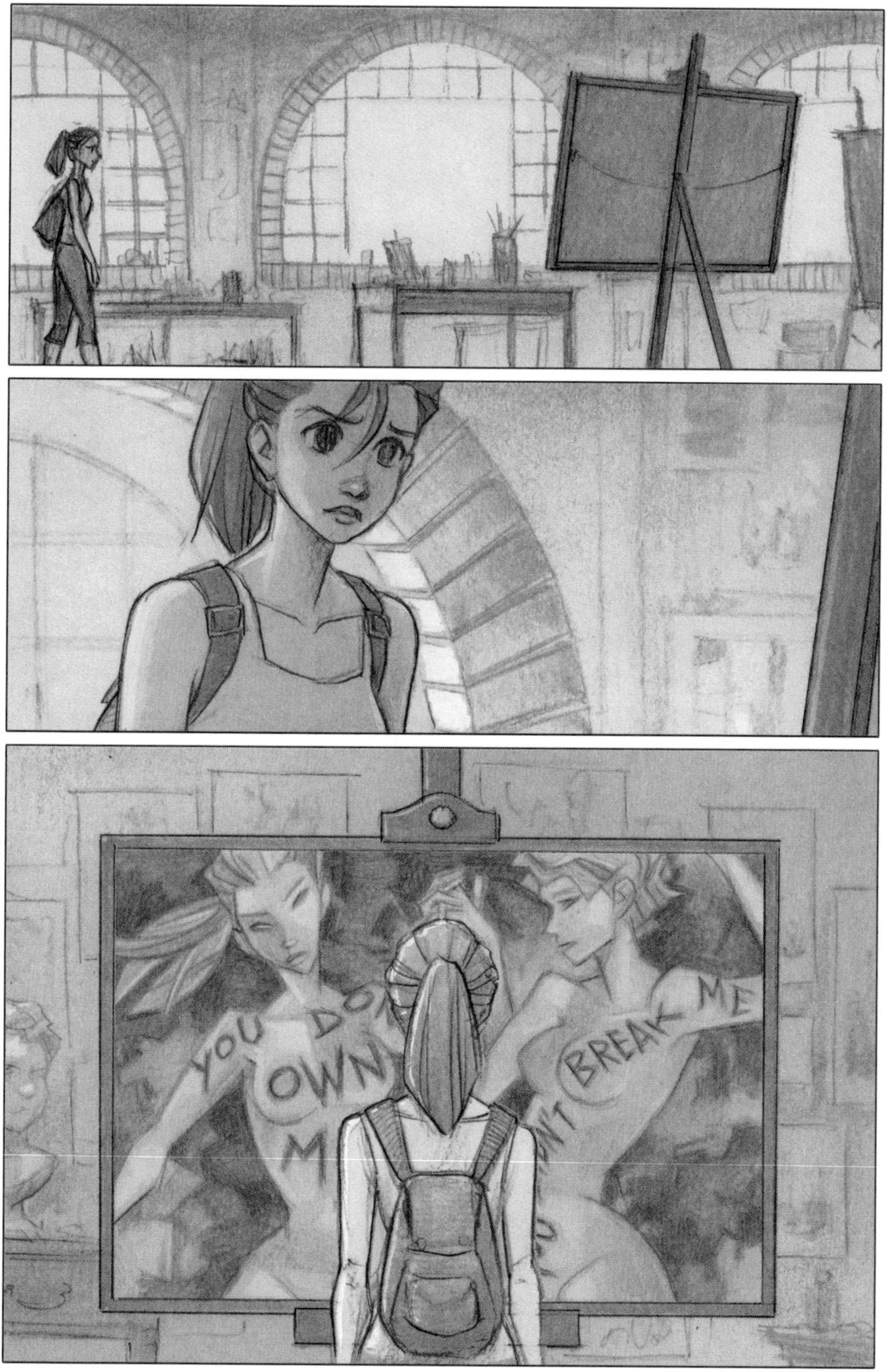
YOU DO
OWN
M
BREAK ME
N'T

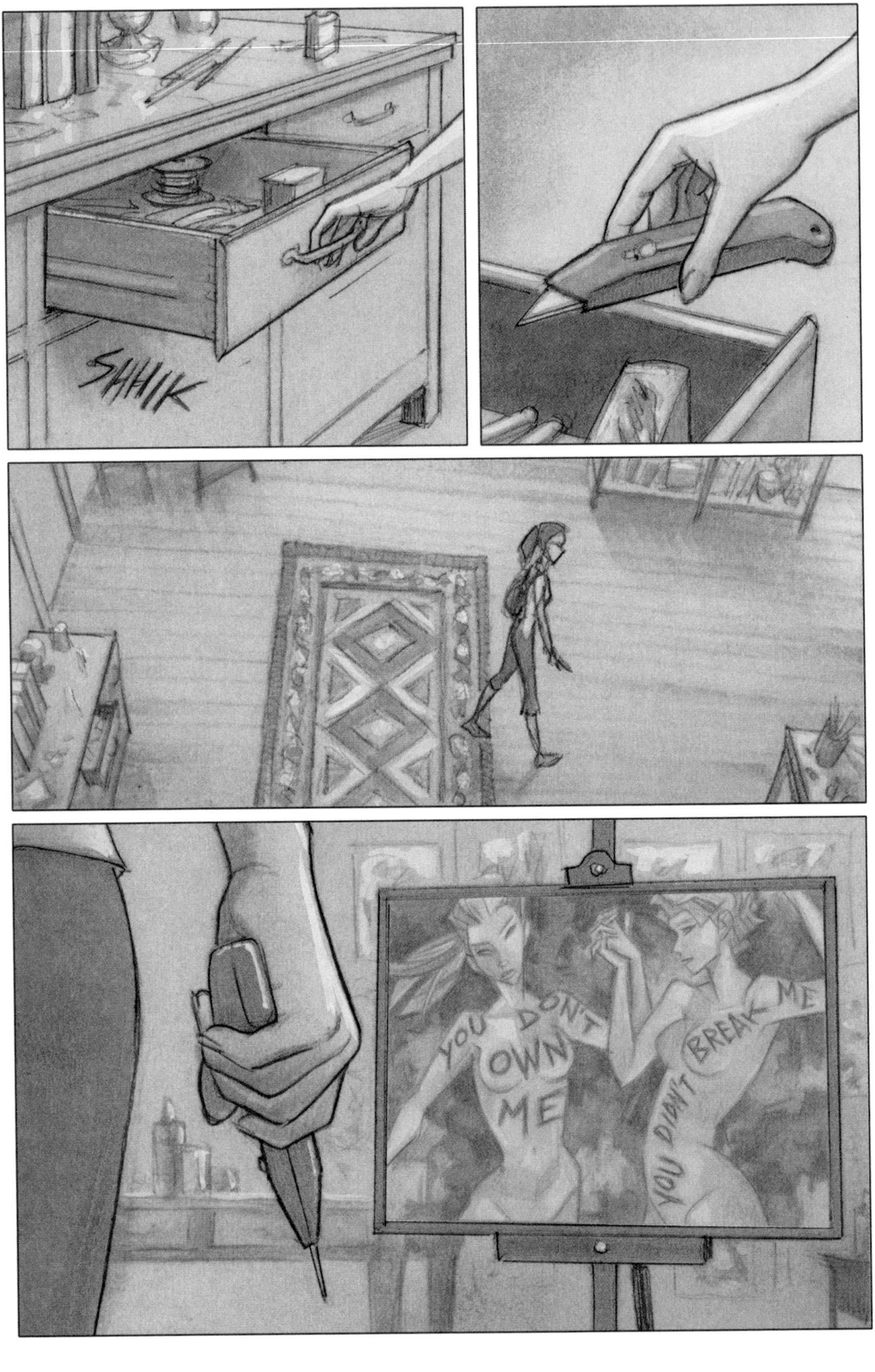
SHHIK
YOU DON'T OWN ME
YOU DIDN'T BREAK ME

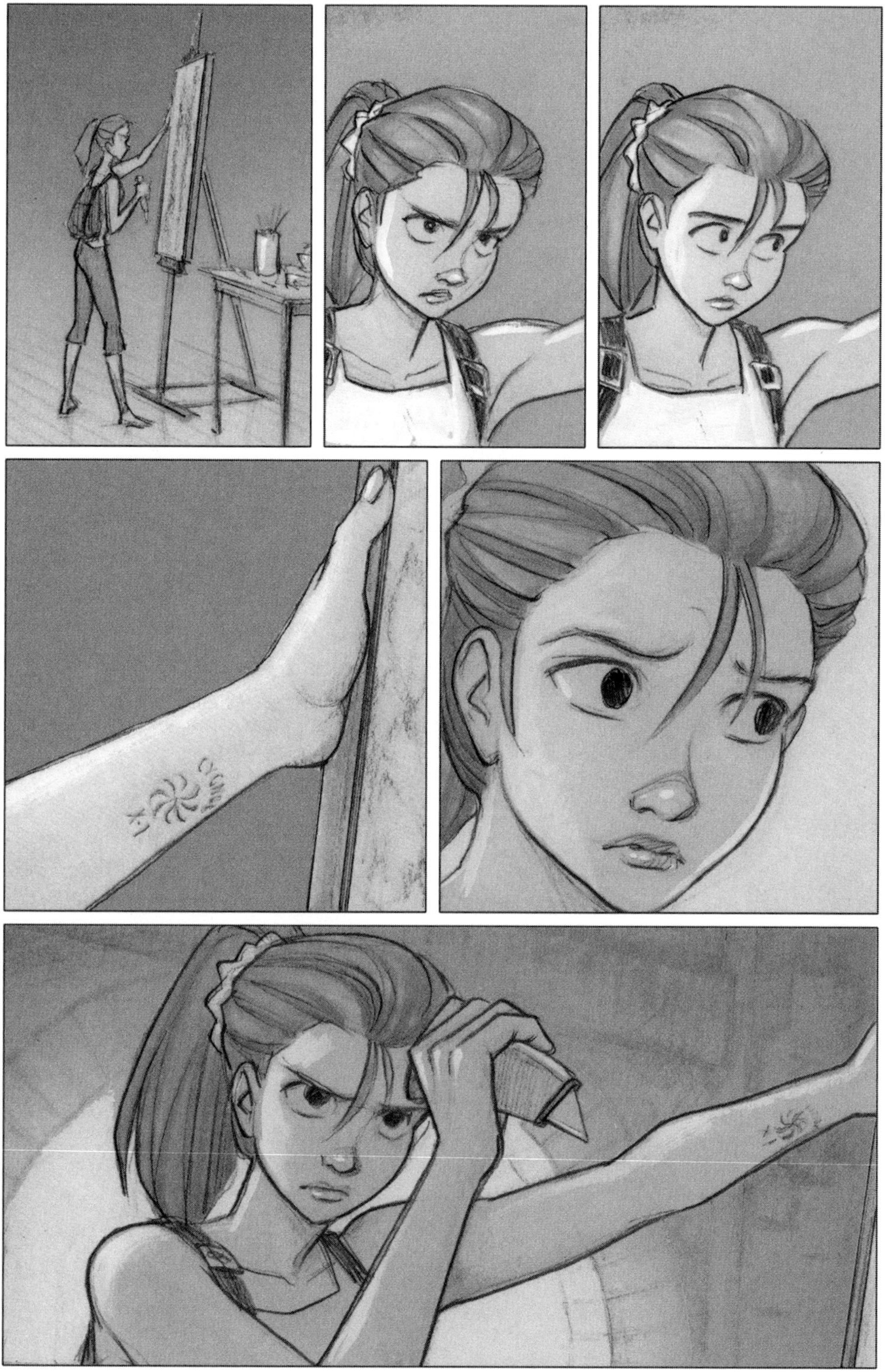

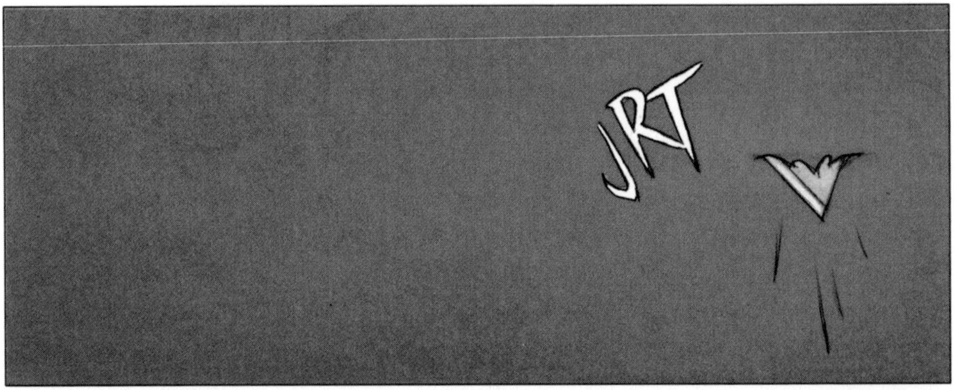
JRT

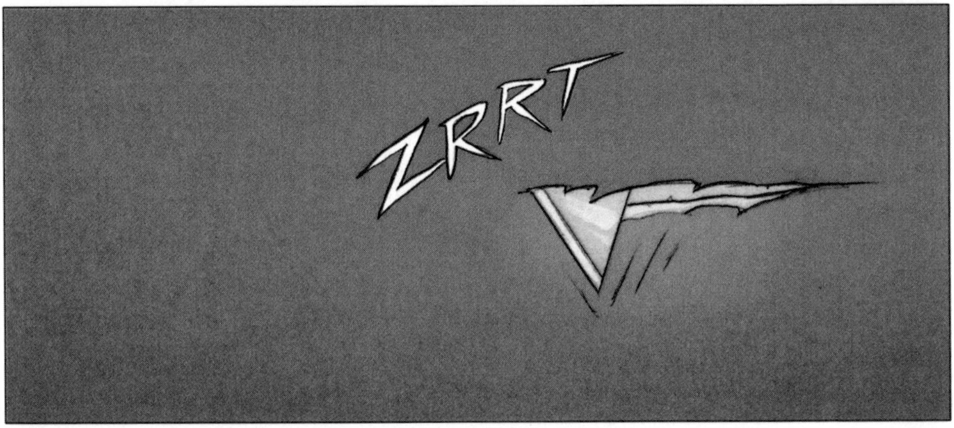
ZRRT

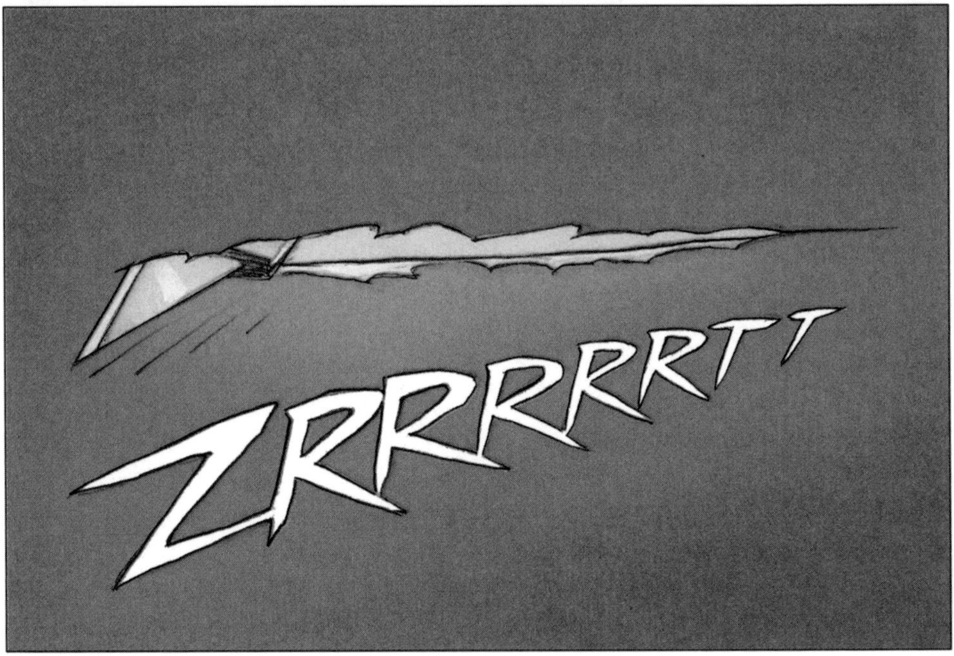
ZRRRRRTT

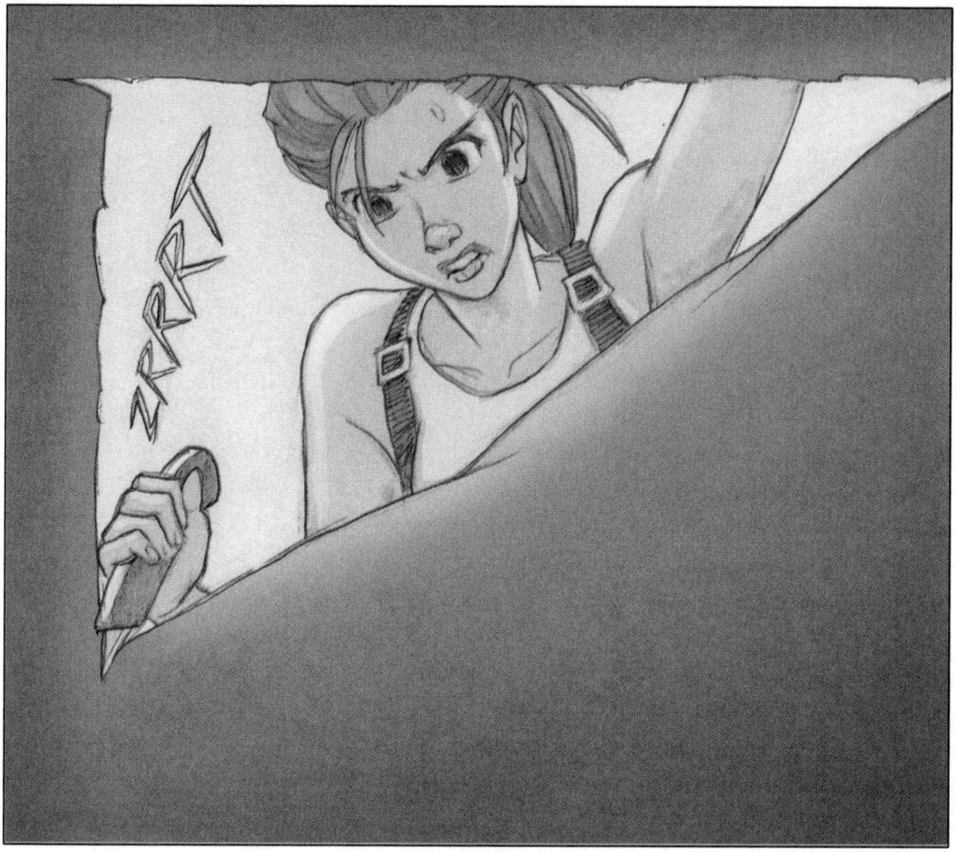
ZRRRT

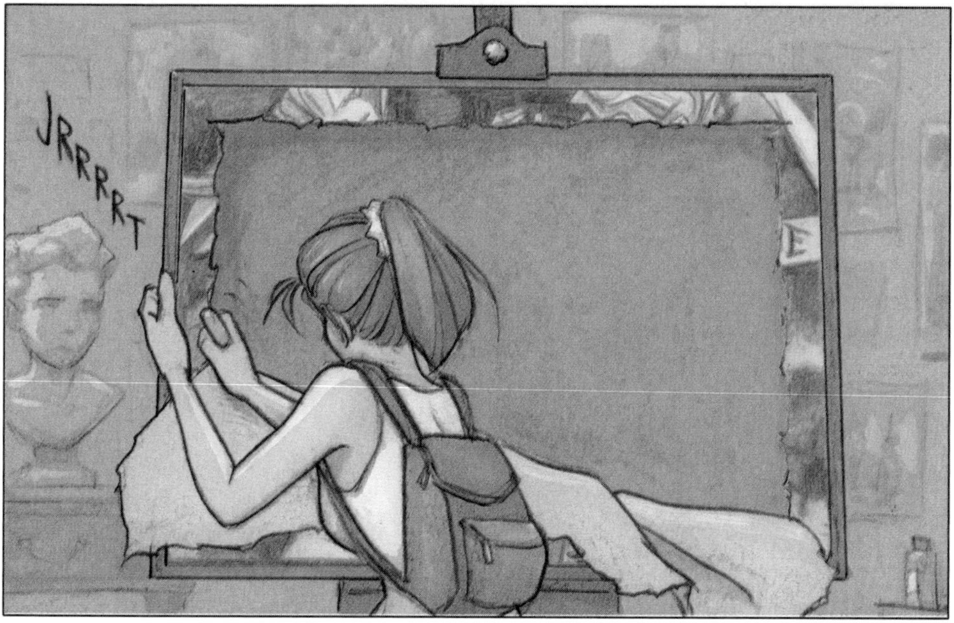
JRRRRT

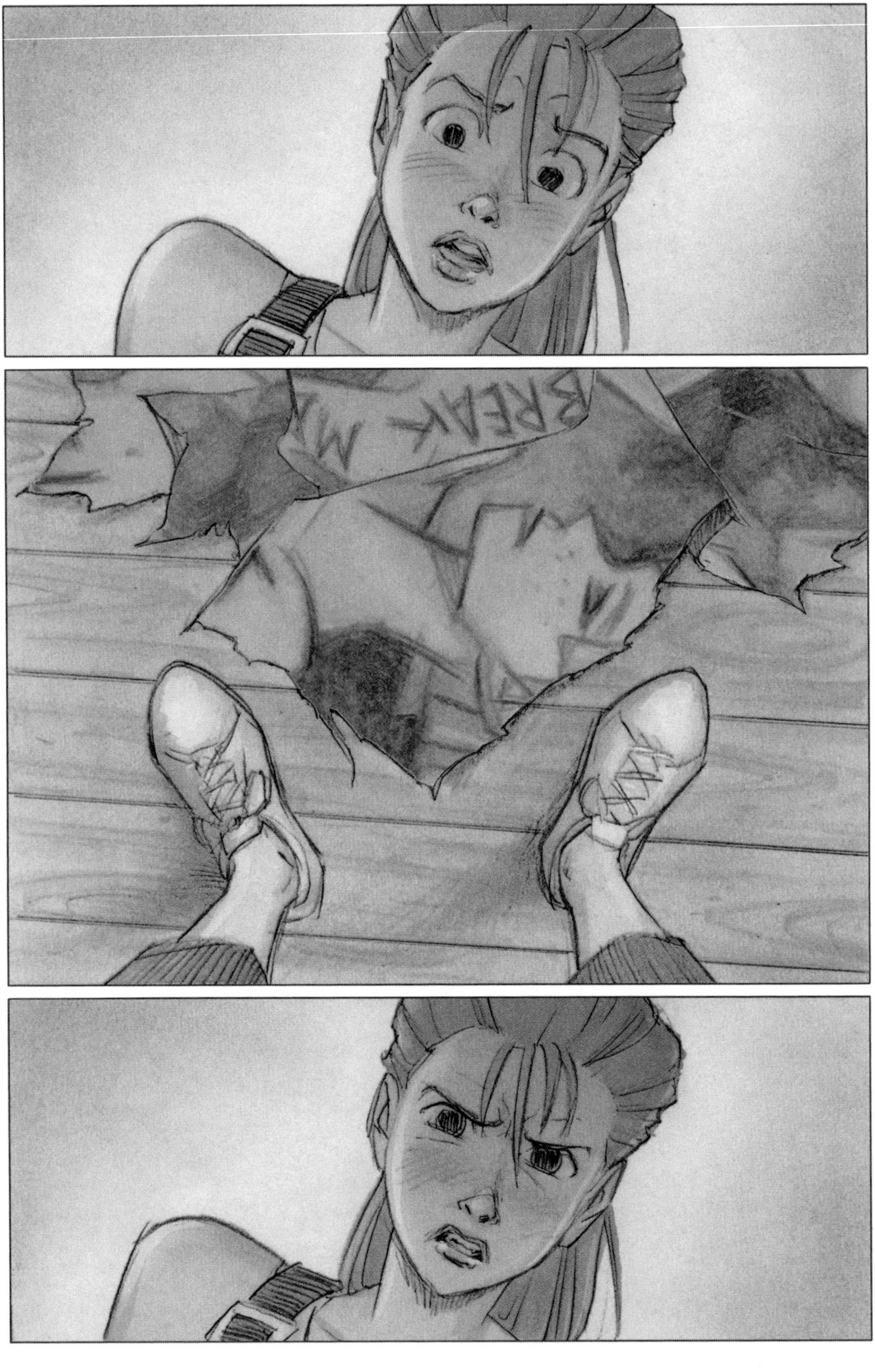
BREAK

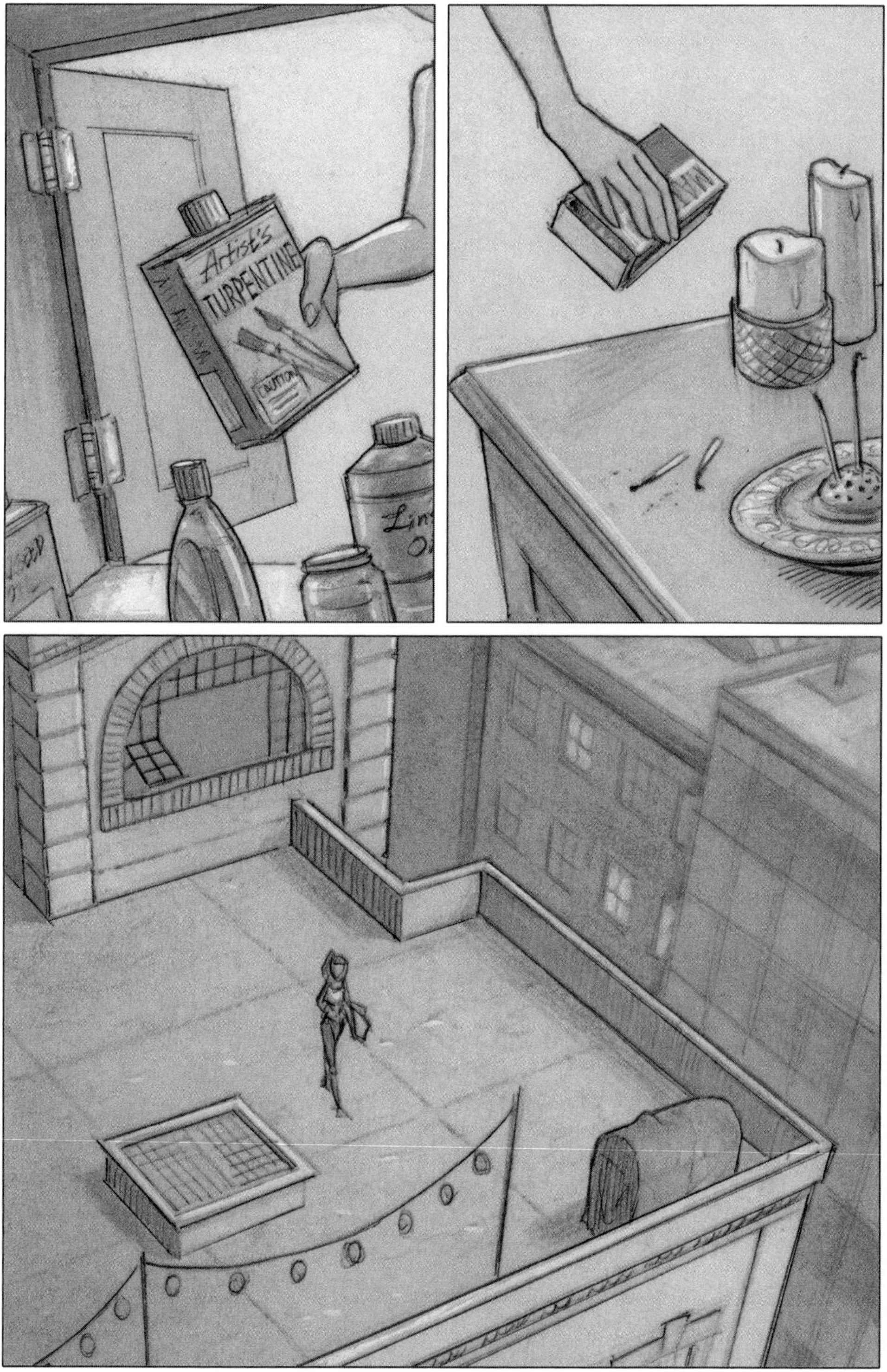
Artist's
TURPENTINE
CAUTION

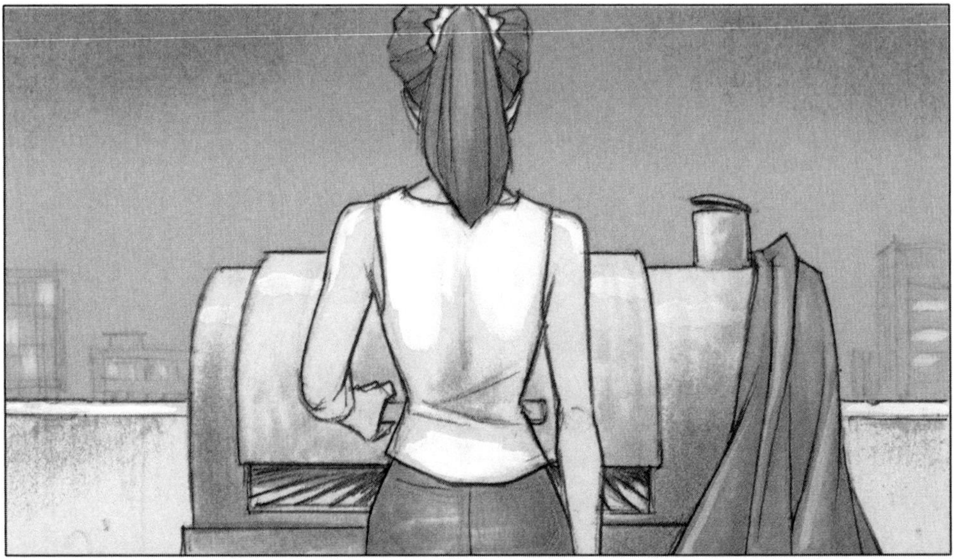

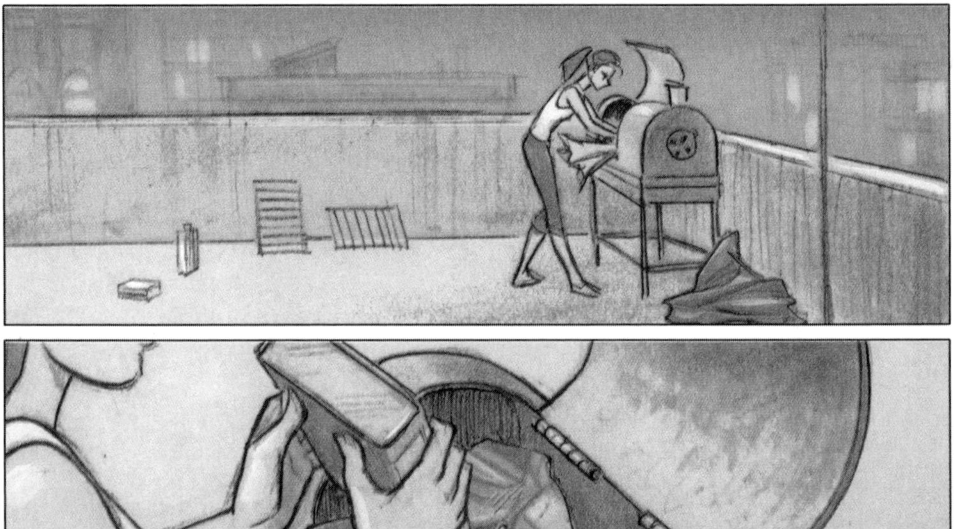

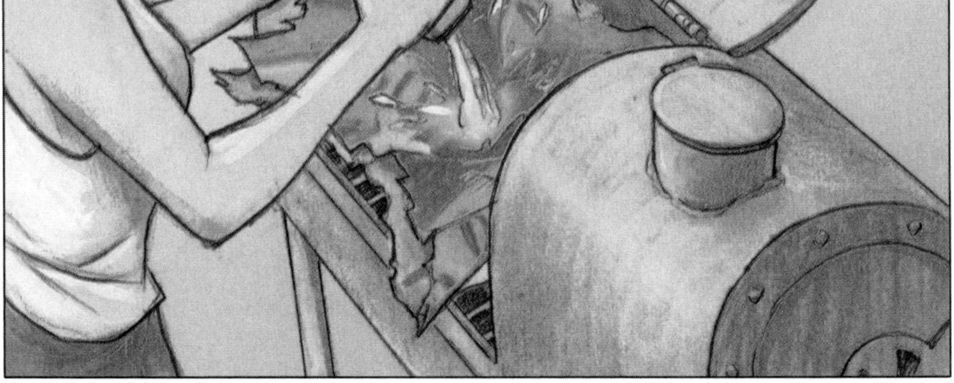

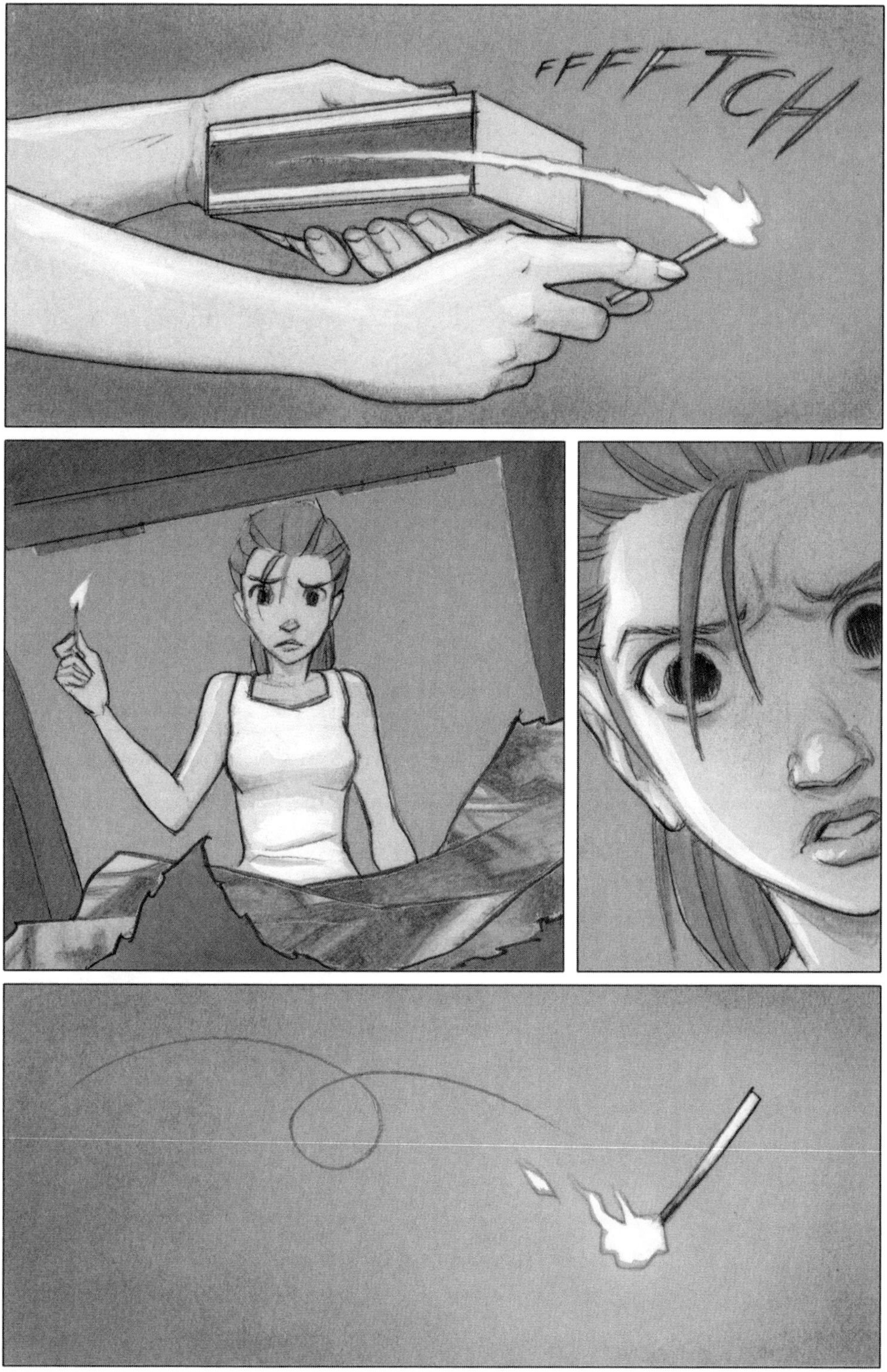
FFFFTCH

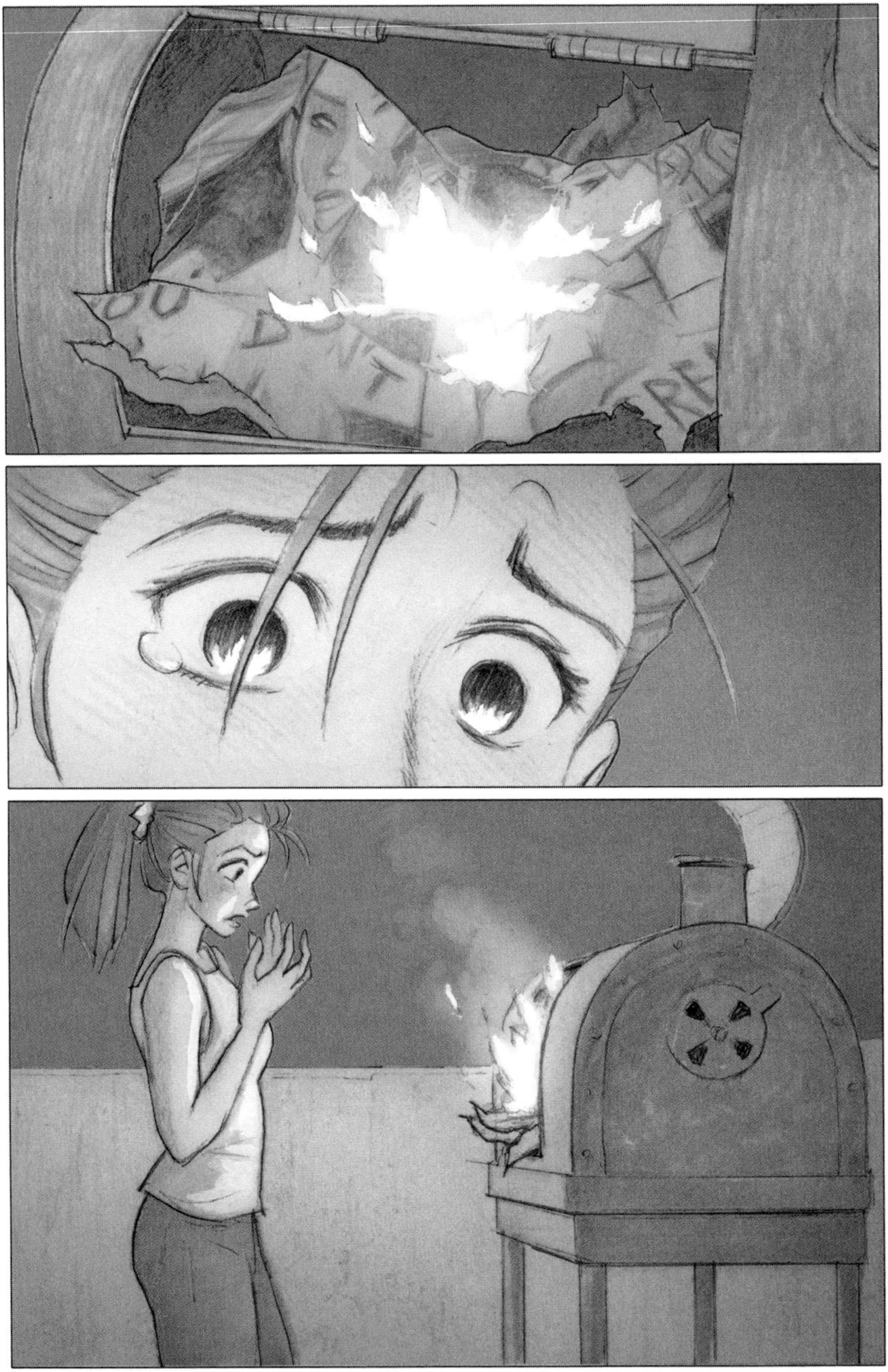

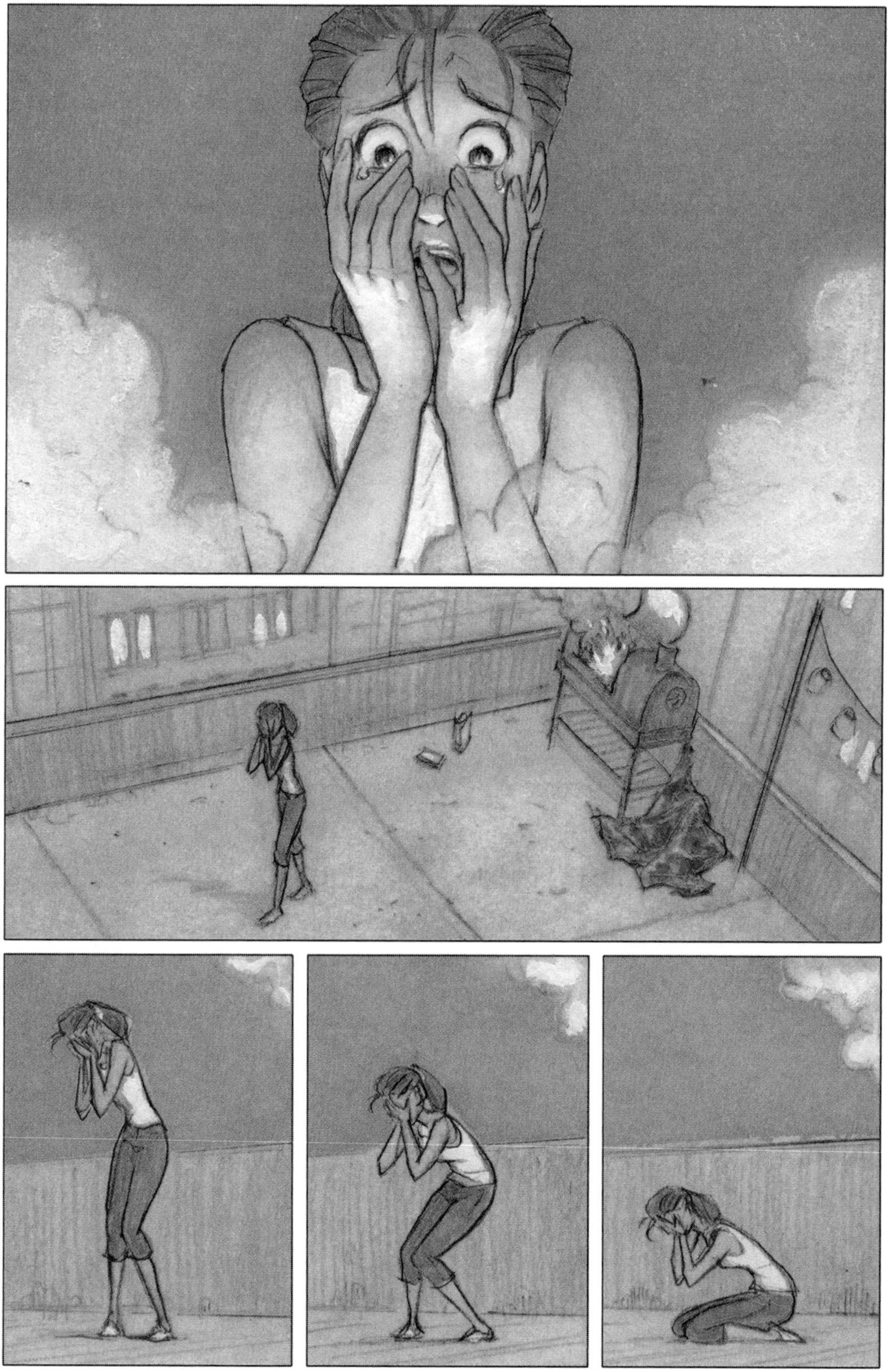

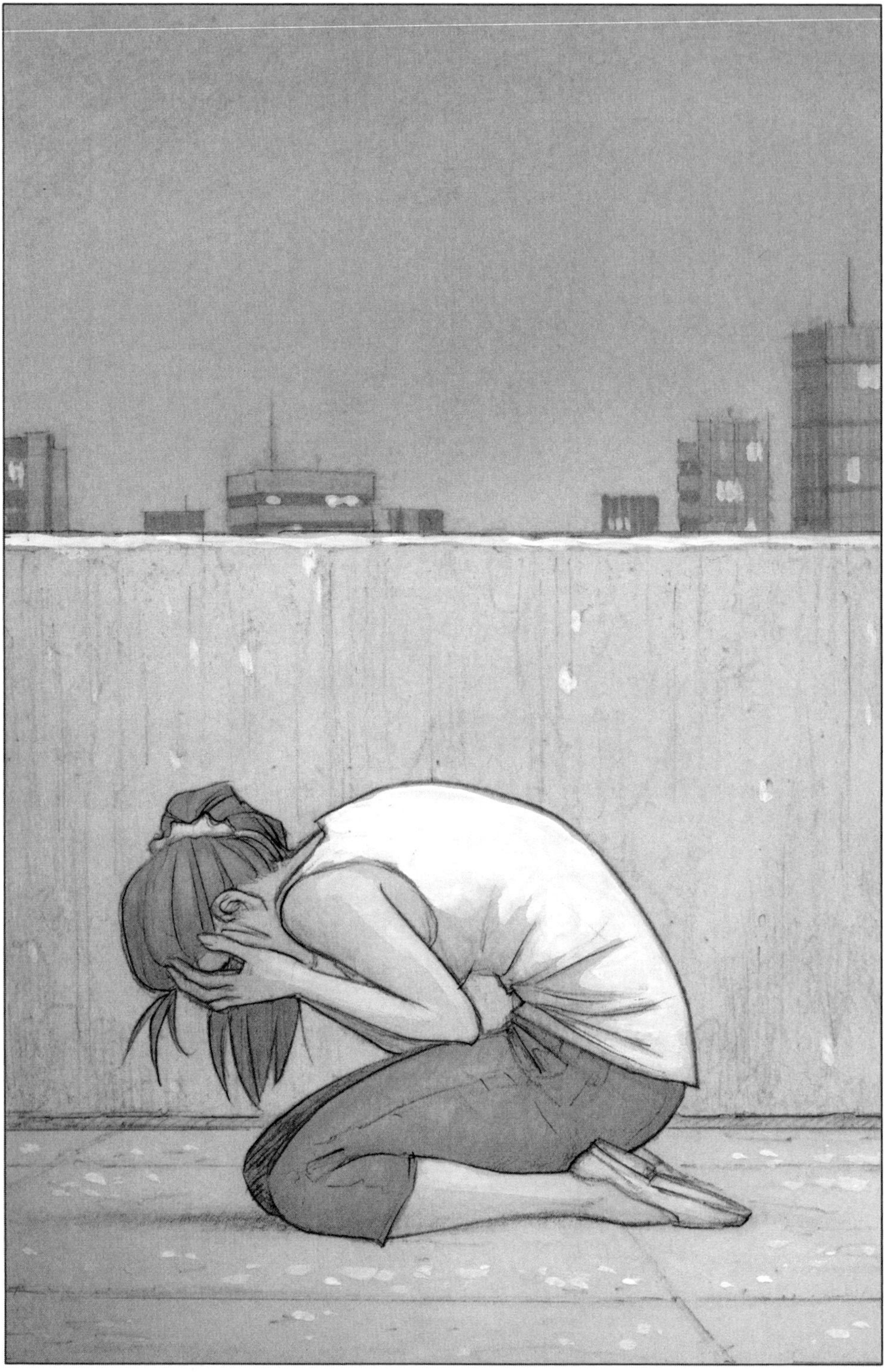

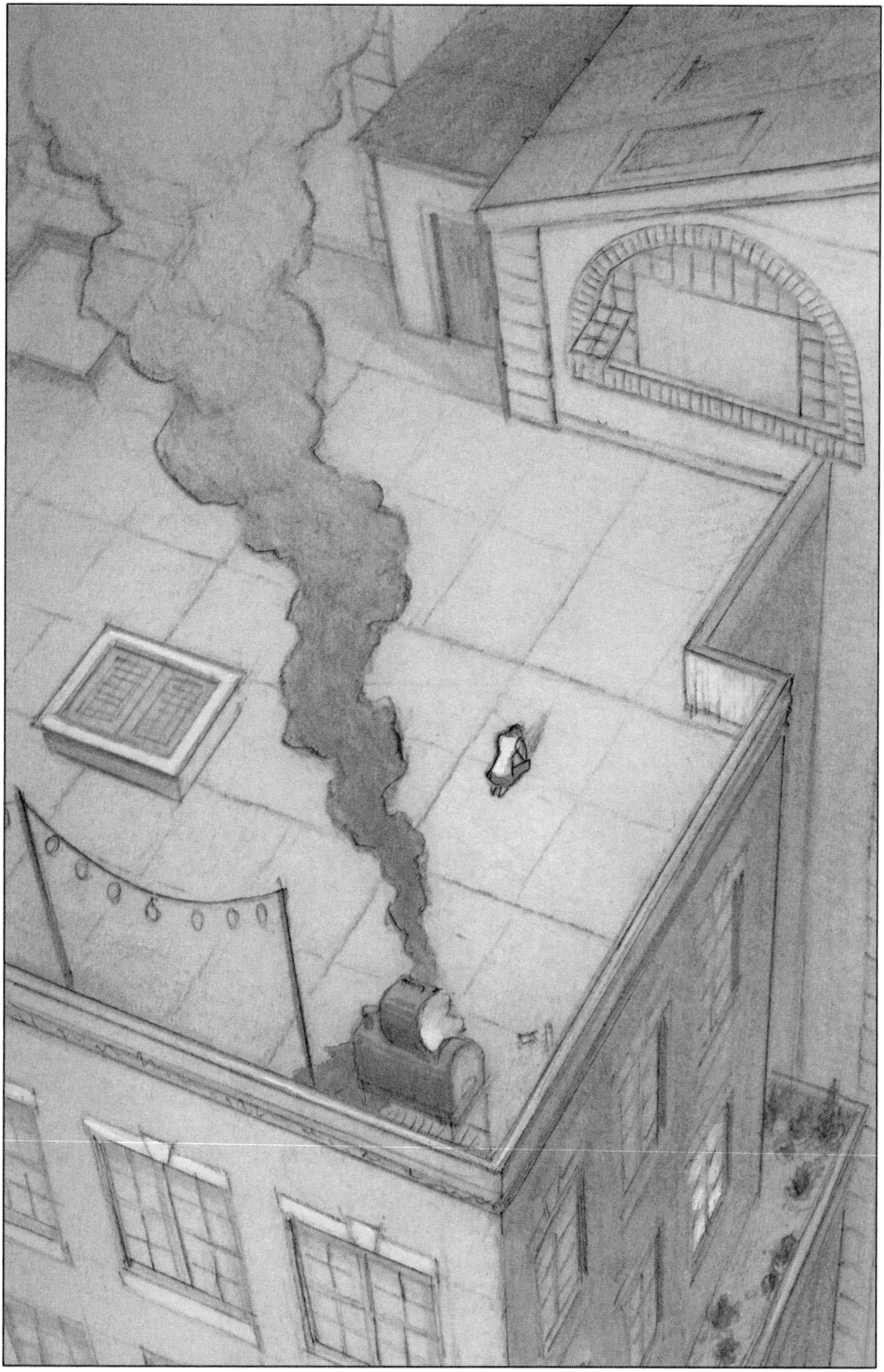

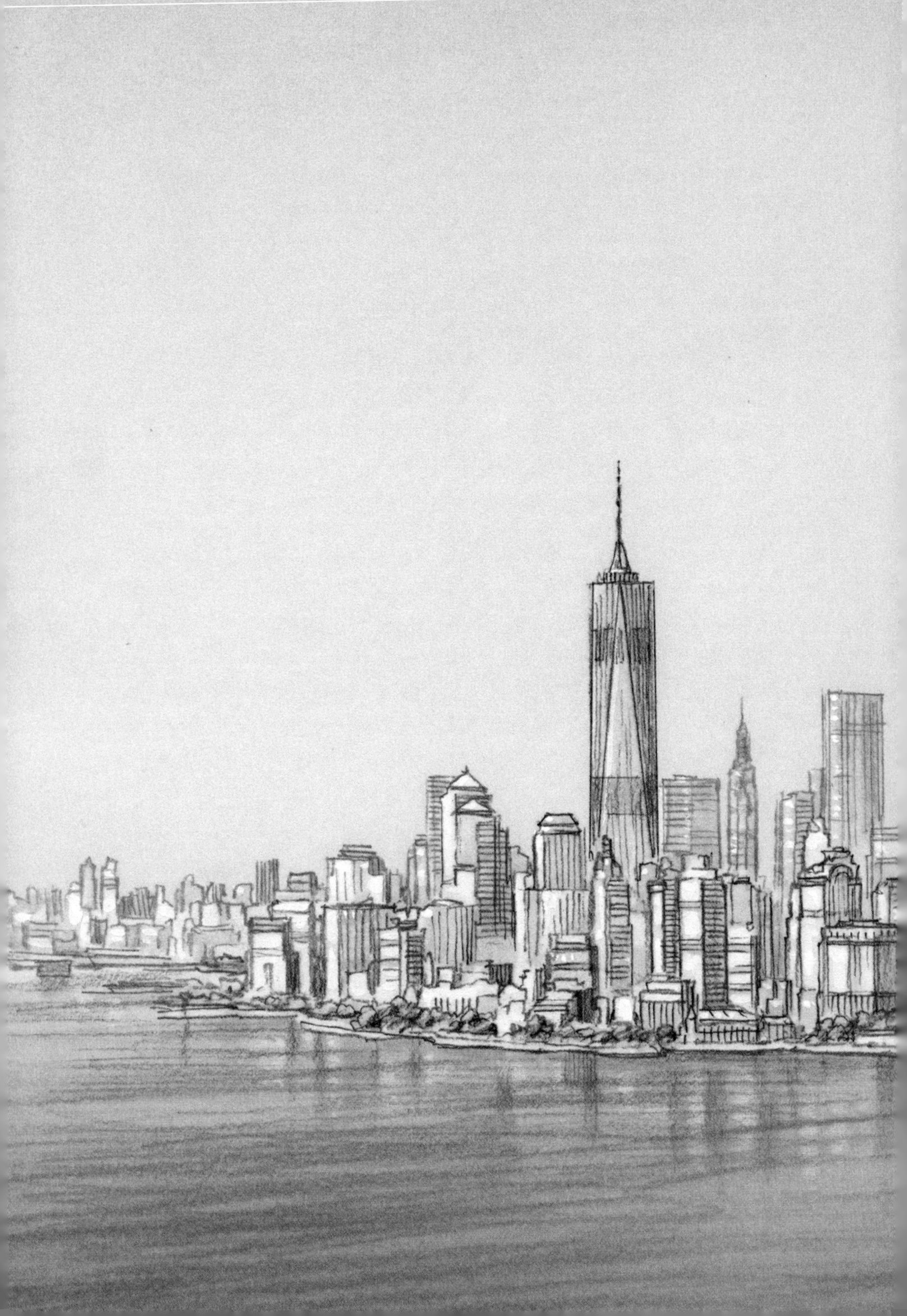

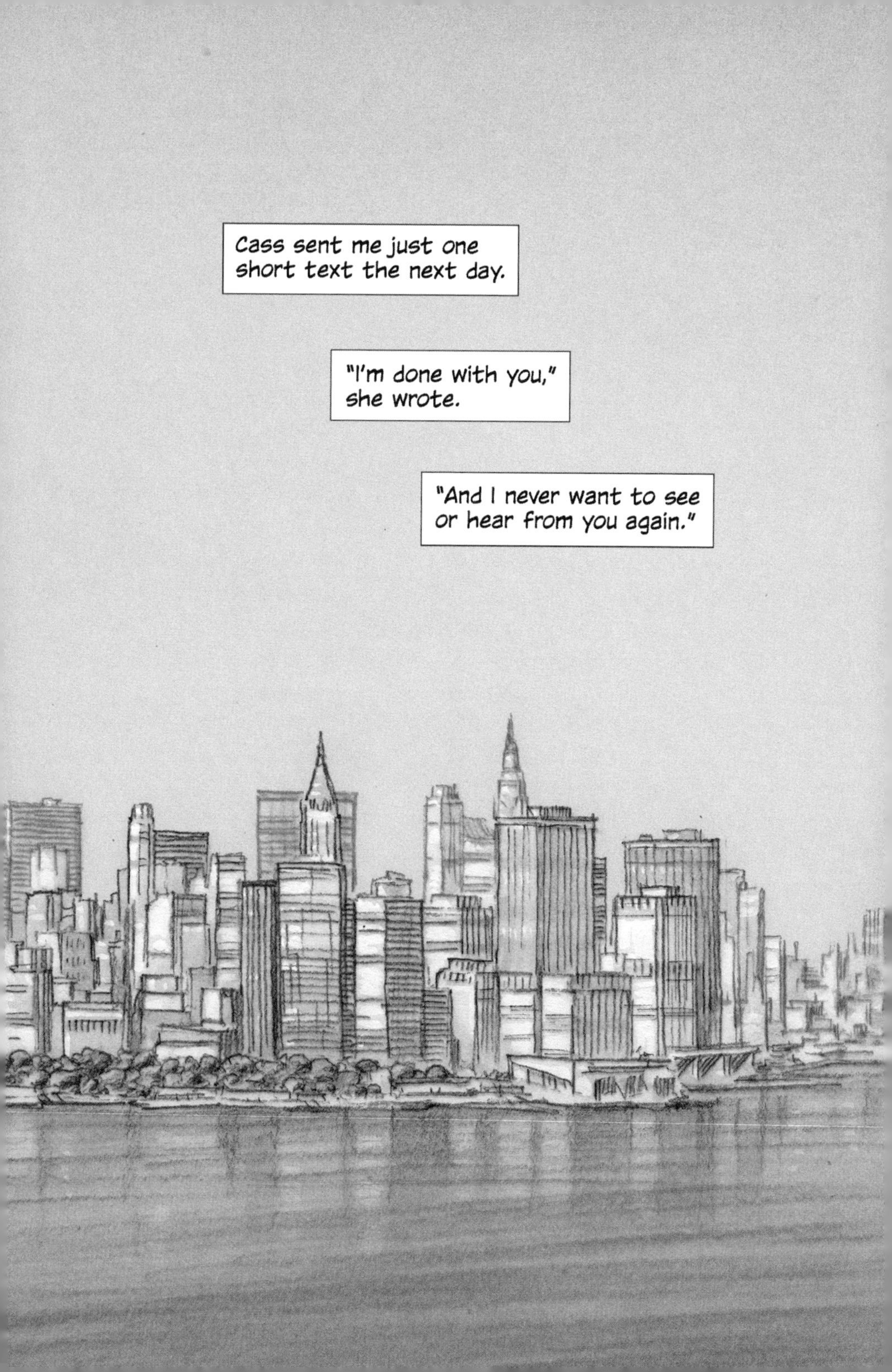
Cass sent me just one short text the next day.
"I'm done with you," she wrote.
"And I never want to see or hear from you again."

Part Three

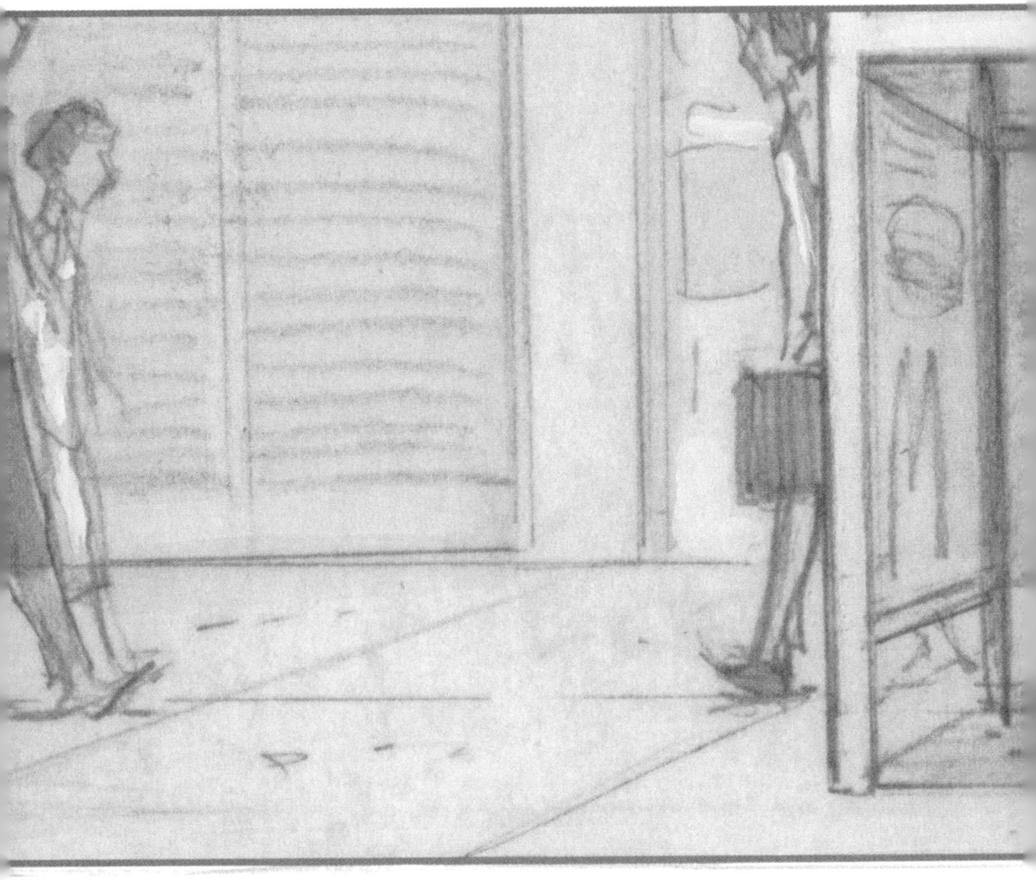

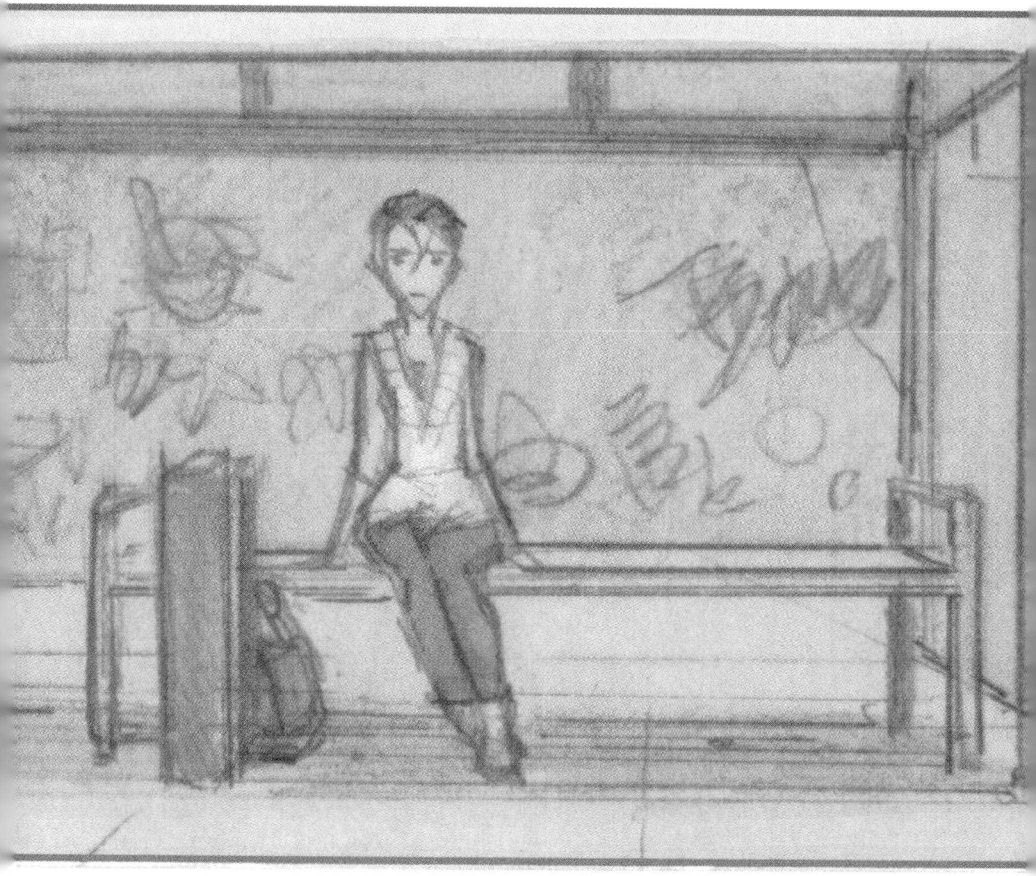

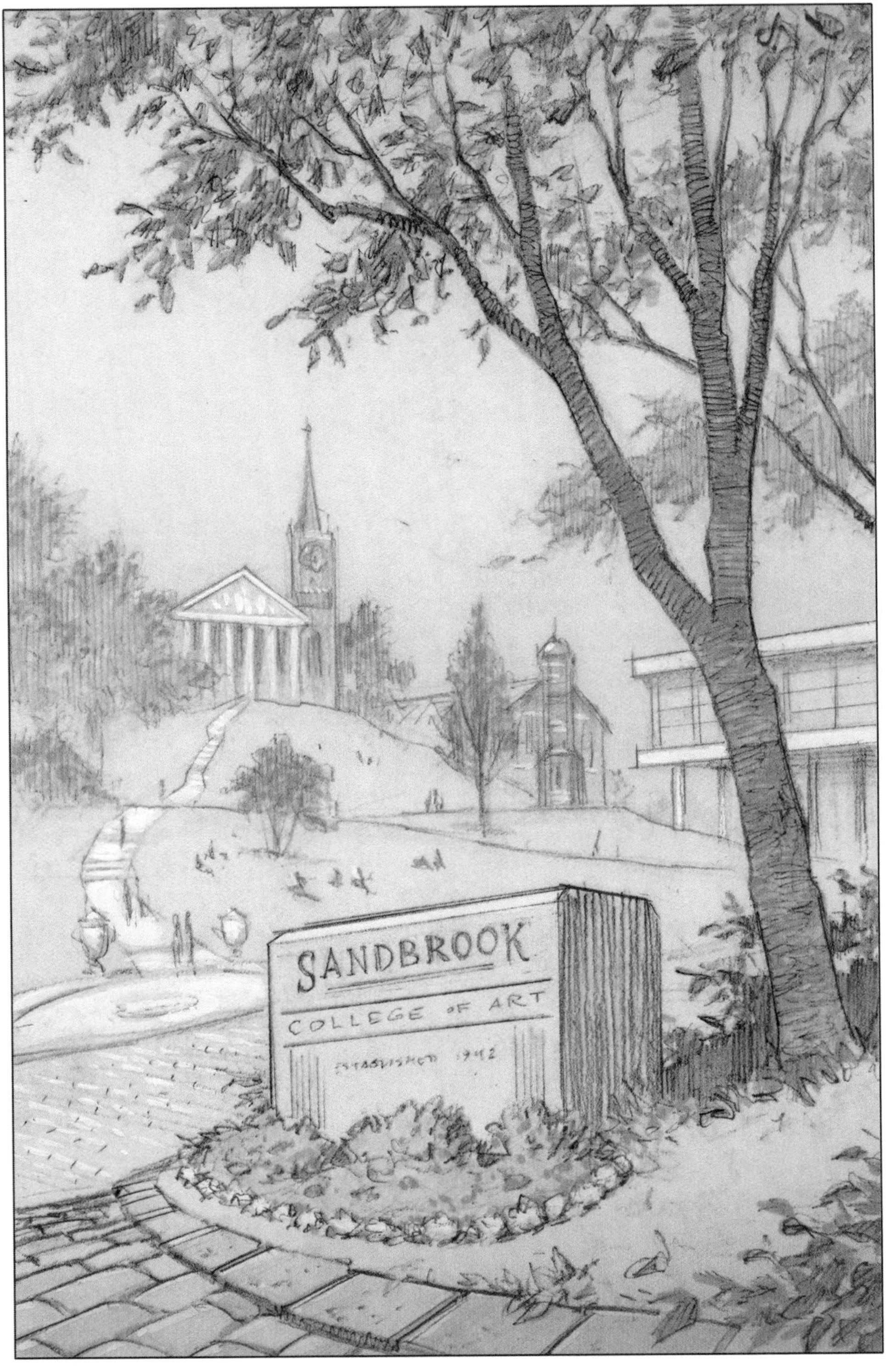
SANDBROOK
COLLEGE OF ART

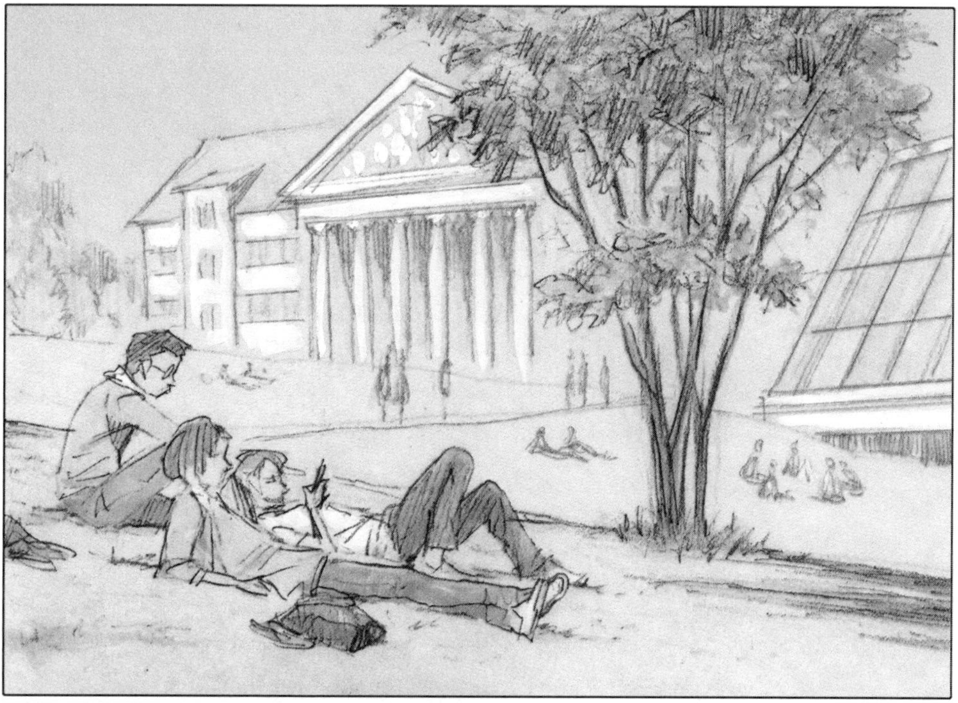

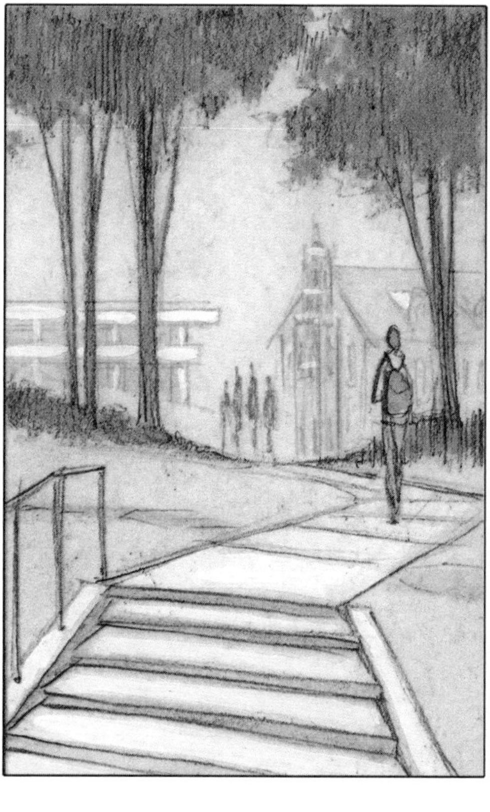

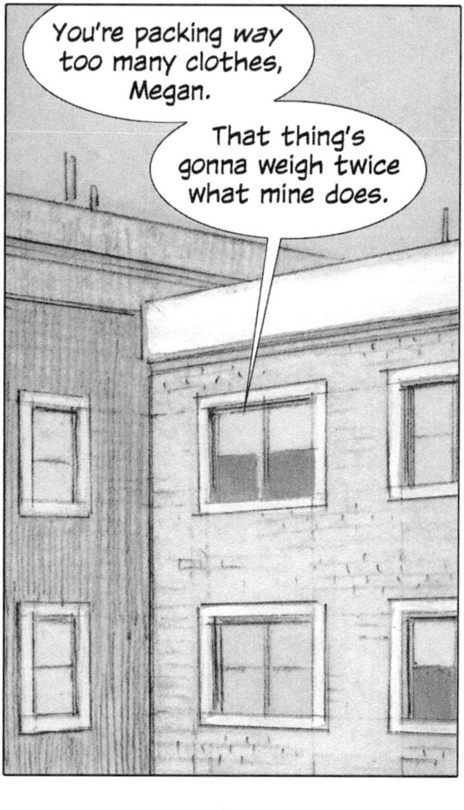
You're packing way too many clothes, Megan.
That thing's gonna weigh twice what mine does.

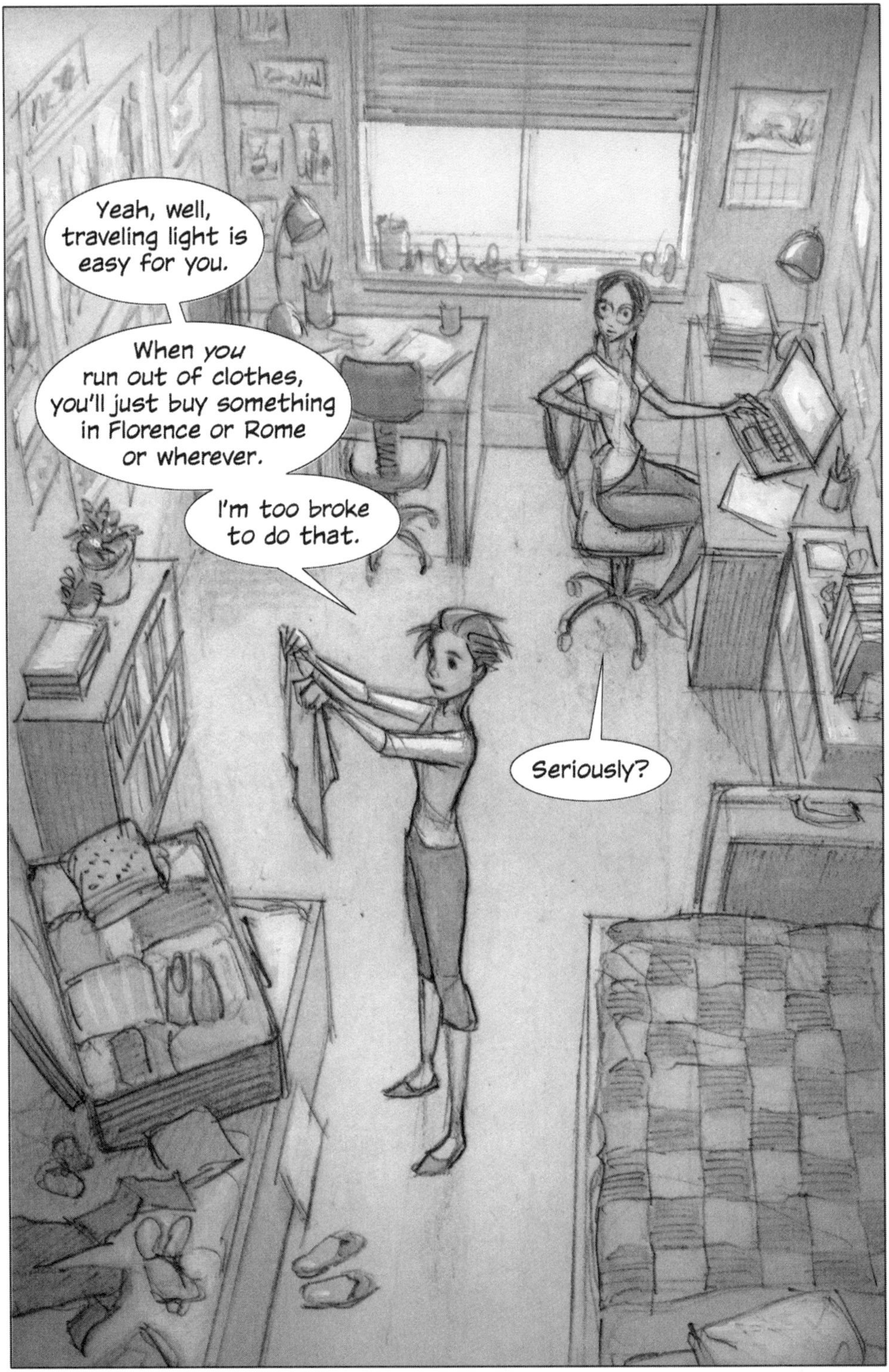
Yeah, well, traveling light is easy for you.
When *you* run out of clothes, you'll just buy something in Florence or Rome or wherever.
I'm too broke to do that.
Seriously?

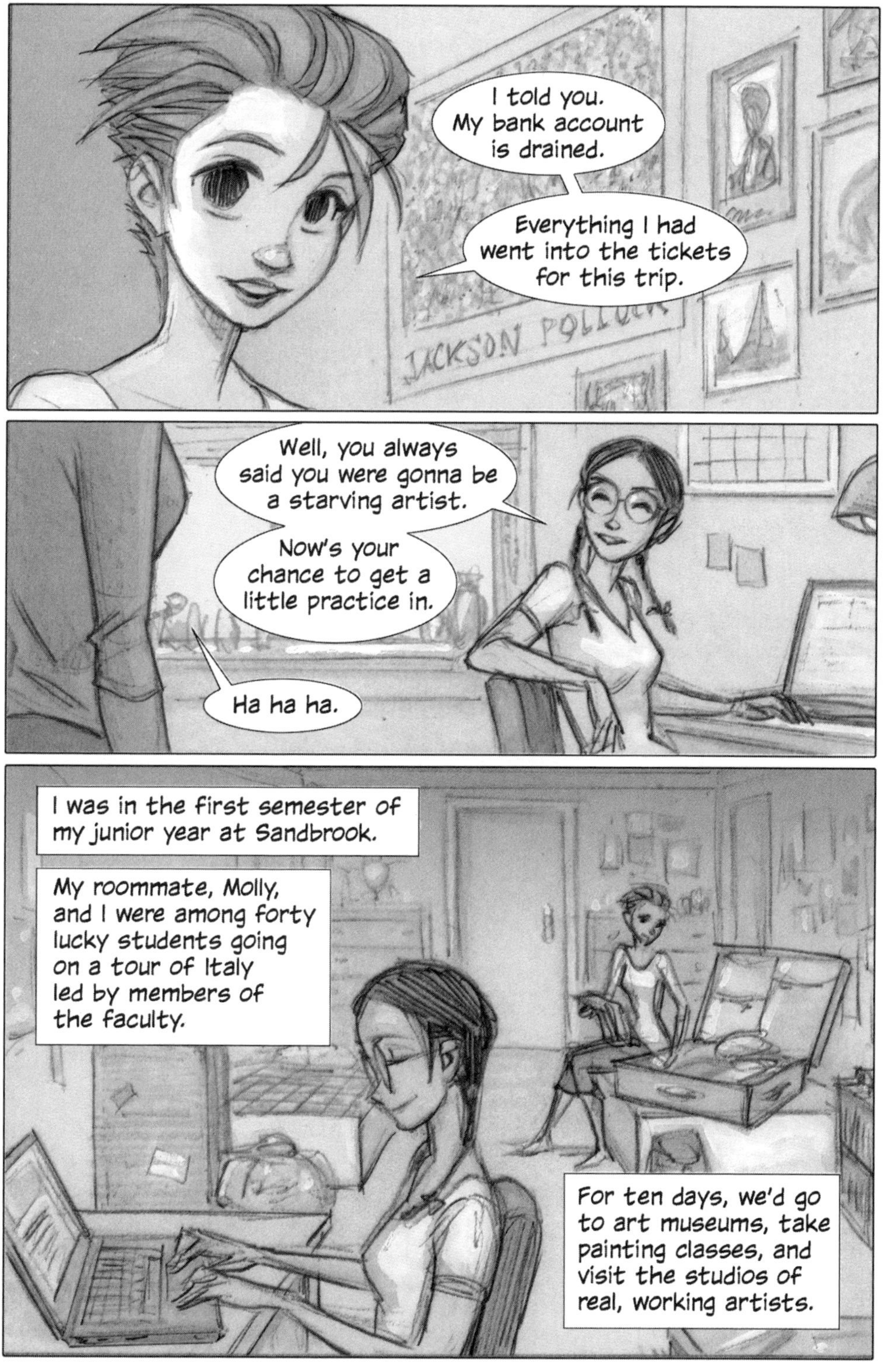
I told you. My bank account is drained.
Everything I had went into the tickets for this trip.
Well, you always said you were gonna be a starving artist.
Now's your chance to get a little practice in.
Ha ha ha.
I was in the first semester of my junior year at Sandbrook.
My roommate, Molly, and I were among forty lucky students going on a tour of Italy led by members of the faculty.
For ten days, we'd go to art museums, take painting classes, and visit the studios of real, working artists.

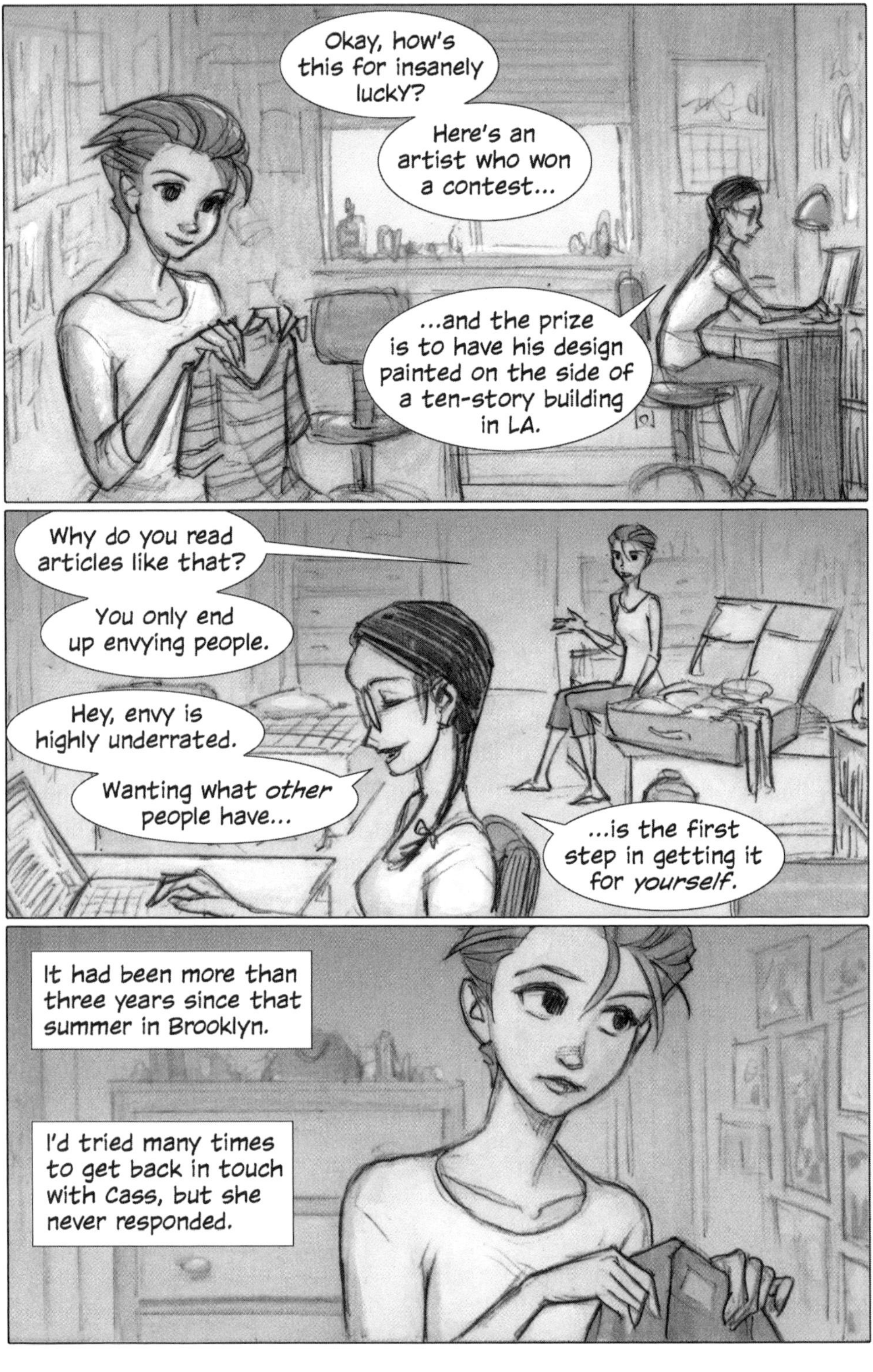
Okay, how's this for insanely lucky?
Here's an artist who won a contest...
...and the prize is to have his design painted on the side of a ten-story building in LA.
Why do you read articles like that?
You only end up envying people.
Hey, envy is highly underrated.
Wanting what *other* people have...
...is the first step in getting it for *yourself*.
It had been more than three years since that summer in Brooklyn.
I'd tried many times to get back in touch with Cass, but she never responded.

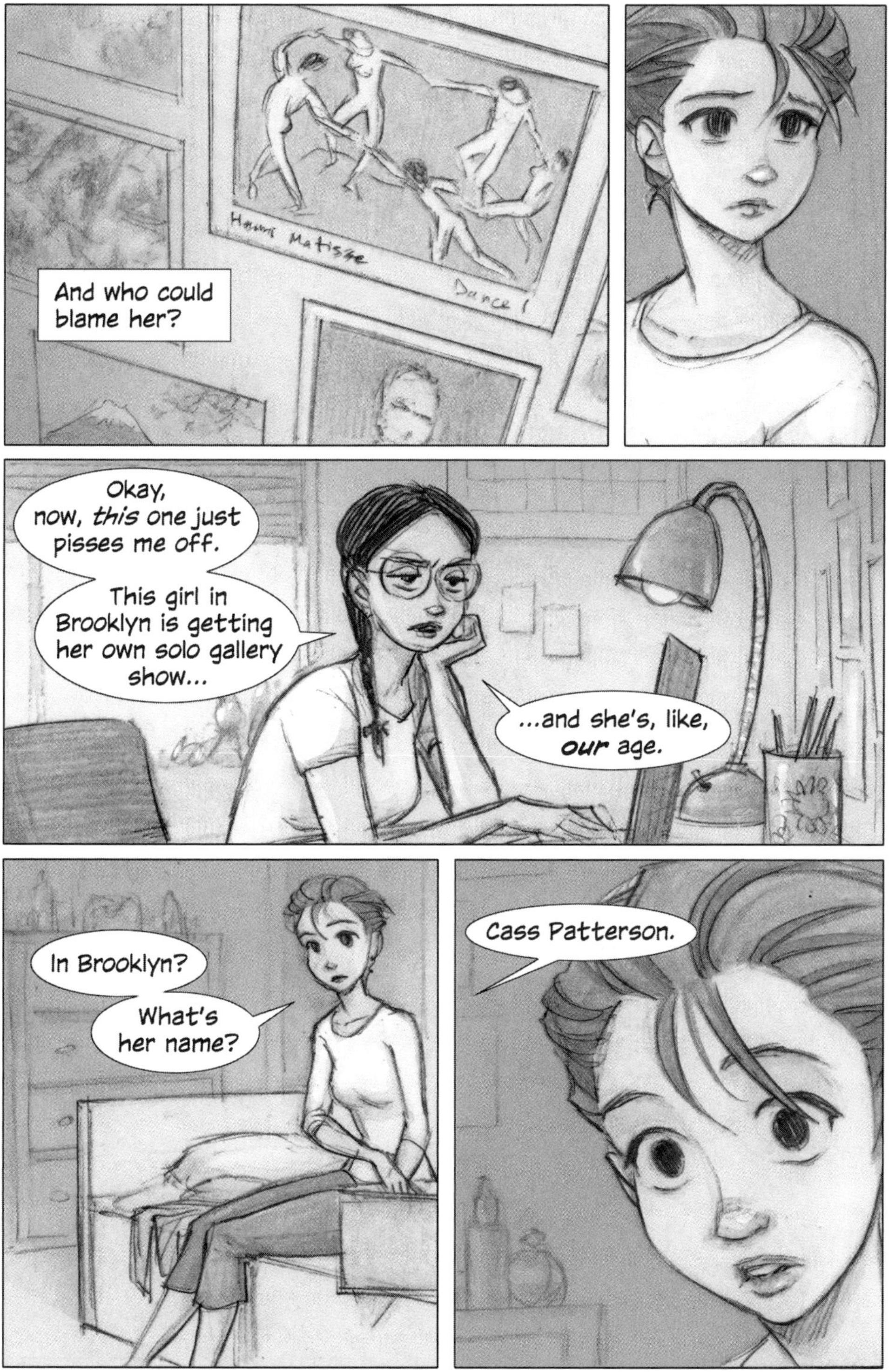
Henri Matisse
Dance I
And who could blame her?
Okay, now, *this* one just pisses me off.
This girl in Brooklyn is getting her own solo gallery show...
...and she's, like, ***our*** age.
In Brooklyn?
What's her name?
Cass Patterson.

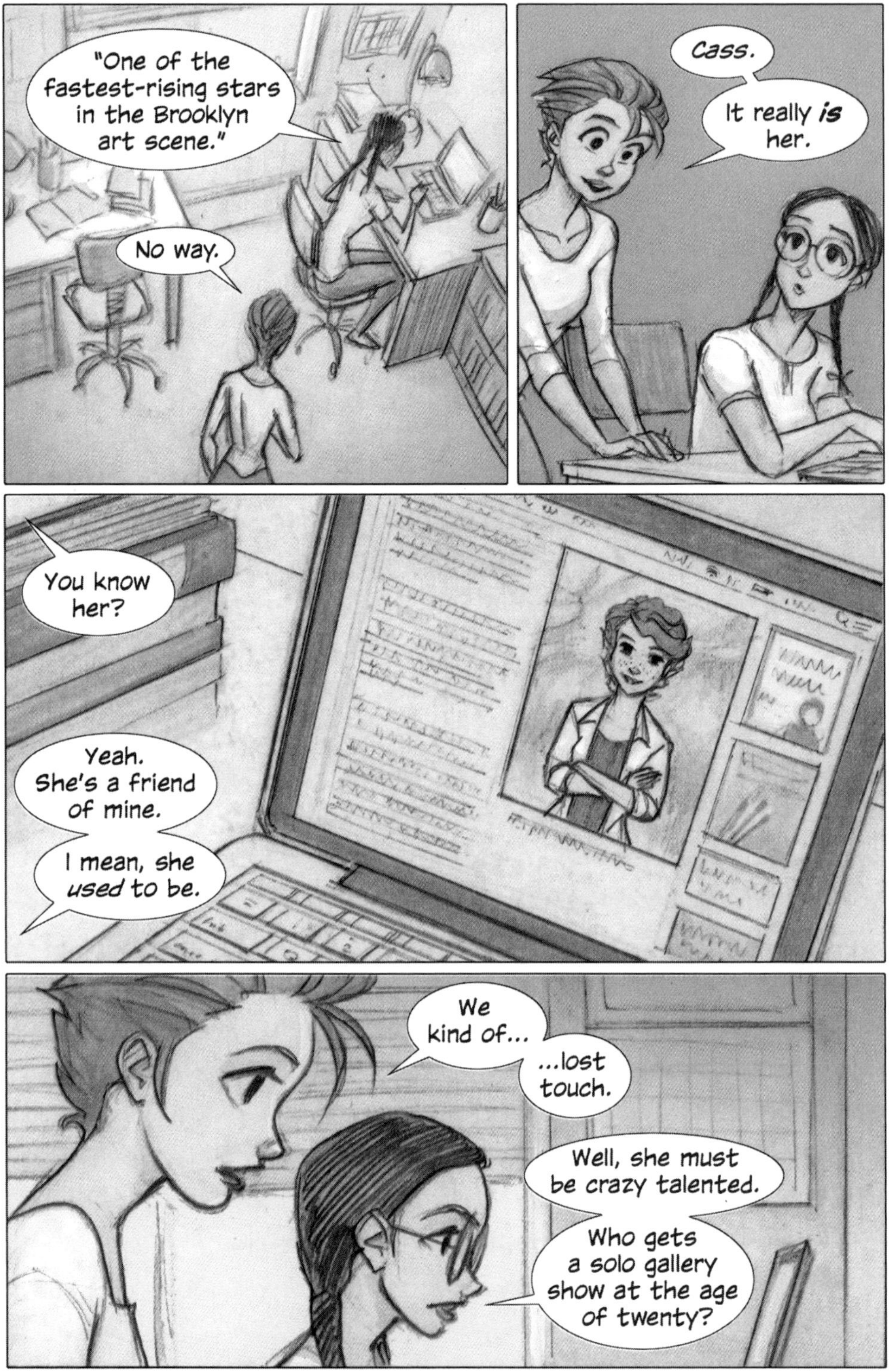
"One of the fastest-rising stars in the Brooklyn art scene."
No way.
Cass.
It really *is* her.
You know her?
Yeah. She's a friend of mine.
I mean, she *used* to be.
We kind of...
...lost touch.
Well, she must be crazy talented.
Who gets a solo gallery show at the age of twenty?

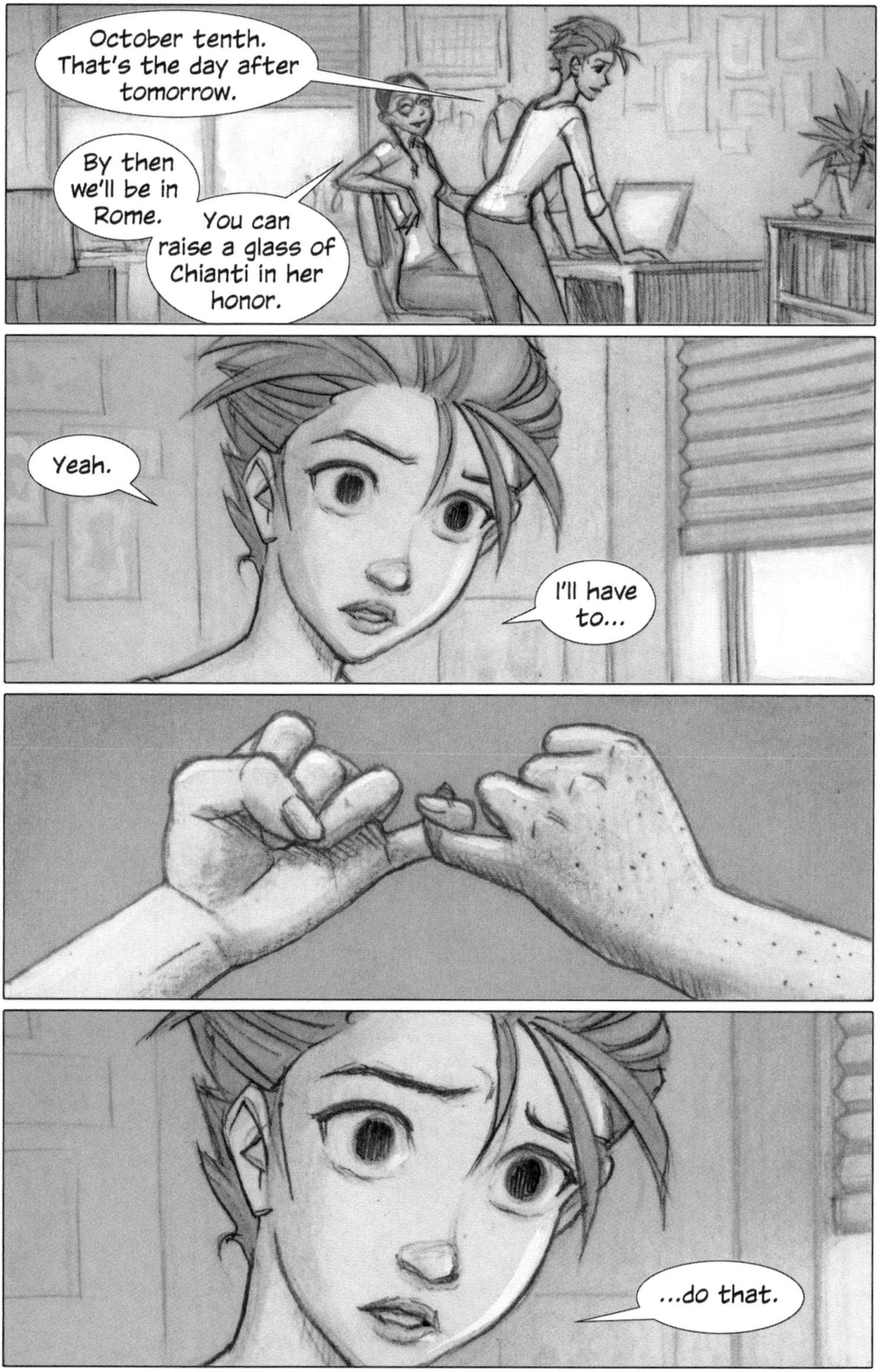
October tenth. That's the day after tomorrow.
By then we'll be in Rome.
You can raise a glass of Chianti in her honor.
Yeah.
I'll have to...
...do that.

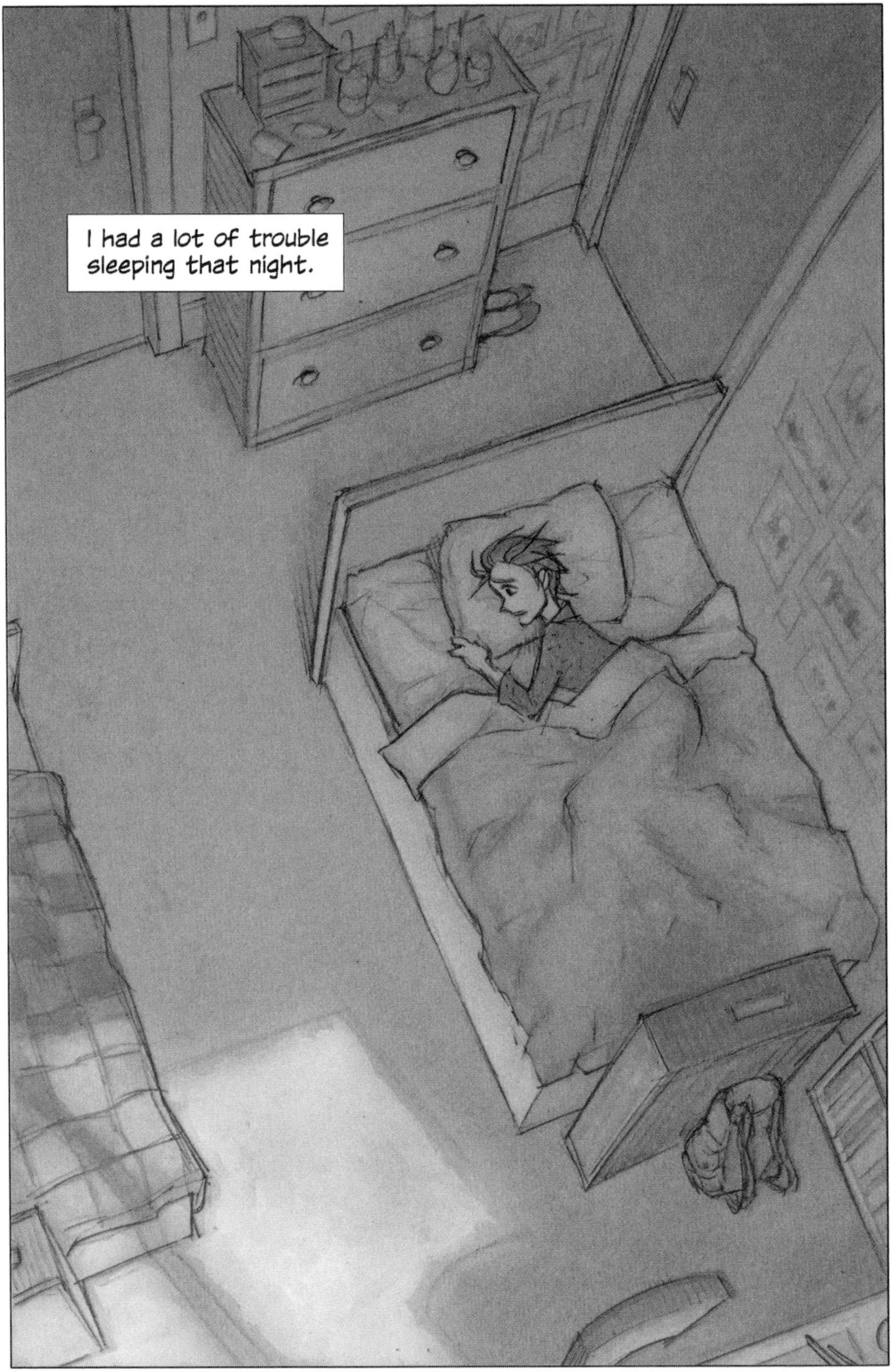
I had a lot of trouble sleeping that night.

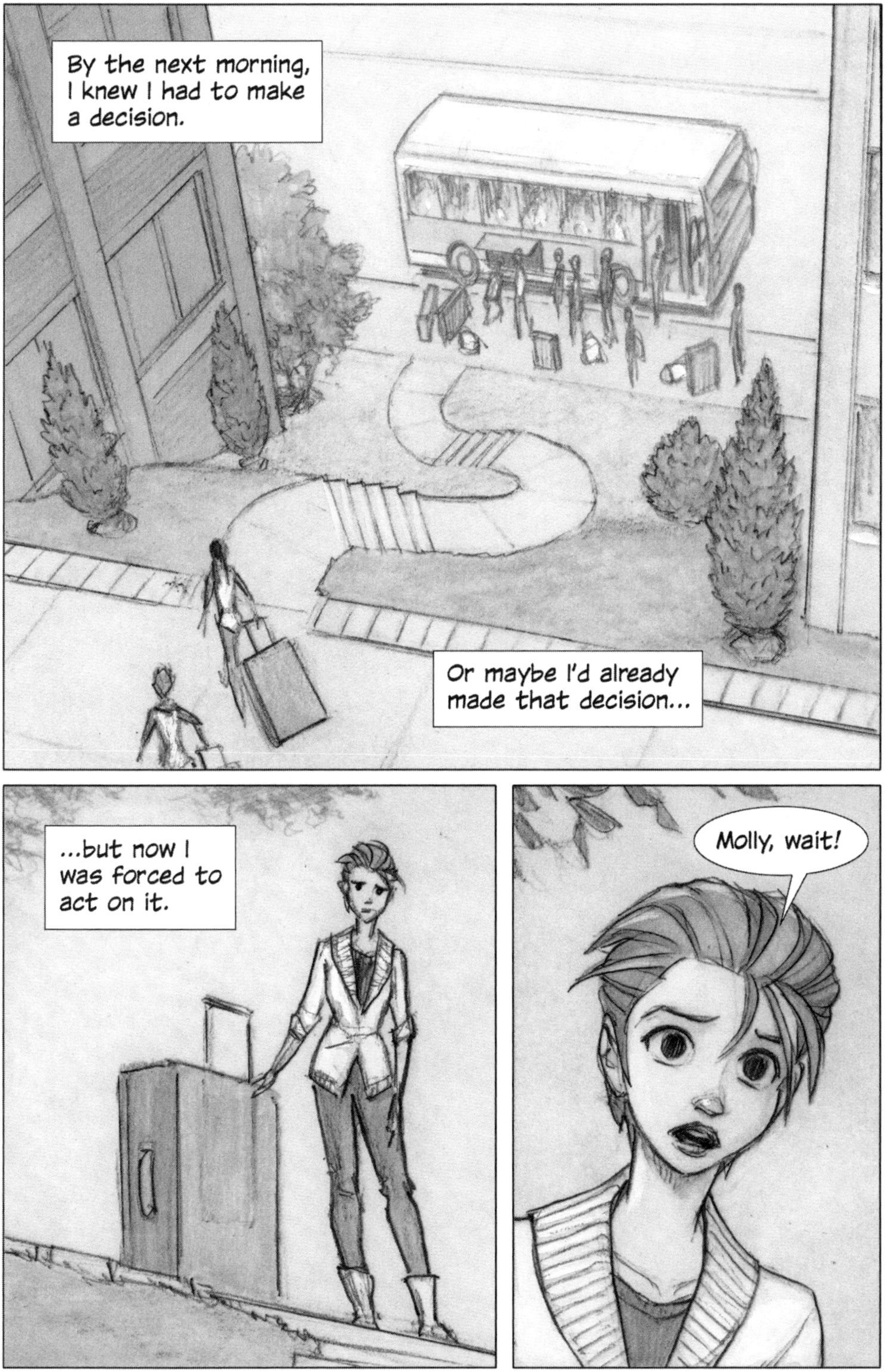
By the next morning, I knew I had to make a decision.
Or maybe I'd already made that decision...
...but now I was forced to act on it.
Molly, wait!

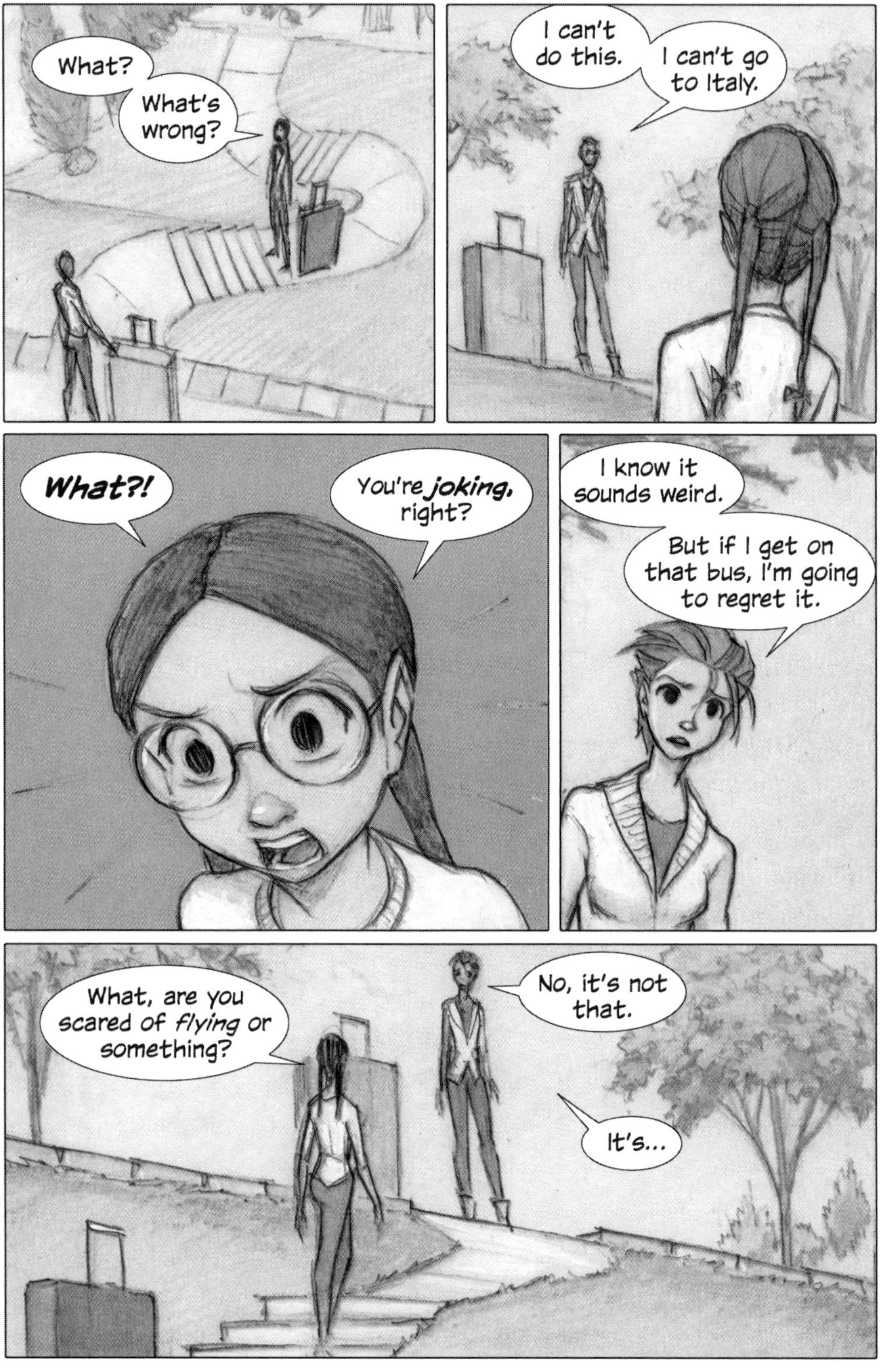
What?
What's wrong?
I can't do this.
I can't go to Italy.
What?!
You're *joking,* right?
I know it sounds weird.
But if I get on that bus, I'm going to regret it.
What, are you scared of *flying* or something?
No, it's not that.
It's...

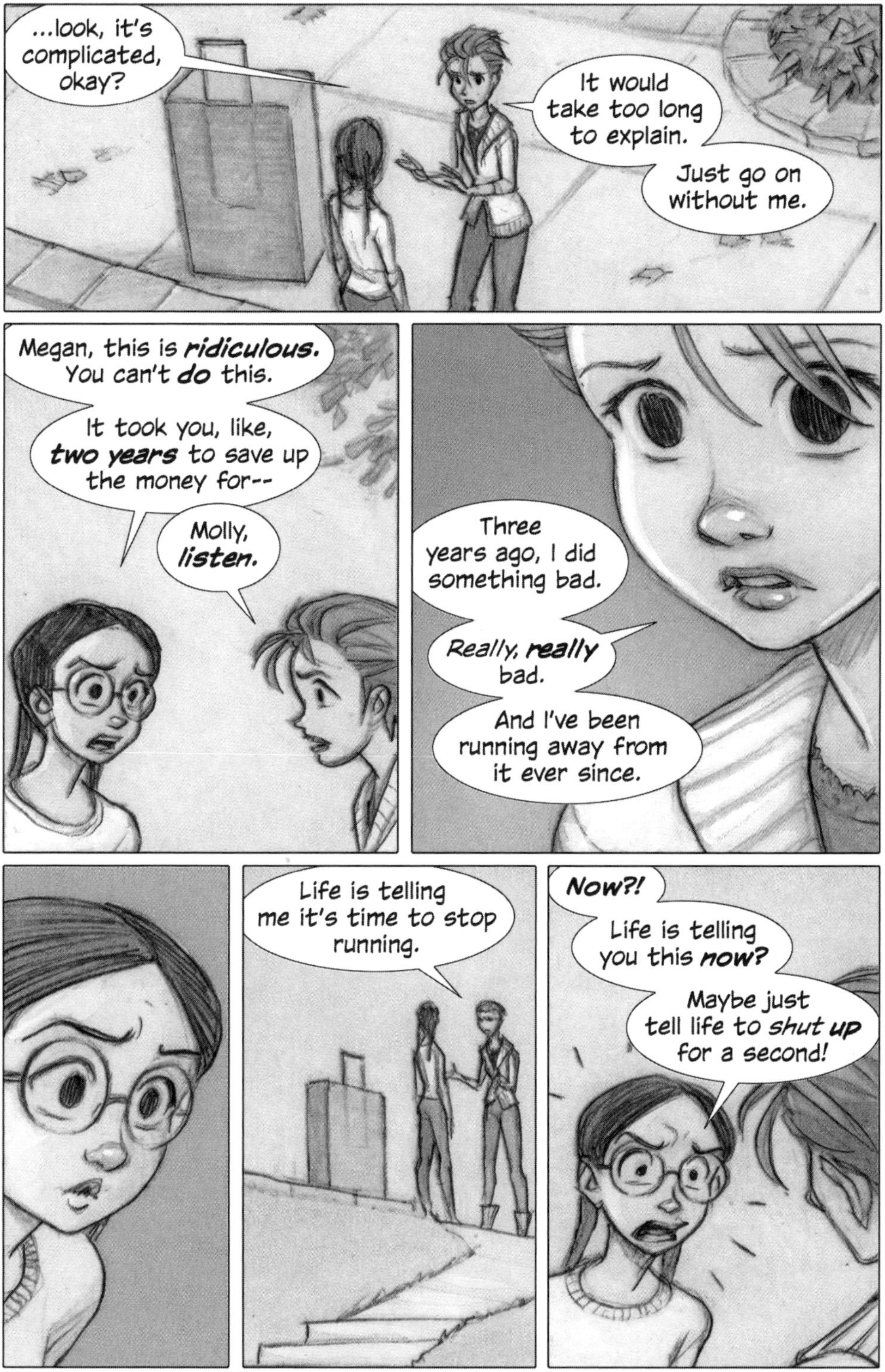
...look, it's complicated, okay?
It would take too long to explain.
Just go on without me.
Megan, this is ***ridiculous.*** You can't ***do*** this.
It took you, like, ***two years*** to save up the money for--
Molly, ***listen.***
Three years ago, I did something bad.
Really, ***really*** bad.
And I've been running away from it ever since.
Life is telling me it's time to stop running.
Now?!
Life is telling you this ***now?***
Maybe just tell life to ***shut up*** for a second!

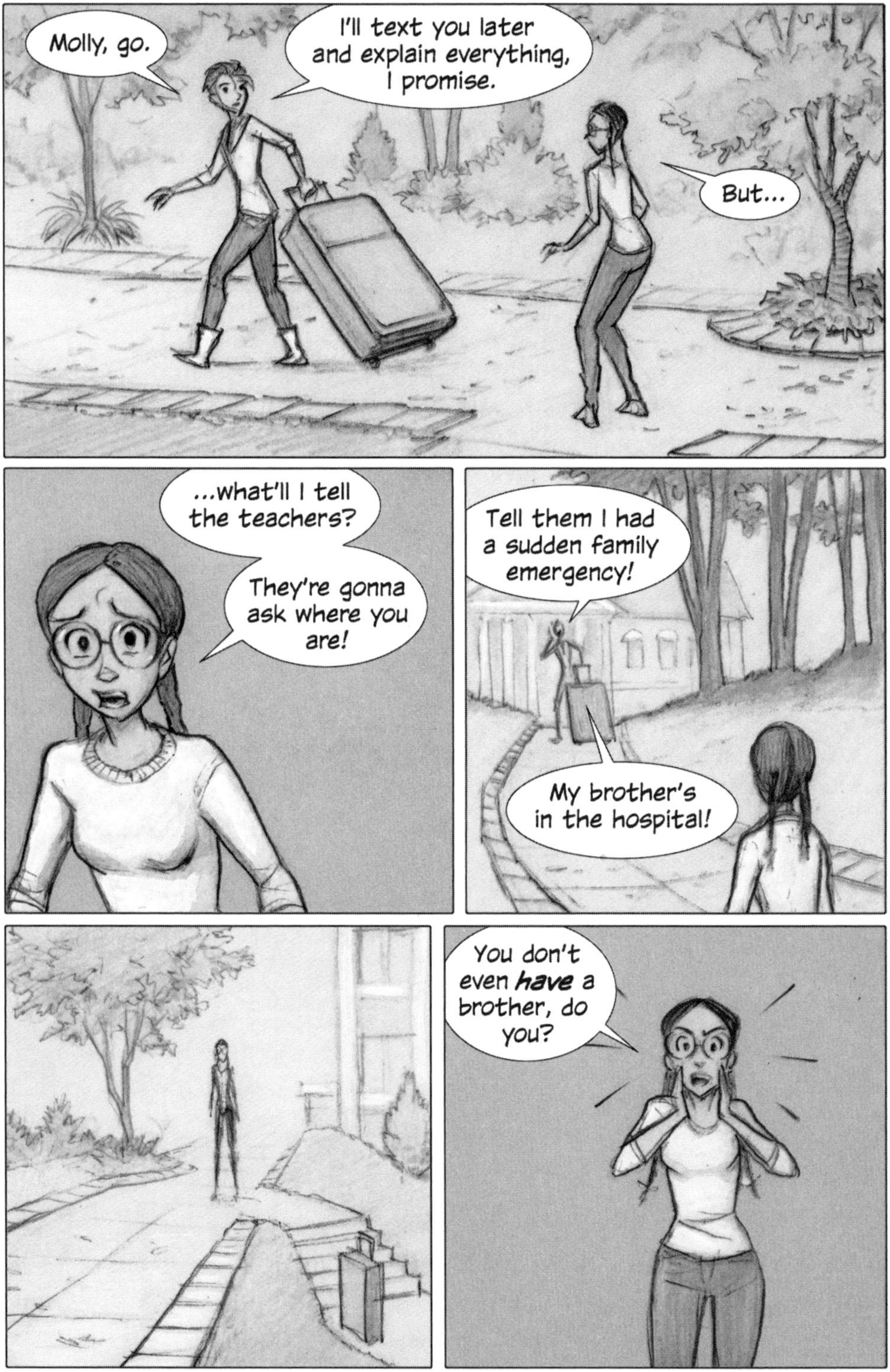
Molly, go.
I'll text you later and explain everything, I promise.
But...
...what'll I tell the teachers?
They're gonna ask where you are!
Tell them I had a sudden family emergency!
My brother's in the hospital!
You don't even *have* a brother, do you?

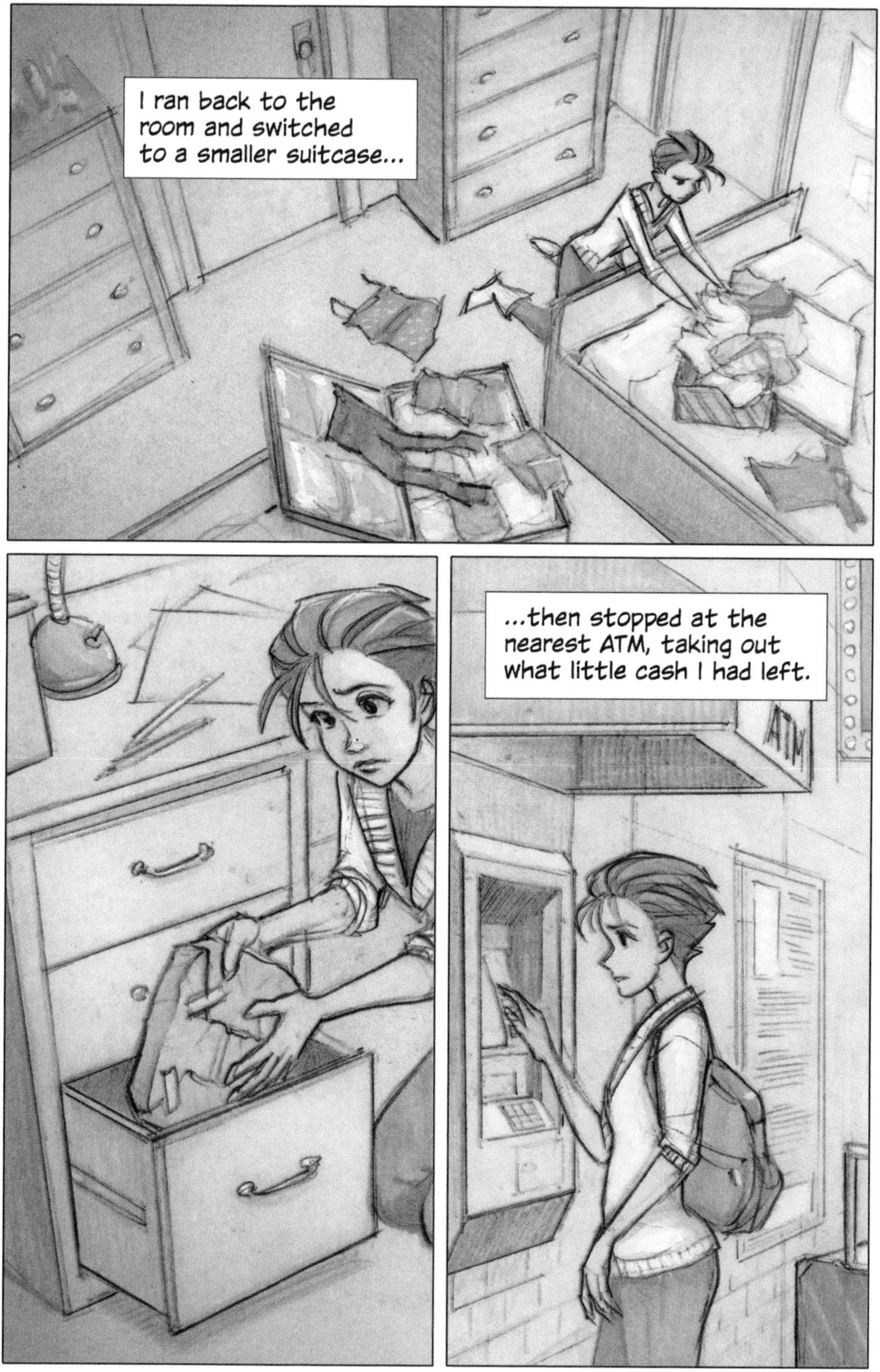
I ran back to the room and switched to a smaller suitcase...
...then stopped at the nearest ATM, taking out what little cash I had left.
ATM

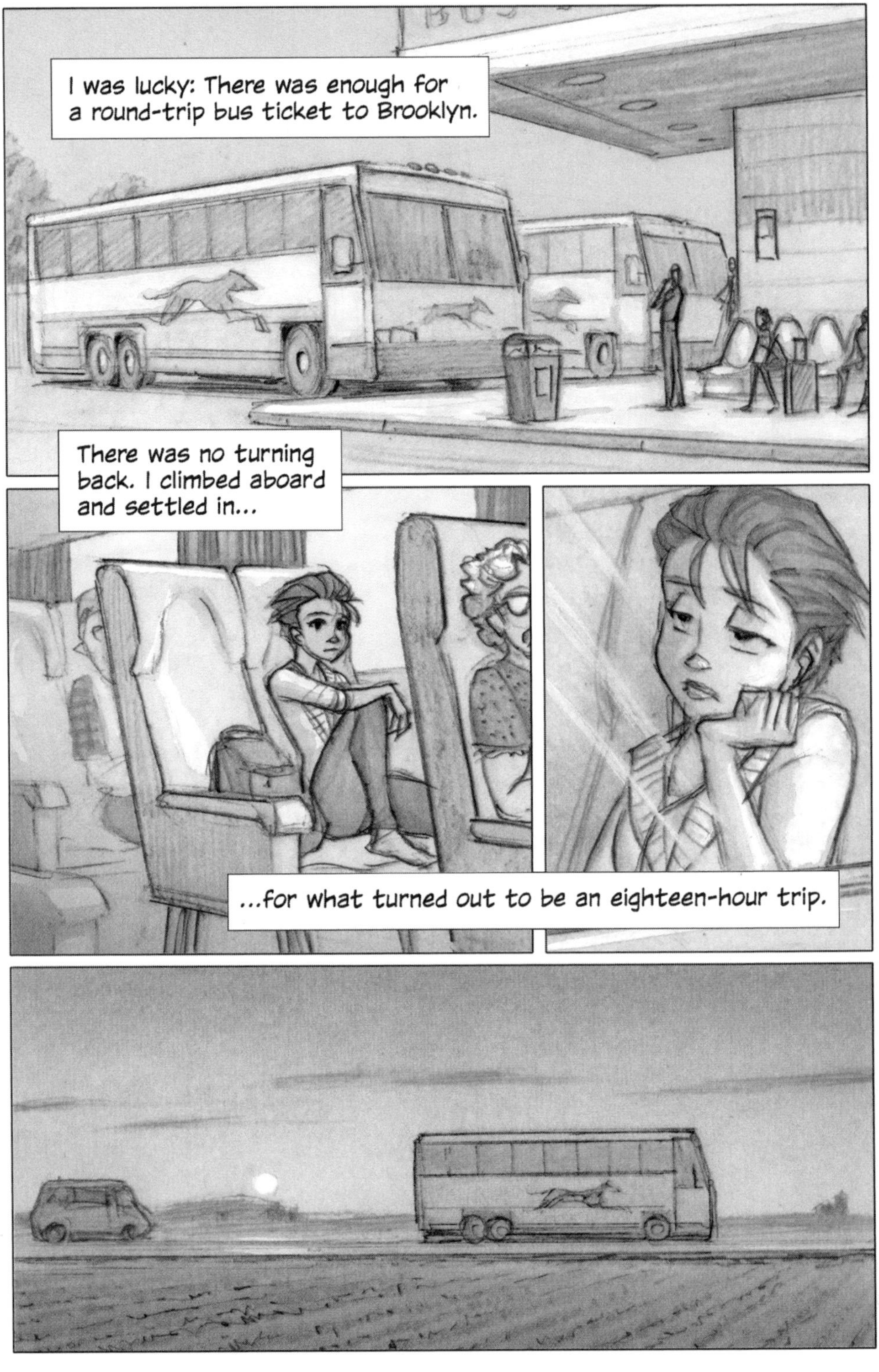
I was lucky: There was enough for a round-trip bus ticket to Brooklyn.
There was no turning back. I climbed aboard and settled in...
...for what turned out to be an eighteen-hour trip.

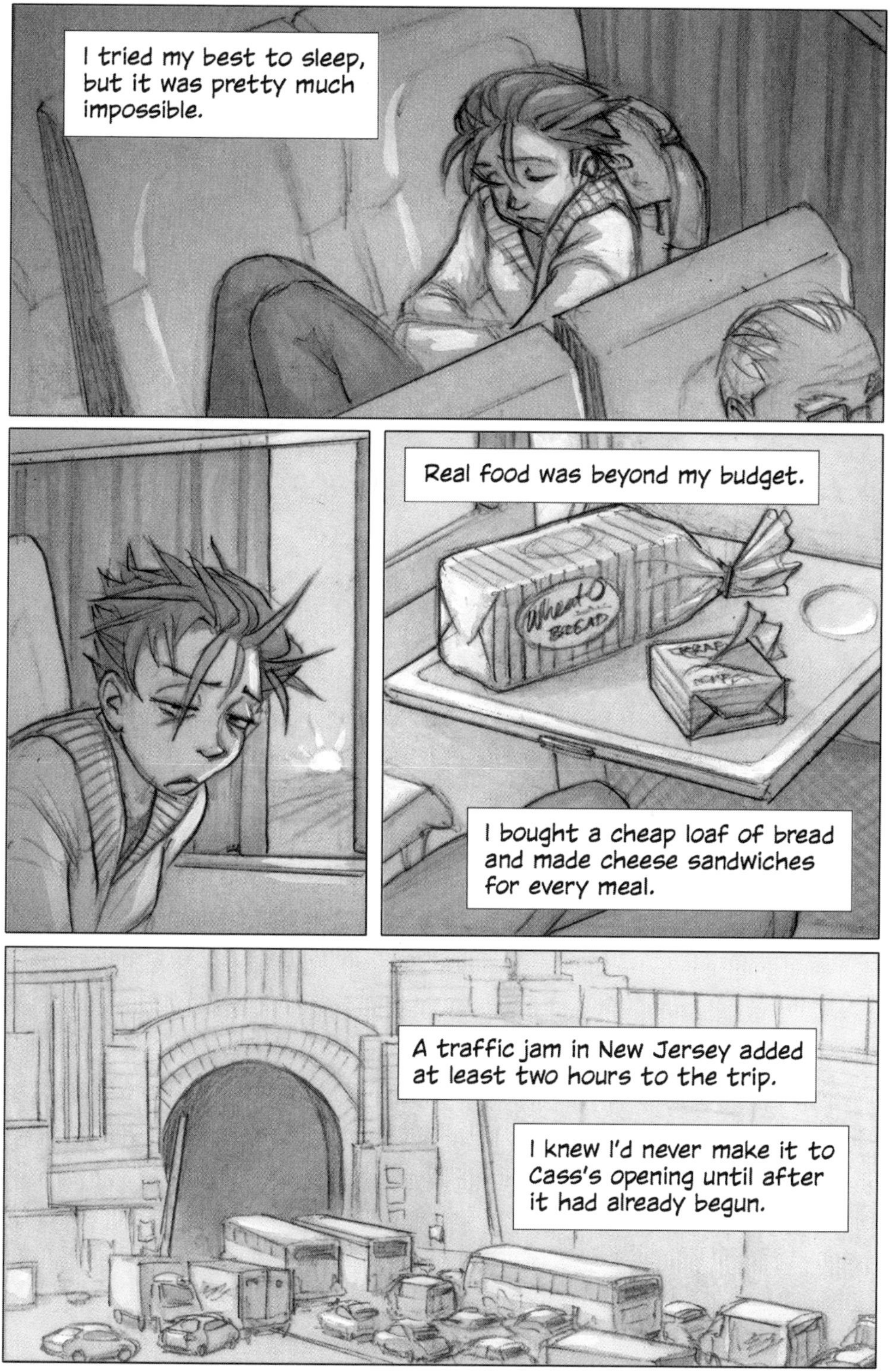
I tried my best to sleep, but it was pretty much impossible.
Real food was beyond my budget.
Wheat-O BREAD
I bought a cheap loaf of bread and made cheese sandwiches for every meal.
A traffic jam in New Jersey added at least two hours to the trip.
I knew I'd never make it to Cass's opening until after it had already begun.

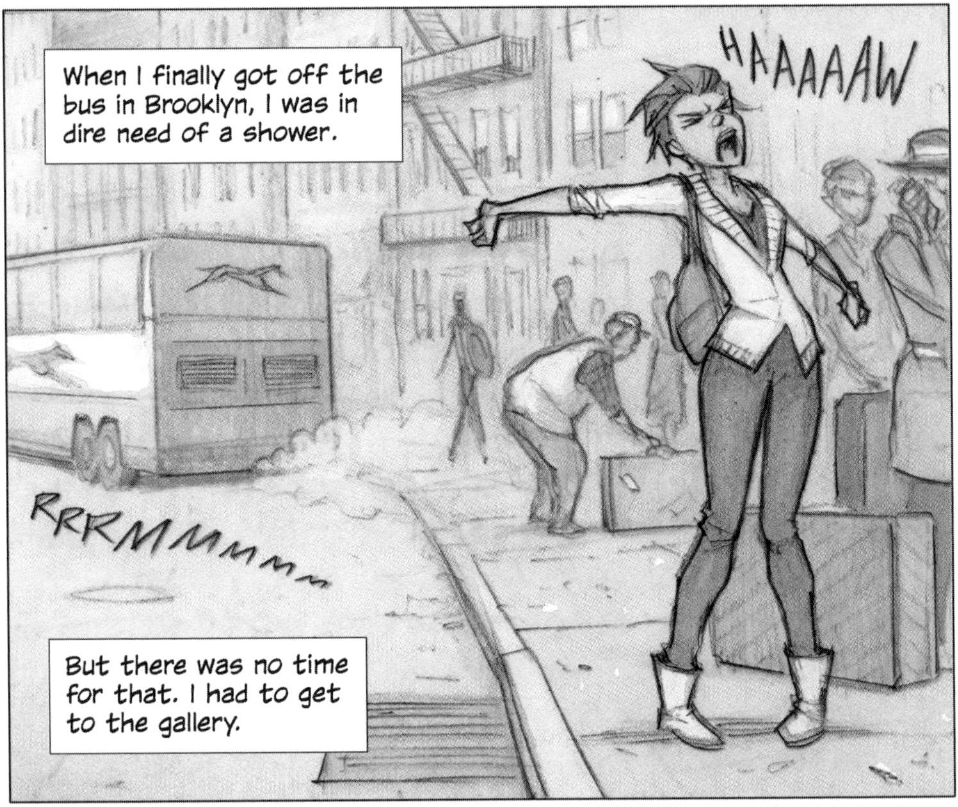
When I finally got off the bus in Brooklyn, I was in dire need of a shower.
HAAAAAW
RRRMMMMMM
But there was no time for that. I had to get to the gallery.

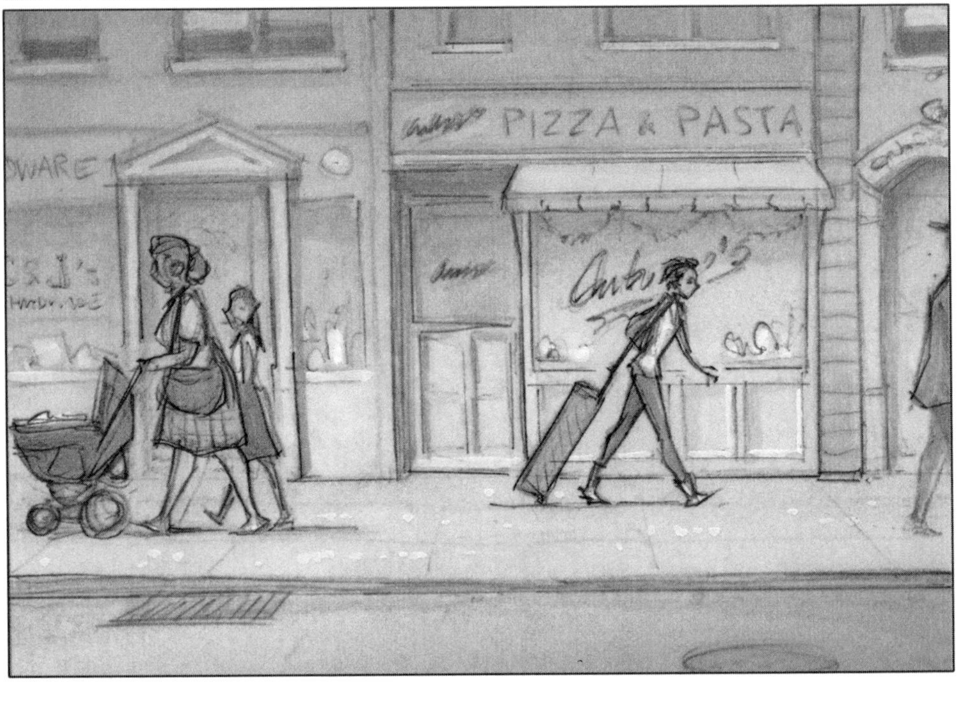
PIZZA & PASTA

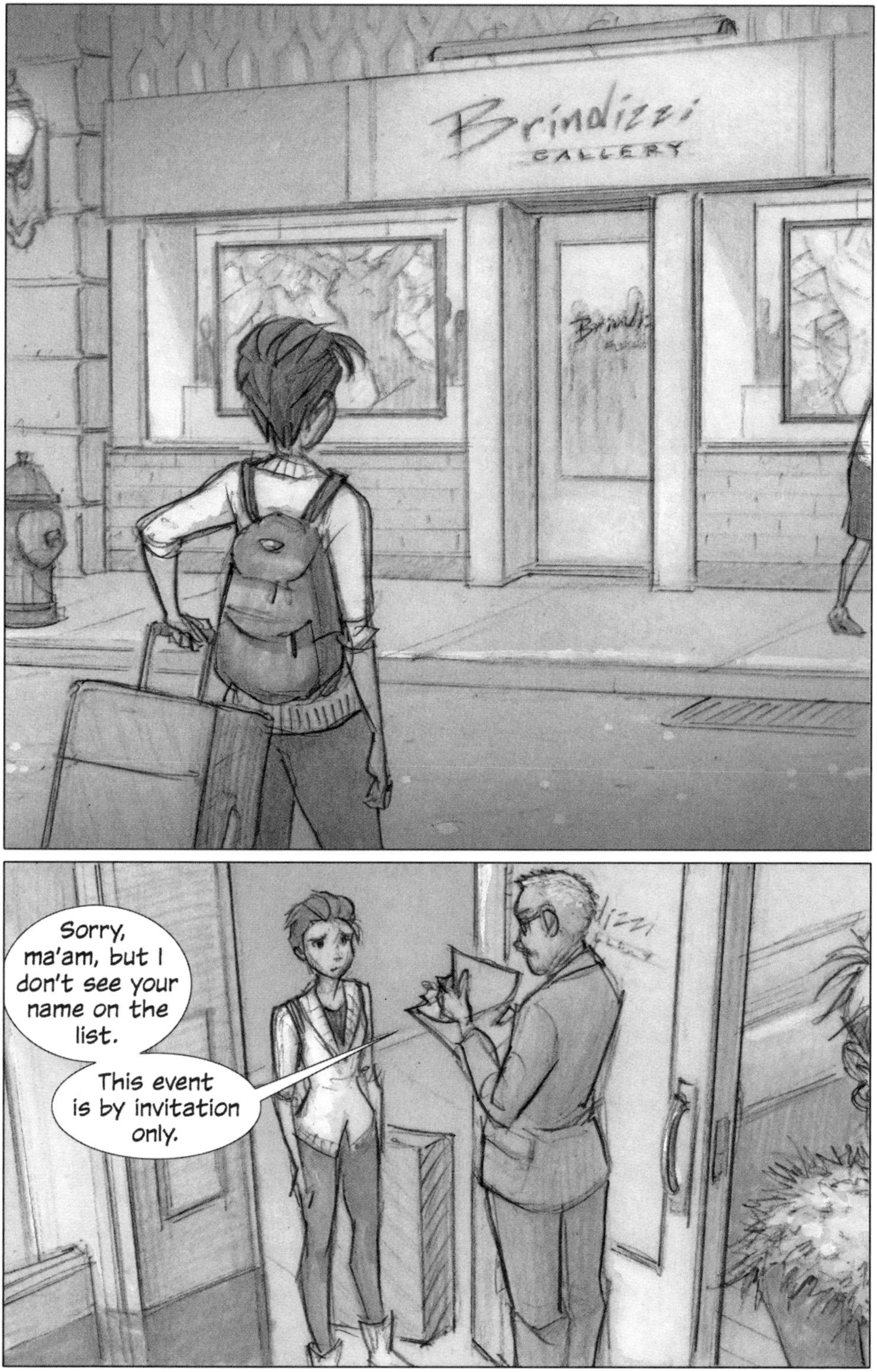
Brindizzi
GALLERY
Sorry, ma'am, but I don't see your name on the list.
This event is by invitation only.

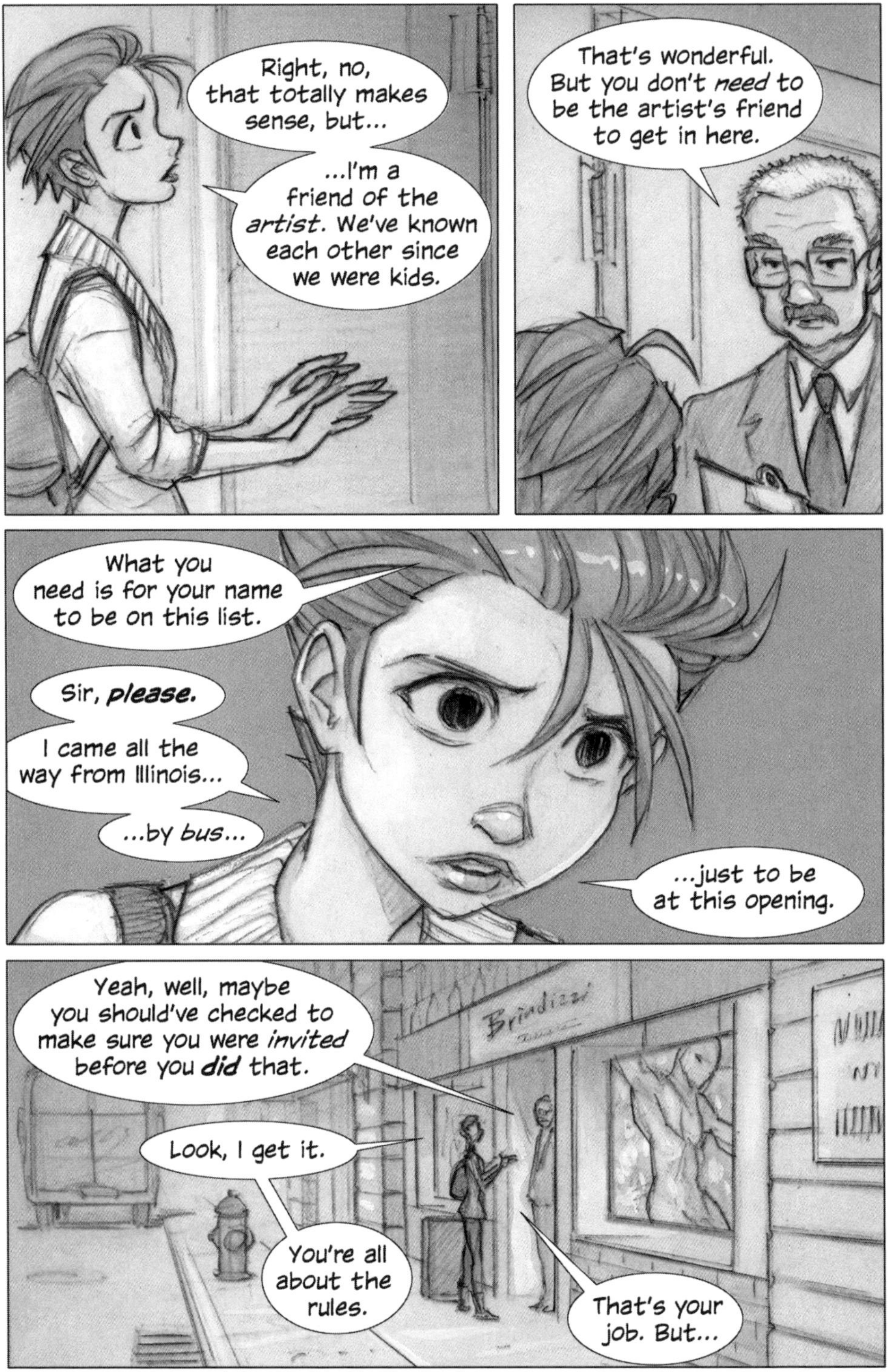
Right, no, that totally makes sense, but...
...I'm a friend of the *artist*. We've known each other since we were kids.
That's wonderful. But you don't *need* to be the artist's friend to get in here.
What you need is for your name to be on this list.
Sir, ***please.***
I came all the way from Illinois...
...by *bus*...
...just to be at this opening.
Yeah, well, maybe you should've checked to make sure you were *invited* before you ***did*** that.
Brindizzi
Look, I get it.
You're all about the rules.
That's your job. But...

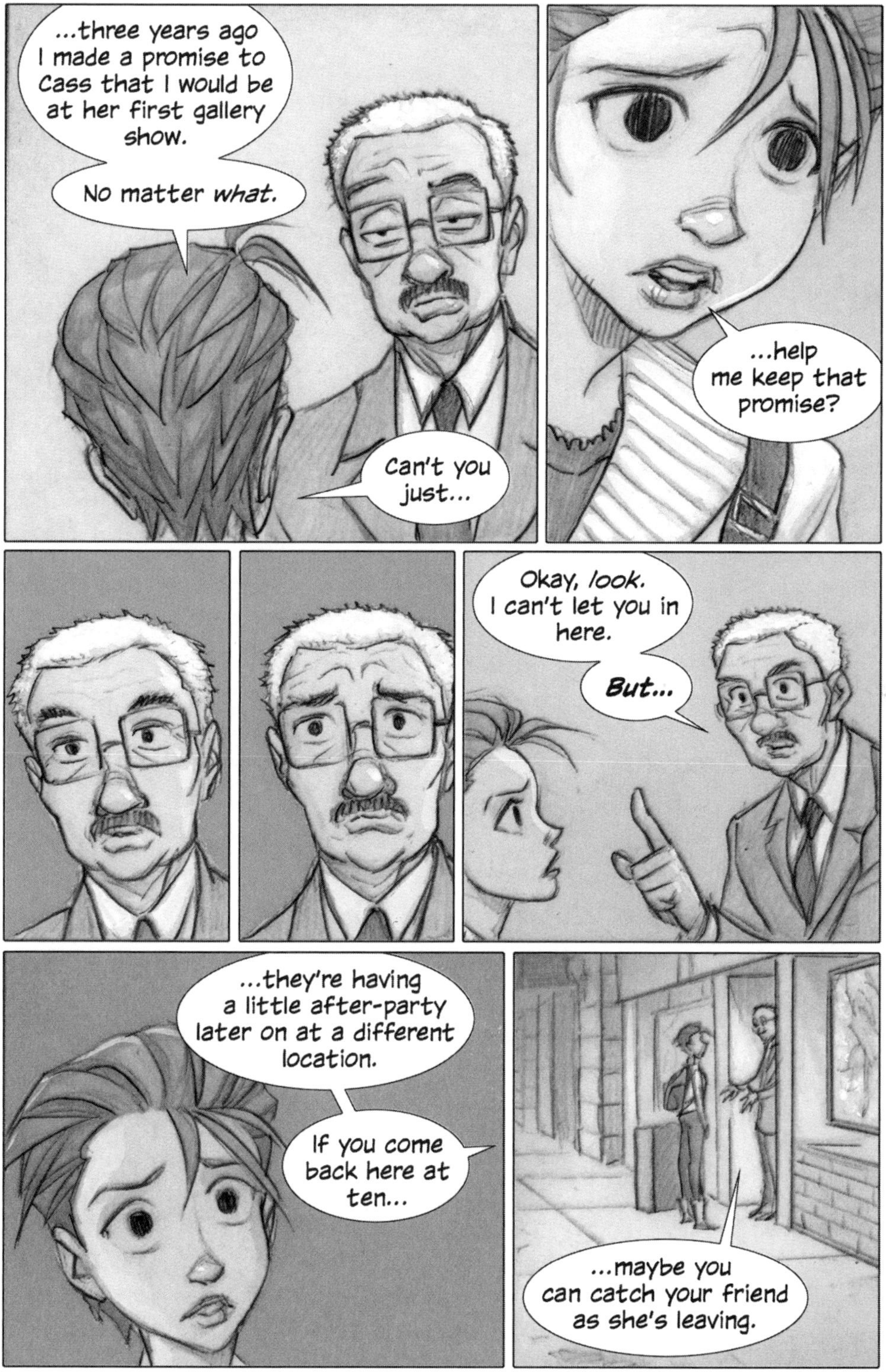
...three years ago I made a promise to Cass that I would be at her first gallery show.
No matter *what.*
Can't you just...
...help me keep that promise?
Okay, *look.* I can't let you in here.
But...
...they're having a little after-party later on at a different location.
If you come back here at ten...
...maybe you can catch your friend as she's leaving.

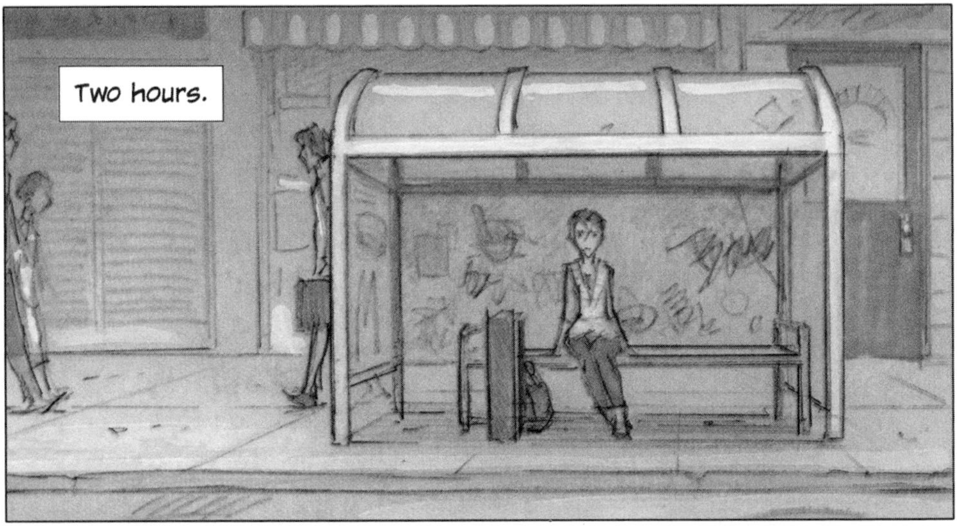
Two hours.

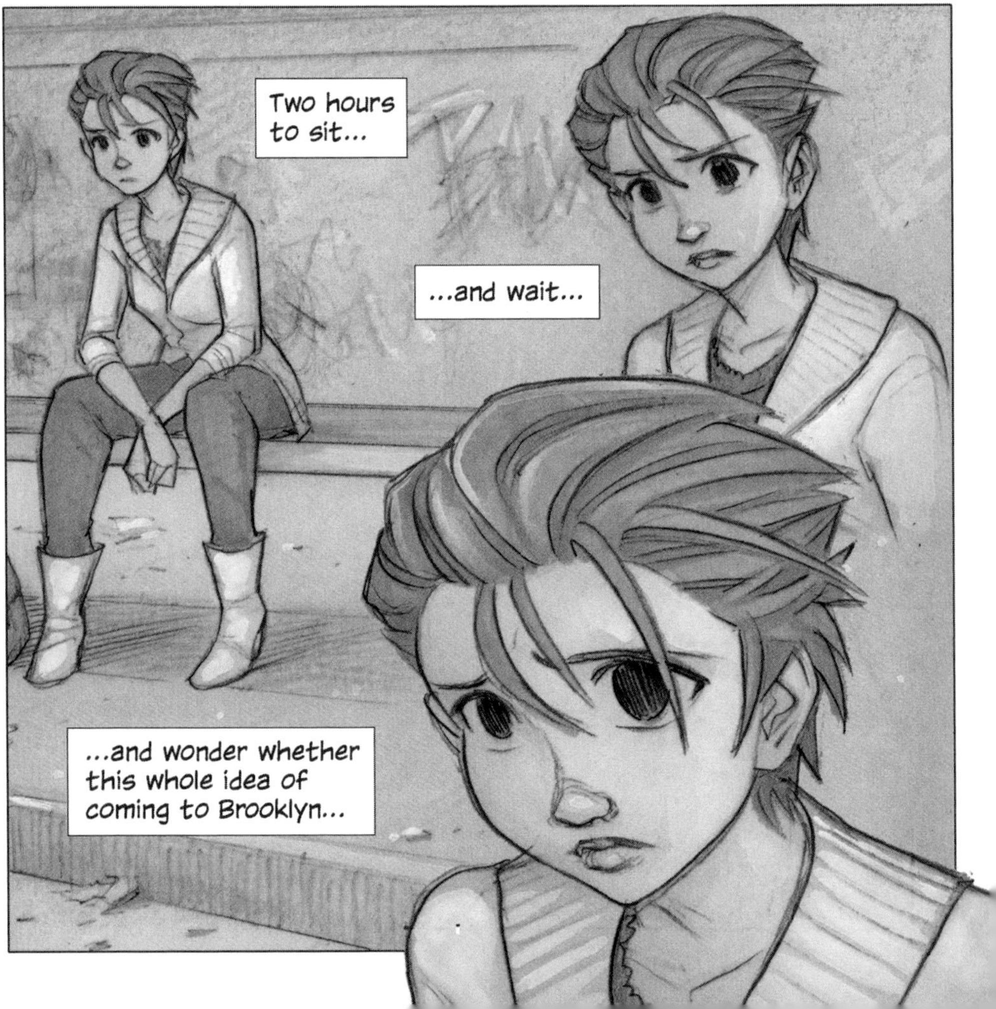
Two hours
to sit...
...and wait...
...and wonder whether
this whole idea of
coming to Brooklyn...

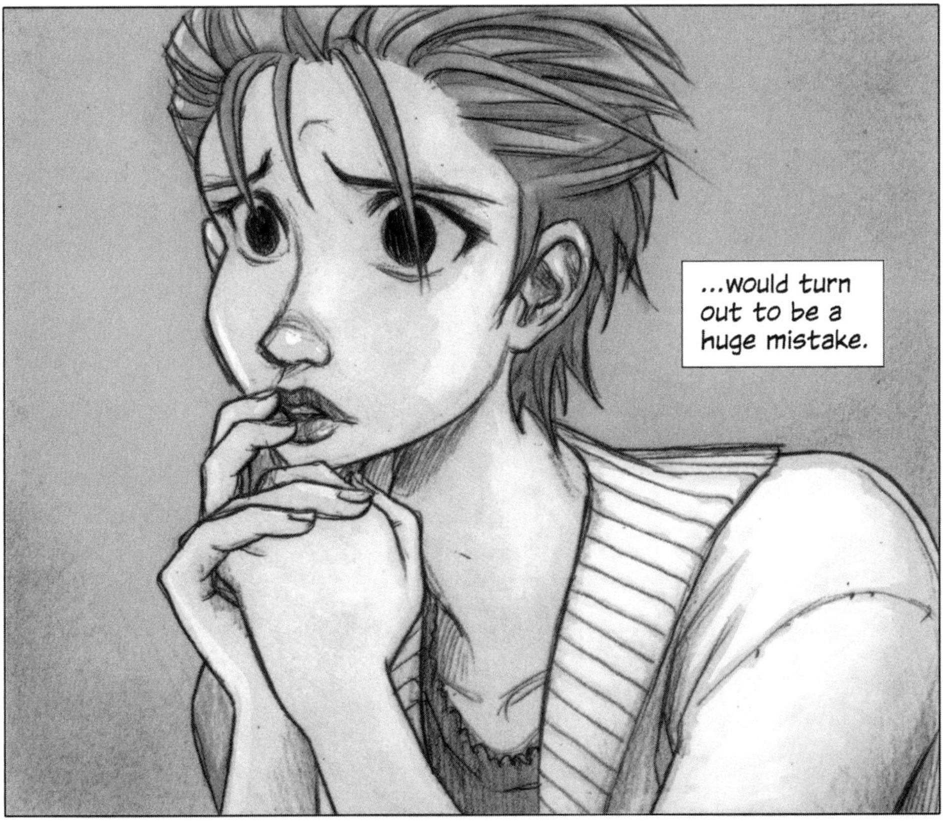
...would turn
out to be a
huge mistake.

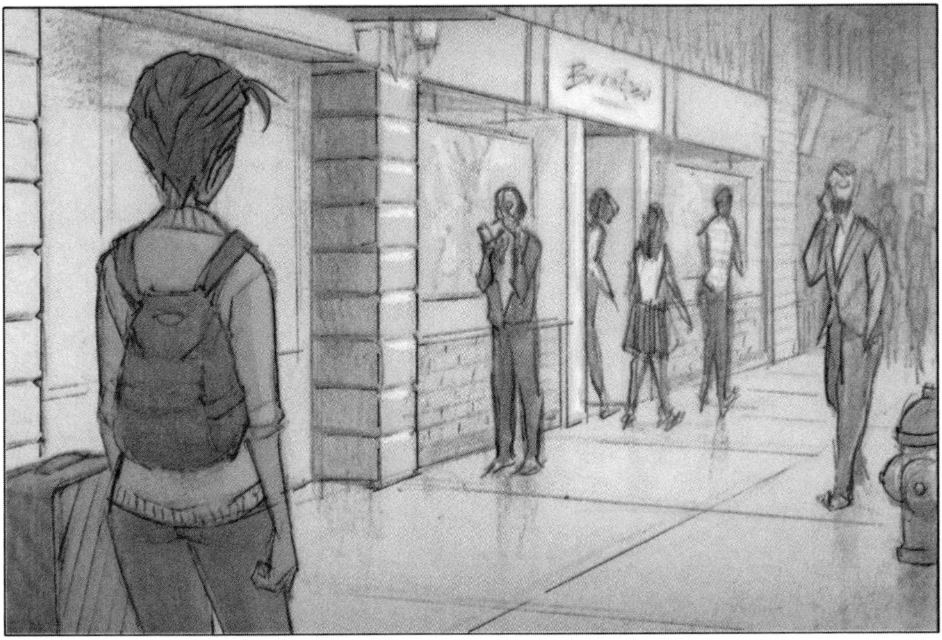

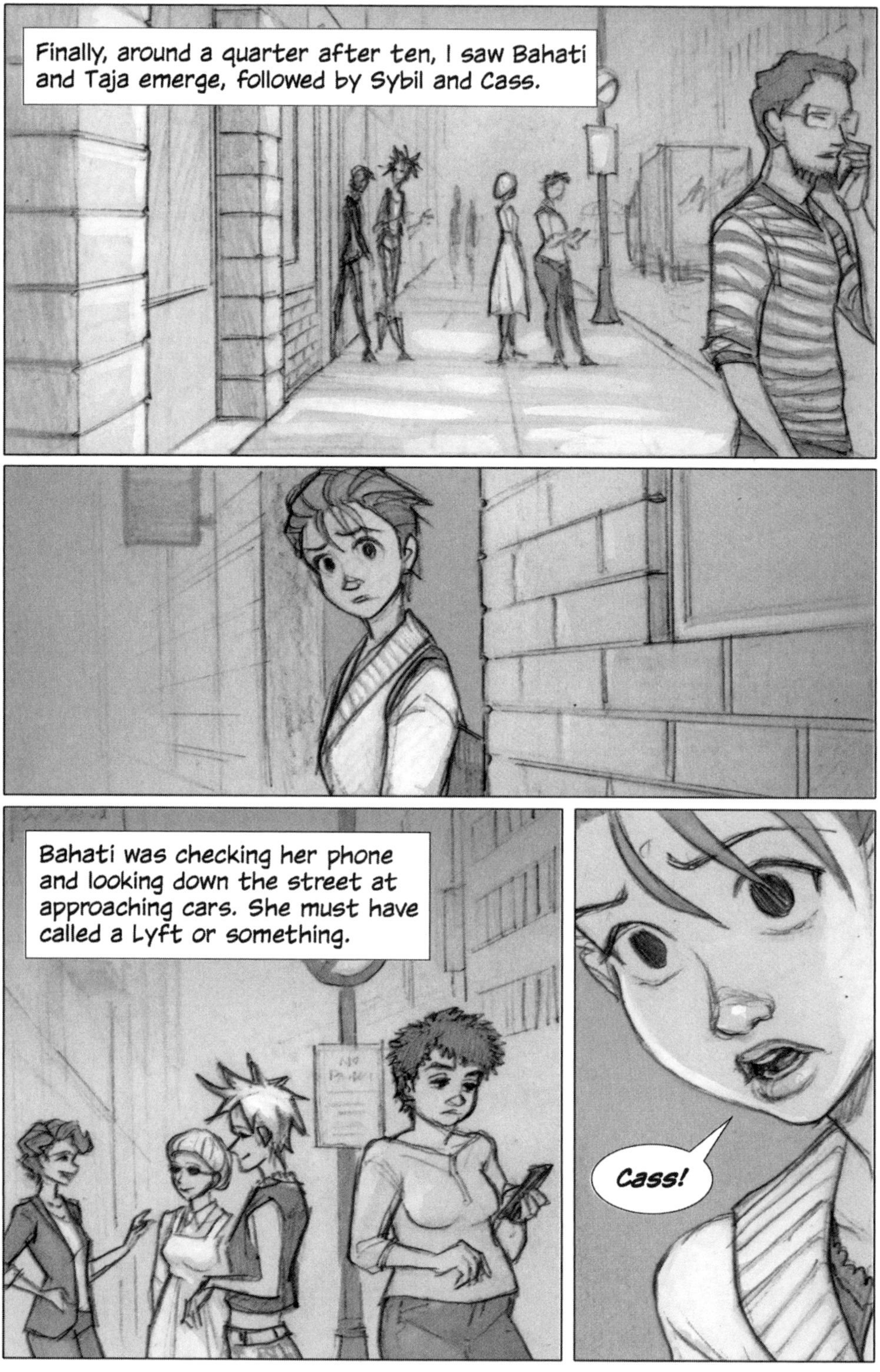
Finally, around a quarter after ten, I saw Bahati and Taja emerge, followed by Sybil and Cass.
Bahati was checking her phone and looking down the street at approaching cars. She must have called a Lyft or something.
Cass!

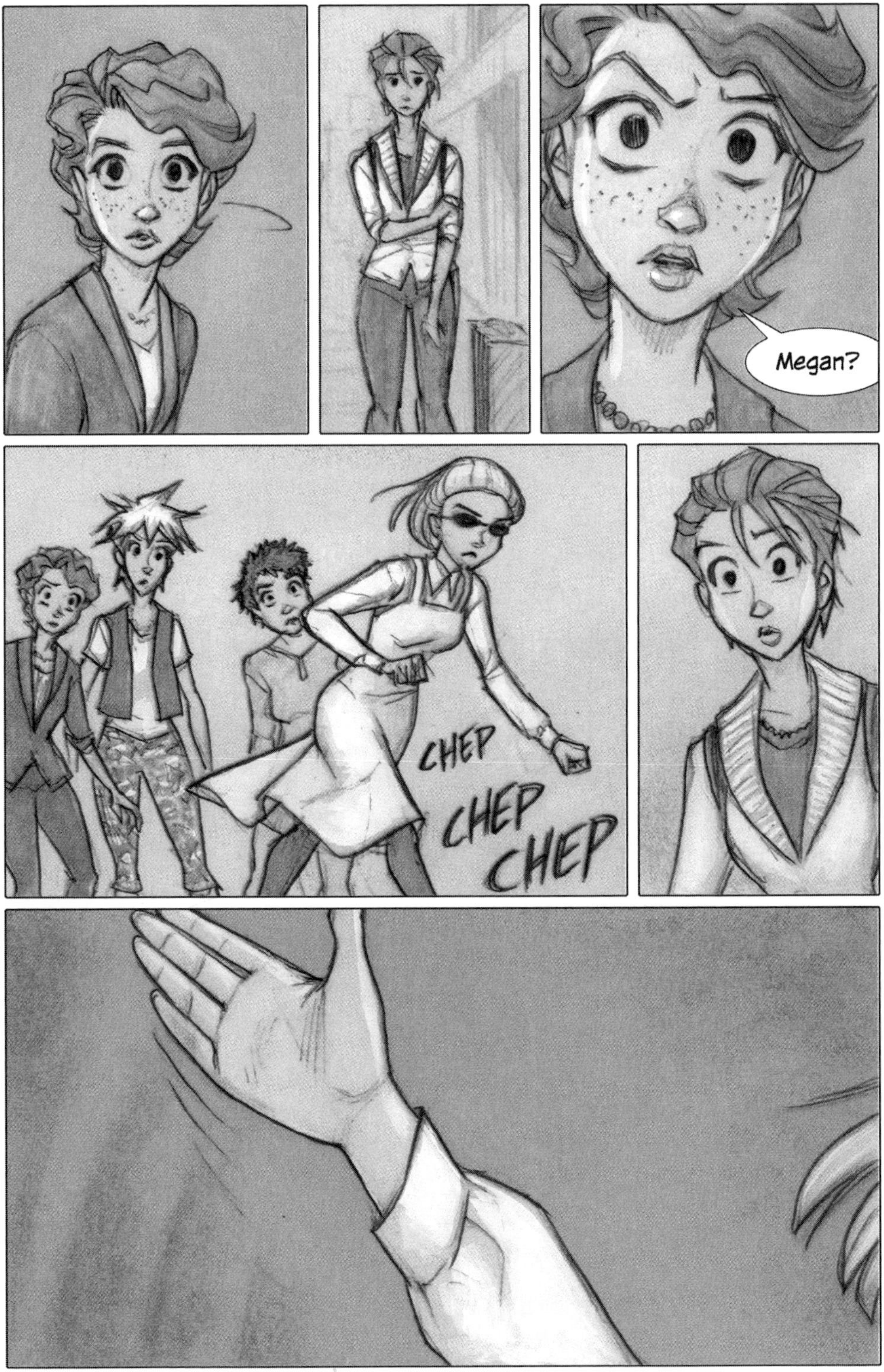
Megan?
CHEP
CHEP
CHEP

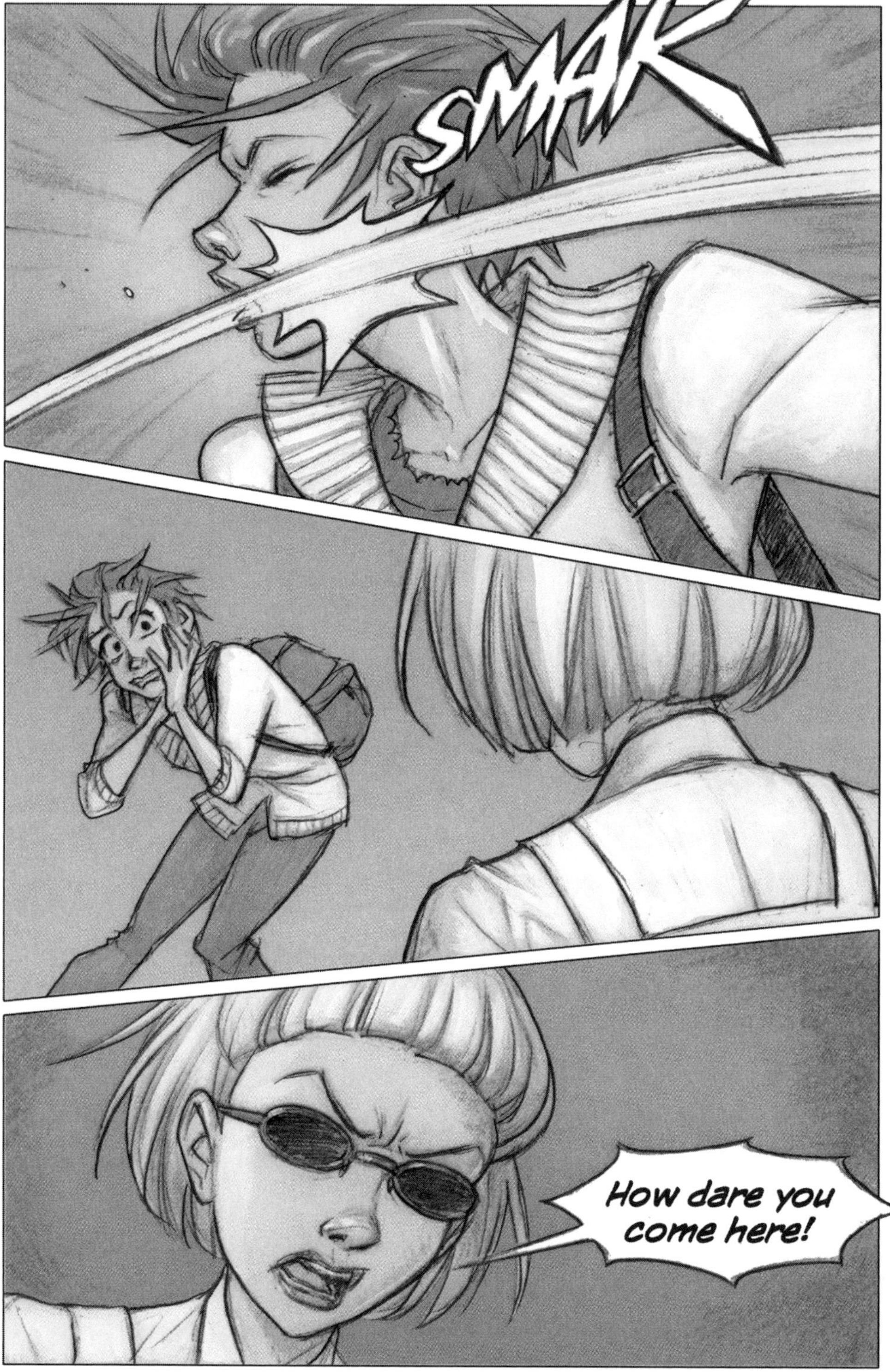
SMAK
How dare you come here!

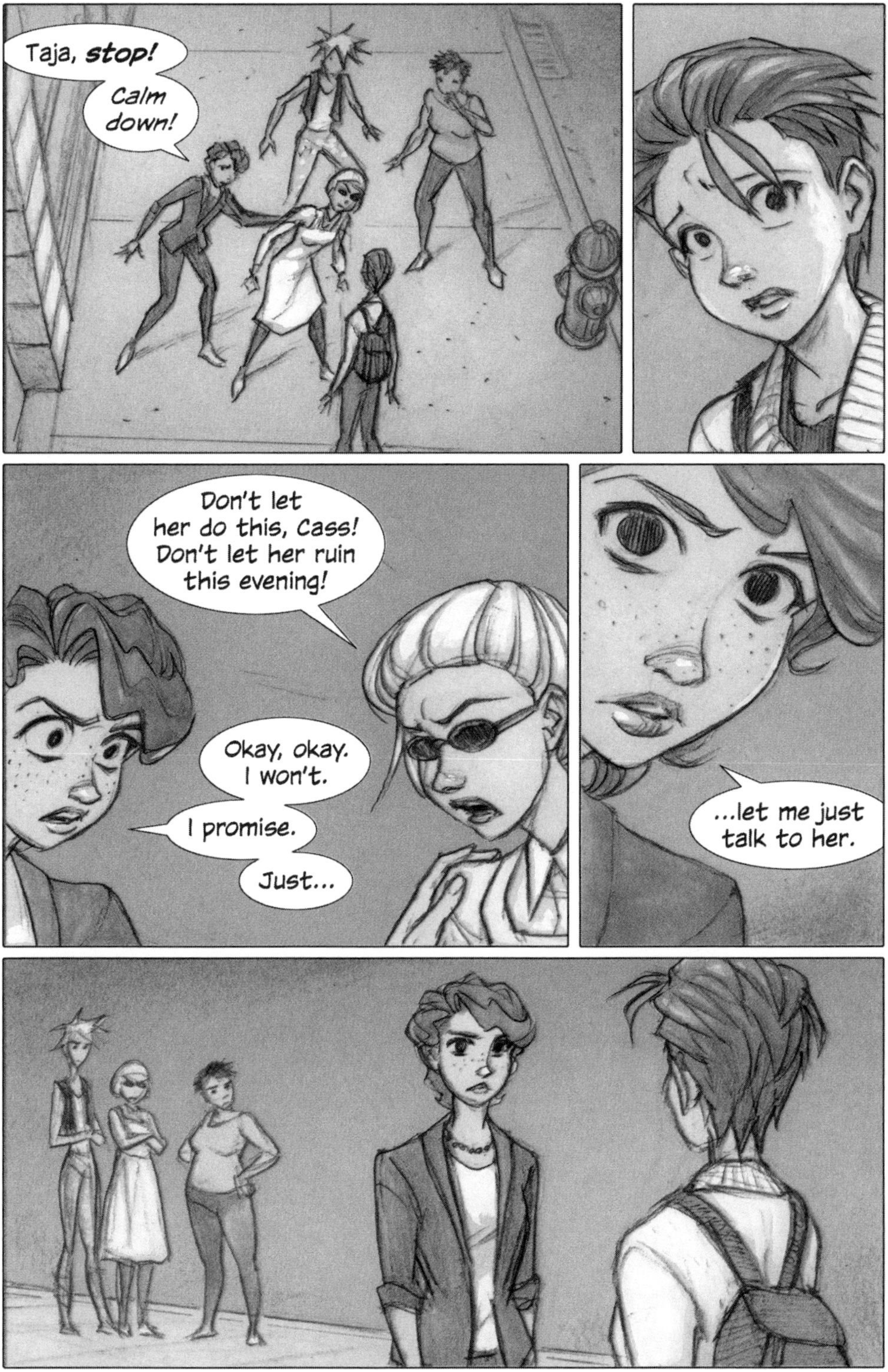
Taja, **stop!**
Calm down!
Don't let her do this, Cass! Don't let her ruin this evening!
Okay, okay. I won't.
I promise.
Just...
...let me just talk to her.

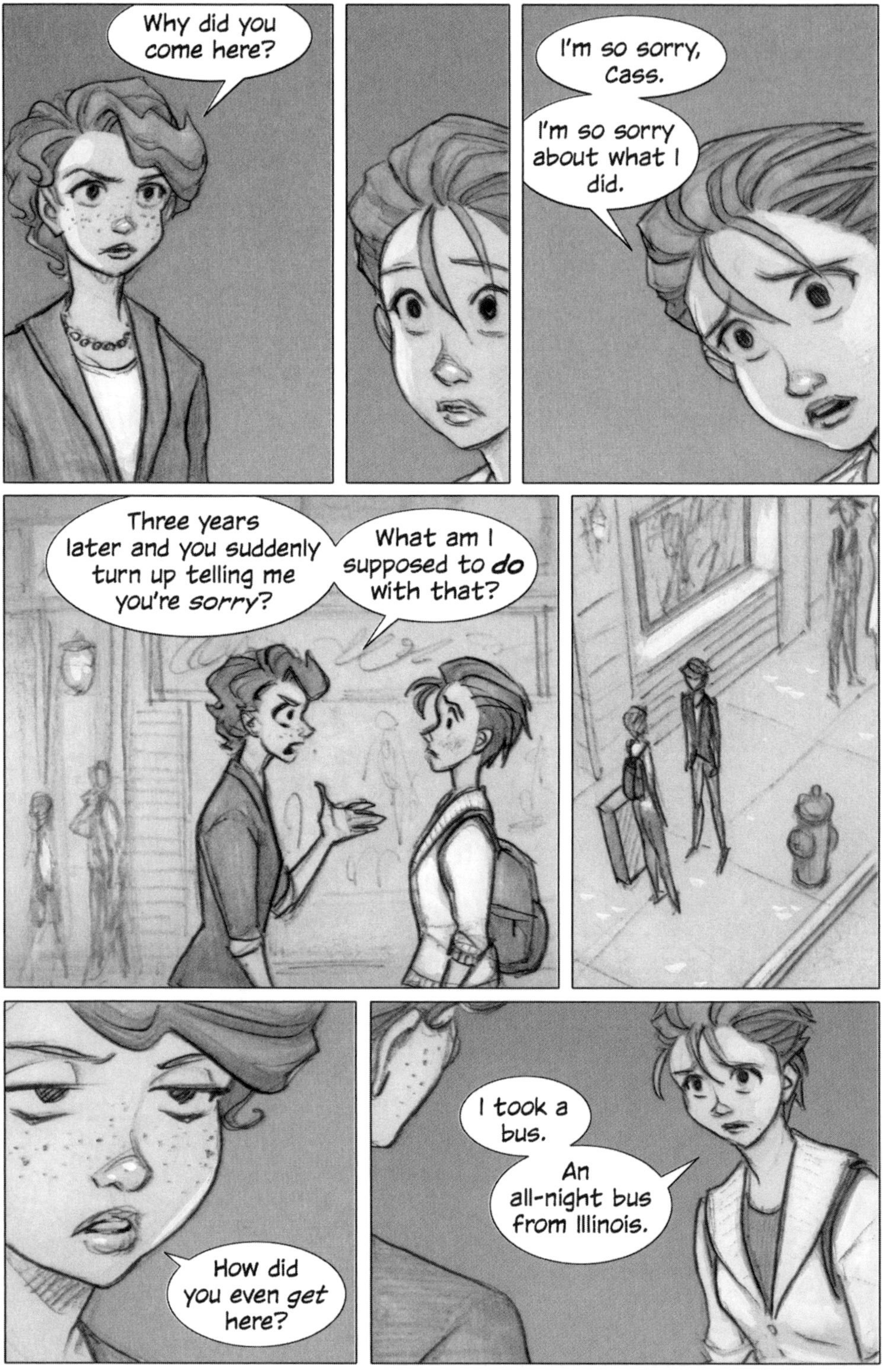
Why did you come here?
I'm so sorry, Cass.
I'm so sorry about what I did.
Three years later and you suddenly turn up telling me you're *sorry*?
What am I supposed to ***do*** with that?
How did you even *get* here?
I took a bus.
An all-night bus from Illinois.

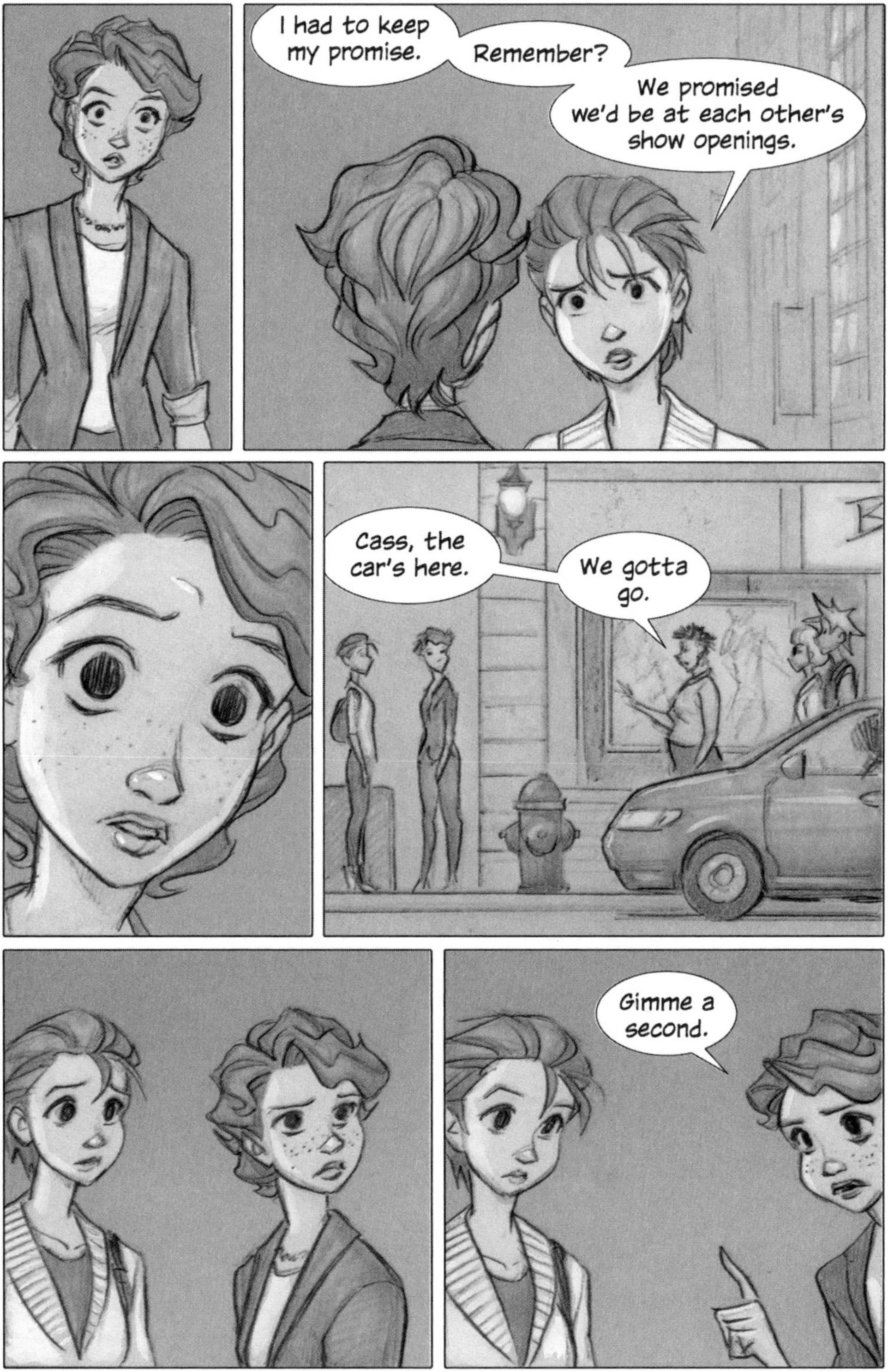

I had to keep my promise.
Remember?
We promised we'd be at each other's show openings.
Cass, the car's here.
We gotta go.
Gimme a second.

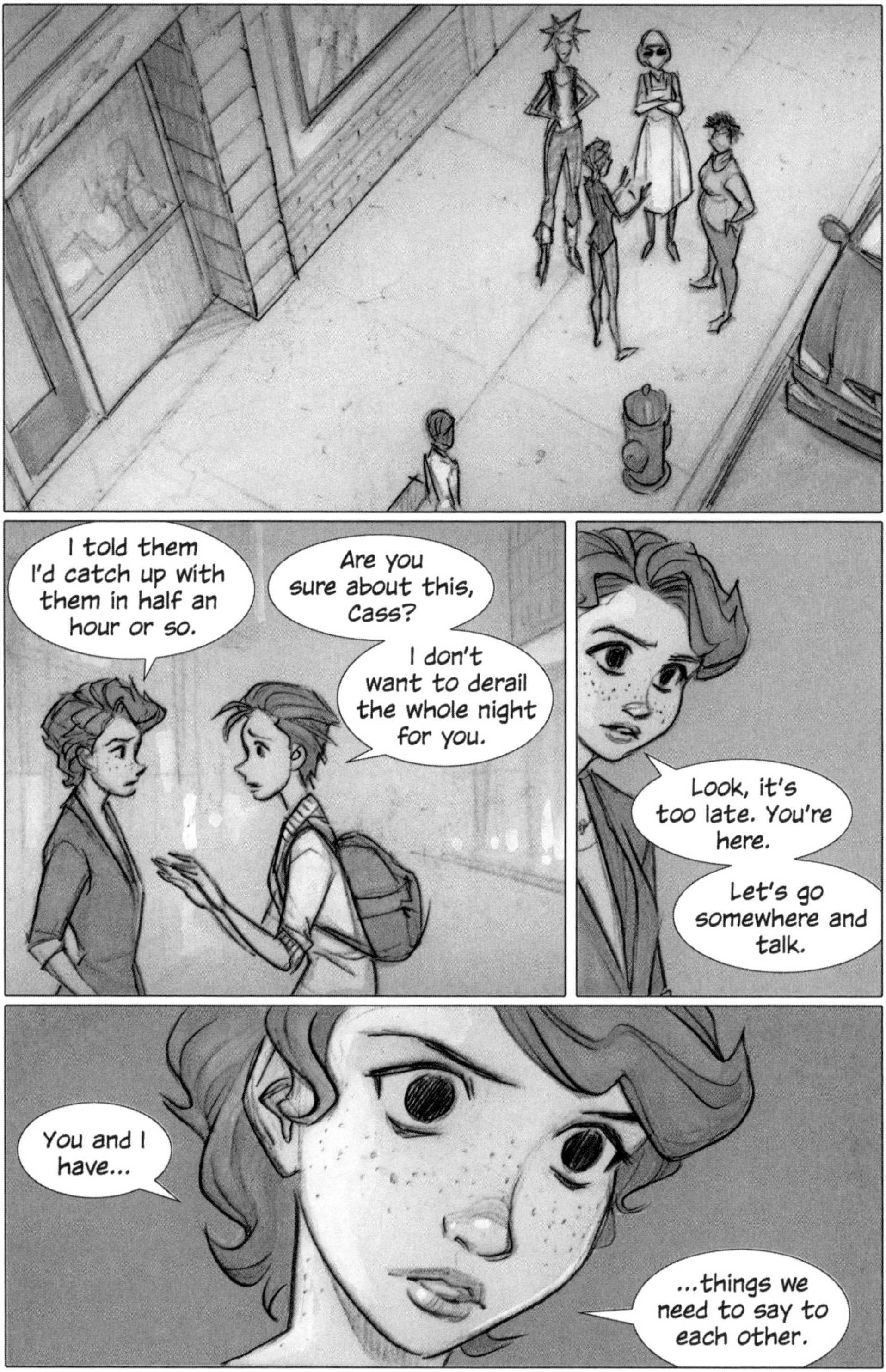
I told them I'd catch up with them in half an hour or so.
Are you sure about this, Cass?
I don't want to derail the whole night for you.
Look, it's too late. You're here.
Let's go somewhere and talk.
You and I have...
...things we need to say to each other.

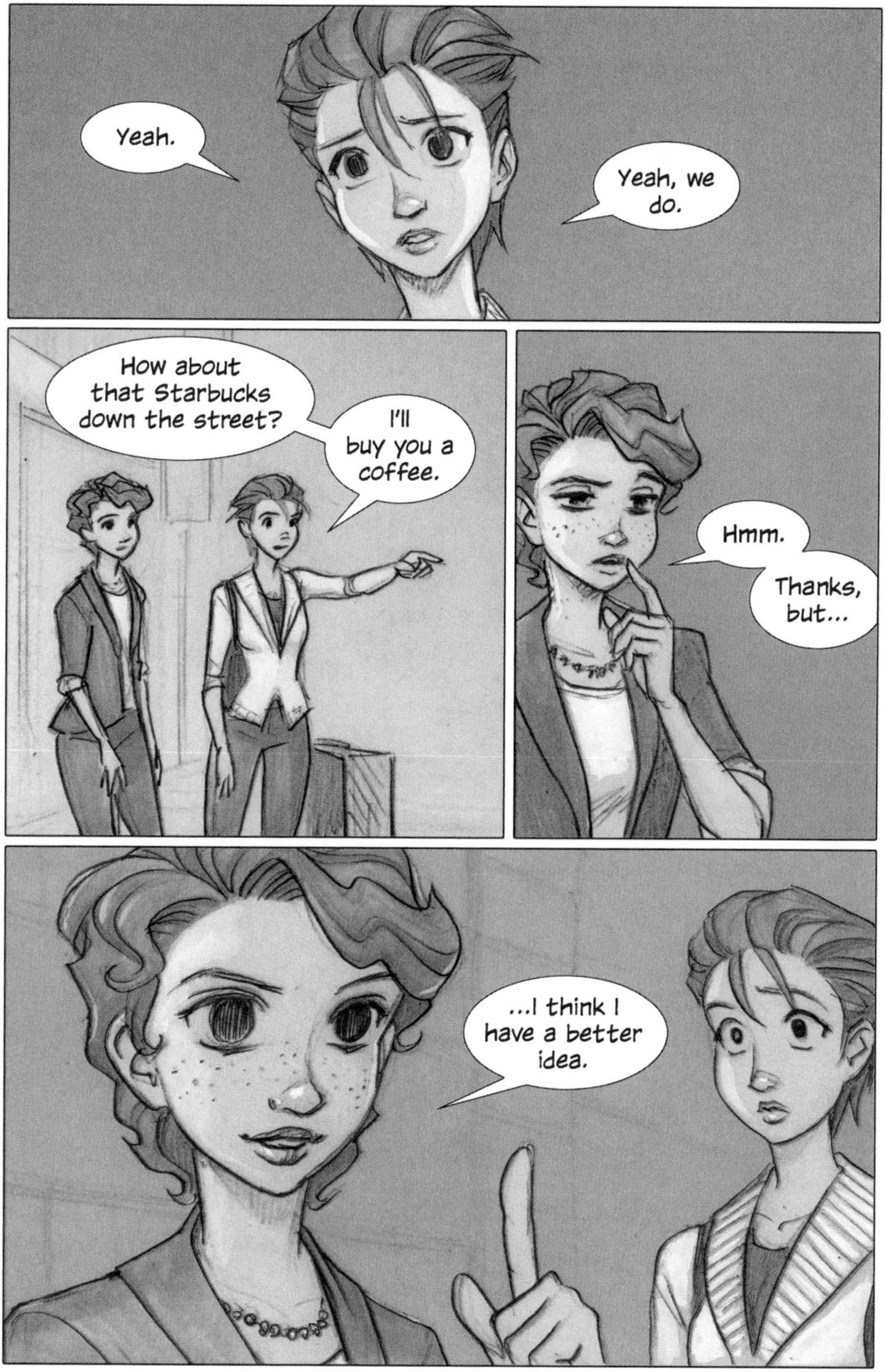
Yeah.
Yeah, we do.
How about that Starbucks down the street?
I'll buy you a coffee.
Hmm.
Thanks, but...
...I think I have a better idea.

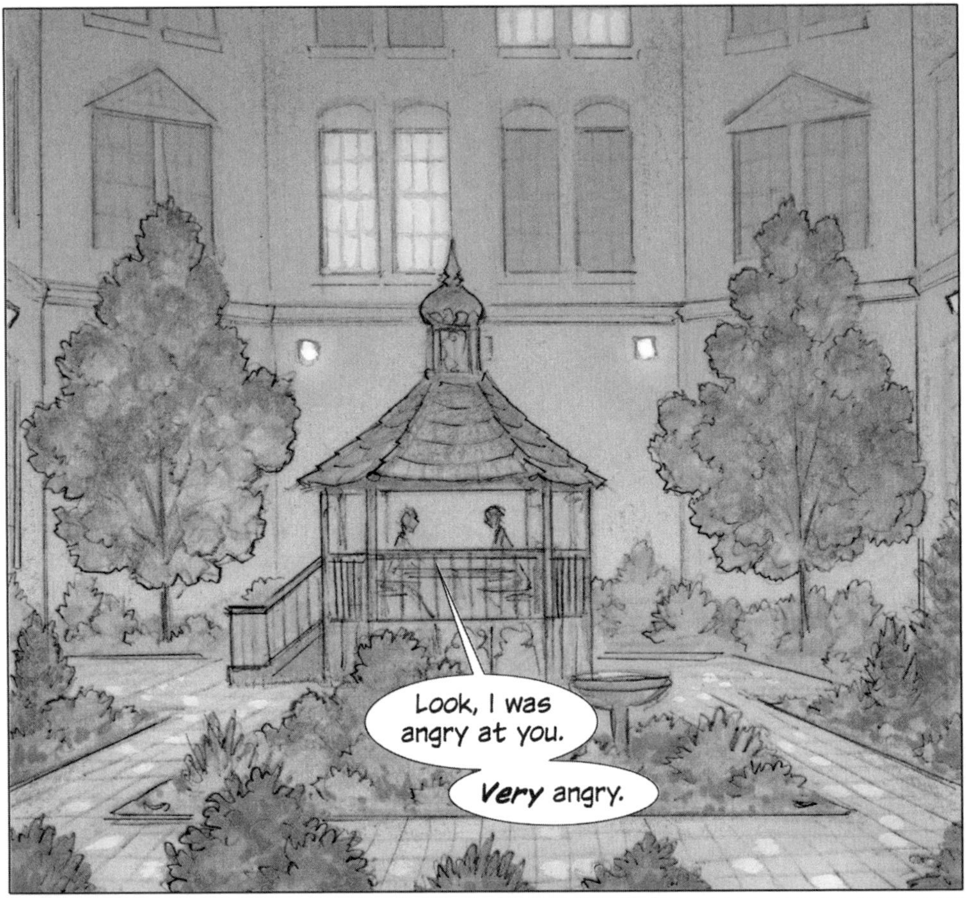
Look, I was angry at you.
Very angry.

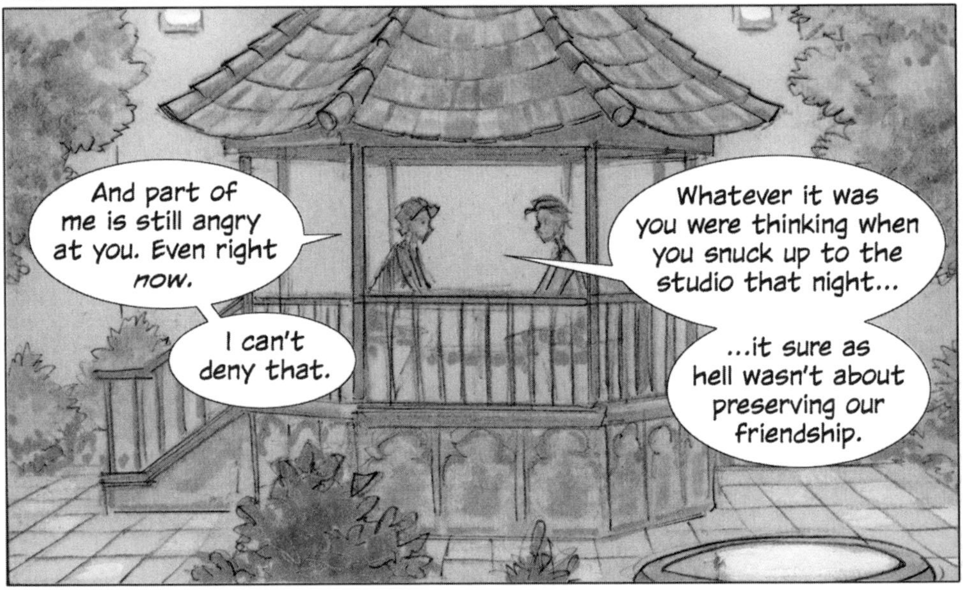
And part of me is still angry at you. Even right *now*.
I can't deny that.
Whatever it was you were thinking when you snuck up to the studio that night...
...it sure as hell wasn't about preserving our friendship.

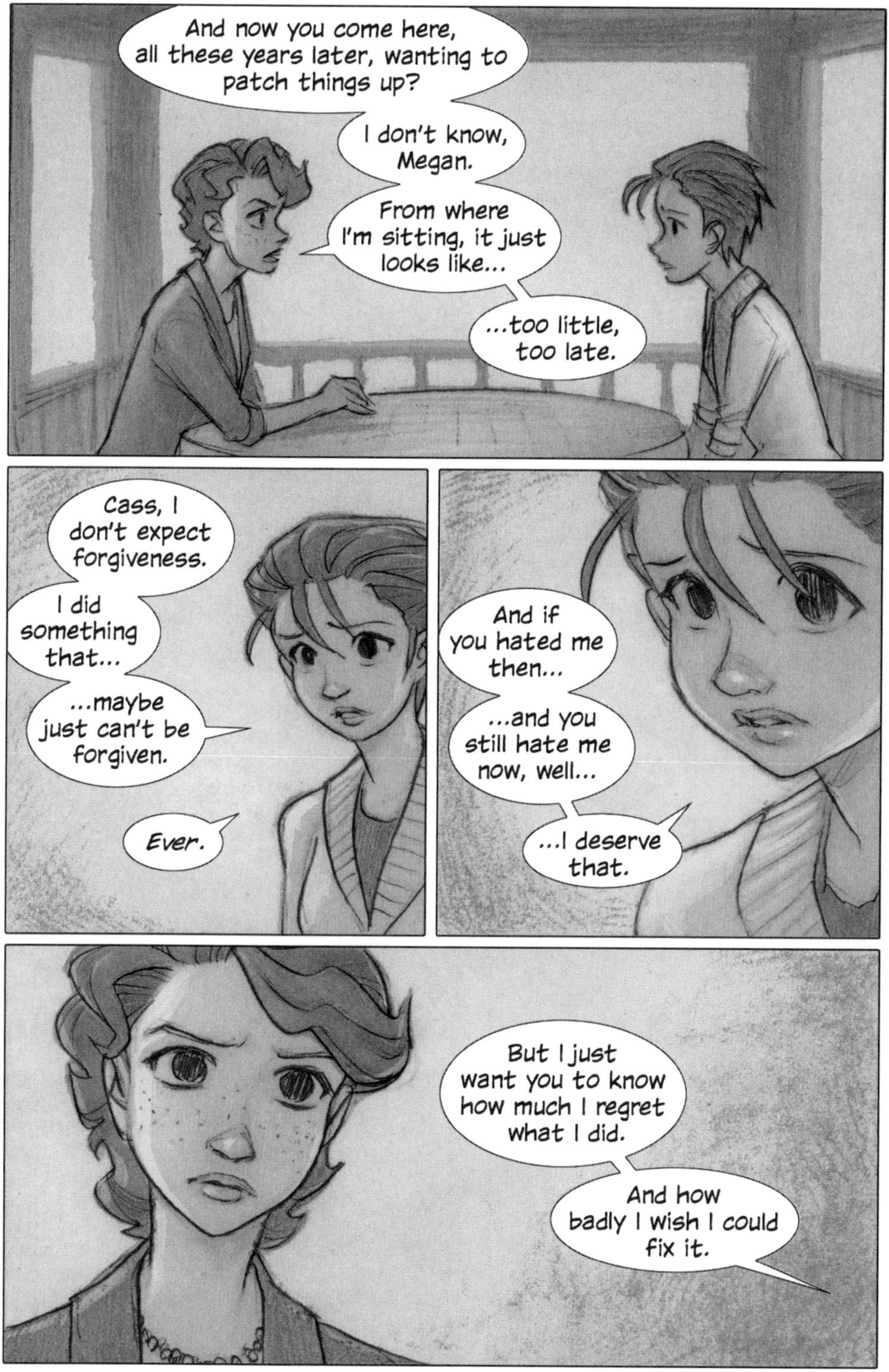
And now you come here, all these years later, wanting to patch things up?
I don't know, Megan.
From where I'm sitting, it just looks like...
...too little, too late.
Cass, I don't expect forgiveness.
I did something that...
...maybe just can't be forgiven.
Ever.
And if you hated me then...
...and you still hate me now, well...
...I deserve that.
But I just want you to know how much I regret what I did.
And how badly I wish I could fix it.

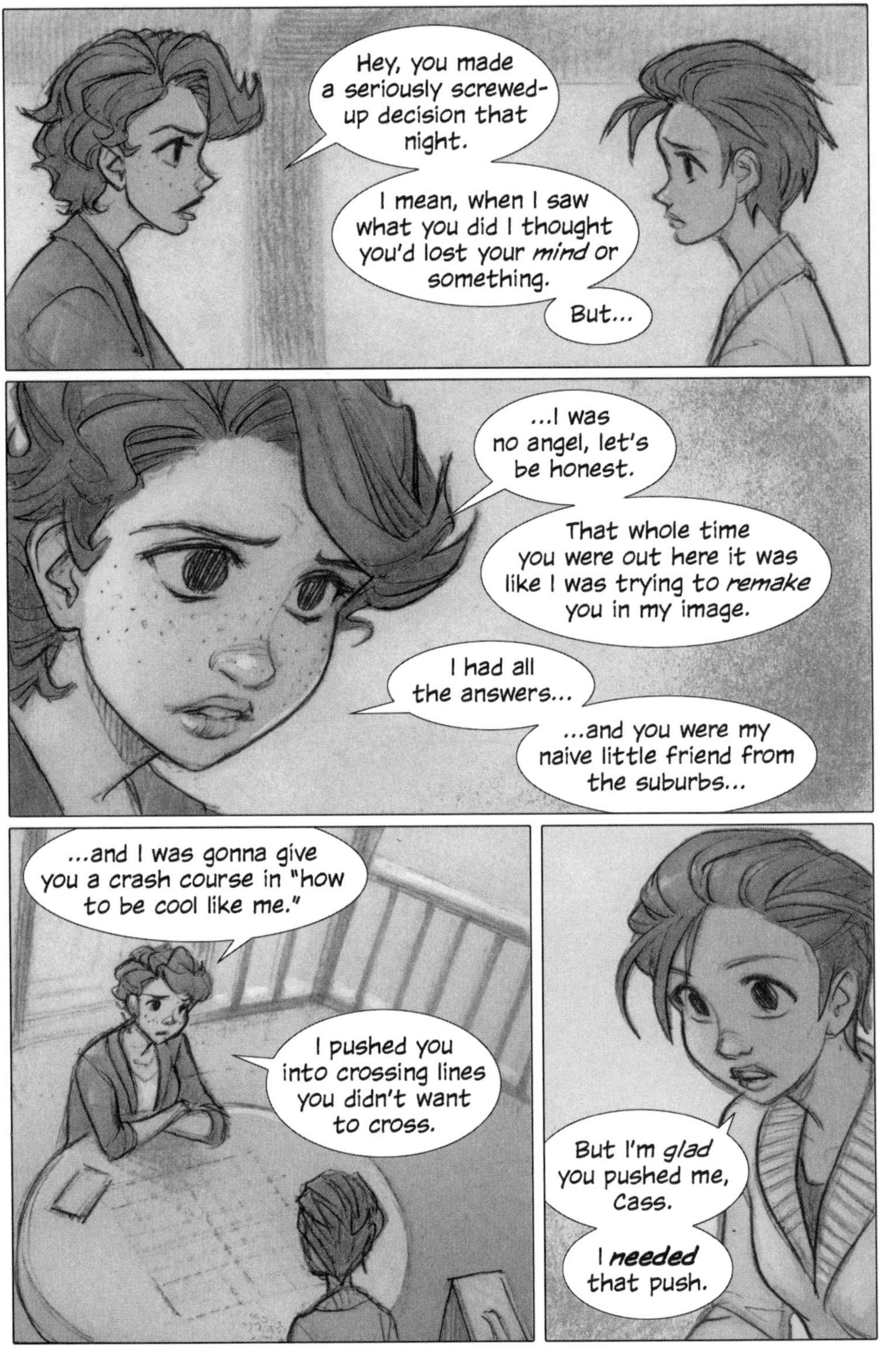
Hey, you made a seriously screwed-up decision that night.
I mean, when I saw what you did I thought you'd lost your *mind* or something.
But...
...I was no angel, let's be honest.
That whole time you were out here it was like I was trying to *remake* you in my image.
I had all the answers...
...and you were my naive little friend from the suburbs...
...and I was gonna give you a crash course in "how to be cool like me."
I pushed you into crossing lines you didn't want to cross.
But I'm *glad* you pushed me, Cass.
I ***needed*** that push.

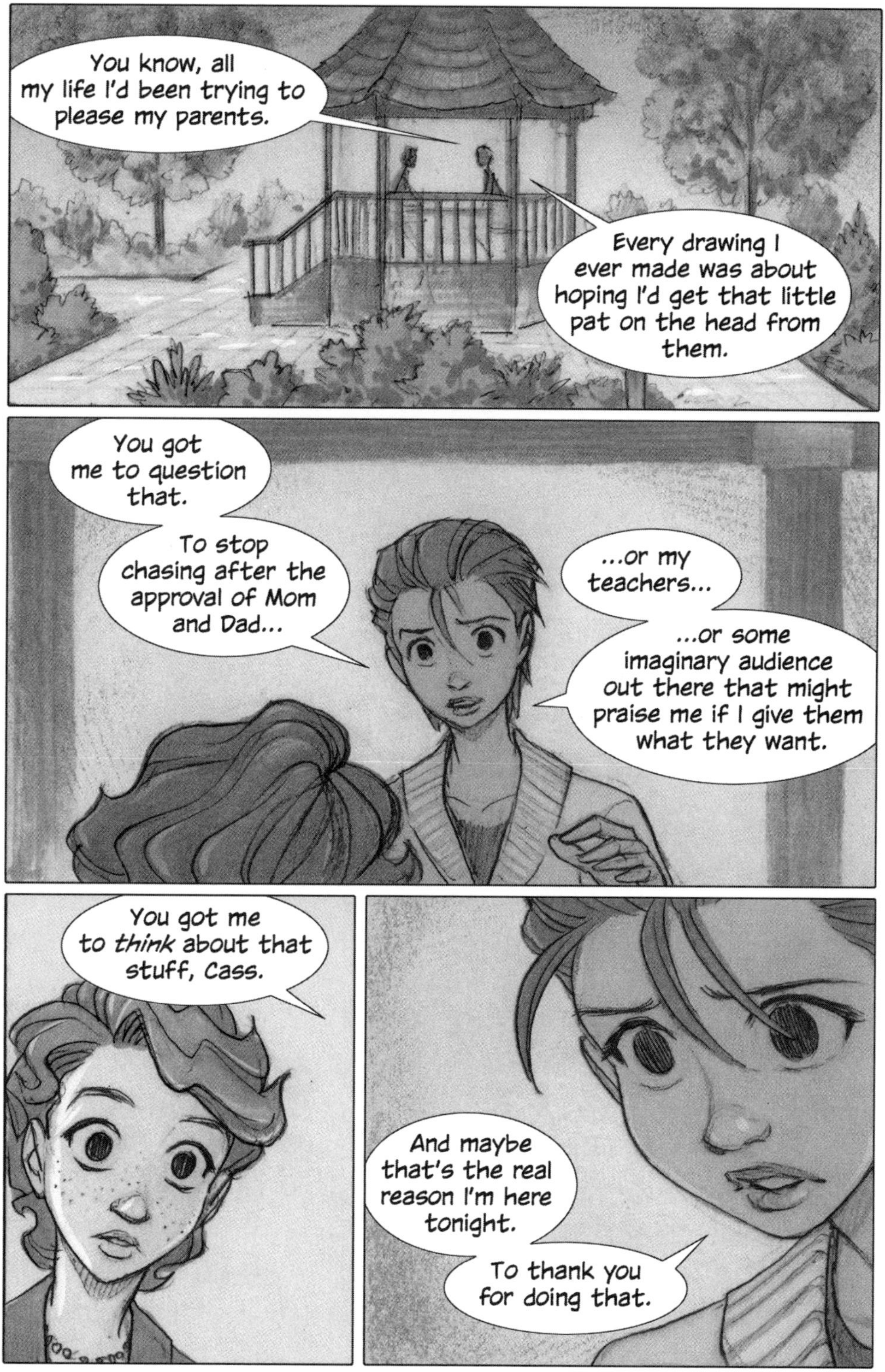
You know, all my life I'd been trying to please my parents.
Every drawing I ever made was about hoping I'd get that little pat on the head from them.
You got me to question that.
To stop chasing after the approval of Mom and Dad...
...or my teachers...
...or some imaginary audience out there that might praise me if I give them what they want.
You got me to *think* about that stuff, Cass.
And maybe that's the real reason I'm here tonight.
To thank you for doing that.

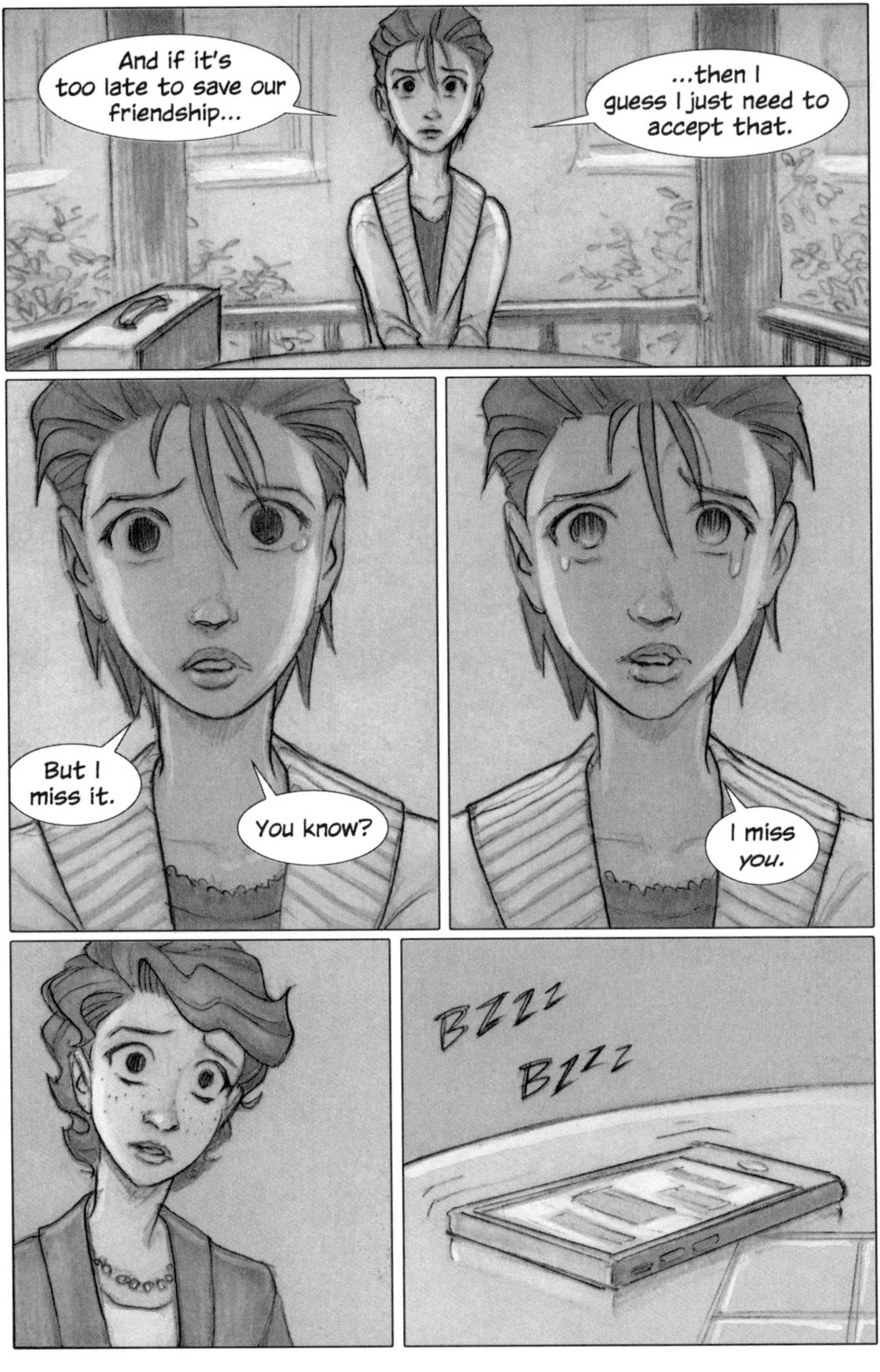
And if it's too late to save our friendship...
...then I guess I just need to accept that.
But I miss it.
You know?
I miss *you.*
BZZZ
BZZZ

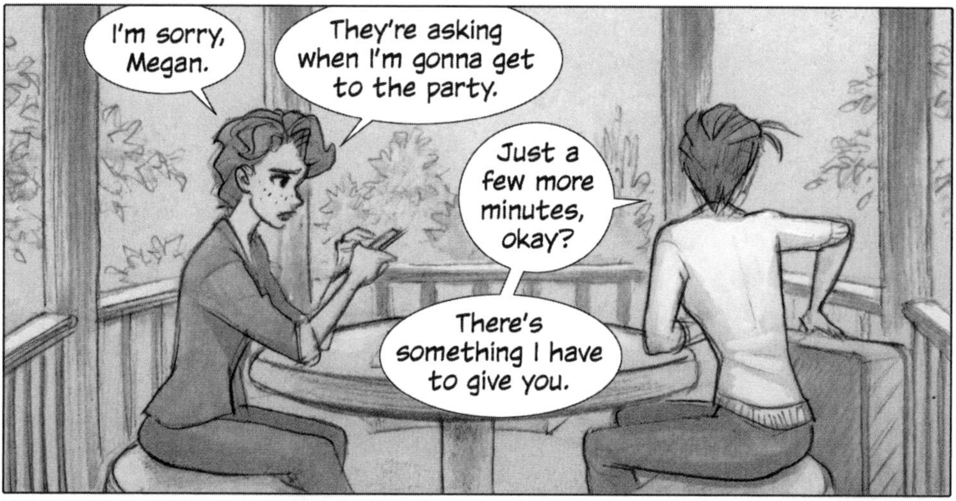
I'm sorry, Megan.
They're asking when I'm gonna get to the party.
Just a few more minutes, okay?
There's something I have to give you.

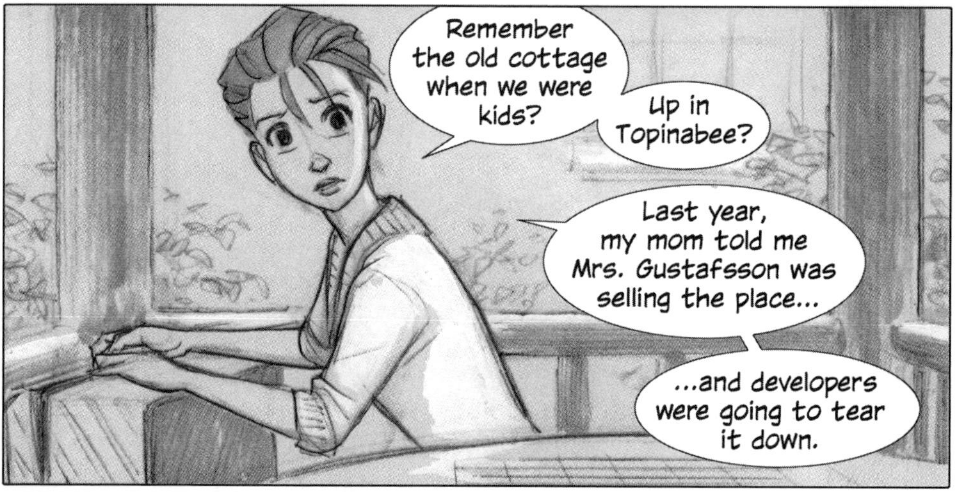
Remember the old cottage when we were kids?
Up in Topinabee?
Last year, my mom told me Mrs. Gustafsson was selling the place...
...and developers were going to tear it down.

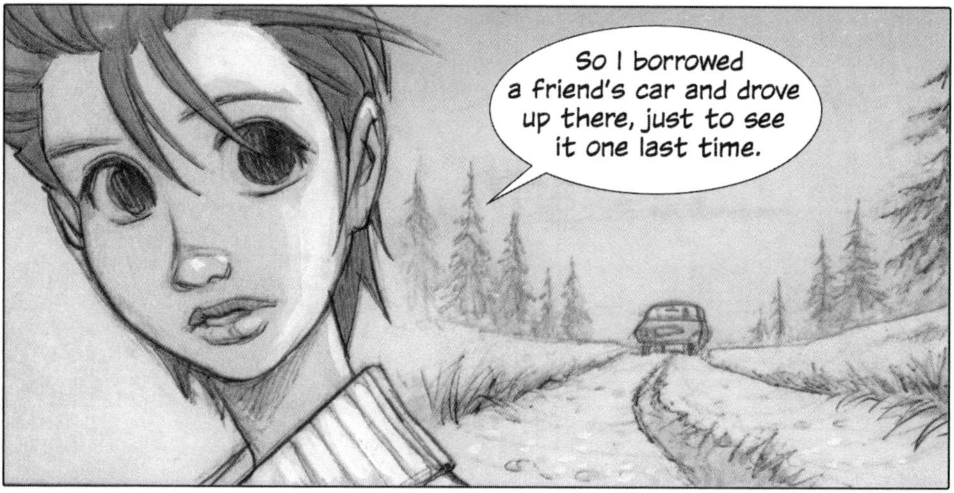
So I borrowed a friend's car and drove up there, just to see it one last time.

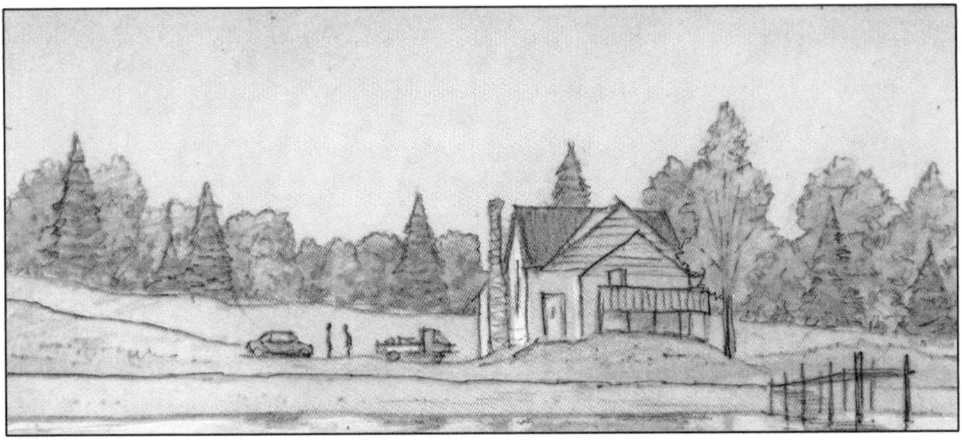

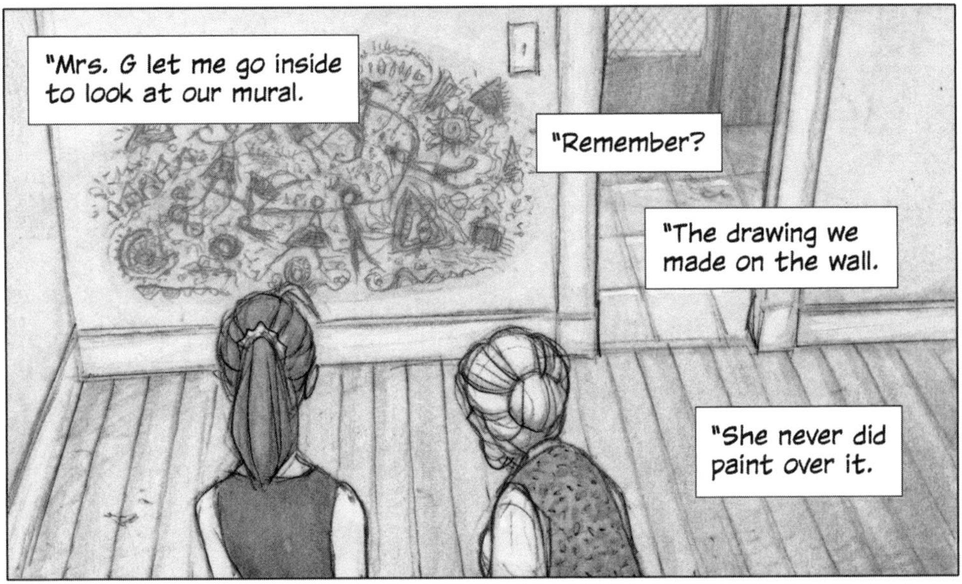
"Mrs. G let me go inside to look at our mural.
"Remember?
"The drawing we made on the wall.
"She never did paint over it.

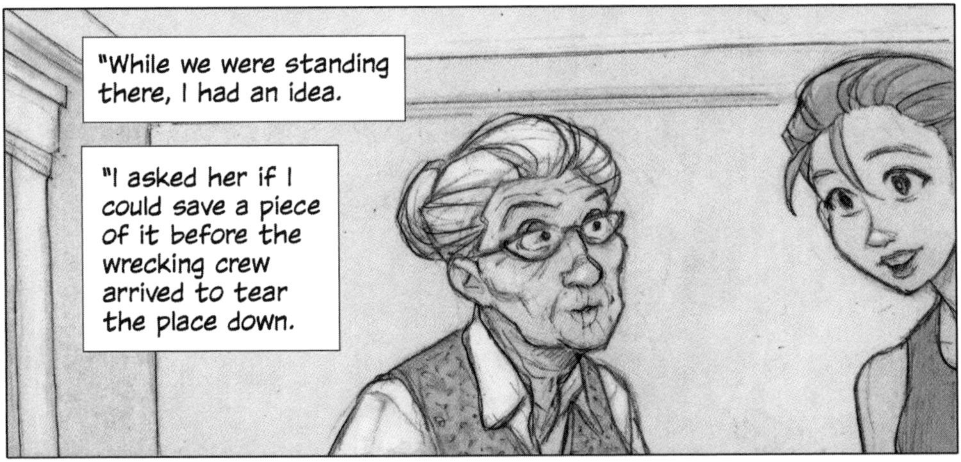
"While we were standing there, I had an idea.
"I asked her if I could save a piece of it before the wrecking crew arrived to tear the place down.

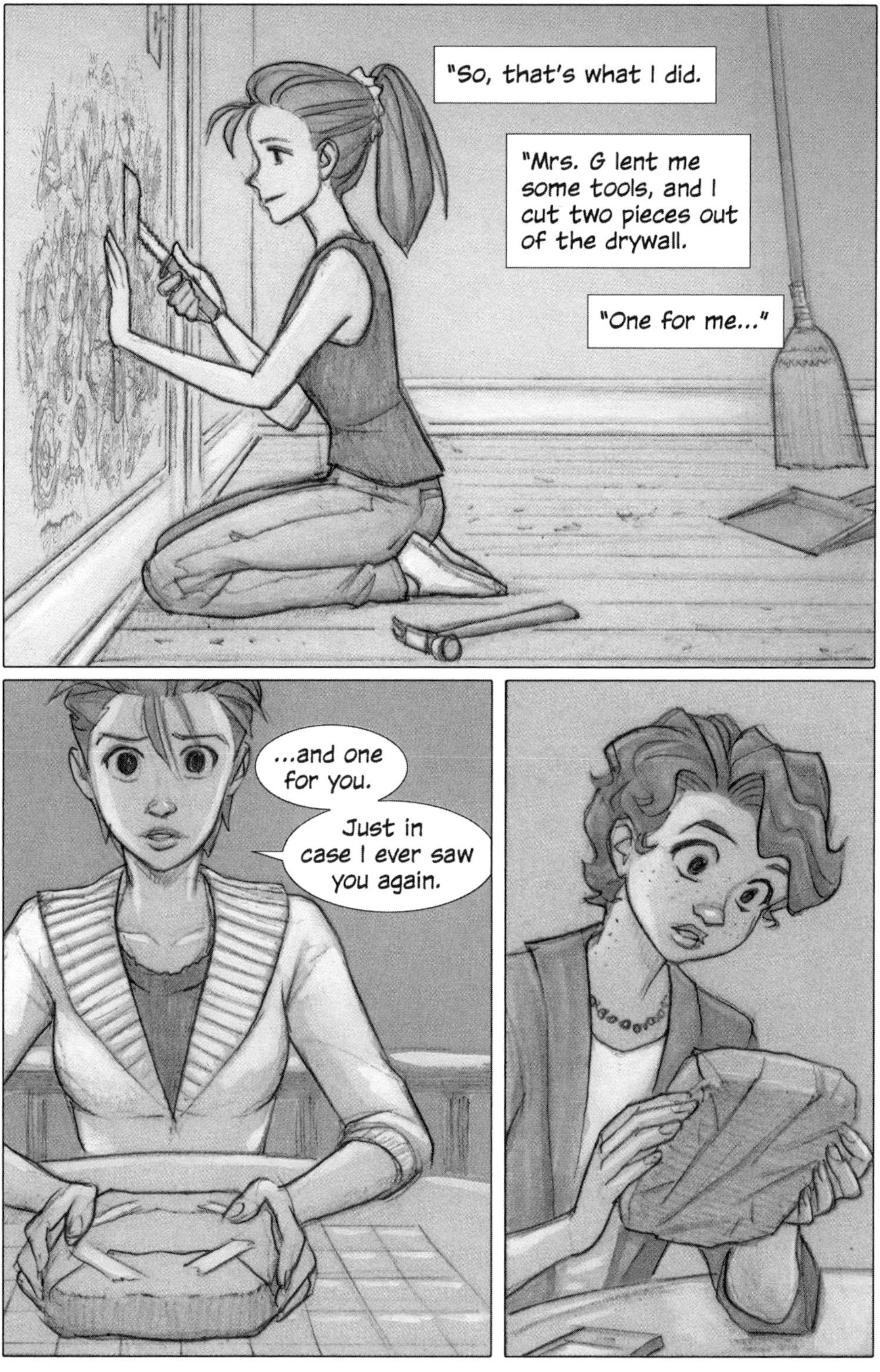
"So, that's what I did.
"Mrs. G lent me some tools, and I cut two pieces out of the drywall.
"One for me..."
...and one for you.
Just in case I ever saw you again.

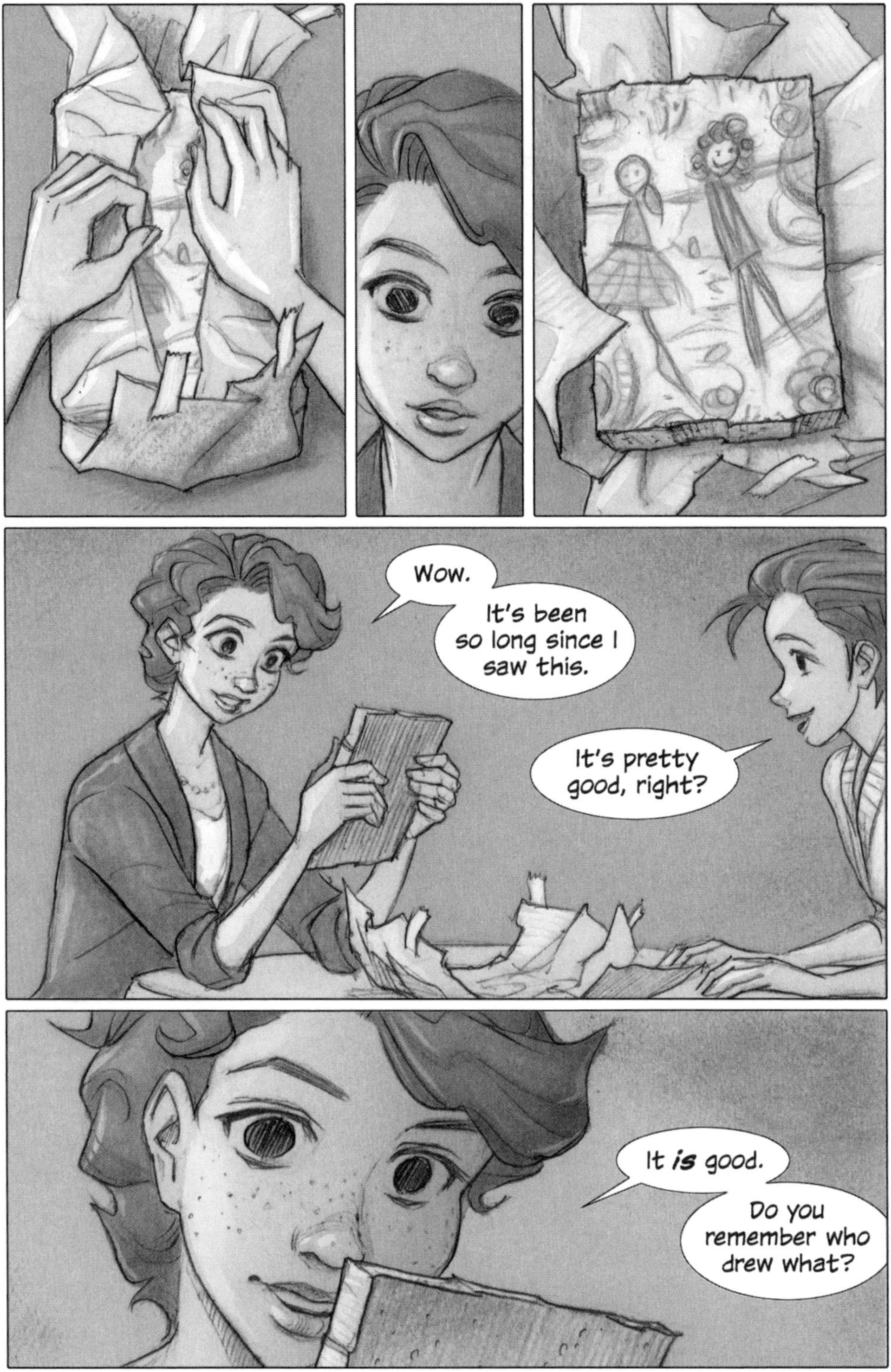
Wow.
It's been so long since I saw this.
It's pretty good, right?
It *is* good.
Do you remember who drew what?

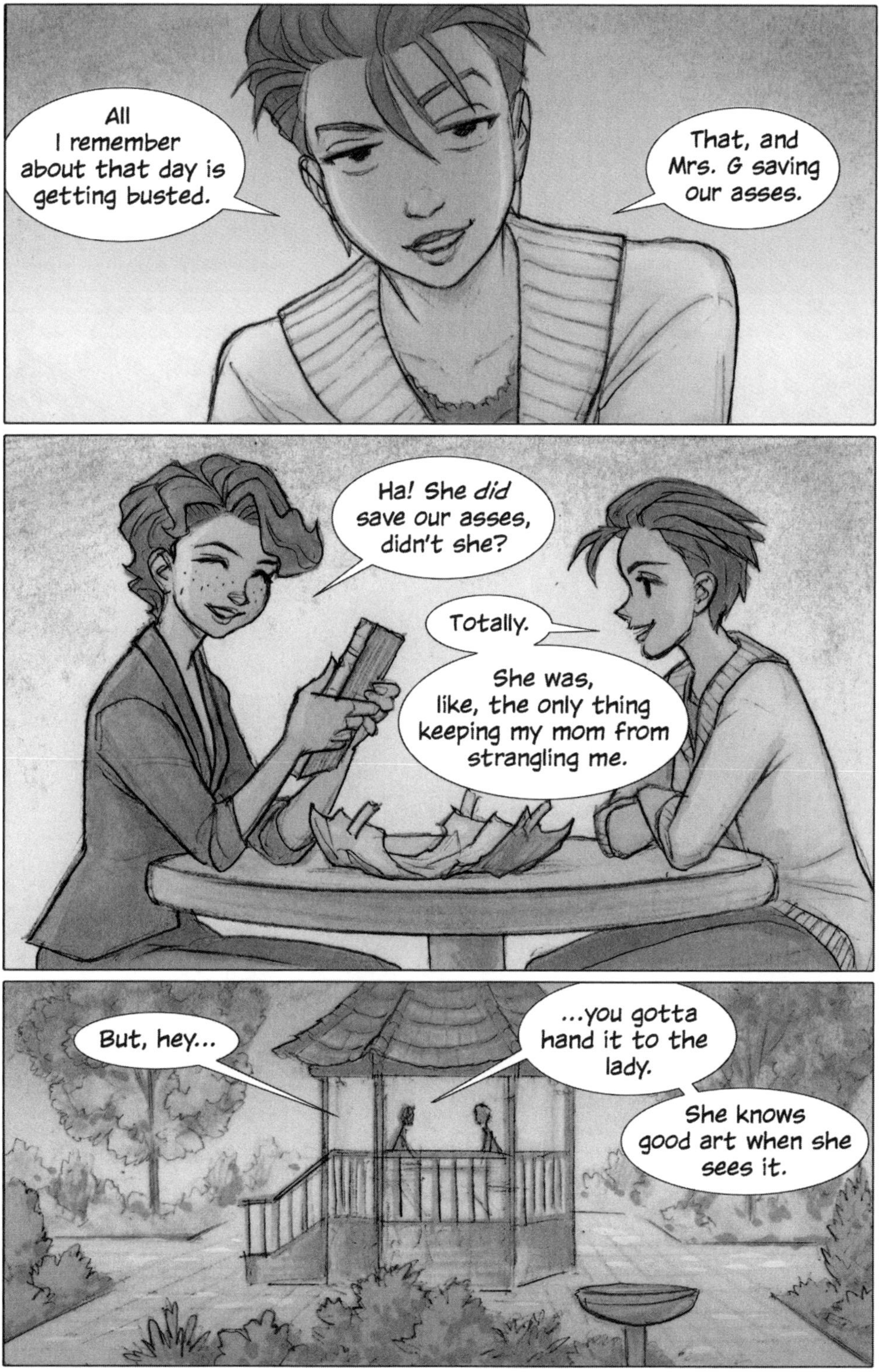
All I remember about that day is getting busted.
That, and Mrs. G saving our asses.
Ha! She *did* save our asses, didn't she?
Totally.
She was, like, the only thing keeping my mom from strangling me.
But, hey...
...you gotta hand it to the lady.
She knows good art when she sees it.

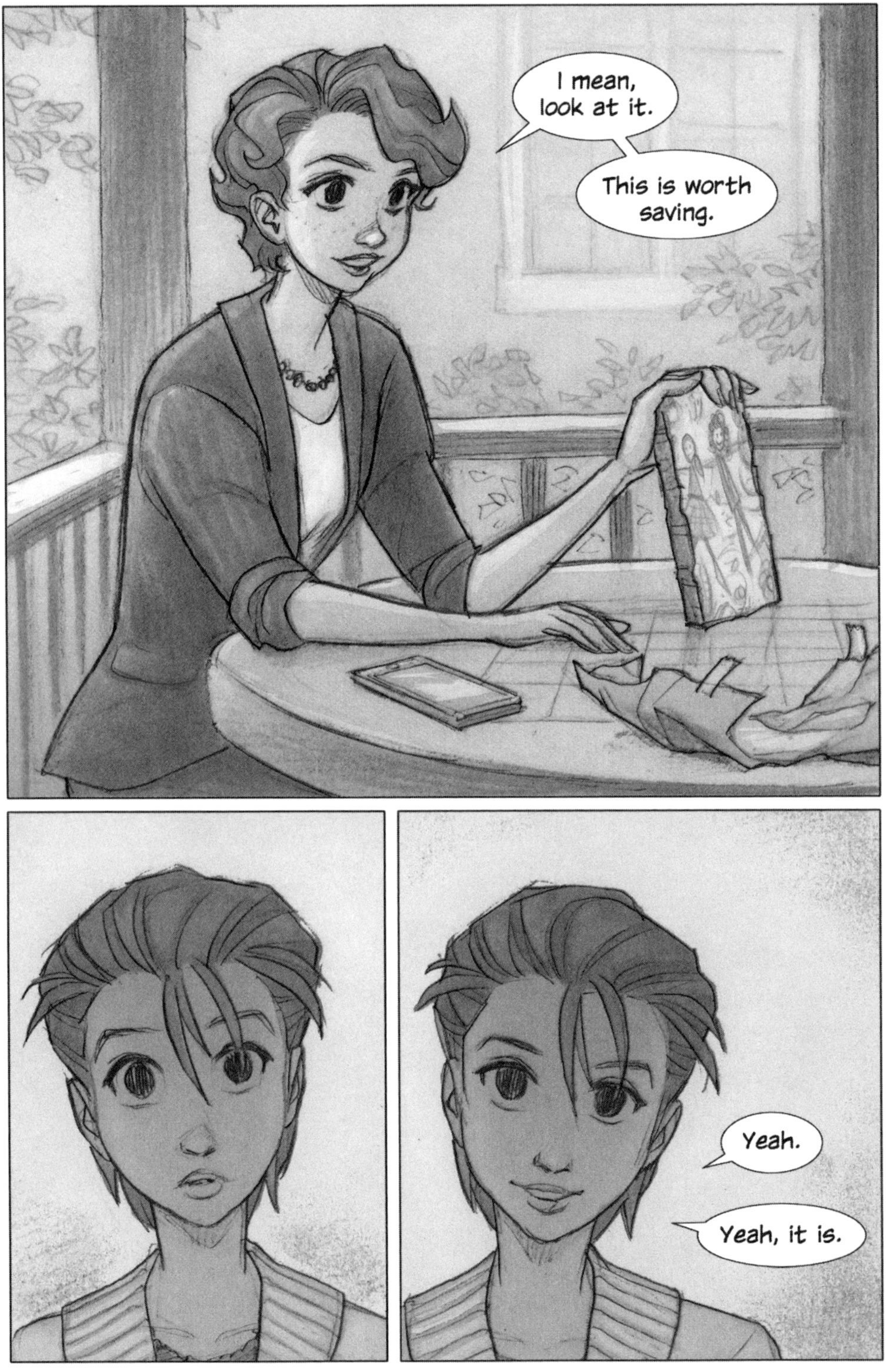
I mean, look at it.
This is worth saving.
Yeah.
Yeah, it is.

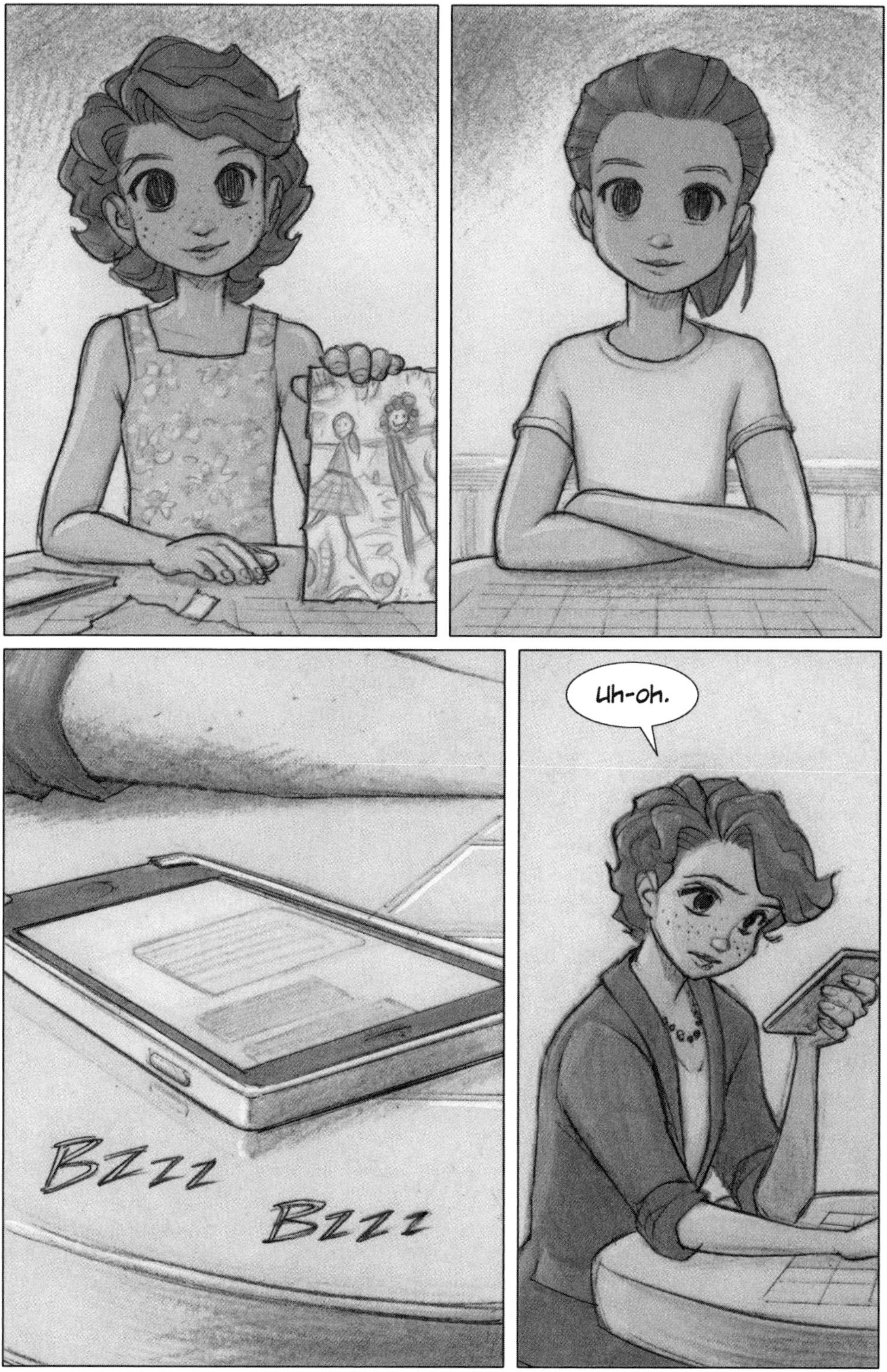
Bzzz
Bzzz
Uh-oh.

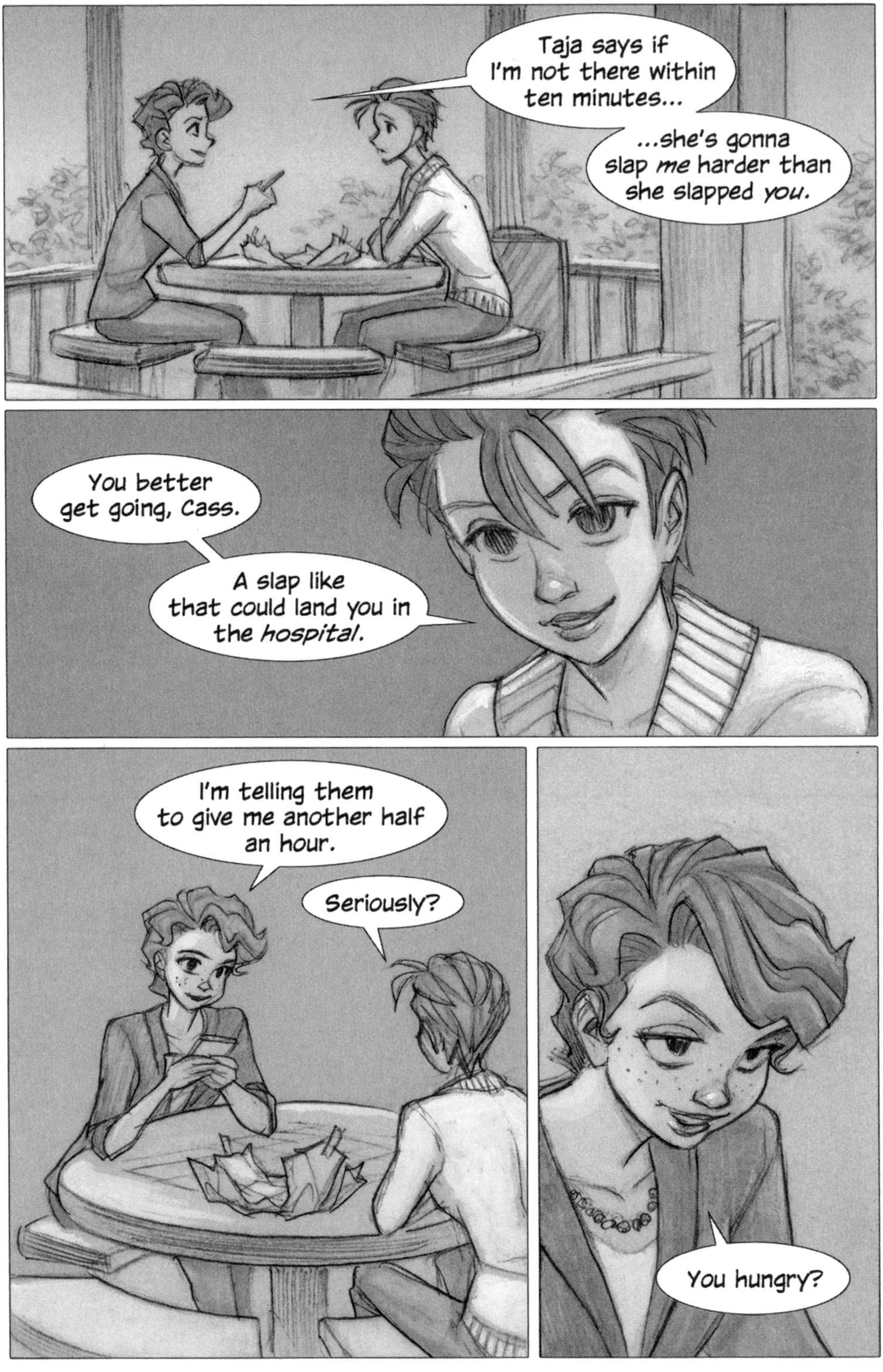
Taja says if I'm not there within ten minutes...
...she's gonna slap *me* harder than she slapped *you*.
You better get going, Cass.
A slap like that could land you in the *hospital*.
I'm telling them to give me another half an hour.
Seriously?
You hungry?

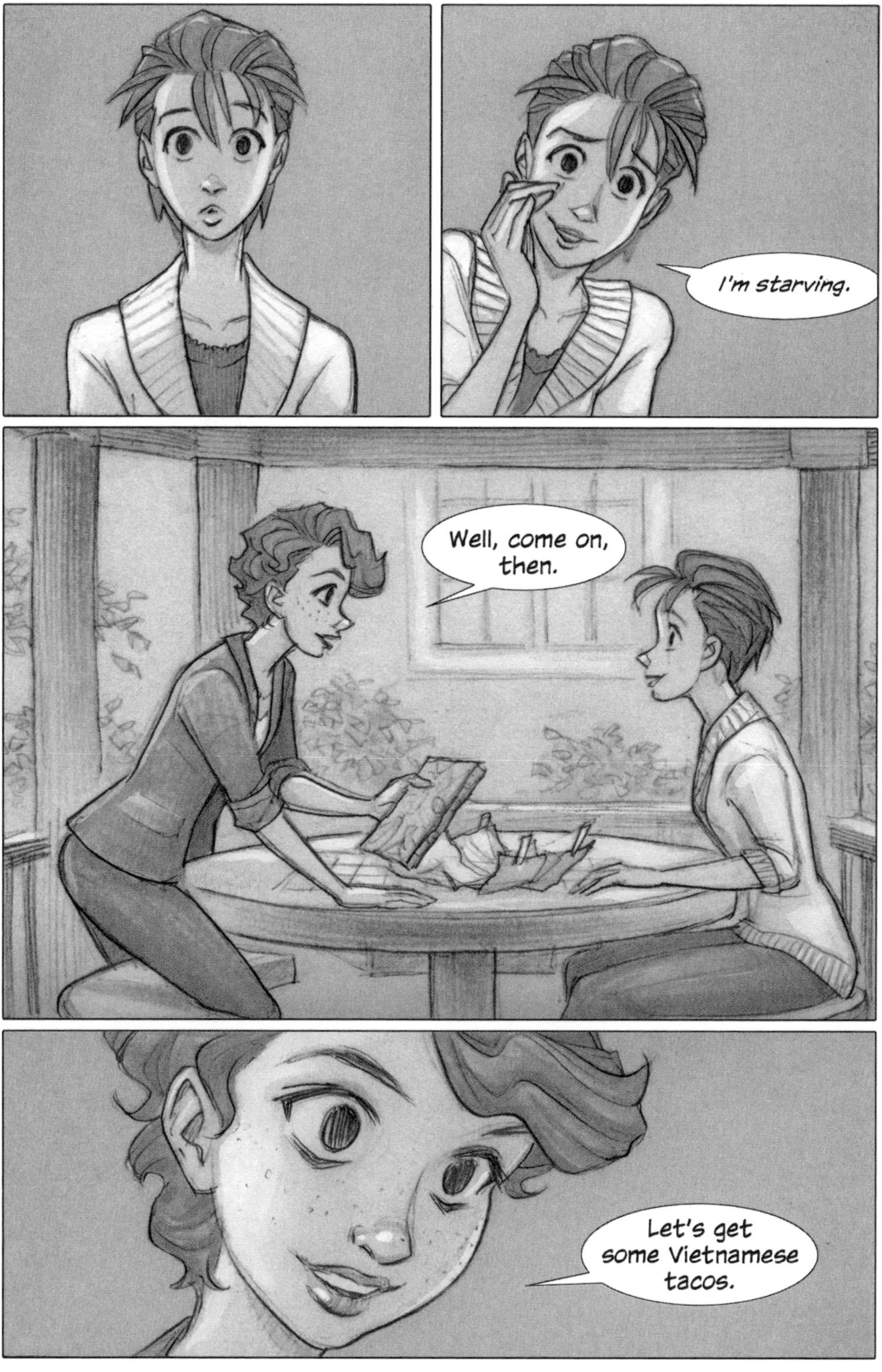
I'm starving.
Well, come on, then.
Let's get some Vietnamese tacos.

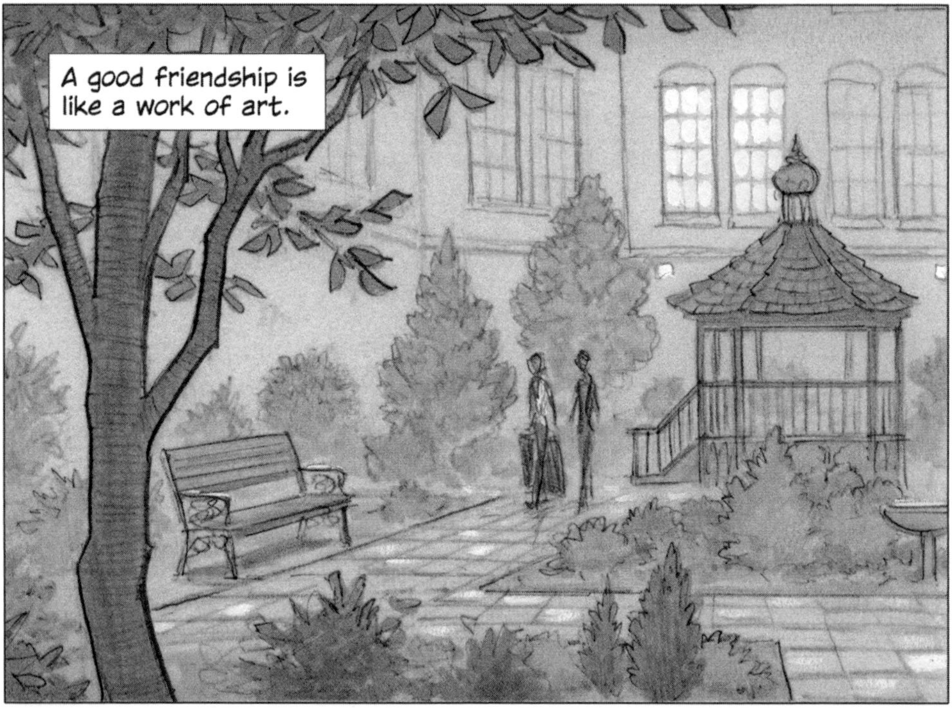
A good friendship is like a work of art.

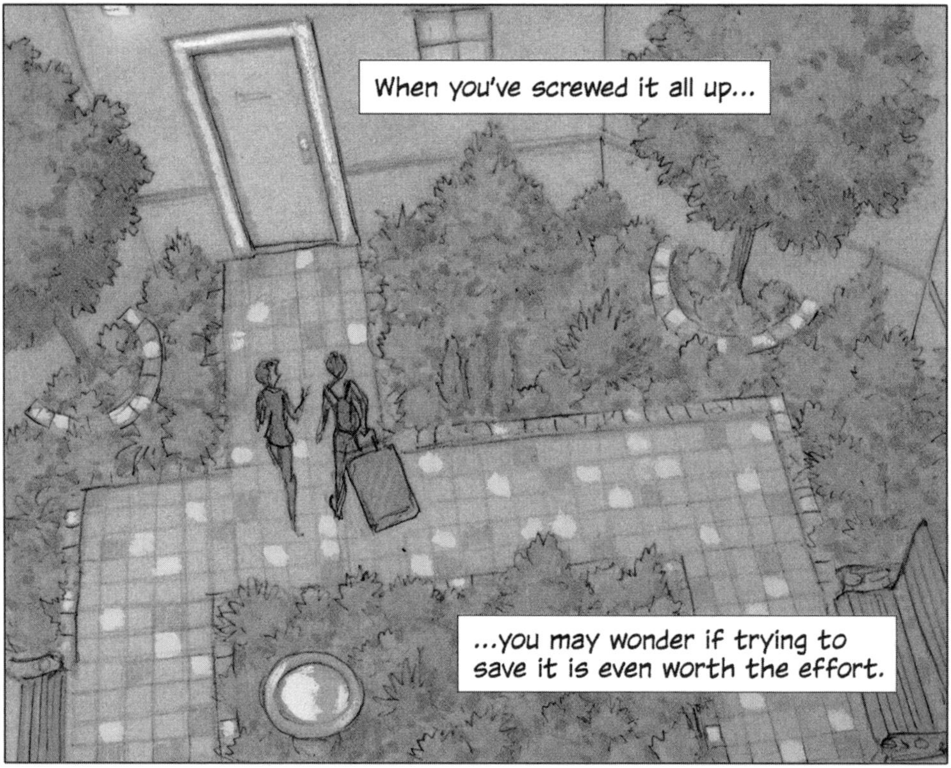
When you've screwed it all up...
...you may wonder if trying to save it is even worth the effort.

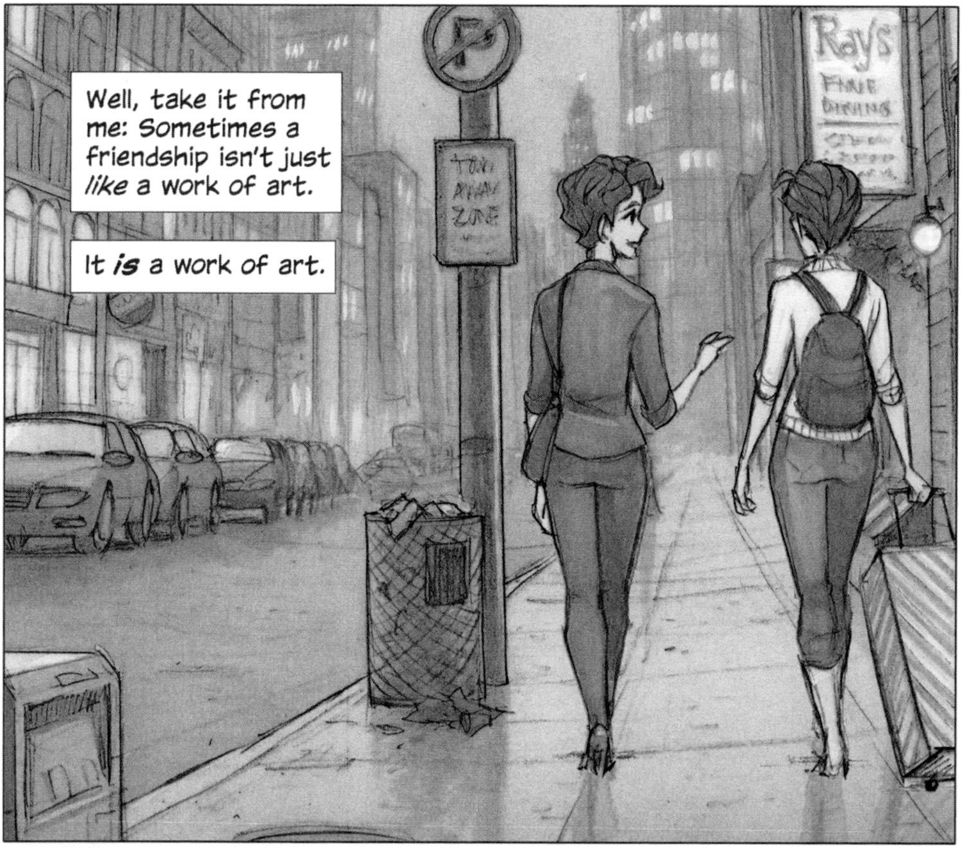
Well, take it from me: Sometimes a friendship isn't just *like* a work of art.
It ***is*** a work of art.
Rays

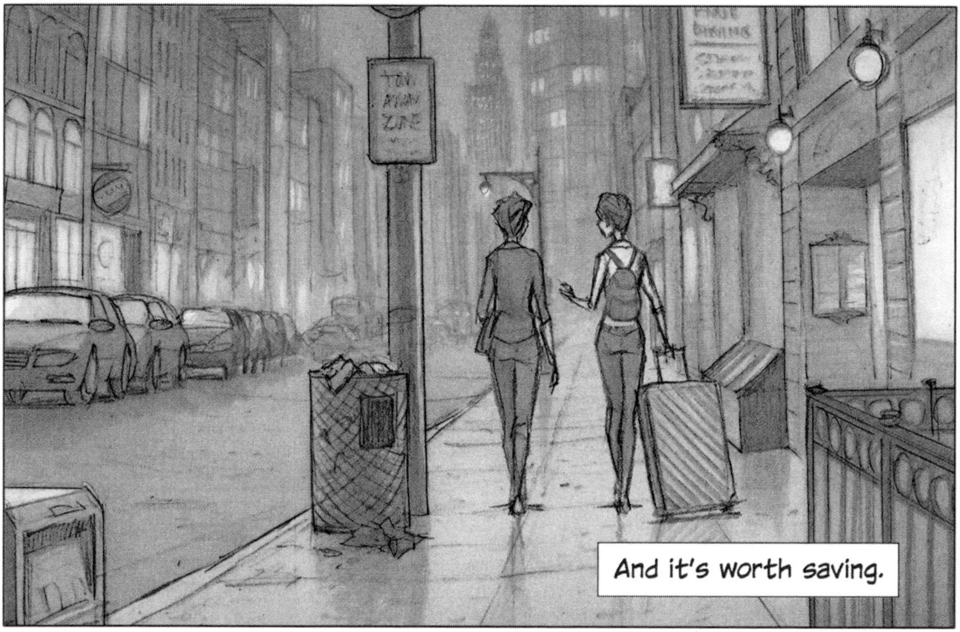
And it's worth saving.

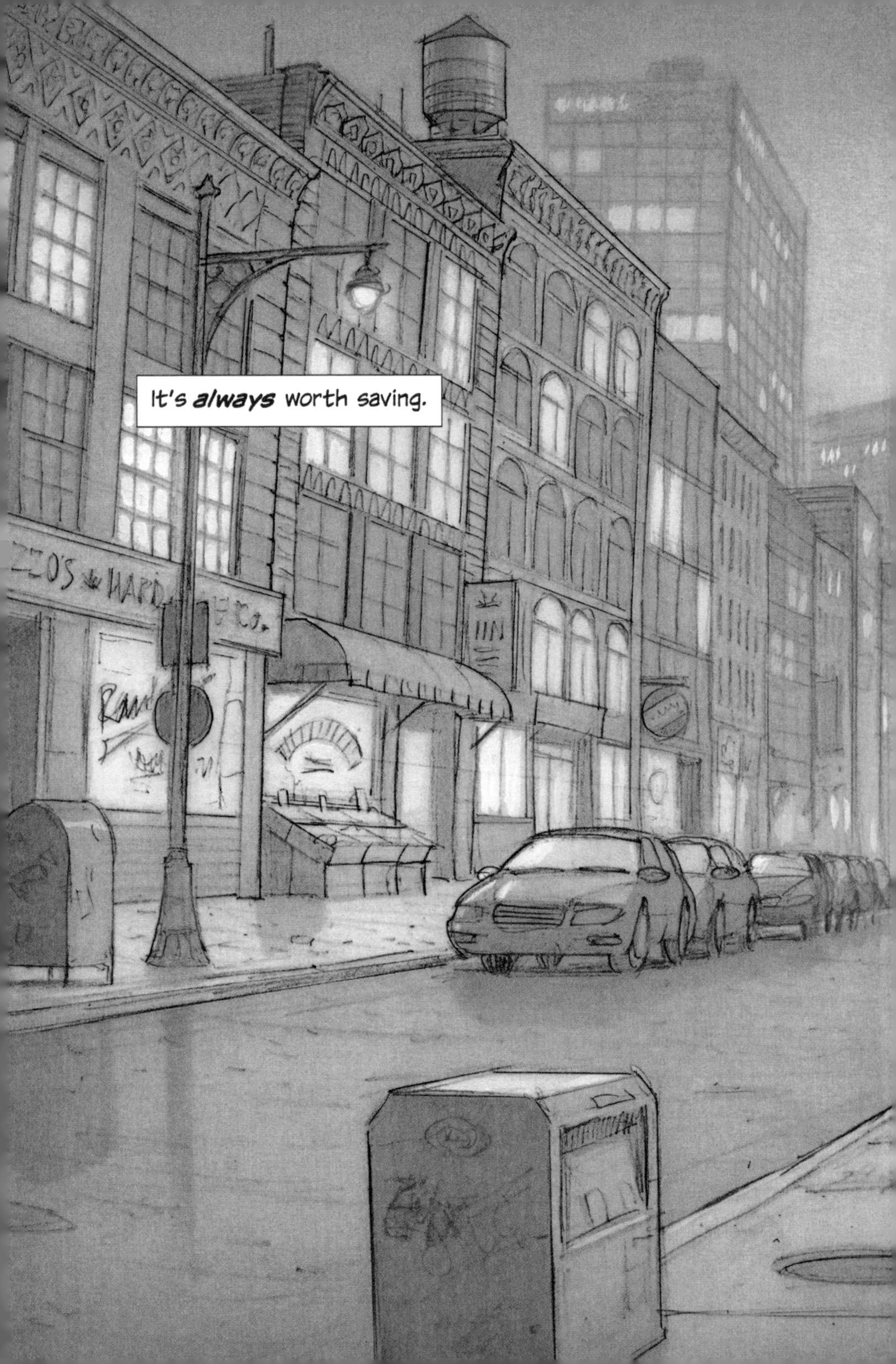
It's *always* worth saving.

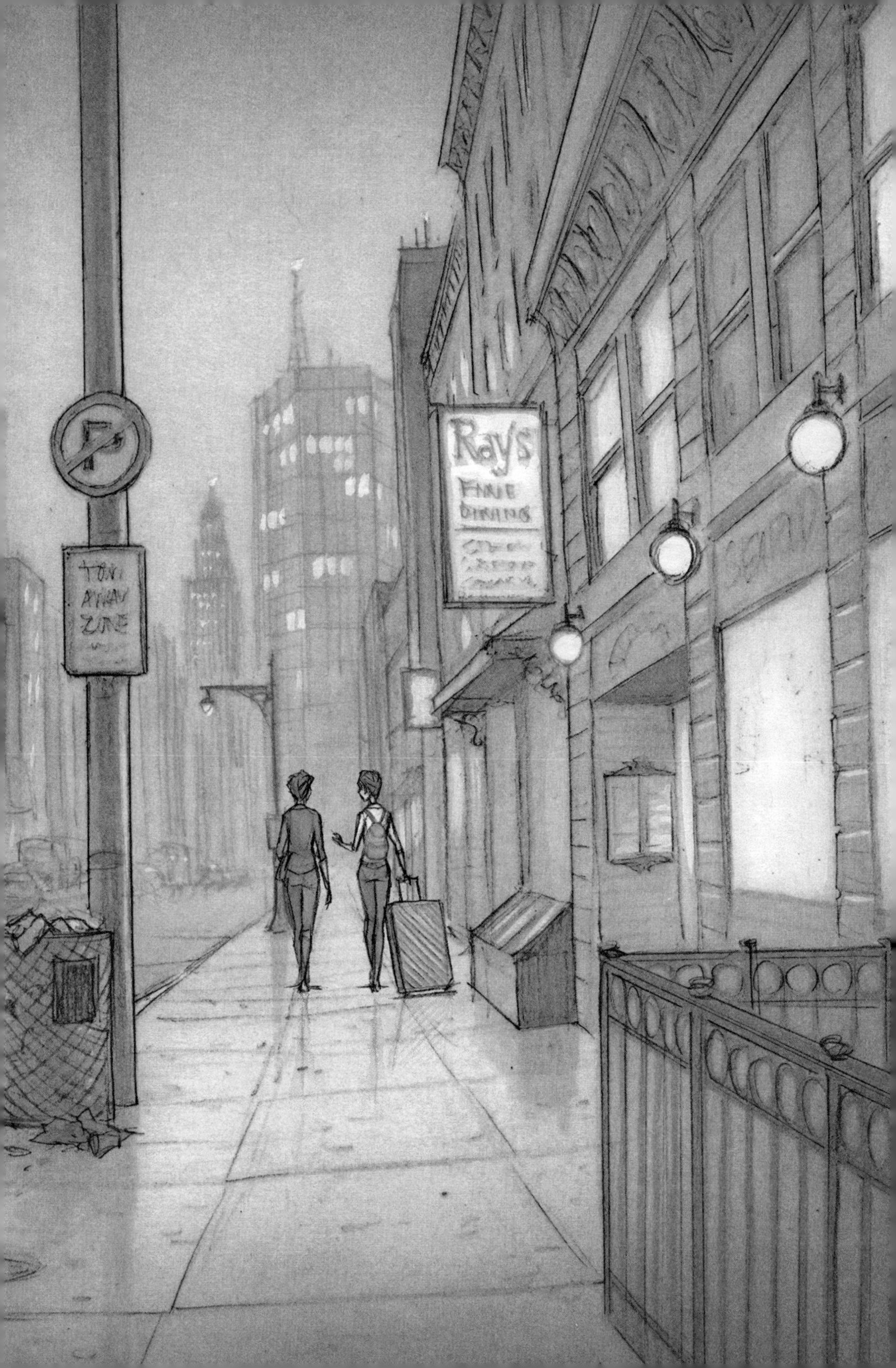
Ray's
FINE DINING
TOW AWAY ZONE

ACKNOWLEDGMENTS Thanks to Emily Meehan and Hannah Allaman, whose editorial guidance made a huge difference in both the substance and the style of this story. Thanks also to Andrea Colvin, whose editorial wisdom really saved the day when it came time for me to bring these pages across the finish line in their final form. I must also thank Jenny Kimura, whose design skills made the finished book as lovely as it could possibly be. I'm very grateful to both Kerianne Steinberg and Lindsay Walter-Greaney, whose eagle eyes spotted an awful lot of embarrassing errors—in both the writing and the art—before they slipped through into the final book. A deafening round of applause is due to Ammi-Joan Paquette, my agent, who believed in this book way back when it was just a vague germ of an idea, and who never stopped believing in it. And finally, many, many thanks to my wife, Miki, whose steadfast support stands behind not just this book, but indeed every book I have ever done.

MARK CRILLEY is the author and illustrator of more than forty books, including several acclaimed graphic novels, for which he has received fourteen Eisner Award nominations. His work has been featured in *USA Today* and *Entertainment Weekly*, and on *CNN Headline News*. His popular YouTube videos have been viewed more than 390 million times. He lives in Michigan with his wife, Miki, and children, Matthew and Mio.